CONTENT

Bound to Fate

bound book one

First Published in Great Britain in 2019 by
LOVE AFRICA PRESS
103 Reaver House, 12 East Street, Epsom KT17 1HX
www.loveafricapress.com

Available as ebook, paperback and audiobook

BLURB

Lara Johnson is coping with the emotional scars of losing both parents in a tragic incident and facing the challenges of starting a new school. Getting involved in a relationship isn't on her priority list. Certainly not this illicit desire for a man, who demands the best from her, yet leaves her breathless in his presence.

All Ike Thomas wants to do is to keep out of trouble and get through the one year internship required for his degree program. But trouble finds him, in the form of an intelligent and brave girl who turns his world upside down. Falling in love is forbidden. So why does it feel so right?

A love like theirs cannot be denied. But catastrophe lies in wait and one night changes their lives forever.

Bound to Fate is a story about surviving tragedy, forgiveness, and the overwhelming love that pulls through against the odds.

Content warning: This book contains scenes that might be triggering for some readers.

ACKNOWLEDGMENTS

Writing can be a lonely process but a group of fabulous beta readers make it a wonderful experience. This story wouldn't have turned out the way it did without the encouragement of Queenie, Henza, Kemi, Chinwe, Bimbo, Sola and Lara. I love you, ladies.

I have to mention my fabulous editor, Zee, who helped me polish the story and make it shine. Every book needs a good editor and she is a fabulous one.

And my family who have learned to be patient with me when I'm in the middle of writing a book and everything else takes a back seat. I love you all.

And of course, I can't forget you the wonderful readers who kept faith with me and picked up a copy of this. You make it all worthwhile. Thank you!

DEDICATION

To my mother.

ONE

T*his is the first day of the rest of your life.*

Lara Johnson chanted the words as she trudged down the stairs from her bedroom, her school bag slung across her shoulder. The phrase had been one her mother had taught her to use when the weight of her troubles threatened to crash down on her.

Hollowness in her chest reminded her that her world had ended three months previously.

The familiar crashing and smashing sounds of the Tom and Jerry cartoon coming from the television drew her into the living room. Lola, her younger sister by two years, reclined on a cream upholstered sofa, her school bag abandoned on the carpeted floor at her feet. In her hands, she held her Blackberry and tapped away at the keyboard with her thumbs. She appeared as if she didn't have a care in the world. Lara sometimes wondered how they could be related, because just as she proved to be an introvert, Lola was the opposite.

The tap, tap of footsteps in the hallway had Lara reaching for the remote control to switch off the television.

"Are you girls ready to go?" Judy called out. As their mother's younger sister, she had become their guardian after their parents died in a car crash.

"Yes, Aunty," Lara replied. "Come on, Lola."

Ignoring everything else, her sister carried on texting for a few more seconds as if whoever was on the other end of the virtual conversation proved more important at this moment. She wouldn't move until the last second.

Lara heaved a sigh and strode across the room. She grabbed Lola's bag and dumped it on her lap.

Lola lifted her head and gave her the evil eye. "What?"

"Aunty's waiting. Or do you want to walk to school on your first day?"

"I don't care. I don't want to go to this school, anyway."

Despite the grumbling, her sister got off the sofa with her bag and headed outside.

Lara shook her head as she followed, switching off the ceiling fan on the way. She had misgivings, too, about starting a new school, especially in her senior year when she needed to prepare for final exams. Neither of them had had any choice but to move after tragedy had befallen them.

Outside, a breeze flapped the admiral-blue skirt around her knees and the rising sun reflected off the small pools of water on the concrete driveway from the rain that had fallen at dawn. She checked her bag for her small umbrella, not wanting to get soaked if it rained again later.

For October, the temperature felt cooler and fresher than the humid heat she'd been used to in Lagos. From what she'd learnt in geography, Enugu lay over two hundred metres above sea level compared to Lagos's eleven metres.

The engine of the silver Honda CR-V revved, making her flinch. Against the background of the quiet neighbourhood, the sound became augmented, especially this early in the morning. Her gaze darted to the car. Judy already sat in the driver's position and Lola climbed in beside her.

"Lara, lock the door," her aunt called out through the open window.

"Okay." Puffing out a breath, she pulled out the bunch of keys she'd been given and did as instructed.

In her old house, she'd been used to securing the premises when going out. As the oldest child, many similar responsibilities fell on her shoulders. She didn't have the luxury of sitting in the car messaging friends on BBM like Lola while someone else did the chores. Then again, these little chores kept her busy with less time to think about the dreadful past. Or scary future.

With the lock in place, she returned her bunch into the bag and hurried to the vehicle now facing towards the gates. She pulled the door and climbed into the back seat.

The grating sound of metal on metal made her wince as the watchman tugged open the gates and they drove out. Today, her senses seemed more acutely sensitive to sounds as her anxiety spiked. Her foot bounced against the floor mat, making her black patent leather shoes squeak. She pressed her palms on her knees to stop the restless motion.

"Aunty, do we really have to go to this school? Can't we go back to our old school?" Lola asked in a sweet voice, finally putting aside the phone. "I'm sure they'll take us back. No problem."

"No, you can't, sweetie." Judy gave her a glance. "We discussed this already. You need to stay with me for now. You'll get used to the new school in no time."

There were a few other reasons they couldn't go back to their old school, even if their aunt didn't say them out loud. For one, it had been an expensive boarding school. Secondly, it lay over five hundred kilometres away in Lagos State while their aunt lived in Enugu State. And according to the bereavement counsellor, they needed to be around family.

"Aunty's house is nicer than boarding school," Lara chimed in. Although she missed the familiarity of her old school friends—not that she ever had that many—she wouldn't swap it for the security and compassion she'd received from Judy, who'd taken them in as if they were her own. Especially as they hadn't seen much of the woman since they were little.

"You say that because you didn't have many friends," Lola said in a sarcastic voice. "I did."

"Honey, I know you miss your friends from your old school, but you'll make new ones here, too. So don't worry about it. You'll both be fine." Judy squeezed Lola's shoulder.

"Okay," her sister said in a resigned voice.

"Lara, you remember where to go to get the registration sorted out?" Judy asked.

"Yes. The school admin office."

"Good. Once you show them the letter, they will let you know where to go. I won't be able to come and pick you after school. But the two of you can take a taxi home together since it's the first day. You will have to take the bus home next time."

"Thank you, Aunty," they both chorused.

Thirty minutes later, they stood in front of the school gates. Tens of kids in blue and white uniform milled around or headed into buildings.

"Hi, Lola!" someone called out.

Lola waved back.

"You know that girl?" Lara asked, astonished since her sister hadn't mentioned she knew anyone in this school.

Lola shrugged. "She lives on the same street as Aunty Judy."

"How do you know anyone already? We've only been in Enugu for a month."

"You're the one who chooses to lock yourself away in the house all the time. Anyway, where's this admin office we're supposed to find?"

Lara breath hitched and she felt as if she'd been hit with a sledgehammer. She bit back a retort and shook her head. She hadn't been locking herself away. She'd been in mourning.

Then again, she shouldn't be surprised about Lola. Her sister was pretty and had been popular at their last school. It looked like she would fit right in at Hillcrest.

As for herself, her goals for the year were simple—pass her exams and gain a university place. She didn't need the attention, and if no one accepted her, she would just have to cope with it as best she could.

"It's this way." She pointed to a sign on the wall and they headed in that direction.

Half an hour later, they'd filled out forms and were directed to their classes. Lola's were in a different building from hers.

"Do you want to meet for lunch?" Lara asked.

Lola shrugged and started walking off.

"If you need anything, just call or text me," Lara said.

"Yeah. Stop fussing, will you?" Glancing back, Lola rolled her eyes and walked off.

Lara couldn't help fussing. Lola was the only member of her family she had left. Okay, she had Judy, but it wasn't the same thing. She'd taken care of her sister since she was a baby and always felt responsible for her, even more so now that their parents were gone.

Sighing, she turned and hurried across the walkway to the class building. Students gazed at her but no one spoke to her. She kept her chin up and her shoulders stiff, determined to project confidence and determination. The truth was, she wasn't very good with change. Unlike Lola who complained about it and seemed to adapt a whole lot quicker.

By the time she arrived at the door to the correct class, it was already shut and the class seemed to be in session. She paused, brushed her palm over her braided hair packed in a ponytail style, and took a deep breath. Then she turned the metal handle, pushed the door open, and walked in.

The class was silent as they listened to the teacher but a murmur passed when she closed the door behind her.

A middle-aged man in brown jacket and trouser suit, white and green striped shirt, and a plain green tie stood at the front. Focusing on him, she walked over.

"Mr. Ejiofor?" When he nodded, she handed over the sheet of paper she'd been given at the office. "I was asked to give you this."

He took the paper and read it.

"We have a new student joining the class today." He glanced at the paper again. "This is Lara Johnson."

Clutching her hands to the back to hide their shaking, she turned to face the class. Big windows sat on the side. The back wall was plain white with a white board over it. On the side wall next to the door was a geopolitical map of the world.

The students sat in columns of two per desk in six columns and four rows. All of them stared at her with different degrees of curiosity.

Lara swallowed, her shoulders tightening. She hated being the centre of attention and even more so to a group of strangers. Her darting gaze caught onto another girl in the front row who smiled at her. There was an empty seat next to her. The only empty seat.

Mr. Ejiofor picked a book from the pile in front of him and handed it over to her. "Take a seat, Lara."

"Thank you," she mouthed and walked over to the empty chair quickly. The sooner she sat down, the sooner everyone else would stop staring at her. She dumped her bag on the aisle beside her and placed the book on the desk top.

The girl next to her turned and smiled. She was the picture of wholesome perfection. Her straight hair was packed neatly into a ponytail, not one strand out of place. Her school uniform was creaseless and fitted, unlike Lara's which needed adjusting around the waist. Her oval face was smooth and lovely, no acne in sight. Even the cheer in her curled lips and the twinkle in her brown eyes showed she was a happy and content girl.

Lara hadn't been happy or content in months.

"I'm Ada Obi. Welcome to Hillcrest School," the girl said in a low voice. "If you need someone to show you around, I can help you."

Lara gave a small smile as some of the tension left her body. Someone was being nice to her. Perhaps she'd make a new friend, after all. "Ada, thank you."

Mr. Ejiofor resumed the lesson in English Literature. Luckily, she'd bought a copy and already started reading the assigned book so she didn't feel too lost in the class discussion although she didn't attempt to raise her hand to answer any questions and the teacher didn't bother directing any queries at her. She managed to sit up straight instead of slumping under the melancholic weight that rested on her shoulders.

Time flew quickly and Mr. Ejiofor left. During the break before the next teacher arrived, the class erupted into chaos.

Shifting in the seat, Lara picked out her timetable and checked the next lesson. Geography—a subject she wasn't so good at.

Flicking the page of the textbook, she glanced at the door. A boy stood there as if on sentry duty, watching for the arrival of the next teacher. The flutter of the sheet did little to calm her nerves as it should. In her old school, she'd acquired the nickname 'Bookworm' because she loved immersing herself into the knowledge hidden between the covers of the printed work.

Shaking her head, she turned her attention back to the words on the page. Aside from noting the topic of the chapter as 'Population Change,' none of the text registered.

First day back at school for a new term usually didn't leave her this agitated. She loved school. But while it was the first day back for her, the school had been back for a few weeks already. She'd missed weeks of lessons and studying.

She sucked in a deep breath and gave another glance at the door. The student standing at the entrance hadn't moved, although his attention was focused on the chaos in class rather than checking if the Geography teacher was on the way.

The churning in her stomach returned, her breathing accelerated. Crossing her arms over on the desk, she lowered her head and started blowing out short breaths.

I can do this. I'm just sitting in a room with other students. Nothing bad will happen.

Breathing in through the nose and out through the mouth, she repeated the calming actions.

Where was the teacher? Perhaps if he turned up, her anxiety would ease just as it had done in the literature lesson.

She'd been having panic attacks since the traffic accident. The doctor had offered to sign her off school for another week or month if she didn't feel ready to be here. Her physical wounds had healed. Mentally, she didn't know if she'd be ever fully recovered.

Tired of hiding from the world, she had to face her life. Face her future, such as it was.

Lifting her head, her gaze swept the class. No one else seemed interested in preparing for the next subject. Not even the girl sitting next to her. She seemed rapt on a lanky male student who was telling a story. His hand and body movements as well as the jokes he cracked identified him as the class comedian. They'd had a similar boy in her last school.

"What's his name?" Lara asked in a low voice. She couldn't be sure Ada heard her above the raucous sound of laughter.

Giggling, the girl turned to look at her. "That's Jimoh. He thinks he's the next Basketmouth."

With a half-smile, Lara's raised a brow in confusion. "Basketmouth?"

"Come on. You know Basketmouth?"

"Yes, I do." She chuckled. "He's good but not as good as a popular Nigerian stand-up comedian." She tilted her head in the direction of some girls sitting in the middle row who'd been staring at her and not so nicely. "What about those girls over there?"

"Oh, that's Princess Gloria and her coterie."

"Coterie?"

"You know? Gang, Pack, Clique, Circle. Don't mind me. I like big words." Ada chuckled again.

Warmth spread across Lara's chest as a big smile filled her face. She liked this girl a lot already.

"Is she really a princess?"

"No, she's not. We call her Princess because she walks around as if her father is the Obi of Onitsha."

Lara glanced at the girl again and she did have a haughty air about her, with the tilt of her raised nose and the group surrounding her.

White paper planes making turbulent journeys above heads bobbing with raucous laughter snagged her attention next. Most of the boys sat on their desk instead of the appointed chairs, either cloistered in smaller groups or listening in on the more general conversation.

"I never thought so many people would sign up to take Geography this year," Jimoh said.

"It's because of the fine boy teacher," another boy chipped in.

"No. You've got that wrong. I know it's because of me everyone is in this class, because no one fine pass me. Check me now." He started doing the vogue pose, causing everybody to break out into laughter.

"What is he talking about?" Lara asked, now curious about why the class seemed to be this full for an elective subject. Geography hadn't been that popular in her previous school.

"Don't worry," Ada said. "You'll understand when you see the teacher. He is something else. Half the class wants to be him and the other wants him as boyfriend."

"He's coming!" shouted the boy standing by the door, and everyone scrambled back to their seats just in time to stand up as the teacher walked in.

"Good morning, Mr. Thomas," the class chorused.

Lara's breath caught in her throat. *This* was their teacher? It couldn't be.

"Good morning, class," the man replied. "You may take your seats."

OMG! Lara couldn't take her gaze away from the man who was going to be her new geography tutor. The world and everything in it seemed to disappear. Just him.

Somebody tugged her arm and she turned to find it was Ada. The rest of the class were now seated down. Her face burned as she picked her mouth off the floor.

"You must be the new student," the teacher said.

"Yes, sir." She swallowed. "I'm Lara Johnson."

"Welcome, Lara." His lips curled in a boyish grin with a dimple on the left cheek.

Her heart thumped against her chest and her skin tingled as if he'd reserved the smile especially for her. She couldn't help smiling in return. Geography would be her best subject this year.

"You can sit down."

"Thank you, sir." Sweeping a hand under her skirt, she turned to sit down and caught the glare coming from Gloria. If eyes could kill, she'd be dead. She lowered her gaze and was glad to have her back to the girl. What was Gloria's problem, anyway?

"Before we get started," Mr. Thomas said in a deep, mellow voice that captured the attention of the whole class. "I want to let you know that the registrations for the exam preparations tutorials are open today. If you'd like extra help with preparing for your finals, then get your name down."

Leaning forward with elbows on the desk, Lara rested her chin in her palms and just stared at the new teacher. She'd had young teachers in her previous school, mostly Youth Corpers, but she'd didn't recall anyone looking this young. Or this *good.*

He stood strikingly handsome and tall. They were all seated but she'd bet he'd tower over everyone around if they stood close to him. His skin, a dark, hickory-brown shade, contrasted brilliantly with his white shirt. The top two buttons lay undone, leading her to look up at his face.

With fascinating almond-shaped mocha-brown eyes, thick curved brows, balanced nose, full sensuous lips, and square jaw line, his face suited the cover of a magazine. Model David Agbodji had nothing on him.

Her mouth watered and she licked her lips. One word whispered in her mind. *Sexy.* She'd heard the term bandied about by her friends, but she'd never used it to describe anyone until now.

She'd never been more sexually aware of anyone until now.

The thought had her straightening her posture as her body warmed. She'd never had a boyfriend before, although she'd attended a mixed boarding school. Boys her age never appealed to her. Also, her parents had been strict about boyfriends. She'd been taught that boys were bad and getting involved could only lead to trouble.

Her focus had always been on academics and getting great results.

All that flew far from her mind as she couldn't look away, absorbing every word the teacher spoke as if he addressed her alone.

"My tutorial classes will run on Tuesday and Thursday afternoons. All those interested should register using the forms on the Year Twelve notice boards." He placed both hands on his desk and leaned forward. "Next week, there will be a test, which will cover everything we've discussed so far this term."

A murmur passed through the class. Lara insides quivered and she swallowed down the panic, surprisingly not at the thought of failing the test but at disappointing her teacher. She'd have to study extra hard this week. Of course, she'd be signing up for his tutorials.

"Sir?" A student at the back raised a hand.

"Yes, Chuma."

"This is unfair. A week is not enough notice."

"Have you been paying attention in class since the start of the term?"

"Of course, sir."

"Then you should have nothing to complain about. If anyone should complain about short notice, it should be Lara."

"That's what I meant, sir. I was complaining on behalf of the new student. It's unfair for her to take a test when she hasn't been in class with us."

"Well, let's ask her. Lara, do you think the test next week is unfair to you?"

OMG! He's talking directly to me. Her face heated up and she swallowed a few times before she could speak.

"Well...um...it is short notice for me, sir." Her voice sounded squeaky. She swallowed again.

"In that case, you are exempted from next week's test, Lara."

Another murmur went through the class and she could hear the disappointment in her classmates' voices. She crossed her arms and shook her head. She didn't want to be singled out for favour and end up being hated by the rest of the class.

"Excuse me, sir." She raised her right hand.

"Yes, Lara," the teacher replied.

"Sir, I want to take part in next week's test."

"Good." He smiled at her again, making warmth spread through her chest. "Now turn to chapter four of the Physical Geography textbook."

The class settled down as the lesson went along. His mastery of the subject and the engaging way he discussed with the class only added to her admiration of him. For a young person who was probably only a few years older than she was, his confidence and ability to keep the entire class active and participating made her want to learn so much from him. Could she stand in front of a class of teenagers and get them to listen?

Before long, the bell rang to signify the end of the class and break time. Mr. Thomas dismissed everyone and the students dispersed.

Lara sighed, disappointed that the class had ended so quickly, although a glance at her wristwatch indicated two hours had gone by since Mr. Thomas had arrived in class.

"Are you going to the canteen for lunch?" Ada asked as she got off the chair.

"Yeah. Okay," she replied and packed up her items.

"Lara, I want to talk to you," Mr. Thomas said.

"I'll wait for you outside." Ada headed for the door.

Lara remained standing on the spot.

Mr. Thomas came around to lean back on the desk, facing her. He was less than a metre away from her. Her heart thudded in her chest, her pulse skyrocketing. If she stretched out her hand and leaned forward, her finger tips would graze the front of his shirt. Would his skin feel warm to the touch? Did he have hard muscles beneath the fabric?

"I'm impressed that you agreed to take the test next week with the rest of the class," he said, his gaze both assessing and amazed, his hand resting on his chest with his fingers splayed.

Cheeks burning, she lowered her gaze and muttered shyly, "Thank you, sir."

"But as you can tell from the protests, my tests are not easy. As this subject is an elective, I'm determined that every student who signs up for it achieves the best result. With that in mind, I'm also aware that you're currently at a disadvantage since you haven't been in school from the start of the school year. I want to level out the playing field for you."

She lifted her head, meeting his gaze. "How's that, sir?"

"I strongly suggest you sign up for the extra weekly tutorials. But for next week, I'm offering you a daily tuition for half an hour during your lunch break."

"All week, sir?" Her brows shot up as her pulse accelerated. She was going to be in a room alone with him for the next few days?

"Yes. Is that a problem?" His brows drew together in a frown as he leaned back on his hands.

"No, sir." She bit her lower lip and twisted her watch around, fretting that he would withdraw the offer. "I'm just worried that you'll be using your personal time to coach me."

"Your concern is duly noted, Lara. But as I said earlier, I'm determined to achieve one hundred percent pass rate for my subject. You have one week to learn topics your classmates have been studying for six weeks. The work isn't optional unless you want to drop the subject altogether."

"No, sir," she said quickly. The thought of not being in his class made her heart sick.

"In that case, go and grab a quick lunch and get back here in twenty minutes so we can get started.

"Thank you." Hands shaking, she pulled her bag off the floor and hurried out of the room.

Ada stood in the hallway, fingers pressing buttons on her phone. "There you are. What did he want?"

"He's going to give me extra lessons to catch up."

As she spoke, Mr. Thomas came out of the classroom. He stared at both of them sternly as if he knew they were talking about him.

She bit her lip and avoided his gaze as she blushed.

"I expect you back in class at the correct time, Lara." He turned and walked away.

"Yes, sir," she muttered and grabbed Ada's hand. "I don't want to get into trouble on my first day. Please show me to the canteen."

"Okay."

By the time they got to the building housing the restaurant, it was already teeming with students and teachers. Lara searched the room for Lola but couldn't find her so she sent her a message. She couldn't stay and eat in there. She bought a meat pie and bottle of Fanta to go instead with the cash Judy had given her this morning. She then bid farewell to Ada who went to queue with another group of girls, and returned to the class.

She sat in her chair and ate her food, checking her phone for messages from Lola. None came.

Right on time, Mr. Thomas strode in. Her respect for this man ratcheted up another notch. It had to be genuine passion for his students and subject that would make him sacrifice his own personal time for her. She'd had good teachers in the past but couldn't think of any who had done something like this before.

She pushed her chair back to stand up.

He waved a hand.

"Don't stand up." He stopped beside the desk.

Pulse racing, she sat forward, her attention focused on him. Would he come closer?

Her shoulders slumped when he remained where he stood. "These sessions are informal. I expect you to be on time. I expect you to pay attention, ask questions, and do the work given to you."

"Yes, sir." Rubbing her clammy hands against her skirt, she licked her dry lips. More than anything else, she wanted to please him. Her foot bounced against the bottom of the desk.

Crash!

The loud sound made her jump back. Eyes bulging, body trembling, she hyperventilated. Shards of broken bottle lay scattered on the linoleum floor, triggering memories of another time and place.

Broken glass shattered on tarmac. Crumpled metal, trapped bodies. The stomach-curdling smell of petrol. Crunching sounds over people's voices. Someone called her name from far away.

A fever swept through her. Sweat trickled down her back and face. She couldn't move. Couldn't breathe.

Someone grabbed her shoulders. Dragged her out of the wreckage. No, the person wasn't dragging her. She was being shaken.

"Lara...Lara!"

She looked up at the person calling her name. The same person shaking her.

What's he doing here? He doesn't belong in this memory.

Slowly, her environment returned to her. She blinked several times as she struggled to get air into her lungs.

"Mr. Thomas?" Her voice came out scratchy and weak, her throat dry.

"Lara, do you know where you are?" He squatted beside her, brow wrinkled.

Blinking again, she swallowed the bile in her throat and nodded. "In school."

His gaze flitted over her body, the frown still in place. "Are you hurt?"

She stared from her hands to the glass on the floor. "No. I'm sorry. Let me clean up the mess."

Shifting, she scrambled to get up.

"Stay there." His tone was gentle and firm.

Stiffening, she didn't move as she watched him stride across the room.

He snatched a sheet of paper off the table and came back to pick up the broken pieces from the floor. He dumped the big chunks in the paper bin, opened the door, and disappeared.

Rubbing her palms down her skirt, she hunched over. First day in a new school and she'd had a panic attack. In front of the most intriguing man she'd ever met, with skin like dark chocolate and eyes like the sky at night.

Oh, God! Heat crept up from her chest to her face. Wanting to get out before he came back, she grabbed her bag.

The door squeaked as it swung open and he returned with a small brush and pan.

Chest feeling tight and frozen to the spot, she watched him.

He worked quickly and thoroughly, sweeping up any last trace of glass and binning them. Striding to his desk, he pulled a bottle of water from his satchel and came back to sit in a chair across from her.

"Drink this." He passed her the plastic container.

She unscrewed the sealed cap, tipped her head slightly back, and drank, glad to soothe her parched throat. When she finished, she stretched out her hand to pass it back.

"You can keep it," he said, his gaze fixed to her face.

"Thank you." She broke eye contact and stared at the desk, clutching the bottle to her side as she wrapped her arms across her body to hide her tremors.

"Lara, why did you have a panic attack?" he asked, his voice low and filled with concern.

Eyes wide, she glanced at him. How did he know? Her foot bounced on the floor. "I...I..." she stuttered.

His hand settled on her knee. Warm. Calming. "It's okay. Breathe in and out slowly."

She followed the instructions of his compelling voice. Her breathing evened out and the shaking stopped eventually.

"Sometimes, I wake up in the middle of the night from a nightmare," he continued. "I'll be shivering and sweating and feeling like I want to crawl out of my skin."

"Really?" Her breath caught and she placed the water bottle on the desk. Why was he telling her something so personal? Something he must be ashamed to share with anyone.

Just as she was ashamed of the bad memories that plagued her.

"Yes. So if something's happened, you can tell me. I'll understand." Withdrawing his hand, he leaned it on the desk beside him, the other on his knee.

She sucked in a deep breath and let it out slowly. Something about him made her want to share her experience, although she hadn't discussed it with anyone after it happened.

Then again, people didn't like to talk about tragedies, afraid of inviting those things into their lives. She was trying to move on from her parents' death, but the memory stalked her. Being in a new school environment didn't help matters.

She glanced up at Mr. Thomas. He nodded as if in understanding as his lips curled in a sad smile. His sympathetic expression bolstered her resolve. She released another slow breath.

"I was in a car crash with my parents. They were killed." Tears misted her eyes and she swiped them with her palms. "Sometimes when I hear a loud noise, I feel as if I'm trapped in that car."

"I'm sorry for your loss."

The stress in his voice made her look across to him. His hands clenched into fists and the skin around his eyes bunched as he gave her a pained stare.

She recognised that expression. It was like staring in a mirror. Staring at a boy who'd undergone suffering. Someone like her. A kindred spirit.

He blinked and the distressed expression eased away as if it was an oil portrait brushed over with new paint.

"Surviving a tragedy like that is tough on anybody. We have a counsellor here at Hillcrest. If you need to talk more about it, she's a good person."

The tormented boy had gone and in his place sat the articulate teacher.

She nodded. But she wouldn't talk to anyone else unless it was him. For one, she didn't like reliving the event. Anyway, no one else would understand what it felt like to carry this guilt around unless they'd been through something similar. Why was she alive when her parents were dead? She'd asked herself the question ever since the accident.

"Good." He lifted his arm and glanced at his watch. "Lunch break is almost over. We'll have to pick up the lesson tomorrow. Read the whole of chapter one from the textbook before we meet then."

She swallowed. "Yes, sir."

Nodding, he strode to the desk and grabbed his satchel.

As she bit her lips and gripped her elbows, disappointment that he was leaving made her chest tighten. Unable to move, she watched him head to the door.

Twisting the handle, he turned back to look at her. "Lara, you're going to be fine. With time, the way you feel will get better."

His lips curled at one corner and he was back to looking boyish in a charming boy-next-door sort of way. Then he was gone.

Butterflies fluttered in her belly. Heat flushed her skin. For the first time in her life, she wanted a boy to notice her. Except this wasn't a boy. He was a man, her teacher, and totally forbidden.

She wanted him nonetheless.

TWO

To whom much is given, much is expected.

Ike Thomas lived those words as if they had been written especially for him. But he hadn't always been so purposeful or honourable.

Once, he'd been a carefree young man whose only concern had been of living a full life and having fun. Then, one reckless moment had sent his world crashing.

The death of this older brother, Obi, had devastated him. Broken him.

There had been several times afterwards when he'd felt he shouldn't be alive. That he should've been the one to die. The one lying six-feet under the earth. The one being eaten by worms and turning into dust.

He straightened his shoulders as he exited the admin building, not allowing his guilt to overwhelm him. He'd become good at hiding beneath his cloak of responsibility. Of pretending everything was okay on the outside, when on the inside, pain shredded through him on a daily basis. It proved tougher maintaining the same strong exterior at the end of a long day dealing with teenagers than it did at the start of the day when his energy levels stood at their highest.

As much as the students drained him, they also gave him purpose. Gave him a reason to get out of bed in the morning. More than anything else, he never wanted to disappoint the people who'd come to rely on him so much. The respect and admiration they projected onto him made him stand taller and even more determined.

On some days like today, the tension returned to his muscles along with a pounding headache. Nothing could shake his self-loathing. Or his wish to go back and change things. A luxury he couldn't be granted.

He settled for making amends any way he could, which included taking this work placement as a teacher, even though it had never been something he wanted to do. His father owned one of the largest property development firms in Nigeria. He didn't need to work elsewhere to earn money. Not to mention that he was studying Architecture and Design for his Bachelor's degree program.

His parents had been adamant; his father, especially. If he truly wanted to make amends for his offences, then he had to do whatever it took.

Perhaps his redemption came in the form of finding love and the right girl in the last place he would've looked. Every time he looked upon her face, he felt as if a star burst inside of him.

"See you tomorrow, Mr. Thomas," Mrs. Bello, another teacher greeted.

As the head of Year Twelve, she mentored him and he reported to her. The woman was like a mother figure to the year group, well-liked and respected. But she insisted on addressing him formally, so he returned the gesture.

"Good night, Mrs. Bello," he replied as he unlocked his sporty, starlight blue Toyota GT Primo. He tossed his satchel on the passenger seat and lowered his body into the car. He was a tall man but he loved the low suspension and riding with his car hugging the tarmac so close. Although his love for fast cars had gotten him into trouble, he couldn't shake this one addiction. He just didn't drive as recklessly as he used to as a teenager.

He pulled out of the parking lot onto the road. It was early dusk, the sun low on the horizon. The air-conditioner hummed gently and Afro beat music from his iPod filled the interior. He cruised towards the junction of the quiet street with the school, slowed further when he noticed a group of male students in the corner. He rolled his window down to instruct them to disperse. It wasn't dark yet but would be in about half an hour. Students weren't permitted to loiter around the premises after school hours.

Just as he leaned across and was about to call out the names of the boys he recognised, he saw the girl they had crowded against the wall.

Lara Johnson.

His blood froze. What was she doing hanging around with these boys? He knew enough about them. Knew they were the notorious boys in school. Jocks with rich parents, who thought they could have any girl they wanted.

His stomach rolled. He'd been one of those boys at their age, so he knew exactly what followed encounters like this one. Bile rose in his throat. He thought he knew Lara well enough to know she shouldn't be in this crowd. As well enough as any good teacher should know his or her student.

The girl with the square-framed spectacles, long braids, and shy smile who worked doubly hard in class, the girl who'd aced the first test he'd given her at nine-eight percent even though she'd only had one week to catch up on six weeks' worth of school work, wouldn't hang around street corners with the wildest boys in school, would she?

Then again, what did he really know about teenage girls? He was hardly an expert on his own life. He hardly had his life together. How could he judge anyone else's?

"Let me go!"

He recognised the shaky protest as Lara's. She had to be in some sort of trouble. Without thinking, he switched off the engine and pushed the door open.

"What's going on here?" he asked in the authoritative voice he used with unruly students as he strode over to the group.

The boys stiffened and moved aside. Lara held her bag to her chest in a defensive posture but her head was bowed and she didn't meet his gaze. Her shoulders stiffened and hunched up, her braids loose over her face.

"Nothing, Mr. Thomas. I was just talking to my girlfriend," Malcolm said. He was a tall and athletic boy who was the captain of the school soccer team where he played as a midfielder.

Lara was dating Malcolm? The back of Ike's throat hurt and he felt as if he'd been punched in the gut. He had difficulty swallowing to clear his voice so his shock didn't seep through.

"Even so, you know the rules about hanging around after school hours," he said when he finally worked the shock down his throat. "You should all disperse immediately, or I'll be compelled to hand out detentions for the next two weeks and letters to your parents."

"We're sorry, sir." Most of the boys decanted immediately, walking away briskly.

Lara remained on the spot, her back to the wall, her gaze fixed to the dusty pavement.

"Lara, how are you getting home?" Ike asked, his voice with a sharp edge. He couldn't shake the bitterness lodged at the back of his throat that she would allow a boy like Malcolm to touch her.

She gave him a quick glance, pushing her glasses up the bridge of her nose, before diverting her gaze to ground again. “I’m taking the bus,” she replied in a small voice.

“Get in the car. I’ll drop you off home.” The tone of his voice indicated it wasn’t a request.

“Sir—" Malcolm was still there, although now at a little distance from Lara.

“Go home or it’s two weeks detention for you, Malcolm,” Ike cut him off. He’d lost his patience with the lad.

Without another word, the boy trudged away, his expression sullen.

Lara scurried to the passenger side and Ike waited for her to get in before doing the same. He instructed her to put her seat belt on before asking for her address. She complied. They drove in silence as his emotions yo-yoed from guilt to betrayal.

The protectiveness he’d felt for her from the first moment he’d walked into class to find her as his new student hadn’t just been out of a sense of duty or even platonic affection.

He hadn’t allowed himself to name the growing attraction he’d felt for her. He’d screwed up his life enough. And he wasn’t about to betray the trust she had in him as her teacher by ever suggesting anything more. At twenty-one, he was older by four years. Not to mention that she was his student and any involvement was prohibited both on ethical and moral grounds.

Now, finding out she was in a relationship with a boy, his heart shrank and he rubbed his hand on the back of his neck. He couldn’t help feeling betrayed, even if he knew it wasn’t fair. His heart didn’t seem to care that she was out of bounds to him and free to choose a boy closer to her age, anyway.

As they neared the street where her house was located, he was about to ask her which turning when he realised her body was shaking.

“Lara, are you okay?” he asked, glancing over at her.

Her head was turned towards the window as if she didn’t want him to see her face. She didn’t answer and her body continued to tremble. The muscles on his neck strained and his grip on the steering wheel tightened.

Had the boys done something to upset her? If so, he would get hold of each one of them and make them pay.

Flicking the indicator, he pulled over the side of the road and killed the engine. He reached down, unclipped his seatbelt, and twisted his body to face her.

"What's going on? Talk to me." He couldn't bear to see her upset but he was afraid of touching her for fear of crossing the line. He scrubbed a hand over his head instead of reaching for her like he wanted to.

"You're...angry...with me." She said the words between sniffs and sobs.

"What? I'm not angry with you." He couldn't believe she was upset because of him.

She peeked at him between her fingers and started crying again.

He heaved out a sigh, his fingers around the steering wheel tightened and loosened. "Okay. I am angry. But it's only because I'm worried about you getting involved with the likes of Malcolm."

He placed his hand on her shoulder, unable to resist trying to sooth away her sadness.

Before he could figure out what she was doing, she'd unclipped her seatbelt, turned around, and fallen against him, her head against his chest.

He kept his arms wide, unsure of what to do. His instincts screamed for him to draw her close, to soothe away her pain. But the sensible part of him warned that this was one of his students. The rules were clear about cavorting with students. If anyone saw them, he would be in trouble. And he couldn't afford any more.

She sucked in a deep breath and snuggled closer to him. His resistance crumbled and he allowed himself to settle his arms around her. He sucked in a deep breath. Her scent filled his nostrils: musk, sandalwood, and vanilla.

He remembered the first day he'd met her and she'd had a panic attack triggered by the sound of her drink bottle smashing on the floor. He'd recognised the fright in her demeanour, as well as the guilt in her anxious movements. It had been like watching a reflection of himself, a projection of his pain and sorrow. In that moment, he'd connected with her on a level he'd never done with anyone else before or since. He'd found his match. His soul twin. The yang to his yin.

He'd seen her at least twice a week for the past five months, excluding the holidays. After the school breaks, he'd had an accelerated pulse rate and adrenaline rush on the first day back to school. At the times, he'd told himself he'd been eager to get back to work and finish his assignment at Hillcrest. Deep down, he'd known the excitement had been for seeing her again after the weeks away.

Sweeping the braids away from her face with his fingers, he caressed the velvety skin on her cheek with his thumb. Strangely, he felt a sense of peace having her close as warmth radiated out from his chest.

For several minutes, they remained in the same position. The world around them continued revolving. It wasn't a busy street. The occasional car and pedestrian went by.

Someone would see them together. He should pull back. He didn't.

Finally, she extracted her body from his arms. He missed her warmth immediately.

"I'm sorry," she said and swiped hands over eyes.

He reached for the glove compartment and withdrew a box of disposable wipes. She pulled out a handful of tissues and cleaned up.

"Why are you sorry?" He searched her face. He wasn't sorry that he'd held her for the few precious minutes even if it would be the last time he ever did.

"I upset you and I didn't mean to. I won't do it again."

Curling one hand around the steering wheel, he pressed his lips together in a slight grimace. "What do you mean?"

She tilted her head and flicked her gaze away. "You're upset that I was with Malcolm. I won't see him again, if that's what you want."

His breath hitched at the temptation she unwittingly offered. Did she even know what she was saying? How much trouble that invitation could lead them into?

"Lara, look at me."

A smile wavered on her face as she looked up.

"This isn't about what I want," he continued. "You're an intelligent girl with a bright future. Boys like Malcolm are trouble. Trust me, I know. If you must date, there are other boys in your year, who should treat you better."

What the hell was he doing? Discouraging her away from one narcissistic teenage boy to a hormonal one? Did he seriously think that any boy in her year group wouldn't be thinking about sex and at least experimenting?

A frown puckered her face and she fiddled with one of her braids, twirling the end around her finger. "Malcolm says none of the boys in school will dare ask me out because I'm going to be his girlfriend sooner or later."

A cold finger travelled down his spine. "Malcolm said that?"

"Yes. I just thought there was no point in resisting him anymore. He'd been pestering me for so long. Today, he said he'd walk me to the bus stop. I agreed, but he brought his friends along with him. He was trying to get me to go over to his house when you showed up."

Ike's chest tingled as she spoke. This didn't sit right with him. Not just because he had feelings for her. He'd told himself he wouldn't act on those feelings, at least not while she was his student.

"Listen to me," he said in a sober voice. Feelings aside, she remained an innocent young girl. "Some boys are like wild animals when they're in groups. They push and dare each other. They do things they wouldn't normally do as individuals. Don't put yourself in the position I saw you in this evening again, especially since you don't seem to know those boys very well. Do you understand?"

She frowned as if she had a question but answered, "Yes, sir."

"And if you have to date Malcolm—"

"No. I won't. I'm going to tell him that I don't want to be his girlfriend. I'll do it now." She pulled out her phone from her bag and started typing on the screen.

A smile tugged the corner of his lips. His heart drummed against his chest. He couldn't help the euphoria bubbling in his veins, but he resisted a fist pump.

Moreover, the victory should be for her determination. He admired her for it. The same perseverance she'd shown from the first day they'd met. She had given him strength on days when the weight of the work had threatened to drag him down.

"Done," she said and put her phone aside. "I just have to find a way of avoiding him, especially after late prep when there are less people around."

"I can drop you off home after late prep," he offered before he could stop himself.

Eyes going wide, a broad smile split her face. She reached across and brushed her fingers against his arm. "You will?"

Beneath the long sleeve of his shirt, his skin tingled where she'd touched him. His throat grew thick.

"Yes." He coughed to clear the lump. "Just on the days you are in school late."

"Of course. Thank you, sir," she gushed.

"You're welcome." The dreamy expression on her large pupils and the steady eye contact told him she was translating his offer as more than it was. He had to maintain the line between them. "You realise I'm just helping you out, right. It's nothing more."

Her smile didn't waver. In fact, it looked like she knew something he didn't. "Of course I understand. You're my teacher."

"Exactly." The word came out more vehemently than he'd wanted.

Eyes shuttered, she lowered her head. Her throat rippled as she swallowed, and her shoulders slumped.

He registered her disappointment and his gut hollowed out. It had to be this way. Her future was at stake, as well as his.

The sky was a mix of purples and oranges as the sun set below the roof tops of the residential houses on the street. As much as he enjoyed her company, he needed to get her home.

"Lara—"

"I know you're my teacher and that nothing can happen between us while I'm at Hillcrest. But don't pretend as if there's nothing between us."

Her directness knocked the breath out of him. For a moment, he just gaped at her as his heart did a jackhammer against his ribs.

"There's nothing between us," he said when he finally worked saliva into his mouth. The lie left a bitter taste but he had no other option.

"Liar." She turned on him, her eyes blazing. "From the moment you came to my rescue the day I had a panic attack, there's been a connection between us. It's been there in every word you've said to me, every instruction you've given, every smile we've exchanged. It's grown steadily."

Rubbing his ear, he opened his mouth and closed it. Everything she'd just said was true. He'd felt their bond strengthen over the past months. But it still didn't make it right.

"Don't you see that what you're describing can't be encouraged?" he asked finally, a heaviness settling over his body. He didn't want to hurt her, but what she was asking for was crossing the line.

"I know what the rules say. I'm not asking you to treat me any differently from the other students or to start taking me out on dates. I just want you to admit to me here and now that you feel something for me. I just want to feel special, to feel wanted. Is that too much to ask?"

His chest tightened and his headache returned. He massaged his temples and shook his head.

"You're asking for too much. I can't do what you want." How could he admit that he'd thought about her as someone other than his student? He'd pictured a future with her in his weak moments. What kind of immoral person did that make him?

"You can't or you won't." She waved her hand. "Anyway, its fine. It's just one more thing to add to what makes me feel shitty about myself. There goes the crazy girl who has a thing for a teacher who doesn't want her in return."

She grabbed her bag. "Thank you for giving me a lift, but I can walk home from here."

"Lara, wait."

She ignored him and reached for the door lever.

Reaching out, he grabbed her arm. He understood her anger but he couldn't let he leave without resolving this issue.

Turning, she glared up at his face and down to where he held her arm. "Are you sure you should be touching your student like this, Mr Thomas? Aren't you afraid someone will see us?"

Her goading rankled. Nose flaring, he released her. "Cut the nonsense, Lara, and don't you dare leave this car until I drop you in front of your house."

He still had authority over her even if he'd dropped a few levels because of their disagreement.

She huffed, dumped her bag on her lap, and crossed her arms over it.

Puffing out a breath, he scrubbed his hand on his head. "Lara, you are a special girl. You're intelligent and I really see a wonderful future for you. But you're not eighteen yet and I'm twenty-one. I'm the adult here and I'm also your teacher. There's nothing between us. Now, I'm going to take you home and we're not going to discuss this topic again. Understood?"

Her gaze darted to him, her eyes over bright.

"But I love you, sir," she replied in a shaky voice before she turned away to stare straight ahead out of the windscreen.

His breath hitched. Tightness returned to his chest and his stomach sank. Tilting his head back on the rest, he closed his eyes. It would've taken a lot for her to make that confession. His admiration for her racked up a notch as the urge to pull her into a hug fired in his veins along with the desire to kiss her and confess his true feelings for her.

Don't be reckless. Think of the consequences. An image of his brother cautioning him loomed large in his mind. His brother had always been the sensible of the two of them. If Ike had listened and complied with the advices, his brother wouldn't be dead now.

Puffing out a resigned breath, he opened his eyes. Instead of responding to her declaration, he turned the ignition and the car kicked to life. As he indicated, checked his mirrors, and pulled into the lane, numbness settled over him.

He'd have to break her heart. It was the only way to save her.

THREE

Lara stared at her hands as the back of her throat burned.

What had she done? Propositioning her teacher had to be the most idiotic thing she'd ever done.

To have him reject her even so politely had to be the most embarrassing of all. How was she going to look him in the face tomorrow during the lesson? She couldn't bring herself to look him in the face now.

She'd worked it out, figured since the first day something had been brewing between them. She could've staked her life on it.

See where the stupid gamble would've gotten her. Dead.

She wished she was dead right now. It had to be better than having to face him again.

She twisted her watch and her foot bounced against the mat on the floor of the car.

What had possessed her to just come out and say it? She'd known coming out with her feelings would be asking for trouble. Students and teachers were not allowed to get involved in a relationship. And throughout the months since she'd met him, he'd never behaved overtly in any way that would make anyone think he felt anything more for her than any other student.

But there had been moments, fleeting as they were, and perhaps more her imagination at the time, when she'd thought there must be more to both of them.

He didn't give her any special treatment in class. But she still remembered her first week when he'd committed half an hour of his free lunch time everyday to teaching her so she could catch up on her school work. She'd scored quite high in the test and she had him to be thankful for it. No other teacher had given her that special dispensation.

Then, there was his age. At twenty-one, he was closer to her age than she'd originally thought. He dressed formally in school, always in a smart shirt and trousers, sometimes with a tie and suit jacket. So the outfit made him look older and authoritative.

She'd found out he was actually a university student on a one-year internship. She would be in university next year when he would be doing his final year. There, they could date. So what would be so wrong with starting a year early? That had been eating at her and it was what pushed her into this revelation here, at this moment.

Now, she couldn't bring herself to look up at him. It had seemed so logical when she'd thought of it. Still, reality proved to be something else. She had overstepped the boundaries, and he was probably angry with her again.

"Lara," he said in a gentle voice.

She froze but didn't look up at him, afraid of what she'd see in his eyes.

"Look at me."

When he spoke so sternly, she couldn't help but respond. She lifted her gaze to his. In the dim car with only the street lamps permeating it, his expression was dark and intense. But he didn't look angry. She exhaled a breath.

"I...I understand that you know how you feel. Your feelings are valid to you and I can't tell you how to feel." He took a deep breath and exhaled. "There can't be anything between us. Surely, you understand that."

His car had the AC humming but sweat still dripped down her back and between her breasts, plastering the white cotton school shirt to her slick skin. Her fingers drummed against her bag as her desperation took over. "Sir, why?"

She was acting like a stupid despondent person but she couldn't help it. His words couldn't be clearer. But surely, his action proved otherwise; coming to her rescue with Malcolm and telling her about his nightmares. They must've meant something.

"The fact that you're addressing me as sir is reason enough. It implies that we're not equals. That I have authority over you. That I can take advantage of you."

She turned to him, hands fluttering, clinging onto this last verge of hope. "But you've never taken advantage of me. You've always taken care of me."

"Lara, it's my job to do so. I've never treated you any differently from the way I treat other students, and I can't treat you any differently now."

She rubbed the back of her neck. "Sir, I'm not asking you to treat me differently. I'm just asking you to love me."

He was the only person she'd connected with in months. This whole school year. Yes, she got on well with Ada. But the girl was the picture of perfection. Perfect home. Perfect parents. Perfect life. Lara sometimes felt inadequate in comparison.

With Mr. Thomas, she knew he wasn't perfect. Knew he hid his troubles beneath the confident exterior. Just like she did.

"Can't you see what you're asking for is too much? Do you even understand what a relationship with me involves? Have you ever had sex?"

Her face heated up and she looked away. She remained a virgin. Was this the reason he rejected her? Did he want a more experienced girl? From the moment she'd fallen for him in her classroom that cool October lunchtime, she'd decided to save herself for him. Would he send her away because of it?

"I haven't. I want you to be my first," she muttered as her body trembled. "I'd never thought about sex, never thought about being with anyone in that way until I met you. You make me feel things I can't explain."

His breath hitched and his grip on the steering wheel showed tight knuckles. The car slowed and stopped. She glanced out of the window. They'd parked alongside the wall surrounding her house.

He tipped his head back and closed his eyes, puffing out a heavy breath.

Her heartbeats became stronger and the sound of whooshing blood seemed loud in her ears. He was going to send her out of the car and leave her hanging. She wanted to climb above the console separating them onto his lap and cling onto him, begging him until he relented.

Opening his eyes, he turned to face her.

Her breath caught in her throat. Her mouth dried out at the consuming expression on his face. It was like that brief glimpse of the tortured boy she'd seen months ago.

This time, his eyes shone as if a light had been kindled behind his irises and his pupils appeared blown out. Leaning forward, he reached across and cupped her cheek, his palm warm and rough against her skin.

Her breath quickened as she pressed her face against his hand, relishing the tingles across her skin.

As he touched her skin, surely, he felt this same craving that vibrated through her body and threatened to drive her insane. Surely, he'd realised her feelings were genuine and he'd soon reciprocate it, sweeping her off her feet.

"This is a beautiful gift you are offering me. But I'm not worthy of it." He dropped his hand, leaving her bereft of his touch. "I don't love you."

His words cut through her like a knife.

"What? You don't mean it." He couldn't mean it. He was just trying to save her, surely.

She gripped his thigh as panic rose. She swallowed excessively, darted her gaze around the car and settled back on his face. *Oh, God. Let him not mean it.*

Her body felt like a dead weight and she couldn't bring herself to let go of him and open the door.

Grabbing her hands off his body, he raised them above her lap before releasing them. "Lara, you understand that what we just talked about can't go any further. You can't tell anyone about it."

A huge lump lodged in her throat and she couldn't speak. She wanted to scream that it was unfair. But she nodded. The tears in the back of her eyes built up. Not wanting him to see her cry again, she grabbed her bag, pushed the door open, and ran across the road to the house gate. She'd disgraced herself enough. She banged on it until the gateman opened. Tears poured down her face as she ran inside.

Lola was standing outside chatting on her phone. But she put it down briefly.

"Is that Mr. Thomas's car...?" She trailed off when she saw Lara tears. "What happened?" Lola asked, now looking worried.

Lara ignored her and walked into the house. Her aunt was already home and sitting in the living room. She called out. "Lara, is that you?"

Lara wiped her face with the back of her hand and cleared her throat. "Yes, Aunty. Good evening"

She took a step towards the stairs.

"Come here. Why are you home late?" her aunty asked.

Lara used the sleeve of her blazer to further wipe her tears so the woman wouldn't see before walking into the living room. "I had late Prep."

Judy glanced up at the wall clock.

"But you're not usually home this late even with late Prep." She turned around and scrutinised Lara's face. "Why are you crying?"

She stood up and walked over to Lara. "What's wrong?"

"Nothing," she replied, biting her lip and struggling not to burst into further tears.

Lola walked in. "It's not nothing, Aunty Judy. She was crying when she walked past me, and one of the teachers brought her home."

"Shut up!" Lara shouted at her sister.

"Don't shout at me! Is it not true? Didn't I see you coming out of Mr. Thomas's car?"

"Who is Mr. Thomas?" Judy asked.

"He's my Geography teacher," Lara replied, swaying her body as she clutched her bag close.

Judy's eyes narrowed. "Why is this Mr. Thomas bringing you home? What did he do to you?"

Fresh tears stung Lara's eyes as she remembered her conversation with her teacher.

"It's nothing." She turned around and ran up the stairs to her room and locked the door, flung herself on the bed, and cried for most of the night.

◆◆◆

In the morning, Judy raised the question of what had happened the previous evening. Lara explained that she'd been harassed by some male students and Mr. Thomas had driven her home to ensure her safety. She managed to convince her aunt there wasn't anything going on with the teacher. Judy bought her story. There wasn't any reason for her story not to be accepted. Lara had never misbehaved before.

For the first time in a long while, the thought of going to school had her dragging her feet and chewing her lips. As they neared the school premises, a film of sweat coated her skin even though Judy's car was cool from the AC.

The first lesson passed without trouble. School didn't scare her—just the thought of seeing Mr. Thomas in her Geography lesson later that afternoon.

Before lunch, she got called into the Principal's office. Mrs. Bello had come to get her.

Her stomach cramped and she twisted one of her braids around her fingers. Had Mr. Thomas reported her for misbehaving yesterday? He'd told her not to discuss it with anyone. Surely, he wouldn't tell on her, would he?

Oh, God, she shouldn't have said what she did to him. Now, she was going to be suspended or even thrown out of school only days before her final exams would start.

The knot in her stomach tightened and she fought nausea. "Is everything all right, Mrs. B? Have I done something wrong?"

"No, my dear. Don't worry." The woman must have seen the apprehension etched on her face and reached out to settle a hand on Lara's shoulder.

She tried to push any panicky thoughts out of her mind. Mr. Thomas wouldn't rat her out. Instinct said he wasn't that sort of person. At least, she hoped so.

The principal's office was a large white room with an oak desk. Mrs. Bello shut the door when they walked in.

"Come and sit down," Mr. Idowu, the Principal, said. He was a stern middle-aged man with salt and pepper hair and a booming voice. None of the students liked to be called into his office.

But from his expressionless face, Lara couldn't tell if she was in trouble or not. She sat on the edge of the chair he indicated and Mrs. Bello sat in the other one in front of the desk.

"It has come to my attention that there was an incident last night involving you and Malcolm Ibeh. Can you tell us what happened?"

Lara's chest tightened and her clenched palms turned clammy. She darted her gaze at Mrs. Bello who nodded with an encouraging smile. Swallowing hard, she narrated what had happened when she'd left the school premises, how Malcolm and his friends had surrounded her, and how Mr. Thomas had come to her rescue sending the boys away.

"Then what happened after you got into Mr. Thomas's car?" Mr. Idowu asked.

Lara bit her lip. She couldn't possibly tell her them what had happened. She'd promised her teacher. "He drove me home, sir."

"He just drove you home? Nothing else happened?"

Lara averted her gaze and lied. "Nothing, sir."

Everything that had happened in the car had been instigated by her. If she confessed, she'd get into trouble. She couldn't ruin her life just because of some stupid crazy things she'd done because she was in love.

"Okay. That will be all. You can return to your class," Mr. Idowu said, waving her out.

Breath rushed out of her as she walked out of the office. It seemed that they'd bought her story. At least, this way, she hadn't gotten herself or Mr. Thomas in trouble.

The hallways were full of students. She glanced at her wrist watch. Lunch time. Although she'd lost her appetite while sitting in the principal's office, she headed towards the canteen. Most day students like her hung out there. The boarders sometimes headed back to the common rooms in their dormitories.

In the cafeteria, she spotted Lola sitting with a group of friends and waved at her. Her sister stood up and came to stand beside her in the line.

"Are you feeling okay?" Lola asked.

Lara nodded, thinking she was referring to last night. "Yes, I'm fine."

"Even after everything going on?" Lola gave her a sad smile and stroked her arm.

Lara narrowed her eyes and angled her body away. Her sister hardly ever spoke to her in school. She certainly never made body contact if possible. "Yes, of course. Why?"

Lola shrugged. "Just checking that my big sis is okay. Catch you later."

Lara's gaze followed her sister as she walked back to her friends. A smile tugged the corner of her mouth. So strange for Lola to be so concerned about her. From the first day they'd arrived at Hillcrest, Lola had made new friends and she'd never needed her big sister.

In fact, Lola was one of the popular girls in her year group, if not the whole school. She was fashionable and pretty. The boys wanted to date her and the girls wanted to be her friend. Lola was in the drama club and the music club and she played netball.

Lara couldn't act, sing, or play sports to save her life. But she was in the debate club and part of the school quiz team, so it wasn't all bad.

She got some yam pottage with fried plantain and found a table to sit at to eat. Not long after she sat down, Ada came to sit beside her.

"I've been looking for you everywhere," her friend said.

"Why?" Lara asked as she picked up a slice of friend plantain with her fork.

"There's a rumour going around school about you. Is it true?"

Lara stiffened and dropped her fork. "What rumour?"

"That you had sex with Malcolm Ibeh."

"What? Where did you hear that?"

"I heard Gloria talking to Christy and the rest of her friends in the ladies toilet. They didn't know I was in one of the cubicles."

The little appetite Lara had rescued vanished and she pushed her tray aside. "You don't believe them, do you?"

"Of course not, but that's not the worst bit. They also said you slept with Malcolm's friends, as well."

Lara's stomach rolled and she felt as if she was going to puke everything she'd just eaten. She snatched her bag and tray and dumped the half-eaten food in the bin before rushing off to the ladies.

What was Mr. Thomas going to think of her when he heard this ridiculous rumour? So this was why the Principal had called her in? They thought she'd had sex with the other students. Well, at least, her teacher was in the clear.

In the ladies', she waited until her nausea passed and she splashed some water onto her face. Ada met her in there.

"Are you feeling okay?" her friend asked.

"How am I going to cope with everyone looking at me as if I'm the school slut?"

"Well, you should ignore them all. You and I know you didn't do it, and anyone else who believes that you did is an idiot."

"No." How dare Malcolm do this to her because she'd broken up with him? She hadn't even kissed, let alone had sex. Lara rubbed a hand over her face as she paced the enclosed space. "I really can't let this go. It's my reputation on the line. I'm going to find Malcolm and make him take back the rumours he started."

"Are you sure?"

"Yes,"

"Okay. I'll come with you."

"Thank you."

They both went in search of Malcolm. Nose flaring, she held her chin up, daring any of the students they met to repeat the rumour to her face. Most of them avoided her gaze as she marched past.

Finding the rumour-monger proved difficult. Although Malcolm was in the same year as them, he was in a different class. They didn't find him in canteen or classrooms, so they headed for the playground. Still no Malcolm or his friends. However, they spotted Gloria with her friends, sitting on a bench.

Ada walked over to them and Lara trailed behind. "Have any of you seen Malcolm?"

"Was he so good that Lara wants round two with him?" Gloria snickered and her friends laughed.

Lara gasped and glared at the girls. "I never slept with him."

"That is a horrible thing to say," Ada snapped, stepping closer to the group and eye-balling Gloria. "We all know that is a lie and whoever started the rumours will pay for it."

"Are you calling me a liar?" Gloria retorted, tilted her nose up.

"If the shoe fits." Ada squared up to her, hands akimbo.

"I'll make you pay for that." Gloria bristled, the smugness wiped off her face.

"I'd like to see you try, Princess. One day, you'll get your just desserts for being such a bitch, and I hope I'm there to watch you fall from your tower."

"Look, it's enough, both of you." Christy, one of Gloria's friends, stepped in between them, raising her palms in each of their directions. "Malcolm is not in school. He's gone home on suspension."

"Really?" Ada asked in a shocked voice as Lara gasped.

"Yes," Christy said. "Apparently, he'd been in a fight with someone. Not sure whom. Anyway, he came out of the Principal's office with a bloody nose. We spoke to him and he said he's been suspended. But we didn't get the time to find out what had happened."

"Wow." Ada turned to Lara. "Karma was swift, wasn't it?"

"It sure was." Lara couldn't help the bemused smile as her friend wrapped an arm over her shoulders as they returned to their classroom. "At least he's not in school spreading lies about me, and I didn't even have to confront him."

At her desk, she slumped into her seat and blew out a shaky breath. She still had to deal with seeing Mr. Thomas in the next lesson.

The empty sensation returned to her belly as she took her book out and started reading it in preparation. She hoped they could move beyond what happened yesterday. Her birthday was coming up in a week's time. Then she'd be eighteen. Her exams would be done in a month and she'd no longer be his student. There would no longer be a barrier between them.

In the meantime, she had to find some time to speak to him after the class and make sure he understood the rumours were a lie. She wouldn't have sex with Malcolm if he was the only boy in school.

When the student at the door announced that the teacher was on the way, Lara brushed back her hair to make sure it was neat and sat up straight in her chair.

Mrs. Bello walked in and the class stood up and greeted her. Lara peered at the door, expecting Mr. Thomas to walk in, but he didn't. Was he running late?

"Good afternoon, class. I'll be your Geography teacher for the foreseeable future," Mrs. Bello said.

Jimoh raised his hand and the woman gave him permission to speak. "What about Mr. Thomas. Is he sick?"

"No. Mr. Thomas is not sick. He is unavailable at this time."

"Is it true, Mrs. B? Has he been suspended?"

Lara's head whipped back as she glared at Jimoh. What was he talking about? Mr. Thomas couldn't be suspended.

Mrs. B sighed. "Yes, Mr. Thomas has been suspended pending a disciplinary hearing."

Lara's heart fell into her stomach as murmuring passed through the class.

"Quieten down. I don't want you to worry about this," Mrs. B continued. "Mr. Thomas is a grown man and he can take care of himself. Now, what topic did you cover last time?"

One of the students answered and the lesson began. But Lara's mind drifted to everything that had happened today. The rumours in school, and the strange way the students had looked at her. Even her sister had come to talk to her when Lola never did before. And now, Mr. Thomas's suspension. It all had to do with her and what happened yesterday. It had to be. It was all her fault.

If she'd found a way to shake off Malcolm, Mr. Thomas wouldn't have needed to rescue her. If she hadn't gone into Mr. Thomas's car and confessed her feelings for him, he wouldn't be in trouble with the school authorities.

He hadn't done anything wrong. All he'd done was protect her, even when she was being ridiculous by confessing her love for him.

She should be the one suspended. She had to see him to apologise. She had to find a way to see him, but she didn't know where he lived.

One person could help her. She glanced in Jimoh's direction. He lifted his head and met her gaze with his brow cocked. She returned her gaze to her notebook.

After the lesson, she grabbed her things and cornered Jimoh in the hallway.

"I want to talk to you privately," she said.

"Follow me to my office," he said and swaggered off.

His 'office' turned out to be a secluded alcove between the buildings that backed onto the sports field.

"What can I do for you?" he asked, his back leaning on the wall and his hands shoved into his trouser pockets.

"I hear you're the man that can get anything," she said in a low voice.

"I am. I can get you whatever you want for the right price."

She leaned forward and whispered in his ear. "I want Mr. Thomas's home address."

Jimoh sucked in a sharp breath and jerked his head back. "That's going to cost you."

"How much?"

"Fifty thousand Naira."

"What? That's too high."

"Well, I'm the one taking the huge risk. If I get caught hacking into the school system, I'll get expelled."

"But I can't afford such a high price. Will you do it for twenty-five K?"

"Okay. I'll do it for twenty-five, but I want all the gist about Mr. Thomas when you see him."

She was so relieved he agreed that she just said, "Deal!" and they shook on it.

It took her about a couple of weeks to save up the first ten thousand that he wanted up front before he would get the information. She had to raid her savings and take it from the money she was given for transportation and lunch. She had to pack a sandwich from home instead of getting cooked lunch at school. And she walked home instead of taking the bus, although Lola paid her fare a couple of times.

Two weeks after Mr. Thomas's suspension, she still hadn't heard any news about him, and he wasn't back in school. Her birthday was in two days and her exams were scheduled to start in two weeks, and she really wanted to see him soon.

That evening, she got a text from Jimoh asking for her to bring the rest of the money into school the next day. She was so excited, she hardly slept.

As soon as she got to school, she sent Jimoh a text and they met up in the library. She gave him the money and he gave her a slip of paper. She tucked it into her pocket.

Throughout her lesson, she couldn't wait for it to be over, knowing that she was finally going to see Mr. Thomas again.

FOUR

"Mum, I understand what you're saying," Ike said into the phone braced between his ear and shoulder as he popped the cap off the bottle of beer he'd just taken out of the fridge. He tossed the opener onto the kitchen counter and the cap into the bin under the sink. "I'm sorry about the stress this is causing you and Dad."

A sigh escaped him. He seemed to be doing that a lot recently. Apologising to people. First, it had been Mrs. Bello, the woman who'd been his mentor since he'd started the placement at Hillcrest. Then to Mr. Idowu, the Principal, who had seemed so disappointed by what he'd done.

Now, he had to deal with his parents. At least, it proved some consolation that he didn't have to face his family yet. Their displeasure measured at a different level, considering his past transgressions.

He had screwed up. Again. And as his screw ups tended to be of monumental proportions, this time was turning out to be no different.

"I know you are, son." The sadness in his mother's voice twisted his gut. "Being kicked off your industrial placement is very bad. Is there nothing that can be done? Perhaps I should speak to the school principal."

He sucked in a deep breath and puffed it out. "I know you're trying to help me, Mum, but that's not a good idea. The parents of the student are insisting they don't want me teaching in the school anymore. They've threatened to sue the school if I go back."

His mother heaved a big sigh. "I can understand their perspective. If I were in their shoes, I'd probably do the same thing. So what are you going to do?"

He took the phone back into his hand and pressed his warm forehead against the cool wall. "I'm going to write the report of my experience during the past few months. Although I'm not due back at University for another couple of months for the presentation, there's no harm in getting the preparation done early."

"What about Hillcrest? Aren't they supposed to write a recommendation for you, as well?"

"Yes, I'm hoping they'll take into account all my efforts from the previous eight months I worked there. And not just what happened in the last one month." At least, that was what he hoped.

"I pray so," she said. "Are you sure you don't want to come to Lagos in the meantime?"

"No, Mum. I'll be fine here." He didn't want to face his father and his wrath. Not yet.

Thankfully, he had this apartment which he'd paid for two years. It came in handy because it was close to the university campus, so he could still live here next year. In the previous years, he'd shared digs with his friends.

Hopefully, by the time he got to see his parents face to face, he would've salvaged the mess of his life.

"Okay. You take care of yourself and call me if you need anything."

"I will. Thank you."

He cut the call after they bid farewell to each other. Leaning against the wall in his kitchen, he closed his eyes and took a swig from the bottle of beer.

Being kicked off the internship so late in the program year was bad. He wouldn't find another placement at such short notice. And if Hillcrest gave him a poor recommendation, it would impact on his degree program. That would be a year's worth of work down the drain.

He rubbed the back of his neck. He'd worked so damned hard at the job only to jeopardise it all in one crazy moment. One stupid mistake.

His fist curled in tight, fingers digging into his palm, the other hand tightening on the neck of the bottle as he remembered what's he'd done to Malcolm.

"Fuck!"

He opened his eyes and walked out, going towards the living room, and took another swig of beer. He didn't usually drink in the middle of the day. But this call to his parent had left him jittery.

With him halfway down the hallway, his doorbell rang.

"What now!" he griped. He really wasn't in the mood for company.

With stomping steps, he marched to the front entrance, turned the lock, and yanked it open.

His body stiffened and his eyes bulged at the sight before him, his senses pealing.

On the level landing, just outside his door, stood the sum of his misery and joy.

Lara.

He was so used to seeing her in the blue and white of the school uniform that, for a brief moment, he didn't recognise her.

Blood rushed in his veins as he took a step back and stared at her from head to toe.

Today, she wore a black tank top, a pair of navy skinny jeans, and black sandals. Her toenails were unvarnished although buffed to shine. He swept his gaze back up, taking in how her clothes hugged her body. She wasn't a skinny girl. Neither was she chubby. But the curves were in the right places.

He swallowed as his knees loosened, desire sparking in his gut, the temptation she presented all too real.

She wore no makeup. Perhaps a touch of gloss that enhanced the heart-shaped plumpness of her lips, making them luscious. But nothing marred her beautiful face. Her loose braids were swept over the left shoulder.

Overwhelming passion fuelled by her presence spread in his veins. He wanted to take the step and breach the gap dividing them. He wanted to take her face in his hands and seal their lips together. His grip on the handle tightened painfully.

The scrape of lock and key brought him back to earth. One of his neighbours would be out before long. They'd see her. She shouldn't be here.

Reaching across, he grabbed her arm and dragged her into his apartment before slamming the door.

"What the hell are you doing here?"

Even as he asked the question, he regretted his abrasive tone. His frustration still rode his blood.

She flinched, taking a step back, her head bowed. "I came to see you. I was worried about you."

"I'm fine. You shouldn't be here. I'm your—" he was going to say 'teacher,' but he couldn't use that term anymore as he didn't have a job any longer.

Turning, she paced four steps down the hall, swivelled, and came back to stand in front of him. Her chest lifted as she sucked in a breath and let it out in a rush. She lifted her gaze up to his face.

"I know I shouldn't. But I couldn't help it. After Mrs. B told us that you got suspended, I knew it had to be because of me." She gesticulated, hands jerking in the air. "So I had to come and see you. I promise you I didn't tell them what happened in the car between us. I swear I didn't."

Taking a step in her direction, he rested his palm on her shoulders to calm her agitated motions.

"I know." His palm scorched and he pulled his hand back. "I know you didn't tell the principal. I didn't get suspended because of you."

Well, at least not directly.

"Oh?" Her forehead creased in a frown. "So why did you get suspended?"

Good question. He didn't like talking about what he'd done. Grimacing, he scrubbed a hand over his face and spun on his heels, walking into the living room. He slumped on a sofa and took another swig of his beer.

She came in and stood beside the sofa opposite. Her gaze flitted across the room before settling on him. Her brows drew together and she twisted a single braid around her finger. She did that a lot when something worried her.

That he could be the source of her unease prickled his spine. He waved at the sofa. "You can sit down."

"Thank you." She walked around tentatively and sat on the edge. "Why did you get suspended, sir?"

His back stiffened. Why didn't he send her home straight away? The plea in her softened eyes made his heart clench, answering the question for him. He took another swig of his beer. "I punched Malcolm."

"You did what?"

The shock and accusation in her voice made his face burn. He closed his eyes. The scene with the boy resurfaced in his mind. His blood boiled.

"He'd been spreading lies about you. Saying he had sex with you." He opened his eyes and leaned his bent head forward against his palms so she couldn't see the shame on his face. "I'd heard some kids whispering about it and went in search of Malcolm. I invited him into a classroom to talk and he started mouthing off. I knew it was all lies and asked him to take it back and go and apologise to you, but he refused. I lost my temper and hit him. Then I dragged him to the Principal's office and reported him for assaulting you. He got suspended because you verified the story when Mr. Idowu questioned you. I got suspended because I struck a student."

She sucked in a sharp breath. "I'm so sorry. You're coming back to school, right? Malcolm is back to school. Why aren't you?"

He lifted his head and met her gaze. Her brows wrinkled and she bit her bottom lip. He'd seen the expression of concern a few times previously. He felt a constriction in his gut. He'd missed seeing her these past few weeks. He'd missed the gestures; the curl of her lips when she smiled, even the furrowing of her brows when she frowned.

"I'm not going back to Hillcrest. I've been sacked as a teacher."

"What?" Jerking back, her frown deepened and tears glassed her eyes. "They can't sack you."

Sighing, he finished the beer and placed the bottle on the small wooden table beside him. "Malcolm's father demanded they sack me. The school doesn't want to have a reputation of teachers assaulting students. They had to let me go."

Fat tears dropped down her face and her voice cracked. "It's not fair. You're the best teacher."

His chest ached. He couldn't stand to see her so upset. Before he knew what he was doing, he'd rounded the table and scooped her up onto his lap on the sofa.

"It's okay," he said softly as he held her close.

She pulled back and looked up into his face. "No, it's not. It's my fault you are in this position. If I hadn't given Malcolm the opportunity to start rumours about me, you wouldn't have been sacked."

His body stiffened. With his right hand, he pulled her glasses off her face. "Can you see me clearly?"

She looked confused for a moment, then nodded. "Yes. I can see things close to me. It's just the things far away that are a bit fuzzy."

"Good. I want you to understand that what Malcolm did was never your fault. Any decent boy or man should know that when a woman says no, it means no. Malcolm is a sociopath. He thinks he can do whatever he likes and get away with it. I simply should've controlled my temper better. Okay? I'm paying for my rash actions. I let all my students down by punching him."

She shook her head, sending her loose braids across his cheek. "No. You didn't let me down. None of the class members think you did a bad thing. We all miss you."

"I miss all of you, too." *You, especially.*

He stared at her face as his thumb stroked her smooth cheek. His heart felt as if it would punch a hole in his chest. The hairs on his arms and nape stood erect.

The last time he'd seen her, he'd denied the affection he had for her. Now, she sat on his lap, the most intimate contact they'd had so far, her warmth wrapping itself around him. She tilted her head up. She had beautiful amber eyes that flared with heat. Her mouth, so lush, so near.

Nights, even days, he'd dreamt about having her like this. Now, he couldn't resist bridging the gap that separated them and brushing their lips together.

The motion, just a caress, proved to be immensely more to his mind and body. Tingles spread through his flesh, longing erupting and spreading with the rush of blood in his veins. His heart thudded against his ribs. All the months, the mental struggles of asserting control, of keeping her apart, crumbled in the simple and powerful stroke.

"I shouldn't do this," he whispered, not pulling back "But I can't help myself."

She gave a small moan. Her hands crept up his chest, creating searing paths through the cotton of his t-shirt. Her movements were so tentative he could swear she'd never been held like this.

Leaning back, he lifted her chin with his fingers. "Have you been kissed before?"

Her lashes feathered her cheeks as she closed her eyes. "Yes, but not like you just did. I...Please kiss me again."

She lifted her lids. Her brown eyes shone bright with adoration and expectation, bringing him to his senses.

He slid off the sofa, dumping her on it, and turned his back to her. "You should go home."

"Sir?"

"I'm not your sir anymore." He froze. That one obstacle no longer existed. The one thing that had kept him in check and demanded he lived up to the respect and admiration of his students. Now, the risk of him ruining her increased with each minute she stayed. "Go home before I take away your innocence. Before I do what I shouldn't."

"It was my birthday last week."

Hesitant fingers feathered his back. Through the fabric of his t-shirt, he felt the burn. His breath caught as his knees jellied.

"Since you're not my teacher anymore, there's no reason we can't be together."

He squeezed his eyes shut. His hands clenched and unclenched at his sides. True. They had no more barriers, except for the ones that surrounded his soul.

When did you become spineless and afraid of living in the moment? Images of the reckless, conceited, and selfish boy he'd once been returned to taunt him. The one who drove carelessly, partied energetically, and fucked rigorously. The one who seized what was on offer with personal gratification in mind. The one who wouldn't turn his back on a woman unless he'd already satisfied his cravings.

Remember your promise. Every action bears a consequence. You are not that boy any more.

His older brother's image overtook the others from his past. His brother had been his voice of reason when he'd been alive. In death, he came back to sit as the angel on Ike's shoulder, when the devil in him tried to take over.

Dragging in a long breath, he puffed it out and opened his eyes. Her fingers still traced his back as if she were uncertain about what to do next. A more experienced girl would press close, making her need blatant. He should send her home for her lack of knowledge alone.

"I'm no good for you. No different from Malcolm. I'm not going to write you love letters and read poetry to you." A girl like her deserved such things. He just didn't do them. The things he wanted to do to her were dirty and naughty and, frankly, pornographic.

He turned around. She stood less than twenty centimetres apart. A little step and there would be no space between them. A little fumble and there would be no clothes separating them. His pounding pulse thundered in his ears.

"When I look at you, especially seeing you in that figure-hugging jeans and top, my body goes crazy and I can't think straight. I want to take all your clothes off and spread you on my sofa. I want to get inside you and cover you with my body. I want to surround you and permeate you. I want to devour you, so that I become you and you become me."

He stared down at her, his hands lifting and dropping by his sides as the intensity of his need threatened to consume him. She didn't look away, the soft flare of heat in her gaze showed her answering lust.

"Do you understand what I'm saying, Lara? The way I feel right now is too deep, too dark, and too intense for someone as young as you to deal with. You should be thinking about your upcoming exams, your results, and your future."

She took a step and closed the distance between them. Reaching out, she took his right hand and placed it on her chest above her left breast.

He squeezed his eyes shut and controlled his breathing, resisting the urge to cup the mound of flesh.

"Can you feel my heart racing?" she asked.

"Yes." The thud, thud, thud came through against his palm.

"It beats so fast because of you. For the past few weeks, I've been so distracted. I haven't been able to study or sleep properly. I've been thinking about you. I can't function without you in my life. I'm ready for you. I love you. Don't send me away again. Please."

He stroked his hand over the bare skin on her chest up to her neck. He laid his hand there, not gripping but loose and flat. Her pulse jumped under her skin.

"Are you sure of what you're saying?" He stroked his thumb across her bottom lip.

"Yes," she said in a breathy voice as her pupils dilated.

"We'll have sex if you stay. You won't be a virgin afterwards."

She shifted from one foot to the other. "I know. I want us to be together in every way."

She had an answer for all of his doubts, demolished the last of his restraint. The corner of his lips tilted in a lopsided grin as he curled his right hand around her nape. He'd always thought her to be intelligent and competent about her school work. Why did he think she'd be any different about her life choices?

"Lara..." He spoke her name with reverence as he wrapped his left hand around her back and pulled her into his arms. He kissed her, properly this time. Their lips fused, hers hesitant, although she clung to him, arms around his midriff. "Open your mouth. Let me in."

She did, parting her lips with a gasp. He swept in, tongue tracing the entrance, sampling her, preparing her, before plunging in. She tasted sweet—bubble gum and Lara.

His left hand slid down her side and cupped the globe of her bum, drawing her close so no space existed between them aside from their clothes. His right hand tangled with the plaits on her nape. He tilted her head back and angled his so he could deepen the kiss.

They both moaned into each other's mouths. Her grip on his shirt tightened as if she would slip to the ground if he let her go.

Passion burned his veins. Any more arguments he could come up with as to why they couldn't be together fizzled away. He broke the kiss, panting for breath, as did she.

He rested his forehead against hers.

"I care about you and I want you. But I can't make you any promises. My life is screwed up right now and I need to focus on getting it back on track."

"I know," she replied in a husky voice.

"And I want you to get the best results in your exams, so that should be your top priority. Promise me."

"Yes. I promise."

"Good." He loosened his grip on her. "Now, we have to talk about sex."

She frowned and dropped her hands, her gaze lowered. "Do we have to? Can't we just do it?"

He smiled. "No, we can't just do it. It's going to be your first time. I want to know what you know."

She pulled away and shrugged. "What's there to know? A man puts his penis inside a woman's vagina."

He burst out laughing. "This is not a biology lesson."

He took her hand and pulled her down on the sofa beside him. "When two people who care about each other have sex, it is more than a physical coupling. Sex becomes an expression of the way they feel about each other. It becomes about giving and receiving pleasure in the most intimate way, not just with their bodies, but with their minds, too. That's why some people refer to it as making love. That's why some wait until they're married. Don't you want to wait until you're married?"

She shook her head, distractedly. "No, I don't."

She sounded emphatic enough to convince him. He stroked a line with his fingers from her temple down to her neck, repeating the action until she shivered. "I don't just want to have sex with you. I want to make love to you. I want to give you so much pleasure that will make you addicted to me."

Her breath hitched. He held her gaze, watching the dark pupils blow out even more. She made him want to be a better person. The person she deserved.

FIVE

"I'm already addicted to you."

Lara didn't know what got into her whenever she was around this man, but her mouth just went loose and spouted whatever was in her mind.

Perhaps it was because she knew instinctively that he felt something similar.

The truth remained that she didn't think she could live without him. The past few weeks had been a ton of misery for her. She'd been honest when she'd said she couldn't sleep or study. Even eating had become a chore forced upon her by Judy, who was getting more worried by the day.

"And I could get so easily hooked on you," he said and kissed her with an intensity that blew her mind.

She writhed in his arms as his hands stroked her body. Then his hand was palming her breast through her bra and tweaking her nipple through the fabric. An arc of sensation ran from her breast down to between her legs. She moaned as her body arched. What was he doing to her? She felt like she was burning up. She'd never felt like this before.

He trailed his lips down her neck. Then, he was tugging her top strap down her arm, exposing her black bra.

He looked up and met her gaze. His eyes were so dark and intense, her breath caught in her throat.

"I'm going to suck your breast. Would you like that?"

He didn't need to ask her. She was happy to hand over her body to him. She nodded as her tongue seemed to be suddenly heavy in her mouth.

He tugged her bra down, pushing up the plump tissue of her left breast. His head lowered and his mouth covered the top flesh which he sucked in.

She moaned long and loud and arched her back and clutched at his shoulders. His tongue flicked over her nipple, licking and teasing while his hand slid down her belly to cup between her thighs. He stroked up and down the seam of her jeans and liquid heat converged in her panties. Just that simple stroke and she wanted to take all her clothes off and have him touch wherever he wanted.

He lifted his head. “Open your jeans. Let me touch you, please.”

Something squeezed at her heart. She hadn’t hidden the fact that she wanted him. Somebody else would take advantage. Malcolm had wanted to jump right in without permission. Even going as far as claiming that he had.

Instead, this man was still asking her permission to do what she’d already offered him. How could she not love him even more? With fingers that barely functioned, she fiddled with her zip and buttons until it lay open.

“Lift your bum.”

She did, and he pulled the denim down to her ankles. He reached down and stroked her through her white cotton panties. She rocked her hips, wanting more. He rubbed her again.

“Do you like me touching you?” he asked, his voice rough.

“Yes,” she replied as she breathed fast.

“How does it make you feel?”

“I feel good. So good.” She couldn’t describe the sensation fully. It was all so new. So foreign. Her body was burning up. Her breaths came in pants, as if she couldn’t get enough air into her lungs. “I...I...”

“Do you want to come?”

He watched her even as he kept touching her, as if assessing her response to him.

“Yes! I want to...come,” she breathed out. She’d never had an orgasm before.

“I can do that for you. Just tell me one thing.” He kept caressing, up and down, teasing her, driving her insane. “Are you my girl?”

“Yes.”

Stroke, up and down. Need flowed through her veins. She trashed about from left to right.

“You can’t let any of those boys in school touch you. Do you understand?”

“Yes.”

“Then, you’re my girl,” he said as he pressed down on the bundle of nerves hidden by her underwear.

Fever spread out from her sex down to her toes and up to her head. She keened and he kissed her then as she trashed about, succumbing to her first ever orgasm.

He held her until her body calmed and she became aware of her surroundings again. Then he pulled her jeans back up. She was a little too exhausted to protest or ask why he wasn't removing it totally. She knew what should come next, him taking his clothes off and filling her up.

But he seemed to be doing the opposite. He tidied up her top and bra, too, so she was looking composed again.

"My name is Ike, short for Ikenna."

Warmth spread across her chest that he'd told her. Still addressing him as Mr. Thomas would've been weird considering what just happened. Now, she felt as if he'd granted her access into his life and they were finally on the same footing. "You have such a great name."

"Thank you." He smiled at her but it wasn't a cocky, self-important grin. No, one side of his face dipped, as if he were saddened.

Her heart thudded. Had she said the wrong thing? She frowned and turned away.

"*Omalicham*." He cupped her face and turned her to face him. "Why is my girl frowning?"

"Why did you call me that?" she asked.

"Because you are my beautiful girl. I got sunshine on a cloudy day. When it's cold outside, I got the month of May. I guess you'd say, what can make you feel this way. My girl, talking about my girl. You remind me of an old song from The Temptations."

"Really?" She couldn't help the massive smile on her face.

"Really." He leaned down and brushed their lips together. "So why was my girl frowning?"

"I thought I said something or did something wrong. You were smiling sadly."

"I'm happy and sad."

She opened her mouth to talk but he placed his finger on her lips.

"You have such beautiful innocence and at the same time, you are bold and strong," he said. "Everything about you calls to me to claim you as mine. But at the same time, I'm worried about spoiling you when there are so many things unclear."

"But being with you feels right."

"It does. I enjoy your company and not seeing you the past few weeks hasn't been easy. I don't know. There's a part of me that feels this could end badly. I don't want to hurt you."

She didn't know what else to say and just leaned her head against his chest.

He scooped her closer and wrapped his hands around her. She listened to the strong thudding of his heart. His skin was warm and firm. In his arms, she felt safe, the worries of the past weeks wiped away, the peace of mind she'd lacked since the death of her parents now restored, perhaps temporarily.

He kissed the top of her head before leaning back. "By the way, how come you're not in school today?"

She looked up at him. "We don't have classes any more, just study periods for revision."

He glanced up at the wall clock. "So you're supposed to be studying right now?"

She nodded.

"And you're here? That's bad, Lara. I can't allow you to miss out on your study time."

"I can study later."

"No, you can't." He stood up. "Do you have any books in your bag?"

"Yes," she replied tentatively.

"Then go and sit at the table and do your work."

"Really? What about making love?"

"Not for you right now. Study first, sex later." He smiled and winked at her. "I'm going to cook lunch."

She grabbed her bag and walked over to the small dining table at the other end of the living room. "You're cooking?"

"Yeah. If I don't cook, I starve. Simple."

She chuckled as he walked away.

She took out her text book and study notes and managed to get into it within a few minutes. The subject she'd been struggling to absorb managed to sink in this time. Perhaps it was because her mind was more settled.

An hour later, the aromatic smell of whatever he was cooking had her stomach growling. She looked up from her books to find him leaning against the door post.

"How long have you been standing there?" she asked as she leaned against the back of the chair.

"A few minutes." He straightened up. "I enjoy watching you study. You have such an intensity that is mesmerising to see when your focus is on whatever you're reading."

She lowered her gaze. Her cheeks heated up.

He pulled out a chair next to her. "I've learned so much from you."

"You have?"

"Yes. I wished I was as studious as you when I was your age. I wouldn't have gotten into as much trouble as I did."

"What kind of trouble?"

"In those days, I was more interested in being popular and getting the girls than I was in studying. When it was time for my exams, my parents had to pay for a private tutor and I had to work doubly hard because they banned me from socialising until after my exams. It was a pain to have to study so hard in a short period of time. To be honest, it was sheer good fortune that I passed my exams."

"But you did well in your exams."

"Not as well as I could have if I'd focused all through the year. It's why I spend so much effort making sure each student understands the subject. I don't want any of them to struggle when it's time for exams."

She reached across and covered his hand on the table. "When I started this year, Geography was my least favourite elective. But I can tell you now, it's the subject I worry about the least. I could walk into the exam hall tomorrow and I'm sure I'll be fine. You laid a great foundation for all of us. Thank you."

"You're welcome." He settled his hand on her nape and pulled her in for a kiss.

She got lost in it, savouring his taste and his scent and the sensations he evoked within her body. She really couldn't wait to get more physical with him again.

"Now, for some food," he said when he broke away. "You can pack away the books for now and set the table."

"Okay." She piled her books together and moved them to the floor beside her bag in the corner. Then she went in search of Ike. A smile curled her lips thinking of him as Ike and not Mr. Thomas.

The kitchen was at the end of the short hallway. It wasn't a massive room, the maple-finished units set up in an L-shape along the wall with a black worktop. A sink sat under the window overlooking the rooftops of the other houses in the neighbourhood. His apartment was on the third floor of the building.

Ike stood by the cooker, stirring something in a pot. He pointed to a drawer. "The cutleries and place mats are over there."

She took out the items and set places for the two of them. He came out carrying two plates of boiled yam, egg stew with shredded cabbage and carrot coleslaw.

"What would you like to drink? There are drinks in the fridge. Just take whatever you want."

"Okay." She returned to the kitchen and grabbed a bottle of Fanta and found some glasses.

The square table had room for four. They both sat next to each other rather than opposite, which was how she'd set it up. She didn't want to be too far from him. She poured half the drink for him and half for her. She took a bite of the food and had to comment on how nice it was.

"You cook very well."

"My mother had two boys first before she had a girl. And she's always worked as long as I could remember. She and my father built the businesses together. Although we had house maids, she always made it clear to us that we needed to learn how to do chores for ourselves. My brother and I would help out in the kitchen with preparing the meals during the weekends. By the time we left home for university, we'd learnt how to cook most meals we ate at home."

"That's impressive. I'm not sure I can cook most things well, but I can cook the basics like rice and stew, egusi soup, yam, beans."

"That's a good start. You'll need the skill when you go to university, otherwise all your money will go on mamaput."

They both laughed and carried on eating.

"So you have a sister?"

"Yes, my baby sis, Ify. She's in Lagos with my parents. She's at IBS in Lekki."

"Wow. That's my old school. What year is she in? Perhaps I know her."

"She's in year 10."

"That's Lola's year. I'm sure Lola knows her. It's a small world, isn't it?"

"It sure is."

Lara stood up and packed up the empty dishes. She put them in the sink and started running the tap to wash up.

Ike came up behind her. “You don’t have to do that.”

“I should. You cooked the meal. It’s only fair that I wash up afterwards.”

“Okay.”

As she washed and rinsed, he dried the plates with the kitchen towel and put them back into the cupboard. When she finished and dried her hands, he covered her back with his body and kissed her neck.

She moaned softly and instinctively tilted her head, giving him more access. Her body warmed up as if he’d lit a fire within her. He kissed her one last time and lifted his head.

Sighing, she turned around. She really couldn’t wait any more.

“You said after I finish studying we could...you know...”

He stepped back. “About that, I’ve been thinking. Come with me.”

He took her hand. Heart pounding, she followed him, thinking they were headed for his bedroom. Instead, he took her back into the living room.

“So I’ve been thinking that I may have a solution that wouldn’t make me feel so bad for wanting you. We’re going to wait until after your exams. That way, you can concentrate on studying without distractions.”

“What? No!” Shaking her head, she crossed her arms across her chest. She’d been waiting for what seemed like forever to get this far with him. First, he’d denied wanting her. Then he’d confessed the intensity of his feelings. Now, he wanted to postpone having sex?

“Think of it this way, it’ll be our way of celebrating completing your finals and leaving high school.”

“No.” She squeezed her face and shook her head again. She couldn’t wait to feel the delicious sensations of orgasm. Remembering what he’d done to her made heat flash on her skin and her panties slick. He couldn’t just tease her and then tell her she had to wait.

“Think about it. It’ll be so much fun because we both waited, and a double celebration.”

She sighed heavily. When he put it like that, then it made sense. Would it be so bad to wait a couple of weeks? She’d waited this long already. Perhaps they could formally celebrate the start of their relationship at the same time and make plans for the future. "Okay."

Grinning, he caressed her right side, spreading tingles all over her body.

"Good girl. Now, you can come here. But just one day a week and we have to pre-arrange it so I make sure there's no one else visiting at the same time. Here—" he pulled his phone out of his pocket. "Give me your phone number."

She called out the numbers and he entered it on his phone. Her phone in her bag started ringing.

"That's me calling you so you can store my number," Ike said.

She walked over, picked up her backpack and took the phone out, saved his number, then heard the sound of someone turning a lock.

"Henry is back," Ike said.

SIX

"Man, you're walking on the wire with this one," Henry Coker said while dribbling the basketball in his left hand as he took steps towards Ike who stood in the defence position of the court.

"How do you mean?" Ike asked as he waited for his friend to make his move. Sweat dripped down his back, his mesh sports vest damp and clinging to his skin. The sun was low in the hazy sky but the heat of the day hadn't faded yet.

Ike couldn't wait any longer. He'd been waiting around too much. He'd finished working on his report. Still, he awaited the final decision from Hillcrest with regards to their recommendations about him.

Waiting was driving him crazy. He had so much energy to expend. Not going to work every day and dealing with highly-strung teenagers meant he wasn't burning off as much energy as before. And his libido was in excess as he hadn't had sex in months. Not since promising to wait for Lara. He hadn't touched another woman.

"This affair you're having with that girl—what's her name?" Henry dribbled to the left.

Ike moved to block him. "You mean Lara?"

His friend bounced the ball into his right and headed in that direction to bypass him. He leapt from the ground, released the ball so that it banked off the backboard and into the basket.

He turned around, grinned, and backed off. "Yeah, her. I wouldn't have made such an easy shot if you weren't distracted by her."

"Whatever." Ike picked up the ball and bounced it a couple of times. He watched his friend and calculated his moves to score a shot. A crossover dribble, euro step, and a lay-up wouldn't work since Henry had already used that move. Then again, Henry was probably thinking Ike wouldn't use it for the same reason.

"Seriously, man, hasn't she screwed up your life enough?"

His friend's words cut into his thoughts.

"You lost your job because of her. If the school finds out you're in a relationship with her, you can kiss your recommendation goodbye. You need that letter, man."

Ike straightened and sighed, holding the ball up in his right hand. "I know. But every time I think about letting her go, it's like I'm ripping out my own heart. I just can't do it."

Henry shook his head. "What have you done with my friend? Is she that great in the sack?"

Ike chuckled, bounced the ball off the floor between his legs, caught it with his left hand, paused, and lowered his voice. "If only. We're not having sex."

Henry stood there mouth agape and Ike took the opportunity. He powered up towards the basket in a jump shot. The ball curved high over Henry, who only reached up at the last minute, and descended into the basket.

Ike walked over to the bench and picked up the towel. He wiped his face and neck before reaching for the bottle of water, unscrewing the cap, and guzzling down half the contents.

Henry walked over to him with the ball in his hand. He dropped it on the ground beside the bench and picked up a bottle of water, too.

"You're not having sex? That's got to be a first," his friend said solemnly.

"Tell me about it."

"This is serious."

Ike shrugged. "I don't know what I'm doing. I know I shouldn't be with her. She's sweet and intelligent. Someone like her shouldn't be with someone like me."

"She's young. She should hang with her age mates. Boys her age."

Henry's words echoed his thoughts.

"Fuck!" Ike flung the empty bottle of water at the trash can. "Do you remember what we were like at that age? We fucked any girl that let us."

"Speak for yourself."

"You know what I mean. It was all about fun. It wasn't about serious relationships. And we weren't even that good at it. More like fumbling and spilling than anything else."

"As I said, speak for yourself." Henry grinned as he wiped his face with a black towel.

A grin tugged at the corner of Ike's lips but he couldn't give in to his friend's ribbing. "Anyway, the thought of any of those boys doing that to her just makes me want to hit something." Which was why he'd hit a student in the first place. "Her first time should be special for all the right reasons. She shouldn't have idiots like Malcolm Ibeh introducing her to sex."

"Malcolm is the boy you punched, right?"

"Right."

"Well, if she's as intelligent as you say, then perhaps, she wants to wait a while before she has sex." His friend tossed his empty bottle into the bin.

"Oh, you don't know her. She's headstrong and knows what she wants. She wants sex. And trust me, she'll do it soon. With or without me." And didn't that idea just make his gut congeal.

"Hmmm. I still say you're playing with your future and not in a good way. Any more screw ups and your father will go ape shit."

"Yeah. I know. I'll be careful." Nothing else he could do short of cutting Lara off. "Anyway, let's go clean up and then we're going out. We haven't hit the town in so long."

They packed up the items they'd brought downstairs for the game and headed to the main entrance of the apartment block. The building was located in a large estate. The sport courts, basketball and tennis, were at the back. A soft play area was located at the side with a slide, climbing frame, and swings for children. The front housed the parking slots for the ten apartments and visitors, all in a walled and gated complex.

The apartments were priced higher than a normal student could afford. But Ike had negotiated the expense with his parents as part of the terms of his placement. He couldn't stay in students digs during his internship year.

Henry had been his friend since their high school days. His friend's family background was totally different from his. But they'd become fast friends once they'd bonded in school. In their first two years at university, they'd shared digs. So when Ike got the apartment, he still wanted to have his friend close. But Henry couldn't afford even half the rent but he insisted on paying his way with everything else. He paid the utilities bills and shopped for groceries.

Ike stopped as he rounded the corner to the front door. Mrs. Bello was stepping out of her car.

"That's one of the teachers from Hillcrest," he said to Henry. "Please take my stuff up. I'll see what she wants."

"Okay. I'll see you upstairs. I'm going to grab a shower."

Ike wiped the sweat on his neck and shoulders as he walked over to the woman he hadn't seen for a few weeks. "Good evening, Mrs. Bello. Are you visiting someone in the building?"

"Hi, Mr. Thomas." She beamed a smile at him. "I came to see you."

"Oh, okay. Come on upstairs."

"No," she said, her keys in her hand but the car door not locked. "Can we talk in my car?"

Grimacing, he stared down at his body. "I've just been playing basketball and I'm all sweaty. I don't want to mess up your car."

She waved her hand dismissively, pulled the door open, and got into the driver's seat. "Don't worry about that. I won't be long."

"Of course." He nodded and walked around to the other side and got in, too. If she didn't mind, why should he?

When he shut the door, she turned on the engine and the AC hummed. Cool air on his hot skin, bliss.

"What did you want to talk to me about?" he asked, feeling a little edge and that something must be wrong for her to drive out to see him.

She turned sideways to face him. "I have good news about your final recommendation letter. I was speaking to Mr. Idowu and managed to convince him that we shouldn't mention the incident with Malcolm Ibeh in there."

Ike closed his eyes and tipped his head forward as he sucked in a deep breath and puffed it out. Leaning back, he opened his eyes. "Thank you so much. I can't tell you how much of a relief it is to hear this."

At last, perhaps his luck was turning.

"Yes, I figured you'd want to know the good news."

Mrs. Bello smiled but it wasn't the full beaming smile he was used to receiving from her. Something sad darkened her face.

"Something else came up," she continued.

His heart thudded in his chest and he just stared at her because he couldn't bring himself to ask the question. What?

She looked away, her gaze fixed at some point outside the windshield. "One of the teachers mentioned to me that she's seen Lara Johnson in your car twice driving past her house. I did a quick investigation and also found out that on those days she mentioned, Lara was not in attendance in school."

She paused, as if to give Ike the chance to absorb his words.

He couldn't even look her in the eyes even if she was looking at him. His stomach rolled and sweat beaded his forehead although the car interior was cool.

Shit. Shit. Shit. He should've known that it was possible for him to be seen together with Lara. His car was very distinctive. Not many people drove a Toyota GT Primo Sports and certainly not in his colour. But he always dropped her back home every time she came to his to make sure she got home safely.

He swallowed several times as he awaited the dreaded outcome of this conversation. The loss of everything he'd worked hard for these past years.

"While I don't want to jump to conclusions as to why a student would be in your car, there is very little I can come up with to explain it. I need to stress that it is inappropriate for teachers to socialise with students. It is easy for simple gestures to be misconstrued.

"I'm not saying that you've done anything wrong. But I will have to insist that you stop associating with Lara or any other student of Hillcrest. I know you're no longer a staff at the school. But I still have to write the recommendation. My reputation is at stake and I won't make the recommendation unless I can get your guarantee that you will have no contact with Lara."

"Mrs. Bello. I..." He trailed off as he couldn't get himself to say the words.

Could he really promise that he would never see Lara again? On the other hand, he knew a threat when he heard it, and Mrs. Bello was threatening to ruin his future if he didn't promise her to keep away from Lara.

"Look, I'm not trying to be difficult or mean," she said when he didn't speak for a while. "I understand what it is to be a young person. Everything seems more urgent than it is. People can make mistakes. But you see, I'm a mother. These students are like my children. Their welfare is very important to me. I want to ensure that when they leave Hillcrest, they leave in a good frame of mind. Lara is a young girl with a bright future. I don't want anything that would derail that future."

The implication that he could ruin Lara's future didn't escape him. He hadn't really thought about it that way. At this age of her life, ruining her meant getting her pregnant. What if they had sex as they'd been planning to after her exams and she got pregnant? What would that do to Lara? Of course, he'd planned to use precaution as he always did, but there were never any guarantees. The only guarantee was abstinence. The only guarantee was to keep away from Lara.

His heart hurt and he heaved a sigh. He had to do the right thing for Lara's sake. "I understand, Mrs. Bello. I promise to keep away from the Hillcrest students."

"Good. I'm glad you understand." She puffed out air as if she'd been holding her breath.

Ike opened the car door and paused. "Gloria Rawlins is a close family friend and her parents expect me to watch over her."

"I'm aware of your existing relationship with Gloria's family, so she's exempted. She's a boarder, anyway, and isn't permitted out of school until the end of her exams."

The knot in his stomach tightened. He didn't miss the skewed message she delivered. He could socialise with Gloria because her parents approved it. But he couldn't socialise with any other student. He suspected the woman didn't want him having a relationship with Lara. Period.

The old him would argue that as he no longer stood as their teacher and as long as they were legal, he could do whatever he liked. Or he'd give her a fake smile and nod but the minute she left, he'd stick his middle finger up in a rude gesture and do whatever he liked.

The old him had died with his brother. The new him nodded, stepped out, and spoke politely. "Thanks for stopping by."

"No problem. See you in a few weeks at your presentation."

He didn't stay to watch the car reverse out of the spot. Instead, he headed inside and up the stairs. His feet felt like they were weighted with lead, each step heavy, and his body felt as if it would crumple in on itself. He opened the door to his apartment, walked in, shut it, and leaned against the wooden slab. Slowly, his legs gave out on him and he slumped to the cool tiles on the floor, holding his head in his hands.

A small creak announced a door opening. Henry stepped out of his room wearing a pair of blue shorts. As soon as he saw Ike on the floor, he hurried over.

"What happened?" Water drops glistened on his friend's head and shoulders.

"I've been banned from associating with students of Hillcrest."

"Shit," Henry exclaimed and sat down on the floor in front of Ike. "How did that happen?"

Ike told his friend about his conversation with Mrs. Bello, expecting his friend to say 'I told you so' at the end.

Instead, Henry placed his hand on Ike's shoulder. "I feel your pain. What are you going to do?"

Ike scrubbed his face. "I have no other choice. I can't see her again. I have to end it."

The phone in his shorts rang and he pulled it out of the pocket. "Speak of the devil. It's Lara. What am I going to say to her?"

"Just tell her it's over. That you guys can't see each other anymore."

"But that will mess her up. She still has exams to complete. I will never forgive myself if she fails her finals because of me."

"Okay." Henry snatched the phone off his hand.

"What are you doing?" Ike sat up straight.

"Let me deal with this," Henry said before pressing the button to answer the call and turned on the speaker. "Hi, this is Henry."

"Oh, Henry. Hi." There was a pause on the line as she sucked in a breath. "Can I speak to Ike, please?"

"He is busy right now. I'll let him know you called and he'll call you back."

"O...kay. I'll talk to him later. Thank you."

"Bye," he said.

"Bye." She hung up.

Henry handed the phone back to Ike. "You're just going to have to avoid her until her exams are done."

***

Lara's foot drummed against the floor of the bus as she rode it the few stops from her house to Ike's. Excitement made her body tremble.

She'd finished her last examination paper yesterday. So she was officially free. Free from high school. Free to date Ike openly.

They'd seen each other whenever possible these past few weeks. Although he made her use most of the time to study, she was still glad that she'd had his company. He'd helped her out when she'd gotten stuck with any subject. Before each exam, he'd sent her a short message wishing her the best.

Now, she couldn't wait to take their relationship to the next level. She planned to surprise him so she hadn't informed him that she would be at his soon. But they'd agreed previously that once her exams were over, there wouldn't be any reasons why she couldn't go to his whenever she was free.

She hadn't seen him for a couple of weeks so she couldn't wait to see him again.

"Good afternoon, oga gateman," she greeted the man who guarded the entrance.

"Welcome." He waved her in.

She walked down the long drive but stopped in her tracks as she saw Ike coming out of his building. With him was a girl she didn't recognise at first. The girl was leaning against him and they were talking in low tones that seemed way too intimate from where she stood.

Lara's heart stopped and her legs became sluggish as she got closer. Another person joined them. Henry, his flat mate.

"Ike," she called out but her voice came out so low, she wasn't sure if he heard her.

Ike looked up and saw her. His expression registered surprise. He extracted himself from the girl whom she now saw was Gloria Rawlins and came towards her.

"Lara, you should've called me before coming over. I'm on my way out."

"I called you several times but you didn't return my calls." She glanced over at Gloria who was staring at her with the usual malice.

Ike pulled her aside. He scrubbed a hand over his face before he spoke. "I'm sorry about that. The thing is, we can't see each other anymore."

"Why?" She glanced at Gloria.

"We just can't."

More distracted with the fact that Gloria was here, she didn't fully absorb his words.

"What is Gloria Rawlins doing here?"

"She's my friend."

"She's your..." Suddenly, the penny dropped and she stared up at Ike. "You are breaking up with me."

He just stared at her with a distant look in his eyes and his voice sounded flat. "I'm sorry."

"You're sorry?" Her gut rolled and she doubled over as she grew sick.

"Are you okay?" he asked, sounding concerned as he reached for her.

"Don't touch me!" She flinched away from his touch.

She'd been such a fool. How could she not have seen this? She'd been so consumed by him that she hadn't seen that he could have any other girl in their school. She wasn't anything special. But Gloria was pretty and popular. Why wouldn't he want her?

Tears burned the back of her eyes and her throat hurt.

She glared at him and then at Gloria. "I hate you!"

She stumbled backwards, turned, and ran towards the gates. Tears fell down her face as she walked on the street. Her vision blurred as her lenses clouded. She pulled the frame off her face and swiped her eyes. Half-stumbling, half-walking, she didn't know how far she walked until she felt the presence of a car beside her and someone called out her name.

She wiped her face again and glanced back with a squint since she didn't have her glasses on to find Malcolm sauntering towards her. She didn't want to talk to him. So she continued walking.

"Hey, Lara," he called out. She could hear his quickened footsteps behind her. "I just want to talk."

SEVEN

Lara didn't stop. Her heart ached and her shoulder slumped as if she carried the weight of the world. She wanted to go crawl into a hole and cry for the next year. She didn't want to talk to anyone, least of all Malcolm.

"Malcolm, leave me alone," she said in a choked voice.

"I'm so sorry, Lara. I really am. Please, just talk to me." His voice sounded pained, as if he were genuinely sorry for the things he'd done in the past.

She stopped walking and clutched her bag to her chest, her head lowered.

Malcolm caught up and came to stand in front of her. "Thank you for stopping. I was just driving past and saw you. I wanted to say that I'm really sorry for all the things I did in the past. I know I was an asshole and you probably would never forgive me. But I'd be grateful if you could."

Lara sucked in a deep breath and blew it out. "I forgive you, Malcolm."

She did. She hadn't thought about him in weeks, anyway. Right now, she had a bigger sorrow to deal with.

"Thank you so much," he said and came closer. "Are you crying? What happened?"

She shook her head. Tears smarted her eyes as the pain of breaking up with Ike crashed over her. "It's nothing."

"Don't say that. You're upset. Did someone do something to you?" He placed his hand on her arm, the tone of his voice concerned.

Perhaps it was just hearing him sound so worried about her when she'd never thought he could be so kind—she broke down in sobs as she spoke. "It's Ike."

"Who is Ike?" he asked gently. "What did he do to you?"

She realised he probably didn't know Ike was Mr. Thomas. She didn't even know his first name until a few weeks ago. But she didn't clarify. Probably best if Malcolm didn't know. "He's my boyfriend. He broke up with me."

"Oh, I'm sorry. Is there anything I can do?"

She shook her head and pressed the heel of her right hand to her eyes. She wiped her glasses against her top before wearing them again. "No. I just want to go home."

"Okay. I'll take you home."

"No. Don't worry."

"I can't let you go home in this state. Let me take you, please. I promise I'll drive you straight home."

She didn't have any energy to argue with him, so she sighed and nodded. Perhaps if she let him take her home, she would get there sooner and have some peace and quiet all to herself. "Okay."

He took her arm and led to the car. It was a small, red, 2-door VW Golf hatchback. He opened the door and helped her in. Then he got in the other side. Lara noted that he was being very nice, much nicer than he'd been to her at the start of the school year. She gave him her address and he drove her straight home. She'd been expecting him to start asking her out like he used to, but he didn't say anything all the way until they got to the front of her house.

"Thank you," she said as she unlocked the door.

"You're welcome," he said. "Take care of yourself."

She was so shocked that Malcolm had been so nice to her without even asking for anything in return. But it didn't take away from her sadness.

Luckily, there was no one home when she arrived. She went straight upstairs to her bedroom and stayed there for the rest of the day.

Each time her phone buzzed, she rushed to pick it up, only to toss it aside when it wasn't Ike calling or texting her. She hoped he would call and tell her it had been a mistake or just a moment of madness. That he wasn't breaking up with her.

Two days later, Lara and Lola were sitting out on the terrace when a visitor arrived. Lara was shocked to see Malcolm walking through the pedestrian gate after the guard opened it.

"What's he doing here?" Lola asked.

"I don't know," Lara replied as she stood up.

Malcolm was carrying a small shopping bag from a popular eatery in the neighbourhood. He came up to them.

"Hi, Lara. How are you doing?" he said, smiling at her.

"I'm okay, thanks. What are you doing here?" she asked.

"I came to see how you were doing. After the other day, I was worried about you. And since I don't have your phone number, I thought I should pop by and see how you are coping."

She was still wary of him. Of men in general. But this caring Malcolm was different from the arrogant boy she'd known in school. Perhaps finally graduating from high school had matured him.

"Thank you for coming by, but I'm okay. You don't need to worry."

"Okay. That's good." He smiled. "Here, I brought this for you." He held out the bag in her direction.

"What is it?"

"It's meat pie and some soft drinks."

"You didn't have to buy anything for me," she said, not reaching for the bag.

"I know. But I went out to buy some snacks for my mum. I drove past your house on the way to the restaurant and I thought about you. So I decided to buy some for you."

Wow. Malcolm was thinking about her, enough to buy something for her? She was speechless for a moment.

"That's really nice of you," Lola said and took the bag from him.

"Thank you," Lara said when she found her voice.

"No problem. Enjoy it. I have to go now. My mum is waiting for her food."

"Okay," she said but didn't move towards him.

Lola nudged her.

"See him off," her sister said in a low voice.

Lara pushed her hand off but followed Malcolm down the drive. At the gate, she bid him farewell and he did the same.

She returned to Lola who was peeking into the bag and taking out the snack.

"What's going on with Malcolm?"

She shrugged and sat down. "Nothing."

"Don't give me that. You guys were squabbling in school and he was spreading nasty lies about you. All of a sudden, he's coming to our house and bringing you meat pie."

Lara puffed out a deep breath. "Malcolm and I have settled our differences. It turns out he can be very nice when he wants to be."

"Really? Just like that?"

"Yes. Just like that."

"So what did he mean by what happened the other day?" Lola took a sip of lemonade.

"I don't want to talk about it."

"Come on. You've got to tell me. You know I won't stop nagging you until you tell me."

"Okay, if I tell, you have to promise not to tell anyone, including Aunty Judy. Promise me."

"Sure, I promise," Lola said.

Lara swallowed. "I had a boyfriend and he broke up with me on Thursday. I was crying when Malcolm found me. He was so nice to me and he brought me home."

Tears welled up in her eyes again. The pain hadn't gone away no matter how much she tried not to think about it.

"Oh, no." Lola stood from her chair and came over and hugged her. "I'm so sorry."

It felt so good to have someone to hug her. Malcolm had tried but she hadn't allowed him to touch her. She hadn't trusted him enough to relax in his arms. When she'd calmed down enough, Lola returned to her chair.

"Who is the boy you were dating?"

"It doesn't matter." She'd promised Ike she wouldn't tell anyone. Even though he'd broken it off and she was heartbroken, she couldn't bring herself to betray him. "He doesn't want anything to do with me anymore. It seems he found a new girlfriend."

"Just like that? Men as such bastards," Lola said.

Lara grimaced. She'd never thought she'd ever allow that word to be used to describe Ike. He had always been good to her until this week. They'd only known each other for less than a year, but he'd had more impact in her life than anyone else she'd met. She wouldn't be forgetting him in a hurry.

"Well, let's forget your ex and enjoy this gift from Malcolm. At least, it seems he has come to his senses and is treating you the way he should've done right from the start."

"What? Malcolm doesn't want to be my boyfriend."

Lola laughed and shook her head. "For my older sister, you are so naive when it comes to boys."

Lara laughed. "What do you know about boys? You're only sixteen."

"I'll be seventeen in a few months. And I know that I've had more boyfriends than you."

That was certainly true. Lola had always attracted male attention. She knew she was a beautiful girl and wasn't afraid of using her looks to get what she wanted.

"Seriously, Lola, you scare me sometimes. Don't tell me you've had sex?"

"As if. I'm not going to give it up to any old person just like that. I'm waiting for my Prince Charming."

"But you're the one who claims to have had loads of boyfriends."

"Yes. I have to kiss loads of frogs before I find my prince. It doesn't mean I'm doing more than just kissing."

"Perhaps that's what I should do. I should start kissing loads of frogs instead of waiting for the prince."

Except, she thought she'd found the prince in Ike. Instead, he'd turned into the big bad wolf.

"Yeah, you should, starting with Malcolm. He wants to be your boyfriend."

Lara couldn't help laughing at her sister's words.

But a week later, Lola was proved right when Malcolm turned up at her house again, this time inviting both of them out for a drive to get ice cream. Because Lola was with them, Lara was able to relax and join in the jovial conversation. She found out that Malcolm was the last child in a family of four siblings, with three older sisters who were either already married or at university. He was close to his mother and spoke quite fondly about her.

"Can I talk to you privately?" he asked when they arrived back at her house.

"I'll see you inside," Lola said as she got out of the back seat. "Malcolm, thanks again for the ice cream."

"You're welcome." He waited until Lola had gone through the gates before speaking. "Lara, I'm having a party next week, and I'd like you to come to it."

He opened the glove compartment and took out a sky blue envelope. "This is the invitation."

"Thank you, Malcolm, but I'm not really a party kind of girl."

"Well, this is a small party to celebrate finishing our exams and graduating from high school. It also happens to be my birthday. I really hope you'll come. Please."

Pressing her lips together in a grimace, she sighed. Going to a party so soon after breaking up with Ike didn't appeal to her. Then again, why should she sit at home and mope around just because he preferred being with Gloria?

Malcolm had been making an effort these past two weeks. His party sounded like it would be great fun. Still, unease weighted her body about spending more time with him.

"Okay, I'll think about it."

"Fair enough. My phone number is on the card. Also, I want you to come to the party as my girlfriend."

Shifting back in her seat, she gaped at him. He couldn't be serious. "What are you saying?"

"I like you very much, Lara. I know I didn't go about it the right way before. But I've changed. I'm serious about you. I've been telling my mum and sisters about you and they want to meet you."

"Malcolm, no." She shook her head and unlocked the door. She couldn't deal with this right now. Not so soon after Ike. Her emotions were still all over the place. Climbing out of the car, she shut the door. Malcolm got out, too, and came around, standing by the bonnet as she walked to the gates.

"Lara, please think about it. I think you're beautiful and I'm serious about making you my girlfriend. But there's no pressure. Whatever you decide, just let me know. I hope you'll come to the party, anyway."

Wow. Her mouth slackened and she cocked her head to stare at him. Who was this Malcolm who was being such a considerate gentleman? This couldn't be the same boy who'd harassed her for weeks, months, to be his girlfriend. Then when she'd rejected him, he'd spread nasty rumours about her.

"Okay, I'll let you know what I decide."

"Thank you." He reached across and squeezed her hand. "Take care of yourself. I look forward to your response."

"Thanks." She opened the pedestrian gate and walked in a daze.

In the house, she found Lola in the living room along with Judy.

"Malcolm just invited me to his party next week." She held up the invitation card.

"Seriously?" Lola snatched the card and gawped. "You know this is going to be the hottest party in Enugu this year, right?"

"That's not all. He wants me to go as his girlfriend. He asked me out."

"Oh. My. God." Lola shouted. "You've got to say yes."

"She doesn't have to say yes, unless she likes him," Judy chimed in.

"Of course she likes him. He's been treating her nice these past few days."

Lara nodded. "He's being the kind of guy I would love to date. And I'm struggling to find any excuses to say no to him."

Except that her broken heart belonged to another person. But she couldn't keep pining for Ike. He hadn't bothered to contact her over the past two weeks. And it didn't look like he ever would.

Would it be so wrong to date Malcolm? He was excited about being with her. At least, their relationship would be out in the open. She wouldn't have to worry about sneaking over to his house. He could come over here. He'd already met Lola. She'd have no problems introducing him to Judy. And he wanted to introduce her to his family. They would have a good healthy relationship. Just like other teenagers.

"Anyway, I told Malcolm I'll think about it, and that's exactly what I'm going to do."

EIGHT

"Are we still going to Rush?" Henry asked.

"Of course. That's where we are headed," Ike replied as he drove the long route that would take him past Lara's house.

"It's just that this is not the most direct way," his friend observed.

"Yeah. I know." He grimaced. "I'm just doing a detour."

When had he become a stalker? How many times had he driven past Lara's house in the hopes of seeing a glimpse of her? For the past few weeks, he'd been doing this at least once a week, perhaps twice. He'd considered stopping once and waiting until someone came out of the house. Hopefully, Lara.

But he'd known that would have been unhealthy. That would actually amount to stalking her. This way was better. At least, if he drove past and caught a sight of her, there would be no harm done because no one would know he'd seen her.

Because he did want to see her. He'd promised not to make contact with her. He couldn't touch her. But nothing prevented him from looking at her.

And like an addict weaning himself off an addiction, he'd had momentary relapses when the urge to be with her had overwhelmed him and he'd gotten into his car and driven down towards her house, like he was doing right now

He approached the building, driving slower than the speed limit, and glanced across. The two sisters came out of the house followed by a woman he presumed was their mother's sister whom they lived with.

Warmth radiated through his body at seeing Lara, and his heart raced. She appeared happy, laughing with her sister as they walked towards a car. He kept glancing between her and the road until she disappeared from view totally. The urge to turn around gripped him. He slowed down and put the car in park.

"Lara lives in that house back there," he said, looking into his rear-view mirror as he hoped to catch another glimpse of her. He hadn't seen her in weeks. Now that he'd seen her, he wanted more.

"She does?" Henry twisted in his seat to look at him and then out through the back window. "What are you doing, man?"

"I'm just looking. Nobody said I couldn't look at her. I just want to know she's okay."

"Did you see her?"

"Yes."

"Did she look okay?"

"Yes. As beautiful as she's always been." As much as he was happy that she looked good, a part of him withered that she could be functioning without him. "I miss her."

"Man, I feel you." His friend placed a hand on his shoulder.

The gates to Lara's house opened and a silver CR-V drove out. It stopped just outside the gate. Lara walked out of the gates. She was wearing jeans, tank top, and sandals, just like the first day she'd shown up at his house. She opened the door to the back, glanced over her shoulder towards Ike's car. His heart stopped as she seemed to hesitate. She must know that he was in there. His car was very easily recognisable. She dropped her hand from the door and started walking towards where he was parked.

He wanted to get out of the car and meet her halfway. He'd apologise and they'd kiss and make up.

Instead, he sat there, watching as she took steps that closed the gap between them.

"Man, you don't want her coming any closer. You won't be able to explain this."

His friend's words prompted him into action. He put the car into gear and drove away in a spiral of tyres and dust. He didn't look in his rear window, for fear of seeing the disgust on Lara's face at his cowardice. Neither him nor Henry said anything until they arrived at Rush. The bar wasn't busy yet. Henry ordered the drinks when they settled in.

Ike took his phone out. He held it in his hands as he thought about sending Lara a message. But he knew that even if he did write one, he would never send it. All the other messages he'd ever written to her since they'd broken up were sitting in his draft folder waiting to be sent. He never would.

What was he going to do to get her out of his mind forever? She'd obviously moved on. He needed to do the same.

"There's a party on campus tonight," Henry said as he looked up from his phone.

"I'm not in the mood for a party," Ike said as he took a sip of his drink.

"That's exactly what you need. You need to get over you-know-who." Henry swirled his drink in the glass. "Think about all the fresh girls who will be there."

Ike didn't want to think about any other girls except the one person he wanted. But he couldn't have her. So perhaps his friend was right that he needed to let go and start thinking about other girls.

His phone pinged and he opened the message from Gloria.

There's a hot party in town tonight. Want to come?

He sent a reply. *Where?*

Gloria was the daughter of Chief Rawlins, a close friend of his father. He'd been like a big brother to her since they both schooled in the same city and their parents lived in Lagos.

Zik Hall. Are you coming?

Zik Hall was one of the guest houses at University. It had a hall that was sometimes hired out for outside functions by non-university personnel. It also had residential rooms that could be used by visiting personnel. But the place was usually full of university students even if they were just acting as ushers. He couldn't leave Gloria alone with all those older boys. She was still only eighteen even if she acted older sometimes. And he knew what kind of shenanigans went on in the Zik hall rooms. It was quite notorious during parties.

Yes. I'll be there, he replied.

"We're going to a party at Zik Hall," he said to his friend when he put his phone away.

"That's the same party I'm talking about."

"Cool. One more drink and then we can head out there. You're driving tonight." Ike pulled his keys out of his pocket and tossed the bunch at Henry. If he was going to forget Lara and get into other girls, then he might as well get drunk while he was at it.

His friend nodded and pocketed the bunch. "I've got your back."

By the time Henry drove them to the event hall, Ike had a gentle alcoholic haze surrounding him that mellowed him out. There was loud music and the place was already buzzing with people.

He sent a text to Gloria to let her know he'd arrived. They walked into the hall. Plenty of girls there. Most of them looked like university students, and a few he recognised. He said hello to some of the guys, exchanging pleasantries since he hadn't interacted with most of them in his year away.

Gloria showed up with her friend Christy. She told him where she was sitting so he said he'd catch up with her later. He got a corner and stood there with Henry as they checked out the talent on offer. He hadn't had sex in a few months and there were a few girls here who he could possibly take home for the night. He wasn't thinking about anything more serious. Just a one night stand. With no strings attached.

"Hi, Ike." A girl strode up to him.

He recognised her from his year group. "Hello, Stella. Long time."

"It has been. How are you doing?"

"I'm doing great."

They chatted for a little while, catching up on the past year. She was a pretty girl. He'd always been attracted to her, but had never really approached her before.

"Do you want to dance?" he asked.

"I thought you'd never ask." She smiled.

He glanced at Henry who smiled at him. It seemed he'd scored, without much effort. Then again, he'd never found it difficult getting girls. He just hadn't bothered since he'd started teaching Lara. Tonight, he would change it all.

They went to the dance floor and one thing led to another. Soon, they were grinding against each other, the girl's bum on his crotch. He pulled her close so that his mouth was to her ear.

"I want to fuck you," he whispered loud enough for her to hear him above the music.

She turned around and smiled at him, before leaning up to kiss him. His libido went up a notch. He tugged her hand and pulled her off the dance floor. Then he headed to the lobby and approached one of the receptionists.

"I'd like a room," he said. He couldn't wait to take Stella to his apartment. Moreover, he couldn't drive because he'd been drinking and he didn't want to cut Henry's night short.

The man shook his head. "All the rooms are booked up."

Ike knew that was just a prelude to negotiation. These rooms were in high demand, especially during an event. So the prices where hiked up and a bribe was usually involved. He put a hand into his pocket and pulled out a wad of Naira. He reeled off two one-thousand naira notes and placed it on the counter top.

"I just want a room for an hour," he said and pulled out another note. "And this one is for you."

The man pocketed the extra thousand and added his name to the register before handing him a key. "Room Five is free."

"Thanks." Ike took the key and smiled. "Come on," he said to Stella.

She followed him up the stairs.

Room Five was a basic room with a bed and a small en-suite. But it was clean and it wasn't like he was going to spend the night here.

Stella shut the door and pushed him onto the bed. He bounced as he landed on his back. She walked over to him, hiked up her skirt, and climbed on top of him.

He liked that they didn't speak to each other but seemed to know what the other needed. He just needed to do this one thing to get Lara out of his system.

Then, they were kissing again. She wasn't Lara but she still felt soft and smelled nice, with nothing hesitant about her touch. She'd done this before. She was exactly the kind of woman he wanted tonight.

Soon, he was pushing her top over her head and palming her bare breasts. She pulled his t-shirt off and licked his nipples before grazing one with her teeth. Then she repeated the action on the other nipple. He groaned and reached for his belt buckle before undoing his fly.

She climbed off him and took her skirt and shoes off. He pushed his trousers down, took out a condom from his wallet, and toed his shoes off. He sheathed himself and lay back down. She climbed the bed and straddled him. Lifting her up, he settled her back down so his tip was grazing her entrance.

With one push, he was inside her. She rocked back and forth. He grabbed her head and pulled her down for another kiss as he drove upwards inside her again and again. Reaching between their bodies, he slid his fingers between her labia lips, stroking her again and again until she trembled with an orgasm.

He took control of her hips, holding her still as he thrust up inside her, seeking his completion. It came fast, washing over him like a fever.

Afterwards, they lay side by side as they both caught their breaths.

He'd done it. He'd had sex with someone who wasn't Lara. Instead of feeling relieved, regret knotted his stomach. He closed his eyes and took a deep breath.

Rolling out of bed, he picked up his trousers, walking into the bathroom. In there, he tossed the condom in the bin and cleaned himself up. He put his trousers on and glanced at himself in the mirror.

He only felt bad because this was the first time he'd touched another woman since Lara. A few more times and he would get used to it.

He walked out of the bathroom to find Stella dressing. He didn't say anything as he pulled his t-shirt on and then his shoes.

"I know this was just a one-off. But if you ever feel like getting together again, you can call me."

He grimaced. He wasn't usually this distracted around women. He tried to make amends and walked over to where she stood and brushed his lips against hers. "Of course, I'll call you. Give me your number."

He pulled out his phone and keyed in her number. Then he dialled it. "Now you have mine," he said when her phone rang.

She smiled up at him. "Great."

They left the room and he returned the key to the receptionist. They walked back to the hall where the music blasted out from large speakers.

As soon as Ike walked in there, his heart stopped at the sight before him.

Lara was dancing in the middle of the room with Malcolm. Arm-in-arm. Everyone else was watching them.

Lara and Malcolm?

Before he knew what he was doing, he'd abandoned Stella at the spot and walked to the middle of the dance floor and yanked Lara away from Malcolm.

"What the hell do you think you're doing?" he snapped.

Lara's mouth dropped open when she glanced up at him.

"I should be asking you that," Malcolm cut in.

"Stay out of this, Malcolm." He dragged Lara's arm. "Come on. I'm getting you out of here."

"No, you're not. Lara is my girlfriend," Malcolm said.

Everything went quiet around them. Even the music. Ike didn't care.

All the blood drained from his head. "Is this true? Are you dating him?"

"Yes," Lara said as she glared at him.

His head would surely explode. She had promised him she wouldn't have anything to do with Malcolm.

"You promised me."

"You mean just like you promised me?" She gave a pointed look to the person standing beside him.

He turned to see Stella and Gloria standing on each side of him.

His face heated. He'd betrayed her by having sex with someone else. Could he blame her for doing the same thing? If it had been anyone else, perhaps. But not Malcolm.

"You don't belong here, Lara. Go home before it's too late."

Her eyes hardened and she glared at him with what he could only interpret as hatred.

"No. You're the one who doesn't belong here, *sir*."

She stressed the last word. This was a different Lara talking to him like this. She injected so much venom into her words, his ears burned.

"Malcolm is my boyfriend and my place is right here with him. You should go home with your girls."

She turned her back to him. Malcolm pulled her into his arms, the expression on his face totally gloating.

Ike's heart fell into his stomach. He'd done this to her. And now, she was in the lair of a predator and there was nothing he could do about it. He couldn't even force her out of there by dragging her out. There were too many people who would report back what had happened to Mrs. Bello and cost him his future.

It seemed they'd both made their beds. They would each lie in it and face the consequences.

"Don't say I didn't warn you," he said before turning around and walking out of the hall.

NINE

Five years later.

"I got the interview," Lara said as she stared at the email. Her laptop sat on the small dining table and she on one of the chairs. Two words jumped out at her, sucking away any joy she would've felt for getting her first job interview after months of searching.

"Congratulations," Ada said, turning around from her position on the three-seater sofa. "Which company is this?"

Lara swallowed to clear the lump in her throat. "Thomas International."

"Wow!" Ada gaped. "That's the same company Jane works for."

"Jane?"

"You remember Jane Benson from uni. She was doing Business Admin. We hung out with her but she graduated a year before us."

"Yes, I remember her. I didn't know that's where she works."

"That's because you don't keep in touch with anyone."

Lara shrugged. She struggled to make friends or keep in touch with people. After what had happened to her, she'd learned not to trust anyone. Ada was the only friend who had stayed constant in her life throughout the years.

Sighing, she glanced around her living room. It was small yet tastefully decorated in warm, natural tones, just like the rest of the flat. There were two cream upholstered sofas with patterned grey/brown cushions, a couple of armchairs on the other side formed a quadrangle with a low, glass-topped centre table, and four matching glass-topped side tables sat between the sofas and chairs. A medium-sized flat screen television and entertainment centre formed a focal point of the room, with family portraits hanging on the walls. In the corner was a large potted Bird of

Paradise plant. Behind the longer sofa was a raised dais with an Iroko dining table and six upholstered chairs that matched the sofas. Two doors led away from the living room—one to the kitchen, another into the hallway with the three bedrooms and a family bathroom, though the master bedroom had an en-suite bathroom.

Despite the modest proportions, it was a flat she was proud of, a place she called home. She'd moved in with Ada when they'd both decided to stay in Lagos after their Youth Service. They'd been together throughout University and it made sense to get a place together afterwards.

The block of flats had just been completed when they'd rented it with the help of Judy and Ada's parents. The area outside the walled complex had been mainly grassland. Since then, the whole area had been developing fast, as commuter families moved from the congested Lagos suburbs. There were now more residential estates, schools, hospitals, shopping malls, and hotels being built within the locale.

"So you know who else works at Thomas International, don't you?"

Lara suspected where Ada was headed but she feigned ignorance. "Who?"

"Mr. Ike Thomas." Ada snorted. "He owns the company. At least, his family are the majority shareholders."

"Yeah. I know." Her foot started bouncing against the floor tiles.

All of a sudden, she was back to the last time she'd seen Ike in that jam-packed party in Enugu. The sharpness of her jealousy at seeing him with that girl. The rawness of his rage when she'd claimed Malcolm as her boyfriend. The price she'd paid for her mistake.

One night that had destroyed her and turned her into a shell of her old self. The young, naive school girl had died that night.

She'd tried so hard to forget that night. To forget that whole year. But there were moments like this when something triggered a memory and she was back there.

Sweat broke on her forehead. She clutched her arms and her body rocked back and forth as she remembered the nightmare.

"Lara..." Somebody shook her. "Lara, you're scaring me. What's going on?"

She opened her eyes and found herself curled into a ball on the sofa with Ada standing over her.

She straightened and sat up. Her arm brushed her face and came away wet. She'd been crying. She hadn't cried in five years.

"What happened?"

"I should ask you," Ada said. "One minute we were talking about your new job. The next, you were curled up in a ball on the floor. I had to lift you and carry you to the sofa. You scared the hell out of me."

"I'm sorry." Lara pushed off the sofa. Her limbs felt heavy as she walked over to grab her laptop. "I'm going to have a lie down."

"Are you coming down with a fever?"

"It's nothing. I just need to sleep. I'll be fine."

Ada didn't look convinced. But there was no way Lara was going to discuss what was really wrong with her. She walked into the kitchen and poured a glass of water before taking it to her bedroom.

She put the glass on the bedside cabinet. Then, she reached into her bag and pulled out the key which she used to unlock the top drawer. She pulled out the bottle of pills, opened it, and tipped out two into her hand. She popped them into her mouth and swallowed them down. Then she lay down on the bed and closed her eyes.

***

Two weeks later, Lara walked into the tall steel and glass skyscraper that housed the headquarters of Thomas International, aptly names TI Tower. She clutched her bag to her side and glanced at her wristwatch for the umpteenth time. The small gold watch had belonged to her mother and was one of the only mementos she had of her late parent. It helped to settle her anxiety as she approached the reception desk.

Cool, air-conditioned air kissed her hot skin and she sighed in relief.

"Good afternoon. How can I help you?" the girl behind the desk asked. She was a dark-skinned slim girl dressed in a frilly white shirt and a black skirt. She wore heavy makeup and long black hair extensions.

"My name is Lara Johnson. I have an interview at three o'clock with Mr. Soneye."

The girl looked her over, as if sizing her up, and then punched a button on the switchboard before speaking into her headset.

"I have a Lara Johnson here for Mr. Soneye." The receptionist spoke in a sing-song voice; the person on the other end said something to which she replied, "Sure."

To Lara, she said, "His PA will be down shortly. Take a seat."

Lara walked over to the sofas and sat down. She picked up a newspaper, although she was so nervous, she couldn't concentrate on the words.

She took in her surroundings instead. The glass and steel skyscraper had recently been completed to critical acclaim. It was a showcase for modern architecture in Africa, the interior a minimalist heaven with clean lines and sleek surfaces. Overtaken by her environment, she couldn't help day-dreaming about working in modern offices like this one.

TI was one of the biggest real-estate developers in Africa and dealt in areas from design and architecture to estate management. Working here would be a dream come true. A chance to use the skills she'd acquired at University. Hopefully, her meeting today would be a step in the right direction.

Feeling a pair of eyes on her, she glanced over to the receptionist and caught her watching, her expression contorted in an almost spiteful sneer.

Lara rolled her shoulders, shaking over the prickle on her skin at the memory of her first day at Hillcrest School and the similar look she'd received from Gloria Rawlins. She hadn't seen the girl in years and she certainly wouldn't let another girl intimidate her in the same way.

She refused to be daunted by the other girl's obvious malevolence. She was dressed in her best skirt suit which, though inexpensive, was still smart and looked the part. She only had a touch of mascara and lip-gloss on, but heavy makeup had never been her thing.

Usually, she paid little attention to her appearance. She preferred to be as inconspicuous as possible. But once she'd had confirmation of the interview, Ada had dragged her over to the hairdresser's to get a haircut as well as a manicure and pedicure. She had even started eating properly again, so that she'd gained a little weight. Anything to get the job, she'd told herself.

The *ding* from the lift brought her attention back into her surroundings. A woman walked out towards her. Lara stood up as she recognised her.

"It's Lara, isn't it?" the woman said in a bubbly voice and with lovely smile.

"Yes. It's good to see you again, Jane." Lara took her hand in a firm shake as she'd been taught to do during interviews.

"I nearly didn't recognise you. You look so different with short hair."

"I hope that's different in a good way." She hoped a certain somebody wouldn't recognise her.

"Of course. You look good. Come on, I'll show you to the meeting room," Jane said and headed back to the lift foyer.

Lara grabbed her bag and joined her.

Jane was a dark-skinned girl with the perfect hourglass figure that reminded Lara of the Nollywood actress Ini Edo. She was in pink shirt and navy skirt that showed off her curves.

The lift doors opened to the swankiest office suites she had ever seen. Everything looked new, shiny, and tidy. A huge, open-plan space sat in the middle, with rows of desks and chairs, glass-panelled meeting rooms decked out with the latest office gadgets on one end, and offices with shielded glass walls on the other. She was struck by the size of it all and the fact that in every direction, the views from the window were amazing because of the floor to ceiling, sun-reflecting glass.

To come to work here every day would be amazing.

"It's this way." Jane continued down the corridor.

People looked up from their desks and smiled as they walked by. The atmosphere looked relaxed. Still, she couldn't shake the edgy energy she felt as she walked into the meeting room where her appointment would be held.

"Jane, could you show me the ladies', please? I just need to freshen up before the meeting."

"Sure. It's on your right as you walk back down the corridor," Jane replied, pointing Lara in the general direction.

As she walked past the people in the rows of desks working away on their laptops or talking on the phone, her anxiety increased. Her steps faltered as she walked into the ladies'. Gripping one of the sinks, she stood still for a brief moment as doubt overtook her composure.

It wasn't that she didn't want the job. She just didn't want to work for a company owned by Ike Thomas or his family. She didn't want to keep reliving her past. She'd paid for her teenage folly in more ways than one. Now, it seemed that fate wasn't done with her yet.

Lara took another deep breath and exhaled. After months of bemoaning her lack of employment, could she seriously walk away from an once-in-a-lifetime opportunity like this one? She may never get another chance at a job like this that involved working with top-level executives. This was her chance; she was strong enough and could do this. She had to. There was too much at stake—too much to lose if she didn't. She would not disappoint herself by letting her nerves get the better of her.

She took another deep, calming breath, checked her reflection in the mirror, and reapplied some powder to her face to take away the shine. Straightening up, she walked out of the ladies' with her chin up and her steps more confident.

I am good enough and I can do this.

She walked back in the meeting room and concentrated on settling down.

Jane walked back into the room. "Olu will be here shortly."

"Who is Olu?" Lara frowned, confused.

"Olu is Mr. Soneye."

"You call him by his first name?" She was surprised; she didn't think the man was that young to be referred to so casually.

"Yes, it's the way we work up here. TI working culture is quite informal and relaxed," Jane remarked enthusiastically.

"It should be an interesting place to work." Lara smiled. "I didn't realise you were the PA for Mr. Soneye, as well."

"I can tell you, it's a great place to work. Olu's PA is on holiday. I'm just covering in her absence. Would you like some refreshments?"

"Just water, please," Lara replied as Jane left to get the drinks.

The door opened and a man walked in.

"Hello, Lara. I'm Olu Soneye, the head of projects at TI."

He beamed a friendly smile as he extended his hand for a handshake, which Lara accepted as she nodded.

"It's nice to meet you, Mr. Soneye." She returned his smile.

"You must call me Olu. We are very informal here at TI. Please, sit down," he returned.

Lara was surprised. Mr. Soneye—Olu—was in his early to mid-forties, old enough to be her uncle. It was unusual in Nigeria to refer to older people directly by their names. He was a congenial man with intelligent eyes and Lara liked him instantly, her body relaxing, losing her initial anxiety.

Jane came in with the refreshments, set it on the table. Lara glanced at her notes to prepare herself.

"Right. I'm ready when you are."

I got the job.

Lara sent a quick message to Ada as she sat in Jane's office, waiting for her to get back. Jane had printed off the job offer letter, terms of employment and job descriptions, and needed Olu to sign them before she could take them home.

Her spine prickled and she looked up from her phone. Through the glass partitioning walls, she observed two men talking in low tones down the hallway from Jane's office. One of them was Olu who was facing her, but the other had his back to her.

The man was tall, with broad shoulders that spanned a well-tailored navy suit.

Instantly, she knew who he was although she couldn't see his face and she hadn't seen him in five years.

But the flutter in her stomach and the rapid beat of her heart were the same as the day when she'd sat in a classroom full of teenagers and met him for the first time. She could never forget that instant attraction. The breathlessness and the need to get as close to him as possible…

It gripped her now.

She couldn't take her gaze away from him as her body heated up.

She should move and hide. She should pray for him to walk away without turning around.

She did neither and sat there as if rooted to the spot.

It was a morbid kind of fascination. It had to be. Because why else would she want him to see her? Why else would she want to remember? When she knew that remembering would be like ripping open a festering wound. A wound that had never healed. Would never heal.

As if sensing her, he glanced back. Mocha-coloured eyes looked directly at her. His dark brows lifted and almost met in the middle, his forehead creasing in undulating lines.

Her world tilted precariously, threatening to fall off the edge into a black hole.

She knew then, she shouldn't have come for this interview. Shouldn't have accepted the job offer.

She could still get out of here before Jane came back with the signed contracts.

But the men stood in her path. She would have to walk past them to get to the lifts. She glanced in the other direction, looking for a fire exit. There had to be a stairwell somewhere. She could use that instead of the lift.

She grabbed her bag and made to stand up when she realised Ike was headed in her direction, his stride confident and powerful, his status apparent for all to see.

She wouldn't make it out of the office in time.

Suddenly feeling like the diffident teenager again, her face heating up appallingly, butterflies fluttering in her belly, she wished the ground would open up and swallow her. *Shit.*

TEN

"Have you got two minutes?" Olu poked his head into Ike's office.

"Sure." Ike stood up and grabbed his jacket from the back of his leather armchair. "I was just heading out for a meeting. We can walk and talk."

"Good," Olu said as Ike headed towards him and shut the door after he'd exited the room. "I just wanted to let you know we've recruited the final member of the Baytown project. I just finished the interview."

"That's a quick decision."

"She is the best of the candidates we've seen and will make a good fit to the team. I didn't see the point in holding off any longer."

"Great. Well done. I'm keen to get the ball rolling on this project. I presume Jane's already onto HR about the contract."

"She is. I told the young lady to wait and pick up the contract. In fact, she's waiting in Jane's office. Do you have a sec to meet her?"

"Of course."

Olu led the way and Ike turned in the direction of Jane's office.

He saw the girl then. She was dark-skinned, with a heart-shaped face and wide brown eyes. Something in the back of his mind prickled as there was something familiar about her.

In a few seconds, he was standing in Jane's office in front of the girl and recognition dawned.

It couldn't be. This person standing in front of him looked so different. For starters, the hair was short and had red streaks in it. The girl he'd know five years ago had long braids and was too conservative and introverted to ever colour her hair such a loud shade. Secondly, the glasses were missing.

"Lara, I wanted you to meet our MD, Ike Thomas" Olu said. "This is Lara Johnson, the new project planner."

It was her.

He'd banned anyone he knew from mentioning that name for the past five years. After the night that everything changed. He hadn't wanted to think of her because he knew he would've gone looking for her if only to make sure she was okay.

And what if she wasn't? He wouldn't have been able to live with himself.

Seeing her now, she looked okay. In one piece. So it had been a good thing to walk away. She'd survived. He'd survived. The world had moved on.

Ike's muscles went rigid as the breath whooshed out of him. It took him a few heartbeats to recover enough to speak. "Welcome to Thomas International. We're looking forward to having you on board."

He didn't stretch out his hand to shake hers, afraid of what physical contact with her would do to him.

"Thank you, Mr. Thomas," she said in a tense tone. "I look forward to working here."

She smiled but it seemed forced.

"There's no need to be anxious," Olu said in a reassuring tone as he noticed Lara's grimace. "Ike here doesn't eat babies for breakfast, although our competitors might think so."

He chuckled at his own joke.

Jane chose that moment to make an appearance and Ike let out air as he took a step back to let her get to Lara.

"I've got a phone call to make," Olu said and headed out.

Ike nodded but he didn't move. Instead, he observed as Jane handed the documents to Lara who picked up the items and thanked her.

"I'll show you downstairs," Jane said.

"Don't worry about that. I'll show Lara down."

It felt strange and right saying her name after so long.

"No. I can find my way down," Lara said, standing rigidly.

"I insist," he said. "I was on my way down, anyway."

Her face fell as she nodded.

He walked out of the office and waited outside the door for her to join him. Then, they walked towards the lift bay. He made sure to slow down so he could match her pace.

He would be the professional. After all, she had come here to see one of his team on a business appointment, not a personal reunion. He wasn't going to bring up the past if she didn't.

They didn't speak as they faced the lift. He pressed the call button deliberately looking out of the window at the view of the bustling metropolis of Victoria Island below rather than at the woman standing next to him, though he was aware of her presence in every other sense. She avoided eye contact as they both got into the carriage and stood side by side although there remained a gap of an arm span between them. He kept his eyes fixed on the brushed aluminium panels of the closed doors as the lift descended towards the ground floor.

Finally seeing her again for the first time in long years, she looked like she'd rather be anywhere but where he was. He should just let her go and forget about her.

Where was the challenge in that, though? Anyway, since Olu had offered her a job, he'd be seeing her often enough, so why not get started right now? He was a business man known for his cool composure and level-headed judgement, the consummate professional. He'd left the follies of his youth behind.

In the enclosed space of the lift, Ike was suddenly more aware of Lara. Her timid smile—which hadn't changed in five years, it seemed—beguiled him, squeezing at his heart. Her glossy short hair, a sassy change from the long dark braids he remembered, he yearned to feel between his fingers. Her light floral perfume tickled his senses, filling him with an urge to draw her closer to inhale her deeply. He clenched his fists to stop himself from reaching out and mentally shook his head.

What's the matter with you? She practically screamed and told you to piss off the last time you saw her.

Luckily, the lift doors opened and this time, he stepped out first, needing the distance to control himself. He sucked in much-needed air that didn't smell of her fragrance.

How could it be so difficult to maintain his composure around her? He hadn't seen her for five years and he'd been fine. All of a sudden, now, he wanted to make physical contact with her. Like they'd never been separated.

Damn.

He waited at the reception area for her to return her visitor's badge and sign out of the register. Outside, surprisingly, he welcomed the heat of the evening sun as he headed to his parked car. The chauffeur had already brought it up front so it was ready to go. It was a Mercedes E63 AMG. His love for sporty, powerful cars remained even if these days, he got to sit in an executive model with a chauffeur up front, and he'd gone from Asian to European manufacturers.

A slight sea breeze blew the flap of his jacket. The beep beep of cars on Ahmadu Bello Way floating in the air.

"Which direction are you headed for? I'll drop you off," he said as Lara headed towards the exit.

"It's fine. I'll find my own way home."

"Lara, I said, I'll take you home," he insisted.

His eyes carried a warning; his voice and his stance would tell her he wouldn't take no for an answer. The driver was staring at both of them and the security guard behind them was watching, too.

"If you are sure," Lara stated, maintaining a level stare at him.

"I am," he replied.

With a short nod, she stepped into the car.

A stirring tension in the air… Ike could feel it, taste it, and smell it, even.

Lara sat next to him in the back seat of his car. They'd departed TI Towers over twenty minutes ago heading towards her block of flats in Ajah, which turned out to be one of TI properties. He'd registered the address as soon as she spoke it. Irony of ironies—his lips tugged in a smirk.

In that time, neither of them had spoken nor stirred. Lara was giving him the silent treatment. Not that he'd made any attempt to break the palpable stillness. They had ignored each other as soon as the car had moved off. She'd turned away to look out of the window—mouth pursed, back stiffened—reminding him of the statue of a belligerent Yoruba goddess he had seen at a museum. He had in turn opened his laptop to read a document in preparation for a meeting with a client tomorrow.

Letting out a deep breath, he closed down his laptop with exasperation, scrubbing his face with his hand. Who was he kidding? For once, the words on the document he was attempting to read didn't make any sense; they were swimming across the screen, teasing him. Even when his brain registered the words, they were quickly replaced by another image. The picture of a sweet, pretty girl with long, dark, braided hair, bright, enquiring brown eyes, and a timid distracting smile.

The same girl sitting next to him in his car.

Lara.

Except she had grown into a beautiful woman with a short, sassy haircut that showed off her unblemished oval face and delicate neck exquisitely, passionate eyes that flashed with flecks of crimson when she was angry and reminding him of the late evening sunshine, and a smile framed by fuller, more sensuous lips.

But there was more to her. None of naivety she had displayed when he'd first met her lingered.

Seeing her again was like seeing a dead person reawakened. He'd mourned her years ago like she'd been dead. To think of her living and walking around without him and maybe with someone else had nearly driven him insane. The only way he had been able to cope was to grieve her loss like he had mourned his father, as if she was never coming back. He had made a conscious decision to forget her, to forge a new life. It hadn't been easy, but throwing himself into work and the business had been a healing elixir.

But here she was, sitting in his car, soon to start work in his firm as an employee. Why was she here? Why now, after all these years? Did she really think she could turn up and they could pretend there wasn't a past? That they didn't have a history together? That he'd never held her in his arms? Never tasted her sweetness?

He watched her; she practically sat as far away from him as possible in the enclosed space of the car. Her eyes trained to look out of the window but he knew she wouldn't see the scenery. She had that distant look about her. Was she thinking the same thing as him? About the past? *Their* past together?

The image of the two of them flashed in his mind and his heart rammed in his chest.

Damn it. Did she plan to just ignore him? Pretend like he wasn't here? For how long? *Like hell.*

"Lara."

Her chest moved up and down as she sighed heavily before turning slowly to face him. Suspicious caramel eyes stared back at him, her shoulders hunched with resignation as if bracing for something unpleasant.

"Mr. Thomas, if you don't want me to work at TI, I'll reject the job offer."

Her voice was strained, and something around his heart softened. He wanted to pull her into his arms, to tell her that everything was going to be okay. However, he couldn't say it, because he wasn't sure everything *was* going to be all right.

She leaned back into the seat and squeezed her eyes shut.

Ike heaved a sigh. She opened her eyes and looked at him.

"I don't want you to quit the job. You earned it." He scrubbed his head with his hand and for the first time today, his cool exterior slipped.

"Then what do you want?" Her wavering voice rose a notch, her hands jerking.

"I just want to talk to you."

"I don't want to talk to you."

"What? You came for a job interview at TI and you expect not to talk to me?" He laughed derisively.

The car had stopped in front of her building.

She pulled back and glared at him. "I went for a job interview. I got offered the job. I'm sure it doesn't say on the contract that I have to talk to you outside of the business. I'm sure you don't want to get sued for sexual harassment."

He flinched. "And I'm sure you don't want to gain a reputation for being unemployable."

"Fine. You want to talk to me? I'm doing it where I'll be more comfortable." She pushed the door open and walked towards the entrance of the building without looking back.

Ike got out of the car and strode after her.

She didn't pause for breath as they climbed the stairs until they got to the first floor. She put the key in the lock and shoved the door open. He followed her in and shut the panel after her.

She tossed her bag on the table in the living room and took her jacket off. Then she walked into the hallway. He used the opportunity to take his jacket off and look around the space. It was tastefully decorated and he wondered if she lived alone. He knew how much the apartments cost to rent, and if she was unemployed, she certainly couldn't afford it.

She came back and headed to the balcony doors which she pushed aside. From the corner of his eye, he saw a light flicker and he turned to face her when he realised she'd lit a cigarette.

Lara smoked?

His mouth fell agape. Would the surprises ever stop today?

"Lara, you're a smoker?"

"Yes. Do you have a problem with that?" she snapped.

"Yes, I do. You shouldn't smoke."

"Well, you can't tell me what to do, and if you don't like it, you can piss off."

"What the hell's the matter with you?"

"You want to know what's wrong with me? You are." She pointed the hand holding the cigarette at him. "You are my fucking problem."

"What?"

"Are you shocked at seeing me like this?" She paced up and down. "What were you expecting? The virginal, naive school girl of five years ago? Did you come to see if you could pick up from where you left off? Well, news flash. That girl is dead. She died that night."

His eyes widened as his stomach rolled and gooseflesh mottled his skin.

"Yes, you killed her that night." She glared at him as if she truly believed her words. "And this is what you're left with." She pointed at her body up and down. "This dirty smoker of a slut. Good news is that you don't have to teach me anything. I can fuck like a trooper."

"That's it. I've heard enough of this nonsense." He strode across to her, snatched the cigarette off her, and stomped on it.

She clawed at him, wrestling with him.

"Calm down!"

"Fuck you!"

They both landed on the sofa with him on top of her. She trashed about but he held her down until she quieted and he realised she had tears on her face.

ELEVEN

What the hell was going on?

The sight of the tears sliding down the side of Lara's face had Ike's entire body freezing for a moment. The old feelings of protectiveness he'd had for her resurfaced, gripping his heart in a clamp and leaving him breathless for a moment.

"Lara, are you hurt?" he asked as he scrambled off her and sat up at the edge of the sofa.

She didn't respond, instead turned to her side and pulled her legs up so she was curled up in the foetal position.

He wrinkled his brow as his mouth dried out. He hadn't felt anything so strong in a long while, and his worry bordered on anxiety. He cleared his throat so he could speak. "Lara?"

Unnerved by her continued lack of response, he got on his knees on the floor so he could look at her face properly.

She stared straight ahead and he had to look back to see if something in particular had caught her attention. The only thing there was the midsized television, currently turned off.

He looked at her face again and realised her open eyes were dull. Vacant. Like she had vacated her body. There were no new tears and she wasn't blinking.

He remembered a movie he'd watched a while back titled *Invasion of the Body Snatchers* where humans were being replaced by clones without any emotions. It felt the same way right now staring at Lara. As if she'd been replaced by a clone or at least by someone he didn't know, if her earlier outburst was anything to go by.

"Please, talk to me, so I know you're okay." He kept his voice soft and pleading. And he couldn't remember the last time he'd pleaded for anything.

She didn't talk. Didn't move. Didn't blink.

He checked the pulse on her wrist and found the constant beat.

Satisfied that she was still alive and breathing, he paced up and down in the living room, regularly glancing at her as he waited for her to do something. Anything.

Nothing changed.

Surely, this wasn't normal behaviour. Something had to be terribly wrong.

After five excruciating minutes of pacing, his anxiety for her wellbeing growing to maddening levels, he pulled his phone out of his pocket and called the only person who he knew could deal with this situation.

"Ike, how are you?" she answered in a sing-song American accent.

"Hello, Jocelyn. I need your help," he said, making an effort not to betray his anxiety in his voice.

Jocelyn Okoro was a medical doctor who specialised in psychiatry. She had studied and lived in the USA until she'd been offered the job as part of TI medical team. She also happened to be a close friend of his.

"How can I help?" she asked, and he could mentally picture her reaching for her notepad.

"I've got a situation here." He sucked in a deep breath and puffed it out. "I'm with someone and she's not responding when I speak to her."

"Hang on," she said, her tone acquiring an urgent clip. "Have you checked her pulse and breathing?"

Ike stared at Lara again. Her chest was rising and falling. "Yes, her pulse is steady but slow and her breathing is regular, so she's alive."

"Good. Are you in TI Tower? I can come to you."

"No, I'm not in the building. I'm in Ajah."

"Oh. It's not Gloria, is it?"

He pictured her forehead creasing in a frown. "No. Lara is an old friend I hadn't seen for a while. I'm just a little concerned about her. Can you help?"

"Okay. Tell me what happened."

He described the encounter when they'd gotten into Lara's apartment. "One minute we were arguing. I took away her cigarette and she scratched my arm. I grabbed her hands to stop her and we fell on the sofa. The next, she suddenly stopped moving and became unresponsive."

Jocelyn went quiet for a little while. He presumed she was assessing her words to understand the scene.

"Ike, without seeing the person, I can't make a proper diagnosis on the phone. But from what you describe, how she went from a state of hysteria to catatonia, she could be suffering from PTSD."

"Huh?" He'd heard about the disorder. But it made no sense in this situation. "What does that have to do with anything?"

"Post-Traumatic Stress Disorder can happen to people who've been exposed to traumatic events."

"Like what?"

"Traumatic events can be anything from sexual assault, rape, physical or mental abuse, to traffic accidents, terrorism, or even war."

He shook his head, gave a glance at Lara, turned his back, and stepped into the hallway before lowering his voice. "Are you saying she could be the victim of one of those things?"

"Yes, and from what you've described, it seems like something you did triggered an episode where her mind thinks she's about to suffer the same thing again."

"What the hell? I would never..." he said in a harsh, low voice. He was about to say 'hurt her' but he couldn't be sure that he hadn't in the past.

"Triggers can be different for different victims. For victims of violence, it could be any action that mirrors violence. So maybe when you grabbed her and forced her down, her mind thought she was about to be attacked."

"Fuck!" He tilted his head back and stared up at the white ceiling. He pictured how he'd snatched the cigarette and gripped Lara's arms when she'd scratched him.

He strode to the living room door and stared at her prone body. Had someone held her down without her permission? Forced himself on her?

He rocked back and forth and his hands trembled. What had she said about the last time he'd seen her in Enugu?

"*That girl is dead. She died that night...You killed her that night.*"

His head became heavy and drooped forward. He leaned it against the wall. Something had happened to her that night and she blamed him for it.

"You're right," he said in a quiet voice into the phone. "I think something happened to her, years ago."

"Something like what?" Jocelyn asked, probably wanting to identify the root cause of the problem so it could be treated.

"I don't know but I'm going to find out." He had to. Not knowing was no longer an option after seeing Lara in this state.

"You do realise that most victims of sexual assault or any form of abuse don't talk about what happened to them."

"Why?" He frowned.

"Because society shames them and makes them a victim a second time. Most try and lock away the trauma. Unfortunately, a lot of them live with PTSD for the rest of their lives."

He sighed. "Can you help her?"

"If she comes to me, I can certainly do my best."

"I'm not sure she'll agree to see you. Anyway, I can't just tell her to go and see a psychiatrist."

"True," Jocelyn said. "That's another stigma that's ingrained into society. People think seeing a psychiatrist means being branded as a crazy person. Mental illness is a disease just like cancer or heart disease. It needs to be treated as such."

"You're preaching to the converted," Ike said. He understood that mental health was as important as physical health, which was why he'd insisted on providing it as part of the health care benefits of TI employees. "I know a way to get her to see you. She's just got a job at TI so she'll be undergoing the usual assessments for the health insurance benefit. I want you to do an extended evaluation while she's with you."

"I can do a full clinical assessment when she comes to see me. You can access the summary report that goes to HR about her overall wellbeing. But you do realise that anything she says will remain confidential. "

Jocelyn was a true professional and he didn't expect anything less from her. "Yes, I know. I just want you to help her."

"Okay. In the meantime, keep an eye on her. The catatonia will pass but it could last from a few minutes to a few hours. When she wakes, she might be disorientated for a few seconds. Call me back if you need to."

Ike sighed. He was supposed to have a meeting. But he wouldn't leave Lara in this condition.

"Okay. Thanks, Jocelyn. I appreciate your help."

"You're welcome. Bye," she said before hanging up.

He cut the line and dialled another number.

"Henry!" He didn't give him the chance to speak when he picked up. "Something's come up. I'm not going to make the meeting. Please extend my apologies to the commissioner."

"Sure. I'll handle things over here," his friend said. "Are you okay?"

"Yes, I'm fine. I'll talk to you later."

They both said their goodbyes and hung up.

Returning to the living room, he sat on the sofa and scrubbed a hand over his face. He had to wait. He didn't know if Lara lived with anyone else but he knew from the layout that this apartment would have two bedrooms. So she could be sharing the place with someone else, at least.

Then again, she could be living with her boyfriend, fiancé, or even husband.

His breath caught and his gaze went to her fingers. She didn't have any rings on. He exhaled in relief and then caught himself.

What was he doing? Surely, he wasn't interested in picking up from where they'd left off as she'd accused him. What they'd had was in the past. It had only brought trouble for both of them. They had both moved on. He had a good life now, the reckless nature of his past abandoned. He didn't want to go back to complicating it.

No. He was only here now because he was concerned with her behaviour. Not because he actually felt anything more for her.

Liar. You know better than to lie to yourself.

Okay. He still felt something for her. But he would have to suppress those feelings like he'd done for years. It was just that seeing her again had left him out of sorts.

A moan came from her and he jerked upright and stood. She blinked a few times and uncurled her body, stretching out. Slowly, she pulled herself to an upright position.

"Lara?" He didn't want to get any closer to her in case he seemed intimidating to her.

She looked up at him and blinked a few times. "Mr. Thomas? What are you doing here?"

He frowned at her question.

"You invited me in to talk," he replied.

She stared at him as if he had two heads.

"Remember, we were arguing and then I snatched your cigarette away," he said in the hopes of prompting her memory.

"Oh, that." She turned away and pushed off the sofa to stand.

Shifting his stance, he swallowed. "Is that all you have to say? You were unresponsive for over an hour. I couldn't get you to do anything."

Staring at the floor tiles, she shrugged, dismissing his concerned words as if they meant nothing. "I'm fine."

"You're not." His words were sharp.

She lifted her head and glared at him. If eyes could kill...

He rubbed his hand on the back of his neck and sucked in a calming breath. "I'm sorry. I didn't mean to raise my voice. I'm just concerned about you. I've never seen anybody do what you did. Has it happened before?"

She grabbed her bag and walked out, her footsteps unsteady.

Great. He rolled his eyes upwards. She was back to ignoring him. He followed her into the kitchen. She opened the fridge and took out a bottle of water.

"You didn't answer me. Has it happened before?" he persisted. One way or the other, she would talk to him.

"Yes," she snapped, and pulled out a small plastic pill bottle from her bag. "You can go now. I'm fine. I'm not going to collapse and die on you, if that's what you're worried about."

She poured water into a glass and took out a pill.

He wasn't so sure she wasn't about to keel over considering how unsteady she seemed on her feet.

"What's in the bottle?" he asked, his concern spiking.

"None of your business," she replied, before chasing the pill down with the water.

"Tell me," he insisted.

"It's just Valium. It helps me sleep." She didn't look at him as she went about replacing the bottle in the fridge.

"So you have problems sleeping?"

She shrugged. "Sometimes. I haven't slept properly for the past two weeks."

"Why?"

"Why do you want to know? And don't tell me it's because you care. We both know that's not true."

He took a step towards her. "I do care about you."

She made a sound in the back of her throat that sounded like she thought his words were a pile of crap.

He resisted moving close to her for more than one reason. Any closer and he wouldn't be able to keep his hands off her, if only to shake her to get answers. Once upon a time, she hadn't been this unreceptive to his words.

He scrubbed his face and puffed out a frustrated breath. "Okay. Let's agree to disagree on that one. Just tell me why you haven't been sleeping properly the past few weeks."

"Why do you think?"

"If I knew, I wouldn't ask you." He couldn't hide his aggravation.

She sucked in a deep breath and puffed it out. "I haven't slept properly since I got the confirmation of my interview at Thomas International. I've been having nightmares about the past."

He jerked back. She might as well have slapped him. Her words had the same effect. She was having nightmares triggered by the thought of seeing him again. Even he could figure that out.

More than anything else, he needed to know what had happened the night he'd seen her last five years ago.

She grabbed her bag and walked around him to head out the door.

For a few heartbeats, he didn't move. Then he went in search of her and found her in a room down the corridor. The room was a mix of cream walls, pastel beddings, and tawny wood furniture.

Lara stood in the middle undoing her shirt, her fingers working buttons through each hole in a slow, methodical manner.

He stilled at the threshold, hesitant to cross the invisible line both physically and mentally. Compelled, he couldn't look away, each of her actions mesmerising. She removed her shirt and tossed it on the bed, revealing the sexy black balconette bra. Moving her hands to her back, she undid the zip to her skirt.

The sound had his heart rate escalating, the rush of blood thundering in his ears.

He'd seen her bare skin before although he'd never seen her fully naked. He shouldn't be looking at her. Any decent man would've turned his back to her or even returned to the living room. He did neither.

Her skirt slid down her hips, past a black lace thong that presented her bum cheeks to him as she leaned over to pull the skirt from her legs.

All the blood in his body rushed south and his dick hardened. Painfully.

She straightened and turned around. He'd never seen her this bare before. His breath caught. She was beautiful. Slimmer than he remembered, but still beautiful.

"You're still here," she said as she walked over to the wardrobe.

Her tone held no surprise. In fact, the corner of her mouth curled in a teasing smile as if she'd known he watched her all along.

His cheeks heated. A lump lodged in his throat so he coughed. "I'm sorry but I couldn't look away."

"I don't mind. I like you watching me." She pushed the left bra strap down her arm, then repeated the action with the right one. Then she reached behind and unclipped it. It hung loose down her arms and midriff, revealing full, firm breasts, areoles like discs and nipples as hard as bullets.

"You do?" He made a conscious effort to look away from temptation before him, up to her face.

"Yes." She flung the bra over a chair and hooked her thumbs into the tiny straps of her thong. "I think you're a very sexy man. I've always thought so. Always wanted you."

She slipped the thong down her legs and flung it aside, too.

"You have..." He lost his train of thought as he stared at her naked body. As if he wasn't painfully hard before. He swelled again.

He met her gaze once more. No shyness there. She wasn't ashamed of her nakedness. She sat on the bed and pushed back until her head lay on the pillow. Then, her thighs fell apart, showing her glistening pussy.

"Can you see how much I want you?" she said in a low voice.

He swallowed and nodded.

She stroked her breasts with one hand while the other travelled down and parted her swollen labia lips.

He suppressed a groan as she gathered her juice from where it dripped and stroked around her clit. She bit her bottom lip as she caressed her pussy from slit to clit again and again, her hips jerking up and down in rhythm.

It took all of his willpower to remain where he stood instead of crossing the floor and joining her on the bed to give her pleasure himself.

"Do you like what I'm doing?"

He swallowed several times but didn't say anything.

"I'm imagining that it's you touching me, preparing my body so you can fuck me hard." She drove her fingers into her channel a few times, pumping in and out repeatedly while her hips jerked. Then she cried out, her body shaking and then stilling.

After a while, she looked up at him with a sleepy smile. "Thank you."

"For what?" He hadn't done anything except watch, and that wasn't a good thing.

"For making sure I was okay earlier and for watching me now."

For the first time since he'd walked into her apartment, he smiled. "You are welcome."

"Will you stay with me until I sleep?" she asked, suddenly looking vulnerable.

Gone was the abrasive woman of earlier. In its place was some of the girl he used to know.

Something clutched his heart. "Yes, of course."

She turned to her side and reached down to pull the top sheet from under her body.

He moved, walking into the room to help. He pulled the light sheet up. "Do you usually sleep naked?"

The thought kicked up his libido again.

"No. Please get my sleep shirt. It's in the top drawer." She pointed at the chest.

He nodded and strode over. This was safer territory. If he treated her as someone who needed his help, they could both stay on different sides of the invisible line. It didn't matter that he'd just watched her pleasure herself.

Well, it did, but if it never happened again, then that was okay, wasn't it?

He took the shirt out and helped her put it on. Then he tucked the top sheet around her and sat on the edge of the bed.

"Do you live alone?"

"No. I can't afford this place by myself. I live with Ada Obi. You'll remember her from Hillcrest."

He smiled. "I remember her. You two are still close friends?"

"Yes." She returned the smile. "We went to the same university. Shared digs. It made sense to move in together since we both live in Lagos now."

She yawned and covered her mouth with her hand.

"Are you in touch with anyone else from Hillcrest?"

She shook her head.

"Just Ada." She yawned again. "Mr. Thomas..."

"You know you can use my first name."

"Are we like friends now?" Her words were slurred. Her eyes drifted shut.

"Of course. We've always been friends."

"No. Friends don't abandon each other." She sighed and turned to her side.

"What do you mean?"

She didn't answer. He heard her gently snore.

He watched her for a minute, stood up, and walked to the door. Then, he went back, brushed his lips against her smooth, soft cheek, and whispered, "I won't abandon you again."

He straightened and walked out of the apartment, shutting the door behind him.

TWELVE

On Monday morning, an empty feeling sat in Lara's belly as she walked from the bus stop towards TI Tower.

Her first day at work. She glanced at her wristwatch. 8.32am. She'd been told to arrive at 9am, and had calculated it would take her ten minutes to walk from the stop to the building, giving her plenty of time.

The sky was a clear blue and the morning sunshine heated the air around her. Pedestrians and cars jostled for space on the pavement and road as people headed to their morning destinations. This street was a crucial part of the business district, packed with businesses, banks, hotels, and shopping malls.

The job offer had been processed quickly and Mr. Soneye had wanted her to start as soon as possible. Since she didn't have any other job to give notice to, she'd been able to start the week after the interview.

Once she'd walked through the security at the gates, she took in a calming breath and puffed it out. Then she strolled into the building.

This time, the receptionist, Mary Ekpo, was courteous, probably taken aback that Lara was now a TI employee, although her attitude was still off.

Jane met her in the reception lobby and took her upstairs, showing Lara to her desk and introducing her to some of the people on the floor she would work on. She was on the top floor, which apparently housed some of the directors and the MD.

Apart from the directors' offices and meeting rooms, the rest of the space was open-planned. Lara was glad her desk was at the other end of the hall from Ike's office. Everything she needed to start her job was available and ready for her when she arrived at her desk.

She couldn't help but admire the efficiency of the team up here and how everything seemed to work smoothly. The people she met seemed to love working here and Jane had plenty of good things to say about the boss.

In the past few days since her encounter with Ike, she had managed to keep thoughts of him at bay for most of the days, but there were moments when her guard was down and thoughts of him would creep in and invade her mind. Worse when she sat in her living room—his inscrutable image always seemed to loom large in that space.

A few things had been set up for her to do on the first day, one of which consisted of going over to the TI Medical Centre. Jane described how to get there and Lara took the lift back downstairs.

At the clinic, she was giving a questionnaire to complete in the waiting room. Once she'd completed it and handed it back to the receptionist, she waited until she was called.

"Lara Johnson?" The woman spoke with friendly American accent.

"Yes," she replied as she stepped into the doctor's office.

"I'm Doctor Jocelyn Okoro, a member of the TI medical team. Please sit down."

She settled in the chair beside the desk to the doctor's right hand.

"I'm sure you read this already in your contract of employment. Thomas International offers comprehensive health care insurance for its employees. As part of this, each employee undergoes a health check when they start work with the company."

"Yes, I read that."

"Good. We are going to give you a physical as well as psychological examination. There's nothing to worry about. If you have any questions about the process, feel free to ask them."

Her stomach quivered and a chill spread down her arms. She always felt uneasy about doctors ever since she'd had to spend time in hospital. Since then, she only saw them when absolutely necessary and they never gave anything more than perfunctory observations, anyway. She always told herself there was nothing wrong. If she kept her mind blank and projected well-being, they picked it up and it'd all be over soon. "Okay. Thank you."

"First, I'll get you to see the nurse who will collect blood samples and a urine sample. Then, you'll come back to me and I'll carry out the physical examination."

The doctor directed her to the room where the nurse gave her a pot to pee in and then drew blood into different vials. She measured her height and weight. Then Lara returned to the doctor's office, went on the examination table, and after the physical, she had to complete two sets of questionnaires.

Afterwards, the doctor started asking her questions. Most of them were easy to answer.

But when she started questions about Lara's family, she got uncomfortable.

"Do you have a large family?" Doctor Jocelyn asked when Lara had returned the completed questionnaire to her.

"No. There are only two of us. My younger sister and me. My parents are dead."

"I'm sorry for your loss. Did you parents die recently?"

Lara shifted in her seat. "No. It's been a while."

"Do you have other family? Uncles, Aunts, Cousins."

"We are close to my mother's sister. She took us in when my parents died. There are other relatives, but we're not in touch with them."

"What about friends? You must keep in touch with your friends from University or high school."

"I don't really have that many friends. Yes, I know people on social media, but they are more acquaintances than friends. I only have one close friend. I prefer it that way."

"Makes sense." Jocelyn scribbled something on her notepad. "Do you get on very well with your sister and aunty?"

"Yes, they are the only family I've got."

"Did you have any problems with them when you all lived together?"

Lara hesitated and swallowed, her mouth dry. Eventually, she shrugged. "Things were okay."

"Good. Do you have a boyfriend?"

It's just a question. Don't think anything about it. She frowned. "Why do you need to know?"

"It's part of a routine set of question. You don't have to answer it if you prefer not to."

"It's fine. I don't have a boyfriend."

Jocelyn scribbled on her notepad again. "We offer contraceptives to women who want them. Here is a leaflet. There are also free packs of condom available from reception."

"Okay. Thank you."

"Okay. That's everything for today. If you have any concerns about your health, don't hesitate to contact me or any one of the team." Jocelyn handed her a leaflet. "There's a twenty-four-hour phone line that you can call in case of an emergency.

"Also, we offer counselling to victims of abuse and sexual assault. I know that most victims don't call the police when they are attacked. But we have a phone number that people can call when they want to talk confidentially. We listen, offer advice, and provide support. Read the pamphlet. It provides advice on how to spot early signs of abuse."

Lara took the pamphlet but she didn't talk.

"I know it's a lot of information to absorb so take your time to read everything I've given you. Also—" Jocelyn reached in the drawer of her desk and pulled out a card, "—this has my personal number on it. You can call me anytime on it. I know what it is like to feel ashamed and hide something terrible."

"You do?" Lara's body hunched.

"Yes, I lived with a physically abusive father. We never talked about it in my family. At the age of nineteen, I got married to an abusive husband. My husband's abuse wasn't physical, but he mentally and emotionally abused me until I felt I had no self-worth unless I was with him. I lost all my friends and had no contact with my family. At the age of twenty-two, I had a mental breakdown."

Lara's mouth dropped open. That couldn't be right. "But you're a medical doctor. You look normal."

Jocelyn smiled sadly. "I'm normal today only because I got the right help. I had to undergo treatment and most of all, I had to tell someone about what had happened to me. It was only then that I started the slow journey to healing. It's the reason I went to medical school and specialised in psychiatry. I wanted to offer others the same opportunity to heal from mental illnesses."

Lara swallowed and nodded.

"So if there's anything, it doesn't matter how long ago it happened. I can help."

"Thank you."

A week later, Lara was fiddling with the leaflet the doctor had given her about the counselling service. The thought of talking to someone about what had happened to her years ago felt daunting.

She'd kept it a secret for so long. What would be the point of sharing it now?

A doctor had told her once that she lacked emotional responses at crucial moments. She agreed because for years, she'd locked everything up inside. She hadn't gotten angry or cried in years until she met Ike again. To be honest, she didn't want to unlock any of those emotions, as she was afraid of the avalanche that would crush her.

She had a good job and her life seemed to be falling into place. Why should she rock the boat? Anyway, it wasn't as if she would ever get justice.

"Good morning, Lara."

At his level, business-like voice, her heart skipped a beat and her head snapped up to see Ike standing in front of her desk. She shoved the leaflet into a drawer as guilt made her cheeks heat up. She didn't want him seeing the pamphlet and perhaps deciphering her thoughts, especially since he'd seen her at her most vulnerable almost two weeks ago.

Anyway, what was he doing here? She hadn't seen him since she fell asleep on her bed with him talking to her.

"Good morning, Mr. Thomas." She stood up, smoothing her skirt suit with her hand. Her lips suddenly felt dry and she licked them worriedly, tasting her strawberry lip-gloss. He had a way of making her feel self-conscious simply by being there.

"Please sit. You have to call me Ike. We are a close team up here and work on first name basis. I'm sure Olu or Jane would have told you that already." He waited for her to sit back down and walked round, sitting on the edge of her desk. "How are you settling in? Do you have everything you need?"

She'd been at TI for a week and she'd managed to avoid seeing him in that time. This morning, he looked especially handsome in his tailored charcoal suit that exhibited his athletic frame superbly. Having him this close was quite distracting and she suddenly found it difficult to think coherently. She diverted her eyes back to her laptop screen before she could speak and hoped her voice wouldn't let her down.

"Yes, thank you. I have all I need." She bit her lip nervously.

"Good. Olu is away on a conference in Abuja. While he is away, I'll be dealing with any issues on the project directly and you would report straight to me. First thing though, I would like you to join us for the leadership team meeting this morning. I want to introduce you to the rest of the directors and divisional heads."

"Oh, sure. When is it?" Her nervousness rose higher. It was worse than she thought. She was going to report straight to Ike! Meaning she would be seeing more of him that she had originally thought. Was she really ready for this? She had looked forward to having Olu as a buffer between her and Ike so that she didn't have to deal with him directly. But no. She was being dropped straight into the deep end—into Purgatory.

"It starts in five."

He stood up, his movement so graceful that momentarily, she forgot where she was as her eyes clashed with his cool mocha ones reminding her of a jungle cat she'd seen on National Geographic channel stalking its prey. The thought of herself as Ike's prey sent shivers down her spine, raising her anxiety level, and she lowered her eyes hastily.

Lara, think...don't get distracted!

Coughing, she managed to dislodge the lump in her throat, allowing her to speak when her brain eventually got back into gear.

"What do I need to bring along with me?" Her voice still sounded croaked.

"Just yourself." He paused and looked at her, smiling reassuringly. "And Lara, don't worry. You'll be absolutely fine."

Glad that he seemed to have confidence in her ability, she hoped she wouldn't let him down. Things had ramped up pretty quickly and she hoped she could keep her mind on the matters of business and not on her enigmatic boss. There was only one way to find out, though. Taking the plunge and praying it paid off in the end.

"Okay. Lead the way," she said defiantly and straightened up. She picked up her notepad and pen, following Ike into the board room, tendrils of excitements twirling in her belly.

***

"Has the quantity surveyor given you his estimate yet?" Ike asked.

He'd taken his jacket off and rolled up the sleeves of his baby blue shirt to just below his elbows. The clothes clung to his lean, masculine body. The sight of him took Lara's breath away.

They were in his office discussing the progress of the project. The more time she spent with him had the old feelings she had for him resurfacing. Now more than ever, she wanted him. Every time she was in his presence, her pulse quickened and her body tingled.

She licked her lips. "Yes, and I've spoken to the suppliers who say they can deliver the materials on time."

"What about manpower? Do we have enough people to complete the project?"

"Yes, I've been talking to the resource manager who has been liaising with the contractors and agencies. We should have everyone on board in time."

There was a knock on the office door.

"Come in," Ike said.

Jane pushed the door open and two men walked in with aluminium trays laden with food and drinks. They set them down on the low table where the bank of sofas was located in Ike's large office.

"Your lunch is ready," Jane said.

"Thank you," Ike said.

The men left with Jane and she shut the door.

"Let's head over to the sofa," he said as he stood up.

"Perhaps I should leave you to have your lunch and come back later," Lara said.

"No." He came around the desk and took her hand. "The lunch is for both of us."

"Both of us?" Her heart lurched. She tried to pull her hand away. "We can't."

"What's wrong with two friends having lunch?"

"It's okay. I'm not really hungry."

He frowned. "You're not? Then perhaps you'll eat a little because I want you to do so."

Excitement flowed through her veins at the possibilities couched in his words. Perhaps this was the opportunity she'd been hoping for. In the aftermath of the disaster that had been their relationship, she was the one who'd lost out the most. Perhaps this was the chance to even out the playing field.

"And if I do that for you, what do I get in return?" She raised her brow.

He smiled the boyish smile that had always made her heart race.

"What would you like?"

"I want you."

That was the truth. Had always been.

He frowned and pulled his hand away. "Me? What exactly do you mean?"

She looked up at his face and met his gaze. "If I eat the food, then as my reward, I want you to fuck me."

"What?" His whole body went still. "You're joking, right?"

She shook her head. "I'm not. I reckon you owe me, anyway. A long time ago, you promised you would after my exams and then you backed out on our deal. This time around, if you want us to be friends—" she did air quotes around friends, "—then you have to fulfil the deal we made."

"No. I'm sorry. I can't do it." He moved away.

She clenched her fists and loosened them. Then she glared at him.

"Then I'm sorry, too, because I can never be friends someone who doesn't keep his word." She packed up her notepad and headed to the door. "Enjoy your lunch, Mr. Thomas."

"Wait."

Ike's word had her freezing by the door, her heart racing.

"I'll do it," he said. "Just don't go."

THIRTEEN

What was he doing?

Ike's breath hitched and his heart raced. Sweat beaded his forehead although the office was cool.

Why did he just agree to have sex with Lara? Hadn't he decided that he wouldn't go there with her? That there was too much at stake again to dredge up all those old feelings?

He closed his eyes and sucked in a deep breath, his mind whirling.

He couldn't let her walk out on him feeling like he'd let her down again. He'd already hired a private detective to investigate what had happened five years ago. He'd given out the names of everyone he could remember who had been at that party, both the university students and the final year high school students from Hillcrest who'd been there. He didn't know where most of those people were these days. But if they were alive, then they would be found, he'd been promised. Apparently, with the popularity of social media and smart phones, it was easier to keep track of people.

The important thing was that he would find out what had happened to Lara, and he would get her justice one way or the other.

Jocelyn had already started the ball rolling in terms of Lara's mental health. And the ball was now in Lara's side of the court to seek the help she needed. Nobody could force her to talk if she didn't.

But he needed to be vigilant and he couldn't do anything that would set her back. He was being brilliantly surprised daily by Lara's eagerness and enthusiasm with the job. She was like a sponge soaking up everything thrown at her, learning at a pretty fast rate, and already producing sound ideas.

Then again, he shouldn't have been surprised. She was an intelligent woman. He had found out five years ago when he was her tutor how smart and entrepreneurial she was. She had topped her class in the subject and won several awards for her projects. Last week, when the pain of seeing her again had gripped him and he'd momentarily lost his bearings, he had wondered at Olu's wisdom for hiring her. However, today, after monitoring her actions for the past few days, he was glad she was a member of his team.

During their meetings, she always presented herself as competent and composed. There was no hint of the woman who'd broken down last week in her apartment. It seemed she had gotten good at hiding the other side of her.

No one else knew about them, their past. At least, it looked that way. She didn't seem keen to talk about it. To talk to him, even. They needed to deal with the past before they could move on. The whole thing had been plaguing him for days. Images of Lara had been whirling around in his mind. Like he'd acquired a virtual stalker—wherever he went, she was there.

It surprised him that after so many years, all it had taken was to see her again and he felt like the young man who had fallen for her.

To think that once upon a time, he'd thought she was *the one*, an angel, the girl to whom he belonged, heart, body, and soul. She had enthralled him, reaching parts of him that were locked to others, showing him the beauty of humanity he didn't think existed. Now, she was back, and he couldn't decide if it was a gift or a curse. Because he was about to risk everything again for her. His peace of mind, most of all. He'd never gotten involved with an employee before. Never mixed business with pleasure. Yet, he was about to do it.

Not to mention that there were other reasons he shouldn't.

He opened his eyes.

Lara stood on the same spot and stared at him, her expression uncertain. He expected her to at least look happy because he'd caved in. Instead, she appeared wary and unconvinced.

"Come and sit down," he said.

She didn't move. "Do you mean it?"

He raised his brow in confusion. "Mean what?"

"Did you mean it when you said you'll do it? You're not just saying it because you think that's what I want to hear. Only for you to change your mind. I won't be manipulated again." She crossed her arms over her chest.

He sighed. "I'm not trying to manipulate you."

"Prove it."

"How?"

"Let's do it right here and right now."

He swallowed as his skin heated up. The thought of taking her in his office excited him, even though he knew it was wrong.

"The food will get cold."

"I don't mind. Anyway, there's a microwave in the rec room."

"Lock the door," he said, his voice low and deliberate.

She smiled the smile of someone who was about to be granted her wish as she turned around to click the keys into the lock position.

Warmth spread through his chest that he made her smile. She smiled so little these days, compared to the young girl he once knew who used to beam sunshine at him with her smile.

He pressed the button on the intercom. "Jane, I'm not to be disturbed for the next hour."

"Okay, sir," Jane replied.

He straightened and turned to face Lara.

"Come here," he said as he leaned against his desk.

What he was about to do, he'd never done in his office before. There was something forbidden about it. A part of him was thrilled at the thought of Lara being the one who would bring out this reckless side of him that he'd locked away. He'd thought he'd outgrown it.

She strode across to him, her hips swaying in a seductive manner. She had a feline grace to her movements. His pulse rate ratcheted up another gear, his heart thumping hard against his chest. Blood rushed to his cock, swelling it, and it strained against the fly of his trousers.

He hadn't even touched her and his body was ready to explode. His fingers itched to touch her.

She stopped at arm's length and he leaned forward, placed his left hand on her arm, and dragged her to him until she collided with his body. His right hand reached for her nape, tilted her head back as he lowered his.

Their lips met in a passionate kiss. In the recesses of his mind, he remembered the first time he'd kissed her. How tentative and chaste it had been.

This time was so different. Nothing tentative about the way her lips opened hungrily for him, as if she'd been starving to taste him. And there was nothing chaste about the way he ravaged her mouth, his lips crushing hers, his tongue thrusting in and out, and his teeth nipping at the flesh.

The sounds of moans competed with the rushing blood in his ears. He wanted more of her. How he wanted more of her.

He tilted her head and deepened the kiss, dominating her with his mouth and his presence. She melted into his arms, rubbing her body against his with unrestrained abandon.

He broke the kiss and they both panted for breath and he lifted her and turned her around, sitting her on the edge of the desk. He settled between her legs and her skirt rode up her thighs as he spread her legs.

He kissed her again, feathering her face and trailing his lips down to her neck. She moaned and ground her crotch against his bulge. Then she reached for his fly and started undoing his buckle.

He froze and closed his eyes. This was moving too fast. Opening his eyes, he straightened and held her hands.

"Wait," he said, his voice husky as he struggled to get his control back.

She looked up at him, her eyes glazed with lust, her lips parted. Although she stopped undoing his belt, she kept her hand on his bulge. Her heat permeated the fabric, making it difficult for him to think clearly.

He sucked in a deep breath and let it out slowly. "You understand that this has to be just once. I can't promise you that we'll do this again after today."

She pulled in the corner of her lip. "Yes, I know this is a one-time only deal. But I've got you for the next hour, right?"

"Yes."

"And you're a fit young man. So I'm sure you can do it more than once in the time we have." She gave him a sexy smile.

The cheeky girl he'd fallen for back then was back. He chuckled. "I'll do my best."

She carried on with his buckle until it came loose. His arousal went through the roof as his anticipation rose. The thought of her touching him was driving him crazy. But he stood still and waited.

Slowly, she slid down the zipper, the sound filling the air. He held his breath as she reached into his boxers and wrapped her slim fingers around him. Heat skimmed his body.

She pulled him out and stroked him gently from the broad head to the root.

Groaning, he closed his eyes and thrust into her hand. This was torture because her grip wasn't firm enough to make him come, but it proved enough to set his veins alight.

Something moist and warm covered the tip of his cock. He groaned again and opened his eyes.

Lara was on her knees, her mouth covering his dick. All his blood went to his cock. He thrust his hips reflexively and he rammed the back of her mouth. She swallowed around his head and he groaned, his hand going to her head and holding her still as he fought not to come.

She didn't let up, though, and she kept working him with her right hand and her mouth as her left hand held onto his right thigh. He felt as if he could feel her all over his body.

"I'm going to come in your mouth if you keep this up." He could barely say the words.

She nodded and moaned around his cock. The action vibrated through him and he lost his control. He pumped into her mouth again and again, his orgasm now within reach as he used her to gain his pleasure. She didn't try to get away. Instead, she swallowed him each time he rammed in and tightened her grip on his base.

"Fuck!" he cried out as he thrust once. Twice. Tipped his head back and his whole body stilled as he emptied his semen onto her tongue.

He stood there trying to catch his breath as she licked him clean and he went soft. He opened his eyes as she released him and stood, giving him a wide grin.

"I've always wanted to do that. Always wanted to be the one giving you pleasure," she said with a tinge of sadness although she was smiling.

His heart clenched and a rush of emotion hit him. He pulled her into his arms and kissed her hard, tasting himself on her. Lara made him feel things he shouldn't. Right now, he didn't care.

He lifted her and carried her to the desk and sat her on it. He leaned back.

"Now it's my turn to give you pleasure."

He reached to the side and pulled down the zip to her skirt. She helped him along, seemingly in a rush, and pushed the skirt down her legs as he pulled it off her. She had on another black lace thong that barely covered her pussy. There seemed to be little air in the room as he hooked his fingers into the straps and pulled it down her legs.

He settled on his knees between her legs and gripped her thighs so he could pull her forward and spread her open. Her pussy glistened just as it had when he'd first seen her naked.

Now, she had her top on, covered from waist to chest, but the rest of her was bare to his gaze. He nuzzled her labia with his nose, breathing in the scent of her musk, letting her juices mark his skin.

His erection reawakened as he parted her labia and gave a slow lick around her clitoris. She moaned and arched off the desk.

"Not too loud, my girl. Everyone on this floor will hear you."

His breath caught and he stilled as he realised what he'd just said. *My girl* had been his pet name for her five years ago. It had shown his soft spot for her and his claim on her. But it had just slipped out now without much thought.

She whimpered, drawing his attention again. He leaned in and tunnelled his tongue into her wet channel before dragging it back up to her clit and pressing down. She jerked her hips. He carried on using his tongue to pleasure her, applying pressure then taking it off, stroking up and down several times.

She arched off the desk and gripped his head, trying to push it down to apply more pressure. He didn't oblige her.

She moaned.

"I want to come," she pleaded.

"What's my name?" he asked as he stroked his tongue around her clit for the umpteenth time.

"Mr. Thomas," she said in grumpy tone.

He chuckled and leaned back, not touching her. "If you want to come, you have to say my first name, like you know you should."

"I don't need you to come." She lowered her hands. "I can do it myself."

"No, no, no." He tutted and gripped her arms. "There'll be no coming for you until you do as I say."

"You're bossy, aren't you?" She sulked.

"Always have been and you know it." He waited.

"Fine. Ike."

"Say it again."

"Ike. Ike. Ik—"

He cut her off when he kissed her hard as he thrust his fingers inside her wet channel. He pumped a few times and then pressed down on her clit with his thumb. She moaned into his mouth, her whole body thrashing for moments on end. Eventually, she quietened and went limp.

He lifted his head. She opened her eyes and gave him a lazy smile of satisfaction. He gave her a brief kiss.

"Now, let's eat that lunch. And if you're good, I'll fuck your pussy before you go back to work."

She beamed an expectant smile at him and nodded. "Yes, Ike."

"That's my girl."

FOURTEEN

Lara floated in a cloud of post-coital bliss as she walked back to her desk, holding her shoulders back and her posture straight. For the first time in weeks, satisfaction coursed through her veins, and she practically bounced as she walked.

Ike had finally fulfilled her wish of making love to her, although it had taken him five years to make it a reality. The affectionate man she'd known had made an appearance as they'd eaten lunch sitting side by side on the sofa.

Perhaps finally sharing physical intimacy with him had thawed the resentment she'd held against him these past five years. She'd relaxed into his arms as he'd fed her pieces of steamed plantain and moi-moi.

Afterwards, he'd settled her astride his lap facing him and had driven into her repeatedly while whispering sweet nothings to her in between kissing her until they'd both climaxed. They'd clung to each other, catching their breaths.

It had felt good to be in his arms finally; she hadn't wanted it to end. Unfortunately, they'd had to untangle and get dressed. They were both still at work. Luckily, he had a bathroom attached to his office, which she'd used to make her appearance presentable again.

Now, she breathed in deeply as she settled back into her chair. A slight scent of Ike's aftershave still clung to her skin. She closed her eyes as she remembered the roughness of his chin where the shaved hair was starting to grow back at it had grazed her thigh. The press of his firm lips as he'd kissed her. She raised her hand and touched her lips. Ike was a great kisser.

She wanted to go back into his office and kiss him again. Her skin tingled in remembrance of all the parts of her body he'd kissed. She wanted a repeat performance.

Then she remembered that he'd said their encounter would only happen once. He didn't want a repeat. Her satisfaction dampened.

Surely, he'd felt the sizzle as well as the certainty that they should be together. The amazing connection between them and his sexy tenderness must prove they could have more times together.

Yes, she knew she wasn't good enough for him to build a future with. She was too screwed up. Too damaged to ever expect him to want her permanently.

But surely, they could enjoy a bit more of each other for a short while.

"Lara, can I talk to you?"

Popping her eyes open, she swivelled her chair around to find Jane standing the other side of her desk.

"Hi, Jane. Of course. Pull up a chair."

"I'd rather talk privately. Let's use one of the meeting rooms."

Something about her tone felt off but she dismissed it. The woman had been nice to her since she started working here.

"Sure." She stood up and followed Jane down the aisle into one of the small rooms. She shut the door when she walked in.

Jane didn't sit so Lara didn't, either.

"What's going on?" she asked.

"Well, I should be asking you that," Jane said.

"How do you mean?"

"Look, I don't have to be a genius to figure out what was going on in Ike's office this afternoon. He had never locked himself in his office with a woman before for that long."

Lara reared back. "What...how did you know the door was locked? He specifically told you that he wasn't to be disturbed."

Jane lowered her gaze, looking ashamed. "I was a bit suspicious so I checked the door."

Lara narrowed her eyes and crossed her arms. She hadn't taken Jane for the interfering kind. "Is this what you do? Go around snooping on your boss's privacy?"

Jane stiffened and pushed out her chest. "I'm his PA. I need to know what he does, especially when he's in the office."

"You sound more like you're his mother. He is an adult, old enough to make his own decisions without interfering personal assistants." She fumed, tired of people who tried to bully her or tell her what to do.

Jane winced and for a moment, she was speechless. Perhaps she hadn't expected Lara to give as good as she got.

"I know he's an adult and so are you, but don't you even care about the person you are hurting?" Jane said finally.

"Look, even if there's something going on between Ike and me, and I'm not saying there is, we are not hurting anyone else."

Jane's mouth dropped open and she stared at Lara as if she'd sprouted a horn. "So you think his fiancée wouldn't care that he is having an affair with you? Do you know how much it hurts when you are cheated on? My ex-boyfriend did that to me for a long time and it was devastating to find out."

"Um. Hang on." Lara swallowed. "Did you just say Ike has a fiancée?"

"Yes," Jane said. "He's been engaged for six months."

She gasped and covered her face with her hands. "No!"

"Are you saying you didn't know Ike was engaged?"

She lowered her hands. "I didn't know. I wouldn't have..."

She didn't complete the statement because she wasn't sure she could trust Jane. She didn't want to confirm the woman's suspicions although her reaction had probably given it away.

On the other hand, she wasn't totally sure she wouldn't have had sex with Ike even if she'd known he was engaged. Their encounter had been a long time coming and she didn't want to regret it.

"I'm sorry your boyfriend cheated on you. But about Ike, his fiancée has nothing to worry about because there's nothing going on between us."

"Thank you. I just didn't want anyone getting hurt."

Shame about that, because she was already hurting. "Good. Now I have to get back to work."

She left the meeting room and headed back to her desk. As she worked, Ike's engagement plagued her mind. Why hadn't he told her? Was that the reason he'd mentioned today being a one-off?

The workload meant she didn't get the time to mull over the issue for too long. But she made the decision to leave Ike to his life and his fiancée.

***

Ike arrived back at his apartment earlier than normal that evening. He'd been too distracted at work after the afternoon with Lara that he'd been unable to work effectively.

Their time together had been special. The glowing smile on her face had been worth the conflict that had threatened to tear him apart for agreeing to fulfil her wish.

It had taken him so many years to finally accept the role he'd played in his brother's death and to forgive himself. He'd learned to accept the responsibility of being in the position of dutiful first child instead of the reckless middle sibling he'd been prior to Obi's fatality.

How could he balance pleasing the woman who had meant so much to him in the past when he owed a great deal to the woman whom he was going to marry and spend his future with?

He'd never been the kind of man to keep more than one woman at a time. He'd never cheated before. As he entered his home, his guilt ate away at him and made his shoulders hunch.

The scent of a woman's perfume hit him before he walked into the living room to find her reclining on the sofa.

"Welcome home, honey." Gloria Rawlings stood up and sashayed over to him. She carried herself with class and sophistication, a woman used to having attention and getting her own way.

"I didn't know you were coming over today," he said, hiding his surprise.

"You work so hard. I thought I'd surprise you."

She draped her arms around his neck. Her high heels meant they were face to face. She pressed her lips against his. He took a while to respond.

She broke the kiss and looked at him with a frown on her face. "Are you okay?"

He sighed. "I'm just a little tired. It's the reason I came home early."

"Poor baby. Why don't you go take your clothes off and freshen up? I'll make sure the chef has something prepared for you."

He tried not to roll his eyes upwards. He was waiting for the day Gloria would volunteer to cook for him instead of instructing his chef. Not that he wanted her in the kitchen cooking all the time. Just that it would be nice if she would at least do it once. Then again, she had never worked a day in her life. Her wealthy parents had pampered her. And he would admit that he indulged her, too.

She was the woman he was going to marry and he could afford to pay a chef to cook his meals, so it wasn't a big deal.

Other domestic staff took care of other household chores. And he didn't expect her to do those, either. When they married, things would continue in the same vein.

In the bedroom, he removed his jacket and tie, folding them over the armchair in the corner. He toe-d his shoes off and removed his socks. Then he strode into the en-suite and turned on the shower before stripping off the rest of his clothes. He stepped under the warm spray and washed himself quickly, scrubbing his body to make sure no part of Lara or her scent remained on his skin.

Then he cut off the water and dried himself with a towel before tying it around his waist and going back into the bedroom.

Gloria came in.

"I hope you're feeling refreshed," she said as she caressed his bare body, starting from his back and then coming to his chest.

His dick gave an unenthusiastic twitch but aside from that, he didn't feeling the usual pre-sex excitement he would have when she did the things she was doing.

She must have noticed his lack of response because she said, "Still feeling tired?"

"I'm sorry. Perhaps later." He hoped his lack of interest would pass quickly.

"Okay." She pouted. "Come and have dinner, then."

She strode out as he got dressed in a pair of shorts and a t-shirt. In the living room, the table was set although the food wasn't out yet. Gloria sat on the sofa flicking channels. He walked to the adjacent sofa and sat down.

"I need to talk to you." He sat with his elbows on his knees as he leant forward, his hands steepled together.

She put the remote on the table and looked at him. "I'm listening."

He sucked in a deep breath and puffed it out. "I had sex with another woman."

Her mouth dropped open. For several seconds, she didn't say anything. Then, she frowned. "Ike, if you're joking, it's not funny."

He shook his head. He felt shitty for doing this to her, but he had to tell her the truth. "I'm not joking. I cheated on you."

"What? When? How?" She jumped off the sofa. When he didn't reply immediately, she shouted at him. "Tell me when you did it!"

"Today. In my office. It's a one-off and won't happen again."

"You expect me to believe that? You just come home and tell me that you cheated on me and you expect me to accept that it was a one-off?" She paced back and forth as she spoke in a loud voice. "How long has it been going on?"

"I swear to you that it only happened once. Today. I won't cheat on you and keep it from you."

"You are sure it was just today?" she asked in a calmer tone.

"Yes. It won't happen again. I'm sorry."

"Okay. I accept your apology. Our upcoming wedding is more important than some woman who can't keep her hands off other women's fiancés."

He stifled a gasp. He hadn't been expecting her to forgive him so quickly, especially after her outburst.

"But I need to know who the woman is," she continued.

"Does it matter?"

"Yes, it does. I need to know."

"It was Lara Johnson."

Her eyes widened and she reared back.

"The Hillcrest Lara Johnson?"

He nodded.

"You had sex with Lara Johnson? That trashy whore?"

Ike was off the sofa before he even knew what he was doing. He gripped Gloria's arm. "Don't ever talk about her like that!"

Her eyes widened.

"You're hurting my arm," she whined.

"Did you hear me?"

"Weren't you there at the party where she threw herself at Malcolm?"

He narrowed his eyes. "That's no reason to call her nasty names. Anyway, what do you know about the party?"

She shrugged. "Just what we saw."

He released her arm and stepped back. "Well, if you want this wedding to take place, don't ever call her a whore again."

She let out a gasp. He left a shocked Gloria in the living room and headed for the kitchen.

FIFTEEN

"Hi, Lara."

Lara looked up from her laptop screen when she heard her name.

"Hi, Femi. How are you?" she replied a bit distractedly as her mind moved from calculating figures to registering the man standing in front of her.

Femi was an accountant from the finance team assigned to work with her to report on the project finances. She had been introduced to him on her first day at work in TI and they had got on quite well. Being in his late twenties, which was not much older than she was, and just slightly taller than her, he was easy going, boyishly good-looking, and always smiled at her anytime they came into contact.

"I'm fine," he replied pleasantly, flashing a set of white teeth. "Have you seen the latest finance report I emailed you yet?"

She smiled back. "Yes, I'm just reading it now. I was going to email you once I had finished reading it. Is there something wrong?"

"Oh, no. It's just that Olu requested to see the report before the sponsor briefing this afternoon. I wanted to run through it with you."

"Okay." She nodded.

"Can we do that now, or should I come back later?" he enquired uncertainly.

"No, we can do it now. Grab a seat." She moved her chair so that Femi could pull up a spare chair from the next empty desk.

They walked through the report, Femi pointing out the key figures Lara should keep an eye on. When they finished, he looked reluctant to get up.

"Eh...Lara. Are you coming out with us next week Friday?" He sounded hesitant.

She frowned and hoped he wasn't asking her out on a date as she didn't want to ruin their friendship by refusing him. "Friday? What's going on?"

"It's the project team social night. Once a month, we go out for a meal and drinks after work. Sometimes, the directors and sponsor join us when a major milestone has been completed successfully."

"Oh, yes. Jane told me about that. I'm not sure yet if I'll be there, though."

"You have to be. You are the newest member of the team and this Friday, we'll be celebrating you joining the team. You can't miss your own party, can you?" he joked, breaking into laughter, and she joined him.

"Of course I can't. Looks like I'll have to be there." She shrugged in acceptance.

Just at that moment, Ike walked out of the lifts across the hall and looked straight at her and the laughter died in her throat when she saw his expression. It looked murderous.

The next thing she noted, he was striding towards her desk. Apprehension gripped her and she stopped breathing and didn't hear the next thing Femi said to her, her full focus on Ike looking so formidable in his dark suit and scowling expression.

By the time he arrived at her desk, his expression was guarded and she couldn't read him.

"Good afternoon, Ike," Femi said when he saw their employer.

"'Afternoon, Femi." Ike gave him a cursory nod, barely acknowledging Femi, his icy eyes focused on Lara as butterflies fluttered in her belly. "Lara, see me in my office in five minutes."

"Sure," she muttered, her voice sounding strained.

He nodded and walked off without another word or a backward glance, and her eyes followed his retreating back.

Femi stood up, reminding her there was someone else next to her.

"I'll see you later and I look forward to Friday night," he said before walking back to his desk.

"Me, too," Lara replied distractedly, her mind already on inscrutable Ike and the reason he wanted to see her.

Ike was pacing his office floor, running the risk of wearing a hole in the carpet. His blood was boiling with rage and he felt like smashing a hole through the wall.

The minute he had walked out of the lifts into the office space and seen Lara and Femi laughing intimately like lovers and sitting so closely, he had seen red. It was like someone had taken a sledgehammer and bludgeoned him with it for the pain that ran through his body.

Was Lara dating Femi? The thought that she could have someone else as a lover was cutting through him like a knife.

He scrubbed a hand over his head.

Why was he getting agitated because he'd seen Lara with another man? He was engaged to Gloria and their wedding day was less than six months away.

He couldn't possibly want anything to do with Lara more than they'd already had. There was no going back.

So why did his heart wrench at the thought of her being with someone else? Why had he felt like grabbing Lara and kissing her in front of the whole floor full of staff so that everyone would know that she belonged to him and was out of bounds?

"Fuck!" He was so screwed up.

He stopped pacing and gripped the edge of his desk tightly, his knuckles cracking in protest. He needed to calm down before she got here; she'd be here in any minute from now. The last time he'd been angry with her, he'd done something he'd regretted. Strange that she seemed to be the only one who drove him to this level of rage, who brought out the beast in him. And always for the same reason, too—seeing her with someone else.

He took a deep, refreshing breath and exhaled. He wasn't a love-struck young adult anymore. He was a grown man, the head of a company that employed thousands of men and women. He had a better control of his emotions and actions; his actions had consequences that affected other people.

He couldn't allow anyone to control the way he behaved. Not even Lara. So he sat down on his chair and stared blankly at his laptop screen.

There was a brief knock on his door.

"Come."

The door opened and the subject of his current headache walked in, looking elegant and smart in her mink-coloured skirt suit and high-heeled shoes, sending all his newly acquired good intentions out of the window. His blood started fizzing again and he decided to stay seated behind his desk to avoid giving himself away.

She stood by the closed door looking balefully at him, obviously not happy to be summoned into his office.

"Sit down."

He indicated the chair in front of his desk and turned back to his laptop screen. He'd let her stew for a while. However, when she didn't move immediately, he looked up and frowned at the chair then up at her. She took a few begrudging steps towards his desk.

"Is this going to be long, because I have another meeting to attend?" She wavered by his desk, glancing at the watch on her wrist impatiently.

Guts. She had loads of it. He'd give her that. His brave, rebellious Lara. She was challenging him, daring him to cross the invisibly thin line separating them. Again.

A smile tugged at the corner of his lips and his fizzing blood settled low in his belly. She needed to know who was in charge here. A lesson was called for; there were still a few things he hadn't tutored her in yet. He pressed the intercom on his desk.

"Jane, can you contact the attendees to Lara's next meeting and reschedule for another time? She is currently in conference with me. Thank you," he said in a matter-of-fact tone like he was rearranging one of his own appointments.

"Sure." Jane's cheerful voice came across on the intercom and he switched it off.

"How dare you cancel my meeting?" Lara snapped at him, her eyes flashing furiously as she stood in front of his desk.

If looks could kill, he'd probably be mortally injured by now. The blood in his veins flared his need again primitively.

***

Lara glared at Ike as he strode casually round his desk like he had all the time in the world. Like he owned the world and could do as he pleased with it. Like he hadn't just cancelled her meeting with project stakeholders.

Stopping right in front of her, he smiled lazily at her, his dark eyes challenging her. She stood her ground but he was so near she could see his pupils dilate and his nose flare with amusement. She clenched her hands to her side to stop herself wiping the arrogant grin off his face.

"What is your relationship with Femi Spiff?" he asked, ignoring her rant, the muscle on his cheek ticking.

"He is a work colleague and a friend, not that it's any of your business," she retorted, glad her voice was cool, though her heart was pounding in her ears, his intense masculine cologne assaulting her senses, and she had to grip the edge of his desk to stop her knees from buckling.

Trying to keep her mind away from Ike, she focused instead on his office. It was a huge room probably the size of her whole flat. There was a round board table and chairs at one end, sofas and low tables at another corner, and a massive desk at the other end. The view was stunning—an unobstructed scene of the blue-green rolling waves of the Atlantic Ocean under a clear sunny sky as far as the eye could see on one side, and the sprawling and bustling magnificence of Victoria Island on the other. It must be quite exhilarating to work in an office with such views.

Ike leaned closer, his breath fanning her cheek and neck, causing them to tingle, bringing her full attention to focus back on him.

"Anything that goes on in TI is my business," he whispered hoarsely before straightening up. "Of course, he could be reassigned to another project. I think we need an accountant for our Ouagadougou venture."

He grinned wickedly.

Gasping, Lara had to pick her mouth up from the floor before she could speak. "You can't do that. You can't just relocate employees at your whim."

"You will find that I can. Travel and relocation is a mandatory part of all employee contracts. We are an international company, after all. Femi is a young man looking to grow his career, and that kind of project will be good for his resume."

She realised Ike was right. He could send Femi off to any project anywhere whether he wanted to go or not, just because of her.

"What's the matter with you?" She glared at him. "Why are you doing this?"

He paced away and came back to face her. "I can't stand the thought of you being with someone else."

Her mouth dropped open. For several seconds, they both stared at each other as the gravity of his words seemed to settle heavily in the room.

Finally, she found her voice. "Let me get this straight. You told me we can't be together. Yet, you don't want me to get involved with someone else?"

He grimaced and averted his gaze. "I..." His voice cracked.

She placed her hands on her hips. "Well, you're out of your mind if you think I'm not going to date other people, especially since you have a fiancée."

His eyes widened.

"Yes, I know. Your busybody PA told me about it."

"Jane told you? I didn't know the two of you were that close."

"I don't know about being close. She was suspicious about what we did in your office the other day and confronted me about it. She said her ex cheated on her and she didn't want you cheating on your fiancée."

Ike frowned. "You didn't tell her anything, did you?"

"Of course not. I told her nothing was going on."

He scrubbed a hand over his face. "Good. I'm going to talk to her."

"I don't want it to seem as if I'm reporting her. But you should know that perhaps, she isn't very discreet about things she hears and sees. This doesn't explain why you didn't tell me you were engaged." She went back to glaring at him.

He strode across the room towards her and she backed up 'til her back hit the wall.

"I didn't see the point of telling you. As you said, I owed you and I wanted the moment with you that was denied us years ago."

He stood so close she could smell his aftershave. He stared down at her with such intensity.

"You were my girl and I wanted to recapture what we had if only for an hour. It felt so good and I don't regret it. Would it have made a difference to you if you'd known I was engaged?"

She swallowed the lump in her throat and shook her head. "No. I have no regrets about what we shared."

His face hovered above hers and her breath caught in her throat. Her eyes locked onto his as intense heat danced in his gaze. He lifted her chin, rubbing her lower lip lightly with his thumb. While she stood rooted to the spot, desire bubbled within her, stopping all lucid thoughts. Her heart raced in anticipation as his sumptuous lips descended and she closed her eyes, expecting his lips on hers any second. Ike was going to kiss her; right here, right now. Whilst her mind rejected the idea, her body welcomed it. All her nerve endings seemed ripened, waiting. She wanted a taste of him.

Still, nothing happened. She opened her eyes as Ike dropped his hands. He sighed and settled his forehead against her.

"I wish things were different. I wish I was free to be with you."

Lara felt so choked up, she was going to cry. She closed her eyes. "It's okay, Ike. I won't hold it against you if you stay with your fiancée."

He leaned back and she opened her eyes.

"It was crazy of me to think that after five years, you would still be single. I really do hope she makes you happy. I won't ever mention the other day to anyone. It will remain our secret."

He smiled sadly. "I told her about it."

"You did?"

"Yes, I felt shitty enough about cheating on her. I couldn't lie to her, as well. She forgave me."

"You really are a good man. You do deserve to be happy. I could never have made you happy. I'm just too damaged." Tears slid down her face.

"Oh, Lara." He pulled her into a hug and stroked her back. "You deserve to be happy, too."

She wept silently at everything she'd lost. Her innocence. The chance of a happy life. The love of a good man.

She sniffed and pulled back, wiping her eyes. He gave her a handkerchief and she thanked him.

"I don't know what happened to you, Lara, but there's help available."

She stiffened and pulled out of his grip.

"Please hear me out." He raised his hands in a placating gesture. "You don't have to talk to me about it. But Jocelyn is great at what she does. She can really help you heal, if you let her. You could live a happy life one day."

She shrugged. "Maybe. Anyway, are you going to promise not to send every male employee off to Kafanchan or Korhogo or some other obscure African town?"

He chuckled. "Yes, I promise. I admit that was a moment of weakness for me. Am I forgiven?"

She smiled at him. "You're forgiven. So tell me about this lovely, soon-to-be wife of yours."

"You remember Gloria, don't you?"

Dizziness made her sway on her feet. "Gloria?"

He caught her shoulders and held her steady. "Are you okay?"

She shook her head. "You're engaged to Gloria Rawlins?"

"Yes. What's wrong?" He appeared confused.

She stared at him in horror. Didn't he know the woman he was engaged to? She was the worst possible person he could marry.

"I've come to realise that there are very few certainties in this life, but one certainty I can swear by is the fact that Gloria Rawlins hates me."

Ike flinched and stared at her as if she'd lost her mind. "You're kidding me."

"I've never been more serious. Gloria hates me. In fact, I'll go as far as describing her as a mortal enemy. She'll kill me if she can get away with it."

"You're imagining things. What reason does Gloria have to hate you?"

She paced away. "From the first day I started at Hillcrest, she hated me. Don't ask me why because I don't know. But she used any opportunity she could get to make my life a misery. Most of the times, I could brush it off until she spread the rumour about me having sex with Malcolm."

"That rumour was started by Malcolm Ibeh."

"Malcolm may have said it. But Gloria is the one who made sure the rumours spread. She was the queen of the playground. Everything she said was repeated readily across the school students."

He frowned as if thinking on her words.

"So why did you never tell me about what she did?"

"Because I didn't know you were involved with her until I came to your house the day you broke off with me. After that, you weren't talking to me, anyway."

"I just find it so difficult to believe that Gloria would do that."

"Okay. What did she say when you told her you cheated on her? I bet she was furious."

"Yes, she was. But that's understandable."

"I bet she went livid when she found out it was me. I bet she called me nasty names."

Ike's eyes went wide. "How do you know that?"

"It's not the first time she's called me names. She used to do that when we were in school."

Ike sighed. "It does seem like she doesn't like you."

"Do you love her?"

He met her gaze. "We have a good relationship and she's been in my life for so long. I love her in my own way. But we're getting married because of my obligations to her family and mine. Her father came to my rescue when I needed help and I made my father a promise on his death bed that I would unite our families."

The back of Lara's throat hurt and she found it difficult swallowing. He had to uphold his family obligations. There was no way around that. She nodded. At least, she had the consolation that he wasn't in love with Gloria.

SIXTEEN

"There's someone at the door," Ada shouted out. "I'll get it."

"Okay," Lara called back as she pulled out the stiff card Jocelyn had given her from her bag. The one with her personal phone number on it.

"Jocelyn is great at what she does. She can really help you heal, if you let her." Ike's words to her yesterday played in her mind.

She flipped the card around in her fingers. She hadn't slept much last night after his revelation that he was engaged to Gloria. Her mind had been all over the place. When she'd gotten home, she hadn't been able to eat, and sleep certainly hadn't come.

She needed to do something. She didn't know what kind of help Jocelyn would offer her. She didn't think talking about what had happened alone would be any good. She just didn't want to relive that night.

But what other option did she have? If there was a chance she would recover and live a normal life like Jocelyn seemed to be doing, then she would have to take it.

"Lara, can you come here a minute?" Ada called out. She sounded annoyed.

"I'm coming," she said and tucked the card in the back pocket of her jeans and took her phone. She would call Jocelyn after she checked out what Ada wanted. Although it was a Saturday, Jocelyn had said she was available any time, any day.

She strode out of her room into the corridor and stopped. She could see the front door from where she stood.

Gloria Rawlins stood outside the door and Ada stood on the inside, blocking her from coming in.

"I'm not letting you into my house unless Lara wants you here," Ada said, one hand on her hip, the other on the door.

"What are you doing here?" Lara asked in a shocked voice.

Gloria looked up and saw her. "I came to see you. We need to talk but your guard dog here won't let me in," she said with a sneer.

"Did this bitch just call me a dog?" Ada stepped across the threshold into Gloria's face. "We're no longer in high school, Princess. There's no gang to protect you."

"If you touch me, I'll get you arrested for assault." Gloria looked down her nose.

Lara stepped forward and grabbed Ada's hand. "It's okay. I can handle this."

"You're sure?" Ada said.

She nodded.

Ada glared at Gloria once more before stepping back. "I'm in the kitchen. If you need me to chuck out the garbage, just call me."

With Ada gone, Lara turned back to Gloria. "What do you want?"

"I need to talk to you. Can I come in, or do you want your neighbours to know that you sleep with other people's boyfriends?"

She raised brow as if she dared Lara to keep her outside.

Lara moved aside and waved her hand.

"You can come in, your highness," she said sarcastically.

Gloria sniffed before walking past her into the apartment. The spoilt daughter of wealthy parents, Miss Popularity who swanked around like her father owned everything and she was a princess. Even now, she still had that nose-up-in-the-air thing as she stood surveying Lara's flat like it was the local rubbish dump. She was very light-skinned, a reflection of the fact her mother was German. Her face was heart shaped, her nose small, her black hair long and straight. Dressed in fitted shift Burberry dress and platform shoes, she could have just stepped off the catwalk runway.

"Gloria Rawlins. To what do I owe the honour of your visit?" Lara couldn't keep the sarcasm from her voice. She must be doing something right for Gloria to feel threatened enough to visit her.

With Gloria's eyes conveying the whole you-are-so-beneath-me attitude and lips twisted in a sneer, Lara couldn't help thinking the other girl had aged dramatically.

"Lara Johnson. I hear you now work for Ike. Well done." Gloria was clapping now as she strutted around her living room like a peacock. "You've finally arrived."

Lara simply watched her calmly. Although she knew Gloria was trying to raise her ire, she finally realised that even with all her finery and bad attitude, Princess Gloria couldn't intimidate her any longer. She was financially independent and had a career ahead of her. She was making her own money, not waiting for her father to die so she could inherit his wealth, unlike the woman standing in front of her. She couldn't help the unpleasant thoughts.

"Well, thank you, Gloria. Ike knows a good thing when he sees it." She couldn't resist the swipe and the haughty smile left the other girl's face.

"And I see you are getting bolder, too. Well, let me give you some advice. Keep away from Ike," Gloria hissed at her maliciously.

"And why would I want to do such a thing? I work with the man." Lara crossed her arms, folded beneath her chest. A feeling of power rushed through her as she realised she was deriving pleasure in seeing Gloria so riled. Strange, because she had never been vindictive towards anyone before.

"Yes, indeed. He told me about the kind of work you do for him, spreading your legs out for him like the whore you are." Gloria sneered at her, her face distorting spitefully.

Lara's face heated up.

"Do you seriously think you mean anything to him?" the other girl continued. "You didn't before, and you are never going to. No one has ever been able to get between us. Ike and I have a special relationship; that's why we've lasted so long. Occasionally, I allow him to catch his fun just to keep him entertained. All men need a bit of distraction once in a while. Something to remind them of their primeval instincts. But eventually, he always comes back to me. Always has, always will. You were just an amusing interlude to him."

Lara felt sick and she clutched her sides as she struggled to stay upright. The other girl's words hit their mark.

"Listen. I'm a woman like you. I may appear more beautiful and wealthier but I have feelings, too, though some people think that I don't." Gloria paused, rubbing her arms before continuing. "Ike is like a child in a sweet shop who wants to indulge in every flavour and shape in plain view and I'm just the obliging parent. You understand that, right?"

Lara just stared at Gloria silently, not believing the nerve of the girl. She wanted her sympathy?

"Well, if you've overindulged him, then you alone are responsible for the consequence. Why should I care?" she said balefully. She was getting tired of this conversation. She had better things to do.

"True. It is my responsibility, which is why I'm here. To rein him in before it causes any lasting damage."

"Well, you are in the wrong place. He isn't here. You're his fiancée so you should know where he is." Lara waved her hand dismissively.

Gloria laughed scornfully. "I'm in the right place. I need to cut off his sweet supply, and you are it."

She couldn't believe her ears, couldn't believe Gloria. The cheek, the gall of the woman. She clenched her hands to her sides to stop herself from slapping the daylights out of the horrible girl. How she could be so vicious and still live with herself, she couldn't understand.

"Gloria, we're not in high school anymore. You don't scare me." She could barely contain her anger now. "You don't come into my house and mouth off. This isn't the school playground."

Gloria reared back as if shocked by Lara's vehement words. They both glared at each other.

"Look," Gloria said, eventually. "I know you have a lot to lose so I'm willing to help you out. To make it worth your while."

"Why do you want to help me?" Lara's mouth nearly dropped to the floor. This conversation was getting ridiculous by the minute.

"Because as I said, I have feelings, too, and I'm not such a bad person. I'm willing to help find you a new job. I can arrange a position for you in my father's company. Or better still. I can give you money to move away."

She took out her chequebook from her bag and wrote on it, tearing out a slip. She held it up but Lara refused to touch it, though she could see the amount was obscene.

Gloria really thought she could buy her acquiescence. Did she earnestly think Lara's feelings for Ike could be traded for money? Could be bought and sold at whim? What was it with rich people that they thought they could buy people and their emotions?

And she'd been genuinely thinking about wishing Ike well with his future. But not now. Not when Gloria had turned up at her door. It proved there was more to what was going on.

Ike had been genuinely shocked when she'd told him about what Gloria had done in the past. It was now her duty to prove to him that Gloria was nasty and didn't deserve to be his wife.

Too much of a coincidence that whenever something bad happened to her, Gloria was always close by.

"I don't need your money, Gloria." She put her hands on her hips and took a gamble. "I wonder what Ike would say if he finds out that his future wife is a manipulative bitch."

The shocked expression on Gloria's face nearly made her laugh, and she capitalised on it.

"Does he know that you manipulated him into getting engaged with you?" she taunted.

Gloria's face contorted and she snapped.

"I did what I had to do to get him." Her voice was so vicious that Lara flinched. "Do you know what it felt like all those years watching him have relationships with other women? I hated it, hated every minute of it."

Lara's eyes widened at Gloria's confession. She could see the hate contorting Gloria's face. And it all clicked.

"It was you!" she accused. "You are the reason Ike split up with me."

Gloria glared at her. "Of course it was me. From the minute you turned up at Hillcrest, you were moping at him like some puppy. I knew it was only a matter of time before he fell for your whole innocent girl act. It's why I got Malcolm to ask you out. But he was so dumb, playing the whole caveman act on you. Of course, it didn't work, and I had to teach him how to act like a gentleman, which eventually worked."

Lara felt like she was going to throw up all over the floor. She felt dizzy and sat on the arm of the sofa.

"You set me up with that psycho just so you could have Ike to yourself." She couldn't hide the shock in her voice.

"I did, and I'll do it again to make sure he doesn't leave me." Gloria sneered.

Lara's hand shook as she picked the phone out of her pocket. Her whole body was trembling as if she had hypothermia. The edges of her vision were starting to blur. She knew what was happening to her and she tried to prevent it. Her mind was trying to shut down again, blanking out everything.

"I'm going to tell Ike about you," she said in an increasingly weak voice. "I may not be good enough for him, but you're certainly the worst person he could ever marry. I'll make sure he never marries you."

Gloria stepped towards her, her hatred apparent. "You do that and you can be sure that what Malcolm did to you will be nothing compared to what I'll do to you. Keep away from Ike."

"Ada!" Lara screamed, knowing she was losing time. She pulled the card out of her pocket as Gloria walked out of the room.

Ada came into the room, gripping her shoulders. "Are you okay?"

Lara swallowed and nodded. "Where's Gloria?"

"She's gone," Ada replied.

She lifted her hand and shoved her phone and the card at Ada. "Call her. Her name is Jocelyn. Tell her I need her help."

Lara was now shaking badly and she rolled into the corner of the sofa and curled up.

"Lara, you're scaring me. What did that bitch do to you?"

"Please..." was all she could say before darkness claimed her.

SEVENTEEN

"Mr. Bode is here to see you."

Jane's voice rang clear through the intercom speaker on Ike's desk.

"Send him in," he instructed before turning to his friend he'd been chatting with. "I'd like you to stay for this next meeting."

Henry nodded. "Sure. What is it about?"

"I'll brief you in a minute," Ike said as he stood up and walked around his desk.

Jane ushered in a smartly dressed man into his office.

"It's good to see you, Mr. Bode." Ike extended his hand and his guest grabbed it in a firm shake. "This is my friend, Henry Coker."

Two men shook hands as he instructed Jane to bring refreshments. She stepped out.

He directed the men to the sofas. "We all need to sit comfortably for this meeting."

The two nodded and took their seats just as Jane brought a tray of malt and beer drinks and tall glasses and set them on the low coffee table. She left and shut the door behind her.

"Help yourselves," Ike said.

Mr. Bode took a bottle of the malt and popped the cap with the opener. Ike and Henry did the same, ignoring the beer.

"So what do you have for me?" Ike said when they'd all had something to drink.

Mr. Bode placed his briefcase on the table and opened it. "We've made some progress on our enquiries. The main person you wanted us to find, Mr. Malcolm Ibeh. We found him."

"Is this the same Malcolm Ibeh from Hillcrest?" Henry asked.

"Yes. I wanted him found to answer some questions about what happened to Lara at that Zik Hall party," Ike said as he sat up straight. "Mr. Bode is helping to track down some of the party guests. Malcolm is top of the list."

"Something happened to her?" Henry's eyes widened.

"Not in a good way," he replied and turned back to the investigator. "You said you found Malcolm?"

The man pulled out a folder and laid it on the table. "Yes, we did. He is in federal prison in the USA."

"What?" Henry asked.

"It's all in the folder," the man replied. "He was convicted for abducting a minor across state lines, sexual assault, rape, possession of drugs with the intent to supply."

Ike picked up the folder and opened it. The first thing was a copy of a mug shot of Malcolm, followed by copies of the court documents that listed what he'd been convicted off.

"He abducted a child?" Ike looked up from the papers.

"Yes. It appears he met and groomed a girl on Facebook. She lived in New York and he lived in Atlanta, Georgia. Apparently, he drove from Atlanta to New York to pick her up and drove her back to his house in Atlanta. The girl was sixteen. He claimed he thought she was eighteen. Although the girl went with him willingly, her parents reported it to the police as he needed their permission to take the girl out of the state, which amounted to abduction.

"Also, he had sex with her. His semen was found on the girl when he was arrested. The age of consent is eighteen, so it amounted to rape. He is now on the sexual offenders' register. And it turned out he was a dealer as they found large quantities of drugs in his house."

"Wow."

Henry's shocked word mirrored exactly how Ike felt. He'd known that the boy Malcolm was would definitely get into trouble with the law at some point. But he hadn't imagined this. And he was still a little disappointed that the man was out of his reach. He wanted answers from him.

"How did you find all this out?" Ike asked.

"I did an Internet search of his name and found an online newspaper mention of a man bearing his name who'd been convicted of abducting a minor across state lines. I wasn't sure it was the same man. But we are affiliated to a PI firm in the states. We had one of them go over to Atlanta and make some enquiries. It turned out Mr. Ibeh was a well-known member of the Nigerian community in Atlanta. He lived in a big house in a nice neighbourhood. People had been shocked to find out he was a drug dealer. In fact, he has some supporters who think he was set up by the police. They say that it was the girl's fault for not telling him her age."

"What?" Livid, Ike chucked the file back onto the table. "How stupid can people be? How can anyone defend such a thing? He was the adult. How difficult was it to ask the girl how old she was, especially since she was living at home with her parents?"

He'd been in a similar situation when he'd met Lara for the first time, although she'd been seventeen and only a few months from her eighteenth birthday. But he'd ensured that all their interactions were platonic. He'd reserved his sexual desires for other women. It wasn't until Lara turned up in his house when she'd turned eighteen that he'd allowed himself to think of her as a woman with sexual needs.

"I don't even know how anybody could defend that kind of behaviour," Henry said, picking up the file. "Unfortunately, there are people who are quick to blame the victim and not the perpetuator."

"As much as I'm glad to see Malcolm pay for any crimes he's committed, this news is a little disappointing. It means we don't get the chance to question him about the party. It was his party and we all know he was with Lara that night."

"We still have options," Mr. Bode said. "One is to question Mr. Ibeh in prison. We can get one of the investigators in the States to pay him a visit. Of course, there's no guarantee that he will talk, but we can certainly try."

"Yes, I'd like you to do that," Ike said. "What is the other option?"

"I also tracked down a man by the name of Jimoh Obalende. He works at the National Theatre, Iganmu. I've got contact details for him." He reached in the briefcase and took out a sheet of paper.

Ike took the paper and pulled out his phone. He dialled the mobile phone number on the sheet. "No time like the present to contact him."

He put the phone on speaker and the ringing sound echoed in the office before a male voice came through.

"Hello?"

"Is this Jimoh Obalende?" Ike asked.

"Yes...who am I speaking to?"

"This is Ike Thomas. I was one of your teachers at Hillcrest School."

"Oh. Of course. Mr. Thomas. Good evening."

"Good evening, Jimoh. How are you doing?"

"I'm doing okay. It's a surprise to hear from you today."

"Yes, I know. I'm trying to contact some of the old students from Hillcrest for a project I'm doing and I was hoping you will help me out."

"Of course, sir. I'm happy to help out."

"Great. Can you meet me today?"

"Um...Sure. I'm just heading to Lagos Island to drop something off. Can we meet somewhere around there?"

"What I want to discuss is a little private, so I would rather do it here. My offices are in Victoria Island. I'm happy to reimburse you for your trouble."

"It's not a problem. I'll be there probably in over an hour, considering the traffic."

"Do you know where TI Tower is?"

"Yes. Just off Ahmadu Bello Way?"

"Great. Just ask for me when you get to the front desk. I'll let them know you're coming. See you soon."

Ike cut the call. "It looks like we'll be getting some answers tonight."

Henry nodded.

"Do you need me to stay for your meeting with Mr. Obalende?" Mr. Bode asked.

"It's not necessary. I can update you," he replied.

"Okay." Mr. Bode closed his briefcase and stood. "I'll keep searching for the other names on the list and I'll let you know what happens with the prison visit."

Ike stood and extended his hand. "Thank you for coming. I look forward to more news."

Mr. Bode nodded and waved at Henry as Ike walked him to the door. After he said goodbye to the investigator and saw him walk to the lift, he turned to Jane.

"There's a Mr. Jimoh Obalende who is coming to see me in the next hour or so. Can you inform reception and security to expect him?"

"Yes, sir," she replied. "Do you need me to stay on?"

"No. You can go." It was already past working hours and most of the floor had emptied out.

He glanced in the direction of Lara's desk and it seemed she had gone home, too. He hadn't seen her today. Then again, he'd been in meetings most of the time so he hadn't had time to dwell on her. But he missed not seeing her.

Dismissing his wistfulness, he headed back into his office and shut the door.

"So what is going on?" his friend asked as he went to the cabinet and took out a bottle of whisky with some glasses.

He returned to the sofa and poured each of them a shot of whisky. He waited until they'd both sipped some before he spoke.

"You remember Lara Johnson, right?"

"Yes, the girl from Hillcrest."

He nodded. "Remember the day I called you to that I wasn't going to make the meeting with the commissioner?"

"You said you would explain later."

"I was with Lara that day."

"You were?" Henry looked surprised.

"She works for TI now. That was the day she came for her interview and I drove her home. Anyway, she was behaving strangely and I called Dr. Jocelyn Okoro who said Lara was suffering from the effects of post-traumatic stress disorder."

"Huh?" Henry's brows went up.

"That was exactly my reaction when she said that. It turns out that Lara could have been the victim of sexual assault, rape, or abuse, and it is linked to the night of the Zik Hall party."

"You mean something happened to her that night?" Henry scrubbed a hand over his head. "Oh, no! And we left her there. What exactly happened?"

"I don't know. She won't talk about it. That's why I've got Mr. Bode investigating. It would've been good to have Malcolm Ibeh to question because I know he has a hand in it. And finding out he'd been convicted of sexual offences only cements my conviction."

"Shit." Henry gulped down the rest of his drink and poured some more. He corked his head as if thinking. "You know, Gloria stayed back that night after we left. She had the car with the driver and claimed she would head off soon after us. But she was there when we got in the car to drive back."

Ike waved a hand in the air dismissively. "She says she doesn't know more than we know."

Henry closed his eyes, sucked in a deep breath, and opened them again. "Look, man, I know she's your fiancée, but don't take everything she says as gospel truth."

Ike narrowed his eyes. "Why would you say such a thing?"

"Gloria has a way of wrapping people around her fingers. I've seen her in action. Just don't trust everything she says."

He shook his head. "If this is because you still have a thing for her, then just stop it. I know she rejected your advances years ago, but you need to let it go."

Henry balled his hands into fists. "You've been my friend for more years that I can bother to count. I've always had your back and I always will. It doesn't matter what happened between me and Gloria. I would never allow a woman to mess up our friendship. I know the reason you're marrying her more than anyone else. So don't accuse me of anything that isn't true."

Ike sighed. "I'm sorry. It's just that it's a shock when people say bad things about Gloria."

Henry raised his brow. "Who else said bad things about Gloria?"

"Well, Lara said Gloria practically bullied her when they were in school together. I know Gloria can be haughty, but she knows better than to bully people."

Henry shrugged. "Well, if you trust me and you trust Lara, then perhaps you should pay a little more attention to your future wife. We can't both be making things up, can we?"

Ike frowned. His friend made a valid point. While he could dismiss Lara's individual accusation or Henry's comment about Gloria not being truthful, when he weighed them up together, they seemed valid enough to investigate.

Also, Gloria had shut down too quickly when he'd asked her about the party. He'd felt at the time she could've been hiding something, but he'd had no proof. And he'd still been feeling guilty for cheating on her so he hadn't wanted to push his luck.

Did she really know more than she'd revealed?

He'd wait for Jimoh to arrive and hopefully give him some more answers. Jimoh had been in the same class with Gloria and Lara. If there'd been enmity between the two, then he'd probably know of it.

EIGHTEEN

"Thanks for coming at such short notice," Ike greeted Jimoh as he exited the lift onto the foyer.

"It's not a problem," Jimoh said as they shook hands.

"My office is this way." Ike led the way down the aisle to his office in the corner. He walked in and waited as Jimoh followed.

Ike introduced Henry and the men shook hands before making themselves comfortable on the sofas. He offered a drink to Jimoh who accepted a bottle of malt.

"So Jimoh, I don't know if you remember in your final year at Hillcrest, Malcolm Ibeh had a party at Zik Hall," Ike said.

Jimoh's lips widened in a big grin. "Of course I remember the party. After our final exams, most of us stayed behind to attend that party instead of heading home to our parents. I was one of those. It was the hottest party of the year."

"Good." He smiled encouragingly. Perhaps he would finally get somewhere tonight. "Do you remember anything specific about that night? Anything unusual."

Jimoh tilted his head. "Well, I remember that it was a fun party. It was packed. Anyone who was anyone around in school or in campus was there that night." He shrugged.

"I'm looking for more specific information about Malcolm and Lara. Did you see them that night?"

"Yes, of course. I saw you two, too." Jimoh nodded in both Ike's and Henry's directions.

Ike's face heated up as he remembered what he'd done that night.

"But yes, I saw Malcolm. I was there quite early. I know that Malcolm didn't come at the beginning. He arrived about an hour after I got there, with Gloria."

"Gloria? Are you sure?" Ike exchanged looks with Henry.

"Yes, they'd both arrived in a chauffeur-driven car. I remember because I was expecting to see Christy, you know,

Gloria's friend, with them. I had a thing for Christy in those days although she never gave me time of day. But I'd been disappointed that I didn't see Christy at that time. But she came not long after that."

"So were Malcolm and Gloria friends, dating perhaps?"

Jimoh shrugged. "Well, I don't know that they were dating exactly. At least, I don't think so. After all, Malcolm declared Lara his girlfriend that night, so it couldn't be possible. But Malcolm and Gloria were very close, anyway. They were both referred to as the king and queen of Hillcrest. Malcolm was the most popular boy and Gloria was the most popular girl; it was easy to pair them. So yes, they were friends."

Henry tilted his head slightly at Ike as if to say 'I told you so.'

This was certainly a new revelation as far as Ike was concerned. He hadn't known that Gloria was friendly with Malcolm. Although they'd been in the same year, they'd been in different classes. And he couldn't ever remember seeing Gloria and Malcolm together alone.

"So tell me more about that night. Did you overhear anything being said about either Malcolm or Lara or Gloria?"

Jimoh thought a bit more. "I remember there was lot of energy in the air, especially among Malcolm's group of close friends. We used to call them the Hillcrest Four gang. Anyway, that night, there was a lot of whispering about them getting fresh meat. But it was a party and there were loads of people popping their cherries that night, so it wasn't a big deal."

Dread curdled Ike's stomach.

"After the big argument between you, Lara, and Malcolm, things quietened down for a while. Malcolm took Lara out of the hall. She looked distressed before they left so I thought he was taking her home or something. But they headed for one of the rooms. After a while, I saw Gloria coming from the directions of the rooms. I don't know if she was with Malcolm or whoever, but after that, I didn't see Malcolm or Lara that night."

There it was. Lara was definitely with Malcolm that night, and Gloria was definitely tied in somehow.

"You don't know what happened between Lara and Malcolm?"

"No. As I said, I didn't see them again until I left."

"Okay. Thank you," Ike said. "You've really been very helpful."

"You're welcome, Mr. Thomas," Jimoh said. "Can I ask why you're interested in what happened that night?"

Ike sighed. He didn't want to betray Lara's privacy. It was tough enough for her as it was. He didn't want her to have to deal with public scorn for something that happened years ago.

He tried a different approach. "I don't know if you know this already, but I'm engaged to marry Gloria in a few months."

"Really, congratulations!"

"Thank you," he said. "I'm just trying to find out as much about my fiancée to help me plan a surprise for the wedding."

"That's interesting. If there's anything I can help with, I'll be happy to do it."

"You've already done so much. Thank you. If you remember anything else, please feel free to call me." He handed Jimoh one of his business cards as he stood up.

"Of course, I will."

The men discussed a little of the local politics before Jimoh headed out. Afterwards, Henry and Ike sat drinking quietly, each lost in his thoughts.

"There's one common denominator in all this," Ike said finally as he put this glass back on the table.

"Gloria," Henry said.

He nodded and headed over to his desk and grabbed his jacket from behind his chair. He lowered the cover on his laptop, unplugged it, and placed it in his chestnut leather satchel.

"What are you going to do?" Henry asked as he grabbed his jacket, too.

"I'm going to talk to her." He pulled out his phone and pressed the button to call his fiancée.

"Hi, honey," she said when she picked the phone. "How are you doing?"

"I'm doing okay. It's been a long day at work. I'm just heading home. Will you be there?"

"No. I'm sorry. I'm with my friends and we're discussing wedding stuff. Not sure when we'll be done. I'll come over tomorrow. Is that okay?"

"Sure. Enjoy yourself. I'll see you tomorrow."

"Bye." She hung up.

"I'll guess I'll have to wait." He grabbed his things and headed to the door with Henry following him. "I'm going over to Lara's house to see if she's okay. I didn't see her all day today."

"Is that a good idea?" his friend asked as they got into the lift.

"Perhaps not, but I just need to know she's okay. I've been a little unsettled all day not seeing her."

"You still have a thing for her."

"I do." He rubbed his face with his free hand. "Seeing her again has been amazing. Touching her. Kissing her. Intense."

Henry stared at him, eyes wide. "You had sex with her?"

"I did." He sighed. "It was a one-off. I told Gloria about it and she forgave me."

"She forgave you?" Henry narrowed his eyes. "You do realise Gloria never forgives anything. If she forgave you, it means there's trouble coming your way later. She has an ulterior motive."

The lift doors opened and Ike didn't say anything as they walked out and said goodnight to the security guard. Outside in the humid night air, he sucked in a deep breath.

"You know, I think you're right. I thought Gloria gave in too quickly after I told her. It was so unusual for her."

Their cars stood ready for them.

Henry turned to Ike. "It's the wedding. You know she will do anything to marry you."

Ike tilted his head and looked up at the dark sky. "Are you saying she loves the idea of marrying me more than she loves me?"

"That's about the sum of it. Be very careful with this one."

He nodded. "I will."

They bid goodnight and he got into his car. He gave the driver the address for Lara's apartment and relaxed back into the soft leather.

His mind whirled with all the information he'd found out today. Malcolm in prison. Gloria's involvement with Malcolm. Gloria's ease at forgiving him. He thought back to his time in Enugu. Gloria had been there the day he'd split up with Lara. She's also been there the night when he'd had the argument at the party.

He was now convinced more than ever that she was involved somehow, which made her forgiving his affair with Lara all the more strange.

His skin prickled and he swallowed. He needed to see Lara and make sure she was okay.

Luckily, the traffic flow had lessened at this time and the drive out didn't take too long. The car pulled in through the gates and parked in one of the visitor spots. He didn't wait for the man to open the door. He strode to the entrance and pressed the buzzer for Lara's apartment.

"Who's this?" a female voice asked.

"This is Ike Thomas. I'm here to see Lara."

There was a pause. "Lara isn't here."

He didn't believe her. "Can I come in?"

"Okay."

The door buzzed and he pushed it open. He took the stairs two at a time until he got to her floor. Her front door was open and a different woman stood there.

"Mr. Thomas, it's a surprise to see you here."

"You must be Ada," he said, smiling.

"Yes." She smiled back. "Lara isn't here."

"Do you mind if I see for myself?"

"Be my guest." She waved him in.

He strode in, glanced into the living room. There was nothing there except the flickering TV. He glanced into the kitchen. The light was off and he switched it on. He kept walking until he got to Lara's room. He knocked on the door. There was no answer. He twisted the knob and opened it.

The room was also in darkness. He turned on the light. The bed was made and the room looked tidy. But no Lara. He opened the wardrobe door and closed it.

He turned around. Ada stood by the door.

"I told you she wasn't here."

"Where is she?"

She shook her head. "I can't tell you."

"Why? What's wrong?" His heart was pounding hard against his chest.

Ada shook her head again and turned away, walking into the living room. He followed, panic rising.

"Ada, tell me what happened," he snapped, losing his control.

"Your girlfriend came here."

"My girlfriend? You mean Gloria?"

"Yes, Gloria. She said something to Lara that triggered her. At least, that's what Dr. Jocelyn said."

"Oh, no!" He remembered how Lara had gone into a catatonic state the last time. "Where is she?"

"You have to call Dr. Jocelyn for that information. But you better warn that girlfriend of yours. If she comes near Lara again, I will kill her and I'll be happy to serve the time. This nonsense has to end."

Ada's vehemence shocked him. She really cared about Lara. And Gloria must have done something bad to trigger Lara.

He gritted his teeth. "Trust me. I'll take care of Gloria. She won't hurt Lara again."

"I hope so," Ada said.

"Thank you." He headed for the door and pulled his phone out as he descended the stairs.

Outside, he called Jocelyn.

"Ike, hi." She gave him her usual greeting.

He didn't waste time on preambles. "Is Lara with you?"

"Not right now."

"Where is she? I went to her apartment and her friend told me to call you."

"Ike, calm down. Lara is being taken care of. Ada called me last week and I had to go over to their apartment. Apparently, Gloria had been to see Lara and something she said sent Lara's mind into shut down. Unfortunately, when she woke up, she went into a manic state. I had to sedate her because she would've hurt herself. We took her to a clinic and she's getting the treatment she needs."

"I have to see her. Tell me where she is."

"I'm sorry, Ike. But she doesn't want you to visit. She doesn't want you to see her in that state."

"No. No!" He was pacing now. "I have to see her. Please."

"Ike, calm down. You know I can't break her trust. Go home. She'll come to you when she's ready. Just give her time."

He deflated, his shoulders humped, and scrubbed a hand over his face. "Okay. But if you need anything, call me."

"I will." She hung up.

He climbed back into the car and slumped into the seat, shutting his eye as all his fears came to roost. He didn't know what he would do if he lost Lara for good this time.

NINETEEN

Ike pulled out one thousand naira note from his wallet and tipped the bellboy who had brought their bags into the hotel suite.

"Thank you, sir," the man said before walking out and shutting the door.

"I don't know why you dragged me out here," Gloria complained as she flounced onto the sofa.

Ignoring his fiancée's complaint, he pulled his phone out of his back pocket and checked for messages. Seeing none, he placed the gadget on the table and sat in the armchair.

"I told you I had to come to Enugu for a meeting," he said, trying not to let her whining bother him. He'd done the hard work of convincing her to come out here with him. The rest should be easy.

"Yeah. But I don't need to be at your meeting."

He reached across and covered her arm with his hand and softened his voice. "My meeting won't take too long, and we'll get some time to spend together without other people interfering."

She smiled at him. "When you put it like that, perhaps it won't be too bad."

"Anyway, Enugu should hold good memories for you. You spent six years here in school."

She shrugged. "I had no choice in the matter. It's because of my step-mother that I came to boarding school here. She wanted me far away from Daddy."

His breath hitched at this revelation from his fiancée. "Are you saying you didn't enjoy your time here?"

"Hillcrest was a good school and I had a good time there. What I hated was being away from my father and giving my step-mum time to get her claws into him."

"Hang on. I thought you get on well with her."

She shrugged. "Yeah, we get on."

"But?"

"But nothing. Forget I said anything."

"If your step-mum did something to you, tell me."

"What? So I can become a whiny, snivelling, helpless victim? I don't think so. There's nothing she can dish out that I can't reciprocate." She dug her phone out of her handbag.

Ike just stared at her. He really was seeing a whole new side to Gloria that he hadn't seen before. He never knew there was animosity between her and her parent.

His phone beeped and he picked it up.

Meet us at Zik Hall in one hour, the message from Jocelyn read.

Okay. See you then, he replied.

"We're going out in thirty minutes," he said to Gloria.

"Where are we going?" she asked, not looking up from her phone.

"There's a new restaurant that opened on Okpara Avenue, but first, I want to stop over somewhere first."

***

Lara's hands trembled and she squeezed them together as she glanced out of the window of the car. City life went on all around her. The cars, the pedestrians, the street vendors. All under a clear blue sky. She knew the temperature was hot out there although in the car, the AC was on full blast.

Jocelyn reached across and squeezed her hand. "You're going to be all right."

She nodded. "I know."

For the first time in years, she truly believed it. The past two weeks had been life-changing for her. Just like the event that had put her on the path to mental breakdown.

Jocelyn had done as she'd promised. She'd started Lara on the road to recovery. No, she wasn't fully healed. Jocelyn's advice was to take one day at a time.

She was undergoing a treatment called Cognitive Behavioural Therapy which involved learning how to control her fears and also unlearning some destructive habits she'd formed in relation to her fears and memories.

As part of the treatment, they were headed to the venue where her life had changed to confront her past. Jocelyn has arranged it along with the psychotherapist who'd been treating her.

As it was, this represented a big milestone. She had rarely visited Enugu during her time at University. Luckily, Judy had gotten a job in Portharcourt and had moved from Enugu. Lola was in Uniport. So Lara had had no reason to come here.

As they neared the university campus, her foot started bouncing against the floor mat in the car and she twisted her wristwatch around and around.

"Remember your breathing technique," Jocelyn said as she covered Lara's wrist with her hand.

She nodded and consciously slowed her breathing down, counting out the beats between inhaling and exhaling. It was a technique that helped her tone down her anxiety attack.

Jocelyn smiled at her when she relaxed back into the seat. The car pulled up in front of the Zik Hall building.

Jocelyn turned to her. "I'm going to be with you every step of the way. Ada is here, as well. You will always be safe. If at any point, you want to give in to your fear, remember that. Going into this building will trigger some memories. Some good and some bad. But remember they are just memories and can't harm you unless you allow your fear to win."

She nodded. "I know."

"Good. Do you remember the traffic light signals? I'm going to ask you at each stage. You tell me if we're at green, to keep going, yellow to take a break, and red to stop and get out."

"Yes, I remember."

"So what light are we at the moment?"

"Green. I want to get in there."

"Come on. Let's go and face your fear."

Lara nodded and pushed the door open. She stepped out. Outside the building, Ada was already waiting with a man who introduced himself as the concierge.

She sucked in a deep breath and closed her eyes. Then she opened them and walked into the structure. Although the place was relatively empty apart from the receptionist who greeted them, snatches of memories flooded her mind. The lobby had been heaving with partygoers the first time she'd been here.

There'd been conversation and laughter, people in a merry mood. She'd also been in a merry mood that day and looking forward to her first adult party.

"The hall that we hire out for parties is down this way," the concierge said, drawing her attention once more.

"How are you doing? What's the status?"

"Green," she said, and followed the man down the corridor.

He unlocked the double doors and pushed them open. Light flooded in from the wide windows that lined the outer wall of the hall. Chairs and tables were packed flat against the edges, and the middle was just an open space.

She'd been led into this room by Malcolm who'd been holding her hand. The middle of the dance floor had been cleared. The DJ had started playing a slow number and Malcolm had pulled her into his arms for their dance since he was the celebrant and he'd chosen her for his first dance.

She'd been elated in that moment although every pair of eyes had been on them and she'd hated being the centre of attention. But it had felt good to be accepted by all the people around there because she'd been seen with Malcolm.

Unfortunately, she hadn't realised her association with him would come with a great cost to her heart and sanity.

She remembered Ike grabbing her arm and wanting to drag her out of there. She remembered the anger on his face and her answering fury and the horrible things she'd said to him all because she'd seen him with some older girl going up to the rooms.

She wrapped her arms around herself and started rocking back and forth.

"Lara, slow your breathing."

Jocelyn's voice penetrated her memories.

She opened her eyes and took a slow, deep breath.

"What light are we on? It's okay if you want a break."

"Green. I don't want to take a break. If I do, I might not finish this."

"Okay." Jocelyn turned to the concierge. "Can we go up to Room Ten now?"

The man nodded and they all walked out into the corridor as he locked the doors again. Then he led the way up the stairs.

Lara's hands trembled and sweat broke on her forehead. She rubbed her palms together and bit her lip. Her anxiety was still there, but at least her mind no longer rushed to shut down as it usually did.

By the time she arrived in front of the open door to Room Ten, she was feeling faint and her feet wobbled like jelly.

"Can I take a break?" she said in a weak voice.

"Are we at yellow signal?"

She swallowed. "Yes. I need to sit down."

"Can you bring us a chair, please?" Jocelyn asked the man who pulled one from the room into the corridor.

Lara sat on it with her back to the wall as she tried to gather her wits and not slip into full-blown panic.

Her life had been changed irrevocably in that room. Once she stepped into it, the memories would all come back.

"Do you mind waiting for us downstairs?" Jocelyn said to the man.

"Of course. Just bring the keys down to the reception when you're done."

"Thank you," she said as he walked away.

It was now just Jocelyn, Ada, and Lara. It showed the level of Jocelyn's professionalism that she wouldn't allow a witness who wasn't part of the therapy team or a close friend to be a part of this process.

"Do you want to talk about anything, Lara?" Jocelyn asked as she squatted in front of her.

She shook her head and sucked in another deep breath as she realised part of her panic had been that she didn't want people she didn't know seeing her in a weak state.

Feeling stronger, she stood up. "I'm ready to go in there."

"Okay. Remember, it's an empty room, and there's nothing in there that can harm you."

"I am safe," she said as she took a step into the room.

It was indeed an empty room, apart from the medium-sized bed covered in a white sheet, paisley throw, and two pillows. A dark wardrobe stood in the corner, as well as a small table. The chair was missing but she assumed it was the same one she'd been sitting on. A small window covered in matching paisley drapes overlooked fields of well-maintained grass. There was a door leading to an en-suite bathroom. She knew that it was made up of white floor and wall tiles as well as white bath tub, WC, and units without going in there to look.

She sucked in a deep breath. The musky smell of the room transported her back to that night; the stuffiness of the room, the feeling of being suffocated, the crushing press of bodies, the hands holding her down, the rip of clothes and skin, the pain flooding through her again and again, crying and begging and still no mercy.

Nausea ripped through her and she rushed at the bathroom door, hearing it bang against the wall as she made it in time to the bowl to heave out everything in her stomach. She slid onto the cool tiles as her whole body shook and she dissolved into tears.

Ada and Jocelyn joined her on the floor, holding her body as she cried.

She lifted her head and pointed into the room. "They raped me in there."

"What?" Ada asked in a shocked voice.

"They held me down and took their turns ripping through my body. I cried and begged them. But they stood there laughing at me. I thought he liked me. He said he did. It was their way of initiating me into the group. That I belonged to them. I was their whore."

"Oh, God." Ada had tears in her eyes.

"I don't know how long I was here for. At one point, he took out a gun and pointed it to my head. Said he would kill me, my sister, and my aunt if I ever told anyone. Said that whenever he wanted me, I had to make myself available. I didn't care about dying. I had lost a lot already. I didn't want him to hurt Lola or Judy."

"Who did this? Who are the people?" Ada sounded furious as she swiped her face.

"It was Malcolm and his gang."

She broke down crying again and Ada pulled her into a tight hug.

They sat on the floor for a while until she was all cried out. Jocelyn gave her a bottle of water from which she drank a little. When she was more composed, they helped her back into the bedroom.

"How do you feel?" Jocelyn asked.

"I'm a little shaky but I'm good. Better than good. I feel as if my system has been flushed, if you get my meaning."

"Yes, I understand. You did very well. Ike is on his way here with Gloria. I can tell him to meet us at the hotel if you don't feel up to facing both of them."

She shook her head. "No. Let them come. He needs to see where it happened."

TWENTY

"What are we doing at Zik Hall?" Gloria asked as the car pulled up in front of the building.

"I told you I had to do a stopover," Ike said before turning to push the door open.

"Wait for us here," Henry, who was sitting in the front passenger seat, said to the driver before stepping out.

Ike stepped out and sucked in a deep breath. This had been his university campus. The familiarity of the setting relaxed him a little, although the dread that had sat in his stomach since he'd boarded the flight to Enugu earlier on that day hadn't gone away.

He hadn't seen Lara in over two weeks and he would be seeing her today. How was she coping with her treatment? Was she fully recovered? It was such a short frame of time to speculate. But the fact that she'd made the trip back to Enugu was a good thing, according to Jocelyn.

Apparently, it was referred to as Exposure Therapy, where the patient was taken to visit the place where the traumatic event happened and they learned to control their fear by exposing them to the trauma in a safe way.

Cold sweat broke on his forehead and a sour taste sat in his mouth. He dreaded walking into the building and finding out exactly what had happened to Lara. But if she was brave enough to come here after so many years to face her fear, then he should also be able to face his.

Gloria came out of the car and crossed her arms over her chest. "What exactly is going on?"

He didn't reply but took slow, heavy steps towards the building. Henry had come along today as support for him and to make sure Gloria did as she was told. He knew there was no love lost between his best friend and his fiancée. Henry was exactly the best person to keep Gloria from misbehaving.

His memories returned as he walked into the reception lobby. That night five years ago, he'd been invited to the party by Gloria. He'd arrived intent on drowning his loss of Lara in booze and women. By the time he'd stepped through the door, he'd already been slightly tipsy.

He strode up to the receptionist.

"Good afternoon, sir. How can I help?"

"Hello. We have an appointment in Room Ten."

"Okay. Take the stairs up to the next level. It's the last room on your right."

"Thank you." He turned around to see Henry holding Gloria's arm. She didn't look pleased, and Henry had a scowl on his face. Ike suppressed a smile.

Those two would make an impressive pair if they ever got over their hatred for each other. He nearly stumbled on a step at the thought. He was pairing his fiancée with his best friend? Had he already decided he wasn't going through with the wedding? How was he going to reconcile that with the promises he'd made?

Sucking in a deep breath, he pushed that thought out of his mind. No need jumping the gun. One step at a time. Right now, he was more interested in seeing Lara.

He walked past Room Five and remembered what he'd done in there with Stella. If he'd known Lara was here that evening, would he have had sex with another girl?

His footstep became heavier as he walked closer to the room and at the same time, his heart raced because he would see Lara.

The door to the room was open. He saw Ada first. She sat on the bed, dabbing her eyes with a tissue.

The tingling sensation in his chest increased. He stepped through the door and saw Lara. She sat on a chair in the corner, and Jocelyn leaned against the table beside her.

Lara's head was bent. As if in slow motion, she lifted it. He saw her red eyes. She'd been crying, too, although there were no tears. His legs acquired speed and he was across the floor before he could think about it. He went on his knees and pulled her into his arms. He squeezed her tight, afraid that if he let her go, she would vanish again, never to be seen.

"Ike." It was Jocelyn trying to get his attention.

He tilted his head to look up at her.

"We have to complete the procedure. There's something Lara wants to say to you."

He nodded and looked at Lara. She met his gaze and smiled weakly. He stroked her cheek. "I'm listening."

She glanced up at Jocelyn and they seemed to exchange a message.

"Ike, can you give her some space?"

He swallowed his disappointment at having to force a distance between the two of them. But he trusted that Jocelyn knew what she was doing. He gave Lara's hand one last squeeze and stood up. There weren't many options of where to sit, so he leaned against the wall by the door.

He heard the footsteps before Gloria appeared at the door. Lara's body stiffened. Jocelyn leaned down and whispered something to her. Her chest rose and fell slowly and then she relaxed again.

Gloria frowned as she glared at everyone in the room. "Ike, what's going on here?"

Jocelyn stepped up and held out her hand to Gloria. "You're here because I asked Ike to bring you. I know you wouldn't have come if you knew this was where you were coming. So I'm sorry for the deception."

Gloria narrowed her eyes. "How do I know I can trust you when you invite me to a place where everyone in it hates me?"

"Surely, you know that I don't hate you, and neither does Ike," Jocelyn said in a placating voice. "Come and sit down."

"Just keep her far away from me." She pointed at Ada.

Ada glared at Gloria before rising from the bed and sitting on the floor next to Lara's chair. Gloria sat on the bed.

"Do you mind having Henry here?" Jocelyn asked.

Lara shook her head. "Don't close the door."

Henry stood just outside the threshold. "I'll stay here and make sure no one is out on the corridor."

"Thank you," Ike said.

Jocelyn turned back to Lara. "Take your time. If you want to stop or take a break, let me know. Okay?"

Lara nodded and lifted her gaze to meet Ike's. "I'm going to tell you what happened the night of Malcolm's party.

Ike's chest felt heavy as he struggled to breath.

***

"I wish I was going to the party," Lola said in a sing song voice as they got outside.

"You're too young for a party on a university campus," Judy said. "I'm only letting Lara go because she's eighteen and Malcolm promised he would bring her home safely."

Lola and Judy got into the car as Lara locked the door. The gateman wasn't around that day so she also had to lock the gates after the car pulled out. She was about to get into the vehicle when something made her look back.

On the road farther down her street was Ike's car. She recognised the distinctive colour as well as the make and model. She hadn't ever seen any other car like it before.

Her hand dropped from the car door and she started walking towards his vehicle. Ike was in it, waiting for her. He'd come to see her. Her heart floated as if in the clouds. She couldn't wait to see him again. Hold him. Talk to him. It had been too long. He'd obviously changed his mind about splitting up with her.

Judy was shouting her name, calling her to come back. But she ignored her. Just as she got within touching distance of the car, it sprang forward and covered her with dust as it sped away.

She shouted for him to stop. But the car didn't, disappearing around the corner. She paced up and down, muttering words she didn't understand as tears rolled down her face.

Then Lola and Judy were beside her, pulling back towards the car.

"Are you okay?"

"Do you want to go back home?"

"I'm fine. I'm not going to miss this party for anyone," she said angrily.

"I'm not so sure it's a good idea for you to go," Judy said.

"Are you going to deny me this one thing? I've never asked to go to a party before. Exams are over. I'm supposed to be celebrating with my friends."

Judy sighed. "Okay. But be careful."

She nodded and they got back into the car as Judy drove her to Ada's house.

She and Ada got dressed in their party clothes. Although she wore a skirt, it was still a decent length. Ada's parents wouldn't let the leave the house otherwise.

She usually didn't wear make-up, but that day, they'd applied mascara and eye shadow and even painted their nails as they chatted excitedly about what would happen at the event.

Ada's older brother, Eloka, drove them to the venue. He didn't stay but he was supposed to come back to pick Ada up. Lara was going to be dropped off by Malcolm.

She texted Malcolm to let him know they'd arrived. As she walked into the venue, she saw Ike. He was with a girl she didn't recognise and he had his arm around her shoulders. They walked up to the receptionist and he asked for a room.

The back of her throat hurt and the area behind her eyeballs burned as tears banked. She'd heard rumours about those rooms. Ike was going up there to have sex with the girl. Nothing else. She turned around, wanting to get out of there. She couldn't stay when she knew Ike was upstairs with someone else. She wanted to curl up into a ball and cry.

"There you are." Malcolm appeared before her. "You look beautiful."

She swallowed her tears back and flashed him a smile. "Thank you. You look good, too."

He was wearing a t-shirt with a designer logo, jeans, and even his belt had designer bling on it.

"Come on. Let's get you something to drink." He took her hand.

She and Ada followed him into an adjacent room where they had bar area.

He took two bottles of Breezers and passed it to them. "These are really nice."

She took a taste and found it to be sweet and easy to drink.

"I'll be back in a minute," he said before walking off.

She stood with Ada watching the other party goers. She saw Gloria with Christy. The two of them were chatting and laughing. When they noticed Ada and Lara, Gloria glared at them before saying something to Christy and then laughing out loud.

"I want you to dance with me," Malcolm said when he came back.

Jimoh was chatting with a giggling Ada as Lara walked off with Malcolm. He took her into the main hall. As soon as they entered, the DJ changed the music.

Malcolm pulled her into the middle of the dance floor. She thought they would dance facing each other but separated. Instead, he pulled her into his arms, making sure there was no space between them.

She felt a little uncomfortable. She'd never danced this closely with a man, never been this close to anyone who wasn't Ike. Then she remembered that Ike was upstairs having sex with some girl. And she relaxed into Malcolm, letting him hold her.

A rough hand gripped her arm and yanked.

"What the hell do you think you're doing?"

Ike was standing beside her, looking enraged. A part of her was glad that he was standing close to her. It was the closest they'd been for weeks.

"I should be asking you that," Malcolm said, putting his arm around Lara's waist to hold her in place.

"Stay out of this, Malcolm," Ike said in a dangerously low voice. He looked ready to put his clenched fist through Malcolm's face. He yanked Lara's arm again. "Come on. I'm getting you out of here."

Malcolm didn't let her go. "No, you're not. Lara is my girlfriend."

Everything went quiet around them as the DJ cut the music. The sound of rushing blood whooshed in Lara's ears.

Ike staggered back one step as if he'd been punched. "Is this true? Are you dating him?"

He was staring at Lara, his eyes accusing.

"Yes," she said as she glared at him. How dare he? Hadn't he been the one having sex with another girl just moments before?

"You promised me." His voice was cold, and a shiver ran down her spine.

"You mean just like you promised me?" She glared at Gloria and the other girl standing beside Ike.

He turned around and looked at them. His gaze lowered as if he was ashamed and couldn't meet her gaze. His shoulders hunched and he seemed deflated.

"You don't belong here, Lara. Go home before it's too late." There was still anger in his voice.

How dare he talk to her like that? How dare he decide that she wasn't good enough to be here among these people when he was here?

She tilted her chin up and glared at him, her anger at him filtering into her clenched fists.

"No. You're the one who doesn't belong here, sir.*" She made the effort of stressing the last word so he would know that from now on, she only saw him as a teacher and he would never mean anything to her again. "Malcolm is my boyfriend and my place is right here with him. You should go home with your girls."*

She turned her back to him and Malcolm pulled her into his arms.

"Don't say I didn't warn you."

She heard his footsteps echoing in the hall as he walked away. His words echoed in her head for moments afterwards.

"I'd like to sit down," she said to Malcolm.

She was suddenly hot and feeling woozy and had the need to lie down.

Malcolm held onto her as he took her out into the lobby. There was no sign of Ike. Malcolm led her up the stairs.

"Where are we going?" she asked, suddenly apprehensive about going into one of those rooms.

"I have a room where you can relax and rest." He tugged her arm.

She was feeling tired and she needed to lie down. "Okay. But I don't want to do anything."

"Of course not." He opened the door and turned on the light. "Just lie down and have a rest. I'll come back and get you later."

She looked around the room. She nodded and lay down on the bed. He closed the door and left her in there. She pulled her phone out of her bag and sent a message to Ada.

I'm just having a lie down.

She must have dozed off because she woke with a jerk.

Malcolm was back in the room but he wasn't alone this time. There were three other of his friends with him. They were drinking and smoking weed.

Her mouth felt like sand paper when she tried to talk and her head still felt woozy. "Malcolm, what are they doing here?"

He beamed a smile. "They are here to party."

She tried to sit up but her body felt heavy and she struggled to move her limbs. Something like a knock sounded and he went to the door. He opened it and she could hear a female voice but she couldn't make out what they were saying.

She tried to shout but it just came out as a croak. One of the men came to the bed, stripped off the cover of a pillow and stuffed it into her mouth, using his belt to hold it in place so she couldn't spit it out. The others just laughed.

Malcolm shut the door and came over to her. "Now it's time to party. Boys, take her clothes off."

She struggled and kicked and scratched as the men pulled her clothes off. But four men against one girl wasn't ever going to be fair. Her top ripped but they did get it off as well as her skirt and underwear.

Malcolm just stood there watching as he smoked, as if they were providing him with entertainment.

Although her mouth was stuffed, she pleaded with her eyes and tears but he didn't seem moved at all.

This man had come to her house bearing gifts and sweet talking her. He'd promised her aunt that no harm would come to her.

Then he was climbing onto the bed. The others still held her down as she thrashed about.

"They say you never forget your first time, Lara. You will never forget me," he said as he gripped her thighs. The other two held each leg while one held onto her hand.

"No!" She screamed as he tore into her body. In her pain, she didn't realise she had broken out of the grip of the person holding her hands. She scratched Malcolm's neck, digging her fingernails into his skin.

He shouted and hit her head, sending it back to the mattress. She fought him as much as he could until his sweaty body slumped over her. Then he was swapping places with the guy holding her left leg.

After the second man, all fight left her. What was there to fight for? They would take whatever they wanted, anyway. They took their turns and when they were done, they left her there and returned to their drinking and smoking.

She lay on the bed, their mixed semen dripping from her body as she curled into a ball, her mind blanked out.

Something cold nudged her temple. She opened her eyes to find Malcolm standing over her with a gun.

With his other hand, he stroked down her body. She felt slimy and dirty where he touched.

"You are now property of the Hillcrest Four. You are here to be used whenever I want you. You know I know where you live. I know where your aunty works and your sister is still at Hillcrest. I still have boys in the school. You tell anyone about what happened here and they are dead. You hear me, dead. Or better still, Lola can get a dose of the same."

She swallowed the bile in her throat and nodded.

"Good. Now go into the bathroom and wash up. Get dressed because I'm taking you home."

She didn't know how she managed to move, but she stood up, removed the gag, grabbed her clothes, and went into the bathroom. In there, she was glad to use the shower to wash off the stench of their sweat and she scrubbed her sex, hoping to clean off any trace of her violation.

When she got dressed, Malcolm placed his arm around her shoulder as he walked her down to the lobby. There were still people around, although not as much as earlier. A car waited outside with a chauffeur. They both got into the back and she didn't say anything on the ride home.

He walked her out of the car to her gates and said, "Remember what I said. Any mention and—" He pointed his fingers at her head in the shape of a gun, "—bang!"

She flinched and nodded. She walked through the side gate not looking back to see if he was still standing there. She eventually heard the car driving off as she entered the house.

"Lara, is that you?"

"Yes, Aunty," she replied but made no attempt to go into the living room. Instead, she headed for the stairs. She didn't want her aunty to notice her torn top.

"Good. Come and tell me how it went."

"I'm coming. Let me just get a drink." She struggled up the stairs as quickly as her achy muscles would let her, into her room, and changed her

top quickly. Then she took a wrapper and covered her body like a blanket before heading back downstairs to the kitchen to get a glass of water.

"Are you okay?" her aunt asked when she saw her all wrapped up.

"I think I'm coming down with malaria. I was feeling feverish at the party."

It wasn't a total lie. Her body felt hot, achy, and feverish although she knew it wasn't malaria.

"Oh, poor you. Go and lie down in bed. I'll get you some painkiller."

Thankful that her ruse had worked, she went back to her room. Her aunt brought her some painkillers and let her to sleep.

But sleep never came.

TWENTY-ONE

As Ike listened to Lara telling her story, nausea rolled through him. His muscles cramped. The back of his throat hurt. He turned away from everyone and faced the wall as tears burned the back of his eyes.

He'd done this to her. He'd left her there for the savages to tear apart and violate. All because he'd been angry and afraid. Angry at himself for not being strong enough to face up to Mrs. Bello, and afraid of losing his recommendation and disappointing his parents.

He'd left the woman he loved behind when she'd needed him. He should've dragged her out of there screaming and shouting, if need be. She'd suffered pain because he wasn't man enough.

He realised the room had gone quiet. Lara had stopped speaking.

He turned around. Everyone was looking at Lara. Their expressions varied. Jocelyn was sympathetic, with a hand on her shoulder. Ada's hands were clenched in a fist, as if she was angry. Gloria swallowed repeatedly and averted her gaze as if she was guilty of something. Henry's eyes bulged in horror.

Yet, Lara wasn't looking at any of them. She was staring at him, the skin around her eyes bunched in a pained stare.

He had difficulty swallowing as he stumbled forward and fell to his knees, his hands clutching the arms of her chair.

"I'm so sorry," he said, his eyes misting over.

"You left me," she said before falling into his arms and sobbing.

"I didn't know... I'm sorry."

His voice broke and he sobbed with her, his heart ripping again and again for everything she'd lost, and everything that could've been avoided. How could he ever make up for leaving her? How did anyone recover from something like this?

He lost awareness of anyone else in the room, only conscious of the woman in his arms. He would give the world to make things right for her.

She lifted her head, her hand swiping at her tears. "I forgive you."

How could she forgive so easily when she had lost the most?

More tears rolled down his face and she wiped them away, her fingers soft on his damp cheek.

"I felt so alone that night, like no one cared about me. For a long time afterwards, I believed it because the nightmare didn't end."

Lost for words, his heart wrenched in pain. What could he say to that?

"You could've told me," Ada said, her voice choked.

"No, I couldn't. I couldn't be sure that Malcolm wouldn't use that gun of his. I'd seen him in action, and there was no way I was going to put anyone else at risk. After he left Enugu suddenly, I was so glad to move on with my life. I couldn't wait to get out of this place."

"I will kill Malcolm, if he ever gets out of jail," Ike said through gritted teeth.

"He's in prison?" Ada asked as Lara's eyes widened.

"Yes, in the States. It turns out he tried something similar out there and he was caught."

"There is a God," Ada proclaimed.

Lara took his hand. "There's more I need to tell you."

She glanced at Gloria.

He turned to look at his fiancée who was staring down at her feet, her chin dipping into her chest.

"What is it?" he asked, the dread returning to curdle his stomach as he turned back to Lara.

"Gloria set me up with Malcolm. She manipulated the whole situation so she could have you to herself."

The sour taste in his mouth returned as he shook his head.

"No. She wouldn't do that." He turned to look at the woman he was engaged to. "Gloria? Is this true?"

"I don't know what she's talking about," she said and pursed her lips.

"She threatened me in my apartment that if I didn't stop seeing you, what she would do to me would be worse than what Malcolm did," Lara said in a surprisingly calm voice.

"Gloria, why would you say such a nasty thing?"

"Are you going to believe what she says over my words? I'm your fiancée!"

Henry marched across the room and dragged Gloria up. "Tell the fucking truth, for once in your life."

"You're hurting my arm," Gloria whined.

"That's going to be the least of your troubles if you don't start telling the truth now," Henry ordered.

"Are you going to stay there and watch him talk to me like this? Do something, Ike!"

He didn't move from the spot and nobody else went to Gloria's rescue.

"Fine," she said finally. "I set the whole thing up."

Everyone stared at her as if she was a monster who'd just walked into the room.

"Look, I didn't know how far Malcolm would go, eventually. He was originally meant to draw Lara's attention away from Ike."

How could she? He was engaged to someone this devious? His stomach rolled. "Tell me what you did, Gloria," he said in a stern voice.

She huffed and sat back on the bed. "I wanted you for myself. But I saw the way Lara followed you around like a lost puppy. So I told Malcolm to ask her out on a date. Of course, Malcolm being Malcolm, he messed it up, which was how you found them outside the school and had to take Lara home."

"You set that up?" He couldn't hide his shock.

"Yes." She scuffed her shoes against the carpet. "You always treated me like your sister while you chased every other woman that came along. I couldn't watch you date some girl in my school, as well. You were always meant to be with me."

He shook his head in disbelief. "You do realise that Lara wasn't even on my radar until that day when I had to drive her home. Your actions drove us together, not apart."

She shrugged. "I realised that, which was why I had to get more help. I convinced one of the teachers you were driving Lara home regularly. She spoke to Mrs. Bello about it. I knew she was your mentor and she would be writing your final recommendation. If she spoke to you, you'd have to listen."

"It was you all along." He scrubbed a hand over his face. "I broke up with her. Why didn't you just leave it be?"

She bit her lip and looked away. "I wanted to be sure that the two of you wouldn't get together after her exams or after she left Hillcrest. So I had to make you believe she was with Malcolm, which was why I taught Malcolm how to woo her with gifts and to talk nicely. We planned that you would be at his party and obviously see him with Lara. I also had to make sure she lost interest in you, too, which was why I paid Stella to seduce you that night."

"What the fuck? Stella was part of your stupid game?" He jumped off from the floor. He pointed a finger at Gloria, clenched his hand, and slammed it on the table.

Everything on it jumped.

"So you let Malcolm and his gang do what they did to her just so you could have me? You are fucking sick!" He spun around. "I'm sorry, Lara. Jocelyn, I need to get out of here. If I stay any longer, I'll kill the bitch."

"Ike!"

"What? I shouldn't call you a bitch? When you could coldheartedly allow Malcolm to do what he did to Lara?"

"I didn't know he was going to do that!"

"Really? Didn't you come to the room? Didn't you see the boys here?"

"I did, but I thought they were just hanging out. They weren't doing anything to her when I saw her. It was only..." she trailed off.

"You can't stop talking now. Spit it out."

"I went to his house once. His parents weren't there. I saw him in his room. She was kneeling on the floor crying and he had a gun pointed at her head while he had his...penis in her mouth."

"Fuck!" Ike braced his hands against the walls. "And you did nothing!"

"Of course I did something. Seeing what he was doing made me feel sick. I told his mother about it. Within a few weeks, Malcolm was on a plane to the USA."

"So that's why he stopped." Tears flooded Lara's eyes. "He just stopped calling. I hoped he'd died in some car accident or something. It was later I found out he'd travelled out of the country. You'll never understand the relief I felt when I heard that. But I couldn't stay in Enugu for him to come back and find me. I had to get away and never return."

She slumped back against the chair and Ike was across the floor beside her.

"Can you help me stand?" she asked.

He hooked his arm under hers and gently pulled her up. When she stood, she dusted her jeans off and smiled at him. "Thank you."

She sucked in a deep breath. "Gloria, thanks for telling the truth. I'm glad that everyone here knows what really happened. I also want to say thank you for intervening when you did with Malcolm. Although you started the whole thing rolling and I can never forget it, I'm grateful that you realised what Malcolm was doing and did something to stop it."

She glanced at Jocelyn, who nodded.

"I've also thought a lot about whether I could ever forgive you. Knowing that there's some humanity in you makes it a little easier for me to say this. I forgive you, Gloria. I'm not saying we're going to be best of friends and hold hands while singing Kumbaya or anything like that."

Ada snorted.

"But I don't carry any grudge against you. I wish you the best. However, I hope you'll take up Jocelyn's services at some point or perhaps seek the help of a counsellor because some of the things you did were sickening. And only a warped mind can come up with all that manipulation."

She sighed.

"Anyway, I'm done talking. I'm exhausted. I'd like to go get some food and then sleep for the rest of the day."

Jocelyn smiled at her. "Well done. We can head out now."

Gloria was off the bed and out of the door quicker than anyone else. Henry followed her. Ada patted Lara's shoulders and then went out.

Ike stayed with Lara as she stepped out into the corridor. "Can I come and see you later?"

"I'm sorry," she said. "Not tonight. We're on a late flight out tomorrow. We can talk in the morning."

"Okay." He swallowed his disappointment. He would've liked to spend more time with her. But he understood she needed to rest after the day she'd had.

Outside, Gloria was already in the car and Henry stood beside it. He watched as Lara, Jocelyn, and Ada boarded their car and headed off before he opened the front passenger door of the vehicle waiting for him. It was best for him not to sit next to Gloria because he wasn't sure he wouldn't strangle her before they got back to the hotel.

They rode back in silence and he didn't wait for either of them when he got out of the car and headed for the reception. He spoke to the guy at the desk and arranged for another room. The man gave him the key to a new room and he headed upstairs to pack his things.

Gloria and Henry were in the room when he got in. He went straight to the wardrobe, took out his overnight bag, and started packing his things into it.

"What are you doing?" Gloria asked.

"What does it look like I'm doing? I'm packing my bag. I'm moving to another room."

"What's wrong with this room?"

He wanted to say '*You're in it.*' Instead, he said, "If I sleep in this room with you, you won't be safe."

"Ah, ah...why are you being so difficult? She forgave me. Why can't you?"

His mouth dropped open. "You are a piece of work. You still don't get it. You've manipulated me for years, and you want me to carry on as if everything is okay between us. Wake up, Gloria. It's over between us."

"You can't leave me." She got up off the sofa and walked in his direction.

"My advice is for you not to come close to me," he bit out and held up his palm in a stop signal.

Henry blocked Gloria from coming any closer.

"Okay. Fine, I'll give you time to cool off, but we still have a wedding in a few months."

Ike gave a cold laugh. "You really do need a shrink. I'm not going to marry you, Gloria."

"Are you really going to give up fifty percent of your business just so you can punish me for something I did five years ago?"

Ike pointed at her. "I'll give up all of my business if it means I never have anything to do with you."

"It won't come to that," Henry said. "I'm going to buy the shares, which will give Ike the money to pay your father off."

Ike's mouth dropped open, same as Gloria's.

She recovered first. "You can't do that."

"Yes, I can," Henry said with a tight smile. "The agreement his father signed with yours means that he can give back the market value equivalent cash instead of shares. I've been waiting for an opportunity just as this. Ike is my friend. He watches my back, I watch his."

Gloria groaned in frustration. "Whatever. You've been waiting for an opportunity to get one up on me. Well, you won't get that chance again. Get out, both of you. I don't want to see either of you again."

Ike grabbed his bag and slung it over his shoulder. Henry held the door open.

Ike turned to Gloria. "Gloria—"

She cut him off with a raised hand. "Unless you're apologising for being rude to me, I don't want to hear whatever else you want to say."

Before she could turn away, he saw the tears in her eyes.

He felt bad for leaving her like this. But she had made her bed and he really wasn't ready to forgive her.

"Take care of yourself," he said before walking out.

"I'll be seeing you around, Gloria," Henry said before shutting the door.

"Do you think she'll be all right?" Ike asked.

"She's got a thick skin. She'll be off harassing another Lagos bachelor before you know it."

Ike chuckled as he put the key in the lock of his door and opened it. "Yes, I'm sure you're right."

"What about you? What are you going to do?" Henry asked.

"Well, I'm going to start by seeing if Lara will have me back. And take it one day at a time."

"That's a good plan. In the meantime, I'm going to let you settle in. Pop over later if you need company."

"No problem," he said as he walked into the room. He dumped the bag on the floor and flopped on the bed. Then he pulled out his phone. There was a message from his mother. He sighed and sat up before dialling her phone number to give her the bad news about the wedding.

TWENTY-TWO

"Wake up, sleepy head," Lara said in a cheery tone as she got out of the bathroom where she'd showered, brushed her teeth, and dressed.

She'd had the best sleep in years, perhaps her entire life. She'd slept the whole night without the help of sedatives. It had been a long, dreamless sleep. She hadn't woken up in the middle of the night hot and shaking from nightmares.

Going through the session yesterday had been cathartic. She'd been exhausted by the end of it. They'd returned to the hotel for a quick debrief. Then dinner and she'd gone to bed at about 8pm. She'd had ten hours uninterrupted sleep not induced by medication.

This morning, she'd woken in a cheerful mood, feeling as if she finally had control of her life, instead of being ruled by fear and nightmares.

Finding a text message from Ike saying he was coming over had added to her cheerful disposition.

The fact that he still wanted to talk to her after the things she'd revealed the past day had to be good. Yesterday, a part of her had been worried that he'd be disgusted when he heard the truth. Instead, he'd been devastated by what had happened to her. He'd cried in her arms. She couldn't remember seeing a man cry before. She'd had to wipe his tears. And then, he'd gotten furious when Gloria had revealed her part in the ordeal.

Ada poked her head from under the covers. "What time is it?"

"Seven thirty," she replied.

"What? It's early," Ada grumbled.

"The early bird catches the worm."

"Eh, I'll gladly skip the worm, thank you." Ada pulled the covers back up and then down again. "Why the hell are you up and dressed at this ungodly hour, anyway?"

Lara grinned. "Ike is coming over at nine."

"He is?" Ada sat up. "I wonder what happened between him and Gloria. He looked ready to kill her yesterday."

"Yes, but I'm sure his friend would've prevented any bloodshed."

"At one point, I thought Henry would be the one throttling her. You know that expression parents have when children misbehave and they are about to pull out the cane?"

She nodded.

"He had it. I thought he was going to spank her or something." Ada chuckled. "Shame he didn't, because I would've paid to watch someone throttle her ass."

Lara burst out laughing. "That would be something to see, indeed. But I don't know if there's any man she couldn't wrap around her finger."

"Henry wasn't taking any crap from her. He looked like he had her figured out already. She needs a man like him to keep her in line. God help him." Ada laughed.

"Yeah, God help him if he decides to take her on. Anyway, enough about Gloria. Are you coming down for breakfast?"

"Do I have to? Breakfast is open till ten o'clock, right?"

"All right then, stay, grumpy. I'll go and knock on Jocelyn's door. She should be up."

"See you later." Ada dived back under the covers.

Lara chuckled as she grabbed her phone and bag and left the room. Jocelyn's room was next door. She knocked and waited a few seconds before the woman opened the door dressed in a white towelling robe.

"'Morning," she greeted. "I wondered if you'd like to come down for breakfast. Ada is still sleeping. I don't think she'll get out of bed before 9am unless there's an earthquake or something."

"Of course," Jocelyn said with a smile. "I just got out of the shower. Give me a minute to get dressed. You can come in."

She stepped away from the door, allowing Lara in.

"Thank you." Lara went over to the chair and sat down.

Jocelyn grabbed a dress from the hanger and went into the bathroom, leaving the door partially open. "I spoke to Ike this morning."

"Oh?" Lara's heart thudded.

"He wanted to know how you're doing."

"He could ask me directly."

"Of course. But he wanted to know my professional opinion. And he wanted to know how to behave so he didn't do anything to upset your progress."

She smiled. "And what did you say?"

"That you've done incredibly well. Your response to therapy continues to be positive. And I told him to be himself. The last thing you want is people tip-toeing around you."

"Good." Her smile widened as Jocelyn came out dressed in a maxi-length blue and black Ankara print dress. The woman always looked lovely. "You look great."

She smiled in return and put her shoes on. "Thank you. So do you."

"Thanks," Lara said and headed for the door. "Come on. I want to have food in my tummy by the time Ike turns up."

Jocelyn grabbed her key and purse and followed her. They went down to the half-full restaurant. They found a table by the window and settled down. The waiter dressed in a white shirt and black trousers took their order. They both went for the hot meals, ordering sausages and eggs with their toasted breads.

"So how do you feel this morning?" Jocelyn asked after the waiter left.

"I feel incredible. I can't remember the last time I felt so carefree. Like I can do anything." She felt so good, she was tempted to stand on the table and shout it out.

"This is fantastic. I'm so glad. It's amazing the changes that happen in the brain when we let go of our fears."

"It's better than any drug I've ever had."

"I'm so proud of you." Jocelyn reached across and held her hand. "Enjoy the feeling and hold on to it. Remember what I said. Don't let other people dictate how you feel about yourself. There'll be some days when something bad will happen and you might feel like falling back on the bad habits and thinking destructively. Use the techniques you've learned."

Lara nodded. "I'm going to take it one day at a time. I'm certainly going to make the most of the way I'm feeling today."

"Good," Jocelyn said as their food turned up.

"Thank you," she said to the waiter who left their plates of food as well as a pot of tea.

She ate the food with relish, savouring every last morsel.

"So how do you feel about Ike coming to see you? Do you still have feelings for him?" Jocelyn asked.

"Yes. I still love him. It will be nice to see him and talk to him, but I'm not expecting anything more from him. It's a huge thing to ask a man to love me after what's happened."

Jocelyn reached out and placed her hand over Lara's. "I know how you feel. I feel the same way about myself sometimes. But we all deserve to be loved, and anyone who can't love us isn't meant to be with us. Ike is a good man. He might surprise you, so don't shut him out. Okay?"

Lara blinked back tears. Sometimes, she forgot that Jocelyn had undergone something similar to what she had.

"Okay," she said just as her phone beeped.

She picked it up from the table and read the message. Her stomach fluttered. "Ike is here."

She typed a reply. *I'm in the restaurant.*

Another message beeped. *Okay. I'm coming in.*

"He's coming here." Her voice squeaked as she clutched her shaking hands on her lap. "Do you think I look okay?"

"You look great," Jocelyn said with a chuckle.

"I feel as if I'm going on my first date." She chuckled. "Actually, it is my first date."

The affair with Ike five years ago had never been dating. Not really. And she'd never allowed any other man close after Malcolm. Casual hook-ups and booty calls weren't dates.

Ike appeared in the restaurant and walked towards her. Her heart raced, her hands still trembling.

"Relax," Jocelyn said.

She nodded and sucked in a deep breath, letting it out slowly. Feeling better, she curled her lips into a smile.

"Hi, Jocelyn. Lara," Ike said as he stood next to their table.

He looked handsome and boyish in a blue t-shirt and dark denims and black sneakers with white soles. He didn't look like the boss she was used to seeing in suits.

"Ike, hi," Jocelyn greeted with a smile as she stood. They embraced briefly and he kissed her on the cheek.

Lara stood, too, her heart still thudding hard against her chest. Ike stepped up to her and wrapped his arms around her. He felt solid and warm. Great, as she sucked in his scent. He brushed his lips against her cheeks and her skin tingled.

"You look great," he said. "Both of you."

"Thank you," they both chorused as they exchanged knowing looks.

"Lara, I hope you don't mind if we go now. I have a few things lined up for the morning."

"Sure." She grabbed her phone and tote.

"Be sure to bring her back in time for her flight," Jocelyn said.

"I sure will," he said and took Lara's hand.

Her skin electrified from the point of contact, and the butterflies in her stomach were certainly having fun. She followed him outside. Warm sunshine greeted them as well as the chauffeur standing in front of the shiny BMW.

Ike ushered her into the back seat before getting in. The man shut the door and got into the driver's seat.

She relaxed into the soft leather as cool air wafted around her. She remembered the last time she'd sat in the back of a car with Ike. She'd been filled with anger and resentment, but none of those feeling came to play now. Instead, her excitement and elation remained. So much had changed for her in the month since she'd started working at TI.

"Where are you taking me?" she asked, watching the scenery as the car rolled out of the gates and joined the morning Enugu traffic.

Enugu wasn't as congested as Lagos, so the flow of pedestrians and vehicles didn't have the same manic quality as there. A part of her missed the sedate life she'd experienced here for the year she'd lived in this place.

"It's a surprise." He squeezed her right hand that he still held onto. "But I'll give you a hint. I'm taking you to somewhere I had wanted to take you to five years ago if we'd had the opportunity to date properly."

She tried to think of places but came up blank. Having never been on a date, she couldn't think. Ada's dates took her to restaurants or the beach, but they couldn't be going to eat since she'd just had breakfast. Enugu was landlocked, so there was no beach.

She turned to Ike with a frown. "I can't think of anything."

He chuckled. "Stop thinking and just relax. We'll soon be there."

She couldn't help smiling back. "Okay."

"Good girl."

Her breath hitched at the term, her heart thudding harder. It was his special word for her. She met his gaze and he held hers. Neither of them looked away. It was as if they were bound in that moment, held in place.

The car went over a bump and jolted them. She looked away, back onto the scenery outside the window.

"How is Gloria?" she asked.

Ike sighed. "She seemed fine this morning when I saw her get into the car to the airport. She's on a flight back to Lagos any minute now."

"You left her to go on her own?" She frowned.

"Henry is flying back with her."

"Oh, that's okay, then." She giggled when she remembered what Ada said. "Ada said there could be something going on between them." She covered her mouth with her free hand. "Oops, I shouldn't have said that."

Ike laughed.

"You're not angry? She's your fiancée."

He squeezed her hand, still amused. "No. She's no longer my fiancée as of last night. The wedding is off. But I agree Henry and Gloria would make a great couple if they don't kill each other first."

She tried to picture Henry and Gloria together, and all she could see was Henry's scowl and Gloria's pout. She broke down in giggles as Ike laughed.

The car slowed down and stopped. She looked around and couldn't help the huge smile spreading across her face.

"You brought me to the fun park?" she asked in awe.

"Yes. Do you like it?"

"Oh my God! Yes!" She scrambled around and pushed the door open. She did a three-sixty degrees spin and ran across to where Ike stood leaning against the car with a grin on his face. She grabbed his hand. "Come on."

He chuckled and she practically skipped to the entrance where he bought two tickets.

"I want to go on the spinning wheel first," she said and dragged him in that direction.

The attendant greeted them and boarded them when a pod became available. The space was small so their sides pressed against each other. She was giddy with excitement as it began the slow journey up.

"You don't know how long I've wanted to do this," she said as she gripped onto the bar.

"You must have come here," he said.

"No. I was waiting until after my exams. But even then, I couldn't because I was always afraid of bumping into Malcolm or one of his friends."

"I wanted to bring you but I was always worried about a student or teacher seeing us together."

"Thank you," she said as they climbed high into the air. From the top, she saw the metropolis as she'd never seen it before. The rooftops of houses, business, cars, people. She held her breath. "The sight is amazing."

"It is. Then again, so are you."

She turned in his direction. He leaned into her and pressed his lips against hers. Her breath whooshed out in surprise. He traced her mouth with his tongue. Her heart thudded faster and she reached for him, clinging on to his t-shirt with one hand. His hand came around to her nape holding her to him, as he continued his exploration of her inner recesses.

The kiss wasn't rushed, every touch a caress that spoke to her of tenderness, of banked passion. Of love. When they came up for air, she opened her eyes. They were almost at the ground level again. Ike didn't move apart until the pod jolted to a stop.

He lifted the bars that held them in place and they climbed out. They walked slowly, checking out the other offerings. She wasn't in a hurry to get on another ride, happy to just stand back and watch other people. There weren't many people here. It was the school holidays but still early morning.

She stopped when they saw a carousel. Except they weren't ponies. "What are those?"

Ike frowned. "They look like donkeys."

"Donkeys don't have antlers. They look like reindeers." She laughed.

He grinned. "They can't be reindeers. It's August. They're donkeys."

"Perhaps they're reindeer-donkey cross breeds." She giggled. "I want a ride."

He chuckled and made a sweeping wave. "Whatever my girl wants, she gets."

That phrase again. He would have her believing she was an innocent eighteen again and had her whole life ahead of her.

He spoke to the attendant who stopped the carousel so they could board. There was no one else on it. She got on and Ike got on the next one behind her. The carousel started moving. The ride was slow and bumpy.

"They certainly move like donkeys." She started laughing and nearly fell off the plastic animal. She turned back to look at Ike who had a twinkle in his eyes as he watched her.

She really couldn't remember being this carefree or this happy. Probably when her parents were still alive and she'd been a little girl.

The ride stopped and they got off. Ike wrapped his arm around her shoulders as they walked to the ice cream stand. He bought two cones and they stood and watched people on the dodgem cars as they ate. Afterwards, he tried the pot shot and won her a white stuffed polar bear.

"I'm going to have to take you back to the hotel shortly, but I wanted to ask you something first of all," he said, looking serious for the first time that day.

Her stomach knotted. "What?"

He took her free hand.

"For the first time since I met you, I'm in a position where I can ask you out without worrying about anyone else or anything else. I'm free to date you, but I really don't know if you want me. So I have to ask. Lara, will you be my girl?"

TWENTY-THREE

Lara left the room where she'd been meeting with the core project team. She hurried to her desk. The meeting had run over. If she was quick, she could pop out and grab a quick lunch before the end of the break time.

She'd been back at work for a few days after the two weeks she'd been away. Jocelyn had signed her off and Ike had approved her absence. But now she was back, she had a whole lot of work to catch up on.

She would've grabbed some lunch for Ike as well, but he was in a shareholder's meeting. Apparently, there'd been some changes to share ownership. They would be served lunch in there.

She got to her desk, grabbed her purse, and headed to the ladies'. She got into a cubicle and shut the door. She heard two people walk in but she didn't recognise their voices immediately.

"Did you read the post making the rounds on Twitter?" one of them said.

"Which one?" the other asked.

"Mr. Thomas's fiancée, Gloria, posted that she broke up their relationship because she found out he was cheating on her. She's been venting her anger on Twitter."

"Omigod!"

"And do you know who the other woman is?"

"I don't know. Who?"

"Jane told me in confidence that it's Lara. Apparently, she caught them together in his office."

"You can't be serious. She only started last month. And she's so quiet."

"Yeah. It's the quiet ones you have to be careful of, you know."

"Some people have no shame, you know."

Lara's cheeks heated up and she wanted a hole to open up in the ground. They were talking about her and she hated for people to discuss her, especially as gossip topic.

She waited in the cubicle for the women to leave before coming out to wash her hands. She'd lost her appetite and wasn't going out to lunch anymore. She dreaded going back to her seat where people could see her directly.

Rushing out of the ladies', she was lucky that most people seemed to be out to lunch. She walked over to Ike's office. The door was locked but she had a key so she opened it and walked in. She was going to work from in here for the rest of the afternoon. Thankfully, he would be out so she didn't have to worry about him coming back and finding her in here.

She tried to work but her mind raced as she wondered what exactly Gloria had posted. Not being able to help herself, she logged onto Twitter and searched until she found Gloria's handle. Her heart sank as she started reading all the tweets and replies. Gloria had turned herself into the offended party and her supporters were in outrage, calling Lara all sorts of nasty names.

She slumped on the sofa, tears welling in her eyes. What did she ever do to Gloria? Even after everything, she'd still forgiven the woman, and it turned out Gloria was not ready to move on.

The door to the office swung open. She sat up with a jolt. Ike walked into the office, surprise on his face at seeing her. Behind him were Henry and an older woman.

She turned her face away and swiped her eyes.

"Lara, what's the matter?" He was already striding across the space.

"It's nothing." She sniffed and bent to pack her things. "I'm sorry. I'll get out of the way."

"No." He tilted her chin up. "Not until you tell me what's wrong."

"Mum, excuse me for a minute," he said and took Lara's hand, pulling her into the adjacent bathroom. He closed the door and held her hands. "Tell me what's wrong."

"It's Gloria. She's been tweeting some nasty things about me." She lifted her phone up. "I know I shouldn't have read them, but some of the staff were gossiping about it and I overheard them."

He took the phone from her and scrolled through the tweets. He sucked in a deep breath and let it out slowly. "The thing about Gloria is that she's jealous of you."

"Jealous? What do I have that she doesn't have?"

"You have strength, you have heart, and of course you have me." He caressed her cheek as he smiled.

How did she get so lucky? He always made her feel good about herself. The past few days of being with him had been amazing.

"When you put it like that, I agree." She smiled. "I'd be jealous, too, if someone else had you."

"So don't worry about her." He leaned in and brushed her lips gently with his. "I love you. I will always love you. Nothing will ever change that. I won't ever abandon you again, no matter what anyone else says. You've got to believe that."

Warmth radiated through her body as her heart raced. He made her feel alive. The girl who'd been excited about a future with him five years ago had been resurrected. She smiled through tears of joy. "I do."

"Then I'd like to take you out there and introduce you to my mum. She's wanted to meet you since we returned from Enugu, but I told her you might not be ready yet. But she came for today's shareholder meeting and I'd really love for you to meet her."

"Your mum? I don't know." Lara swiped at her face, wondering how she looked. Her stomach tensed. "I must look horrible."

"You look lovely, like you always do."

Sighing, she bit her bottom lip. "But she's used to seeing Gloria who always looks immaculate."

Ike pulled her to the front of the mirror and stood behind her. "Look in the mirror. What do you see?"

She shrugged.

"I see you, and you are the brilliant woman I love. My mum will see that, too."

Smiling, her limbs tingled and the tension in her body dissipated. "Thank you."

He pressed his lips to her cheek, spreading more heat and tingles through her body. "Come on."

He took her hand, opened the door, and led her out to his office. His mother and Henry sat on the sofas talking.

"Mum, I'd like you to meet the love of my life. Lara, this is my mum." He pulled Lara to stand in front of him.

Although she felt a little nervous, it didn't overwhelm her as Ike's love for her shone through boosting her confidence. She curtsied. "Good afternoon, Mrs. Thomas."

"It's great to finally meet you, Lara." Ike's mum took her hand and pulled her onto the sofa and hugged her. "I've heard some wonderful things about you."

"You have?" She glanced at Ike, who just chuckled.

"Yes. You are a brave young woman, and I'll be so glad to have you as my daughter-in-law."

Her mouth dropped open and Ike grimaced.

Henry chuckled.

"What? You mean you haven't asked her to marry you? What are you waiting for?"

"We're taking it one step at a time, Mum," he said.

"It's my fault. I want him to be sure he wants to be with me," Lara said.

"I understand that. But I can tell you that by the way he's been singing your praises, he's pretty smitten and pretty sure."

"Mum!" Ike protested.

It only made Lara laugh. She loved the woman already. It seemed all her Christmases had come at once. For Ike to still love her knowing that her body had been violated was one thing but to have this kind of genuine affection from his family was the cherry on top of a very sweet cake.

"You're right, Mrs. Thomas—"

"You must call me Mum." The woman squeezed her shoulder.

Lara's heart filled, ready to burst with joy. "You're right, Mum. I would marry Ike if ever asks me."

She raised her brows at him, teasing him.

He leaned back. "It's like that, huh. You see how the two of them just ganged up on me so quickly," he said jokingly to Henry.

Henry chuckled. "Well, they're both right. You've got to get your act together. It's been five years coming."

"You, too, huh?" He chuckled and reached for his satchel. "Well, I have a surprise for all of you."

He pulled out a small box and Lara's mouth dropped open.

"No, you didn't?" She gasped and covered her mouth with both hands. Her body trembled and her heart thumped so hard against her chest, she feared it would punch a hole.

"Yes, I did." He grinned at her as he went on his knees and took her trembling left hand. "You are bold, brilliant, and beautiful, and nothing would make me happier than having you as my wife, Lara. Will you marry me?"

How was this thing even possible? How could she go from almost losing her mind to being absolutely ecstatic within such a short time? Whatever this was, she didn't want it to ever end.

"Yes, I'll marry you," she said in a choked voice.

He took out the most beautiful ring she'd ever seen and slipped it onto her finger.

"Congratulations!" both Mrs. Thomas and Henry said at the same time as they pulled them into hugs.

"You can bring the champagne in now, Jane," Ike said into his intercom before pulling Lara in for the most blissful kiss ever.

This was the first day of the rest of her life.

Thank you for reading Bound to Fate. If you enjoyed this book, please leave a review on the site of purchase.

Check out the books in the Bound series

Bound to Fate
Bound to Ransom
Bound to Passion
Bound to Favor
Bound to Liberty

ABOUT KIRU TAYE

Kiru wanted to read stories about Africans falling in love. When she couldn't find those books, she decided to write the stories she wanted to read. Her stories are sensual, her characters are flawed, and sometimes she adds a dash of exciting suspense.

Her debut novella, His Treasure won the Love Romance Café Book of the Year in 2011. The stories in her popular Essien series are international bestselling novels.

She believes this is the time for African writers of pop/genre fiction which is why she founded the publishing firm Love Africa Press. She is a USA Today bestselling author and also a co-founder of Romance Writers of West Africa, a support organisation for African romance writers.

Connect with Kiru
Website: http://www.kirutaye.com/
Facebook https://www.facebook.com/AuthorKiruTaye
Twitter https://twitter.com/KiruTaye
Instagram https://www.instagram.com/kirutaye/

VEGAS NIGHTS
BY
UNOMA NWANKWOR
BILLIONAIRE PACT BOOK 1

This is a work of fiction. Names, characters, businesses, places, events, locales, and incidents are either the products of the author's imagination or used in a fictitious manner. Any resemblance to actual persons, living or dead, or actual events is purely coincidental.

First published in United States of America in 2019

Kevstel Publications
info@kevstel.com

Dedication

Thankful to God from Who the gift comes I dedicate this to my readers. I love & appreciate you.

Author's Note

This series features friends Darius, Hakeem & Brice. They grew up rough, so made a pact to never go without. What they didn't bargain for was love. An *unexpected possession*, a *fumbled play* & a *slipping friendship*, will they eventually get it right? Enjoy this a fun, flirty, sweet romance under my Afro Luv Bites Collection.

1

"I'm about two seconds from strangling you!"

Safiya Nadar narrowed her eyes at Layla Assan, her best friend. She intended the look to be intimidating, but it didn't work. It only made Lay, as she called her, cackle. Rolling her eyes, she returned her focus to the treadmill to get her mileage in.

"You should know by now that I'm not scared of you," her friend replied.

Safiya shook her head and stopped the machine she'd been on for the last several minutes. She turned to her side and looked at Layla. They had been best friends since elementary school. Layla and her mother migrated to Atlanta from Ethiopia when she was nine. Safiya met Layla when she stuck up for her while she was being teased about being the newest kid in school. An experience she knew all too well since she, her grandmother and her dad had migrated from Tanzania two years prior. The little girls hit it off immediately and had been inseparable ever since. They had experienced almost everything together – lots of laughter, tears, arguments, heartbreaks and death. Their friendship stood the test of time. They were both the only children of their parents, opposites in behavior, but blood couldn't have made them any closer.

"Lay, I can't just go running off to Vegas."

"Who said anything about running off? We're strolling through the airport and getting on a plane." Layla gave her an incredulous look.

"You know what I mean—"

"Actually, I don't." Layla cut off her machine and turned. Her chest rose and fell, trying to fill itself with oxygen. She stepped down and wiped her face with a towel.

Safiya smiled. She always admired how well put together her friend was. Her long, honey-dyed hair was in a bun on the top of her head. Loose springy tresses fell all over her face. Her mocha skin shone and had a glow that was enhanced by the perspiration from her workout. Compared to Safiya's slender, five-foot, six-inch frame, Layla was a curvaceous five feet four, but her personality and confidence made one think she was well over six feet tall.

"Remember my dad? Who will take care of him while I hop off to Las Vegas with you?"

"I've told you we're not running or hopping anywhere—"

"Be serious, Lay."

"I am being serious. You know your dad loves when you take time for yourself. Unc is always complaining how you're so bogged down taking care of him, even though the nurses do their jobs well. He's not an invalid. Stop making him feel like one." She rummaged through her backpack and retrieved her wireless ear pods case.

"It's just for the weekend."

Safiya massaged her forehead.

"Or, I'll tell my mother to check up on him. You know he'll hate that, but I'll do it."

Safiya widened her eyes and shook her head. She remembered the last time she had Layla's mom check in on her dad. He didn't let her hear the end of it. He said she nagged him more than her late mother.

Layla laughed. "Okay then, stop making excuses. It's been a year since your divorce. And might I remind you, Justin is in Boston enjoying his newfound freedom and you're here wallowing as if the world has come to a halt."

Safiya creased her eyebrows. The excitement she used to feel in her heart at the mention of that name had been replaced by a hollow of regret. She and Justin had been college sweethearts. Layla had never liked him, but tolerated him because of her. She thought Justin was trying to create a wedge between them. And although that was true, it wasn't something Safiya shared with her best friend. She wanted her man and her girl to get along. Like most love stories, theirs was a match made in heaven, until it wasn't. They had gotten married barely six months after meeting, against her father's wishes. A month later, her dad became sick and she was all he had. Justin knew that, but her having to sacrifice time to take care of her dad angered him. Let him tell it, he was being neglected.

Justin was a budding musician and he was used to Safiya being able to bar hop with him and go on impromptu trips to pursue opportunities he felt would lead to something more. With a dad recovering from a stroke, she just couldn't do that anymore. As time went by, Justin sought the comfort and support he claimed she wasn't providing from another woman. It wasn't until two years into that relationship that Safiya found out.

"Look, you need to live. Life is short and things don't always go as planned, as you know. All you've done since the divorce is go to work, take care or rather smother your dad and repeat."

"That's not true," Safiya said.

"Name one thing you do that I don't have to force you to do. I'll wait." Layla put one hand on her hip and shifted her weight to one leg.

Safiya knew her friend was right, but she didn't want to admit it. The failure of a divorce weighed so heavily on her that she shielded herself from the public. Even though the circumstances of the demise of her home wasn't her fault, she couldn't help but wonder if she should've done things differently to save her marriage.

A beat passed between them. "I thought as much," Layla said. "Look, I have to write this article about the grand reopening of the *Walden Luxury Hotel and Casino*. Come with me. I'm scheduled to talk to the owner on Friday afternoon, then we'll have the whole weekend to ourselves. Sunday, we'll be back."

"I have to work Friday," Safiya countered.

"Call in sick. You hate that job. The only reason you're still there, is we haven't hit the lottery." Layla laughed.

Safiya rolled her eyes. "Let's go, cause you're seriously wrecking my nerves."

The two friends walked toward the exit of the gym they visited twice a week.

"You know I'm telling the truth." Layla stopped walking and placed her hands on her hips. She cocked her head to the side and creased her brows. "And how many times will I tell you I'm not scared of you."

As they stepped out into the cool March evening, Layla's phone rang, interrupting their conversation. With the smile on her face, Safiya knew immediately it was Todd, her fiancé.

She walked ahead to give her friend some privacy and let her mind wander to the comment about the lottery.

"When will that be?" she muttered to herself.

Hitting the lottery was a standing joke they had about being free to buy a building so they could open their own businesses. Layla, who was a journalist for *Lifestyles of the Wealthy*, had a dream of starting her own media house. A place where she could write articles about things that mattered and not the frivolous lifestyle of the rich and simple, as she called them. Safiya, on the other hand, worked for *Fragrance & Things* as a mixer and tester of fragrances for candles. She had the dream of opening her own candle making business where she could make products with ingredients that were healthy and smelled good. Opening her own business would not only give her something she was happy with creating, but it would allow her to properly care for her aging dad, make a real difference in her community and have the flexibility to spend more time doing things she once loved.

"I see you smiling. Todd must have been his nasty self on the phone," Safiya said as Layla approached.

"And you know this." Layla raised her hand for a high five, which Safiya gave.

"I love the two of you together. You took your time and got to know him. He treats you like a queen and I'm so happy for you."

"I know you are, and I love you for it. However, I'm tired of not telling you about the freaky stuff, so we need to find you a man and quick."

"Nope, we are not looking for a man. There's so much I have to focus on right now and a man isn't one of them. I'm happy living vicariously through you." Safiya walked over to her grey Altima and pressed the key fob to unlock the car. She opened the back door and threw her gym bag in.

"Whatever. So, Friday are we on?"

"Only if you promise it's just a girl's trip and you won't try to set me up with anybody."

Layla sighed and shrugged. "Okay, whatever…your loss. Ms. Kitty will soon close up with the way you're going."

"Oh my gosh. On that note, I'm going home." Safiya opened the car door. Layla naming her body parts shouldn't be new to her, but it still shocked her every time.

"Hmm, yeah, bye. Talk to you later. Kiss my Uncle poo for me. I'll come get you from work early on Thursday. We need to go shopping."

Safiya looked down at the old tee and black leggings she was wearing. She bugged her eyes, looking back up at her friend.

"Yeah, don't look at me like that. You're not going to Sin City like…ugh. I don't even know what to say. But yes, we're giving you a makeover *rafiki*."

"You do know I don't own my job, right? I can't just leave whenever."

"And you do know I don't care. Figure something out. Before Justin, you were daring and resourceful. I don't know how he sucked out your soul, but we're getting it back. Love you, *dada yangu*." Layla strode off to her Jeep Cherokee, not waiting for her response.

Safiya sighed and got in her car. *Vegas, here I come.*

She started her car and pulled out of the parking lot headed to her dad's house. She had been pulling double shifts a lot lately, so she looked forward to spending the day with her favorite person.

2

"You're a freaking genius!"

Darius Gray raised his champagne flute in salute to his best friend and investment advisor, Hakeem Richardson.

"Cut it out, man. I only brought you the deal. It was your signature ruthless business strategy that made it all come together."

The friends clicked glasses and took a sip. Standing at the huge window of his penthouse suite, Darius took in the view of the city he had spent a lot of time in over the last year.

"So, you ready for tomorrow?" Hakeem asked, taking a seat on the couch.

"As ready as I'll ever be. It's going to be lit."

"It wouldn't be you if it wasn't." Hakeem chuckled.

"You're as bad as I am, so don't throw stones."

"I never said we were bad," Hakeem grinned.

Both men shared a laugh. Darius met Hakeem and his brother Brice in an orphanage during their preteen years. The three of them grew up together and formed a strong bond in the process. Darius and Hakeem, who were closer in age, naturally gravitated towards each other and became best friends. The three of them went through so much together. Right before an angel took Darius in, they agreed to stay in touch. And they did, resulting in a brotherhood spanning more than a decade.

Darius pulled out his phone. He needed to call his assistant to make sure everything was in place. Julia was always on top of everything, but the perfectionist in him always had to be sure. He looked at the reminder notification he'd just received.

"Oh, shoot."

"What is it?"

"I forgot I have this interview with some reporter from that lifestyle magazine."

"When?"

"Tomorrow at noon."

"So, what's the problem? Still gives you plenty of time for the opening in the evening. Is Vanessa going to be back by then?"

Darius ran his hand over his head he kept clean shaven. In the early days, he loved the press and interviews, but now he shied away from them. One wrong quote and his stock would plummet. He learned that the hard way a couple of years ago.

"You know I don't like this press thing. I don't know why I agreed to this one."

"Because it's the magazine you vowed to get on the cover of," Hakeem replied. "Speaking of, how does it feel?"

"What?"

"Hitting the billion-dollar mark before thirty-five. That was your goal and you did it. All by yourself." Hakeem paused. "I'm proud of you, man."

Darius who was now the Owner and CEO of *Gray Holdings* remembered the day he told Hakeem he would be a self-made multi-millionaire by thirty and would hit the billion mark by thirty-five. In fact, all of them had made that pact. They each landed in the orphanage due to their parents not making the best decisions. The desire to leave a legacy and be there for their own kids, when they had them, propelled the friends. It was a mission they had all accomplished.

For Darius, after being rejected for adoption so many times, he became a runaway and lived on the streets. He knew what it was like to go hungry for days. He also knew the torture of sleeping on hard surfaces with little or nothing to shield him from the cold. He remembered days when he saw a rat and wished it was a juicy steak. He'd experienced hunger pangs so painful, it felt as though his intestines were feeding on themselves because there was no food for them to feast on. He survived by pick-pocketing to buy what he could, or shop lifting food and others essentials. It was during one of his thefts that he met the angel who would make a lasting impression on him. Although she was with him for a brief time, she gave him what he'd always longed for – a home.

"None of this would have been possible if you didn't invest in my first venture," Darius said.

The friends, though poor, were smart. They ended up getting scholarships and attending college together. Hakeem, who dabbled in trading stocks, made a huge profit right after college and agreed to invest in Darius's first flip job.

"You were good with your hands. So, when you talked about flipping houses and I could help, why wouldn't I?" Hakeem finished off his drink. Then stood and walked to the bar to refill his flute. "Now look at you, acquiring and flipping real estate all over the world."

"You didn't have to invest in me…so thank you."

Several moments of comfortable silence passed between the pair. Darius was lost in his thoughts of what the weekend held. He would finally be done with Las Vegas for a while and could head back to his home base in Georgia. His schedule rarely kept him in his ten-bedroom mansion located in the city of Johns Creek, but that was also where his center and real heart was and he was looking forward to spending some time with her.

"You've avoided two of my questions now."

Hakeem's voice brought him back to the present. "What questions are those?"

"Vanessa and how does it feel." Hakeem counted off his thumb and index finger.

"I feel accomplished. And Vanessa man…I don't know. I think she's beginning to want what I can't give and that's my cue to let her go."

"You're telling me as beautiful as she is and all the years you guys have been doing this off and on thing, the fear of loving someone trumps trying to make it work?"

Love? That was a taboo word for him. Love made a person weak and vulnerable. It made one relax and not take precautions, thinking the one you love will have your back. His angel had loved and look where it left her. Six feet under. So, yes, he'd pass on the weak emotion.

Darius took a deep breath. "That's exactly what I'm saying."

"One day, the money won't be enough. You'll want more."

"And until then, I'll keep acquiring the money. With a clear head." Darius studied his friend. "What's with all the love talk? Are you ready to settle down?"

"I don't know. Some days I am. Bed hopping every night is getting old." Hakeem rubbed his arm absently.

Darius watched as his friend's eyes sunk with regret, as they always did with this topic. That could only mean one thing – Mariama Niang. Over the years, Darius had become convinced she was Hakeem's true love. Darius swallowed a lump in his throat. If he could wish for anything, it would be to go back to that night and make it right for his friend. But even he couldn't. He'd advised Hakeem to move on, but he didn't seem to be able to do it.

"Who knows? You might meet her tonight at the after-party." Darius winked.

Hakeem groaned and Darius laughed. In his opinion, they were still young, but if his friend wanted love, who was he to tell him different? As long as cupid knew to stay miles away from him.

◆◆◆

"I said no cheese and no onions!"

Darius heard the raspy voice as he walked into the hotel's restaurant the next morning. His newest luxury hotel had a soft opening two weeks ago, and guests have been arriving by the thousands since then. Later in the evening was the grand opening, so now was not the right time to have dissatisfied customers.

"We're so sorry about that—"

"That's what you said the first time you brought me the omelet with cheese. You went back to fix that and now you're bringing me the omelet with onions. I told you the first time I didn't want either in my omelet."

Darius stood against the table in the back as he noticed the two women. He was walking over to diffuse the situation, but something in that sultry tone halted him.

"Safiya, I know you don't joke about your food, but calm down." The woman sitting by her laughed.

Darius observed the scene as the chief chef came out and apologized profusely to both women. He then took her plate and hurried back to the kitchen. Darius took in both women. Since they were seated, he couldn't get a full view. However, the one he now knew as Safiya had him intrigued and his loins tight. The curiosity to see the face that went along with that voice had him sauntering towards their table.

"Good morning, ladies," Darius greeted.

Both ladies looked up at him, but only one of them showed signs of recognition.

"You are—" the other lady started.

He quickly cut her off. "Darius Gray, pleased to meet you." He nodded at the pair.

"Ummmm, you're more than Darius Gray. I have an interview with you later," Safiya's friend spoke again.

Darius nodded and smiled, his eyes resting on Safiya, who hadn't yet said a word. She had briefly acknowledged him with her eyes before refocusing on her food.

"I look forward to it Ms...."

She stretched out her hand "Assan. Layla Assan."

Darius shook her hand.

"And this rude one over here is Safiya Nadar." She nudged her friend with her elbow. Her friend growled back at her.

The sound sent an unfamiliar sensation up Darius's spine.

"Excuse her. Something about not getting her food right sets her off."

"Well, I hope the issue has been fixed to your satisfaction."

Safiya looked up at him. In that moment, the trip over to their table was worth it. The right words to describe her beauty eluded him. The wrong adjective would be a disservice.

"Yes, it has. Thank you," Safiya said, and immediately went back to scrolling through her phone and eating.

"I'm glad." Darius turned to Ms. Assan. "I'll see you in a couple of hours. You ladies enjoy your meal."

Darius walked away and went straight to guest services. He wanted to know if they were staying in the hotel or if they just came for breakfast. He had an interview with Ms. Assan soon and needed to know how cooperative he'd be based on what he needed her to do.

3

"Tell the pilot there's been a change of plans. We leave for Atlanta tomorrow night, not tonight."

A couple of hours later, Darius paced his office as he rattled off instructions to his assistant. Pleasure never came before business, but this time, he was willing to make a tiny exception.

"Call Mr. Chang in Hong Kong and tell him I have another obligation, so we'll have to push our meeting out. Tell Mr. Patrick he should head to Miami after he leaves San Diego. He has to represent me for the Realtors Annual Gala." Darius walked behind his desk and flipped through his iPad. "And lastly, call the florist. Instead of the usual white roses, send Grammy pink roses."

With the information he'd just gathered, he had to do some swift adjustments. His curiosity had been piqued and when that happened, he chased whatever it was until he got it. The mocha beauty currently staying in his hotel had his attention.

"Yes, Mr. Gray. Is there anything else?" Julia asked.

Darius leaned back in his leather seat and tented his index fingers under his chin. A few seconds later, he looked up at Julia. "No, that will be all. Thank you."

Julia gave him her signature warm smile and walked toward the exit. Darius attempted to refocus on the day's activities, but try as he might, his mind wandered back to Safiya Nadar. In the moment he was in her presence, all the senses in his body came alive. He allowed his memory to recollect her features. Her mocha skin smelled like strawberries and coconut. Her lips were perfectly outlined with deep burgundy lipstick. As he watched her lips wrap around the fork, he almost let out a moan. Her hazel-brown eyes were shrouded by long black eyelashes. Her jet-black hair was straight and stopped right at her shoulders. He found it so sexy that she kept tucking loose strands behind her ears when she leaned into the plate in front of her. The black t-shirt she wore showed cleavage he'd love to bury his head in.

Over the years, women had come in and out of his life. Some as just bed partners, others as dates, but none could stake claim to him. After their time was up, he compensated them heavily, and they went their separate ways. He was no stranger to beauty. On his arms, he'd had models, actresses, white-collared professionals, you name it. But there was something about Safiya that pulled him in. If he had to move his flight several hours to find out what it was, that's exactly what was going to happen.

"So, how do you relax?" Ms. Assan asked.

"Relax? I have no idea what that is," Darius joked.

Ms. Assan had arrived in his office an hour ago for the interview and they were now finishing up. At least he hoped they were.

She had begun by asking him about his childhood. He never really shared his story in detail except the stuff the media already knew; he was an adopted orphan. He never shared the truth that he was abandoned before he became orphaned. The fact that his parents left him at a fire station like yesterday's trash and walked away was something he wasn't proud of. For years, the rejection made him hang his head in shame and fueled his rebellious phase. If he wasn't good enough for them, he didn't see how he could be good enough for anyone.

He'd continued that way until he met Jacqueline Gibson aka Ms. Jackie. That day he was in a store, stuffing essentials into his baggy pants. He bumped into her and everything fell to the floor. He was busted and furious at the same time. As he ran from the store, he cursed her as bad luck and hoped he'd never see the woman again. Fate had something different planned. A week later, she turned up in his orphanage to get some papers signed by the director. That was the beginning of his adoption journey. Darius winced at how much hassle and pain he had given her.

At the time, his goal was to shield himself from her love before she abandoned him like the other woman in his life had done. The reverse turned out to be the case though. She had cared for him unconditionally, making him a part of her family that just consisted of her mother. And when she died a few years later, he almost lost it, but Grammy, as he called his adopted grandmother, wouldn't let him. She put aside her own grief to make sure he was okay. She was his heart and he would move the world to give her anything she desired. Luckily, she hadn't asked him anything he couldn't provide.

"Mr. Gray?"

Darius blinked his eyes and returned his attention to the woman in front of him. "I apologize. You asked about relaxation, correct?"

"Yes. You're an astute billionaire, owning several chains of hotels and casinos around the globe. This year, you added team owner to your belt by acquiring the *Peach Heights* – the Atlanta Baseball team. I'm sure your schedule is extremely busy, but you know what they say, all work and no play…"

"For me, work is relaxing. I've come to find out an idle mind is a terrible thing. It can take me into dark places, so I like to remain occupied. However, I do find time to step away from it all, especially when I go back home to Atlanta."

"What do you like to do?"

"Let me start by saying not golf." Darius laughed and Ms. Assan joined him.

"There's a lake in my backyard and I love sitting there looking out into nature and meditating. I also like to work in my woodshed. Building unique fixtures."

"Oh wow, that's an interesting fact. Pieces you sell?"

"No, it's a hobby of mine and are for my eyes only."

Woodwork was something Jacqueline encouraged him to do to channel his anger. When she died, he stopped and resumed his rebellious behavior until Grammy had a heart-wrenching talk with him. He picked up the hobby again but now, the shed was where he worked and had private conversations with Jacqueline, alone.

"Got it." Ms. Assan looked at her watch. "We're at the end of our time. But I can't let you go without asking you the question on every single woman's mind."

Darius knew it was coming. She hadn't asked it and he dared hope she wouldn't, but here it was.

"We all know you're a very private man, but there has to be a girlfriend somewhere. Is there?"

Darius chuckled. "I'm still a single man. No significant other that I know of."

"Are you adverse to marriage?"

"Short answer…no."

"Long answer?"

"Women need attention and commitment, neither of which I have the capacity for presently."

"Well, at least you're honest about it and not leaving a trail of broken hearts." Ms. Assan smiled.

"Never that."

Several moments later, Darius walked back over to his desk while Ms. Assan packed up her camera and notepad. They'd wrapped up the interview, but she wanted a few pictures of his office and its view.

"Thank you again for talking to me. The interview should be out in next month's issue of the magazine."

"It was a pleasure." Darius extended his hand for a brief handshake. "I'd like to invite you and your friend to the grand opening of the hotel as my special guests tonight. As a rule, I never allow reporters in my private suite. However, I'll make an exception for you."

Just as he expected, Ms. Assan's mouth fell in shock. *Bingo, she took the bait.* He had quite a reputation over the years for being no-nonsense when it came to his privacy, so to invite a camera into his personal space was a major exclusive.

"What? Really?"

"Yes." Darius shoved his hands into his pockets. "Julia will give you the necessary information."

"Thank you so much, Mr. Gray." Ms. Assan made her way to the door and just as she was about to touch the doorknob, Darius called out.

"Ms. Assan."

She turned to face him.

"I do expect to see both of you tonight."

He saw the exact moment in her eyes when she understood what he really wanted. To his surprise, a huge grin took over her face.

"You will," she responded and made her exit.

4

"You cannot be serious."

Safiya cradled her face and took in a breath. She exhaled and glared at her friend as they walked through the upscale boutique.

"Will you stop being dramatic." Layla looked at her. "The interview went well, and the man invited us to be his guests. What's the big deal?" She lifted a dress from the rack and put it beneath her chin. She stepped in front of the mirror to inspect the outfit.

"The big deal is, you promised it would be a girls' trip. Come on, Lay, I'm not in the mood for a man," Safiya whined.

"A man is definitely in the mood for you," Layla snickered.

Safiya remained silent, a sign that she was serious and most likely frustrated. Layla got the message and turned to look at her. The stare-off lasted only a few second before Layla put the dress back and walked up to Safiya. She took her hand and they sat down on one of the benches.

"Remember that time in Middle School when your pet parrot died?"

Safiya creased her eyebrows, wondering what Slinky had to do with her not wanting to be at a loud party with a billionaire and his other rich friends.

"I hope there's a point to this."

"Stop being difficult and follow me here," Layla scolded.

Safiya nodded with a faint smile. Slinky was very dear to her. Her grandmother gave him to her right before she passed away. When the bird died, she was devastated.

"Remember you mourned that darn thing for weeks…"

"He was special."

"And so was Justin."

Safiya rolled her eyes.

"What I'm trying to say is that after a while, you got a dog and now Rex is like a member of the family."

"He *is* a member of the family." She loved her golden retriever.

"Exactly my point. You got over Slinky and were able to give Rex a chance and love again." Layla paused. "Yes, Justin messed up. Yes, you were hurt. But you must live your life. I'm not telling you to get married. What I am telling you is, have a good time tonight before we go back to our boring lives tomorrow."

Safiya sighed. "You have a whole fiancé. How would he feel?"

"I'll be there partially working. Also, I told Todd and as long as they don't touch or breathe on me, he's cool. You, on the other hand, have no restrictions. And I'm telling you now, Mr. Gray has a thing for you. Please don't be weird."

A few hours earlier, while Layla was conducting her interview, Safiya was lounging by the pool, taking in the Vegas sun while enjoying the company of her Kindle. As she sipped on a mimosa, she berated herself about not taking time off for self-care. She was getting to the erotic part of the book when Layla's loud squeal interrupted her. Several minutes later, Layla had run down how the interview went and told her about the extra pictures she could get tonight. But then there was a catch.

They had always had each other's back – doing anything for the other. That's just the kind of sisterhood they had, but Safiya didn't think she could pull this off. She hadn't been on any dates since Justin broke her heart and as she told Layla before, she had big short-term goals and men were nowhere in her immediate sights.

"Can you please get out of your head?"

"Uhhh...sorry."

"What had you so zoned out?"

"Just thinking about the future."

"There won't be any future if you don't start living for today."

"You know I'll go with you even if I don't want to."

"Yes, I know you will. But I'm asking more than that. I'm asking you to live a little. Don't be weird. Where's the woman I once knew? Daring, confident. Come on, Justin shouldn't have that much power."

In that moment, something snapped in Safiya. He had no power unless she gave it to him. All the lies and deceit came flooding through her like a wave that hit shore. She had pushed the hurt down so deep that she had begun to act like it wasn't so bad. But it was. She rode hard for that man and at the end of the day, he abandoned her in her time of need, and moved on to have a whole new family. That was it. Love was nowhere on the radar, but there was nothing that said she couldn't have a good time.

"What's that smile? A yes?" Layla asked.

"Yes."

Layla squealed and the two friends hugged. They stood up and walked through the store and picked up dresses they wanted to try out for the events of the evening. Since it was a grand opening and they were also relaxing in VIP for the night, they opted for classy and chic. As Safiya tried on the different dresses she took to the dressing room, her mind wandered to the man…Darius Gray.

After the breakfast fiasco and Layla told her who he was, she decided to Google him. Safiya knew from being with Justin that everything you read on the internet was not true. But there was never smoke without fire.

Darius Gray had the most alluring, chestnut colored eyes she'd ever seen. His smooth, hairless scalp, perfectly trimmed moustache and beard oozed dominance and authority. His face showed signs of a hard life that had been spruced up by money. From looking at him earlier, he probably stood at least six feet, five inches. There was still something about him that intrigued her. Especially when she saw the photo shoot he did for GQ.

The images of him flooded her mind and caused her body to tingle. He was cut to perfection, displaying a gorgeous six pack.

His muscles rippled against one of the polo shirts he wore in another shot. The image that stuck with her most of all was his taunt ass in the last shoot. It looked like you could break something on it. He was exquisite.

Darius was six years older than her, and had numerous luxury hotels and resorts and other ventures. He came from a lowly background, but now lived in the opulent Johns Creek. Safiya sighed as that was a long way from her modest DeKalb County. What stuck out though was the abundance of information about his social life. He never seemed to keep one woman for long. She wouldn't exactly call him a playboy, as there was nothing about any kind of scandal with any of the women, and they were far and few in between. What was glaring was that none of them lived like her: normal. They were all actresses or models.

There was a knock on the dressing room door. "Girl, get out here. Let me see how the dress fit."

Safiya looked at the emerald gown she had on and smiled. She opened the door for her friend and stepped out.

Layla's mouth fell open. "They ain't ready, *rafiki*... nope they are not ready."

"You like it?"

"I love it! I can't wait until tonight."

"Let me see yours."

Layla lifted the black and white sequined dress. Safiya gave her a smile of approval. They already had their nails done at home, so all that was left was make-up and Layla did a mad face beat. Now all they had to do was enjoy the rest of their day and be ready for tonight.

As they paid for their dresses, Safiya thought about hers. It was a bit more daring than anything she would normally wear, but she was now determined to live a little. Even it was for just one night. The next day she'd be back home, to her boring job and her boring life. Besides, what happened in Vegas stayed in Vegas.

Mr. Gray wanted her company? Her company he would have.

5

He was used to the opulence, the crowd and people vying for his attention. He was also used to people trying to fulfill his every desire. He was, after all, a very wealthy man, and not to be egotistical, but he was also aware of his charm and looks. But what Darius wasn't used to was being ignored by the person he wanted the most.

The ribbon cutting happened a couple of hours ago. After some speeches by him and key high-ranking members of the hotel's staff, dignitaries were taken on a tour of the hotel. After that, they retired to the massive dining room for a light lunch provided by the one and only Chef Perez he had flown in from Paris. Although he never got sidetracked when business was concerned, he couldn't keep his eyes off a certain Ms. Nadar.

When he saw her and Ms. Assan enter the lobby earlier, his breath literally caught in his throat. The dress she wore brought out the animal in him. It was a shade of green. He wasn't sure of the name, but the color against her sepia toned skin was magic. The dress stopped at her knees, showing her shapely legs and hugging her curves like a glove. She had on light make-up, but those lips. Those lips, lush and glossed, looked so soft. He longed to press his lips against them to test his assumption.

He was okay, until she walked across the room. Her exposed skin almost made him choke on his drink. The dress had a plunging back that stopped right above her waist and he could see the inscriptions of a tattoo across the base of her neck. The desire to trace his tongue over it was so strong, he had to put distance between them immediately. There was a time and place for everything.

But their time was now. Ms. Nadar had done everything she could to keep away from him. But now her time was up. Darius, Hakeem and some of his business associates and their significant others were in his private lounge above the hotel. He sat in the corner with Hakeem, nursing his drink.

"I've seen that look. So are you going to do something about it or mope all night?" Hakeem said interrupting his thoughts.

"Shut up, man."

Hakeem lifted his hands in surrender with a laugh. Darius never knew it was possible, but he was nervous about talking one on one with Safiya Nadar. Something about her told him she wasn't easily impressed. Lifting his glass, he threw back his drink, and grimaced at the burn of the liquor as it went down his throat. He set his empty glass down, and sauntered toward the women, who were laughing over drinks.

"Good evening, ladies, I hope you're having a nice time," Darius said.

"Ah! Mr. Gray—" Ms. Assan started.

"Call me Darius."

Safiya smiled and lifted her champagne flute in acknowledgement before taking a sip. *She isn't ignoring me. Progress.*

"Okay, Darius, this place is simply divine. I have no idea how people can afford to stay here for long periods of time. But then again, apparently a whole lot of people can."

Darius chuckled.

"Thank you. I'll be sure to pass your glowing compliments to my architect." Darius glanced at Safiya. "Ms. Nadar are you always this quiet?"

"I'm not quiet. Just observing."

"And what are your observations so far?"

"That there's a whole other world than the one I'm used to."

"How so?"

"Well, it's definitely not this."

"So tell me." Darius paused when he saw her hesitation. "That's if it's not too uncomfortable for you."

"It's not like the one you grew up in, for sure. This hotel is like something I think heaven would look like."

Darius laughed again, but didn't forget the insinuation that he'd always had it good. "You'd be surprised at how I grew up."

Darius glanced at Ms. Assan who smiled at him.

"Ms. Assan…"

"Please call me Layla and I'm giving you permission to call her Safiya."

Safiya rolled her eyes at her friend and laughed. Darius turned to her with a raised brow, non-verbally asking for her permission as well. She nodded and he turned toward Layla.

"I'll call over the hotel manager to walk you around to get some of the pictures I promised you." Darius looked around and summoned Mr. Wringer over.

"That would be fantastic." She patted her bag which Darius assumed had her camera. "While I'm gone, take care of my friend."

"You do know I'm standing right here." Safiya raised her hand.

Darius watched as Layla gave her friend a stoic look and returned her eyes to him. "You seem like a really nice man. But I also know that if I make one wrong move, your security will tackle me like a ball player. I want you to know, though, that if anything happens to her, I'd gladly go to jail."

Darius was both stunned and pleased by her threat. He could already tell the dynamic of the friendship between the ladies. Normally quick on his toes, her words left him speechless, so he simply answered. "Noted."

Safiya shook her head and closed her mouth that had dropped open in shock.

Darius's hotel manager walked over. "Yes, Boss?"

"Ms. Assan here would like to take some pictures of the private lounge areas. Please show her around."

"Sure thing." He turned to Ms. Assan. "This way please."

Safiya followed them with her eyes until they disappeared around the corner. She then turned to Darius.

"I know you don't want to stand here by yourself. Please come with me. My area is over there. Then you can tell me all about how I grew up in a world so different from yours."

"You're not gonna let that go, are you?"

"Nope." Darius winked.

"So we might as well get started now."

A while later, Darius and Safiya were sitting on one of the plush couches in a secluded part of the club. She'd become more relaxed and he was enjoying her company. He still couldn't believe how strikingly beautiful she was. They'd talked a little politics, television shows – not that he really watched a lot of television – and sports. To his amazement, they shared some of the same interests. The more she spoke, the more he wanted to know. Why, he couldn't place, so for now he'd say she fascinated him.

"You've told me your favorite team, show, and political affiliation, but I still think there's so much more," Darius said.

Safiya took a sip of her drink. "Because there is, as I'm sure there is with you." She uncrossed her legs and then crossed them again. The rise of her dress had Darius's throat constricting. He had tried to ignore the pull between them all night, as he didn't want to scare her off. But the more comfortable they became with each other, the harder he found it to contain the desire that was growing within him.

"So why hotels?"

Darius thought about his reason and didn't know if he wanted to be that vulnerable with her.

"Let's make a deal. I provide an answer, and you grant me a personal question of my own."

"Can I reserve the right to decline to answer?"

"Yes, but you have to offer up something else."

"Offer? Don't you mean answer?"

"No, I mean offer." He winked at her.

Just as he expected, she hated to be challenged and took the bait. "Shoot."

"Okay, I was homeless for a period in my early teens. So, I guess subconsciously I wanted to own houses in excess. Homes that were like homes away from home."

"But why for the rich and not for the less privileged?"

Darius felt his anger rise at that question. Why people automatically assumed he didn't do anything for the less privileged always amazed him.

"Have you heard of Now Living?"

"Uhhh...yes. I love the work they do for the downtrodden. Is that you?" Safiya's eyes bugged out. She looked at him with remorse and astonishment.

Darius simply nodded.

"I'm so sorry for assuming. I should know better."

"That's okay. Let's just say you can make it up to me later." Darius paused and decided to pursue what she was saying. "Why should you know better?"

"I mean people make assumptions about me that aren't true."

"Like?"

"When I got my divorce…"

"You're divorced?"

"Yes," she whispered.

"How long now?" Darius wanted to ensure there wasn't a crazed ex running around somewhere.

He had lived his life scandal free and needed it to stay that way. One, he couldn't stomach scandals and two, he couldn't do anything that would affect his reputation, stock and eventually his money. Poverty was never ever going to be an option where he was concerned. This time, however, the mention of an ex brought out another feeling – possession.

"Over a year."

"I hope he's not lurking around somewhere trying to get you back."

Safiya raised her brows. "Why? Will you protect me?" She tilted her head back and laughed, showing her perfect, white teeth.

Her elongated neck begged for a kiss. When she noticed he wasn't sharing the moment, she calmed down.

"I'll do more than protect you if you let me." His voice was low.

She raised her hand and tugged her earlobe, something he noticed she did any time she was nervous.

"I didn't know that you had to wait for anyone to let you do anything."

"I usually don't, but you're different."

"Why? I'm sure you have women falling at your command."

"But I have a feeling, not you."

"You got that right." Safiya looked around the lounge. "This is all nice, but it isn't the real world.

He noticed her attempt to change the topic and indulged her. "Just because it's not your world doesn't mean it's not real."

"You do have a point. The more reason I'm not trying to get caught up in it."

Darius studied her. He made her nervous and he was conflicted about it. On one hand, it confirmed her attraction to him. While on the other, she was doing everything to fight it. All he wanted was for her to trust him enough to relax. He was used to women throwing themselves at him for what he had. The woman beside him couldn't care less and he was enjoying that.

"Tell you what? Let me make it your world for the night."

Safiya stood with an infuriated look on her face. Darius knew immediately that she had misconstrued what he meant to say. He stood. Despite her height, he still towered over her.

"No, no, I meant for you to allow me show you the town. The view of the city is exquisite at night and I'd love to show you around."

"Oh." Safiya used her hands to smooth down her dress that had risen with the haste in which she stood. "Ummmm…. let me go check on Layla."

"Ms. Assan is in good hands. I promise." Darius stepped closer to her, deliberately invading her space. Unlike before, she didn't back away. She was a far cry from the woman who didn't even look him in the eye at breakfast the previous day. He was grateful to whatever was responsible for the change. That and the liquid courage in her glass.

Safiya gave him a skeptical look. Darius chuckled when she took out her phone and called her friend. After a couple of "oh's", "that's nice", "sure", and "goodnights", Safiya hung up the phone and returned it to her purse.

"I told you she was fine. You ready?"

She nodded. "Lead the way tour guide. I have to be back early because my flight leaves pretty early in the morning."

"That's new. I've never been called that before."

"Well, Mr. Gray, there's always a first time for everything."

"Oh yes. Yes, there is."

6

"I can't believe it. Are you serious?" Safiya asked. She was barely able to hold her laughter in as she waited on Darius's answer.

His face was flushed. "Scout's honor." He raised his hand.

She swatted his hand. "You weren't even a scout."

He shrugged and laughed along with her. "You know what I mean."

For the past couple of hours, they'd been riding round the streets of Las Vegas in his stretch limousine. They shared drinks and stories about themselves that no one else knew. He had taken off his tie and jacket and rolled up his sleeves, while she was bare feet.

"Butt dialing her grandma has to be a classic." Safiya took another sip of her drink. Her tolerance meter was telling her she shouldn't, but she was enjoying herself. Darius had told her stories from his rebellious youth, even how he met his best friend, Hakeem Richardson and the rest of the gang; Brice and Aiden. This story about him and his teenage crush having sex, not knowing they had butt-dialed her grandmother took the cake.

"Okay, stop laughing at my pain, woman."

"Okay, okay…my bad."

Darius pulled her legs up and draped them across his knees. He began gently massaging her feet. Earlier, when she complained about them hurting, he had encouraged her to do away with her shoes. She hated heels. This was all Layla's idea, and they started to do what they always did; hurt her feet. At first the gesture seemed harmless, but now she wasn't so sure. Nevertheless, the will to repossess her feet eluded her as she let out a moan.

"Be careful, you won't want me to think you enjoy my foot rubs."

Safiya narrowed her eyes at him. The need to prove to Layla and herself that she still had what it took to attract any man had been on the rise all night. Before Justin, she was like Layla had said, daring and resourceful. So, just for tonight that's exactly what she'd be. After all, what happened in Vegas stayed here.

"Why Mr. Gray, supposing I do. What are you going to do about it?" She adjusted herself, propping herself up with her elbows.

"Supply your heart desires."

His eyes roamed her body, leaving a trail of fire in their path. Her breathing hitched, causing him to grin. He continued caressing her feet, then calves, slowly moving up to her thighs. The atmosphere around them was charged with lust, desires and, dare she say, greed. All night long, with his wit, charm and humor, he had slowly chipped away at the invisible wall she had put up. She actually liked him. The evening felt very intimate. Over and over, she chided herself that this was wrong, but then consoled herself that after tonight, she'd never see him again.

Darius caressed her jaw, then his fingers wrapped around her neck, pulling her flush into him. She straddled him with her hands flat on his rock-solid chest. They stayed locked in an intense gaze for a minute. It was as though Darius wanted her to register what was happening between them.

"May I?"

Safiya nodded.

"I need you to say the words, beautiful."

"Yes," she whispered.

The word was barely out when his lips hit hers. Like clay in the hands of a potter, her body melted and molded against his. Of their own accord, her arms wrapped themselves around his neck as her palms caressed his smooth head. His tongue invaded her mouth and tried to set up camp. Soon after, their tongues began to do battle as she held on for dear life. She had never been kissed that way before. He was on a mission to claim her soul. He nipped her lip and she moaned. His hands roamed her body and blood rushed to her head, making thinking impossible.

"Perfection," he whispered.

The tingling in her body made her weak. Now she understood the term, earth-shattering kiss. He gave her several light kisses along her face and neck. He gathered her into his lap while she came down from her high. She laid her head on his chest. Darius's fingers stroked her hair sending her straight into a sleep coma.

"Mr. Gray. Mr. Gray."

Darius felt nudging. He stretched his body and opened his eyes. Standing before him was a fully dressed Safiya Nadar. He blinked to gather his bearings. They weren't in the Walden, rather in another one of his hotels in a different part of town. He returned his eyes to her. She lowered her eyes and stepped back. A move he found cute considering all the things he'd done to her body over the last several hours.

"Good morning, beautiful. And I think we're way past the formalities." He sat up against the headboard and folded his arms across his bare chest.

Safiya twisted her fingers together. "Ummm…Darius, I'd like to explain—"

Darius raised his hand to stop her. They'd been very reckless, but he still needed his ego intact. And her trying to tell him this was a mistake less than a couple of hours later wasn't the way to do it. Yes, it was a slip-up, but he was going to consider it the side effects of spur-of-the-moment Vegas nights.

"Can I at least freshen up before you start laying down the regrets?"

"Um, yeah sure."

Darius glanced at her again with a smile. Picking up the phone by the bedside, he made a quick call. Securing the sheet around his body, he walked toward her. He kissed her forehead and proceeded to the bathroom.

Darius stared at his reflection in the mirror. In the solitude of the room, he chided himself for being so careless. He'd always made sure he was cautious and strategic with everything he did. Getting drunk around the town with a stranger and ending up somewhere other than where he stayed was something he had never done. There was a uniqueness about Safiya, though. He couldn't shrug it off even if he wanted to.

He made up a plan to satisfy both his lust and curiosity; keep her around until she was out of his system. It would be a win-win. He'd offer to take care of her, and she'd be his companion. His lips turned up in a smile when they caught the hickey on his neck. Yes, she was one of a kind and he didn't want to let her go just yet. However, he had to think of something convincing enough to get her to stay.

Minutes later, Darius walked back into the bedroom. Safiya was no longer in her dress from yesterday, but a simple white tee and jeans he had the boutique downstairs bring up for her.

She was so preoccupied with something on her finger that she hadn't looked his way. Darius cleared his throat and she looked up at him.

"I see the clothes fit. I thought you'd prefer them to the dress you wore last night."

"Yes, thank you."

"Would you like to order breakfast?"

"Uhhh, no I really should be going back."

"Running away from me so soon?"

"Mr. Gray..."

The scowl on his face made her correct herself.

"Darius, this was fun. I have no regrets, Really, I don't, but I have to leave now."

"At least have breakfast with me first."

She looked at her watch.

"What time does your flight leave?" he asked.

"Soon."

"And you're going back to Atlanta, correct?"

"Yes."

"So, let's eat. You'll have ample time to make it." Even if he had to convince her to travel on his jet with him, he would.

She placed her hand on her hip and smirked. "Does anyone ever say no to you?"

"Not if I can help it. Could you please order us breakfast?" Darius wiggled his brows.

Safiya giggled. "Sure."

Darius walked back to the bag that held the clothes from the boutique and retrieved the brown khakis and a pink polo shirt. He quickly dressed as Safiya talked to someone on the phone. He presumed it was her family or Ms. Assan.

Soon after, there was a knock on the door. Darius opened the door to the waiter. The smell of eggs, waffles, sausage, ham, grits and coffee hit his nose, causing his stomach to rumble. Moments later, the pair had settled down to their food.

"So, did you have a good time in Vegas?"

"Yes. I had never been before, but I know for sure I can't live here. It's a little too fast paced for me." She raised her index finger. "But, I did meet a certain billionaire who showed me a nice time."

"Glad to be of service." Darius chuckled. "Supposing I told you I wanted to see you again?"

"This time I'd be firm on my 'no'." If she didn't have a flustered look on her face, Darius would've laughed.

"You hurt me. Am I that terrible?" He feigned pain.

"On the contrary. You're a decent human being, but like I've been telling you the past twenty-four hours, our worlds are very different." Safiya lifted her cup of coffee to her lips.

She stared down at her left hand with a puzzled look on her face. "Do you know why I have this soda ring thing on my finger?

Darius took her hand in his and studied it. It was the ring from the mouth of a soda can.

"I'm not sure, but I can't remember half of what happened yesterday. Maybe you tried to open a soda." Darius shrugged.

"Yeah maybe. I've been trying to take the darn thing off, but it hurts. When I get back to the room, I'll use some cocoa butter."

The rest of their breakfast was eaten with light chatter. They both talked about their other interests in the community and personal aspirations. Darius noticed that Safiya made him think a little deeper than he normally would. His whole focus in life was conquering the now and focusing on the next. That made him think about his deal in Paris coming up in the next couple of weeks.

Darius excused himself and walked over to the dresser to retrieve his phone. It was almost ten a.m. He had to return to the hotel and get on with the day. He glanced over at Safiya who was tucking a loose tress of her hair behind her ears. He winked at her and she bit her lip and lowered her head, trying to hide her blush. His mind wandered to their sexy escapade and he adjusted himself. His phone rang, interrupting his thoughts.

"Hey Hakeem, what's going on?" he answered the call.

"Is there anything you want to tell me?"

Darius frowned and removed the phone from his ear. He put the device back against his ear. "Who pissed in your Cheerios this morning?"

"A certain billionaire who's acting out of character."

"What has Brice done this time?" Darius asked.

The Richardson brothers, as they were known, were totally different in character. Hakeem was the more reserved one and Brice was the reckless one.

"Just turn on the TV man. We have to fix this because…"

Darius zoned out of the rest of the conversation. The frown on his face must have alerted Safiya. She stood and walked to him.

"What's wrong?"

"I'm about to find out." Darius looked around for the remote and couldn't find it. "Do you know where the remote is?"

Safiya did a quick search and found it behind the television. She handed it to him, and he powered on the television.

Darius placed the phone back to his ears. "What am I supposed to be looking for?"

Before Hakeem could speak, the headline splashed across the screen. *Billionaire Darius Gray is off the Market.* Darius's eyes bugged while Safiya let out a gasp. The presenter went on to say that he and an unidentified woman were seeing coming out of a chapel in the middle of the night after a quickie wedding by an Elvis impersonator. In the blurred footage, Safiya's head was down so no one could see her, but Darius was on full display. It went on to say that they were working on finding out who the woman was.

Safiya plopped down on the bed. Darius turned the television off and sat beside her. He took her hands in his. Neither of them said a word for several minutes. The memory of the previous day came flooding back to him. After their make-out session in the car, he'd ordered his driver to cruise around the strip while they soaked up the high. Sometime later, Safiya stood on the seat and stuck her head through the rooftop while the wind flowed through her hair. She encouraged him to join her and he did.

It was carefree and spontaneous. In that short time, that's exactly how she made him feel—lighthearted. They came across one of those chapels and she wanted to see what a real one looked like. Her wish was his command. He couldn't remember them getting hitched, but the reports claimed they did. He made a mental note to get Julia to obtain any records the chapel had.

"You still there?"

Darius heard Hakeem's voice come through the speaker. He hadn't hung up. He picked up the phone and told Hakeem to meet him in fifteen minutes in his suite. After hanging up, he called Julia, gave her some instructions and told her the same. He took in a breath, exhaled and faced Safiya.

"Please do something. We must get this annulled before they identify who I am. I can't do this. I can't." She was sobbing.

Darius knelt in front of her. He cupped her face in his hands. "I'll protect you. This will be annulled before the end of the day."

Her gaze bored into his eyes, probably searching for the truth of his words. He was extremely attracted to her, but he'd never kept a woman against her free will. And he wasn't going to start now. Besides, him wanting to see her again wasn't the same as wanting to be married to her – by a long shot. They were definitely on the same page. Annulment.

"I guess that answers the mystery of the soda ring on my finger," she whispered.

"I can't believe I was so cheap. You deserved a better ring." Darius joked, trying to make light of the situation.

Safiya nudged him playfully. He smirked. There was nothing light about the situation, but he couldn't stand to see her upset and panicked.

"You're so silly. But I'm serious, you'll take care of this? My dad and I live a very quiet life. I can't bring this spotlight to him. Not when he isn't feeling good."

"Scout's honor."

"Do I need to remind you again that you're not a scout?"

"Depends on how you want to remind me."

Ugh…move I can't take you seriously. That's how we landed in this mess in the first place."

7

"Just slow down a minute and think," Hakeem said.

Darius was growing frustrated with his friend's ridiculous idea. He buried his head in his hands and let out a growl. He had taken a quick shower and changed into some of his own clothes. He couldn't get in his second cup of coffee before Hakeem came barging in. Granted, he was his best friend and investment man, but what he was proposing was utterly ridiculous. Darius plopped down on the couch in the sitting area of his penthouse suite. He cradled his arms on his knees and leaned forward.

"I promised her that I'd get this thing annulled by tonight. The more I waste time with you, the possibility of that happening is slipping through my fingers."

"But listen to me. You're one of the very few billionaires that have been free of scandal. Your shareholders have come to rely on your sound judgement, meaning they and your investors trust you."

"And…"

"The world is still waiting on you to give a statement about this marriage. Now you want to give the statement and say it's a mistake?" Hakeem frowned. "You could lose your credibility; your stocks would plummet, and investors will pull out. It speaks a lot to how reckless you can potentially be."

"You and I know that I'm not reckless. It was a drunken mistake; one I plan to fix. More importantly, marriage is nowhere on my radar. So, no, I will not be forced into one because of what people would say," Darius emphasized.

"You and I are not the ones that lace your pockets. This could seriously affect your bottom line. Is it something you're willing to risk?"

Darius stood and walked over to the balcony. He opened the sliding door and walked out. His chest started to tighten. Logically, he knew that nothing the shareholders did would do any significant damage to his net worth. But fear was nagging at him. He vowed that he would never be poor again or be looked at as that orphan that wasn't of value to society. This wasn't the same thing, but it had the potential to be strikingly close.

Losing money or spoiling his name was a trigger for him, and Hakeem's words had begun playing mind games on him. But marriage? Even a fake one was nowhere in his cards. He was not averse to love…why was he even thinking about that word? This was purely lust. All the same, he wanted no parts of it on a permanent basis.

"Look man, it's not permanent. You like the chick—"

"Her name is Safiya." Darius snapped.

"You see, that proves my point. You like Safiya, so it's not that bad." Hakeem paused. "You said it yourself, you wanted her for a steady companion, so why not just ask her?"

"Wanting her for a steady companion and being married to her for convenience are two different things. I'm just setting myself up for…"

"For what? The possibility that you might actually fall?"

Darius clenched his jaw. "I think you have you and I confused. I'm not falling for anything. I'm just not trying to inconvenience myself or her."

"Well, you gotta figure it out. Is doing anything other than, at minimum, six months to a year of discomfort worth you potentially putting a dent in all that you've worked for?"

Darius frowned. Try as much as he could, he couldn't totally dismiss Hakeem's concerns. But why would she want to pretend to be married to him?

"Offer to pay her." Hakeem blurted out, as though he could read his thoughts. "Money can do anything, my friend. Persuade her by offering money. A cool million will do the trick."

Darius contemplated for several seconds. How could he tell her that because of his stocks, she should stay married to him for a while? The lady he had come to know in the last twenty-four hours would for sure tell him what he could do, and where he could go with his reputation and money. It wouldn't be pretty.

Darius toyed with both options. Do nothing and give her the annulment he promised her or be self-centered. The latter bothered him because it was all about his ego, but up until now, when it came to his reputation and money, that's exactly how he guarded it.

His phone buzzed in his pocket, breaking him away from his thoughts. It was his heart. He looked at his watch. He should've been on the jet by now, headed home to her.

"Hey, my favorite lady," Darius greeted his grandmother upon answering the phone.

"How are you doing, baby?" She paused. "But then again, I don't know how favorite I am if you couldn't call me first."

"Grammy, what are you talking about? You know I'm on my way back to you. We'll spend the whole week together."

"Don't you dare. That wife of yours deserves a proper honeymoon. When you get back, then come see me and then you can tell me why I had to hear it from the church instead of you."

Darius didn't even have the ability to formulate words to respond to her. *This can't be freaking happening.* He had gotten TMZ to pull the story earlier. Apparently, it wasn't done early enough to stop his grandmother's nosy friends from seeing it. He desperately wanted to tell her the truth, but she was still recovering from open heart surgery she'd had some weeks ago.

"Are you there, Darius? Did you hear me?"

"Uhhh, no Grammy. What did you say?"

"I said I'm happy you finally settled down. I want to see my great grandkids. You know I'm not getting younger. But I wasn't going to badger you about it. I knew you'd come around."

"Ummm, yes ma'am."

"So where are you going for the honeymoon? Do you know how long you'll be gone?" She fired questions at him. "Oh, never mind, take as long as you like, but bring my granddaughter-in-law back to me as soon as you get back," she instructed.

Darius was ready to respond when he heard coughing. The nurse he hired to take care of her could also be heard in the background. Moments later, she came to the phone.

"Mr. Gray, Ms. Elise needs to take her medication and rest now. Can she call you back?"

"Yes, sure. How is she doing?"

"She's doing great. I make sure to keep her stress and worry free. Soon she'll be out of the woods and back to her regular activities."

"How long will that take?"

"With the progress she's making, six to nine months tops."

"Okay, let me say bye to her." Seconds later his grandmother was back on the phone. "I love you, Grammy."

"I love you too, baby, Take care of my granddaughter-in-law for me."

After they hung up, Darius remained silent. With that single phone call, the dynamics of his situation just changed. He had to convince Safiya. Now it was personal.

8

"I said come to Vegas and have a nice time." Layla fussed. "I said nothing about coming here and getting your behind married."

Safiya and Darius had returned to the Walden a little while ago. They left the other hotel through an exit she didn't even know hotels had. On getting here, they entered this one with the same secrecy. She always knew rich people did too much, but this was just extra. In this situation, though, she appreciated it.

When they arrived, two burly men met them. They didn't speak, but one carried her bag and the other carried his. Julia, his assistant was also there and was rattling things that Safiya couldn't keep up with. What she did hear – words like court, press and annul – satisfied her.

Darius didn't take her number, but told her that someone would be in touch. He brushed his lips lightly on her cheeks and wished her well. Safiya didn't want to admit it, but the gesture stung. Something had changed from when they were alone to when they were around his staff. She knew he couldn't be overly affectionate with her, but his coolness created a twinge in her heart.

"Lay, chill out. I told you Darius said it would be annulled before the day is over and the record sealed."

"Oh, so we're calling him Darius, now." Layla teased.

"Stop it. I'm stressed out enough." Safiya threw her clothes into her suitcase. They had to leave for the airport in the next hour.

"You wouldn't be stressed if when I tried to get you to have fun, you did." Layla walked to the dresser to pack up her hair products. "If you had fun on the regular like any normal twenty-nine-year-old, you wouldn't have gone all the way to the left when a little fun was dangled in front of you."

"Says the woman that bartered me off for some pictures."

"Sure did, but no one told you to give up the cookies. That was all you." Layla giggled. "I'm fine with that though, because despite all your fronting, you like that tall glass of cocoa."

Safiya tried but couldn't hide the heat that crept up into her cheeks. That man's body should be in a museum somewhere on display. When he was dressed, he was a thing to remember but naked, that physique should be studied in colleges.

"Oh Jeez, that look on your face!" Layla shook her head. "I'm glad he got you together. But again, did you have to marry the man?"

"I don't know why you're still carrying on. I should be the one panicking. But I'm not, because I know he'll fix this."

"No, you're not panicking because you're still under the trance of his charm." Layla placed her hand over her heart. "You gonna drive my pressure up."

"Stop being silly. I told you everything will be fine."

"And if it's not. Do you like him?"

"Like as a person, yes. Attracted even…yes. Do I want to be married to him? Hell nah. Do you know what kind of headache that would be? A real marriage to a billionaire? Not even a fake one. We barely know each other."

"But your lady bits know him." Layla winked.

Safiya waved her off. "Yeah and you can see what kind of asinine decisions came as a result."

The two friends laughed as they checked around the room to make sure they didn't forget anything. Putting their suitcases on the floor, they picked up their purses and made their way to the door. Safiya's eye widened at the two bodyguards she'd seen earlier, standing in front of her door.

"May I help you gentlemen?" Layla asked before Safiya could form the same question.

They glanced over at her. At least she assumed they did since their heads moved and their eyes were covered by dark shades. Safiya always found that dumb since there was no sun in a building. Once again, too much.

"Ms. Nadar, Mr. Gray would like to see you," one of them said.

"For what? We have a plane to catch."

"Those are our orders, Ms. Nadar."

"Well, you can tell your boss I have a plane to catch," Safiya said, fuming at the way Darius was summoning her. *Who does he think he is?*

"We can't allow you to leave."

"Can't?" Safiya seethed.

"Ms. Nadar, we're only doing our jobs. Mr. Gray requested your presence. If you just follow us, you'll make it easy on us all."

Safiya was about to say something else when Layla touched her arm. "Girl, I'm not trying to be on the news. Let's go see what the man wants, and we'll be on our way."

"He asked for just Ms. Nadar—"

"Well, that's where he messed up. Because she isn't going anywhere without me," Layla responded. "So, what's it gonna be Hercules? You wanna go back and tell your boss she's not coming because you won't let me tag along?"

The two men looked at each other and shrugged. "Follow us."

"You're banned from giving out the cookies. You were generous one night and now we're being escorted to the upper room by Hercules and Mr. T over there," Layla said in a hushed tone.

Safiya would've found the joke hilarious, but her face was flush and the vein throbbing in her neck had her mind on one target. Darius Gray. No one summoned her. She didn't care how much money they had.

9

"Are you out of your mind? You want me to do what?!"

Safiya could almost feel the imaginary smoke being emitted from her ears. She stood on the opposite side of the chair and glared at the object of her rage. Seconds later, she lowered her eyes, disengaging from their stare-off. Although she could snap his neck right now, Darius was still the sexiest man she'd ever seen. *Get it together, Safiya. Focus!*

She and Layla were escorted to his suite several minutes ago. She met his friend, Hakeem. After she dug into him about summoning her, he apologized and politely asked Hakeem and Layla to give them some privacy. What she thought he wanted to say could never rival what he actually said.

"Safiya, I'll pay you two million dollars to stay married to me for nine months."

"Lower your voice, beautiful," he said calmly.

"Don't tell me to lower my voice. You're proposing to turn my life upside down so I can pretend to be your wife? Do you have any idea what you're asking me?"

"I do. And it's not my intention, but there are other variables to consider now. I can't make the annulment happen."

"Can't or won't?

"A little bit of both." He paused and walked towards her, she stepped back. He stopped and raised his hands in surrender. "Look, if I didn't really need you, I wouldn't ask."

"I have a life. Can you guarantee that it will go on without any changes while we're pretending?"

This was just crazy to her. One minute she was assuring Layla that he would be true to his word and ensure the annulment would go through. And the next, he's asking her to stay married to him for the next nine months. What about her dad? What about her job? Her quiet life? All of that would be interrupted just so he could please his grandmother. His grandmother was sick, and she felt bad. She wouldn't be human if she didn't, but why must her life change so that his could be good?

Since his grandmother had a heart condition, Safiya would not only have to pretend in public, but also in private. Darius was proposing that Safiya would move into the same mansion his grandmother lived in.

"No, your life will change drastically. You will be moved into my mansion. You can't go back to your job. As my wife, you'll have to head several charities, attend charity dinners and fundraisers, important events and, of course, travel with me as often as I require you to be there. But I promise you, the minute our contract is up, I won't keep you a moment longer.

"Wow! And your life, remains as it is. This is unfair. What will my dad say?"

"He can't think that it isn't real. That would do more harm than good. The only people that will know that this is an arrangement are Layla, Hakeem and my lawyer."

Safiya placed both hands on the back of the couch and bowed her head. She wasn't sure she could do this. She wanted to make a better life for her dad and herself, but not like this. He had a ton of medical bills and she had school loans. She was making little to nothing in a job she hated. Nevertheless, was exchanging that for money worth what her life would become? Could she endure the scrutiny she'd be under? Not to mention the flock of women she was sure would come after her for snagging one of the most eligible billionaires in the country. She was deeply attracted to Darius, but in no way was she willing to put her heart on the line for him to potentially trample upon.

"You're a billionaire..."

"That I know."

"You can get anything you want in the world."

"Almost anything."

"I'm sure you can have any woman pretend to be married to you."

"I'm sure I can."

"So why me?"

"Because you're the one that my grandma saw."

"But she didn't see me. My head was bent."

"That's true, but she saw the color of your skin."

"So? You can get any other black woman to pretend to be your wife."

"None that I know are Safiya Nadar."

"Now you're just playing with me. Why me?"

Darius moved closer to her. She stepped back, but unlike before, he continued his approach until her back was against the wall. He leaned against her. Her breath hitched and her heart rate accelerated. His cologne made it impossible for her to breathe. Their eyes locked, as his fingers made a sensual and slow accent up her thigh. He lifted her and her legs immediately circled his waist. He captured her lips. Safiya groaned as his tongue invaded her mouth, ready for battle. Moments later, he set her lips free.

"I don't know any other Safiya, whose kisses drive me insane. I don't know any other Safiya, whose eyes have me ready to give her the world. I don't know any other Safiya whose raspy voice sends shivers down my spine. I don't know any other Safiya who makes me throw caution to the wind. Do you want me to go on?"

She shook her head, speechless. She was caught up in euphoria by his words and the feel of his hands caressing her back. She closed her eyes, and leaned her head back exposing her neck. He buried his head in the nook of her shoulder before setting her ablaze with light kisses.

Darius set her down. She looked up at him just in time to catch the smirk on his face. It jerked her back to reality. He had used her desires to his advantage. The right thing to do would be to push him away and stomp off. The will to do it, however, was missing. She liked him and he was willing to pay her. And she was sure she'd have some fun during the deal.

"Did that change your mind, beautiful?" His body was still flush against hers.

"You do know money and sex can't get you everything."

"Yes, I'm aware of that. If not, we would've been on our honeymoon by now and not wasting the past hour arguing."

"So, nine months, two million dollars and that's it?"

"Scout's honor."

Safiya rolled her eyes and pushed him away. "Jeez, I'm in trouble. There you go with that Scout's crap again."

Darius let his head fall back in laughter and pulled her close. He nipped her ear. "Behave woman. Don't push your husband away."

Safiya rolled her eyes. *Please, let me come out of this with my heart intact.*

The next day, after a painful interrogatory phone call with her dad – who was still not pleased - a draining talk with her best friend convincing her that she'd be okay; and the intense scrutiny of a lawyer, Safiya was finally on Darius's private jet headed to Tunisia in North Africa for their fake honeymoon. Not only had his grandmother insisted on it, but his lawyer, Layla and Hakeem had suggested that if they were going to do this, they might as well make it believable.

She was seated next to the windows as she scrolled through Instagram. Darius's lawyer released a short statement a few hours ago and already the press had dug up everything there was to know about her. Not only that, but she was now being compared to every woman he had ever dated. She rolled her eyes and continued to scroll through her feed. She hated the internet sometimes. She was so engrossed in reading the good and not so good posts that she didn't feel Darius standing by her side until her phone was being taken out of her hand.

"Stop reading that smut. The media will say whatever it takes to make people click on their links.

"So, they'll do anything for clout."

"Huh?"

"You have no idea where that line came from, do you?"

Darius shook his head, turned off her phone and slipped it into his front pocket. Safiya giggled at his confusion.

"Have you heard of Cardi B and Offset?"

Darius creased his brows. "Of course, I've heard of them."

Safiya narrowed her eyes. "But not that song?"

"No. Not really a fan."

"I am. The line is off their "Clout." song. Basically—"

"Safi baby, I know what clout is. I'm not that removed."

"Okay, just checking," she chuckled. "Can't believe you don't know the song though. It was so popular. Hmm, I guess I'll let you slide."

"Don't tease me, woman. Because you know exactly what I wanna slide in."

"Get your mind out of the gutter." Safiya giggled and turned her head so she could look out the window. Needing a break from his intense stare. His eyes, if she stared at them too long, she'd find herself trapped in a trance. She hoped that at the end of this she wouldn't find her heart trapped in limbo, because despite their attraction to each other, he had paid her, and she had accepted. She had to remember that.

The pair settled in for the seventeen-hour flight. They had casual conversation over their meal, played cards, talked some more, and watched a couple of movies before settling in for the night.

Safiya woke up to a kiss on her forehead "We're here, beautiful."

She stretched her body, it seemed like she only went to sleep a minute ago. Not wanting to share her stale breath with him, she made her way to the bathroom.

"No kiss?" His deep chuckled tailed her.

Moments later, they deplaned at Djerba Zarzis airport and were whisked away by a long, black car with tinted windows. Darius placed his hand on her thigh as they rode through the small, quaint town. Being from the eastern part of Africa, she had learned about the other regions of Africa. Her dad made sure of that. She had never however been anywhere in North Africa. She was so excited about being able to see some of it in person.

They were spending the next three weeks in Djerba, the largest island in North Africa, which was in the Gulf of Gabes. According to Darius, he bought a villa in Houmt El Souk, which was the main city on the island about a year and a half ago.

"So, how did you find this place?" Safiya asked.

"I came here once with a business partner. I knew instantly I wanted to own property here. In America and almost all of Europe, I'm known as Mr. Gray. When I come here, I'm just Darius," he said. "And sometimes I need to be that."

"I'm honored you decided to share this place with me."

He responded by squeezing her thigh. Safiya turned her body slightly to get a good view of the scenery.

"I know it's going to be a lot when we get back. So, I figured this will be a good place to be without all the chaos."

"I appreciate it." The only problem was that with only the two of them and little or no staff, she wasn't sure how she'd be able to avoid him. Which she had come to realize was something she must do.

Once they arrived at the guarded residence, Darius gave her a tour of the place. The ground level of the two-story villa had a full kitchen, a patio, pool, an office and a total of five bedrooms, each with a balcony and an adjoining bathroom. Half of what he was telling her about the history of the place, was lost on the opulence of the villa.

Even if he didn't want others to know who he was, I'm sure this house will give them an idea.

Moments later, they made their way up the stairs and came to a halt in front of a room down the hall. Darius opened the door, allowing enough space for her to enter. It was huge, probably the size of her one-bedroom studio apartment. The décor was crème, pink and grey. With such feminine colors, she immediately wondered how many women he'd brought here. She walked over to the balcony and opened the double doors. The view and the sunshine hitting her face was heaven. The air seemed to be saturated with the smell of the Sahara Desert mixed with waters of the Mediterranean Seas. She took in a deep breath and exhaled.

"This will be your room. I'd rather you stay with me, but I understand this may all be too much, so I'm willing to give you options," Darius said, after he'd tucked her bags neatly away.

"Willing? Oh, how kind of you sir," Safiya snickered.

Darius shook his head at her. "My room is at the other end of the hall. Make yourself at home and I'll come check on you later."

Left by herself, Safiya checked out her room. The details were outstanding, the bed linen was certainly 100% silk. The pink and grey tiles in the bathroom were so intricately put together, she wondered how long it took and the patience to see it through. She took out her phone and called her dad and Layla to let them know she'd arrived safely. A few seconds later, still sitting on the bed, Safiya yawned. It was Tuesday evening and in just seventy-two hours, her life had completely changed.

She decided to take a shower so she could relax on the king-sized bed, even though it looked too good to lay on. As she went into the bathroom, she remembered she had nothing to wear. She had packed extra light for Vegas, and never made it home.

She went in search of her bag in the closet. Her mouth gaped and her eyes widened at the sight before her. Quickly gathering herself, she walked into the expansive space. There was every piece of clothing a woman could need – jeans, dresses, shorts, skirts, blouses, formal wear – you name it. There were also belts, bags, hats, purses, sneakers and heels. Safiya's mouth hung open in awe. There was a note on the island located in the middle of the closet. Her hands shook as she walked over to retrieve it.

I hope everything is to your liking.

See you later

DG

When did he have time to do this? Safiya's mind travelled back to the phone calls Darius had made right after she signed the contract two days ago. She overheard him mention Tunis, but assumed he was telling someone to get the house ready. Not buy up the whole mall. Safiya picked out a cute loungewear set, took a quick shower and hopped into bed for what she thought would be a quick nap.

10

Darius opened the cabinet and got out two plates. He dished out ojja. It was a traditional breakfast he tasted a while ago and had become very fond of. It was basically eggs poached in a deliciously spicy tomato sauce mixed with spicy lamb sausage and local spices. He sliced a fresh baguette and set it on the side. He hoped she'd like the staple Tunisian breakfast, if not he could easily whip up an omelet. He walked over to the boiling hot water and poured it into a tea pot over mint tea.

The three days since their arrival in Houmt El Souk were spent in the villa. Safiya introduced him to Nollywood movies on Netflix. The Nigerian movie industry, which to his surprise was the third largest movie industry in the world, behind Hollywood and Bollywood. She was adamant about him not checking his phone or any of his gadgets. In her words, they needed to get with the business of getting to know one another so they could convince his Grammy that the marriage was legit. The last thing he wanted to do was rattle her even further, so he complied.

Relaxation.

It was a strange feeling since he didn't really believe in the concept. He had work to do, deals to close. Time and circumstances were constantly changing, so he made it a point to use his judiciously.

Darius was sorely mistaken when he'd thought that since they were indoors, they'd spend most of their time reacquainting their bodies. Safiya vetoed that, along with them sharing a bed. When he gave her a separate room, he didn't really believe she'd use it. Today, he was working on changing that. True, this was a phony marriage, but there was nothing fake about the way his body craved hers.

Setting their food in the middle of the island, he turned to the refrigerator for the juice, then poured her a cup of tea. He smiled when he remembered the first morning they woke up and she frantically searched for a coffee pot. He didn't drink it, so had no use for it. Safiya he noticed couldn't do without it. Darius rectified that within the hour. Today however, she lost in their game of scrabble the day before, so she was drinking tea.

"A man who knows his way around the kitchen. I like it."

Darius turned and was stunned at the sight before him. Her hair was in a messy bun on her head, her face was bare, and she had on the shirt he discarded on the couch last evening. The shirt stopped halfway down her thighs, displaying her toned legs. He'd never seen anything sexier.

"You do know that coming in here like that will have you hemmed up against the wall."

"I'd like to think you can show restraint and at least feed me first." She winked.

Darius smirked. "Be careful, beautiful. Here, sit. I made you breakfast."

Safiya walked closer to the island and the first thing she did was lift the cup of tea and take in the aroma. "Smells good. I guess I'll be a good sport." She took a sip from the cup.

Darius sat opposite her. Safiya took his hand as she had done with every meal and blessed the food.

"What's this?" She picked up her spoon.

"You don't know?" he asked.

"Why should I? Please don't tell me you are one of those?"

That quickly, Darius saw her smile disappear, replaced with tight eyes and a head cocked to the side.

"One of who?" He had an idea what she might mean but was buying time to come up with an explanation that would get his foot out of his mouth.

"Those that think because I'm from the Continent it means I should know everything African."

"I'm educated enough to know that's not the case. But I admit sometimes our unintended bias rears its head. My apologies." He reached over and placed his hand over hers.

"None, necessary besides, you're right. Just how I assumed you don't have problems because you are rich, or you should know Cardi B and Offset's song because you are Black American."

"We have to be more aware and be willing to offer grace." Darius didn't mean for them to get so deep so early so he quickly ended that line of conversation by explaining the meal he made. He watched her pick up her spoon for a taste.

"Good, but where's the pepper?"

"You see I tried not to assume—"

"You're not assuming. Those are facts, Africans love spice."

Both of them shared a laugh as she walked to the cupboard to retrieve the paprika and add it to her bowl. He remembered the day Hakeem's girlfriend, Mariama, who was Senegalese prepared them some yassa chicken, and they had to drink a ton of milk to get that spice off their tongue.

A few minutes later, Safiya spoke. "Okay, I know you're tired of being cooped up all day watching movies. So, I was looking online and there are a lot of things for us to do. Are you up for it?"

Before he could respond, she spoke again. "Oh, I forgot you don't have security with you. Can you go out?"

Darius smiled at her flustered expression. "Relax beautiful, I do have security. You just can't see them. However, with or without them, we can explore the town. What do you have in mind?"

In response, Safiya clapped her hands, jumped off the stool and ran from the kitchen. Darius smiled at her goofiness. He'd stayed in this home only once. That was when one of the companies whose Board he sat on, invited all its board members to participate in a ceremony which took place in one of the mausoleums at Borj El Kebir castle. All he did then was attend the festivities, agreed to host an after-party, and flew back to Atlanta the following day.

Moments later, she came back with her iPad in her hand, scrolling through what he assumed was some tourist site.

"Today is Thursday so we can go to the one of the souk markets. Did you know we can take a ride from here to Camp Yadis Ksar Ghilane? Or we can explore the Yasmine Shopping Center, there is a gourmet coffee house. You know I wanna check that out. The museums, did you know it was around the Ajim port they shot some Star Wars scenes? Obi-Wan Kenobi's house is here. The one in the original movie…here…in Tunisia. Layla would kill me if I don't take pictures. She's a huge fan." Safiya rattled off.

Before Darius could respond, she started talking again. "There's even an ancient castle here—"

"Borj El Kebir. Yes, now that I know." Darius looked at her in amazement and admiration. Over the past couple of days, this carefree attitude had become his kryptonite. Every woman he had ever dated was as serious as he was. But with Safiya, it was different. He would've attributed it to their six-year age difference, but he had also seen the serious side of her. The part that wasn't moved by him and his money and deeply passionate about her ambition in life. The side that put her father's needs ahead of her own. The one who wanted to know about the ugly parts of his life as well as what made it pretty now.

Her laughter brought him out of this trance. "So, tell me, what else do you know?"

"I know that in this island, Djerba, according to legend used to be the land of lotus eaters where Odysseus was stranded on hos voyage," he said.

Safiya raised her brow. "You're talking Greek mythology?"

"Yep."

"Well, that I know nothing about. This island however from the little I saw online is gorgeous. Now let's see if reality matches up." She tore a piece of her baguette and scooped her ojja.

He lifter his tea to his lips. "I'm sure it does, but I'll let you tell me."

She chuckled, covering her mouth with her hand. His heart twanged. The uncomfortable feeling intensified the more he remained in her presence. His chest tightened at the fleeting thought that what he felt was past lust. But what was the feeling past lust, because it couldn't be love? He barely knew her, but his adopted mother's words entered his mind. *Time doesn't matter. When cupid hits you, it just does.*

Darius blinked his eyes to rid himself of the useless sentiment. Cupid was not hitting him. They had come to that agreement a while ago. It was Cupid's stupid arrow that made his mother blind to the red flags of love until it was too late. After these three weeks and another two weeks in Atlanta, he'd dive into work so deep that Cupid's arrow wouldn't even be able to find him.

"Are you listening to me?"

"I'm all yours, Beautiful. We can do anything you want."

Darius stood and took their empty plates to the sink. He discarded the scraps and filled the sink with soap. That was another thing Safiya got him to do, wash his own dishes. He hadn't done that in ages. His hands were immersed in the soapy water when he felt her warms hands creep under his shirt. She massaged his abdomen and he bit his lip, holding in his pleasure.

"Anything?" her raspy voice sent a tingling up his spine.

Darius turned, leaned against the sink, and encased her in his arms. He pulled her against his hard body. Narrowing his eyes at her full breasts, Darius bent his head and took her mouth with his. He tried to swallow her whole with his passion. Their tongues entwined, stroking each other to a feverish pitch, a clear indication that for three days, he hadn't felt the softness of her lips. Breaking away from their kiss, Darius hoisted her up on the island and stood between her legs. Safiya stared at him with pure desire that matched his.

"As much as I want to let you have your way with me, if we start, we won't be going anywhere today." Darius leaned his forehead against hers.

Smiling, Safiya ran her hand over his head. "Okay, husband. But you owe me."

Darius cupped one of her breasts and squeezed. "Your wish is my command, wife. Now go get dressed. I need to make a few calls."

Several hours later, Safiya sat between Darius's legs as they sailed the open seas. Darius stroked her cheek as she rested her head on his chest. She had the perfect day planned. Except when they found out that Yadis Ksar Ghilane was a luxurious camp that offered tents in the oasis of the Sahara Desert. He promised to bring her back so they could spend a couple of nights and go camel back riding. Safiya quickly changed course and they took a trip to the castle, shopped in the souk market, visited the museum and finally they ate lunch in a private secluded booth at Restaurant Dar Hassine. She gave him the attractions, he made it happen. The last part of the day however was put together by him. When she talked of Ajim earlier, he didn't want to tell her he had a yacht docked there. After they visited and took pictures at the Star Wars house, he brought her here. Her reaction was worth the surprise.

"This view is fantastic."

Darius tried to contain her hair that was flying in his face. "Yes, it is." She had tied her hair up in a ponytail before, but he had insisted she let it down.

"I still can't believe you own a yacht here that you barely use. I went on a vacation tour in Florida once and we were told that just parking the boat, set owners back like twenty grand a day."

"You went on this vacation, alone, right?"

"Out of all I said, that's what you picked up on." Safiya giggled. "Don't you think we're a little late in the game for you to be thinking or worrying about whether I have a significant other?"

"Who says I'm worried? Even if you did, it became insignificant the minute you entered the limo with me."

Safiya turned her head to the side to look up at him. "You're joking, right?"

"I never joke when it comes to you. I was going to pursue you regardless." He kissed her hair. "Fate made my job a whole lot easier by you marrying me."

"Don't you mean a drunken night?

"Not really. I wanted you and I wasn't ready to give you up just yet." When he said it out loud, it did sound less than romantic.

"Oh." Her low whisper confirmed his thoughts.

Darius could feel the atmosphere shift. He didn't mean to make her sad, but he would always be truthful with her. He wanted to make sure they were on the same page, so she wouldn't end up hurt when their time was up. They sat in silence for a while before they were interrupted by one of the attendants, who brought them the food and drinks they had ordered. They ate in silence for a few minutes before they began to chat on safer topics like her job and plans. He let her in on his upcoming deals and travel plans after they arrived Atlanta.

Hours later, they were back at the house, showered and retired on the bed. His bed. He lay his head on Safiya's lap and looked into her eyes. She was watching reruns of *Martin*.

"I didn't mean to upset you earlier," he said.

She picked up the remote and paused her show. She looked down at him. "You didn't upset me as much as you brought me back to reality."

"Meaning?"

Safiya shrugged. "In the days I've been here with you, away from reality, I kinda got caught up that this really was a thing. I'm here to do a job, after which, you'll pay me for my services."

Although he was now sure they were on the same page, to hear her say it out loud was like a sucker punch to his gut. Before he could voice his opinion, she spoke again.

"But that doesn't mean we can't satisfy our bodies. And if I remember correctly, Mr. Gray, you owe me."

Safiya lowered her head and captured his lips. Raw passion took over and whatever he had wanted to say moved to the back of his mind. This conversation was far from over, but in the moment, talk was the last thing on his mind.

11

Safiya looked out the window and took in the familiar sights and sounds of downtown Atlanta. The driver Darius insisted on her having was taking her to the restaurant where she was meeting Layla for lunch.

The last eight months were like a blur. Who knew the life of the rich and famous was so busy? The three weeks she and Darius had spent in the Tunisia seemed like light years away. While in Djerba, they had gotten closer and the cares of the world seemed to be a distant thing.

After the awkward conversation they'd had the first week, Safiya's resolve to live in the moment but guard her heart became greater. Before their return, Darius had bought her the most expensive ring set he could find. Very quickly, she had gotten settled into her new abode. Just like in Djerba, everything a woman could need and desired was set up in the bedroom she now shared with Darius.

Over the course of the first couple of weeks, they'd visited her father. Just as he did on the phone, he expressed his displeasure and suspicion of their hasty nuptials. To her surprise, Darius spent time trying to convince him otherwise. They went out fishing and golfing, but what totally got her dad to calm down was when he was treated to owner suite privileges at the Atlanta Heights game. It also helped that Darius was genuinely attracted to her, so his hands never stayed to himself.

His grandmother was an easier sell. She had her own smaller house on the property, but as Safiya soon learned, she popped in wherever she felt like it and when it was least expected. Safiya was now fond of the little older lady, but she knew the woman watched her like a hawk. It was undeniable that the older woman was thrilled her grandson was now married. Safiya still doubted that she believed Darius's story that he decided to keep their relationship a secret, hence the suddenness of their marriage. Since she was being paid two million dollars, Safiya took it upon herself to convince her. Her thoughts went back to the dinner they had on the second night they arrived home.

"Ah, young love, tell me again. How did you two meet?" Darius's grandmother had a huge smile on her face as she asked the question Safiya was sure they had answered up to three times already.

Safiya felt her piercing eyes rip through her soul. Was she just messing with her or did she know the truth? Safiya smiled and glanced over at Darius who wiped the corner of his mouth with a napkin and placed his hand over hers.

"Grammy, we've told this story more than enough times now. Safiya and I met during a business meeting, but decided we didn't want the media in our business. When the time was right, we both agreed we were ready to take the next step."

"Oh, right that's it." His grandmother took her eyes off her grandson and turned her way. "Well, Safiya welcome to the family."

"Thank you, Mrs. Gibson."

"No, around here I'm Grammy." For the first time in the last forty-eight hours since she'd met the woman, her smile was warm and genuine.

"I want to get to know my granddaughter in-law better, so I'll move back into my old room."

For the six months that followed, Grammy kept her eyes on them like a hawk. Well, her mostly, because Darius resumed business travels a month after their fake honeymoon. He made sure he wasn't gone for more than a week at a time, but he was still gone. Safiya, on the other hand, quit her job and was assigned an assistant who helped her get acclimated to her new duties as the billionaire's wife.

The waiter brought over their cheesecakes and placed them on the table. For the past couple of hours, she and Layla caught up over lunch. The friends still talked on the phone almost every day, but hadn't seen each other for a while.

"While I loved you feeding me and what not, I also know something is on your mind. Can you tell me what it is while I work on this cheesecake?" Layla lifted a piece of her dessert to her mouth.

"Why does something have to be wrong for me to see my friend?"

"I didn't say something had to be wrong for you to see me. I'm saying something is bothering you… now."

Something was wrong, something she hadn't told anybody because she still couldn't believe it was real. She'd taken all the necessary precautions.

"I'm pregnant," Safiya blurted out.

Layla remained silent. She lifted her lemonade to her mouth and took a loud sip. Her dramatics were driving Safiya insane.

"Please say something."

"What I have to say, you've heard before, but you and your fake husband are the most prideful people I've ever met. So, I'll say what I know you want to hear."

"And what's that?"

"I know where you can get an abortion." Layla shrugged.

Safiya frowned. "What?! Stop joking around."

"I'm not."

"You're serious?" Safiya hissed. "Come on Lay, this is serious business. I don't know how it happened, but I think in all the—"

"I'll tell you what happened. Love. Look, I know this thing started off as a sham, but even a blind man on the street can see that you and Darius love each other. You can act, but not that well. Social media has you and him as hashtag couple goals. The way he looks at you in public, the way you can't keep your hands off him. You guys have stopped deceiving the public long ago. The only people you're deceiving are yourselves."

"Okay, okay. I admit it. I love him. Gosh, how can I not? But I will not force him to love me or beg him to let me stay – baby or no baby." Safiya took a sip of her drink.

It was true that sometimes she forgot that they were in a fake marriage. The way he treated her, she was sure he forgot, too. However, he had made no mention of feeling anything deeper for her or wanting her to stay. The last thing she was going to do was tell him about the baby and be a charity case. A man like Darius would never let her take the baby away, so he would force her to stay with him out of obligation and that would kill her more than anything.

"Darius is different. I don't know what it is, but in the last several weeks, he's become distant. We still share the same bed and make love, but something is missing. I did ask him what was wrong, and as usual, he said nothing. Then I told him that I was going to start looking for a house to move into once our deal was up. Do you know what he said?"

Layla shook her head.

"He said he'll get Julia to help me. I love him, but I won't be a fool for him. But now this baby complicates things." Safiya bowed her head. "But I can't kill it." She rubbed her flat belly.

"How far along are you?"

"Eight weeks."

"You've been to a doctor already? How did you manage that, being Mrs. Gray and all?"

"It wasn't easy, but money is a powerful thing," Safiya said wearily. "It must have happened when we went to Europe two months ago."

"Look, my friend, you're happy. You didn't plan this life, but you've been blessed with it. Good thing the man is not stuck up either. Plus, he is all types of cocoa-shake fine."

"Watch it," Safiya warned playfully.

Layla waved her off. "Whatever…don't nobody want your man. What I'm saying is, don't make any hasty decisions without at least talking to him. Sit him down and tell him how you feel. Most of all, tell him about the baby. There's no need assuming and then walking out of a great life you could've had."

Safiya took in her friend's words. Darius was due back from Milan tonight. She would plan something special and then tell him in the morning over breakfast.

"Okay, even though I have three more weeks until the contract is up, I won't be able to stay there and face him if he dismisses me."

"And the money? You'll miss out on two million dollars?"

"He gave me the check last month. I haven't cashed it. However, he also opened an account for me, and I've been taking care of any other things from there." Safiya paused. "I don't know Lay. All I know is now."

"Please be smart about this."

Safiya nodded and the two women went back to enjoying the remaining part of their afternoon, which also included some retail therapy.

12

Darius's flight arrived a couple of hours ahead of schedule. He'd come home to a quiet house. He searched for Safiya but didn't see her anywhere. One of the housekeepers informed him she'd gone out for lunch. His first instinct had been to call her, but lately he had found himself in self-preservation mode. She was with him just for the money and sex, nothing else. He had to keep reminding himself. That part was made pretty clear when she told him she would start looking for a place.

Granted, he hadn't said the words, but couldn't she feel that he loved her by his actions? Well, his actions before she let that sentence come out of her mouth. He shouldn't have let himself get carried away by the breath of fresh air she brought him, or the fact that she provided the piece of sunshine that had been missing since his adoptive mother died. He always knew love was a weak emotion and he had allowed himself to fall and the joke was now on him.

He was in the den watching a repeat episode of *Ozark*, a show she had introduced him to. Yes, he was a glutton for punishment. His phone rang. He let out a breath and picked it up. Not wanting to hold it to his ear or put in his ear pods, he put the phone on speaker.

"Hey Hakeem," he answered.

"Hey man, I know you just got back from your trip, but I was calling to tell you about this new property in Australia. I think it would be a good investment."

Darius contemplated. He just got home and wanted to spend some time with Safiya before they said their goodbyes. But then again, he was doubting his ability to be present as she walked away.

"Tell me about it."

Briefly Hakeem talked him through the history of the hotel franchise they were potentially going after, the pros, cons, and how long it would take before he saw a return on his investment. Darius decided it was worth a shot.

"Good man, I'll prepare everything," Hakeem said. "So, we haven't talked in a while about you. How are you doing?"

"I'm good. And we talk almost every week."

"You know what I'm referring to you. You and Safiya. I saw Vanessa try to slither her way into your VIP lounge two nights ago. What was she doing there? Are you and Safiya okay?"

Darius took a deep breath and decided to ignore the Vanessa part of Hakeem's statement. She was in Milan when he was there celebrating with some business associates. She tried to immerse herself into the party in his VIP suite, but he quickly shut that down.

"It's been good, but it has to come to an end, right?" Despair laced his words.

"Not everything. I've never seen you this happy or carefree, so what's stopping you from making her yours, permanently? Her dad and Grammy seem to be happy with the union." A beat passed between them. "You guys are happy. That's if you'd stop avoiding the truth."

"It's not that simple…"

"Yeah, that's because you choose to complicate it." He took a breath. "Look man, I know this started because we needed the shareholders to maintain their faith in you. You've done that. So, what seems to be the problem?"

"I don't think she feels the same and I won't expose myself only to be rejected."

"Now you sound like a coward. I know this is a touchy subject for you, but regardless of what you think, Ms. Jackie loved and was happy. What ended up happening to her isn't her fault but that jerk."

Darius's nostrils flared. It was a touchy subject for him and that was why love was an emotion he'd never allowed himself to feel. He finally messed up, but he was going to fix it.

He'd been living with Ms. Jackie and Grammy for about two years when she got a boyfriend. At first sight, Darius hated him; something about him seemed off. He couldn't place it, but about eighteen months into the relationship, the man's violent tendencies started to show. One day during dinner, he got upset and slapped his mother, and she hit her head on the table. She was taken to the hospital and was diagnosed with a concussion. Somehow, they missed that she was bleeding internally, and she died some days later. If she wasn't so much in love, she wouldn't have had blinders on and would've seen her so called boyfriend for who he really was. A monster.

"I don't know man. I just don't know," Darius said. "Send me the packet for the Australia thing so I can review it and give you my final decision."

He disconnected the call and lifted his legs onto the settee. He twirled the drink in his hand and he mulled over the last several months. Safiya had opened his eyes to life, not just checking things off his list, but living it. He loved coming home to her in his bed. Her dark long thick hair pilled across his pillow was always a sight to behold. She wanted to wear a bonnet, he bought satin pillows instead. She wasn't only a beautiful and very adventurous and satisfying wife and lover, she was kind, caring and compassionate.

He had never seen his staff laugh so much since he hired them. There was an airiness to the house that she brought with her and they were all better for it. Even his grandmother had a glow having someone to talk to. She'd made his house a home. All of her made him happy, and he realized that it was more than a euphoric feeling of something new. He loved her.

The idea of loving her and making this a permanent arrangement didn't sound bad, but he didn't have the courage to believe she felt the same way about him. He refused to let down the last piece of guard that surrounded his heart, especially when she hadn't said anything to even give him a tiny hint she felt the same. He wasn't ready to put what was left of his heart on the line. If she rejected him, he wasn't sure he could bear it. He'd been let down by the first woman in his life – his biological mother. He wasn't ready to be let down again.

◆◆◆

"You guys are happy. That's if you'd stop avoiding the truth."

"It's not that simple…"

"Yeah, that's because you choose to complicate it. Look man, I know this started because we needed the shareholders to maintain their faith in you. You've done that. So, what seems to be the problem?"

Safiya backed away from the den's door not waiting to hear Darius response. She made a beeline to the bedroom. She couldn't stop the tears from falling. On her way back to the estate, her phone wouldn't stop buzzing. She checked it out and discovered she got several Instagram notifications. She loved the app; it was about the only social media platform she knew she probably couldn't live without. She'd gotten tagged on several photos showing Darius and Vanessa in conversation in Milan. Not only was Vanessa potentially a thing, but to hear that the reason he asked her to stay married to him was for some stupid shares. Some shares? She felt stupid and betrayed. All this while, she thought it was because of his recovering grandmother but he used her as a pawn for his business. He was a billionaire for goodness sake. What could the shareholders have ever done to him that he needed to come in and turn her life upside down?

Some months ago, she would've brushed it off. But the way things were with them now, she wasn't so sure. Or was it this baby that was making her insecure? Safiya got to meet Vanessa several weeks after their nuptials. That day she wanted to surprise Darius with lunch in his downtown office. The person who ended up being surprised was her. On Darius's previous instruction, Safiya was never to be stopped from entering his office. She still however, as a courtesy, respected protocol.

That day, as she approached his door, she could hear a female voice that was far from calm. Safiya entered and Darius made the introductions. After Vanessa left, he promised her that she wasn't that important and so would never be someone she'd have to worry about. Now she wasn't so sure.

Safiya plopped down on the sofa in the sitting area of the bedroom. She cradled her head with her hands. She felt her heart shatter for the second time in about two years. During this marriage, she had undoubtedly gained things along the way. But then again, what she had no knowledge of in the first place, she couldn't miss. Now he made her get used to all this, and she was just a pawn in a cause that didn't make any sense. The more she tried to contain her tears, the more they fell. This wasn't her; she was never this emotional. Safiya placed her hand on her tummy and rubbed, her emotions conflicted. Her heart swelled with love at the being they'd created. But also angry at herself and the situation.

For minutes, she sat in silence pondering her next course of action. He had lied to her. What else had he lied about? Was it over with Vanessa or was he good at covering it up? In the last eight months of being in his world, she knew for a fact money could keep anything hidden. At least for a while.

Safiya didn't know how long she sat playing out different scenarios in her head. The plan to do something special for Darius suddenly left a bad taste in her mouth. She would never be one of those women that kept their child away from its father. She was too close to hers to ever deprive another of the feeling. But she needed to get away from here. Even for just a while.

Trust. Could she still trust him? What did they have without it? Her eyes travelled to the picture of them that hung above the dresser. The joy…that couldn't all be a lie. She knew they needed to talk but, in this moment, she didn't even have the strength.

With her game face back on, she stood up and opened the door. Darius stood there, mid-knock. No matter how hurt and angry she was with him, her body yearned for him.

"Hi, beautiful. I didn't know you were back." He moved closer to her and placed a kiss on her lips. As was the case lately, it lacked the passion it once held. It felt like he had taken back pieces of him he'd given her.

"Oh, I came in some hours ago. How was your trip?" She struggled to keep her voice clear and light.

"Boring, but very productive."

"At least it was productive." Safiya mustered up a faint smile

"I guess so. Have you found the building you want to rent yet?" He asked, loosening his belt, walking to the bathroom, and starting the shower.

She followed. "Yeah, there's one in Atlantic Station that would be perfect." Her eyes roamed his body as each piece of clothing came off.

"Awesome," Darius yelled from the under shower.

Safiya sat on the sink and they proceeded to discuss what Safiya would consider safe topics while he showered.

Several minutes later, Darius held her close in bed. It felt like she was floating on cloud nine. As always. He ran his fingers through her hair, listening as she discussed her dad and plans for her business. She loved this man. Deeply. Did he love her? Did he want a child? Over the past couple of months, he'd taught her to demand more. But what if that more was something she couldn't have? How much different would life be if their foundation wasn't built on lies? Being with him like this made her want to woman-up and confess how she felt about him, inquire about what she'd overheard. She opened her mouth to spill her guts when he spoke.

"I have to make a short trip tomorrow."

"But you just got back," her tone was accusatory.

He kissed her temple. "I know but I have to go to DC. I should be back in three days."

She remained silent.

"You could come with me if you like."

Safiya thought about it. Everything she wanted to say flew out the window. He was leaving so soon. He never did that. Was he trying to tell her this arrangement had turned back to business as usual? Her earlier resolve returned. This would be the perfect time for her to leave without all the emotions. Even if she did go to DC, she'd still return to face her problems. It was better to make this as painless as possible.

"No, that's okay. Since its just three days. I'll be fine."

Safiya needed answers to her questions and some clarification before she told him how she felt. With him leaving again, that wasn't going to happen soon. Just in case she didn't like his answers, she needed to be ready.

Darius cuddled her close, placing warm kisses on her nape. Their passion escalated. His hands roamed her body at a feverish pace. A tear formed in the corner of her eye at the impending loss of his warmth. He rolled her over and made love to her all night long.

13

"I never figured you to be a coward."

It was approaching noon when Safiya and Layla walked into the building that would be the future home of Kupendeza Scents. She ignored her friend who stomped behind her, trying to assert her point. Safiya smiled, pleasantly surprised at the progress that was being made. The mixing room was finished, and the display section was coming together nicely. The registers she'd ordered were still in their casing because the contractor had to redo the sales area again.

After she and Darius got married, he couldn't stay away from her for so long, and she travelled with him almost everywhere. Being with him, representing him in events and sitting on boards didn't give her much time to get started on her dream, but now she was seeing it come to life and her joy knew no bounds.

"Safiya! I think you're going about this the wrong way," Layla said.

Safiya placed her hand on her hip and turned to face her brooding friend. "Look Lay, you aren't the one that has to deal with a broken heart. I do—"

"I get that. What I don't understand is, why you couldn't have a simple conversation with him and clear everything up?"

Safiya was tempted to let the debate end there, but she knew the rest of her Saturday would be hounded with questions.

"He lied to me. The whole reason I thought we were doing this was a lie."

"But the whole thing started off as a lie."

"That's not the point. The fact is if I knew this was about some silly shares, I wouldn't have agreed."

"The lies you tell." Layla rolled her eyes. "You want me to believe you would have turned down two million dollars?" A furrow lay between the lines of Layla's brows.

Safiya shifted from one foot to the other. She needed to use the restroom. This baby growing inside her wasn't even a full three months and was already controlling her body function. "Well, you're right, but I also know you understand what I mean. Besides, I did want to talk to him. But like he's been doing for the last couple of months, he ran away. And you know I'm not going to chase after any man."

Safiya noticed the moment the unspoken challenge left Layla's eyes. She was grateful for that because she really wanted to enjoy this moment. "Tell me what you think?"

Her mouth twitched on the verge of a smile. "I'm so proud of you, Safiya."

"Aww, thank you *rafiki*. I really should be thanking you. If you hadn't dragged me along…"

"I just want you to be happy. I saw what your breakup with Justin did to you." Layla looped her hand in Safiya's.

"I am happy. Besides, he's just another man."

"The lies you tell. He's a wealthy, fine man. If I wasn't happy with Todd, I'd give his friend Hakeem some play." Both friends laughed.

"Hate to break it to you, but Darius told me he and his one true love broke up in college and ever since then, he hasn't taken any woman seriously. And you know I can't let my friend go out like that."

"That's why I love you, *rafik*i." Layla paused. "Now finish showing me this place so you can feed me. Since you're the one with the money and all."

In palpable silence, the women strolled around the ground floor, which was the sales and display area, then took the elevator to the second floor where the storage and mixing areas were.

A few notes and a call to the contractor later, the women where in the car to one of their favorite stores. They discussed Layla's upcoming wedding and things they'd buy for the baby. Safiya pulled out her phone to check in with her dad. He was at a baseball game. It was something he did often since Darius got him season tickets. The car pulled up to prime parking space by the side of the store. Safiya placed her hand on the door handle when she felt Layla tugging her back slightly.

"Hold on, Safi. I'll say this only once and I promise I won't bring it up again, but I'll always be there for you with whatever you decide to do. You moving out of your home is a coward move, especially when you didn't have a conversation with him. You and I grew up with one parent each and we vowed that would never be the case of our children. It's just not you."

"I agree, but I needed a breather, so I left. I didn't totally move out. Also, I would've talked to him if he came back two days ago like he said he would. That man has been gone another week. We talk every night, but our conversation is so strained. I'm not trying to force him to be where he doesn't want to be." Safiya rubbed her stomach. "Maybe this is his way of detaching, but I tell you this, this baby won't grow up without two parents because of my feelings. I'll tell him about the child soon. I'm not one to use a baby as a pawn. If Darius decides to be there, fine."

"Okay, that's all I can ask for," Layla said, stepping out of the car. "I'm so surprised your dad hasn't said anything yet about you not being with his beloved Darius. Where's his grandma? She hasn't noticed you left?"

"Grammy is on a retreat with her church, so, she's not in town. And I'm surprised about my dad too. You know how he was when I told him we got married."

Layla gave her a knowing look and they walked toward the store.

Later that evening, Safiya had changed into comfortable loungewear and was seated on top of the island in her dad's kitchen. He had prepared his famous boneless barbeque. Earlier, she and Layla had parted ways after spending money on things Safiya now felt were totally ridiculous. There was no telling what she was having, but Layla had coaxed her into buying unisex baby clothes. It way too early to be shopping and despite everything, she wanted her baby's father by her side. She fully expected for her friend to be by her side, but today, she really wanted her man – her husband.

With rising frustration from the second unanswered call, Safiya opened the Safari icon on her phone and typed Darius's name in Google. This is what her life had turned into, stalking her husband on the internet in case he turned up with Vanessa. Her eyes scanned the links. Nothing recent. She tossed the phone and walked up to her dad.

Safiya placed her hands on his shoulders and looked while he brushed the meat with his secret sauce. "*lijē*," he said with a smile.

"Hey, Papa, I see you still got it."

"Yep and I'll never lose it."

She grinned and he twisted his head to kiss the back of her hand. He returned to what he was doing, and she leaned against the sink next to him, observing. He had single handedly taken care of her after her mother died. No matter what was going on, he'd been there for her. He always said he promised her mother when she was on her sick bed. Safiya knew for a fact that if they had remained in Ethiopia, he would've remarried and probably bore a son due to family pressure. Minutes later, she watched him put the meat on the indoor grill. He turned to her and adjusted his glasses on his nose. Her body stung from the judgement she sensed. In the seven days she'd been staying at his house, he had let her be, but in this moment she knew that reprieve was over. Layla just had to go and talk him up.

"I know you know what I'm about to say." Her dad traced the brim of his shot glass with his thumb. "What are you still doing here?"

Safiya gave a wave. "Daddy, I did tell you that I came to spend time with you."

"When I married your mother, the love of my life, there was no way she was sleeping anywhere without me. I was skeptical on this rushed marriage with Darius, especially after the last jerk." He pulled out the stool near the island and sat.

"Dad, Darius is out of town, so I decided to spend a little time with you. Are you saying you've not enjoyed my company?"

"No, I'm saying that you could've come during the day and still gone back home."

"We live on the other side of town and there was no way I was driving that long." Safiya moved to the fridge and removed the potato salad they had prepared earlier. She felt her dad's eyes follow her, but she avoided them.

"You are grown, and I won't get into your business. You're always welcomed here, but if you have problems with your husband, my expectation is you try and work it out before seeking cover."

Safiya wanted to come clean with her father. Tell him what was really going on. He would be the best one to talk to from a male's perspective. But she couldn't disappoint him again. She did when she married Justin. That man made a fool out of her, making her and her dad the laughingstock of their circle. How could she now tell him that for the past several months, she'd been in a marriage of convenience? With one of the most sought-after billionaires in Atlanta. It was still bad that their arrangement was coming to an end and she would be a divorcee twice over, but at least she had a few more weeks before that happened.

She slid past him and placed a kiss on his forehead. "We're fine dad. Now can you please check on the barbeque? I'm starving."

An uncertain smile spread across his face as he studied her for cracks. She remained unfazed. Soon after, father and daughter set the table and sat to eat. Over the meal, she updated him on the progress the contractors were making, and he informed her of a new lady friend he met at the library a while ago. Safiya's mom had been dead now for twenty years and in that time, her dad never dated anyone that she knew of. It was time for him to be happy again. His eyes twinkled when he spoke of his lady friend, so she figured she must have made an impact on him.

After the dishes were washed and the kitchen cleaned, her father took his nightly cup of Tetley tea and headed upstairs for his room. Ever since she could remember, that had been his routine. Safiya double checked the doors and headed for her old room, located in the lower level of the house. Despite her pleas, he'd refused to move from this house when she asked him to some months ago.

There was a light rap on the door. Her eyes went to the clock. It read 9:05 PM. She checked for her phone, but remembered she hadn't picked it up since she tossed it earlier. The knock came again but it was louder this time. With calculated steps, she reached the door, looked through the peephole and her heart jumped. She leaned her back against the door. The knock came again, startling her. Quickly coming to terms with the fact that she couldn't let him stand outside all night and curious as to what he was doing here, she opened the door.

"Are you seeing him?" Darius seethed, waving what looked like a magazine in his hand. Her eyes followed it for a moment, then she gazed at him. His eyes were darkened with rage. What the heck did he have to be angry about?

14

"What's wrong with you and who are you talking about?" she asked. Instead of giving an answer, Darius brushed past her into the house. Safiya closed the door and turned to face him. He was pacing like a wild animal in a cage. His mouth moved with what she assumed to be expletives, but he never voiced them.

He stopped and observed her as she stood by the wall with both arms folded across her chest.

"Why are you here and not in our home? Did you need somewhere where you could go undetected?" he growled.

She placed her hands on her hips. "First, I need you to respect my dad's house and lower your voice. We can go into my room and talk like adults. And home? Ha! That place hasn't been a home for a couple of months now."

"Which way?" Darius asked.

Safiya turned and went to her bedroom. His light footsteps indicated that he'd fallen in line. She entered and turned to face him standing with his hands balled. He closed the door. He still had the scowl on his face that had greeted her earlier.

Her eyes roamed over him. This was the most inopportune time, but she couldn't contain her love or attraction toward him. He was the sexiest man she'd seen. Her body ached as she recalled the last time he was in control of it. They needed a vacation for how much work they put into guaranteeing the other's satisfaction. Instead, he left before she woke up and now, they were here fighting.

"Now answer my question," his voice boomed, bringing her out of her revere.

"Your question makes no sense. Who are you talking about?"

Darius moved closer to her and placed the paper he held earlier on her vanity and shoved his finger at a picture on the front page. "Him!"

Safiya looked at the paper. It was a sleazy tabloid, one she hadn't heard of before, but what was most shocking was they photoshopped a photo of her and Justin from years ago and made up a ridiculous headline about Darius Gray not being able to keep his wife. She looked back up to her husband. If he didn't look like he was about to blow, she'd laugh. Upon further thought, it occurred to her. Why was he so angry? Did he want her? Well, of course he wanted her. The chemistry between them was never an issue. It was the heart.

"It took this to bring you home?"

"I've been working."

"You were working when I met you."

"Safiya now is not a good time to play with me. Answer my question."

"You're the master of games and your question is absurd."

"Safiya, don't—"

"Besides what does it matter if I am seeing him?"

Darius's eyes sent daggers through her. He walked closer. "It matters because you belong to me and I told you in the beginning; I don't share."

Cold shivers danced along her spine. She was turned on by his possessiveness, but enraged at the same time. What gave him that right when he was living foul himself?

"Under false pretenses."

"What the heck is that supposed to mean?"

"You lied to me."

"I've never lied to you…now—"

"Give it a rest. I'm not seeing him. That's an old picture. If you weren't so busy avoiding me, you would know what I've been up to," she said. She could see the unspoken relief in his eyes. She rolled her eyes. All this was about his bruised ego. "Now you got your answer, you can leave."

"Not without you."

"I'm not going anywhere with you. We have three more weeks before the contract ends. I'll just stay here."

"That wasn't the deal."

"Consider this an amendment." At this point, the questions she had for him didn't even matter. For a moment, she was under the illusion that he came here to fight for them. He just wanted to make sure appearances were kept. Probably to make sure his name didn't get muddied.

"I don't do amendments. Either we go home, or I sleep here with you tonight. Whatever sound bites your dad gets are totally up to you." Darius sat on the bed and began to take off his shoes."

"Why are you here, Darius?" The fight in her had left.

"Because you are." His tone was nonchalant.

"You're being a jerk?"

"I hate you feel that way. But when it comes to you, I'm irrational." Darius took his shirt out of his pants and leaned back against her pillows. "And don't ask me to apologize for it."

Safiya shook her head and sat on the opposite side of the bed. The two of them remained in silence until Safiya decided to lay everything out in the open.

"Darius, I came here to think and you're not making it easy."

"About?"

She sighed. "You. Us. Me. I need to get my thoughts together."

The bed creaked and soon after Darius was kneeling in front of her. Despite her melancholy, a wave of excitement made her heart leap. His head briefly rested in her lap. Then he looked up at her. She looked into his eyes, which now seemed softer. The hunger in them was undeniable. They roamed her body as though it was a treasure map. He lifted his hand to her face, and she snapped out of her trance. She had to protect her heart. Sex was never their problem and she had to remember that and not mistake this for more than it was.

"You lied to me."

"You mentioned that. When?" The sincerity in his question tugged at her heart.

"When we woke up in the hotel, you promised to get the marriage annulled. Then you changed your mind and came up with this contract. Why?"

Darius stood, sat next to her and lifted her to his lap. She prayed he didn't lie to her now. She didn't know whether they had a future together, but if he lied to her, the probability was closer to none.

"When I was a young boy, my mother died. I had no idea who my father was, and I guess there were no relatives because I ended up in an orphanage. My childhood was extremely hard. As fate would have it, I met a woman in my early teens who loved me through everything, took me in and changed my life. Until hers was cut short. In my mind, her death meant the comfort I'd come to know was going to be taken away from me again. The way she died also closed off a part of me. Now two women I loved and depended on were taken away from me, by love."

Safiya's hands that were on her lap itched to pull him in for a hug, but he needed to say this. She needed to hear it. It was the only chance they had.

"My biological mother was taken away because of a broken heart. My dad passed before I was born. When I was growing up, she'd say things that made me know she pined over him. He was the love of her life. Sometimes I think she worked herself to the bone just to be away from me. I'm told I'm his carbon copy. I knew she loved me, but I could also tell I brought her pain. My adoptive mother was taken away because she stood up for me against the man she loved. Love gets people killed. From then on, two things drove me; avoiding love and making money."

"I'm so sorry to hear that, but it still doesn't answer my question."

"From the moment I laid eyes on you, I wanted you. It's that simple. But Hakeem did persuade me to stay married to you by reminding me that I hadn't had a scandal to my name and quickly getting an annulment could equate to bad publicity, which would affect my stock. But then Grammy solidified the decision."

Safiya shot to her feet. Somehow the fact that he needed her to prove his character made her feel dirty. She shouldn't, as she was getting something out of the deal. If she wanted, she could buy all the soap in the world to wash herself clean. She knew it was silly, but she had to admit that the only reason she was angry now was that she loved him. Things were different.

Darius eyes followed her as she paced.

"Why didn't you tell me?"

"It wasn't necessary." He searched her eyes. "Does it matter?"

"It shouldn't, but it does…"

He closed the distance between them. "Why?"

Safiya open her mouth to respond, instead she stumbled back as a wave of nausea hit her, sending her scrambling for the adjoining bathroom. She flung her head over the toilet seat and let the contents of her stomach spill. She felt the gentle grip Darius had on her hair to keep it out of her face. He rubbed her back in a circular motion. She hated him seeing her like this, but nothing was as she liked when it came to this life growing in her. After a couple more elongated dry heaves, she wiped her mouth with the back of her hand and proceeded to the sink.

"I can't smell that bad." He joked, leaving the bathroom.

She brushed her teeth and dabbed her face with cold water. Darius came back in with her nightwear. She stretched her hand to take the clothes from him and he dismissed her. "Move, woman. Let me take care of you." Safiya leaned against the sink as Darius carefully undressed her and redressed her in her night wear.

"Are you ill?"

"No, it must be something I ate."

"Okay. I can always call Dr. McNair and he can fit us in."

"That won't be necessary." *Because I know what's going on with me. You and your child are stressing me out.*

Darius picked her up and placed her on the bed, and got in with her. Safiya wanted nothing more but to rest in his arms, but knew she couldn't. She wiggled to get free, but he held her tighter and caressed her hair.

"When I saw that paper, I was in rage, but when I went home and you weren't there, I went crazy. All sensibility left me. I'll admit I have issues with love and dependency, but in those moments, I came to the quick resolution that I had to take a chance and see if you feel an inkling of what I do."

"And what do you feel?"

With bated breath, Safiya waited on his response. She could feel his breath on her nape and the thumping of his heart beating against her back.

"I love you, Safiya Nadar Gray. I love you. I know this contract ends soon, but we must figure something out. My existence will cease to have meaning without you in it."

Her rib cage expanded with each syllable he spoke. Her brain scrambled to find the right words. This was what she wanted, but there was still something nagging at her. Vanessa and the fact that he hadn't asked that they stay married. Figure something out – what did that mean?

"What about Vanessa? She seemed to have all your attention."

Darius's head jerked up. "I don't care about anybody's attention but yours. Besides where did Vanessa come into play?"

"When I saw her with you in *The Socialite Magazine*."

Darius's brows furrowed. "You shouldn't believe everything you read."

Safiya raised her brow and pointed to the magazine he brought in earlier.

"Touché, but I did say when it comes to you, I'm irrational." In the next few moments, he explained the Vanessa situation to her. As he got to the end, she couldn't contain her smile.

Safiya straddled him and his hands went around her waist. "I love you, too. So much. But explain this 'we gotta figure something out statement'."

Darius brushed his lips against hers. "It means for the rest of my life, I want to wake up, roll over and kiss the love of my life good morning."

"Hmmm, that can be arranged. But am I giving you back your last name?" She struggled to stifle her smile.

A scowl appeared across his face. "Not on your life. I'd never had a dream come true until I met you."

"Not even when you made your first billion?"

"That pales in comparison to the way you make me feel." His lips caressed her neck and roamed her body.

Safiya stretched her neck to give him better access. "When…we started this, I thought it was gonna be…a huge mistake." She moaned.

"Woman, are you done talking? I have other things that need my attention." He squeezed her bottom.

"Quit it. Not under my dad's roof."

"I gave you the option to leave with me, but you didn't take it." He captured her lips with his. His tongue invaded her mouth, sensually caressing it with love.

"Darius, wait, I have something else to tell you…"

"Tell me later, I told you I have things to do." He rolled her over and began to lift her night dress, relegating her next words to the back of her mind.

For the next couple of hours, Darius made love to her body in ways she never knew was possible. It was a good thing her father's room was on the other side of the house. Her body tingled from the aftermath. She shifted to get up. Her bladder was about to overflow. He squeezed tighter holding her in place.

"Where are you going?"

"Your child is sitting on my bladder," she tossed out. Through the sliver of the streetlights entering the room, she saw his eyelids fly open. She grinned at his expression.

"My what? When did you find out? Why didn't you tell me?" With each question, his hand moved over her stomach and his eyes bounced between it and her face.

"Your child, some weeks ago. I was going to, in fact I tried to some hours ago."

His lip came crashing down on hers. Moments later, he set her free and cupped her face. "I promise to do my best to make myself worthy. Thank you."

"You already are…but I really need to pee now." She scurried from the bed and headed to the bathroom.

"Hey," Darius called out. She turned to him. "We might have been a spur of the moment thing, but that warm Vegas night was the beginning of the best nights of my life."

She blew him a kiss. "You promise?"

"Scout's honor," he raised two fingers.

Safiya rolled her eyes and pushed the door open. "Oh jeez, here we go."

EPILOGUE

Thirteen Months Later,

For a lavish wedding in the beautiful Saint Joseph's Catholic Church in Houmt El Souk, Safiya and Darius's celebration had been beautiful. With their adorable six-month-old daughter, Nia, sleeping peacefully, Safiya gazed into the magnificence of the stars above. She lifted her wine flute and took a sip, sighing deeply as the liquid made its way down her throat. She closed her eyes and leaned back into the lounge chair near the pool of their Jones Creek Mansion.

The memories of Darius's spectacular proposal two weeks after he found out she was pregnant still made her tingle all over. They'd been at a final championship game for the *Peach Heights*. Right before half time, he slipped away. Before she knew it, a stage rose from the middle of the field with Darius standing on it and a boy's scout group behind him. After the sweetest serenade of words, baring his soul before thousands, the boys lifted placards to their chest that formed the words, 'Will You Marry Me, Again?' Tears had rushed down her face and she hadn't noticed the microphone that had been placed by her side.

The whirlwind of events between that day and their wedding were a blur. She hadn't wanted to walk down the aisle with a protruding stomach, so she wanted to wait after she gave birth. Darius cancelled the idea immediately; he gave her ten days and that was it. Since money talked, it took seven. She was surprised at how many of his closest friends attended on such short notice.

"That smile on your face better be about me."

Startled, Safiya opened her eyes and took in her husband. He'd changed into his swimming trunks and held in his hand a platter of cheese, grapes and assorted fruits.

"Always baby," she responded. Even she could hear the lust that laced her tone.

He set down the tray, picked up a bunch of grapes and sauntered over to her. He held her throat lightly and placed the fruit above her mouth. She bit off two, so did he and quickly bent to capture her lips, his hand gently applying pressure to her throat. Their tongues tangoed, both enjoying the juice from the grape. He released her when it became apparent, they had to breathe.

"Come take a swim with me Mrs. Gray." He stretched out his hand.

She placed her hand in his. "Your wish is my command."

"Hmmm, really now." Darius swooped her up and walked toward the pool. "Don't punk out when I cash in on that comment." He winked at her.

Safiya smiled back, thankful for spontaneous Vegas Nights.

Final Note

I hope you enjoyed Safiya & Darius's story. Please don't forget to leave a review.

We'll visit Hakeem Richardson & Mariama Niang next in Second Shot.

Other books in the Billionaire Pact series

Second Shot

Pretend Bae

Biography

Unoma Nwankwor writes Christian and sweet contemporary romances that span Africa and the Diaspora. She weaves romantic tales for readers who enjoy stories centered around faith, family, and the rich culture of Africa. Through the pages, she promises humor, tight hugs, forehead kisses, plus redemptive, sacrificial love. She's the recipient of the Nigerian Writers 'Award 2015 Best Faith Based Fiction Writer. In 2017, she was short listed for the Diaspora Writer of the Year and has received two awards of Excellence from Romance In Color. The co-owner of KevStel Productions & Publications and founder of Expectant Living, Unoma is also a wife and mom. You can catch her writing from the comfort of her bedroom nook with a pack of pepperoni slices and a cup of java.

Awards & Accolades

1. NWA's Best Faith Based Fiction Writer Award 2015
2. The Scepter Award for Brilliance in Entertainment 2016
3. NWA's 100 Most Influential Writers 2016
4. NWA's shortlist for Diaspora Writer of the Year, 2017
5. Romance In Color Award of Excellence 2019

Newsletter:
https://landing.mailerlite.com/webforms/landing/g0c9j9

Website: http://www.unomanwankwor.com/

Twitter: http://www.twitter.com/unwankwor

Facebook: https://www.facebook.com/UNwankworAuthor/

Love and HIPLIFE

First Published in Great Britain in 2020 by
LOVE AFRICA PRESS
103 Reaver House, 12 East Street, Epsom KT17 1HX
www.loveafricapress.com

Available as ebook and paperback

ACKNOWLEDGEMENTS

My gratitude overflows to Love Africa Press for believing in the story and publishing it.

I've said it once and I'll say it a million times more, my editor Zee Monodee is the absolute best!

I'd like to thank Empi Baryeh and Amaka Azie for your honesty as beta readers.

Thanks to Estelle Kramo who helped with the Cote d' Ivoirian French lines in the story and for introducing me to her beautiful country when I went to visit.

The Arabic lines were initially vetted by my good friend Mario Iseed, who has wanted to be a character in one of my books ever since he learned I was a writer. Maybe one day.

DEDICATION

To the late Professor Joseph Kwesi Ogah. He will always be one of my favorite educators.

CHAPTER ONE

Climbing Mount Afadjato, the highest mountain in West Africa, wasn't the grandest objective Lamisi Imoro had ever come up with but at this point, she'd die before she got to the top. If only she could suck in enough air, she'd be able to at least take another step.

"Oh, God. Oh, God. I … can't …"

She planted both hands on her knees so she wouldn't crumble to the ground in a heap of blubbering sobs. How many people had the young guide seen keel over in their pursuit of the climb? Why the hell did he have so much energy to leap up the incline when taking four steps knocked the wind out of her?

Her best friend, Precious Kpodo, turned and retracted the few prized paces she'd gained towards the top to return to Lamisi's side.

"I told you we should've waited until your cold cleared," Precious said as she her chest rose and fell with her own heavy breaths. "To be honest, with all of that yellow mucus you said you were bringing up last week, I think you have a touch of bronchitis."

Now able to stand without pain slashing through her ribs with every inhale, all Lamisi could do was glare at her friend. "You're a physiotherapist, not a doctor."

Precious was right, but Lamisi hated being sick and would go to any length to make sure it didn't disturb her life. Ignoring it helped it to go away faster.

She kicked at a stone on the ground. "I swear this mountain has plotted to kill me so it can reign victorious over my downfall."

Precious laughed. "You'll be all right. Take one step at a time and think about dancing on the highest point in Ghana."

Her body, now caught up with its much-needed oxygen supply, gained vigour with the desire to accomplish her task. She thrust her shoulders back. "I can do this. I can do anything I set my mind to."

She clambered up the near-vertical gradient that should've been outlawed for people to climb. Each forward motion turned into a burden that brought fire to her lungs as she breathed in what should've been cool forest air.

Always searching for unique and fun things to do in Ghana, she'd arranged the weekend trip to the Volta Region.

No more mountain climbing. Ever.

She tugged her sweat-drenched T-shirt away from her chest as she stopped again, panting with the effort to catch her breath. "We're almost at the top, right?"

The guide's empathy must've disappeared after her nonstop complaining because he didn't look the tiniest bit sorry when he pointed straight up and replied, "We've gone a quarter of the way. It gets steeper from here."

Earlier, he'd mentioned winning a competition last year amongst all the guides by climbing and descending the mountain the fastest.

Lamisi released a whimper of anticipated torment.

"I can't go on. You two can leave me here. I'll be fine." She waved a hand towards the scenery. "I'll enjoy nature."

And inhaling without effort.

Precious and the boy shared a look. "You know we can't do that. They told us at the information desk that we had to stay together. If you want us to go back down, we'll do that. This was your goal, not mine."

Damn. Precious knew just how to get to her. Holding in her grumbles of complaint, she trudged forward.

What had to be an hour later, she paused and glanced at her watch. Only a miserable five minutes had passed.

Heavy footfalls caught her attention as another group trooped up behind them. She recognized the trio of men led by their own guide—they'd left them at the hotel. How had they climbed so fast?

She'd never been one to go fan-crazy, but her first sight of Bizzy, ingeniously pronounced *Busy*, one of the most fascinating hiplife artists to catch her ear, had left her speechless. The musical genre blended Ghanaian culture with hip hop beats.

Being in the same room with him had had her hands trembling while her heart beat out of sync. Her face had most certainly turned all shades of reddish brown with the effort it had taken not to bounce up and down while screaming.

Not even seeing him in concert several times through the course of his career had caused such a reaction. Watching his videos captivated her like no other musician ever had. Not that she spent much time gawping at his tall, muscular body as he did things with his hips that had saliva easing out the side her mouth. Once. It had happened just once.

He'd winked at her when their gazes had caught and held in the hotel lobby. Hadn't it been enough that her belly had done some kind of crazy flip and she'd gotten dizzy? She'd transformed into a flirtatious, bold woman as her eye had repeated the motion. Never in her thirty years had she winked at a man.

During the brief interaction, she'd wanted to run to him and gush about his music and then ask for a picture with him, of him, near him.

It hadn't happened. She'd taken the coward's way and swiped the smile off her face and endeavoured to put on an aloof air with her head high and shoulders thrust back. So what if that move had made her breasts lead her out the door and his eyes had fallen to them?

It wasn't the Ghanaian way to throw oneself all over stars.

First of all, it created way bigger egos than they needed. Second, she wasn't a groupie trying to get into his bed. Although thinking about what those hips could do made her want to reconsider the stupidity of not introducing herself to him. Who didn't like having fans?

Not that she'd know. Her life revolved around teaching languages and doing research for her PhD. No fandom there.

The tall, broad-shouldered man possessing brown eyes with the clarity of a Malta Guinness glass bottle caught her attention while still a few feet below her. His decadently full lips rose at the corners, revealing white teeth that contrasted with the richness of his russet-brown skin. Judging by how his eyes narrowed as his cheeks pushed them up, his smile must be genuine.

She couldn't breathe for a different reason other than climbing the wretched mountain.

Lamisi pivoted to face her nemesis and trudged upward. To relieve her mind from her inability to take in full breaths, she counted each step. Maybe by the time she got to a hundred, they would've reached the top. Wishful thinking.

She'd made it to twenty before grabbing onto the backpack she'd thrust at Precious when things had started to get rough. If the woman could drag her to the top, everything would be fine, but Precious swatted her hand away.

"I'm not a cart donkey, Lamisi. I'm barely able to get through this ordeal myself."

Lamisi had trouble believing the words. Precious' skin glistened while Lamisi had gone through three face towels—one of them Precious'—and removed the bandana she'd used as a headband to cover her twisted natural hair in order to dry her face.

Precious continued up the pathway, and just as Lamisi was about to do the same, the second party walked up behind her. Having lost the competitive edge to make it to the top before them ten steps ago, she did nothing but shift to the side as they proceeded.

They didn't pass. Bizzy himself stopped next to her.

"Good morning," he greeted in an ultra-sexy voice.

Maybe the exertion of scaling this beast of a mountain wasn't so bad if it could make his voice a bit huskier and breathier than his singing voice. Not a huge difference, but her ears caught and wanted more.

"Are you all right?"

Lamisi tore her gaze away in an attempt to not stare like some silly school girl with a crush on the most captivating man she'd ever encountered. "I'm fine. Just taking a breather."

Before he could respond, one of his companions spoke in Hausa, a language of some people from northern Ghana. Individuals from ethnic groups in the middle and southern areas of the country didn't tend to speak it. He obviously presumed neither she nor Precious understood.

Lamisi looked down at her chest and crossed her arms over her breasts. *Crap.* Exercise plus cool mountain air equalled nipples which could double as headlights through her T-shirt. Why hadn't she thought to wear a padded bra?

Bizzy chastised the guys in Hausa about their rude behaviour and warned them to cut it out.

The giggling men continued to gossip about her, but she was happy he'd tried to stop them.

She sucked in a lungful of the cool air before speaking her next words in Hausa.

"I would appreciate it if you would stop talking about my breasts as if it isn't a natural phenomenon for them to react to the cold." She felt a moment of pride over having pulled out the equivalent of a word in a language that wasn't her first, or even her sixth. "As your friend pointed out, it's rude to talk about people in a language you *presume* they don't understand." She thrust a finger into the air. "It's impolite to talk about people in any language."

She hoped bird poop would land in their gaping mouths as she turned her back to them and climbed with the renewed intention of reaching the top.

The run-in had ignited her temper and reminded her that she was a strong woman. She might not be able to control every aspect of her body or her life, but her mind was another matter. Where her thoughts went, her body would follow. Right then and there, she mentally catapulted herself to the peak. Nothing would stop her now.

Blaise Zemar Ayoma, known to the world—or at least the hiplife-listening crowd of Ghana—as Bizzy, snapped his mouth closed and stared at the retreating back of the curvaceous woman. Her facial features and accent when she'd spoken to him in English had delineated her as someone who wasn't from his ethnic group or at least hadn't grown up among them. Yet, she'd understood and spoken Hausa fluently.

He whipped around to his friends and spoke in English. "How many times have I warned you about discussing people in front of them in Hausa? Now you've upset her."

Their raucous guffaws bounced off the trees.

Abdul, his oldest friend and trusted bodyguard when the need arose, cupped his hands a few inches from his chest. "But her nipples within her perfect breasts were pointed straight at you. Didn't you notice?"

He certainly had. His semi-aroused state would attest to it, but he'd never admit it. Her smile and wink that morning at the hotel had charmed him. He'd decided to introduce himself when her demeanour had changed. A scowl had contorted her face before she'd huffed out of the place.

Both women were striking, but in very different ways. The speaker of his native tongue was shorter, the crown of her head reaching the top of his shoulder. Standing at six feet, he'd been born the runt of the family. Even his mother towered over him.

The woman's compact body and flawless skin presented as someone who took care of herself. Anyone who understood that natural hair was beautiful was the kind of woman for him. Not that he'd decline someone who used relaxers or wore weaves, wigs, or extensions in their braids, but he had an affinity for the confidence it took for a female to wear her hair in its original state.

Her bright dark eyes had spoken to him, called him. Unfortunately, his friends had messed it up before anything could get started.

"You need to apologize," he ordered.

Musah ignored him. "Maybe you excited her, and that's why she was showing them off."

He tried again. "I know you heard me. We'll march up there, and you'll apologize."

Abdul nodded his agreement while Musah mumbled something about women being nothing but temptation.

"Don't you even think about making her your third wife, Musah."

The man tilted his head and looked to the sky as if contemplating it, and then shook his head. "Kadijah and Hawa would kill me. Besides, the woman isn't my type. Much too severe and talkative for my liking."

More like bold and brave for addressing something that bothered her. Qualities that appealed to Blaise.

"It makes no difference." Abdul pointed to his skull. "Her tight, short-sleeved shirt, jeans, and lack of hair covering indicates she doesn't share our religion. I don't believe such a woman would be persuaded to become a Muslim."

"You know that not all women wear hijab, so she could be Muslim." Blaise grinned. "If you two apologize, then perhaps I have a chance with her. At least to go out on a date."

Both men scoffed. Musah clapped a hand against Blaise's shoulder.

"You don't have a chance, my brother. Don't forget that you are also a Muslim, although a backsliding one. Besides, that woman would deliver you to an early death with her words alone. My ears are still ringing from the inflection she used in our dialect.

And you know she's not from our area. Imagine what would happen to you if she chastised you in her own language?"

Abdul shook his head. "My friend, it would deteriorate your manhood. You need a calm woman to suit your laid-back personality. One who will support your career and not put her own above yours. A good Muslim woman like your parents expect you to marry."

Blaise's heart sank. How many times had he heard the same edict about marrying within his religion, his culture if possible, from his mother?

He longed to push aside his friend's words, but he knew them to be true. He didn't need a dramatic woman who would trouble him. Not with the media trying to dig up information on his lifestyle that wasn't any of their business.

Although he hadn't practiced the faith consistently in years, he shivered at the thought of his parents' reaction to him bringing home a woman who wasn't Muslim. Their support over the years had been immeasurable. He never wanted to disappoint them. He had a certain image to uphold as the child of a chief. His father had been generous in allowing him to fulfil his passion of becoming a hiplife artist. He wouldn't push the boundaries. His wife would be a Muslim, with no argument.

The woman with peaked nipples and the contagious smile had interested him. Not just with her fluency in Hausa, but her initial friendly response to him at the hotel before shutting down. But his friends were right.

"You still have to apologize," he reminded them.

Musah dropped his hand to his side. "Rightly so. That's if she doesn't collapse by the time we reach her."

The two men laughed while concern made him want to get to her faster.

CHAPTER TWO

Lamisi allowed her outrage to carry her battered muscles and tortured lungs to the top of Mt. Afadjato with only one more break. She refused to let the uncouth men catch up with them.

When they finally reached their destination, she stumbled to the rock formation where the signpost announced the altitude of eight-hundred-eighty-five metres and allowed her legs to buckle.

Precious snapped a few pictures of Lamisi's final demise before handing the camera to the tour guide and posing for her own pictures.

The stunning view left her mesmerized. Had it been worth a near-death episode to experience one of Ghana's natural wonders? She'd have to ponder it once oxygen had replenished her brain.

Precious took the camera from the guide and settled next to her. "Now that you can breathe, tell me what happened with those guys."

When Precious had asked her on the way up, Lamisi had chosen to focus on placing one foot in front of the other. She now told the story of their rudeness.

Precious laughed. "I didn't even notice."

Lamisi blew out a gust of air. "It's not funny. It was embarrassing."

"At least you have nice breasts."

They glanced down at her chest. She'd placed a couple of tissues over her nipples to keep them hidden.

"I do."

"The guys were cute," Precious said.

"For bush men."

Lamisi bristled when she noticed them clear the corner to reach the top. Hand slapping ensued among them.

She gathered the strength to stand. "Time to go."

Precious turned her attention to the copse of trees leading to the end of the climb. "Don't let them spoil your victory of making it up here. Relish it. How about taking pictures where you don't look as if you've passed out?"

"You're right. I must look victorious for social media." She stood next to the signpost, placed her fists on her hips, and focused straight ahead at the clear blue sky. "Snap away."

The trio headed in their direction, looking as if they'd taken a stroll on flat land rather than the gruesome incline Lamisi had endured. She tried to ignore them, but had a tough time keeping her gaze away from Bizzy's commanding presence.

After more than enough pose changes and a few pictures taken by the guide with them together, she hooked her arm through her best friend's and walked to the edge overlooking the town. "I wonder if the people down there think anyone is watching them."

Precious chuckled. "We can see houses and cars, but the humans are dots from this distance. I'm trying to figure out how many of them have ever climbed this mountain."

"I'd guess very few."

The sudden presence of a voice smooth as whipped shea butter made them both jump.

Bizzy held up his palms. His crooked grin did more to increase Lamisi's heartbeat than his sudden presence in their conversation.

"I'm sorry. I didn't mean to scare you."

Not feeling charitable towards him or his crew, her tone came out harsh. "It's not polite to eavesdrop."

He dipped his head forward in acknowledgement. "It seems that our transgressions against you are piling up."

"This is your first offense." She waved a finger at the two men standing on either side of him. "Unlike them."

The one with the lightest skin amongst them all stepped forward. "We're sorry to have offended you. If we knew you understood our language, we would never have done it."

Lamisi fought the upward twitch of her lips at the withering look Bizzy shot his friends. She craned her neck to look into his eyes. The men held the characteristic height of those from the most northern regions of Ghana.

"Is it right to talk about people in a language they don't understand?" she probed. "I was taught that it was bad-mannered."

Before either of his two friends could speak and dig themselves further into their trench, Bizzy shook his head.

"What he meant was that he shouldn't have been speaking about you at all, especially about something so—" His eyes twinkled as his tongue flicked out to lick his tantalizing lips "—sensitive."

Lamisi feared she'd collapse with the sudden thinness of the air. She refrained from looking down at her breasts to make sure her hardened nipples weren't poking through again. With one word, he'd aroused her. Well, one word said in the sexiest voice she'd ever heard.

Unnerved, she'd gain control by informing him that he shouldn't be the one apologizing, but Precious pinched the back of her arm.

"She accepts your apology."

"Thank you." He spoke to Precious before turning his attention to Lamisi. "My mother always tells me that only people with big hearts are able to forgive. My name is Blaise Ayoma. These are my friends Abdul Fobil and Musah Adongo."

Lamisi allowed Precious to be their spokesperson since she wasn't as ready to forgive as her friend had indicated. She'd rather put the men on the hot seat and enjoy watching them squirm for a little while longer. At least until they realized their offense.

Precious touched the tips of her fingers to her upper chest. "I'm Precious Kpodo, and this is Lamisi Imoro."

Blaise looked into Lamisi's eyes when held out his hand. "It's a pleasure to meet you."

She wiped her moist palms on her sweat-soaked jeans before sliding the right one against his. An unexpected electrical current coursed its way up her arm and down her spine. She swallowed hard, enjoying the odd combination of pleasure and awareness inviting her to move closer.

"It's …" She cleared her throat when it came out raspy. "It's nice to meet you, too."

After longer than what seemed normal, they released each other, and he offered his hand to Precious. Lamisi extended hers to the other two men in turn. She noted that the contact with them didn't do anything but make her want to wipe their dampness from her palm. There was no desire to bask in the attention of their gazes like she'd wanted to do with Blaise.

Standing within arm's length to one of the greatest hiplife artists in Ghana, her tongue loosened. "I'm a fan of your music."

And you.

No need to reveal the silly crush she had on him. As a musician, not a person. She didn't know him like that.

A lopsided grin appeared. "That's good to hear."

Not what she'd expected. His modesty elevated her attraction to him. As an artist, not a man whose handsomeness stole her breath.

Precious pointed and squeaked. "Oh my goodness. You're Bizzy."

Her friend had never been good with faces, but it had taken her long enough to recognize him.

All three men beamed, making her wonder how the sun reflecting off their teeth at such a height didn't temporarily blind her.

"My friends call me Blaise, so feel free."

Lamisi bit the inside of her cheek to keep from laughing at Precious' besotted gaze.

She fought her own giddiness as she thought about his accomplishments. He'd struggled for years before making the charts two years ago with his hit song, *I dey gaya da nokwrƐ*. The translation of *I tell you the truth* didn't sound as rhythmic as when he sang in the four languages he'd used.

English, Pidgin English, his own mother tongue of Hausa, and Twi, the most spoken local language in the middle and southern portions of Ghana.

The song impressed her more each time she listened to it. Not only did the beat have her wiggling her hips, but the lyrics were insightful in a way that few people could understand unless they spoke all four languages. Which she did, with an addition of seven others.

His songs tended to possess a powerful depth that most people had limited understanding of because of the mix of languages.

On the surface, his music appeared light and fun as he sang about a love which has been lost or found, enjoying life, or some other frivolous theme. Those who could interpret the words understood that he incorporated politics, issues of social justice, and even the overuse of religion in the system as undercurrents to his lyrics.

She hadn't wanted to know if he wrote all of the songs himself. Already holding him in high regard, she didn't need her awe and fascination of him rising to the stars.

She turned to Precious and tugged at the hem of her shirt to stop from lifting her friend's chin to close her mouth. "Are you ready to go?"

It took a few more seconds of staring before Precious turned her attention to her. "Pardon me?"

"Let's head back down."

Never shy, Precious held her phone to Lamisi before asking Blaise, "Can I please take a picture with you?"

"No problem."

Precious pointed to the signpost. "Over there."

Once they reached the spot, Blaise draped an arm around her shoulders.

Lamisi placed a hand over her stomach at the surprise burn of jealousy in her stomach. She stood rooted in place and snapped several pictures instead of charging to the pair to pull them apart.

"That should do it," she announced.

Relieved when they separated, she reached out to hand Precious the device.

Blaise stayed in place and nodded at Lamisi. "Would you like a picture, too?"

Saying no would be rude, wouldn't it? She handed Precious her phone. With each step, she hoped he would loop his arm around her, too. But then, she recalled her sweat-soaked shirt and recanted the wish.

He didn't seem to mind her sopping-wet clothing because he tucked her into his side. She snaked her arm around his waist and gripped his shirt as she leaned into him. Despite a height difference of at least half a foot, her curves fit into his firm body as if they'd been pieced together in a puzzle. Heat burned the side in direct contact with him, and she snuggled in closer as he squeezed her shoulder.

A part of her hoped the photo session would never end. The muskiness of his perspiring skin blended with the spiciness of the cologne that clung to his shirt had her inhaling deeper. If he smelled this amazing after having climbed a mountain, he'd be irresistible when freshly showered and dressed.

Women threw themselves at the star for a reason. Hell, she'd become one of his groupies for a moment. Who was she trying to kid? She still was. Yet, no matter how friendly, handsome, or talented he was, they came from two different worlds within the same country. He lived for people to watch and admire him while she preferred to stay in the background, observing. She'd do best to remember how different they were because their relationship would never last.

As if there was a miniscule chance of him thinking about me in that way.

When Precious announced that she was done, Lamisi released her arm from around him and started to move away, only to be held in place.

He handed his phone to Musah. "Take some with mine."

Lamisi craned her neck to look up at him. "I'm not famous, like you. What do you need my picture for?"

The intensity in his eyes softened her knees.

"It's only fair," he stated in Hausa.

He had a point.

"And you feel too good against me to release just yet," he added.

He couldn't be serious. The line would work on one of his younger groupies. Her maturity kept it from going to her head. "I'm sure you say that to all the women you pose with."

His brows drew together as he canted his head in thought. "No. Never. You're the only one."

A warmth that had nothing to do with the sun radiated out from her chest. The ego of a simple woman who spent all her time with her head buried in journal articles researching for her PhD and teaching language courses wanted to believe him. Her rational mind kept her connected to the reality of him being a charming man who knew how to weave words into entrancing spells.

"Share your beautiful smile with the camera. And me."

His whispered words breezed into her ear eliciting a delicious shiver.

She looked at him to see if he'd taken his own advice. Her lips complied with his instructions when she discovered him focused on her. Smiling.

"I've snapped at least twenty pictures. I'm done," Musah said with a scowl directed at Blaise that hadn't been present before he'd been given the job of photographer.

Lamisi shuffled away from the electricity of Blaise's touch. She regretted the loss of contact.

"Thank you for the pictures," she said in a rush to leave the man who set off an unfamiliar desire in her to plaster herself against him. Possibly press her lips against a mouth which sang lyrics that had the power to touch her heart with their conviction.

She pointed towards the centre of the earth with her left hand and waved with the right as she back-pedalled to where they'd come to flat ground.

"We're heading back down, so enjoy the rest of your stay."

Blaise caught up to her. "Would you ladies like to join us for lunch when we reach the bottom?"

He'd used the breathier, huskier timber from when they'd first spoken on the way up. If exertion hadn't caused it like she'd thought, what had? Was he flirting with her?

Goosebumps erupted at the possibility. She had to get away before she begged him to say her name. Maybe whisper it and then have his tongue trace along the shell of her ear. She shivered and crossed her arms over her chest to hide any evidence of her reaction.

Her enamoured state came to a screeching halt. Hadn't she read or heard somewhere that he was getting married to a Nigerian heiress?

She answered his invitation before Precious could. "Thanks, but we have to get home. It's a long journey."

"Where do you live?"

She looked at Blaise from the side of her eye. "Why do you ask?"

His muscular shoulder rose in a shrug. "If you're going to Accra, you could ride with us. Unless you drove."

His friends stepped to either side of him.

"There's no room," the tallest said. "Not with our wives."

She had her reasons for getting away from Blaise; what was theirs? "We drove, so there's no need for the ride."

"Thank you, though," Precious said with a huge grin. "It was generous of you to offer."

Blaise's gaze never left Lamisi's face as he held up his phone. "Can I have your number?"

She blinked several times. *What the hell for?* She'd never been and never would be a home wrecker. She didn't believe in disrespecting herself or her fellow sisters.

She snarled in disgust. "I'm sure your girlfriend wouldn't appreciate that."

She grabbed Precious' arm and called for their guide who stood watching the scene.

Lamisi led the way, not waiting for anyone's response to her comment. She would've loved the chance to interrogate him about his insightful lyrics, but knowing he'd be willing to cheat on his girlfriend, a beautiful heiress who ruled social media, set a blaze of ire in her belly.

What a philandering jerk.

CHAPTER THREE

Lamisi found the descent a hundred and fifty percent less tiring than the climb, yet more treacherous. She slid a few times as the stones and dirt shifted under her feet, before wizening up and slowing her pace rather than rampage down the mountain to get away from a certain womanizing hiplife artist.

A patch of dirt loosened as she stepped down, causing her foot to resist gravity and kick into the air with the other soon to follow. A strong grip stabilized her and kept her from hitting the ground. Heart beating with a bounding so intense that it hurt her ears, she looked up to thank her rescuer. The words got stuck in her throat as she met the handsome face of the man she'd stormed away from.

Forgiveness for the way he'd disrespected his girlfriend with his blatant flirtation had yet to enter her consciousness. She pulled her arm out of his grip and mumbled, "Thank you."

Then, she turned … only to slip again. *Dammit*. This time, she regained her balance without help.

"Take your time. There's no rush."

Ignoring how his presence, to her annoyance, made her stomach flutter, she took more careful steps.

He hitched a thumb behind them. "We were getting along well. What happened up there?"

A direct man. Of course he was, because how often did talented, outrageously gorgeous, communicative men drop into her life?

"Why did you ask for my number when you have a girlfriend?"

"I'm a single man."

He was a performer—the sound of surprise and conviction in his voice could be an act. Yet, he hadn't hesitated for even a second before answering. It wouldn't be the first time she'd come to the wrong conclusion about a person, but her source had been reliable. Kind of.

"That's not what the entertainment news report." She placed a hand on her hip as he stepped closer to her so that Musah could get past. "Deola, the Nigerian oil heiress? Remember her?"

Abdul laughed as he slapped Blaise on the back. "I told you that escorting Deola to those functions would come back to haunt you."

And then, he continued on his way, leaving them planted on the side of the mountain.

Lamisi watched the others meander towards their destination as she waited for Blaise's answer. Precious was in the midst of pointing at a tree as she chatted with the tour guide. The woman loved all things science.

He shook his head. "I'm not dating Deola. Or anyone else right now."

"So she's not your girlfriend like the tabloids say?"

Why should she even care? They'd just met, and unless she attended another one of his concerts, they wouldn't see each other again.

"It was a misunderstanding."

By this point, she had heard enough. She turned to make her way down the mountain so she could get as far away as possible.

"We aren't dating, but we sort of use each other."

She nodded as she tried to convince herself that she didn't want to hear the whole story. "Thank you for clearing that up. I wish you two a happy life together."

He skittered past her and blocked her path. "Please, let me explain."

She crossed her arms over her chest and tapped her foot out of annoyance, but disappointment held a bigger portion of her current emotional state. She'd rather have never discovered that her hiplife hero was a plain human male who made bad decisions without caring who he hurt.

"What for? I'm someone you just met. It's not necessary. Besides, I'm hungry."

His full lips spread into a smile as he took off his backpack. Curiosity got the best of her as she watched him open it and pull out a chocolate bar.

Blaise waved it in front of her face. "I'll give it to you if you listen to my explanation."

Her stomach grumbled loud enough to scare the hidden wildlife as she eyed the candy with longing. What would it hurt to hear him out? She'd get some gossip directly from the source and a snack to tide her over. No negative in that equation.

He reached for her hand and placed the chocolate in it. The tingles skittering up her arm from the contact overtook the sensation of hunger.

He hesitated for a moment before shaking his head with a deep frown. "I'm sorry. I don't know what got into me. I should've just offered it to you without the bribe. It was nice meeting you, Lamisi."

Then, he swept his hand to indicate that she should walk ahead of him.

She hesitated for a moment before opening the candy bar. "You're invited."

He chuckled and shook his head to decline. "Thank you."

The tradition of offering to share food tended to be a source of entertainment. What was the saying about sharing being caring?

She took a bite and moaned as the flavour of the peanuts, caramel, nougat, and chocolate merged onto her tongue as the most decadent treat she'd ever eaten. Hunger made everything taste incredible.

"Thanks," she said around the confection still in her mouth.

His Adam's apple bobbed several times. "My pleasure."

Never had words felt as if they'd stroked her most intimate places as delicious warmth settled low in her abdomen. She glanced at her chest to ensure that those well-placed tissues were still doing their job. Barely.

The quicker she got away from him, the better.

"Look, your life is none of my business." She pointed in the direction they were supposed to be headed. "How about if we complete the descent so we can go home?"

He didn't speak as he stared into her eyes, seeming to consider her for a moment.

After long seconds of his direct attention, her mouth went dry as she longed to close the gap between them and feel his body against her again. Tilt her head up and stand on her toes so she could kiss him. Just once because her tingling lips needed to know.

A photo of Deola, resplendent and regal in a splendid silver gown while she hooked her hand into the crook of Blaise's arm at a gala, burst into her mind.

She averted her gaze and set her feet to walking.

"How do you understand Hausa?" he asked after a few minutes of their feet crunching against the earth.

Heat infused her face despite there being no exertion as they strolled. The question never failed to embarrass her when it should be a source of pride. People tended to question her honesty when she discussed her language skills so much so that she never wanted to. Explaining that she was a genius when it came to linguistics was too much of a hassle.

"It's one of the languages I speak. I picked it up when I spent a few months in Nigeria. Bauchi State in the north." A short and simple answer that should lead to no more questions.

His jaw dropped, exposing all of his teeth. "You learned Hausa in a few months?"

She nodded, ignoring his astonished tone. "I've always been good with languages."

"How many do you speak?"

She sighed in resignation at having to carry on with the conversation. "I speak eight languages fluently. I'm not counting pidgin."

She kept the fact that she understood a total of twelve to herself. That part tended to freak people out.

She snuck a glance at him as she waited for his reaction. Would he call her a liar? Or try to test her with any of the other languages he might speak?

The corners of his lips were downcast as he nodded and kicked at a stone on the path with his shoulders hunched forward. "More than the five I know."

It sounded like he might be jealous. The man had talents that transcended hers in so many ways, and he was envious of her ability with languages. She transitioned her snicker of delight into a cough.

She expected at least one question from him about her language skills. But nothing broke the silence apart from the crunch of the ground caused by their steps.

Her curiosity made her ask, "What's your fifth language?"

He rubbed his chin. The combination of the trimmed beard with the faded haircut suited him.

"French."

Her love of his music and languages got the better of her. "Ah. *As-tu déjà pensé à l'intégrer à ta musique?*"

A slight horizontal crease appeared on his forehead when his brows rose. "I understood the word music."

She spoke in English. "I asked if you had ever thought of adding French into your music. You don't speak any French at all?"

He shrugged. "I started taking lessons with a private tutor a couple of weeks ago. I'm moving into the next phase of my career by having French be the base of some of the songs I'm writing. It'll make me more accessible to the Francophone countries."

Did she dare ask? "So, you write your own lyrics?"

His shoulders appeared broader as his chest expanded. "I do."

She pursed her lips to the side, not quite believing him. "You wrote the songs on all three of your albums?"

"You really are a fan. People remember two. That first one went nowhere."

"I know, but in my opinion, it was the best. The nuances you put into the lyrics were insightful. More than just a beat. Even though those were catchy." She ignored the slight slip of her sneaker. "You didn't answer the question. Did you write all of the songs yourself?"

"Every single one. No artist is an island. My producers had input when it came to laying the tracks."

She looked into his eyes. Did she believe him? Why shouldn't she? Not as if she found him to be unintelligent, but to be so graceful with words, not just in one language, but three or four in the same song, was beyond belief. It must be similar to the astonishment people experienced when they learned about the number of languages she spoke.

A few paces passed before a melodious tune swirled into her ear and captured her attention.

"When I looked into your eyes for the very first time, I was swept away by their intensity. They were so open one moment and then shuttered closed the next. I wanted to get to know you, but you were gone. Until we met again on the mountain climb."

Her body became weightless she got a sense of floating. Bizzy had just serenaded her with a song she'd never heard before. He'd created it on the spot about their encounter. Three languages interwoven into one beautiful set.

"How did …" Incredulous at his amazing ability to weave words on the go in a way that sent chills down her spine, her extensive vocabulary vanished.

He shrugged. "Creating songs is my gift."

Gazing into his eyes with admiration, she didn't see the tree root jutting out in the middle of the path until it was too late.

Considering he was staring at her instead of where they were going, for once, he was the one to trip over the obstruction.

She reached out to grab him liked he'd done so many times for her. But the contact she made with his muscled arm wasn't enough.

Relativity kicked in as time moved in super slow-motion.

Rather than reversing his downward momentum as she'd hoped, she descended with him.

With a turn of his head, he must've realized she was chasing him down on the ride. Then, he did the most incredible thing.

In one fluid movement, Blaise grabbed her with both arms and pulled her close. His solid bulk took the brunt of the interminable fall when they landed.

Still, gravity wasn't through with them as they rolled a few times together … until they finally stopped.

CHAPTER FOUR

Blaise opened his eyes with a start once they stopped tumbling. On any other day, a beautiful woman lying on top of him would be welcomed. Concern for her wellbeing hit him harder than he had the ground.

"Lamisi." He loosened his arms from the tight hold and lifted his head to look at her. "Lamisi," he said a little louder.

Her groan caused a sense relief that had him taking full breaths again.

"Are you okay?" he asked.

He winced as she adjusted herself against his chest and raised her upper body to look into his eyes.

"As far as I can tell. What about you?"

His buttocks throbbed, but he wouldn't share that. "I'm sure that even with my brown skin, I'll be bruised tomorrow from the fall."

She reached a hand to the ground to help push herself off of him. He held her in place with a light hold. The warmth of her soft lushness had the effect of some sort of anaesthesia against any pain he hadn't assessed yet.

"If you release me, I'll get up. I know I'm not light."

He stared into her eyes. "You're just right."

Her heart thumping hard against his chest increased its pace, and her breathing became shallow and rapid as her gaze dropped to his mouth.

Electric shocks swarmed along every inch of his skin. If nothing else ever happened in his life, he had to taste her. Relish the fullness of her lips. Lose himself in the reality that made up the woman he'd just come to know as Lamisi.

He raised his head to meet her flesh. The spark at their contact shot into him. But he only had the chance to experience a lingering soft brush of her tantalizing lips as she pressed against him for too short a time.

Then, she scrambled to her feet and shuffled backwards.

He sprung up to make sure she didn't fall again. Bad move. The pain had him seeing full daylight under the canopy of trees as his ankle gave way. He landed back on the ground.

Lamisi rushed to him and knelt. "Are you all right?"

He sucked in a breath. "My ankle. I think I may have twisted it. How are you?"

Other than kissably gorgeous.

"You broke my fall, so I'm fine." She touched his shoulder. "Thank you."

As a man, he couldn't let her get hurt for attempting to help him when she didn't have to. "Anytime."

When the warmth of her hand seeped into him, he realized just how much he meant it.

Once again, she was the one to break the intoxicating moment between them. "Let me look at your ankle."

She shifted down to his foot, pulled the hem of his jeans up, and then grazed her fingers along the area just above the rim of his sneaker.

A red-hot tearing pain bounded around the spot. He tried to stifle the hiss, but it escaped as he pulled his leg away from her.

"It's already swollen. It could be a severe sprain or a break. I'm not sure. I'll run down and get Precious so she can check it out." Her hand landed on his knee as if to reassure him. "She's a physiotherapist."

Terror clawed at him as he thought of her going down alone. Possibly getting injured. "It might be nothing. I might've just been surprised the first time I stood. Let me see if I can put pressure on it."

Her eyes went wide and her twists shook with the swing of her head side to side. "I don't think you should. You saw how well I did trying to stop your fall. Neither of us needs to take another tumble like that again."

Unless it's into my bed. He shook the intruding thought away while the creative side of him made a mental note to write a song using the word tumble.

"I'll be okay." There was no harm in trying.

Blaise ignored Lamisi's extended arms as he pushed himself up onto his strong leg. He did accept her shoulder to rest against as he lowered his injured one onto the ground.

He closed his eyes against the excruciating shards of pain and lifted his foot before he could place his full weight on it.

"Oh, dear Allah in the Heavens," he said in Hausa.

"I would've thought you'd be using some swear words," Lamisi said.

Grateful for the support, he glanced down at her. "I don't curse."

"Is it a side effect of following Muslim rules?"

He grinned. "If you want to call my mother's chastisement and punishment of uttering it a side effect, then so be it."

She laughed as she helped him sit on the ground.

He grunted as he gingerly settled his leg in front of him.

"Keeping my language clean was one of several stipulations she gave me when I told her I wanted to go into the music industry." He caught her gaze. "That, and making sure to respect all women."

"Sounds like she's strong and instilled some good values into you."

Proud of his mother's achievements when it came to educating the women in her town and those surrounding them in the Northern Region of Ghana, he smiled. "She is."

Lamisi pulled out her cell phone. "There's no signal. I'm going to get Precious and the tour guide."

Having no other choice but to let her go, he grasped her hand and squeezed. "Be careful."

"I will. I'll be right back."

He watched as she descended. Out of sight, he tested the ankle by moving it. He let out the growl of pain he hadn't been able to express in Lamisi's presence.

And then, he relaxed or tried to while he waited for help to arrive.

Sure, he'd just experienced agony like he couldn't recall in years, but he'd also just had the ultimate of sweet kisses. Something that wouldn't have happened if he'd been paying attention to where he'd been going rather than staring into her enthralling dark eyes.

His lips still tingled from the brief touch. He wanted more. To make it a deeper encounter and have her respond to him rather than run away.

As much as she might want to deny it, she liked him. At least, she'd been impressed with his music. Always a plus.

Already, she'd inspired him to write. Tumble was the word she'd thrown at him. Which language would he use to describe his plunge into her eyes and seeing straight to her soul?

He'd always been told, especially by his stern disciplinarian of a father, that he was emotional. He'd learned over the years how to take advantage of it through poetry, and eventually, his lyrics, rather than be ashamed. He understood his feelings, and with Lamisi, he'd definitely toppled into something he'd never experienced before.

CHAPTER FIVE

Lamisi rubbed her arms as the sensation of needles pricked into her skin. She had to look down to make sure they weren't real. She hated hospitals. No, not even close to the word. Detested, deplored, despised all rolled into one would better suit her feelings about the institution. She still hadn't gotten over childhood incidences of treatments and injections which had supposedly been meant for her own good.

"Are you okay?" Precious asked as they sat in the waiting area of the Emergency Room while Blaise's two friends had gone to his bedside.

She lied with a nod while clasping her trembling hands together. She wouldn't be okay until the disgusting antiseptic scent left her nostrils.

Precious shook her head with a deep frown altering her beauty. "I'm surprised you volunteered to join us."

"What was I supposed to do?"

She kept her voice low, out of earshot of Abdul's and Musah's wives. The youngest one kept glaring in her direction. Not the first time a Ghanaian woman had given her nasty looks she didn't deserve. It wasn't as if she'd pushed Blaise and laughed over him in victory. Lamisi ignored her.

"The guy broke my fall by letting me land on top of him." For a moment, her nausea receded as she recalled his heroic action along with a kiss she'd never forget.

For those few seconds in his embrace, she'd allowed herself the luxury of believing that only they existed in the world. The craving she'd experienced to get even closer had magnified by a thousand as she lay sprawled on top of him. That kiss had been inevitable.

Or so she allowed herself to believe because her stomach roiled with the wretchedness of her guilt. She'd kissed another woman's man. If he couldn't say outright that he wasn't dating

Deola, then it meant they were. Having been cheated on by two guys in the past who she'd thought she'd been seriously involved with, she never wanted to make another woman experience the same type of detrimental betrayal at her hand.

"Let's go." Her friend's voice jogged her mind into the present. "I came to make sure he got the X-ray. We don't need to wait." She raised a finger and moved them left to right in Lamisi's face. "Your phobia of hospitals is making your eyes look glazed."

Lamisi blinked several times.

"I don't have a phobia." She rubbed damp palms against her jeans. "Just a debilitating fear."

Those last words had come out as a mumble.

Precious considered her.

"And yet, instead of staying at the hotel, or even in the car, you decided to come in. Interesting," she drawled out.

"You had to be there to see the acrobatic feat he performed." Lamisi rolled her hands around themselves, failing to replicate with their motion what had happened. "Escorting him here was necessary."

Precious nudged her shoulder with her own. "You've had a crush for years. He's gorgeous, successful, and from what I observed, seems to like you, too. A guy doesn't stare at someone like he did you unless he appreciates what he sees."

Wait until she told Precious about the kiss, the impromptu song, and Deola.

Her shoulders slumped at the last. "Let's stay a little longer. I want to find out how his ankle is. I hope it isn't broken."

What could she do for him if it was? Nothing. Why was she fighting nausea and a possible fainting spell by hanging around?

"I doubt it, but it's better to be sure. You look more green than brown right now. Let's go see how he is so I can get you out of here."

Every muscle in her body had become sore as if she'd been, well, climbing a mountain. She wasn't sure if her jittery legs would be able to support her if she stood. She shivered as sweat meandered down the side of her face from the terror threatening to drown her.

"I hate hospitals."

Precious looped a comforting arm around her shoulders. "I know. That's why you being here for him is so shocking. You like him, don't you?"

"I respect his music. It's incredible. Most people don't recognize that he's taken a social stance while dancing to his songs. Not until he gives his interpretation during an interview. Plus, he protected me when he didn't have to."

Precious raised a brow. "Weren't you the one trying to stop him from falling when he tripped?"

She wasn't having that conversation again. Nor would she admit that she liked him. It didn't matter, anyway. He was making his way up the music charts while she'd be completing her doctorate within the year. They lived completely different lives, and other than being multilingual, probably had nothing in common.

Then why was she still sitting in this dreaded hospital waiting for him?

"Help me up. That mountain did bad things to my legs, and I'm not sure I can walk anymore after sitting for so long."

Precious laughed. "What makes you think I can get up myself?"

Lamisi's breath snagged as her attention caught the hiplife star hobbling down the corridor. "Here comes Blaise with his friends."

At the sight of him without plaster of Paris on his lower leg and supported by Musah alone, she forgot the soreness of her body, stood, and went to him.

"So, it isn't broken?"

His charming crooked smile eradicated the misery she'd suffered through while waiting.

"No. Badly sprained, though."

Relieved and unable to keep her hands to herself when she'd been so worried, she reached out and touched his arm. She wasn't sure who passed the current, but she took a moment to enjoy it before letting her arm drop. "That's great to hear. Much better than a break."

His eyes captured hers and refused to release her. "You stayed?"

"Yes." She ignored the heat creeping up her neck and hitched a thumb at Precious. "She wanted to make sure they treated you well."

Precious cleared her throat.

So what if she'd just revealed her true feelings to her best friend with that tiny lie? She'd deal with the teasing later.

He shifted his eyes away, leaving her with a longing to bask in them.

"Thank you, Precious."

"No problem. It was actually—"

"We need to go." After years of friendship, she knew when Precious was about to rat her out. "It's a long journey to Accra. And you should get off your feet. I hope you'll be able to elevate your leg while you drive back."

"He'll be fine," Musah said. "Let's go."

Blaise raised his leg. "Lamisi has a point. The doctor instructed me to keep it up and iced."

Not wanting to leave him, she lunged at the opportunity. Nothing prevented her from getting to know him. As her favourite musician.

"Since it's just Precious and myself in her car and yours is full. How about if we give you a ride?"

A choking sound came from Precious.

Blaise cut off anything Musah had opened his mouth to say. "I accept. It'll give us a chance to finish our discussion."

CHAPTER SIX

Blaise lounged in the back seat of the Kia Sportage SUV. That new car smell permeated his nostrils as the air conditioning cooled the atmosphere. He had his long leg extended along the backseat without it touching the door as an ice pack sat on top of his ankle.

The medication they'd given him had taken the edge off the pain. He no longer winced each time he adjusted his leg. From his vantage point behind the driver's seat, he observed Lamisi's profile while she kept her sights on the road. Her forehead sloped into a pert nose that shadowed a slightly smaller and darker top lip than the pinkish-brown bottom.

His lips tingled as he recalled the pillowy softness of hers during their fleeting kiss. He wanted more. Not just physical encounters, but to get to know the beautiful woman. He had no doubt her personality would be gorgeous, too.

"Tell us *all* about Deola," Precious said after she'd gotten them fifteen minutes into their journey.

He glanced over his shoulder to find Abdul still on their tail in his Land Rover Discovery. He anticipated a heated lecture for the stunt he'd pulled. It would be worth it if he could get Lamisi to go out with him on a date. His instincts screamed in a way he couldn't ignore that getting to know her would change his life.

They could hang out and indulge in the heat of attraction that ignited when they got close. Perhaps if they fell in love, she'd be willing to convert so they could marry. The possibility pleased him.

As if ice water had been thrown in his face, he realized that he'd never visualized marrying anyone before. He'd just met Lamisi and knew little about her. The medications must be stronger than he thought to allow him to have such ridiculous musings.

"Are you okay?"

He snapped out of his thoughts to find Lamisi's concerned gaze focused on him.

"Yeah." He grimaced as he rubbed his thigh, hoping they'd think it had been pain that had let his mind stray. What had Precious asked? Oh, yes. About Deola. There isn't much to tell about Deola. She's all over social media and what you see is what you get. High fashion and travelling."

He'd leave out the negative aspects that she didn't show everyone. Her persistence in having her way all the time rivalled that of a manipulative politician. She was spoiled, rich, and controlling. Not a good combination for anyone who had to deal with her.

Precious clicked her tongue. "I meant about you and her. It's rumoured that you're together."

He was sure Deola had started it, but he had no proof. It was ironic that they'd come out after she'd started dropping hints that she liked him in more than a platonic way.

"We're friends. The media made more out of our attending a few events together than they should've. As you know, she's the heiress to an oil empire. With me being the son of a prominent chief, they called me a prince. The concept of a royal romance in modern West Africa appealed to them, and obviously, their audience."

He caught the way the women tipped their heads towards each other and exchanged a glance. He didn't question it. The media had promoted the rumours with enough verve to make it seem believable.

Lamisi angled her body with her shoulder propped against the back of the seat. Her eyes narrowed as if she had the power to see through him like the X-ray machine they'd used on his ankle. "The tabloids say that you're dating exclusively and are on the cusp of getting engaged."

He maintained eye contact to help provide support to his words. "That's not true. We're only friends. Nothing more."

"Benefits?" Precious asked.

He shrugged. "That's none of your business."

The women exchanged another poignant look.

"But no," he admitted. If he wanted to see Lamisi again, he had to be transparent. "We're two people who hang out every once in a while when there's a special occasion with press hovering."

No need to tell them about the time Deola had kissed him. The memory still left a sour taste in his mouth. Her beauty and elegance hadn't stirred anything in him. Attraction had to be present—in their case, it proved missing.

"At glitzy events," Lamisi muttered as she settled into her seat, facing the windshield.

"It helps to hang out with someone who knows the business. Her father may be an oil mogul, but she's into hanging out with celebrities. Her social media numbers are through the roof. It never hurts to be seen with her."

Precious' brow rose as she glanced at him in the rear-view mirror. "Are you using her?"

"Not at all." He had difficulty finding a way to explain. "We've just never addressed the rumours with the public. Denying anything to the media triggers them to latch onto it. We both know it'll die down."

Unless Deola feeds into it.

Lamisi returned to looking over the side of her seat. Probing him. When she seemed appeased with the truth in his answer, her lips curved up into a smile. A good sign.

"How did you meet?"

"At a party Wander threw in Nigeria about a year ago. He introduced us, and we got along."

The car swerved towards the left before Precious corrected it. "*The* Wander?"

Blaise chuckled. "The one and only."

He'd had similar reactions when he'd met his favourite artists for the first time. The humbling experiences had given him the insight into why people stumbled over their words when they came in contact with him.

Lamisi's eye roll before she resumed her proper seating position showed just how impressed she was with his name-dropping.

"Who is the song 'A friend forever' about?" She carried on with the interrogation.

His lips puckered into a frown, and he blinked several times at the mention of a single from his first album that never got radio play. The fact that she was able to rattle off the title so readily let him know how much she appreciated his music. Warmth swirled beneath his ribcage and settled in the centre of his chest.

"It was released years ago, so it couldn't be about Deola." He skirted the question.

She nodded. "True. Precious, please pull over."

Her friend did a double take in her direction. "Why?"

"I'm getting a crick in my neck from turning so much. I'm going to sit in the back with Blaise." She looked at him. "If that's okay with you?"

The anticipation of having her closer elicited tingles all over his scalp similar to what happened every time he went on stage.

"Sure," he said in as casual a manner as he could manage.

Precious slowed down and pulled over to the side of the road. Women carrying one-man-thousand and abolo on their heads ran to the vehicle. The miniscule fried fish paired with the steamed corn and rice flour wrapped in banana leaves were popular in the area.

Lamisi climbed out of the vehicle, opened the back door, and assessed the situation.

With a twinge of pain, he moved his leg to the floor to give her space, and she got in. Once settled, she patted the top of her thighs. "I'll be your pillow."

For someone who knew how to create and spit out lyrics with the ease of breathing, he sat speechless.

"It's okay," she coaxed. "I know one of your legs probably weighs as much as both of mine, but I'll be fine. If it gets to be too much, I'll return to the front."

"The added elevation is good for your ankle," Precious contributed as she removed her wallet from her bag.

He placed his limb on her. Electric shocks infused into him from the heel of his bandaged foot to where their contact stopped mid-calf.

For the first time, he thanked Allah for the injury he'd sustained. This might end up being the best car ride of his life.

CHAPTER SEVEN

The intimacy of them in the backseat ensconced in a way that people who had known each other for years would engage in should've been uncomfortable.

Not even a little bit. The weight of Bizzy's leg settled on her thighs set off a familiarity that she wanted even more of, so she took the liberty of resting her hands on top of his lower leg.

The tantalizing sparks of awareness where they touched made her breathing shallow and rapid. She'd hyperventilate if she didn't gain control of her body, so Lamisi ducked in deep inhales and releasing them slowly.

What had she been thinking by getting so close to him? Her heart hadn't settled into a normal rhythm since they'd sat in the same car. Now, she doubted that any part of her body was getting enough blood with the speed the organ was racing.

That's right—she had wanted to ask her favourite artist questions regarding his work that she was sure no one had ever queried him about before.

Precious caught her attention in the rear-view and smirked as if she understood the lies in the excuse her mind had created.

Now that she knew he didn't have a girlfriend, she'd ceased fighting the magnetism pulling her closer to him as if they were each tied to an elastic cord that had reached its peak stretch. A wonder she hadn't crawled on top of him already.

Precious waved towards the sellers surrounding them. "Do either of you want abolo and one-man-thousand?"

Lamisi snapped out of her daze of sensation. "I almost forgot that Alhassan asked me to get him some. He can eat two big bags of the one-man-thousand in one sitting. Please get me enough of the fish and of the abolo to keep him happy."

She didn't miss the tightening of Blaise's calf muscle against her. When she gave him her attention, he was staring at her with a tight frown.

Without thinking, she rubbed her fingers along his shin. "Are you in pain? Should I go back to the front seat?"

His muscles clenched again at her touch, and then relaxed.

"No pain," he said in the husky voice from their mountain encounter.

His fingers as they grazed her arm spiked a barrage of incredible sensations that caused goose bumps to burst out onto her skin.

"Stay," he whispered.

The dry state of her mouth made it difficult to speak, so she nodded.

Oblivious to the fireworks going off in the backseat of her car, Precious asked, "Blaise, do you want anything?"

His gaze remained steady on Lamisi. The passion that filled his eyes as the tip of his tongue licked his lips enticed her. Of its own accord, her body leaned closer to him. One more taste wouldn't hurt. Their first kiss, although nice, hadn't satisfied.

Halfway toward her destination, Precious' throat-clearing jarred her out of the craziness she'd been about to indulge in, and she sat straight up.

"Fish or abolo is what I meant by *anything*."

"Nothing for me. Thank you." His low tenor voice brought to mind hot nights entwined with a lover who could satisfy.

Lamisi tore her gaze from those succulent lips to view the cement buildings outside her window as she fanned her face. The same woman who was quick to remove her hand from a person's grasp during a handshake had been about to initiate a kiss. It had to be the combination of physical exhaustion and the remnants of oxygen deprivation that had her acting so out of character.

Or she'd finally come into contact with a man she had a hard time resisting. Considering that his upper body had risen towards her as she'd closed in, it had been a mutual moment of yearning.

Precious looked between them with a grin before ensuring that the food she'd placed in the passenger's seat was secure. And then, they were back on the road heading to Accra.

"Who's Alhassan?"

The hardness in his voice caught her attention more than the inquiry. Was he jealous? It would explain the initial scowl and the tension in his muscles when she had mentioned the name.

She'd asked him quite a few personal questions already. Only fair she reciprocated. "My older brother."

His head jerked back as if surprised. “Alhassan is an Arabic name.”

“It can be.” Just because she’d give him the information didn’t mean she’d make it easy to learn more.

“Are you Muslim?”

As always, the question asked by someone she barely knew irritated her. What did it matter what name she called God or how she chose to worship as long as she treated people with respect, love, and dignity?

“My mother was a Muslim before she got married.”

She’d asked her mom several times why she hadn’t maintained her religion. Her answer had always been about love and sacrifice. She’d discovered a better life by converting in order to be with her husband rather than to live without him and remain a Muslim.

“She insisted on naming her children, though.”

He leaned closer with interest. “Your name is popular in the north of Ghana.”

“She’s Dagomba from the Northern Region.”

“Do you speak Dagbani as part of your language repertoire?”

Precious interrupted with her laughter. “Don’t even bother asking her that again. Any language you can think of, she probably speaks, understands, or can pick up in like two minutes.”

Lamisi denied with a shake of her head. “That’s not true.”

“Close enough.”

Blaise’s grin took the sting out of her embarrassment.

“If I had your skill for languages, I’d—”

“Become an international spy? A quadruple agent?”

He chuckled. “I was thinking more along the lines of writing songs in lots more languages. But being a spy might be fun. Are you one?”

Making sure her face remained neutral, she cocked her head the slightest bit as she stared at him.

“Do you think I could tell you if I was?” And then, she giggled. “I can’t lie to save my life. With me, what you see is what you get.”

“I’m pretty sure there’s a lot to learn.” He winked. “I’m looking forward to taking up the task.”

Either he was a great liar or he really did like her. Would he ask her out when they dropped him off, or was he all talk? The real question raced within her bounding pulse. Did she want to see him again?

To her credit, Precious kept her mouth closed.

"Back to your siblings. How many are you, and what are your names?"

It was as if he knew she didn't know how to handle the flirtation.

"We're five in total. The eldest is Alhassan, then Miriam." She pointed to her chest. "I'm right in the middle. Then comes Ras, and the baby is Amadu."

"What do you all do for a living?"

She raised her right hand from where it rested on his leg. Her palm cooled when a second ago, it had been absorbing his heat.

"Your turn. Remember that's why I came back here in the first place?"

Precious' snicker was the only indication that she'd been paying attention to them. Where was a divider when you needed it? Lamisi wanted Blaise to herself.

Realizing the possessiveness of her thoughts, she rested her hands at her sides, limiting their contact. She needed to keep a clear perspective, and touching him any more than necessary blurred her reasoning.

He raised a brow while the corner of his lips twisted towards the side in confusion. "What was the question?"

She laughed at his adorable expression. "Since your memory is so poor, I'll refresh it. Who did you write 'A friend forever' about?"

And are you still in love with her? Pining for a woman who doesn't return your affections?

She wouldn't hold it against him if he didn't answer. It wasn't any of her business. She chewed the inside of her cheek as she willed for him to appease her curiosity. The song beheld a haunting melody, and the lyrics had touched her at a time when she'd fallen in love with a man who never saw her as more than his student.

Time had healed her from the, but regret still lingered at what could've been whenever she saw him.

Had Blaise gotten over his own heartbreak, or was his heart still beating for another?

"What if I just made up the song?" he asked.

"I could be wrong, but I don't think that's your process. Your music sounds personal." *And touches my spirit with their depth.* "Nothing can convince me otherwise, especially after hearing the song you created before we fell."

His dark eyes seemed to consider her. Or had his mind wandered to the past?

"It's about someone I loved and lost."

Precious snorted. "Is that how you're going to play it? Lamisi picks up nuances in languages like the skin absorbs sun rays on a bright day. She likes your music because of the meaning you attach to it. Unlike most people, we don't understand every language you sing in. She does."

Lamisi nodded at her friend's support.

"Besides," Precious continued. "If you haven't guessed, you've just met your number one fan."

Those appealing lips rose into a smug smirk, adding a gleam to his eyes. "Is that so?"

Her face heated to feverish levels as she ducked her head.

"She is. She's been following you ever since she heard the first song you released. I'm surprised you don't recognize us from your concerts. She's dragged me to at least five of them."

Not needing any more mortifying truths to spill from her friend's mouth, she gathered her courage and looked Blaise in the eyes. "It was for research purposes."

Not a complete lie, if years ago she'd been to a psychic who had foreseen coming up with an idea for her doctorate based on his music.

"Uh huh." The disbelieving murmur from the front seat wasn't helping her case.

"Your songs inspired me to write my PhD dissertation on the use of mixed languages in music and the impact on the listener."

His smile broadened.

"I don't know what impresses me more: myself for inspiring you, or the fact that you're studying for your PhD."

"Since I have your injured ankle in my lap, if I were you, I'd praise me going for my doctorate."

He touched his hand to his chest. "But my magnificence brought it out in you. I deserve the credit."

Lamisi giggled. "You're right. It's all about you. Years of coursework, intensive research, writing, and disappointing mishaps that waylaid my progress with a year left, if I'm lucky, before I stand against a panel to defend my work means very little."

"When you put it like that … How about we share the accolades?"

She tipped her head from side to side as if considering. “Sounds fair.”

“Have you really been to five of my concerts?”

“Yes,” Precious answered. “We flew out to Lagos for one of them. She knows all of the lyrics and could sing your songs if you ever got sick.”

“Precious,” she hissed. “Please don’t let me inform Blaise about some of the adventures I’ve had with you over the years.”

Her oldest friend caught her gaze in the mirror and clamped her lips together. The smile of mischief stayed in place.

“So, Lamisi Imoro is my number one fan.” He reached out to her. “It’s nice to finally meet you.”

She glanced down at his palm and then back at his earnest eyes before shaking it.

Without warning, he tugged her to him and whispered, “Gorgeous and intelligent, with a great ear for music. A magnificent combination. It would be my pleasure to get to know such a spectacular woman better.”

Her heart took off at a gallop as electric currents shot up her arm and charged her whole body. A slight turn of her head would place her lips against the bristles of his short, well-kept beard.

She struggled to haul in a breath. What was the response to someone she’d crushed on from afar for years?

“Um ...”

His mouth against the shell of her ear sent feathery flames along the area with every movement of his lips.

“It’s okay. We can take our time and see what happens. I wanted you to know that I like you.”

His withdrawal left her filled with longing. For once, a man’s direct approach hadn’t irritated her. In the short time she’d known him, he’d done nothing but impress.

CHAPTER EIGHT

Lamisi had asked him to share one of his deepest secrets. That took confidence. For both of them.

"You asked me about 'A friend forever'."

She nodded.

He wiped a hand down his face. Was he really going to do this?

"Most people presume it's a song about friendship, but there are two lines within the lyrics that reveal the truth."

"*One day, the time will come when …*" she recited in English then continued in Ewe as he'd originally sung it. "*My broken heart will mend.*" Then, "*From your inability to love me as more than a friend,*" was completed in a perfect Nzema accent.

Did she realize that she'd placed her hands back on his leg? Her gentle touch exposed how lost she was in the words.

She looked into his eyes. "They were the only lines I have ever heard you sing in Ewe and Nzema. As if you'd learned the languages just for the song."

He grinned, proud of her ability to comprehend more than the lyrics, but the depth of them. "I wanted to sing about my unrequited love, but not have people truly understand."

"Give me the full translation in English," Precious ordered.

Instead of speaking the words, he sang the song in English the way he'd written it, but then hidden it with Ewe, which he spoke fluently. The words sung in Nzema, spoken by an ethnic group in the Western Region, were all he understood of the language.

"Awww. That's so sad," Precious said with a hand at the centre of her chest. She took a second to turn to Lamisi. "I can see why it hit you so hard back then."

Blaise shifted his gaze between the two. "One-sided romantic experience?"

Lamisi cleared her throat. "I'll share if you will."

Did he really want to hear about her past loves? Could he afford not to? What if she were still hung up on this guy?

"Mine was nothing major," he said. "One of my college classmates saw me as nothing more than a friend."

"You wrote a song about it and veiled the lyrics in languages you don't use. Doesn't sound minor to me."

He shrugged. "What's in the past is done."

"What happened to her?" Precious asked.

"I don't know. We didn't maintain contact."

Because I couldn't watch her go out with other guys knowing one of them would be the lucky one to win her heart.

Lamisi looked at him. "Are you still hung up on her?"

He chuckled.

"Not at all. It happened years ago. What's that saying about time healing all wounds? It surely does." He pointed at her. "Unless it didn't for you. Are you still in love with the guy?"

Her twists shook along with her head. "Not at all. Time truly is a cure-all. At least for relationship issues."

One question pressed on him that he needed an answer to. "Are you involved with anyone right now?"

She snapped her eyes to his. He expected an indignant refusal to answer.

"No."

His chest collapsed as the air he'd been holding in rushed out. "I can't tell you how glad I am to hear that."

Blaise's talent as a musician had always been obvious to Lamisi, but she wouldn't have guessed he'd be quick-witted and hilarious. The banter between the three of them had her ribs hurting with laughter. The return trip had taken much less time than when they'd driven up.

Wasn't it always the way that the journey home seemed shorter than when heading out to an unknown destination?

Precious parked in front of a house set in an estate complex in Tema that Blaise had directed her to. Aside from the differences in colour, the homes, from what she noticed above the protective wall, appeared similar. The area was pretty, with trees planted along the sidewalks and clean, but bland. At least on the outside.

The interiors of the properties were probably as unique as the owners.

What would Blaise's home look like? She'd guess cool and comfortable. Like how it felt to hang out with him. Then the practical part of her brain smacked down her romantic one, and the word *flashy* came to mind. He had the means, so why not show it off, right?

Lamisi looked down at the weight on her lap. Her own legs had gone a little numb, but she'd refused to give up the proximity.

"How's the ankle?"

"For right now, I'll say its fine. I have a feeling that as soon as it touches the ground, the pain will be excruciating."

She stroked the top of his foot and said a silent prayer for healing. "You'll be better sooner rather than later."

"Thanks."

A knock sounded at his window. His friends and their wives were lingering outside.

He pressed the button to slide the glass down. "Give me a minute."

Not waiting for a response, he rolled it back up, pulled out his phone, and placed his thumb on the finger scanner to open the screen.

"How about we exchange numbers?"

Filled with uncertainty, her hand flew to her hair and smoothed down the twists on the right side of her head. "I don't think that's a good idea."

Precious opened her door. "I'll be back. I'm going to stretch my legs."

She got out and closed the door, leaving them alone.

Traitor.

He rotated the device end to end several times. "I thought we were getting along."

Rejecting him might be easier if he wasn't still resting on her.

Who was she kidding? The necessary task of declining his interest would be difficult regardless. She lived a life of complete privacy. From what she knew about the stars in Ghana and the world, they existed in the spotlight, seeking attention everywhere they went. She had no desire for that.

"We were."

He raised his phone and wiggled it. "Then can we chat?"

Only one way to shut it down. "Look. You're a fantastic musician, and I love your work. Meeting you has been wonderful. Thanks for answering my questions about your songs, but we live in two completely different worlds."

He turned his head side to side and looked around. "Aren't we still on Earth?"

An exasperated sigh hid her entertained smile.

"You know what I mean. Your lifestyle is all flash while mine is as simple as khaki trousers." She flung her vision to the front to avoid the heaviness of his gaze. "I'd like to keep it that way."

"My life isn't as crazy as you're making it out to be. For the most part, I'm a normal guy when I go out in public. Ghanaians don't make a big deal about seeing me unless I'm on stage. They have more important things to concern themselves with, like their own lives."

He had a point. And he would know his lifestyle way better than she would.

"I already told you that I like you, Lamisi. It would be great to get to know you better."

His words had hit her straight in the chest. She liked him, too. Beyond his musician status. He was a down-to-earth man who was easy to talk to.

Yet, the fear in her gut churned. She couldn't risk the pain that getting to know such a man would eventually entail. As stereotypical as it sounded, she didn't doubt that he had more than his share of women and was able to toss one out when bored because so many others had lined up to fill the role. She had no desire to compete. Would she even be able to?

"You should let your friends help you inside and put some ice on the ankle."

His shoulders slumped. "So I can't convince you to give me your number?"

Already regretting her decision, she gave him a negative shake of her head.

"How about if I give you mine? There's no harm in that, is there? If you want to ask me more questions about my music, I'm at your fingertips."

A risk-free venture. "Aren't you afraid that I'll sell it to the highest bidder?"

"Just make sure you give me my share of the profits if you do."

Back to being comfortable with him, she grinned. Maybe she'd given him enough negative responses for the day. What would it hurt to have his number? She grabbed her cell from the space next to her. With her mind a little hazy from excitement, it took two attempts to slide the pattern onto her screen to unlock it.

Where was that *contacts* icon again? She located it and tapped. "I'm ready."

She input the number as he rattled it off. *Blaise.* What more did she need to add as she saved it?

"It was a pleasure meeting you, Lamisi. I hope you call and we get to see each other again one day. If we don't and you're ever at my concert, please come backstage."

Her mouth went dry with the temptation of the offer.

"By the way," he said and then paused.

"Yes."

"Let it be known that your lap doubled as the absolute best pillow. If you happen to hear it in a song, you'll know where it came from."

She laughed. "Just as long as you give me my share of the proceeds."

The joviality they'd experienced on the ride lingered until he tipped his head towards the glass. "My friends aren't the most patient people, and I'm sure they're exhausted."

"You must be, too."

He lowered his leg to the floor of the vehicle. Try as he might, he wasn't able to hide his gasp, and she felt for him.

"My body might be a bit sore, but thanks to a beautiful, strong woman who kept me distracted from the pain, I've never felt more energized."

Wouldn't he stop his stream of lovely words so she could leave him without feeling the need to use the number he'd given her?

"Take care, Bizzy."

Just like when he'd first met her, he winked. "You, too Lamisi Imoro, master of many languages. I really hope I hear from you."

Unlikely, but she did, too. Sometimes, she longed for things that weren't good for her. He'd been flung to the top of that category.

They opened their doors. When she stepped out, she held tight to the metal as her legs buckled for a second. A quick glance over her shoulder revealed that no one had noticed because they were too busy helping Blaise.

She walked to his side to get some blood circulating to her weakened muscles. Getting one last glimpse of him.

Hobbling with support, he waved. “I’ll be waiting for your call.”

She raised her hand in a goodbye gesture before they escorted him up the walkway to his front door.

Misery over leaving a man she’d known for less than a day trumped the joy she’d felt while being with him. There was one thing she knew for certain. The man had captivated her.

CHAPTER NINE

A week had passed since Lamisi's trek up the mountain had ended in a roll down its slope with a stunning man to break her fall.

Blaise still stayed on her mind. It might be easier to forget him if she'd stop listening to his music on repeat. Each song fascinated her with the strength of his lyrics and the artistry involved in their creation.

Much to Precious' annoyance, his number sat unused on her phone. Lamisi had stared at it enough to memorize it. Yet, she never pressed the button that would have his smooth, low tenor voice sending tingles traipsing across her skin as he spoke.

She shouldn't be focused on a man when she had a doctorate to complete. Since she'd registered for the programme, the process had been thrown off the tracks not once, but twice.

Her principal supervisor had been brilliant—a linguistic studies professor who was knowledgeable, kind, and direct. Lamisi had always known where she stood with Professor Ogah who never wasted her time. Efficient and dedicated to academia and helping others to progress to their highest level. After a year of coursework, she had been assigned to him.

Towards the third year of her PhD and blissfully working on her dissertation, he had died after undergoing a minor surgery. She'd mourned him with the intensity of losing a beloved father figure. A tragedy not just for her, but the world because he had been such a spectacular individual.

Her second supervisor of the three she had been assigned had had to step up. A stressful time that she never wanted to repeat. It would've been better if her new supervisor hadn't even taken on her project because a year later, the woman had transferred to a university in Spain.

Where was the justice? Lamisi had been shot down so low that she'd spent a full week in bed crying, whining to anyone who would listen, and contemplating her educational goals. A master's degree wasn't something to sneeze at. It wouldn't get her to the level of academia that she desired, but she could live with it.

No, she couldn't.

She had set a goal of obtaining her doctorate, and nothing would stop her. As long as she had breath in her lungs, she would complete her dissertation, no matter how much time it took.

By the time her third supervisor had made himself available, she'd had to extend her program, which meant paying an extra year of tuition. Her doctorate would take five years instead of four. Not fair, but what could she do?

Professor Amartey was the kind of person who didn't want anyone rising up the ranks to meet his own. He hadn't thought her original topic was good enough and had wanted her to adapt her theses into something that would suit him.

Lamisi had been driving home, dejected after a meeting with Professor Amartey, when a Bizzy song had come on the radio. She'd wondered how many people understood the three languages he'd sung in.

The brilliant topic idea would appease Professor Amartey without her having to completely change her dissertation. She'd never forget the joyous desire to hop out of the car while dancing to the music as the vehicle moved forward, just like in those video challenges.

When she'd presented the idea to him last month, his frown hadn't seemed as negative as usual when he'd nodded his approval.

To this day, her hands still trembled when she walked into his office. The man hadn't become less intimidating in the least.

Between hospitals and having to see Professor Amartey, she wondered which one she hated more. At least, hospitals made it their mission to help a person feel better. Not so much for her supervisor.

Taking a deep breath to help calm her racing heart, she knocked on his office door.

At his gruff "Come in," she forced her feet to move.

"Good afternoon, Professor Amartey."

"Sit down," he grunted without looking up from whatever he was reading.

Not put off by his lack of greeting, she walked to the closest chair, swept her dark blue, knee-length skirt under her legs, and lowered herself down, placing her ever-present research notebook on her lap, and waited. Sometimes, it took up to five minutes for him to address her again.

In an ideal world, she would've requested a new supervisor who showed more respect for her and her work. Heck, in a model world, Professor Ogah wouldn't have died, and people would be calling her Dr. Imoro by then. She just had to endure for a short while longer.

He slammed the draft he had insisted she print out each time she submitted her work on the desk. "Your dissertation lacks depth."

She gripped her notebook instead of grabbing the stack of papers and kept quiet. He would explain in his own time.

"You mentioned an artist in the background of your work as influencing the topic of your research." Professor Amartey rested his forearms against the surface of his desk. "Along with the interviews of music listeners, you need to add interviews from performers as an aspect of your research."

Standing and screaming at the top of her lungs while taking her work and beating his desk with it wouldn't begin to satisfy her rage. Her nostrils flexed in ways she had no control over as she huffed in breaths to control her temper. She glanced down at her notebook to find it twisted.

Interviews with artists meant having to undertake analysis that took up so much time and energy that it would leave her fatigued for a full week once she completed it. Her mind blanked out for a moment to stop from thinking about the amount of work the man had added to the pile already on her head, ready to compress and then break her spine.

She flexed her fingers, hoping it would be enough to keep her from diving towards the man and placing her them around his neck. The university looked down on counts of assault and battery. It would better than letting the burning in her eyes give way to tears of frustration. Professor Amartey fed on weakness, so she sat with a stiff spine and kept her eyes dry.

"It's a great idea," she said without enthusiasm or honesty. As she'd experienced previously, there would be no point in arguing with him. "I also think it will add another dimension to the research."

Which was true. Even though it would suck up her time and brain power when she was already running on fumes.

"Bring the questions to me this week so I can review them, and you can get the interviews done as soon as possible."

Had he given a viable time-saving suggestion instead of grunting a goodbye? If she had heard the word e-mail in the sentence, she would've run out of the room screaming about an alien abduction.

"Yes, Professor."

Now to find some way to get in contact with the artists. It wasn't as if she ran in their circles.

Her breath hiccupped as Blaise's face grinning up at her just before their lips brushed hers sprang into her mind. Her heart pounded out his name in rapid succession.

Lamisi's brain whirled with the new development. Working tirelessly on a dissertation for so many years had made her a bit jaded. Just like that, her interest in her research had been rejuvenated.

Or is it the chance to talk to Blaise again?

She ignored the inner voice.

Would he connect her with other artists and allow her to interview him after the way she'd blown him off? She sure hoped so because she had no contacts in the music business.

Self-preservation had been a good-enough reason for her to stay away from Blaise. Completing her dissertation represented a greater incentive to call him.

It didn't mean anything would happen between them, though. For the sake of her doctorate and avoiding bias, nothing could.

◆◆◆

Blaise sat with his French tutor, bored out of his skull. He'd been deceiving himself when he'd presumed that the language would be easy to learn and incorporate into his music.

The six weeks of these three-hour lessons four days a week had been a waste of time as his mind swirled with the differences in tenses. Why would they torture people by assigning a gender to each noun?

The man he'd hired from Côte d'Ivoire to teach him the ins and outs of the language had been pleasant and patient. Mostly. At the end of their sessions, Blaise wasn't the only one whose eyes had glazed over.

Possessing a fluency in the language would be more ideal than having the words translated into his lyrics and singing them. He'd thought jacking into a few lessons with a French-speaking native, watching lots of French movies with subtitles, and listening exclusively to music from Francophone African countries would help him to understand the language within months.

He'd been kidding himself. The vocabulary had been more difficult to pick up than any other language he'd learned, and he didn't sound anywhere as authentic as his teacher when he spoke.

Running barefoot under the scorching sun of his hometown while a pack of wild dogs chased him for hours on end appealed to him more than having the conversations that Armand forced him to speak in French. On a daily basis, he thought of hiding in his walk-in closet when the doorbell rang with Armand standing outside.

Blaise put a stop to the repetition of the tenses of *run*. He rummaged through the vocabulary in his brain to find the French words he needed to send the man packing for the day. Nothing but *au revoir* came to him. He'd need to say more than goodbye to keep from sounding rude.

"Let's end the session early," he said in English.

Armand flipped his wrist over and glanced at his watch. "We still have an hour and a half remaining."

Blaise rubbed his short beard, ready to throw down a lie before he realized it wasn't necessary. His tutor would still be getting paid for the whole session. "It's been a long week, and I'd like to get some rest."

It didn't take any more explanation as Armand bent his head and gathered his things. Was he grinning?

Blaise pulled out his wallet and handed Armand the money due him. Quality French lessons weren't cheap. And the way things were going with his inability to grasp onto it, they wouldn't be worth the trouble.

He limped a little from the slight throb still present in his ankle as he walked the man to the door.

"I'll see you next *Lundi*." At least, he'd gotten the word Monday correct.

Armand grimaced. "*Oui, Lundi*."

He'd pronounced the word in a one-eighty degree different way than Blaise had.

"*Lundi*," he corrected himself.

It didn't drive away the sour pucker of the man's lips. "*Au revoir*."

"*Au revoir.*" He frowned at how unalike his own version had sounded to Armand's before he closed the door.

If he were any type of quitter, he'd tell his tutor to never return because he was giving up on making French the base for some of his songs with English thrown in to accentuate. Unlike other hiplife artists from Ghana, he wanted to take the Francophone countries by storm with a fresh, unique style.

The lyrics were ready; he just needed to jam the new language into them in a way that didn't make him sound like an idiot.

Blaise stumbled to the couch and flopped into it, resting this arm over his forehead. There had to be an easier way to learn. Fatigued from the mental exertion, he'd started to drift off to sleep when his cell rang.

He grunted after a quick glance at the screen. Deola. She'd been clingy over the past few weeks, her new habit of daily calls annoying. The hints she kept dropping about them taking their friendship further had thrown him off. The woman's vindictive nature wouldn't allow him to decline in a direct manner, so he'd found ways to change the subject.

There had been rumours of her shutting down a popular photography studio in Lagos when the owner decided to break up with her. He had no idea how true it was, but he wasn't willing to risk everything he'd worked so hard for by allotting her an outright rejection. He'd just have to ease her out of liking him. In the meantime, he'd continue to ignore her advances.

Other than friendship, he felt nothing for Deola. Where the woman he felt nothing for wasn't afraid to show it, the one he was drawn to her like rivers to the ocean had refused to contact him. He'd contemplated stopping by the only university in Accra that offered a doctorate program to make enquiries in the language department about his mountain woman.

Reason had kept him from making a fool of himself. Maybe she wasn't a student in the language section. Didn't she say that her dissertation had been inspired by his multilingual songs? Was she a music major?

Rather than tease himself about the possibility of stalking her, he answered the call.

"Good morning, Deola."

"Hi, Bizzy." She let out a sigh. "It took you long enough to answer. Why do you sound tired?"

He'd asked her to call him Blaise on several occasions, but she never did. "I just had a French lesson."

"I don't understand why you insist on forcing yourself to learn that language." As always, the poutiness in her tone pervaded. "If people don't speak English, that's not your fault. Besides, what do places like Benin and Côte d'Ivoire know about good music? If they had any kind of clue, your songs would be skyrocketing on their music charts." She giggled. "That's even if they have them there."

For an educated, wealthy woman who'd travelled to many countries throughout the world, she still held a limited viewpoint about, well, everything. For her, no country was as good as Nigeria. Considering they treated her as royalty there, he could somehow understand her reasoning.

He often wondered why she communicated with him. If he didn't speak Hausa like her, would she have any interest?

"For years, Côte d'Ivoire was considered to be one of the leading countries of West Africa with its advanced infrastructure and economy."

"Oh, darling." Her condescension came through loud and clear. "That was forever ago and no longer worth mentioning. Aiming to impress those people with your music is a waste of your talents. Focus on writing in English and maybe Hausa so you can catch the eye of an American artist who will be willing to collaborate with you. That's when the huge sales will come."

He definitely wouldn't shun an international collaboration. His gut told him that French lyrics would help get him there.

He ignored her unsolicited advice. "What's going on?"

"Sweetheart, does something have to be happening for us to speak? I've gotten rather addicted to our daily calls and look forward to them. You could do better by picking up the phone and ringing me every once in a while."

Her habit of manipulation infuriated him. Yet another reason they wouldn't make a functional couple. Deola needed someone she could control. He wasn't the one.

At his lack of response, she continued. "Anyway, what are you wearing to the VGMAs? It's only three weeks away. I'd like to choose a gown that matches you."

Blaise sat up straight. Had he forgotten that he'd asked her to escort him to the biggest music awards ceremony in Ghana? He raked through his memory only to come up with a no. She was continuing with their prior arrangement. If he ever wanted a real relationship to blossom with a woman he liked, he'd have to cut Deola off. Gently. Which meant with a lie.

"I hadn't planned on going."

"Don't be ridiculous." Her voice rose an octave. Quite the feat considering how high-pitched it already was. "You're up for four awards, one being Artiste of the Year. I'd like to adorn the arm of a winner. Which I know you will be."

He thought about how the tabloids would continue to splash false information about their platonic relationship. "I don't think—"

"It's okay. It's not necessary for me to know your colour. I'll wear black. It goes with everything, and I look fabulous in it. I'll be staying at Rema Resort. Same bungalow as always. Pick me up at seven. We want to make a splash with our entrance. I wouldn't be averse to you renting an upscale car. A Bentley or Jaguar will do. Get a driver, though."

She took a breath that wasn't long enough for him to get a word in.

"This is going to be so much fun. According to social media, everyone is going to be there. I'll arrange for the photographer because my posts have to be on point. My fans will expect nothing but the most glamorous pictures of us. Do you have your acceptance speech written? Don't go up there unprepared. Stumbling over your words would be beyond embarrassing. I wouldn't be able to stand it."

If he were going to get out of the date, he'd better do it now. "Listen, Deola. I appreciate the—"

"No need to thank me, babe. You're welcome. We complement each other. Beauty and talent mix perfectly together. I'll be flying into Ghana on that day because you know I don't like spending too much time in other African countries. Except for SA. I love the beachfront hotel I stay at in Cape Town. See the comfort I'm willing to sacrifice for you? By the way, in a week, I'm traveling with Daddy for two weeks onto an oil rig. He insists that I learn at least a little bit about the business. I want you to know because he told me the phone reception would be bad."

She heaved out a sigh. "Can you imagine two weeks without speaking to me? I know it will be difficult, but you'll manage. As for myself, I have no idea how I'll survive without social media. How will people be able to adore and copy my amazing fashion and style sense if they can't see me? Anyway, I'll figure it out. I always do. The stressors of my life. Not everyone would be able to handle it. Bye, honey."

The phone went dead. His breath had been stolen with it. How did he always allow her to outtalk him? Wasn't he the master of words? He had half a mind to call her back and tell her they wouldn't be attending together.

But then, who would he go with that would be comfortable with him and the paparazzi? Lamisi came to mind. The woman had been respectful, but hadn't appeared awestruck.

Time to man up. Snatching his phone from where he'd tossed it across the couch, he tapped Deola's contact.

It rang several times, and just when he was about to give up, she answered.

"Miss me already, dear?"

"Deola, I can't go with you to the VGMAs." Just like she'd done to him moments ago, he didn't give her a chance to speak. "I'm looking for a relationship, and as wonderful as you are, we aren't well-suited. I can't find someone if I'm always seen in public with you and newspapers are throwing around the rumour of us being a couple when we aren't."

He paused then to let the words sink in. "I hope you understand."

What was going through her mind? Was she planning some sort of revenge? He rolled his eyes. What could she do to his career even with her social media influence? He'd risen to the top because of his talent, not because of anything she'd done for him. When they'd met, he'd already been well-known. That's why she'd clung to him.

She was a woman who could sense potential, and he had it in eighteen-wheeler tankards.

After the longest time, she spoke.

"You've made your feelings clear." Where was the inflection in her tone? "I thought we were going as friends. Nothing more. I understand your point. Are you seeing someone?"

"Not right now, but it's good to keep our options open just in case the right one drops into our lives."

Speaking multiple languages and being beautiful even though she doesn't have any makeup on and is sweating like three grown men.

"Are you sure? You hesitated for a moment."

There it was, the harshness in her voice that he'd anticipated.

"I'm positive. I'm flying solo these days. Working on my French and my career."

Her heavy sigh seeped into him. “I understand. Thank you for your honesty.”

Did she? This wasn’t the way he’d expected the conversation to go down. He’d anticipated bleeding from the ear with her screeching and yelling. Lucky for him she was being civilized.

“Good. I hope you have a safe journey on the oil rig.” What else could he say? Have a great life?

“Thank you, I’ll talk to you another time. Take care.”

The phone went dead. Blaise stared at it for a minute before getting up and doing part of the choreographed dances for one of his songs.

He’d dodged a bullet. From what he’d heard, no one told her no, but he’d gotten away with it.

More dancing.

Now, to find that special woman who sparked his soul. Someone he’d want to spend the rest of his life with. Had he already met her and let her go without even trying?

CHAPTER TEN

Lamisi procrastinated calling Blaise after the meeting with her horror of a supervisor by completing the interview questions he'd requested. Then she'd researched and compiled a list of Ghanaian hiplife artists who would suit her project if they were available. Her hips were loose and flexible from all the dancing she'd done while listening to their music.

When that task had been completed, her parent's house, where she would continue to live until she received her doctorate or got married—whichever came first—absolutely had to be cleaned from top to bottom. It didn't matter that they had a cleaner come in once a week to do that task.

Exhausted, she showered and lay on her bed. Maybe seven at night was too late to call him.

She scoffed at her own state of ridiculousness.

What if he refused to help her? Even worse, hung up?

Nerves rattling enough to make her stomach squeamish and her mouth so dry that she didn't think she'd be able to speak if he did answer, she stared at his number for the billionth time. Good things never came to those who didn't try, so she squeezed her eyes shut and touched an index finger to where the blue phone icon should be.

The phone flew away from her ear when a voice said, "Hello," on the third ring.

She caught her cell with the opposite hand before it could slam onto the floor, breaking yet another protective glass cover.

"Hello?" Definitely Blaise's entrancing voice.

"Um, hi. This is …" She placed a hand on her chest in an attempt to calm her palpitating heart and took a quick breath. Professionalism was the key. She was calling him for help with her dissertation, not to ask him out. If he said no, she'd find someone else. Simple as that. "Hello Blaise, this is Lamisi Imoro."

His turn to go silent. Maybe he had no recollection of her.

"We met climbing Mt. Afadjato a few weeks ago. I understood when your friends were speaking in Hausa. We drove you home when you sprained your ankle. My friend, Precious, told you that I'm your biggest fan."

Shut up already! How many other people had he met on that mountain?

"Yes. I remember."

His emotionless tone told her he no longer had an interest in her. Why did that fill her with so much disappointment?

"Good. How are you? And how's your ankle?"

"I'm well and on the mend. Not at a hundred percent yet, but much better. Thanks for asking. What's going on?"

She wiped away the sweat dripping onto her phone as she held in her standard reply of being fine herself. He hadn't asked of her welfare in return. May as well get it over with.

"I'm working on my dissertation for my PhD."

"I recall that I was your inspiration for the topic."

She heard the smile in his voice, and her tight muscles relaxed in response. "You were. I met with my supervisor, and he suggested that I add interviews from a few multi-lingual artists."

"You'd like to interview me," he said without any type of inflection to let her know how he felt about it.

"If you could make time in your schedule for me to ask you some questions, I'd really appreciate it."

The line remained silent. The whooshing of blood through her arteries filled her ears as she angled her body forward, hoping he'd say yes.

"I'd also venture to guess that you'd like me to get in contact with some of my colleagues to arrange interviews with them."

She didn't miss that he had neither accepted nor declined the interview.

"Actually, that would be very helpful." She hated being on the receiving end of a favour.

"I'll do the interview."

She let out a sigh of relief. "Thank you. Anything you can do about getting me some artists that are almost as great as you?"

"Good one," he said with a chuckle. "I'll see what I can do. How about if we get together and discuss it in person?"

They'd be meeting for research purposes, she reminded herself as she tugged on one of her twists and chewed the corner of her bottom lip. It wasn't a date. Not even close.

"Sure," she said with a casualness that made her proud. "When are you available?"

"I have a meeting in the morning, so how about in the afternoon?"

"Tomorrow?"

Where was the time she'd need to mentally prepare herself for seeing him again? Her body needed strong warnings to keep from reacting to him.

"If you're available." Was that hesitation in his voice? "It would be best to schedule with the other artists as soon as possible."

He was right. She'd just have to get over herself and put her education at the forefront. Unsolicited physical responses to Blaise be damned.

"Tomorrow afternoon would be fine. Where should we meet and what time?"

"I'll be in Accra. Where do you live? I could pick you up."

And have it feel like a date? No way. Her heart wouldn't be able to take it, and her mind would lose the necessary focus to get through the encounter with him. She'd spend the time zoning out that he'd said he liked her rather than concentrating on her project.

Who was she kidding? That would probably happen anyway while looking at him. His eyes were hypnotic with their intensity. And his lips. Full, dark, and soft. Irresistible.

"Hello? Lamisi? Are you still there?"

"Hello, can you hear me?" She played into the consistent network problems that plagued the phone network systems. "Hello?"

"I can hear you," Blaise said. "Can you hear me?"

"Yes. I live in East Legon. I could meet you at Cool It in Legon Mall." The place wasn't as crowded as the bigger restaurant in Accra, so she wouldn't have to watch throngs of his fans snatch his attention.

"I don't mind picking you up. I'll be at Circle."

"That's okay. I have an appointment with my supervisor in the morning, so I'll be in the area of the mall. What time?"

"How about at one?"

Professor Amartey should be done berating her research skills long before then. "Sounds good."

"Okay, I'll see you at one."

Tempering down her squeal, she kept her voice level. "Okay. Bye."

"Bye." He sang rather than spoke, bringing a huge smile to her face.

She pressed the end call button and sighed. Not only would she see him again, but he'd agreed to help her. If she hadn't had a major crush on him before, it would've started right that minute. Something she had to guard against now that he was involved in her research.

She couldn't afford to have her doctorate disapproved because of bias due to a personal relationship with one of the interviewees. Not after everything she'd gone through to get to that point.

Blaise finished his second drink of ginger beer within the hour he'd been waiting at the restaurant for Lamisi. She'd sent a text saying she was running late.

When had he last waited an hour for someone? It tended to be the other way around. At least, she hadn't cancelled. She'd only called for a favour, not because she liked him. And yet, he got the sense that she did.

He hadn't gotten jittery at hearing a woman's voice in a very long time. He'd wanted to keep her on the phone last night, chatting about nothing and everything.

What was it about her that he found so special? He could find beauty, charm, and intelligence in so many women in Ghana. Lamisi possessed a quality he had yet to identify that had caught and kept his attention when others hadn't. Probably why he was still lingering around with his stomach growling when he could've eaten and left.

The door to the Jamaican restaurant opened. His breath caught when Lamisi stepped in and looked around the place. Finding him, she walked towards his corner table. He slid out of the booth as she reached him.

Wearing a light green, button-down dress shirt tucked into a navy-blue straight skirt, she got into the booth. "I'm so sorry to have kept you waiting."

"That's okay." Glad to finally be together after two weeks of missing her, he smiled. "At least you called. More than I've gotten from others."

She shook her head. "I hate wasting people's time. It's just that my supervisor held me up."

Her eyes started glistening. If that wasn't enough to concern him, her sniffles were. "What's wrong?"

She fanned a hand in front of her face.

"Nothing. I'm just ..." She swallowed hard before pointing to his glass. "May I?"

Not waiting for an answer, she reached for the water and took several sips. It didn't seem to help as the tears escaped her eyes and trailed down her cheeks.

The bench squeaked as he shifted closer to her. His fist clenched with the urge to eradicate whatever or whoever had upset her.

"Lamisi, what's wrong?"

Taking a tissue, she swiped her face with a force that left him surprised she hadn't caused herself injury.

"My supervisor is such an arrogant know-it-all ass." Her eyes kept filling. "He makes me so angry, I could punch him."

She banged the bottom of her fist against the table, making the glasses shake.

He waited for the reason behind the tears. Minutes passed with her silence. "Why are you crying?"

"I told you, I'm upset at my supervisor's behaviour." She sniffed and drank more of his water. "From the first moment I got assigned to him, he's given me a hard time. He's the kind of professor that wants to be the only one at the top of the pyramid. He makes things difficult so I'll want to give up on attaining my doctorate."

He had to be missing something. "And?"

"I'm not going to quit." She blew her nose. "I've come too far."

The tears had stopped, leaving her eyes red and him still not understanding. "Did he make you sad?"

"No. Why?"

He'd never had a more confusing conversation in his life. "Because you were crying."

She stared at him with her brows drawn as if she were the one confused. And then, as if comprehension dawned, she laughed.

She couldn't seem to stop. He'd missed the sound as much as he had her.

"Thanks, Blaise. I needed that."

"You're welcome?" He could accept gratitude even though he had no idea what he'd done.

"It's embarrassing, but I cry when I'm exasperated." She shrugged. "I guess it's better than throwing things, but people end up thinking that I'm sensitive."

"You aren't."

She rolled her eyes. "Not at all. I'm pretty sure that if I didn't cry when I got angry, I'd end up in jail for beating someone, or at least trying. It's as if God infused me with that annoying trait to save His people from my wrath."

Intriguing. "Then what do you do when you're sad?"

"Cry. But it's different."

"Okay."

She looked him in the eyes.

"I'm sorry. I didn't mean for you to see me like that. I've held it in for too long. My supervisor would've never let me live it down if I had cried in front of him." She stuck her tongue out and looked down at it. "I thought I'd bitten it so hard that it might be swollen."

He chuckled, still not clear about what had just happened, but glad to have the lighter version of Lamisi back.

The server came over. "Are you ready to order?"

Without looking at the menu, Lamisi said, "I'll have oxtail with beans and rice, and a glass of ginger beer."

"Curried chicken and plain rice," Blaise said.

"Anything to drink?"

"A big bottle of water."

The server left with a nod.

"Why don't you get a new supervisor if this one is frustrating you?"

The sound she made lay somewhere between a whimper and a grunt. "He's my third. My first supervisor was amazing. Just before the end of my third year, he died."

Blaise hoped he didn't set her off with the depressing conversation. "Sorry to hear that."

"Me, too." Lamisi smiled. "Professor Ogah had a great influence on how I viewed linguistics. He spoke more languages than I did and gave me a better understanding of how I learned.

He changed my life and way of thinking about languages." Her shoulders slumped. "He's in a better place now."

"Yes." What else could he say?

"Long story short, my second supervisor moved to another country, and then the third one in line, Professor Amartey, took her place." She said the name with teeth exposed in a snarl. "He makes writing my dissertation a living Hell."

The muscle in his jaw ticked as rage at the injustice Lamisi had faced brought out a growl. "That's not right. Do you need me to talk to him to ease up?"

Her head flinched back.

Had he said something wrong?

"No, but thanks. I can handle my own battles. He hasn't crossed any type of line into abuse or anything like that. He just doesn't appreciate how much work I've been applying to the dissertation and is highly critical about everything I turn in. Including the interview questions for the artists I submitted. He had me wait for two hours in his office while he attended a meeting before he gave me his suggestions."

Not ready to stand down with his offer, he leaned in. "Let me know if anything changes. I can be quite influential."

She nodded and grinned. "I can handle it myself. Thanks for the offer."

His heart expanded at the sweetness of her smile, making him feel even more protective of her. Blaise held his index finger and thumb a centimetre apart. "Just a little chat with him? He'll be as kind as a puppy to you afterwards."

Her incredible brown eyes twinkled. "As much as I'd like my supervisor to be docile, I decline."

His head and shoulders slumped with the drama of his heaved grunt of a sigh. "Okay. Fine."

Little did she know that the next time her supervisor made her cry, for whatever reason, he'd be in the guy's office so fast that plaster would fly off of the walls.

She deserved to be treated well. By everyone.

How had he come to care so much about a woman he had only recently met?

There was only one answer. The same thing that had kept him thinking about her. She was different. He'd be an idiot to not realize it. An even bigger fool to let her slip away from him again.

CHAPTER ELEVEN

Having skipped breakfast due to fear of vomiting in her stress-inducing supervisor's office, Lamisi downed her oxtail and rice as if it had been a week rather than all night since she'd last eaten.

The whole episode of her fury-induced breakdown in front of Blaise had more entertained rather than humiliated her.

She'd found the fact that he'd offered himself as her protector to be both horrifying because he didn't see her as someone who could take care of her own problems, and sweet because it showed that he cared. The man had a way of chipping away the resistance she'd built against him.

She took a break from her food and glanced around at the full restaurant. "I'm surprised no one recognized you."

He tipped his head towards one of the tables across the room. She twisted her torso to observe a group of women stealing covert glances in his direction and whispering to themselves.

"They aren't sure if I'm who they think I am. I rarely get approached when I'm out. For those bold enough to do so, I appease them with a conversation, sometimes a photo."

She shook her head. "That's not how I imagined your public life to be. I thought it would be more like we see on television."

"Very few Ghanaians have a reaction to me one way or the other. They're too busy trying to find their own way through life to worry about me. You're my number one fan, and yet, you ignored me when we first met."

"That's not true. I smiled and winked back."

"Ah, yes," he said in that breathy voice that made her shiver. "That moment is imprinted in my mind forever. Just as I was about to approach you, your face went all sour."

She laughed when he scrunched his features together and sucked his cheeks in.

"I wasn't that bad."

She bowed her head for a second before facing him with the truth.

"I didn't know how to handle your attention." Starting with his head, her hand waved to where his torso met the table. "You're a handsome musician with successful albums to your name, and I'm … me. The encounter wasn't what I expected."

Hinging at the hips, he leaned closer, propped his elbows on the table, and gave her a lopsided flash of teeth that made her want to crawl over the barrier to close the space between them.

"You think I'm handsome?"

An eye-roll accompanied her drawn-out teeth sucking. The man knew his appeal, so his joke fell flat.

"How about we discuss the interviews I need for my research?"

She reached into her bag and pulled out a printed sheet of paper which included the title of her project, its objectives, and the names of the top fifteen Ghanaian multilingual hiplife artists who best suited the parameters of her dissertation.

Blaise was number one. Professor Amartey had agreed to the list of artists. She got the sense it was because he didn't know who they were; otherwise, things may have gone in a more harrowing direction.

The server came to remove their plates and asked if they wanted dessert. They both declined.

Blaise read through the list. "Ambitious, aren't you?"

She shrugged. "Since I already knew the greatest of the greats, I figured you'd have no difficulty hooking me up with at least seven of the others."

"Slick. When would you like to conduct the interviews?"

"Since my supervisor has approved the interview questions, anytime this week or next would be perfect. Each interview will take about an hour, and I can meet them anywhere they want."

"Can I be with you for the interviews?"

She kept her face from morphing into a look of surprise at his request. Why would he want to be?

"Between travelling and the interview itself, that would take up a lot of your time, which I'm sure you could spend on more worthwhile ventures, like writing fabulous chart-climbing songs."

She hoped she'd been diplomatic enough for his ego.

"Besides, your presence might skew the artist's answers, which wouldn't provide a true evaluation for my research."

"In that case." He picked up the pen she'd placed on the table. "Is it okay if I write on this?"

"Yes."

Blaise struck out two of the names on the list.

"Why did you do that?"

He tapped the pen between the two names he'd cancelled out. "I wouldn't trust these guys alone with a beautiful woman. So, I won't even ask them."

Heat crept up her neck and resided in her cheeks. With all the women he must encounter, he thought her beautiful? Would she sound as if she were begging for a compliment if she asked him to repeat himself?

For the next forty minutes, Lamisi watched him contact his musician colleagues. His ability to smooth-talk them into accepting to do the interview had her mesmerized. If she could speak to people like that, she'd probably want for nothing ever again.

Eight confirmations had her clapping and kicking her legs under the table with excitement.

"Thank you so much, Blaise. I'll be a busy woman this week with interviews every day until Friday, but it'll be worth it. *And* I get to meet some of the best hiplife artists in Ghana. Thank you. Thank you. Thank you. What can I do to repay you?"

He rubbed his chin. "Well, there is one thing."

"Name it."

"Can you help me to learn French?"

Not what she'd been expecting. Their conversation on the mountain came back to her. "You said you wanted to use it in your next album. Haven't you started to learn?"

He tugged at his ear, something she'd never noticed him do before.

"I have a tutor, but it's not going very well. I thought I was good with languages, but French seems to be the exception. Those tenses are impossible to learn."

"Wouldn't my teaching you be the same as the tutor that you already have?"

"Not exactly."

She had so much to do to get her dissertation written and ready to defend against a panel that would tear her apart if she didn't complete the work well. She'd taken a one-year leave of absence from her job as an assistant lecturer at the university, but she didn't want to squander her time by becoming a private tutor when she could be writing her research.

Yet, she owed him. Big time. Saying no would be rude, but she had to think of herself first. Didn't she?

◆◆◆

Lamisi's excitement from only moments ago had decelerated when he'd presented his request.

The idea had bounced into his brain that he'd have a more enjoyable time learning the language if she were to teach him.

"What do you mean, not exactly?" she asked. "A tutor is a tutor. When you do the work, you get the results."

The woman was tough. He needed that if he were to reach his goal.

"Believe me, I've been studying all the time, but something's missing." *You.* "I'll be going into the studio to start recording in about six weeks, and so far, my lyrics are still all in English."

Since he'd been having such a hard time with French, and Lamisi didn't seem keen on helping him to learn, he needed to take a different tack. "How about rather than me trying to learn the language in that time, which would be impossible, you help me translate some of it?"

He'd thought about just doing a translation before, but knew that being fluent in the language would make him sound better while singing it. This way, as she translated the lyrics, he could learn the language from a more practical level.

She looked at him from the corner of her eye. "Why can't your tutor interpret for you?"

When was the last time he'd faced so much resistance from someone? People tended to fall at his feet wanting to make him happy. He appreciated Lamisi's style of staying true to herself. A respectable quality that mirrored him. How much more did they have in common?

"Let's just say that Gospel is more his style of music. I don't think he's ever listened to a secular song. If I asked him, he'd probably clasp a hand against his chest, raise the other one while bowing his head, and exclaim, 'Jesus take the wheel!'"

Her laughter held the same huskiness of her voice, pleasing his ears. He needed more.

"My tutor would exclaim it in French, and he'd add backward hops to emphasize his point."

"Oh … my … goodness," she said between her guffaws and smacking the table. "Stop it. I can totally see it."

He chuckled. "I haven't described him, so someone in your life must have left a strong impression."

Her laughter ended with a sigh. "Definitely."

"What he's teaching me is practical for if I travel. When will I ever sing about asking where the toilet is? Can you see why he's out of the running for lyrics translator?"

Getting her to agree was paramount, so he rushed on with his argument. "He may be technically knowledgeable about the language, but I don't hear a flow in him."

Her head dipped to the side as an indent formed in the middle of her forehead. "A flow?"

Blaise nodded and undulated his arm in a wave-like motion. "The tempo that will translate in the music so it doesn't sound straight or stilted."

"You've lost me."

He rummaged for a term she'd relate to? "He's monotonous."

"No up or down rhythm in his speech." Her head bobbed. "I get it now."

Not everyone did. "You possess the flow, and it will help me to decide which lyrics should be sung in French and which should be in English. And …"

He paused to pique her interest.

Her eyes widened. "What?"

"Who would be better to help me create my first French/English album than my number one fan?"

She burst into laughter. "Damn, you're good."

He thought so. "Does that mean you'll help me?"

"How long do you think it would take to do the translations?"

At least, it wasn't a no. "It's only for six songs. I can't see it taking more than a couple of days."

She rotated the empty glass which had contained her water while she thought.

"Please say you'll help to make me the king of French/English hiplife."

"Considering that hiplife is based in Ghana, it's doubtful. You may need to go with the term they use in Francophone countries for similar music. Closer to zouglou, zouk, or Coupé-Décalé. Have you decided which style you'll sing in?"

His jaw dropped. “You’re one impressive woman.”

She plucked at her shirt. “I sure am.”

He chuckled. “I’ve got the musical styling covered. We’ll discuss it if you decide to help me with the translation.”

“Since I owe you and it won’t take too much of my time. Okay.”

Blaise pumped a fist in the air.

“How about this weekend so we can get it out of the way?” she asked in a dry tone.

“Your enthusiasm is contagious,” he teased.

“Sorry, but I’m very busy,” she said with one side of her mouth quirked upward in a partial smile. “Working on albums that will expand the scope of music in Africa, maybe the world as we now know it, is not my main priority.”

His chest swelled with the confidence she had in him. “I see. I won’t take it personally then, Dr. Imoro-to-be.”

A full smile bloomed on her face, raising his spirits even higher.

He shifted closer to her as his gaze fell to her lips before rising to her eyes. “How about we seal the deal?”

Her mouth rounded. “Oh?”

He descended his head slowly to give her the opportunity to decline. Her lids hovering at the closing point encouraged him on.

The brush of their lips caused a shock to travel through him, just as it had on the mountain. He’d anticipated this moment since she’d stormed into the restaurant. No—since they’d last seen each other.

He moaned when she raised a hand to his jaw as their lips merged.

Drenched in her scent of sweet roses, his greatest desire was to deepen the kiss. He did the gentlemanly thing and backed away. They were in a public place, even though most of the lunchtime diners had cleared out.

He stared into her eyes with her hand still moulded against his cheek.

“Sealed with a kiss,” he said once his mind had cleared enough for words to form.

He knew without a doubt that he’d turn it into a song one day and dedicate it to her.

CHAPTER TWELVE

Three of the most incredible days of Lamisi's life had gone by in a whirlwind of heart-racing excitement. How many times had she pinched herself when in the midst of such extraordinary Ghanaian musicians? They had all been gracious and generous with their time and answers. A few of them had even wanted her to contact them about the results of the research, which had elevated her exhilaration into the outer galaxies.

Other than receiving several calls from an unknown number with someone breathing on the other end of the line without speaking, it had been a perfect week.

She'd gotten Blaise's interview out of the way first. After the ease of conversing with him about his music, she'd found the interactions with the others to be more of a comfortable chat than a strict interview.

She smiled when Blaise answered his phone on Friday. For the past few days, she had called and gushed her gratitude for having set her up with the artists. They'd end up talking about their day, which she enjoyed. Talking to him was like conversing with a friend who had the ability to make her core pulse with a need that hadn't been fulfilled in a very long time.

"Lamisi, if you thank me one more time, I'm going to turn each of the interviews you did into their own favour."

The giggle tripped out of her. "Okay. Okay. No more. How was your day?"

"Stressful."

She sat up in the seat at her desk, ready to take care of whatever had worried him. "Why? What happened?"

"My manager wants a few of the new songs ready by the VGMAs."

Lamisi watched the most popular music awards held in Ghana every year. "When are they holding them?"

"In three weeks. They asked me to perform. As my manager pointed out, it would be the perfect platform to introduce the new sound."

It certainly would since the ceremony was broadcast all over West Africa. "Can you have them ready by then?"

"Yes. The tunes and the lyrics are set. At least the English version. I just need my star translator to transition them into French. Are we still on for tomorrow?"

After having his voice in her ear all week, nothing could keep her from seeing him again. "Yes."

"Great. I can pick you up and bring you to my place."

A loud 'no' resonated in her head. She couldn't be alone with him in his home. She'd kissed him in a restaurant and had longed for more. What would her traitorous body allow him to do if they were alone? They hadn't known each other long enough. "Can't we meet somewhere more public?"

"I have recording equipment in my home that we'll be using."

"Oh."

"How about if you bring someone with you? As long as they don't tell the world about my project, it'll be fine."

Had he read her mind, or had she been so conservative in her dealings with him that he'd guessed why she'd hesitated? A smile spread across her face at his ability to make her feel at ease.

Tomorrow being Saturday, she could ask any number of people to join her. Her youngest brother Amadu had completed his exams; he'd be perfect. Precious had a wedding to attend—otherwise, she'd have been her first choice. "Okay. What time?"

"I'm under a bit of pressure to get this completed. How about eight? We'll get some work done, and then, I'll feed you lunch."

"Sounds like a deal. See you then. Can you send me the address?"

"Will do. Have a good night."

"You, too."

Just like every time she'd spoken to him, she hung up first. Lingering on the phone would be too telling of how much she liked him.

Whether anything would come of it, only time would tell.

CHAPTER THIRTEEN

Lamisi parked in front of Blaise's estate house and got out of the car. Two doors clicked closed before hers. Amadu had jumped at the opportunity to meet Bizzy, and so had Precious when she'd mentioned it.

"I'm going with you. It's only a wedding I'm missing out on," Precious had said. "Besides, I barely speak to my colleague. She won't even know I'm not there. I can't miss an opportunity to experience musical history in the making."

Lamisi hadn't been able to talk her friend out of joining them. So instead of one guardian at her side, she was flanked by two, both much too excited about hanging out at Blaise's place.

The front door opened before they reached it. He'd known they'd arrived in the estate complex when they'd needed his permission to clear security at the front gate.

Blaise stepped out of his home wearing a pair of well-worn jeans with a yellow T-shirt that outlined his muscular chest and arms. The strength of his body stayed imprinted on her own. The consistent memory of the gentle brush of his soft lips still stirred butterflies in her stomach.

Lamisi's mouth went dry at the sight of him. His beard remained trimmed and his hair was the same low-cut style it had been when she'd last seen him a few days ago. Yet, his handsomeness had quadrupled. If such a thing could be tallied.

"Welcome."

The moment he opened his arms out to her, she skipped forward to ensconce herself into them. The sun blazing down on them had nothing on the heat her body absorbed when she looped her arms around his waist and melted from chest to thigh into his solid strength.

She closed her eyes and clung tighter to his perfect form as her body buzzed with an awareness that curled her toes. Her senses overloaded with his presence as his unique smell wafted into her nose. A mix of … She took a deep whiff to discern the scent. Leather and citrus. She could get drunk from the combination.

He released her before she was anywhere near ready.

The hug with Precious wasn't as intimate or long as the one they'd shared. Her insides danced at that.

"Hello, Precious. How have you been?"

"Hi, Blaise. Life's been busy, but good. How's the ankle?"

"Mostly healed. Every once in a while, I get a twinge of pain, but it's manageable."

Lamisi introduced the men.

A clap of hands introduced their handshake before their palms slid along each other, ending in a snap of their fingers.

Blaise's lips rose with a smile. "Good to meet you, Amadu."

Her protective little brother displayed a polite reserve which was unlike his bold personality. "You, too. I'm a big fan of your music."

A huge understatement.

"So far, it sounds like I have a solid fan base in the Imoro family."

"Not everyone, man." Amadu's honest nature came to the forefront, as usual. "My father won't listen to anything but old school high life, and my eldest sister is Gospel all the way. The rest of us, even my mother, are more eclectic in our music tastes."

Blaise glanced at her with a brow raised and a twinkle in his eyes. "Gospel, you say?"

Lamisi giggled at their inside joke.

"Nothing but," Amadu responded with a curious look at Lamisi.

He led them into his home.

"Oh, my goodness," Precious whispered with more than a touch of awe.

Lamisi whole-heartedly agreed as the air-conditioned atmosphere hit her. Dark brown leather couches and chairs cradling light yellow and orange throw pillows filled the perimeter of the living area. The tan and white rug below the coffee table met the edges of the seats. A plasma screen television took up a third of the opposite wall.

The rust colour of two walls gave the room a warm glow while the light grey in the dining area and the barrier which held the door they'd just entered appeared to expand it.

He'd given the space a Ghanaian feel with a few carved wood masks and vivid paintings of scenery of their homeland.

"Make yourselves at home," Blaise said. "I'll be right back.

They settled side by side onto the couch. Lamisi held back a groan as she ran a hand against the buttery soft material while being enveloped in a seat with the perfect amount of firmness and sinkability.

Amadu hadn't stopped gawping at the flat screen. "This place is inspiration."

"Is it just me, or is the house massive?" Lamisi asked.

"I wouldn't have guessed how far it extended. And this is just the living and dining room." Precious pointed towards the staircase. "Did either of you notice a second floor from the outside?"

"No. I thought it was a single story." Then again, she'd been too busy basking in Blaise's embrace to notice much of anything other than him.

Amadu twisted his upper body. "Is that a swimming pool in the back?"

They stood as if attached by a wire and looked out of the windows protected by an intricately designed metallic burglar-proofing system. A gleaming, crystal clear in-ground swimming pool met her gaze.

"I don't see a wall enclosure. How big do you think the property is?" Precious asked.

"It's six plots," Blaise announced as he came into the room with a tray of bottled water.

Never in seven lifetimes would she have guessed that he'd be the one to serve them. Didn't he have a house help? He couldn't maintain this incredible home by himself. Could he?

Out of habit, she stepped forward to take the tray from him.

"Please sit. You're my guest."

She sank into the seat, once again impressed by him.

They each plucked a bottle of water from the tray with a word of thanks.

Blaise sat in an armchair. "How about a tour of the grounds before we start work?"

"If it isn't an inconvenience." Lamisi kept her voice light instead of letting the eagerness come through.

"Not at all."

They formed a queue behind him as if on a school excursion.

He swung right when they reached the dining room into a kitchen that made Lamisi's knees weaken with envy.

Light brown wood cabinets broke the cream-coloured theme of the walls and marble-looking countertops.

He reached for one of the tall cabinet handles and opened it to reveal a full refrigerator. She'd only seen such a beautifully hidden panel on television shows.

Saliva filled her mouth at the eight-burner stainless steel range making up part of the centre island.

"Do you enjoy cooking?" Precious asked.

"Yes, but for the most part, I leave the task to my Aunt Vida who prepares my meals. She's amazing."

Lamisi raised a brow at Precious when Blaise turned his back. A man who knew how to cook and openly admitted it. Intriguing.

They walked to the far side of the home past the swimming pool, guest house, and a massive garden. A shelter housed two vehicles and a motorcycle.

Lamisi's body thrummed with memories of rides that had left her invigorated. Her hands had gripped the handles as the motorcycle vibrated beneath her. The engine had revved with the hum of a lion as she'd taken to the road, owning it. It had been much too long since she'd controlled the kind of power that left her feeling free and uninhibited.

As if hypnotized, she ambled over to the red and black Suzuki and stroked the sleek machine from its cool metallic handle bars to its elevated seat which would sink as soon as her ass sat on it. Such a fine vehicle. Could anyone else hear it begging her to straddle it and show it love by taking it out for a spin? She raised her leg to obey.

"If you don't get her away from that motorcycle—" Amadu warned, "—you'll never get your translations done."

Lamisi's foot hit the ground as she looked up from her trance to find Blaise standing next to her.

He stepped closer. "You're kidding, right?"

Amadu shook his head. "Not even a little. She learned how to ride one when we visited our family in the north."

"Makes sense," Blaise said. "Considering that it's a common mode of transportation along with bicycles."

"She kind of got obsessed with the speed aspect." Amadu rubbed a hand over his head. "Turned my parents prematurely grey when she flew by their car one day. As much as she pleaded for one when we returned to Accra, they refused."

Lamisi waved her hand in her brother's face. "Hey. I'm right here. That was a long time ago, Amadu. I've gotten over it."

Mostly. She wouldn't brag about having gotten a motorcycle license and borrowing one of her friend's bikes every once in a while. The exhilaration of the wind rushing past never got old.

Precious grunted. "Once a speed demon, always ..."

She let the rest of her words hang.

Lamisi took one last, longing glance at the motorcycle that would feature in her dreams tonight. She looked up at Blaise who seemed to be considering her. Too bad mind-reader wasn't on her list of talents.

By the time they'd finished seeing the house, she had lost Amadu to the video game collection and Precious to the gym. At least, they wouldn't be too far away in the unique basement space.

Her jaw dropped when they encountered the mini studio he'd spoken of.

"This is not small, Blaise," she accused while taking in the hardwood floors, a closed-in booth with clear glass or plastic—she couldn't tell—and equipment she'd only seen on shows or movies about music.

"Compared to professional recording studios, it is."

Lamisi touched the panelled wall. "Is it sound-proof?"

"Yes. If I were hard-pressed, I could create an album here, but I use the place to tinker around and get my creative juices flowing. I leave the work of blending to my producer since he's so good at it."

Where was the cockiness she'd expected from someone who'd made it big in such a competitive business? Maybe they weren't as different as she'd initially thought.

CHAPTER FOURTEEN

Blaise refused to let liking Lamisi get in the way of business. He'd handed her a non-disclosure agreement before exposing her to his work. The pain of past betrayals had served as a lesson. She didn't seem to mind as she scrolled her signature onto the form after listening to his reasoning for it and then reading it.

They settled into the seats at the desktop computers he'd set up in his studio. Keeping his hands to himself during their session would be a feat of Mt. Afadjato proportions so he'd left the door open as an added incentive to behave.

She hadn't exposed her breasts or legs in the overkill manner other women used to catch his attention, yet her jeans and loose-fitting red dashiki top tempted. Her hair had been freshly twisted and framed her face. Unlike the day they had met on the mountain and the restaurant, she wore makeup that enhanced her beauty. Especially her exotic, angular eyes. Breath-taking.

In the past few moments alone, he'd sucked in discrete deep breaths to take in more of her sweet yet somehow spicy rose fragrance. He'd have to set his mind to concentration mode in order to get the work done.

"I have six songs I'd like to translate."

"Will they be the only ones on the album?"

He clicked a folder on the desktop.

"No, but those are the ones which will be mixed with French. If I can pull it off," he mumbled the last.

Her hand on his shoulder sent a simmering buzz into him. When would he get used to the fact that their attraction was inevitable and electric?

"You can do it," she assured. "To the best of my knowledge, it's never been done on such a grand level by a Ghanaian artist, but if anyone can pull it off, you can."

His chest puffed out with pride at her confidence in him. Support was a treasurable thing. The fact that she gave it out so freely and believed in him said a lot about the kindness and generosity of her personality.

He clicked on the song he'd entitled 'You're the One for Me.'

Lamisi scanned the words that popped up on the page. "How's this going to work?"

"You asked me about the style of the songs." He clicked on the bottom of the screen and opened his music player. His voice came through the speakers singing the English lyrics to the song he'd set to a rough beat he'd created.

Lamisi bopped her head and shook her shoulders. A good sign.

She crossed her arms over her chest and sighed when the song finished.

"Oh my goodness, those lyrics are beautiful. You've combined hiplife with zouglou." She grabbed his forearm with her eyes wide. "Blaise, you've created a whole new style of music. That's so incredible."

He blinked at her several times. Not for the first time, he wondered about the incredible woman sitting next to him. "I'm impressed. You really know your music styles."

She tucked her hair behind her ear and avoided his gaze by staring at the computer screen. "I'm a fan of all genres of music. Like languages, I recognize them easily."

The woman wore modesty like a light jacket during the cool dry Harmattan season. She possessed gifts that would make most people walk around with their nose stuck in the air looking down on everyone who didn't come up to her level.

How much more would he discover about her that would astonish him?

Rather than embarrass her further, he got to work. "Which of the lyrics will flow well in French to the beat?"

Time to see if he'd made the right choice with her, at least when it came to his career. Their personal relationship would be determined later.

Lamisi startled at the knock on the door.

A woman about the same age as her mother stood with her hands clenched together. "I'm sorry to disturb, but lunch has been ready for over two hours. Amadu and Precious have already eaten."

Lamisi extended her body in a stretch that loosened tight muscles. "What time is it?"

Blaise displayed the face of his watch by flipping his wrist over. "Two o'clock."

Grabbing his hand, she twisted his arm with disbelief to look for herself. "We've been at this for five hours?"

"It would appear that way." He rotated his chair towards the door. "We'll be up in a minute, Aunty. Thank you for coming to get us."

The older woman's smile pulled out a dimple on each of her chubby cheeks. "I know how you can go all day without eating when you're in here. It's not good for the body to work without sustenance."

Not waiting for a reply, she turned and left.

"Five hours?" Lamisi still couldn't understand how so much time had passed.

His laughter didn't diminish her incredulity. When had she ever done anything where time flew by so fast? Sleeping didn't count.

Focusing on the task had been impossible at first with her heart racing at his nearness. The occasional brush of knees when they swivelled their seats in the same direction happened too often to be coincidence.

And then, the job at hand had taken over, and that's when everything but translating the lyrics had possessed them.

Getting to her feet, she tipped her neck from side to side, and then rolled it around. "This happens to you a lot?"

He towered over her when he unfolded himself from the chair. "It does. Losing myself in the music is what makes me so good."

She bumped his shoulder with her fist. "Here I was, thinking you were humble."

Hands crossed over his chest as he arched backwards, he widened his eyes and gasped. "Who, me?"

"I don't remember you being half as dramatic during your shows as you are in real life."

"That's because my manager said I had to tone it down."

Their combined laughter filled the studio. No longer jittery about being near him, she could definitely get used to hanging out.

She may not get the chance again because they only had two songs left to translate. Now that they'd developed a rhythm, it shouldn't take long. Would they remain friends? She'd really like that.

Who was she kidding? She wanted more.

She placed a hand over her stomach when it rumbled.

"Sounds like I overworked you. Let's go eat."

She followed him out of the secure haven she'd discovered in the studio. Would working on her dissertation in this room make time fly? She doubted it. The combination of being with such a talented man while creating something new and inventive had to be a contributing factor.

They walked in on Amadu fixated on a football video game in the entertainment room and left him to it.

Now, she prayed that Precious would also be occupied so she'd have Blaise all to herself for a little while longer.

CHAPTER FIFTEEN

It didn't take ten minutes for Lamisi to empty her bowl of the eba and okra soup. She sighed in contentment as she rested against the seat. "Please don't tell my mom, but that was the best okra soup I've ever eaten in my life."

The eba, as they called it in Nigeria, made from gari, a dried and then fried cassava, had been mixed with hot water to give it a more solid yet sticky consistency for shaping and scooping out the stew-like soup by hand. She hadn't been embarrassed to lick her fingers once the food had disappeared.

Blaise placed a single finger over his lips. "Your secret is safe with me."

"What do you do when your mother comes to visit?"

"I warn Aunty Vida not to cook as well."

The older woman laughed as she came to the table. "As if I could downplay the gift Allah has graced me with. Besides, my cousin comes to visit just to eat from my hand. Would you like some more food? There's plenty."

She struggled to sit up from her lounged position in order to show respect. "No, thank you, Aunty Vida. It was absolutely delicious, but I'm full."

She was even too replete to hide the slight bulge that made an appearance over the waistline of her jeans. If she were home, she'd unbutton them, but in Blaise's house, she brought her chair closer to the table, hoping he wouldn't notice.

The woman picked up their bowls before Lamisi could offer to help and swooshed out of the room whistling a happy tune.

Eating a Ghanaian woman's food and then complaining about how stuffed you were tended to bring out all sorts of joy.

"She's your aunt by blood?" she half-whispered.

"Yes." He kept his voice as low as hers. "Not only is she my cook, but she's my parents' spy."

"Interesting."

"More like annoying. But my parents didn't want someone they didn't know preparing my meals. Being a chief, my dad can get paranoid. The good thing is that she doesn't stay in the house with me."

"I've heard about the fighting that goes on in the north when chieftaincy is called into issue. Not pretty."

He held her gaze. "My father came by the stool peacefully. No one contested."

She smacked hand over her eyes and groaned. "I've just eaten a meal like a glutton with royalty."

His chuckle warmed the inside of her chest. Would she ever get accustomed to his joviality and how her body responded to it?

"I'd rather one day be called the King of Hiplife."

She hated to disappoint him, but reality had to be faced. "Sorry, but that title belongs to—"

"Me."

"Nope, but how about you being the King of Frenafrohip, considering that you just created a new style of music that's going to be huge."

"Frenafrohip. Frenafrohip." He rolled the word around his mouth as if tasting it. "A combination of French, Afro, and hiplife, right?"

She nodded, impressed that he'd caught on. "It just came to me, but now that I hear you say it, it sounds too heavy. What about Francohip."

"Francohip. I like it even better. How about creating a dance to go with it?"

"You're on your own with that one." Grunting with the stiffness in her joints after sitting for so long, she stood. "Let's finish the last two songs, and then, we'll head home and give you some privacy."

"Or we could relax now and complete them tomorrow. Maybe after you finish church? If you're free."

Before she could answer, Precious yelled from her place on the couch. "We're coming over."

It took her the speed of light to reach the dining room. "I'm sure your poor brains are in need of a rest today. A good sleep will have you refreshed and ready for more work tomorrow."

Lamisi lurched forward when her friend shoved her shoulder.

"Lamisi, Amadu, and I will be here bright and early so you can finish the work." Precious tipped her head to the side and squinted up at Blaise. "Eight in the morning will do nicely."

Who knew her friend could be so easily bought? Give her a gym and a remote control to an enormous plasma screen television, and she took over two people's lives.

Blaise didn't help by smiling. "Eight is fine."

Aunty Vida strolled out of the kitchen. "Wonderful. I'll have breakfast prepared for you, so don't eat before you come."

Precious clapped the cupped palms of her hands together.

"Great." She turned her upper body, but then twisted it back. "By the way, is it okay if we take a dip in your pool tomorrow?"

Lamisi slapped a hand over her mouth with embarrassment while Blaise chuckled. "You have free reign. Enjoy yourselves."

"You're the best, Bizzy. In that case, we have to get going right away. We have some bathing suit shopping to do before the stores close. I'll go get Amadu."

"I'm so sorry," Lamisi muttered. "It looks like your toys are too much for them to resist."

"It's no problem. I hope you're available tomorrow, though."

His voice pitched up with what she took to be concern.

She waved a hand down. "I'm free. Sundays are rest days for most of my family."

"No church?"

The ring of a phone interfered with her answer. She glanced down at the table to see Deola's beautiful, heavily made-up face flashing bright and broad on his screen.

He snatched the phone from the table and swiped it so the ringing stopped.

Air rushed out of her as if she'd been punched in the stomach. He'd claimed that he and the heiress were friends. Then why not answer the call in her presence?

She shook off the sense of betrayal and jealousy. She had no right to either. An ex complaining about her hounding jealousy claimed it had been the reason he'd broken up with her. She'd later discovered that he'd been a lying, cheating, manipulative bastard who had her thinking she might be going crazy when he really had been seeing someone else. She'd been grateful to her ex for inadvertently teaching her the signs of sneakiness in a relationship and that she should always trust her instincts.

Precious and Amadu came trooping up the stairs, discussing the best place to shop for swimming costumes.

Lamisi forced a smile. "We'll see you tomorrow."

They each went to the kitchen to thank and said good bye to Aunty Vida.

The tension between them remained as Blaise walked them out. Her useless chaperones were loading into the car when he leaned down and hugged her close. Her body and mind were not of one accord when she wound her arms around his shoulders and melted into him.

“Thank you, Lamisi. Now I understand why you couldn’t stop with expressing the gratitude last week.”

He released her before she was ready to leave the nest of his muscular arms.

Tomorrow. She’d committed to helping him, and she would. He owed her nothing, not even the truth about his relationship with Deola. Once she did him this favour, they’d be even, and she wouldn’t have to see him again.

CHAPTER SIXTEEN

"Everything had been going well," Blaise complained to Abdul on video chat as he paced the living room an hour after Lamisi and her crew had taken off.

He'd sensed a sudden annoyance in her when Deola's face had come up on his screen. Had she been jealous? He liked the idea of her caring enough about him to be.

His reaction to the call could've been handled better. He'd been taken off guard by how much he'd enjoyed Lamisi's company and hadn't needed Deola's pushy presence disturbing their good time. It had happened anyway.

"Not only is Lamisi magic when it comes to knowing which lyrics need to be translated, but she's cool to hang with. Easy." He kicked the leg of the coffee table hard enough to jiggle the vase of fake flowers. "Deola, on the other hand, only cares about herself and instinctively knows how to ruin things even when she's not around."

Why couldn't he see it before? Even her supposed friendship was toxic.

"What did Deola want?"

He'd returned her call because not doing so would have resulted in a catty, never-ending lecture about phone etiquette. When had he started to allow her have so much control over his life?

"She wanted to convince me that going to the VGMAs together would be better than me going alone or with anyone else because she looked fabulous on camera and knew how to handle the media."

Abdul's frown brought out the brackets at the sides of his mouth. "I told you not to mess with her. Your head got so big when she gave you a little of her attention."

"Whatever, man. I need to get her to back off without hurting her feelings."

"That's a tough one. No one has ever broken off a relationship with her without severe repercussions."

Blaise clenched his fist and tried to keep himself from yelling.

"We aren't dating. We never were. She kissed me once, and it was horrible." He shuddered at the experience. "Wet, sloppy, and I swear that a mouthful of sugar wouldn't have made it any better."

Abdul chuckled. "Sounds disgusting."

"There's absolutely no attraction. No chemistry. Nothing between us."

Unlike with Lamisi. One touch from her, and his skin buzzed. All he'd wanted to do when they were working together was get closer. Nibble on her perfect ears. Slide his lips along her smooth cheek before meeting her mouth, sparking the flames between them.

"Not sure what to tell you. Maybe you should meet with her face to face and let her know how you feel."

"I've already told her. She's a smart woman; she should've gotten it."

Abdul snorted. "Smart and spoiled rotten are two different things. You've heard the stories about what happens when the oil heiress doesn't get what she wants. She had a clothing boutique shut down because they didn't have anything she liked in her size."

Blaise ran a hand over his head and grunted. He'd heard the rumours and even believed that most of them were true. That's what freaked him out. Someone who had everything going for her shouldn't be so vicious. Damn his ego for getting caught up in wanting to be seen with her.

"You'll figure something out, Blaise. You always do. Now tell me a little more about the new album. Did Lamisi really tear it up with the translation?"

The air became easier to breathe with the change of topic. "Not only that, but she came up with a name for the style."

"Really?"

"Yeah. Check this." He paused. "Francohip."

He could see the wheels in Abdul's head grinding as his friend tipped his face to the ceiling. Blaise knew he'd gotten it when Abdul pumped a fist in the air.

"Aw man, that's hot! A combo of Francophone and Hiplife."

"Exactly."

"She's done well." As if remembering something, Abdul brought his squinting eyes closer to the screen. "Did you sleep with her?"

"No."

Not that he hadn't wanted to since the first moment he'd lain eyes on her. Everything about her appealed to him. He knew without a doubt that she was attracted to him also; yet, she'd stayed away from him instead of calling right away. It would've been for ever if she hadn't needed the favour.

"Blaise." His friend extended the name the way his mother did with a hard hit on the s when trying to draw out the truth from him.

"I haven't."

"Good. Keep it that way. She's not the one for you. She's not Muslim, and your parents wouldn't approve."

The thought of disappointing them was his Achilles heel.

Getting into relationships had never been an issue. Until Lamisi. He hardly knew her, but she made him think of a future as her children's father. His mother had always encouraged that when he found the one, he'd know. Maybe he shouldn't have rolled his eyes at what he now might believe to be sage wisdom.

"Lamisi's mother was a Muslim before she converted to Christianity to marry her father. That should count for something."

Abdul huffed out a sigh. "Unless she's one herself or is willing to convert, then you know as well as I do that it doesn't count. You mentioned you'd be finishing the translations tomorrow."

Blaise murmured his agreement.

"I suggest you cut ties with her after that. Neither of you owe the other anything. The way your eyes glaze over when you mention her name isn't a good sign."

Done with the topic, Blaise asked about Abdul's security firm. His friend delved into the latest development of his new venture, leaving his personal life alone. At least for the time being.

***

Unlike the excitement on the last day of school when she'd been younger, having this be her final time hanging out with Blaise didn't thrill her.

The feeling of unworthiness which had initially kept her away from him had crept back in last night and stuck. He was down to earth and friendly, but he was also a star, accustomed to the glamourous things in life. She was a simple woman who didn't belong in his world. Not like the fashionista Deola.

With good reason, she was sure that women threw themselves at him. She wasn't the sort to share her man. Ever. He'd tire of her and move on—may as well do it before he got the chance.

Why couldn't he be a regular guy living a normal life?

As soon as she parked in front of Blaise's home, he came out.

Amadu stepped up to him first. They shared a handshake ending with a snap. "Hey, man. Thanks for letting us stop by again."

"I owe your sister big time, so enjoy yourself."

"Hi, Blaise." Precious got a short hug while Lamisi hung back.

"How are you doing, Precious?"

"A little sore from my workout yesterday." She held up a bag. "That won't stop me from hitting the gym again. I washed your sister's clothes. Thanks for the loan."

"You're welcome. Breakfast is ready and on the table. Help yourselves."

Precious and Amadu went in without a backwards glance at her.

Unable to resist, despite her newfound resolve, Lamisi initiated the hug. Damn, he felt good. Solid, strong, and right.

"I have a surprise for you after we eat."

Curious, she released him. "What is it?"

His eyes glimmered with mischief. "You'll see."

What could he have planned?

Seeing the buffet spread on the table, all thoughts of his surprise were pushed to the back of her mind as her mouth watered. She filled her bowl with Hausa koko, a smooth porridge made from millet. Skipping over the fried eggs, toasted bread, and oatmeal, she forked koose onto her plate. She held back a moan when she took a bite of the spicy, fried black eyed bean cakes. She had to get the recipe of the best koose she'd ever eaten from Aunty Vida before she left.

The conversation was sparse as everyone focused on the succulent meal. Once plates were empty and multitudes of thanks given to Aunty Vida, they took off to their play spaces.

Lamisi turned to Blaise. "What's my surprise?"

He grinned and stood.

"Follow me." He stopped mid-step. "Bring your driver's license."

She raised a brow. "Why?"

"We don't need issues from the police if they stop us driving the motorcycle."

She clutched her hands to her chest as she looked back and forth between back door and Blaise. Letting out a squeal, she ran in place before crashing into him with a tight hug. "Thank you!"

She hustled to the living room where she'd left her pocketbook, rummaged through her wallet, and pulled out her valid motorcycle driver's license.

"Do you want to see it?"

He chuckled. "No. I trust you."

It must run deep if he was willing to let her drive his motorcycle after the stories Amadu and Precious had told him yesterday. An opportunity should be grasped, not questioned.

With one more leap onto him and a smacking kiss to his cheek, she grabbed his hand and bolted to the side of the house.

Little did he know that he was about to have the most amazing ride of his life.

CHAPTER SEVENTEEN

As they worked on the last song to be translated, Blaise's body still hummed from the residual adrenaline from the motorcycle ride. He'd given Lamisi free reign to go where she wanted. She'd taken to the longest stretch of highway she could find. Being Sunday, the Tema Motorway had been free of the standard traffic found during the week. And then, she'd surprised him by taking the George W. Bush Highway straight to its end in Mallam.

The ride had been as exhilarating as if he'd driven the motorcycle. Her merger of speed and safety as they'd zipped along the road had set him on a natural high. Three hours of driving hadn't seemed to be enough for her when they'd gotten back to his place and removed their helmets.

Her skin glowed, and she couldn't seem to shake her smile. His own had been plastered on his face at having made her so happy.

The translating went smoother than planned. Their minds refreshed, they didn't just complete the last two songs, but went over the ones from yesterday and improved them.

Blaise relaxed with his hands propped behind his head and legs crossed at the ankles.

"We work well together."

"Yes. Well, I'm a language genius."

He nodded. "And you have the flow. I told you."

She hopped up, raised her arms above her head, and flexed her back with a groan.

He rotated to the left as the desire to nuzzle her exposed abdomen threatened to take over good sense.

The chair squeaked as she flopped into it. "It just hit me that I haven't heard you sing the complete songs with the French. We've been doing it all piecemeal."

His moment of embarrassment had come. "I told you that I'm not the best at pronouncing the words."

"Not a problem. We'll go through it line by line."

The faith she had that he wouldn't butcher the language bolstered him.

He pulled up the last song they'd worked on since it was fresh in his mind. For this piece, they'd decided that the chorus would be in French and would start the song. In English, the lyrics were gorgeous, and he did say so himself. He'd been thinking about the woman he'd one day fall in love with as he'd written it.

He looked into Lamisi's dark eyes. Had he unknowingly written the song for her?

Don't be ridiculous. He barely knew her. Although he liked everything he'd discovered so far. Mostly. Her stubbornness could be irritating, but then again, who liked everything about anyone? It would be unnatural.

Just like in his lyrics, her smile made his insides go wobbly.

Hanging out with her felt … right.

Your love sets me free, allowing me to grow
The light in your eyes brings me to my knees
I will love you forever because
with you is where I'm meant to be
I will love you forever because
with you is where I'm meant to be

Lamisi sang it in French to the tune he'd created. He repeated the stanza.

Even to his own ears, the words came out stilted.

The way she bit her bottom lip and grimaced as she listened sent a trickle of sweat gliding down his back.

"That was a nice try," she said with the hesitancy of a teacher to a pupil who'd messed up the answer. "How about if I sing it once and you repeat it?"

She didn't wait for a response. Her sweet, melodious voice did justice to the song, and he got lost in it.

"Now you."

A repeat performance brought on that same disappointed expression.

"Okay." She stretched out the word. "You really need to work on your French. It's a soft language, and you're using it more like a battering ram than a feather."

Ouch. Didn't he like her honest nature? Maybe not at this moment, but he'd learn from her harsh teaching style.

"Let's take the first line and work from there."

Fifteen minutes later, her hair was standing straight out from how often she'd run her hands through it.

She sprang to her feet. "Your lyrics have been translated. I think I've done all I can for you."

"What's wrong? I don't understand."

"Do you want my honest opinion?"

Would his ego survive more of her blatant candidness? "Always."

"Your French is awful. Have you ever heard anyone sing one of your songs and they mess up the language completely, but they joyfully think they've gotten it right?"

He chuckled at her analogy even though he knew where she was going with it. "Many times. Especially when they don't understand the language that it's being sung in."

She rotated her wrist once before presenting her hand palm up with fingers pointing at him. "That's you when you sing in French."

"Come on, I can't be that bad."

"Record yourself and see."

Blaise accepted the challenge. When he played the verse back, he cringed. Horrible. If this had happened in any of the Ghanaian languages or even English, his career would've never gotten off the ground.

He rested his head against the back of the chair and scraped a hand down his face until it rested over his mouth. "What am I going to do?"

His transition into French shouldn't be this difficult. He was a man of rhythm and languages. He'd finally found something that he truly stank at.

The hand she placed on his shoulder brought a comforting warmth.

"From what I can tell, you have three options."

He waited for her to share.

She settled into her seat. "First of all, you could scrap the idea altogether. The songs would sound fabulous in English and the languages you're loquacious in."

Just as he was about to speak, she placed a finger against his lips. He willed himself not to suck it into his mouth and let his tongue sweep over it.

As if realizing what she'd done, she removed her touch and clasped her hands together on her lap.

"I'm spouting ideas. It doesn't mean you have to take any of them."

"Fine. I'm listening."

"The second option is to collaborate with a Francophone singer."

Not bad. It had occurred to him to do it with a couple of the songs, anyway. He'd feel like a fraud if he let someone else sing all of them. It wasn't as if he was starting a boy band or anything. He was a solo artist and would continue to thrive as one.

"The last is that you practice until you speak French like it's your first language. Or at least sing the lyrics as such."

After what he'd just heard come out of his mouth, he wasn't sure about that option, either. "Do you think it's possible?"

She shrugged. "It depends on how much work you're willing to put in."

"Will you help me?"

She snapped her neck so far back that her chin became double. "Um. I'm busy with my dissertation, remember? Busy, busy, busy PhD woman here. No free time."

"Please. I'm willing to put in the work. I really am. I just need a little of your time. Not all of it. Just some."

The fact that it would keep him seeing her was secondary, yet worked out well. He didn't doubt that the more she got to know him, she'd find him irresistible. Just as he found her.

Her twists shook with her vehement rejection. "You should be taught by someone from a Francophone country or get immersed in the language or something like that. That's how I learned how to speak it. I studied French in senior high school and had a couple of classmates from Togo and Côte d'Ivoire who I used to harass into speaking with me. I even followed one of my friends home to Côte d'Ivoire during one of our long vacations. Such an amazing experience."

He'd thought about taking a trip to Côte d'Ivoire, but the idea of going to a non-English speaking country by himself didn't appeal. He grabbed her hand as an idea caught hold.

"I know you're working on your dissertation, but I desperately need your help. Will you travel to Côte d'Ivoire with me?"

With her eyes wide and mouth gaping, he didn't anticipate a favourable response.

CHAPTER EIGHTEEN

Lamisi's parents had taught her to say what she meant because the truth would serve her. She'd learned over the years to soften her words with kindness.

The latter left her current sphere of existence only to be replaced by pure exasperation.

"Are you right in the head? Why would you ask me for such a huge favour when I just told you how busy I am? Why don't you ask Deola to go with you instead?"

She clamped her lips closed at what her temper had let escape. What had gotten into her? A jealousy she shouldn't be experiencing over a man she hardly knew.

It didn't matter. Rather than deal with the issue she'd created, she picked up her things to take her mortified self home. She'd accomplished her mission. It wasn't her fault he couldn't speak French in a manner anyone would understand.

He clasped a hand to the back of his neck and growled.

The action made her dash towards the door.

"Lamisi, please wait."

She stopped and turned at the pleading in his voice. What was she doing running away like a bunny facing a hunter? She was stronger than that.

"As I told you before, Deola is just a friend."

"Okay."

"I should've taken the call when it came through yesterday, but we'd had such a great day, and I didn't want to ruin it."

She crossed her arms over her chest to emphasize her response. "Okay."

He sighed. "The truth is that she likes me, but I only see her as a friend."

"I knew there was something going on between you two. The media doesn't always lie. Everything is based on at least a kernel of truth."

"Except when it comes to anything going on between her and me." He took a step closer. "The attraction is purely one-sided. It's just that she's spoiled and likes to get her way."

Lamisi snorted. "Not surprising for a billionaire oil heiress. She probably gets everything she wants just by raising a finger. What makes you think she won't have you?"

"Because I don't want her." He closed the distance between them by another step. "I never have. I hate to admit this, but I initially saw her as an ego and possible career booster. I was wrong. But then, we got to know each and became friends. Nothing more. It turns out that I really like someone else."

Her heart threatened to hurdle into her throat with its fierce beating. The smouldering gaze he captured her with gave her the answer, but she had to ask anyway. "Who?"

His lips rose in a smirk that made her stomach dip as another agile step brought him even closer. "A woman I recently met. I used to call her mountain woman. After experiencing how she handles a motorcycle, she's now thrill-seeker."

"Oh?"

She'd never had someone be so genuine and forward at the same time. Was she crazy to believe him, or had the charm he'd embroiled her in stolen all of her good sense?

"It turns out that she's my number one fan, even though I would've never guessed it by the way she ignored me the first time we saw each other from across the room."

That brought on an unstoppable grin. "Maybe she'd heard that stroking a musician's ego never turned out well. Better to keep celebrities grounded."

"Yeah, well, I haven't been able to stop thinking about her, and when she called me, I was so excited that I nearly forgot my own name."

Her breath stuttered when he reached out and caressed her cheek with his fingertips. She really should back away.

"Things got even better when this amazing, smart, beautiful woman agreed to help me create a new brand of music. It took a lot of willpower on my part not to touch her while she sat within reach."

Eyes heavy as desire flared, Lamisi stared at his mouth, watching his lips cease their speech as he lowered his head.

The first touch was electric as his lips glided over hers. Her lids closed as she savoured the softness of their firmness. The simple touch turned her inside out with its magnificence. Their lips nibbled and teased in exquisite sweetness.

She'd wanted this moment since the first time she'd lain sprawled on top of him on the mountain.

Blaise's hands spread across her back, pulling her closer to the hard planes of his body. She moaned as she gripped his muscular arms to keep herself upright.

His tongue brushed against her lower lip, and she opened for him. What she'd considered extraordinary just moments ago became earth-shattering as his tongue slid against hers. She circled him, taking in his taste mixed with the fragrance of leather and citrus. A heady, enticing scent.

The earth could implode, and she wouldn't care as long as he never stopped.

Wrapping her arms around his shoulders brought her flush against him.

She whimpered in protest when he slid his mouth to her cheek. The kisses down her jawline brought him to her neck. She stroked the back of his head as he nipped and sucked flesh she'd never known to be sensitive until that moment.

Sliding her hands to cup his cheeks, she raised his head until their lips met again. Passion ran rampant as their tongues swept each other's mouths as if the secrets of life were hidden within.

Her body grew increasingly fevered with the need for more.

When Blaise slid his large palms up her ribcage and touched the undersides of her breasts, she moaned with encouragement. She didn't think to question. Only feel.

His thumbs honed in on her nipples and flicked them, sending a hot flash of desire straight to her core. She lifted her leg to wrap around his thigh. His hardness meeting her centre ripped a groan from her throat.

She hadn't been a virgin for many years, but she'd only just met him in person. It wasn't her style to move so fast with a man. Months, maybe a year, would pass before deciding to make love to a man she'd dated exclusively. Sometimes not at all.

Her logical mind had shut down, replaced with instinct and raw passion. Her body found antiquated societal rules obsolete as she rolled her hips against him. Her hands roamed over the broad expanse of his strong back, gripping his shirt to give her leverage.

"Hey you guy—Oh my goodness!"

Precious's sudden appearance brought reality back to the storm of pleasure.

With only one foot planted on the floor, Lamisi lost her balance when disentangling herself from Blaise. If he hadn't still been holding her, she would've fallen. Another save for him.

When he released her, she smoothed her hands over her top to hide her exposed midriff and help control the jitters.

Mortified that she'd been caught kissing a virtual stranger, she avoided Precious' gaze.

Precious wouldn't let her get away with it. "Lamisi?"

The smirk she witnessed when she looked up matched the amusement in Precious' voice.

She'd get her friend back one day, and revenge would be sweet.

She cleared her throat. "Yes?"

"I'm *really* sorry to disturb. You have no idea how much, but Aunty Vida sent me down to drag you two up for lunch." The grin never left. "She said she'd be leaving early and wanted to make sure you both ate."

Precious pointed towards the entrance. "I could tell her that you're, well, busy."

Lamisi would pay Precious' hair dresser to wash her friend's hair with bleach. That would be a good enough payback for the onslaught of humiliation she kept piling on.

"Please let her know that we'll be there in a minute."

Blaise's voice sounded normal. Unaffected by the torrent of heat still raging through her body.

Rather than leave, Precious stood in the same spot, smiling as if she'd been handed a million Ghana cedis just for being there.

"Precious," Lamisi hissed with a head tick to the side.

"Oh. I'll see you two upstairs."

The finger guns with the corresponding clicks enflamed Lamisi's face even further.

Horrified at her behaviour, there was only one thing she could do. Spine straight, she turned to face Blaise. All shame washed away as she looked into his heated, hooded eyes. She swallowed the apology that had sat on the tip of her tongue.

She wasn't sorry it had happened. His lips called out to her, and angels help her, she wanted to answer.

She took a step back to keep herself from catapulting herself at him. Or was it to give her a better running start?

"We'd better get up there." She winced at her nervous giggle. "We wouldn't want to take up Aunty Vida's free time."

Two steps, and he was within reach. "To be honest, all I want to do is kiss you again."

The flutters in her stomach couldn't be mistaken for hunger. She dropped her gaze to his chest. The same one which had been pressed so firmly against her breasts.

"There's no point."

No longer because of her dissertation. The kiss had disqualified him from including him in the paper. It would be impossible to listen to his voice on the recording of their interview and not remember this encounter. Her work would be filled with bias.

He hooked a finger under her chin and raised it so they were once again eye to eye. No hiding from him.

"Why not? I like you. And I know you like me." One corner of his mouth rose. "You're bad at hiding it. I can see it in your expressive eyes."

Once again caught up in a haze of need, she fought it and removed herself from temptation.

"Deola aside." No, she wouldn't let that issue go. "We're too different."

He cocked his head as his gaze remained steady. "How can you tell? We've only had a couple of days to get to know each other, and most of that time was spent working. I want the chance to acquaint ourselves. Obviously, our bodies know what they want."

Even then, her core throbbed with the desire to be with him. Why was she fighting it so hard? What was she afraid of? Would it be so bad to learn more about him?

"How about if we take things slow?" he offered.

A corner of her mouth tucked between her teeth, she narrowed her eyes to study him. "What do you mean?"

"We go on dates. Chat on the phone. See how things go between us. Just as long as you don't close me out." He sighed as if the truth weighed on him. "I like talking with you, Lamisi. You're interesting and real. When you laugh, it makes my heart do somersaults, and all I want to do is make it happen again. And again. I like seeing you happy, and I'd appreciate the chance to understand you better. And to have you do the same with me."

The man had a way with words, but then after falling in love with his lyrics, she already knew that.

"Can you guarantee that you'll keep me out of the media?"

He shook his head in outright refusal. "Are you kidding? After catching this small glimpse of who you are, all I want to do is show you off to the world. You're amazing. We can keep our personal lives as private as possible, but I can't hide you. It would be like concealing a masterpiece of artwork when all it longs for is to be appreciated. Impossible."

She got lightheaded with the pleasure his declaration induced. Who could say no? Certainly not her. "I can accept slow."

He lifted her. Feet dangling, arms clutching him while she giggled, he swung her around.

"Slow it is."

CHAPTER NINETEEN

For the solid, down to earth man Blaise considered himself to be, he'd somehow transitioned into light and airy since Lamisi had agreed to date him. Even gravity had released its hold to allow him to float. At least in his mind. Magnificent sensations bemused him, eliciting fresh songs that he took the time to jot down when they came to him.

What had happened in the studio with Lamisi before lunch had blown him away. Their honest conversation had changed everything between them. They'd been on fire. From her skittishness, he got the sense that ketchup from a freshly opened bottle would get to its destination long before their relationship got beyond the friendship level.

What was she afraid of? Had someone hurt her?

He'd discover and eradicate her uncertainty. At least, she hadn't shied away from the chance to get to know him.

If only he could use his power of persuasion to influence her in speaking French with him. "Your garden is peaceful and lush."

He snapped out of his thoughts as Lamisi's sweet voice brought him back to the outdoor sanctuary she'd lead him to after lunch.

"Thanks. Being out here gets my creative juices flowing."

She plucked a leaf from a plant next to her when they settled on the wooden bench. "Let's hope it has an impact on your French. Since I'm stuck with you after Precious and Amadu's temper tantrum when I told them we'd leave, we'll try again."

The glimmer in her eyes and the slight upward lift of her lips softened her words.

Did going slow mean he couldn't lean in and kiss her cheek at random moments when he found her adorable? Only one way to find out, so he brushed his lips along her soft skin.

She smiled and touched her fingertips to her face. "What was that for?"

"Because you're beautiful."

A snort wasn't what he'd expected.

"You're going to have to tone it down with the flattery. I know who I am."

Her denial hit harder than a punch to his solar plexus, knocking the wind out of him. He lifted her hand and placed it over his chest.

"I'm not one to flatter anyone, Lamisi. What I mean, I say. Who you think you are and who I see you as seem to be two different people. Your eyes draw me in the same way looking at the ocean does, deep and unfathomable, yet gorgeous to behold. Your nose—"

She waved her free hand in front of his face and sniffled. "That's enough. I don't want to cry in front of you again."

He rested his forehead against hers. "These are tears of …"

"Overwhelm and happiness that you think I'm beautiful when there are gorgeous women who—"

He cancelled the rest of her words with a quick kiss to the lips. He pulled back so she could see the sincerity he presented.

"Don't compare yourself to anyone else. You are gorgeous, intelligent, witty, strong, and all other sorts of things that I can't wait to find out about. I'm not trying to drive you away, but I know for a fact that you can get someone better than me. I just happened to find you first."

"I doubt that. You're pretty impressive."

He rolled his eyes. "Now who's being charming?"

She giggled and shocked him by tapping her finger on the tip of his nose.

"Do you want to practice your French or not?"

"Not." He laughed. "Let's do it."

"Okay. This time, we'll start saying the words instead of singing them."

As ready as a star pupil wanting to please his teacher, he nodded and waited for her to present the words.

"*S'il te plaît, ne me casse pas les oreilles.*"

"What did you say? I understood please." He pulled at her earlobe. "And ears."

"I said, please don't make my ears bleed."

He laughed. "So that's how it is? I see."

"*Oui.*"

She repeated the sentence.

He mimicked her words.

"Again," she ordered.

Her mouth broadened into a smile after the tenth round of say and repeat.

"That last time sounded just like yours."

She waved her hands like a football match referee calling for the stop of play. "Not at all. It was terrible, but I now understand your problem. You're trying to speak like we do Hausa or even Twi."

"I don't understand."

"French is a soft language. If you don't produce the r's in the back of your throat as if you're rolling it, it will sound flat. And you need to keep your mouth small when you say the vowels."

"I still don't get it."

In her enthusiasm to get her point across, she grabbed his arm. The tingles from her touch distracted him.

"Ewe! To my ear, French sounds more like the language of the Volta Region than any of our other language in Ghana. At least the ones I've heard." Narrowed eyes focused on him. "I've only heard you sing in Ewe once. Do you speak it?"

"As if I was born in Kpando. That's what I spoke with the tour guide on Mt. Afadjato."

She grunted. "I must've missed it when I was trying not to die."

"You made it. At least, you can claim that as your badge of honour."

The removal of her hands left his skin cool. He preferred her warmth, so he entwined their fingers.

Her hand stayed in place. A good sign.

"Say something in Ewe."

He obliged.

"You are a lovely woman who I could stare at all day." He stroked the back of his fingers down her cheek. "Your skin is as soft as the petals of an orchid."

Unable to stop the draw pulsing between them, he brushed his lips against hers and let his breath fan them as he continued in Ewe. "And your mouth causes me to lose concentration and focus on the pleasure of tasting you."

She squirmed out of his arms after her telling shiver and placed both hands against the sides of her face.

"Yeah. Well … Um." She shuddered out a long breath. "Your Ewe is perfect. And …" She shifted her eyes to the side and then returned them back to his. "Thank you for the compliments."

Amadu's blessed presence in the car on the way home prevented Precious from talking about what she'd witnessed in the studio. Her grin hadn't faded for the whole ride. Amadu had inquired about the lunatic expression, but neither of them had explained.

"Tomorrow. Meet me at *The Cake Boutique* at four," were Precious' parting words when getting out of the car. No option to decline.

The next day, Lamisi adjusted herself on the turquoise seat cushions before taking a sip of the cookie dough and brownie milkshake. None of it made it to her mouth as she drew in her cheeks to suck harder. Giving up, she went into the shop and requested a spoon for the viscous drink.

In the minute it took her to get back to their table, Precious had finished her caramel cupcake.

"Mmm hmm," Precious hummed as she chewed.

Lamisi's eyes drifted closed as the sweet spoonful of milkshake hit her tongue. Precious had made the right call to meet there. It'd been a long time since they'd gotten hyped up on sugar together.

Her phone rang. An unknown number flashed on her screen even through the TrueCaller identifier. Since it could be her supervisor, she picked the call. "Hello."

"Lamisi Imoro?" the feminine voice asked in a harsh tone.

When would people learn basic phone etiquette? "Who is this?"

"Don't worry about it. Are you Lamisi Imoro? Never mind. I know you are. My sources are never wrong."

Sources? She sat up straighter. Could this be related to the heavy breathing calls she'd been receiving? Refusing to confirm the caller's suspicions, she repeated in a sterner voice, "Who is this?"

"All you need to know is that if you keep seeing my man, I'll make your life miserable."

What the hell?

"I have no idea who you are or what you're talking about?"

Precious raised her brows.

"Don't play dumb. You know exactly who I'm talking about. I'm tired of your nasty home-wrecking behaviour. I won't have it. Leave him alone, or completing your dissertation on time, if at all, will be the least of your worries."

Before she could respond to the threat, the line went dead.

Not one to tolerate nonsense, Lamisi called the person back. Beeping sounded before an operator informed her of the number being out of service. She tried once more and got the same response.

She glared at her phone wondering what had just happened.

Her heart beat loud and fast in her ears. Hands trembling, she placed the phone on the table. "That was odd."

"What's going on?"

She relayed the conversation word for word. "I have no idea who she was talking about."

"Could her man be Blaise?"

Lamisi discounted him after the discussion they'd had. She'd believed him when he said he wasn't seeing anyone. "She called me a home-wrecker. I figure the guy is married. Besides, we only just met up again, so no one would ever connect us. Her mention of my dissertation makes me wonder if it's about a guy I assisted with a postgrad course last semester."

"Could be," Precious said with a single shoulder shrug. "Or the woman's man is cheating on her with someone else and she thinks it's you." She leaned in. "Is it you?"

"No," Lamisi growled out.

Her friend laughed. "I didn't think so. You're too much of a stickler for the rules to get involved with your students."

"You're right about that. Plus I had negative zero interest in any of them."

"Doesn't mean they didn't have any in you. And what about your co-workers?"

Lamisi ate her milkshake as she pondered the phone conversation. Could it be a colleague? She rarely engaged with anyone outside of discussing work. Minding her own business was her main priority.

Precious ignored the strawberry cupcake on her plate. "Tell me about what happened with Blaise."

The hairs on her arms rose with exhilaration at the mention of his name. "We kissed."

"I saw that part. Good thing the air conditioner was on because you two would've driven us out with the heat you were generating."

Lamisi shook her head. "It wasn't that dramatic."

"Huh. Your leg was curled around him, Lamisi. And don't think I didn't see where his hands had landed." Precious giggled. "Who knows what piece of furniture might have gotten broken with your activities if I hadn't come in when I did."

She scooped a spoonful of the chilled dessert into her mouth to help cool her embarrassment.

"You know I'm not judging you. In my opinion, you're way overdue for romance. And from what I've learned about Blaise, he's a good guy." She rested her elbows on the table. "What shocked me was that it happened so quickly. One minute, I was harassing you to call him and you're sticking to your guns. The next, you're slathered on him like Nutella on bread."

Lamisi confessed everything that had gone down in the recording studio, including the suggestion to travel with him to Côte d'Ivoire and how she'd been willing to accept his offer of taking things slowly.

"Slow?" Precious screeched. "You two?" She swiped her hands through the air. "No. Never. Not at all. What made you agree to that? Even the hug you guys shared when we left his place sparked up the room. I had to hold Amadu back from flinging you two apart."

Lamisi's leg jiggled under the table as she breathed out through palms cupped over her nose and mouth. Admission time. "He scares me."

Precious tipped her head to the side. "How?"

"He seems too perfect, you know? Plus he's a star who's accustomed to dating stunning, glamorous women. Not someone simple like me." She stirred the spoon in the milkshake, remembering how uncomfortable she'd become when he'd told her about how he saw her. She longed to exemplify the woman he'd described. "Even though I believe him about Deola, I still get a sense that there's more to the story than he's telling me."

"First of all, don't downplay yourself. You're a beautiful, intelligent woman. And you have excellent taste in friends. That says a whole lot about how fabulous you are."

Lamisi chuckled. No one could ever knock down Precious's self-esteem. Her name ensured it.

"You're like a superhero with all the languages you speak and understand. It's not a gift anyone else I've ever met possesses. And you're helping him by using it. Didn't you say that his French is a little better because of how you compared it to Ewe? Who else would've been able to do that? Your skills are saving his musical behind."

Lamisi knew better, but kept her mouth shut. The man was determined, and he would've gotten the work done. It just happened that she'd been around to help him.

She chewed on a chunk of brownie from the milkshake.

"You forget that I've known you forever. He's not like any of your exes." Precious held up a hand when Lamisi opened her mouth to speak. "Those guys who cheated on you were useless scum. They didn't deserve you, and I could see it from miles away. You know me, though. Live and let live."

Lamisi cranked up a brow. "Is that what you were doing when you told me to dump the military man?"

Precious held a palm to her chest. "In my defence, that was the first and only guy I mentioned was bad for you."

Her friend's memory must be slipping with age. "What about the teacher? You butt your nose into every relationship I have. Live and let live, my ass."

"That's neither here nor there. You have to admit that I was right."

The reluctant grunt sounded as her answer. Her friend knew her too well.

"Lamisi, you can't stop dating because you think a man *might* cheat on you. You've declined every guy who's asked you out in the past year."

The go-to excuse came to her lips. "I've been busy with my doctorate."

"You realize who you're talking to, right? That won't fly with me."

She was glad she had someone to hold her accountable.

Precious peeled the paper from her remaining cupcake and took a bite.

"So good," she mumbled around the confection. "Can I make a suggestion?"

As if anything Lamisi said would stop the outspoken woman. "Go ahead."

"You getting your PhD is like me receiving one, too. That's how invested I am in your success. You're too efficient for even me sometimes. I know your schedule of progress. Take him up on his offer to go to Côte d'Ivoire. You'll have a rested brain to tackle the last leg of your research. Spending time alone with him will be good for both of you."

Lamisi blinked several times. "What?"

"I'm not saying you should sleep with him." Precious winked. "Not saying you shouldn't, either."

"Oh my goodness!"

"I want you to loosen up and have a good time. Get to know him on a level you wouldn't while on home turf. I'm sure he's not as well-known there, so you'll be able to roam without worrying about him getting recognized like he would here."

She had a point.

"You'll get to visit Melanie and her family in Abidjan like you've been promising to do for years."

A smile crept onto her face at the mention of their mutual friend.

"And you can stay in the hotel of your choosing. I'd go for one with five stars myself. Take in a couple of concerts so he can get a better ear for the music. You need the break. The tail end of this dissertation has been stressing you out, which has been stressing me. We both need you to go away on vacation and relax."

They broke out laughing.

"He's a good guy, and you can glam up like the best of them when you want to. Give him a chance."

"Are you done with the lecture, Professor Romance?"

She held up a finger. "Just one more thing."

After several seconds of silence, Lamisi gave in and asked, "What is it?"

"Listen to your instincts. If you had done that when you first met him, you two would probably be married and pregnant with triplets by now."

Lamisi sucked her teeth at her friend's silliness. Her point was valid, though. Listening to her gut had never steered her wrong. Where her instincts had wanted to get to know him better, fear of sustaining heartache by the man every woman wanted had made her stay away.

From here on in, she'd trust her heart and see what happened. She'd still be cautious, but at least, she'd give him a chance. Hopefully, he wouldn't disappoint her.

CHAPTER TWENTY

The flight landed in Côte d'Ivoire the Thursday after Lamisi had surprised Blaise with the offer of escorting him. She'd reminded him that the cost of the venture would be on him. Yet, she'd taken things in hand by organizing the flight and the hotel.

He'd appreciated her consulting with him before confirming any bookings. As if they were a team in making the decisions.

"I'm only here for the weekend," she'd told him. "That's enough for you to get accustomed to the place so you'll be comfortable staying longer if you want to. I think the baptism by fire will allow you to acquire an accent that won't cause your French listeners to curse you out for defiling their language."

He'd laughed at her joke while understanding its seriousness. His career depended on this excursion. At least Armand, his French tutor, had told him he'd been impressed by his improved intonation during their sessions.

In the taxi, on the way to their hotel, Blaise took in the city. He hadn't expected it to be so advanced. After the country's civil wars, he was glad to see that the political strife they'd experienced hadn't damaged too much of the infrastructure, at least in Abidjan.

War could never rival the benefits of peace.

He pulled out his phone and recorded the words. He'd flesh out the song later. In the meantime, he listened to the conversation between Lamisi and the driver like she'd suggested. Understanding everything was impossible, but he wasn't completely lost, either. When he joined in, the driver smiled while Lamisi leaned close and gently corrected him with a whisper.

Tingles coursed from the top of his head down his spine every time it happened. He resisted the temptation of drawing her to his side and seducing her with words that would have her dropping her guard and initiating kisses.

He'd honour their agreement of taking things slow. It was probably better. His parents wouldn't approve of her being a Christian. This had become blaringly clear when he'd presented such a prospect to his mother the other day. She hadn't been happy.

Maybe it would be better if he backed off. An impossible concept to sell to his racing heart when he looked at her. He'd just have to see how things went. Lamisi didn't seem disturbed by him being a Muslim. Maybe she'd be willing to convert before they got married.

Whoa. They hadn't known each other for a month, and he was thinking of marriage? Way too soon.

He shook his head and returned his attention to the view outside the window. This street in Abidjan reminded him of Accra with the hawkers walking amongst the vehicles and selling their wares as they sat in traffic. He looked forward to playing the role of a proper tourist.

The hotel Lamisi had chosen sat in the heart of the city.

The stylish lobby of the multi-story building impressed him—the kind of place that charged in US dollars instead of the local currency of franc.

Having been in his home and learning how much he enjoyed the comforts of life, she'd decided that only the best would do. Yet another positive quality about her. They kept adding up.

After getting settled into their rooms, they met in the hallway thirty minutes later.

"Where are we off to?" he asked as the elevator carried them to the lobby.

"To visit my friend and her family. I haven't seen her in ages. And it will give you a chance to listen and practice in a comfortable setting."

He could handle that. An intimate group to practice with would be better than speaking in front of strangers.

They got into a taxi waiting at the front of the hotel. Lamisi gave the address. The driver programmed it into his phone and then took off.

She turned to Blaise with the biggest smile on her face. "Repeat after me. *J'adore parler français. C'est une langue tellement expressive.*"

He did it ... only to have the driver glance at him in the rear-view mirror and chuckle. He knew it wasn't the statement he'd repeated about him liking to speak French because it was such an expressive language.

The driver hadn't blinked when Lamisi had said it.

She slipped her hand into his and squeezed. "Don't mind him. You really are getting better," she proclaimed.

He squeezed back, letting the ego that had gotten kicked in the teeth recover as he relaxed in her reassurance.

◆◆◆

After years of promising to visit her friend, Lamisi had finally ended up on her doorstep in Côte d'Ivoire. All because of Blaise.

The conversation with Precious had freed up whatever had bound her. She'd determined herself as worthy of everything and everyone she desired, including the soon-to-be King of Francohip. Not all men were the same. She needed to keep that on a loop in her mind, and everything would work out.

Melanie's screams when she opened the door brought out Lamisi's own squeals as they hugged.

The French flowed fast and furious as the world dropped away.

"It's so good to see you again. Why did it take you so long to get here?" Melanie asked as she held both of Lamisi's hands and cut off the circulation to her fingers.

"I could ask the same." Lamisi pushed her bottom lip out into a deep pout. "When was the last time you stepped foot in Ghana to visit me?"

"Oh, no, my friend, you will not turn the tables. All blame goes to you."

Lamisi giggled.

"It's so good to see you. You look magnificent." Her gaze fell to Melanie's pregnant belly and then up to her rich dark brown skin. "You're glowing."

Melanie turned in a circle.

"Thank you. My baby is fantastic. I feel good most of the time, and I only have two more months to go." She rubbed her abdomen. "I can't wait to meet her."

"Me, too."

A clearing of the throat brought the women's attention to the entrance.

Two pair of eyes stared at the chocolate-skinned, tall, athletic, heart-wrenchingly handsome man flashing his gleaming teeth at them.

Lamisi took the couple of steps to reach him and rested a hand on his arm.

"Blaise Ayoma, this is my good friend, Melanie Ettien."

The two shook hands.

"It's a pleasure to meet you, Melanie," Blaise said in French.

At least, it no longer made Lamisi's eye twitch.

Melanie smiled when she responded in her colonial language. "You, too."

Her gaze didn't wander from Blaise's face for several seconds as her brows creased together.

An unfamiliar sense of possessiveness drove Lamisi to lean in close enough to him so their arms touched. She ignored him when, from her peripheral vision, she noticed him glance down at her.

Melanie shook her head and blinked.

"Please," she said in English. "Pardon me for staring. It's just that you look familiar." And then, her eyes lit up, and she snapped her fingers with excitement. "Oh, my. You're the Ghanaian hiplife artist Bizzy."

She reached out and took his hand, shaking it so hard that the strong man's body vibrated. "My friends won't believe this."

"How about a picture for proof?"

"Okay." Melanie picked up her phone from the table, tapped the screen a few times, and thrust it at Lamisi.

Amused, Lamisi took the photos. So much for him not being recognized in Côte d'Ivoire. "It seems your reach is farther than you thought."

"I'm glad to hear it," he said.

Melanie touched the hair she'd bunched into a loose bun and looked down at herself. Then she turned hot eyes in Lamisi's direction. "*Oh mon Dieu, Lamisi. Pourquoi ne m'as-tu pas dit que tu amenais quelqu'un? Regarde-moi, je suis dans un piteux état.*"

"On the contrary." He said in the sexy voice that held a catch of breath. "You're as far from a mess as can be. You're radiant," he replied in English.

Lamisi laughed at her friend's gaping mouth. "He understands some French. He doesn't speak it as well as he should … yet. That's why we're here. And of course, to visit you."

"Yes." The English had returned. "You are more than welcome. Bizzy, where are my manners? Have a seat."

"Please, call me Blaise."

Melanie nodded with an unrelenting grin. "Blaise."

They settled in the living room of the cute single-story home.

"Excuse me while I bring you some water."

Hospitality, just like in Ghana, reigned with their neighbouring country. No one came into their home without receiving water. The choice was up to the guest whether they'd drink it or not, but it was always presented.

"Melanie is a bit vain. I'm shocked she agreed to the picture. In her excitement, she must've forgotten that she wasn't dressed to the nines," Lamisi gossiped. "I'm sure she'll return in a floor-length sparkly evening gown and a fully made-up face."

Blaise laughed. "I can't believe she recognized me."

"Me, neither. Considering she spent her senior high school years in Ghana, maybe she follows the music."

She shrugged to downplay it, the selfish part of her not wanting him to be famous here. A nice, normal time of getting to know each other would suit her better.

"It would be helpful if I had a fan base here. It'd make breaking into their music scene easier."

She waved down a hand. "Don't worry, with the songs you've created, you'll have no difficulty getting the people of this, and all the other Francophone countries, to love you."

His eyes softened as he slid closer to her. The kiss on her cheek was unexpected. Heat flushed her face.

"What was that for?" One day, she would become accustomed to his random acts of affection rather than questioning it.

He caught her fingers in his. "I appreciate your support. Not once have you told me I couldn't make it. Or told me I should give up."

She hadn't been perfect. "I presented it as an option."

"As part of the truth I needed to acknowledge because you were right about me sucking at French. But then, you helped me."

He kissed the back of her hand.

A spiral of warmth settled in her chest.

"And now, you're spending time you could be using to work on your dissertation to help me even more. I can't express how much I appreciate it."

She wasn't as altruistic as he made her out to be. Should she tell him about the need she had to get to know him? The part about gaining a temporary break from school to relax and refresh her mind? A mini vacation that he was privileged to pay for?

She didn't get the chance. Her mouth was silenced when his lips brushed against hers, reminding her of their first kiss. If she were going to start something with him, she may as well be completely honest, at least physically.

She reached her free palm up and grazed his cheek as he dove back in. His lips, full yet firm, nibbled hers. Demanding, yet yielding. She could kiss him for the rest of the time they had together, but the throbbing at her core told her it would lead to more than she was ready for.

The sound of something banging pulled her out of the magical experience of his touch.

Prying her eyes open, Lamisi held back any sense of awkwardness as Melanie hovered above them holding a tray with a large bottle of water and two glasses beside it.

The woman had changed into a red sequined top that stretched over her extended belly, a black skirt that flirted with her knees, and heels that her doctor would most likely warn her against wearing in her condition. And yes, the makeup was present and in full force.

Holding in her laughter to the point where she thought she'd burst a major blood vessel, Lamisi stood and hugged her friend. It was nice to know that while Blaise was disrupting her world, some things never changed.

CHAPTER TWENTY-ONE

Blaise and Lamisi had spent the taxi ride back to the hotel in silence. He figured she was all talked-out after the hours spent with her friend. He'd intermittently watched French-speaking television shows and listened to their conversation. Most of both had been lost on him.

They hopped out of the taxi at their temporary residence.

"Thanks for taking me to meet Melanie," he said when they met up on the sidewalk. "I feel like I intruded on your time with your friend."

"No worries. We talk all the time on the phone. It was just a matter of seeing her after so long that hit us."

He rubbed his stomach. "She didn't have to feed us so much."

"That would be like telling Aunty Vida not to do the same. Melanie is one of the most gracious people I've ever known. You'll never leave her home without needing to spend the night, or at least take a nap, because you're so stuffed." She winked at him. "I saw you dozing for a few minutes there."

"Guilty. I still need to burn off some of the food. Want to take a walk?"

"Sure."

The sun was starting to sink in the sky, casting a golden pink light to view their surroundings. Abidjan reminded him of the main areas of Accra with the human and vehicular traffic trying to get home after a long day.

Competing with restaurants, vendors sold food at the roadside. Grilled fish and fried plantain scented the air. Instead of the hot kenkey made with corn dough that was an evening staple at home, the residents here preferred attiéké.

He'd been wary of the pellet-like food made from cassava when Melanie had presented it to them after they'd washed their hands. It had been complemented with fried fish and a concoction created from peppers, onions, tomatoes, oil, and spices.

He'd watched how the ladies ate. Just like with many foods in Ghana, no utensils were necessary. He'd liked the mild flavour of the steamed cassava and hadn't refused when Melanie had offered more.

Music came from Lamisi's bag. She dug through it and pulled out her cell phone. Her lips flattened into a tight line as she slammed her finger into the face of the screen, making the ringtone stop.

"Who was that?"

Did he have a right to ask? The fact that the call had irked her dropped a boulder of dread in his stomach.

She flicked a hand. "Someone calling from an unknown number. I've blocked it every single time, but she calls from different lines because it always comes through."

The hairs on the back of his neck stood as the skin of his scalp tightened. Was he just feeling her own irritation? He'd always been sensitive, but never this empathetic. "Maybe they're coming from different people."

"I doubt it. I answered once, and the woman threatened me. I'm pretty sure she was crazy because I had no idea what she was talking about. Ever since then, I don't pick up unknown calls."

His agitation heightened as thoughts of Deola pinged across his brain. It couldn't be her. As an unknown in the entertainment world, Lamisi was off everyone's radar. He tamed the idea of Deola's involvement. It seemed unlikely.

The mystery still needed to be solved.

"What did she accuse you of?"

"It doesn't matter because it isn't true." She crossed her arms over her chest with a definitive nod. "I don't want to talk about it anymore. I'm sure she'll get tired of playing her idiotic games if I don't indulge her. She'll realize the truth of her mistake soon enough."

The protector in him roared inside with the need to take care of her problem. Find a solution that wouldn't leave her stressed each time her phone rang. The independent woman had made up her mind to handle it her way, and he'd respect her decision even if he didn't like it.

The least he could do was offer his assistance. "Let me know if you need me to do anything. I'm always willing to help."

"Thanks."

He budged her shoulder with his. "You're saving my career. I'm in your debt."

"Language is my life. It's my pleasure to assist."

"Thanks for the lesson you had Melanie give me on my French. I think it helped."

She smiled up at him. "With each encounter, you're improving. Soon, you'll sound like a local."

Her encouragement swelled his heart. "I hope so. By the way, I don't mind if you ditch me to spend time with Melanie. I didn't realize that coming here would be so much like Accra. Now I know and can handle it. You don't need to be my guardian."

"You're stuck with me and my tutorials, Bizzy. Melanie and her husband are travelling to visit her parents in Lakota early tomorrow and will return on Sunday. We'll stop by before our flight back to Accra."

"I don't mind." He downplayed his excitement at being able to spend time with her. "What do you have planned for us?"

"I read somewhere that you're Muslim. If you agree, since tomorrow's Friday, I thought we'd attend *ṣalāt al-jum'ah* at the Mosque of Plataea. It's a gorgeous structure."

"Technically, yes, I am, but not practicing," he answered. "Well, other than not eating pork or drinking alcohol. Along with the basic principle of respect ingrained within the religion, I'm not a practitioner."

"Oh." The sides of her mouth drooped. "I didn't know that."

At least, he'd been able to keep one thing away from the public.

His heart raced as a revelation clicked. He stopped walking to look at her in the light transitioning from natural to artificial. Someone behind them almost rammed into him. He was happy to have recognized the insult thrown at him in French.

Blaise pulled Lamisi closer to the building they'd stopped near. "You said we'd attend service there. Is that for my benefit?"

She blinked up at him. "I may not be the most devout Muslim, but I like to attend *jum'ah* every once in a while."

His legs threatened to buckle. The one thing he'd worried about had been a moot point. Better to clarify just in case his stomach using up most of his blood in food digestion had left him delusional.

"Are you a Muslim?"

"Yes."

Amazed, it took him a beat to speak again. "How? Why?"

She shrugged. "It's the religion I identify with most. My parents raised us as Christian, but they encouraged us to explore and find our own spirituality. My mother was a Muslim who chose Christianity when she married my father."

"Why did you pick Islam over Christianity?"

"I didn't. Not really." She spread her arms out wide and formed a circle with them by linking her hands. "It's all the same thing. The same God with different names and too many misunderstandings between the people who practice their faiths to let them comprehend this."

He nodded in complete agreement. "Even within religions, there are differences and disagreements."

"Exactly. It would be better for the world if we realized that we're all one."

She'd spoken the words he'd been trying to live all his life. "True."

"I've practiced as many religions as I could discover. Islam resonated within me." She held a palm towards him as if to halt him from speaking. "I'll be the first to admit that it's not perfect. After all, it's a religion. But I like the way it respects the beliefs of others because Allah is the God of us all."

She lifted a slim shoulder and let it drop. "It's what I've been practicing ever since. Perhaps not as well as I should, but I try. Sometimes—"

Blaise leaned over and kissed her hard on the lips. Even that brief touch stirred a yearning in his chest. He wanted more, but held back.

The country had been colonized by the French, but Africans in general tended to be conservative. Kissing in public, especially the way he longed to delve into the warmth of her mouth, would be frowned upon.

Her tongue flicked out and licked her lips, keeping his attention there. Her gaze flittered to their environment before returning to his eyes. "Why'd you kiss me?"

Because you're extraordinary in every conceivable way and it hurts my muscles to restrain myself from touching you.

"It's a celebration of you being Muslim."

One more reason to appreciate that they might belong together. They'd only know for sure with time, but so far, he could envision being with her long term.

Now to make her see it.

CHAPTER TWENTY-TWO

The colossal mosque held a magnificent glory that Lamisi had never experienced before in a place of worship. Inside and out. Did Blaise being by her side before they'd split into their designated male and female areas have anything to do how her spirit had lifted with excitement?

She stepped out of the women's area of the mosque feeling fulfilled and connected to Allah and his creation. It took a while for her to catch sight of Blaise's wide-shouldered stance, towering height, chocolate skin, and defined features among the exodus of males. Her breathing hitched when he came into view. Stunning.

His dark eyes searched the female portion of the crowd. When his gaze met hers and he smiled, time stood still. Her heart threatened to lurch out of her chest with the force of its beats. She took her time descending on shaky legs to meet him at the bottom of the stairs.

"Hi," she managed to get out in a low, breathy voice, caught up in the fact that this man wanted to be with her.

"Hey. How was the service?"

"I loved it. Almost makes me want to become completely devout." She held up a finger knowing it would never happen. She enjoyed spirituality more than the religious aspect. "Almost."

He chuckled.

"I understand what you mean. The place is spectacular. The energy in the atmosphere transcended me to a state of being ethereal." He held out his hand and it quivered. "Even now, I'm having trouble acclimating to my body."

He'd expressed her sentiment in such an articulate manner. If they weren't at a mosque, she'd be the one to plant a kiss on him. "Me, too."

Ready to leave the space where people continued to flow around them, she stepped to the side and bumped into someone.

Lamisi recognized the man's Arabic roots when she looked at him.

"*As-salāmu'alaykum. Ana asfeh.*" She greeted in Arabic and then apologized.

The man stopped and cocked his head before returning her greeting of peace. "*Wa'aleikum salaam Wa-rahmatullahi wa-barakatuh.*"

He then asked if she spoke Arabic.

"Yes, I do," she responded in his language and watched as his bearded face smiled. Before he could ask her any further questions, she added, "One of my former colleagues in Ghana was Lebanese. When we became friends, I picked up her language."

The handsome man, somewhere in his early thirties, stepped closer. Blaise's heat touched her from behind.

If the man's wide eyes were any indication, he was impressed. "You learned Arabic by ear?"

"Yes. Languages are a gift of mine."

"No matter what else you may speak, Allah has blessed you abundantly with the language of Arabic."

Laughter sprinkled out of her.

"I see." She continued the conversation in his language. "My friend told me something similar."

Blaise cupped a hand over her elbow. A show of possessiveness that elicited a bubbling giddiness in her chest.

She glanced up at him. His narrowed eyes and snarled upper lip were directed at the stranger.

"We should get going," Blaise said in English, his voice deeper than normal.

She recognized jealousy when she saw it. She probably shouldn't be so happy about it, but when had anyone cared about another man's response to her? Never.

"It was nice speaking with you," she said in English to keep Blaise in the conversation.

The man's eyes rose to Blaise's face, and he stepped back with a nod. "*Etsharafna, ma' el salameh.*"

With a contagious grin and a lift of his hand, he left.

Blaise stalked the guy with his eyes. "What did he just say?"

She shrugged to keep the situation light while her insides danced. "That I'm the most intriguing woman he's ever met, and he wished my overbearing bodyguard weren't around to block his chances."

He stepped closer, towering. "He didn't say all of that."

"The language is word efficient." She took off down the street towards the hotel with her hijab still covering her head as the mosque mandated for women to worship. She needed to change out of her long-sleeved top and ankle-length skirt into something more heat-friendly.

He strode down the street with her. "You can stop playing now. What did he say?"

"He told me it was nice talking with me and that I should take care."

"Huh. On the mountain, you told me that you speak eight languages, but what are they? I don't want to be shocked the next time one comes flying out of your mouth."

She chuckled. "Let's see. I'll count Twi and Fante as one because they're both Akan. English, French, Hausa as you very well know, Ewe—which I picked up from Precious, Ga which is my father's tribe, Dagbani, from my mother's people, and Arabic."

No longer afraid to boast for fear of overwhelming him, she smirked. "I understand more languages than I speak, so please don't think you can talk about me in front of my face and get away with it."

His shoulders shook with his booming laugh. "I'm sure that even if I created my own language, you'd be able to understand. You have an uncanny way of reading people, not just understanding what they say."

She stared at him in wide-eyed awe. He'd noticed that about her? What else had he gleaned? Maybe that she was still scared about getting involved with him although she thought she might almost be ready.

Shaking fears from the past proved harder than people who said, "Get over it," made it out to be.

"What if I told you to your face that I find you to be incredible?" he said in Hausa. The language streamed beautifully and resonated within her. "From what I've encountered and seen of you, you're generous with your time and soft-hearted towards those you love. You smile freely at people you don't know, which I'm sure brightens their day as much as it does mine." He tapped the centre of his chest. "It has the ability to make my heart flutter."

She bowed her head, cheeks bunched with her grin. The man was too much. No one other than him had ever spoken to her in such a poetic manner before.

Not the time to act shy. Raising her head, she pulled her shoulders back and looked up into his eyes. “Thank you.”

“My pleasure.”

They reached the hotel a few minutes later.

“After I change, I thought we’d get something to eat. Melanie recommended a few places in the same area. We could check them out and see which one is the best.”

“Cool.”

They headed up to their rooms. At their doors, Blaise reached out for her and pulled her into a hug. She wound her arms around him and leaned her head against the strength of his shoulder.

Hadn’t she wanted this for the past week? The security of being in a man’s arms thrilled her. She willed him to hold her for the rest of the trip. For the rest of her life.

She snapped her eyes open as terror clawed at her. Thoughts of the future with someone she was still getting to know weren’t supposed to be in her scope of thought. Maybe heat had gotten trapped in her skull from wearing the hijab. She released him, and he followed suit.

The kiss to her cheek eased her trepidation. Moments like this made her feel as if he cared and could also see them progressing through life together. If she were more confident, she’d capture his lips and kiss him as if he were the last thing her mouth would ever devour.

He pulled away, leaving her body to cool.

“Whenever you’re ready,” he whispered. “I’m here.”

She didn’t need to ask what he was referring to. Taking things to another level would require more than a few days of interacting. The prickly warmth of her skin at his offer told her differently.

Listening to her body would make things complicated when she wanted simplicity.

Too late.

CHAPTER TWENTY-THREE

Lamisi flopped across her hotel room bed at the early hour of nine p.m. and let out a huge yawn. The day spent with Blaise had been perfect. Not only did the locals no longer do a double-take and snicker when he spoke their language, but they'd had fun.

Blaise's talent wasn't limited to constructing song lyrics. Jokes also featured on his specialty list.

A day of exploring Abidjan had included a beautiful walk on the beach and a dinner of fresh grilled red snapper paired with her now favourite attiéké. She hadn't wanted the day to end. To be apart from him.

Serious, PhD-oriented Lamisi disappeared when they were together, replaced by the giggly teenager she'd once been. Anyone who knew her would be surprised at how laidback she was when with Blaise.

It must be the fact that he didn't seem to take much seriously. Granted, he was a focused man and knew how to handle issues. Yet, his main priority seemed to enjoy life.

"What's the point of worrying when it won't solve anything? Live in the here and now. The rest will take care of itself when the time comes."

He'd spoken without diverting his gaze from the brilliant clarity of the sea when she had complained about how much more work she still had to do on her dissertation.

A philosophy she could totally get with. And would. Maybe even when he wasn't around.

The sparks kept passing back and forth with each touch, accidental or otherwise. A delicious warmth had found a new home tucked under her ribs when he gazed into her eyes. She'd focused a lot of her attention on his mouth when he spoke, not only wanting to hear his words, but feel them against her lips. Proof that entering his room tonight when he'd invited her to watch a movie and hang out would've been a bad idea. One that might've led to a physical intimacy she wasn't yet ready for.

She'd barely started to trust him—sleeping with him this early was out of the question. At least, that's what her mind kept reiterating. Her body, on the other hand, wanted to climb all over him and finish what they'd started in the studio last week.

A gentle knock on his door wearing a robe with nothing underneath would lead to an invite inside.

Her core throbbed as her fantasy went into overdrive as she slid her robe down her body so it pooled on the floor before she stripped his clothes off.

She hopped out of bed, clearing her mind of him kissing her into oblivion as his hands roamed over her body, driving her to the pinnacle of need that compounded the one she already had for him.

The water would relax her while washing away the sea salt that the refreshing ocean air had deposited on her skin.

Thirty minutes later, she was sure the residents below her would come up and tell her to cut out the pacing. The activity kept her hands from twisting the metal handle that would release her from the room. She strode the few steps it took to get to the wardrobe cabinet where she'd stored her laptop.

A muffled noise came through the wall on Blaise's side. When his voice got louder, curiosity wriggled under her skin. What had happened to make him sound so upset?

Not my business.

Then why was her ear against the cool painted plaster, being incredibly rude by eavesdropping?

"How did you find out about Lamisi?"

The mention of her name was the sole justification for continuing to listen when she knew better.

"Don't try to change a subject that you brought up, Deola. I asked you a direct question."

She covered her mouth to keep from gasping as her heart clanged against her ribcage. She'd never make a good spy. Why was his *friend* talking about her?

"I told you before that I'm not taking you to the VGMAs. In fact, the way you've been behaving lately, I think we should take a break from our friendship."

A low feminine screech reached through the wall.

"I'm not someone in your command. If you can't respect me and my decision not to get involved with you, then we can't continue as friends. Lamisi has nothing to do with you, so you'd be better off forgetting her name. I'm *not* your man. I never have been and never will be. It's time you understand that."

His voice sounded strained, as if attempting not to let everyone in the hotel know his feelings on the matter.

This time, the pause lasted for much longer than the previous ones. Deola must be having her say. Was she the type of woman who'd beg? If she were anything like Lamisi, she'd let Blaise go.

Then again, he was an extra type of special. Would she fight for him?

She didn't know.

When Blaise finally spoke, his voice was too low for her to hear. Lamisi looked around for anything that would amplify sound. Where was a stethoscope when she needed it?

What was that creaking noise? She leaped away from the wall with her hand on her chest when a door slammed shut.

Okay. The conversation hadn't ended to his satisfaction. Had Deola been convincing enough to retain a position in his life?

And then, a red bulb went off in her head. Was Deola the one stalking her through calls and texts? Had the woman been so threatened by her that she'd stooped so low?

Given the situation, Lamisi smiled. She'd never been anyone's object of envy before. Much less a wealthy, world-famous heiress. She thrust her shoulders back with pride and strutted to the side of the room she should've been on the whole time rather than listening to Blaise's conversation.

Now that she was at least eighty-five percent sure of who'd been behind her stress for the past couple of weeks, it no longer held her captive. She could look at the phone, give the petty woman a millisecond of her time, and then carry on as if it had never happened.

Lamisi would wait Deola out. She'd get tired of playing her petty games.

CHAPTER TWENTY-FOUR

Blaise swayed his upper body to the beat while listening to a zouglou song by an Ivoirian artist that he admired. The lyrics held more meaning as he repeated them as Lamisi had instructed.

So far, their weekend had been the best he'd had in a long while. Being with her was like breathing in the fresh, clean air from his hometown.

Easing her into his more affectionate manner put a strain on him when he wanted to shower her with kisses, random caresses, and words that would melt her resistance. He'd kept things light by brushing her hair off her face when the wind blew as they walked hand in hand on the beach yesterday.

The hug they'd shared at the end of the night before separating to their own rooms had stoked a strong desire to stay by her side. To hold her all night while they talked, nothing more.

He refused to let himself recall how responsive her lips had been the week prior. It would've just driven him insane with a need he couldn't fulfil.

Deola's call last night had perturbed him. She'd been tenacious about attending the music award ceremony together as if he'd never told her they wouldn't. He'd been firm in his rejection. Even though her outrage had vibrated through the phone, he hadn't back-tracked.

And then, she'd mentioned Lamisi by her full name in a casual comment which had aimed to manipulate. His head had nearly exploded with rage when she'd refused to reveal her source. She'd either been having him followed, or one of his boys had betrayed him.

Protecting Lamisi had become his main priority. He'd deal with how Deola had discovered her information later. No longer caring about upsetting the heiress, he'd broken off their friendship.

Or at least tried to. Her tearful pleading had touched his sensitive side.

He'd given her one more chance. Although the woman lived a privileged life, she had few friends, and when her guard was down, came off as lonely.

He'd ended up putting stipulations on their relationship. She wasn't to mention Lamisi. Had to keep things platonic. And there would be absolutely no manipulation.

Thinking back on the conversation, he should've let her drop. If the rumours were correct, Deola's lack of friendships was due to her controlling, vicious, and vindictive nature. He didn't need the hassle.

He'd stormed out of his room to stretch his legs and exhaust his ire with a walk. When he'd returned long after midnight, he'd raised his knuckles to rap on Lamisi's door, but had stopped himself at the last second. His feet had dragged along the carpeted floor to his room.

Now he stood at her door at a reasonable hour, looking to take her out on another tour.

Lamisi swung the panel open wearing a sleeveless pink, blue, and cream-coloured batik print dress that hugged her waist and flowed out over her hips to her knees. She had applied a light layer of makeup that brought out her cheekbones, dark eyes, and full lips.

He leaned against the wall as she stared, hoping he looked cool instead of a man whose knees had just gone weak.

She touched her fingertips to hair she'd pinned away from her face. "What?"

"You look wonderful."

"Thank you. Are you ready to go? I have a full day planned."

No trying to get him to gush over her. No denying her own beauty. Just a confident answer from a strong woman. He looked forward to the experience of falling more in like with her.

After eating breakfast in the hotel restaurant, they went to the local market and interacted with the market women. His ears picked up a lot from the atmosphere. When he repeated snippets of what he had learned to Lamisi, she beamed up at him.

"You sound good."

The feeling of pride would last until he messed up again.

"It's a process," she reassured with a pat on the arm. "Keep trying. I know you'll get it."

The confidence she had in him made him want to succeed for her almost as much as for himself. Once again, he slid down the slippery slope of admiring her even more.

Following the local market, they went to a shopping mall. The interactions with the people in the modern space weren't as frequent, but he did get some practice in.

During their lunch at the food court, they released the student-teacher role, enjoying the meal and each other as they talked about their family and childhood. Many of the stories they told had them laughing to the point of drawing attention from their neighbours.

After one more round through the massive mall to help settle their food, he tugged her to the glass and metal railing where they watched people going about their business. "How about we return to the beach and relax until it's time to head off to visit with Melanie?"

Lamisi shook her head. "Not on the agenda."

He wished he could add some kissing onto the list of things planned to do. He had trouble focusing on anything but her reapplied gloss over such luscious lips.

"Then what is?"

She tipped her head, exposing the side of her neck. He brushed his lips against the area. From the way she leaned into him, she had also forgotten about the public space they were still in.

Blaise flicked his tongue against her soft skin, eliciting a moan from her. He raised his head to find her eyes closed with her mouth slightly parted. He gripped the railing until his palms hurt and faced the other side of the mall to prevent himself from breaking further social norms and kissing her full on the mouth.

His heart slowed to normal as he focused on people-watching.

Lamisi positioned herself to face him head-on. "As much as I'm appreciating the air-conditioning, we should get going."

"Where to?"

She grinned and wiggled her brows. "You'll see."

He appreciated her teasing, but not her announcement. "I'm not a fan of surprises."

"Okay, then let's call this an examination of sorts."

When she took off towards the end of the mall, he stayed in place, watching her hips sway and making the dress flounce around the back of her cinnamon-hued skin.

She glanced over her shoulder to find him observing her. Halting mid-step, she pivoted and returned. "I promise that you'll like it."

"How do you know?"

"A gut feeling. Besides, it's better that you know this about me now."

Interest had him standing at his full height, making her tilt her chin to look into his eyes. "What?"

"When it comes to languages … and one or two other things, I tend to be right all the time."

He smirked, piqued by curiosity. "Is that so?"

"Come with me and see."

The one invitation was all it took to accept her challenge.

CHAPTER TWENTY-FIVE

Lamisi took him to the last place he'd ever expect to end up while in Abidjan. A barber shop.

He ran a hand over the short bush on his head. "I don't need a cut."

"It's not about the haircut. It's about the interaction." Grasping his shoulders with both hands, she caught his gaze. "Your mission is to go in there and speak only French. No other language will be allowed."

"Why a barber shop when we can do it anywhere? What if they butcher my hair?"

Unable to help herself, she reached up and smoothed her fingers over his head. The dark coils sprang under her touch, and he shivered when she caressed the base of his hairline.

What he'd started in the mall lingered, and her neck tingled with the memory of his kiss. His lips the only thing in sight, she stepped closer to diminish the unnecessary gap between them.

The door to the shop opened, letting out raucous laughter from inside.

Disappointed, she hung her head and dragged in a deep breath. She turned to the glass panel to see that men and a couple of women were looking at them, hooting. Head on fire, she dropped her hands to her sides and stepped to the left, out of their view.

Lamisi risked looking up into Blaise's face and found him grinning. She'd met the most irresistible man in the world. Either she learned how to deal with it, or she'd end up falling into their attraction every time they were together. Privacy be damned.

She cleared her throat. "This is where Melanie's husband has been getting his hair cut for the past fifteen years. As you witnessed from the number of people waiting inside, it's a pretty popular place. I called the owner and told them Bizzy would be stopping by for a cut and chat." She flung up a finger. "In French only. The guy said he was a fan of yours. Do you want to disappoint a fan?"

He chuckled. "Since you put it that way …"

"Good. Don't worry. I'm sure they'll take it easy on you. When you're done, we'll head over to see Melanie."

He tugged her deeper into the shadow of the building. Her mouth dried at the passion in his eyes just before he lowered his head to her and slid his lips against her mouth. "When do we get to be alone?"

Lifting her heavy lids, she gazed into his eyes, her mind hazy. "Um."

"Hey, Bizzy."

The familiar voice of the barber shop owner asking if he was going in lulled into her head.

Blaise kept his gaze glued to her for a moment longer before pivoting his head to the left. "*Oui, j'arrive.*"

Lamisi regained strength in her legs and followed him into the shop to observe the magic of black men bonding over the buzz of clippers and snipping scissors.

◆◆◆

Blaise and Lamisi sat side by side in the taxi for the late-night ride back from Melanie's place.

He skimmed a hand over his head. The barber had done as he'd asked and faded him out on the sides. The conversation flying around him at the barbershop had made him laugh so much that he'd forgotten about being self-conscious of his French and had participated when he could. Glimpses of Lamisi grinning as she flipped through a magazine had told him he was doing well.

The guys at the shop had been accommodating and gracious when he'd messed up. They'd stayed for an hour after the owner had removed the cape and dusted off the excess hair because the positive vibes of the place had been conducive to learning.

"Good job today," she said once they'd packed into a taxi to head back to the hotel.

"Thank you. Since it was an exam, what grade will you give me?"

She cocked her head and tapped her chin as if thinking. "An A for effort and being a good sport. And a B minus for your pronunciation."

"I'm impressed with myself. It's better than the F you would've given me last week." He intertwined their fingers. "I couldn't have gotten this far without you, Lamisi. Thank you."

Her grin squeezed his heart.

"Glad I could help."

He heard the residual tension in her voice. She hadn't been herself, at least what he knew of her while they'd visited with Melanie and her husband. Instead of the intense focus she could give to a conversation, she'd seemed side-tracked and a bit jumpy.

"You seemed a little preoccupied with your phone this evening." Blaise broke the comfortable silence. "Is everything okay?"

"Since you asked." With a sigh, she untangled herself from him and pulled her cell from her bag. A couple of screen slides later, she held the device out to him.

"This message slipped through my radar before what I was reading registered."

'I told you to stay away from my man. Since you don't know how to listen, bitch, I'll just have to show you what happens to people who cross me.'

Not believing his eyes, Blaise read the message again before giving her his attention.

Lamisi twisted her hands together. "I've narrowed down my stalker to one person."

Ready to do damage to whoever was causing her such turmoil, he asked, "Who?"

She stared at him in a way that made him question if she thought he was the guilty individual. "Your friend, oil heiress Deola Olajumoke."

He believed her. Deola mentioning Lamisi during their conversation last night gave him no other choice. He rubbed a hand over his face.

"After what I heard you say through the wall last night," she continued, "I don't doubt that it's her."

"What?"

She dropped her gaze. "I didn't mean to eavesdrop, but you were loud at some points."

He had to fix this. "I think you're right. I'll call her and tell her to stop."

Her hysterical laugh drew the driver's attention in the rear-view mirror.

A deep frown replaced her joyless laughter. "Have you heard the same stories about her that I have? Crashing cars while drunk driving and not being punished. Getting people fired from their job because they didn't serve her fast enough? The woman is a holy terror who can get away with anything because her father is a billionaire."

She slumped into the seat. "She's delusional enough to think that you're her man. After what you told me, I know it's not true, but still … The woman wants you and is willing to threaten me to have you."

"But she can't have me. I've told her that several times, and I'll do so again as soon as we get to my room." Fearful that Lamisi would give up on their new relationship before it even got started, he gripped her hands. "This is the last time she'll threaten you. I won't allow it to happen again."

"How can you stop her? She's money and power. That combination means she can do whatever she wants no matter who it hurts without consequences. God knows what she has planned for my dissertation. Not only have I had three advisors, but my current one already stalled me several times out of spite. If Deola whispers into his ear, I may never get my doctorate."

Lamisi bowed her head and rubbed her temples.

"I can't give up my dream, Blaise. I've worked too hard to get here, and I refuse to get pulled back." She raised her head and held his gaze. "By anyone."

A heaviness settled in his chest at her ominous words.

The taxi came to a halt. He looked out the window to find that they'd arrived at the hotel. Discussing how to handle Deola ranked high on the schedule for tonight. Just as Lamisi wasn't willing to jeopardize getting her PhD, he wouldn't lose her.

CHAPTER TWENTY-SIX

Lamisi's hand trembled as she pulled the cab's handle to let herself out while Blaise paid the driver. She'd been off-kilter ever since reading the horrible message. Melanie had pulled her to the side and asked what was wrong. She'd claimed nerves about being so close to the end of her dissertation.

And now, she'd confronted Blaise. His offer to talk to Deola was sweet, yet ridiculous. Whatever the woman wanted, she got, not matter who suffered in her acquirement of it. Was he strong enough to withstand Deola's wrath if he got in her way?

Doubt lingered as she waited for him to join her on the short path into the hotel. When he'd caught up with her, a man wearing a dark hoodie jogged towards them.

The guy called out, "Here's your lesson, bitch!"

Within the blink of an eye, he untwisted a bottle and aimed it.

In slow motion, liquid squirted towards her face and splattered before she could raise her hands to protect herself. She pushed out a scream just before Blaise ran and tackled the guy to the ground.

Their rolling scuffle didn't take long as she yelled at the anticipated burning of her face from the acid the man had sprayed her with. She would be scarred for life. Her howls brought people sprinting out of the hotel.

"Lamisi," Blaise said, out of breath. "Are you okay?"

He tugged at her wrists to bring her hands down from her face.

"Madam, what happened?" One of the hotel's attendants squatted next to her and asked in French.

Lamisi gulped in the cool air that hit her skin. Where was the sizzling agony of flesh melting that should've had her writhing on the ground? With gentle fingers, she tentatively touched her cheek where the fluid had landed. No pain. No caustic smell of chemicals. Nothing but moisture.

Heart racing, she looked at Blaise while answering the attendant.

"My face. He threw liquid at it." She swallowed hard. "Is it … disfigured?"

Brows furrowed together, Blaise took out his phone and turned on the flashlight. She squinted at the beam of light as he assessed her. "Not at all. Are you feeling any pain?"

She slumped and let out a sob of relief. It hadn't been acid in the bottle. Whatever it had been, she needed to wash it off. Struggling to get to her feet, she fell as her knees buckled. Blaise helped her up.

"Bathroom."

He assisted her inside with an entourage of gossiping hotel workers and a few guests following. He insisted on getting her into her room. Rather than wait for the elevator, she took the stairs two by two. Her hands too shaky to slip the key card into the slot, he took it and opened the door.

Sprinting in, she tore into the bathroom, stripped off her clothes, and rinsed her face.

Siphoning in a deep breath, she gathered courage to look into the mirror. She clutched the sink to keep from sliding to the floor when unmarred skin reflected back at her. Gratitude filled her chest. The back of her hand to her lips stifled the wail of relief that shook her body.

Not knowing what had been squirted at her, she dragged her crying self into the shower. Her nearly full bottle of face soap didn't hold enough for the number of times she scrubbed her face, neck, and chest. So she continued with her body soap.

A knock against the barrier startled her.

"Lamisi, are you okay?"

She swallowed back her tears and palmed the tiled wall for support.

"Yes," she choked out as the water continued to stream down her face.

Air ruffled the shower curtain as the door opened. His voice reached her ears clearer although he hadn't entered. "Are you sure? We should go to the hospital to have you checked out."

The last place she ever wanted to be. "No … no hospital. I'm fine. I think it was only water the guy shot at me."

"Not acid?"

"No."

"Are you sure? We should still get to the emergency room to confirm."

"My face isn't burning. If it had been acid, the skin would have become warped."

"But what if—"

"I'm fine." The ferocity in the words bounced off the shower walls. Taking in a shaky breath, she spoke at a reasonable level around the lump that had formed in her throat. "Give me a while. I want to make sure to wash off whatever he got on me. You should do the same."

Seconds ticked by, and she feared he wouldn't leave.

"My door is open if you need anything. I'll be right back."

As soon as she heard the closing click of the door, tears mixed with the water sluicing over her, the drain collecting the residue of the nightmare she'd just endured.

◆◆◆

There was nothing Blaise could do for her at that point, so he limped to his room. The fight with the assailant had led to soreness in the ankle he'd injured on the mountain. He'd wanted to chase the guy down when he'd escaped his grip, but taking care of Lamisi had been more important.

Worried about her, he took a quick shower. Her "fine" hadn't sounded it at all. Who would be after being attacked? Thank God it wasn't acid. Not only her beautiful face would have been marred, but her whole life would've been affected. Her outgoing personality might've taken a huge hit.

Her strength of will would have gotten her through it, especially since he'd have stayed by her side the whole time. She meant more to him that being a pretty face. Her intelligence, sense of humour, huge heart, talent, and determination made her special. She brought a unique light to his world that hadn't been there until he'd met her. Scarring wouldn't frighten him away from someone so extraordinary.

He hopped out of the shower, dried off, got dressed in a pair of shorts and T-shirt, grabbed his phone, and left his room to rap on Lamisi's door.

The barricade between them cleared, with her on the other side of the open threshold. Eyes puffy and red, the sight of her both made his heart clench and had him sending up a prayer of gratitude that her face hadn't been disfigured.

"Can I come in?"

She swept a hand into the room.

He took in an area almost identical to his, varying with a colour scheme of light orange and cream. Fighting the need to wrap her up and hold her for the rest of the night, he lowered himself into the only chair as she sat on the edge of the bed. Space might be the best thing for her. For someone he was strongly attracted to, he really didn't know her all that well.

"How are you doing?"

She shrugged, and her lower lip quivered.

He sprang from the chair onto the bed and wound his arms around her. Her tears poured onto his shoulder until her sobbing transitioned into intermittent shuddering breaths and sniffles.

She pushed herself up and walked across the room to grab the box of tissues. After blowing her nose, she kept her head bowed. Needing to soothe her, he went over and rubbed her back.

"Do you want to go to the police?"

"Ha. And say what? That a guy called me a bitch before squirting me with water? I can hear them having a big laugh and saying, 'Madam, when we have murders to solve, you expect us to care about this bit of nonsense?' just like they would in Ghana. No, thanks."

She had it right on point.

The guilt hit him once again. His association with Deola had caused this misery for Lamisi. "I'm sorry this happened to you."

He pulled out his phone from the cargo pocket of his shorts.

She grabbed his arm, her eyes glimmering. "Who are you calling?"

If it was the last thing he ever did, Blaise would make Deola pay for what she'd done. But first, to flush out her informant.

"There's only one way Deola could have known where I was and who I was with."

"You believe me that she's responsible?"

"Yes."

She closed her eyes for a second, inhaled so that her chest and shoulders rose, and nodded. "I wasn't sure if you would. I have no real proof."

"Your instincts are good enough for me."

"Thanks."

He hit send on Abdul's contact and waited. He would've never thought his friend would betray him.

Abdul's smiling face popped up on the screen when he answered. "Hey, man. How's Franco land treating you?"

Blaise held back a growl. "Lamisi got attacked. What the fu—"

She pinched his side.

He clenched his jaw, rubbed his chin, and counted to three. "Tell me what you know about it."

Mouth slackened, Abdul blinked several times while craning his neck closer to the phone. "*Me ya faru*?"

The Hausa flew naturally out of his mouth.

Blaise narrowed his eyes. Abdul had done a great job at looking confused, but he wasn't buying it. "You know what happened. And speak English."

"I don't know what you're talking about. What happened to Lamisi? Is she okay?"

"Someone has been harassing her over the phone, and tonight, they threw acid in her face."

Lamisi clutched his arm and squeezed.

"That's terrible. How is she?"

Blaise ignored the question. "You're the only one I told about my trip to Côte d'Ivoire with Lamisi. You're the only one who could have told the attacker where we are."

Abdul gave a fierce shake of the head with a hand over his chest, as if swearing like they used to do as children. "I told no one of your trip."

Blaise assessed his friend's mannerisms with a critical eye. "Are you sure?"

"I promise on all that I hold dear that I told no one. I would never betray you, my brother."

Either Abdul had been taking acting lessons from top actors in Nollywood, or he was telling the truth. If that was the case, then how did Deola find them?

"I believe him," Lamisi whispered.

He gave a single nod of both acknowledgement and agreement. "Then how could Deola have known where we were?"

Eyes once again as round as clay bowls, Abdul's mouth dropped open. "You believe Deola did it?"

"Yes. She called me last night reminding me about the music awards. When I insisted that we weren't going together, she mentioned Lamisi."

Abdul set his mouth in scowl and waggled his finger. "I told you she wasn't a good person. I could sense it in her. Besides, young rich people who don't work for their money have too many issues. That one especially. Alima is always telling me that Deola is misunderstood, but I don't believe her. Being spoiled is never a good thing."

Blaise's spine straightened at the mention of Abdul's younger second wife. A memory niggled in the back of his mind but refused to clarify itself.

"Alima speaks highly of Deola. When Salifa or I contest her opinion on the woman, she becomes outraged. If I didn't know that they've never met, I would figure Alima to be a friend of hers."

A revelation announced itself in Blaise's head louder than the call to prayer. "When I told you about my trip to Côte d'Ivoire, I remember Alima hovering behind you."

He hadn't thought anything of it because the favoured wife was always around her husband.

It took Abdul a few seconds to make the connection before he bellowed out her name.

Alima jogged into view.

Lamisi leaned closer to Blaise so that her face was in the small section at the bottom of the screen. "She's the one who kept shooting me dirty looks and whispering while glaring at me at the hospital the day we met."

When Alima looked to the screen and noticed the faces staring at her, she narrowed her gaze and emitted, "*Karuwa.*"

The word whore couldn't have been meant for Blaise.

"Alima! What has gotten into you, spitting out insults as if raised in the gutter? Apologize." Abdul had switched to Hausa since the woman didn't speak English as fluently as his first wife.

With militant defiance, she folded her arms so viciously under her breasts that it pulled at her hijab. "I will not."

"Why not, Alima?" Blaise asked on a tone much kinder than the one he wanted to dish out. He would play good cop today. "Has Lamisi offended you?"

"Yes." Spitting with indignation, she continued. "By trying to steal you from my friend, she has become my enemy."

Guilty. It wouldn't hurt to get more evidence. "Who is Lamisi trying to steal me from?"

"Deola. You have agreed to marry her. She has told me that the announcement will be made at the music awards where you two have planned a public proposal. My friend has told me all of the details." She sighed. "Very romantic." Her eyes sharpened with a flick towards Lamisi. "She will not ruin it. You belong with Deola."

The occupants in both rooms stilled with silence and confusion.

"I'm not marrying Deola," Blaise shouted. The woman had gone too far.

"How are you and Deola friends?" Abdul asked at the same time.

Alima grinned at her husband. "She responded to me when I left a message on her page a few months ago when Blaise and she initially met. I was proud that Blaise had finally met a woman worthy of him."

At least, she'd had his best interest at heart. It still didn't dispel the anger keeping him on the cusp of crashing his phone against the wall.

Lamisi rested a hand on his upper thigh.

"Did you tell Deola that Blaise had travelled to Abidjan?"

"Yes. We are the best of friends and talk about many things." The young woman's smile lit her face. "When she asks about Blaise, I inform her. She always takes my calls. She was pleased with me when I told her about your weekend trip to Abidjan." Alima shot daggers from her eyes at Lamisi. "Even if it was with *her*."

Lamisi's low growl hit his ears, but didn't reach the phone's speaker. He had no doubt that blood would be shed if the women were in the same room.

"You have not done well," Abdul chastised in a strict tone, leaving no doubt that Alima would learn the error of her ways. "Leave me."

Alima opened her mouth as if to protest, but then seemed to think better of it when she looked into her husband's scowling countenance. She scurried away.

Blaise had heard more than enough. He returned to English. "I'm sorry I blamed you, my friend."

"No worries, Blaise." Abdul averted his gaze to meet Lamisi's eyes before bowing his head. "I apologize for the actions of my wife. I assure you that it will never happen again." The screen filled with his face. "I'm glad you weren't injured."

"Thank you."

Blaise turned to look at Lamisi's profile at her softly spoken words devoid of any irritation. Her features no longer held the tension they had just moments ago. Could she have truly forgiven that quickly? He knew that she had when she turned and her dark brown eyes caught his gaze and held.

He was honoured to have met such a remarkable woman.

Abdul cleared his throat.

Resistant to lose the link he had with Lamisi, it took him longer than it should have to return his attention back to the screen. He entwined their fingers to keep the connection.

His friend rubbed his full beard. "What will you do about Deola? The woman is crazier than I thought."

"That's a fact. I'll talk to her. By the end of the conversation, I know she will back down."

Abdul raised a brow, but didn't ask any further questions. Once again, he gave a slight bow to Lamisi. "I am truly sorry for the stress you have suffered and my wife's role in it."

He must really be feeling the guilt to elicit two apologies.

"*Na yarda da uzuri.*" Lamisi accepted the apology in Hausa, revealing that she held no ill will towards Abdul.

"Just make sure she understands that what she did is wrong," Blaise added. "My business is no one else's but my own."

"Yes. I'll talk to you later, my friend. Have a good night, Lamisi."

"You, too."

The screen went blank with the cut call.

Blaise pinched the bridge of his nose and released a mouth full of air, glad that his friend hadn't betrayed him. Now to shake Deola from his life.

CHAPTER TWENTY-SEVEN

Over the shock of being assaulted, a wild hunger of fury took its place. Abdul's idiot wife wasn't the one to blame.

Deola was.

No matter what Blaise said to her, nothing would change. The woman with the kind of power and money Lamisi couldn't even fathom would come after her again. And again. The prima donna wanted Blaise, and there was probably nothing she wouldn't do in order to make it happen.

Scenes from too many Nigerian and Ghanaian movies where a woman was kidnapped by a jealous ex came to mind. The ideas had to be initiated from somewhere. She had no doubt that Deola could and would make her disappear without getting caught.

Was she willing to risk her life for a man? Not just any man, but Blaise. The one her heart seemed to beat for. They hadn't known each other for long, but he was so comfortable to be around that she had no difficulty being her true self. That had to mean something.

Didn't it?

No one else could live for her. Being with Blaise would be a wonderful experience, but she came first. If she were to continue down a path of having a relationship with him, she would live in a constant state of fear. Watching over her shoulder, waiting to be attacked from any and all directions. What kind of life would that be even if she were with the man that made her feel amazing and special?

Their romance had to end even before it had started. Yet, she couldn't leave him without experiencing what they could have been together. She would have no regrets about leaving him. But first …

Bolder than she'd ever behaved, she looked into his eyes and closed the space between them. Mouths met with zips of electrical charges. At the slight parting of her lips, he deepened the kiss.

His solid muscles beneath her hands flexed as she caressed his back and pressed closer. Not close enough to satisfy. Everything disappeared at the onslaught of their explosive passion. Consequences no longer existed, only the pleasure they could experience. Together.

With the acceptance that this night would be their first and last together, Lamisi released all inhibitions and pulled Blaise with her when she lowered onto her back.

He released her lips. Panting, he stared down at her. "Lamisi?"

He'd given her the time to back out. She wouldn't. The moment went beyond anything she had ever experienced. She longed for him more than even her next breath. She raised her leg to hook around his hip.

"Make love to me, Blaise."

Brows arched over eyes that held her bound and mesmerized. "Are you sure?"

If tonight had left her one lesson, it was that life was worth living right now.

She reached up to smooth a hand over his cheek. He was her present. Nothing else mattered. A nod of affirmation later, his lips crashed down onto hers, permeating her with the slick heat of his mouth. The spiciness of his scent and the pressure of his muscular body on top of hers—he filled her with a desire so strong that any concept of regret became inconceivable.

He lifted himself off the bed, leaving her skin cool and wanting, and reached his hands down. When she clasped them, he tugged her to her feet.

With a deliberateness that she'd only experienced in her fantasies with him, he stripped off her clothes, trailing kisses and suckling sensitized flesh as he exposed her.

As he removed his clothes in a more hurried manner, Lamisi's practical side kicked in. On wobbly legs, she went to her bag and pulled out an unopened box of condoms. Thank God for a best friend who worked in healthcare and had insisted that she buy them.

She pivoted to face him. The box slipped from her fingers when sumptuous chocolate skin covering lean muscle met her gaze. She picked up the condoms and reached out for him. Her hands smoothed over the light dusting of coily hair on a solid chest and rippled over his defined abdomen.

Before she could reach her target, he grabbed her wrists and brought them up to his mouth. The light graze of his lips at the sensitive areas just below her palms sent tingles down her spine and moist heat to her core.

He held her arms away from her body and looked her up and down with a glint in his eyes. "Lamisi, you're gorgeous."

Foregoing any kind of shyness, she returned the favour over his body. "You, too."

Blaise moved to her, and they touched skin to skin from chest to thighs.

"Are you sure?" he repeated.

His warm breath over her ear sent a shiver through her.

More than she was of anything she had ever done in her life. "Yes."

He removed the box from her hold, ripped it open, and took out a single packet. Lamisi stood motionless as he opened it and slid it over his rigid length.

A shadow passed over as the reality of the moment invaded. This one-night experience would have to last her for the rest of her life.

She led him to the bed and tugged him down with her. Fingers stroked intimate places. Lips and tongues caressed as kisses drove their unyielding hunger.

When their bodies joined, she knew their souls had, too. Their oneness became her world as they moved together in gratifying strokes.

Stars exploded behind her eyes as her climax took her to the heavens and beyond. Blaise called out her name with his explosion within her a moment later.

They lay entwined for the longest time. He kissed her shoulder before getting out of bed and heading towards the bathroom.

Lamisi covered her naked body with the sheet as questions bombarded her. Two stood out as the most prominent. Why did she miss him so much when he was close enough to throw a shoe at the door he'd just walked behind? The second tore at her heart—did she have to let him go?

After their spectacular love making, she felt even closer to him on all levels. Her skin tingled, and blood pulsed at the recent memory. What they had shared couldn't be considered normal. More like destined. Dare she even think it when she wasn't sure she believed in it?

Shadows silhouetted Blaise as he came out of the bathroom. He eased onto the bed and hovered over her. The sweet kisses to her lips as his body pressed against hers teased.

He settled a pillow under his head, facing her profile, and sighed as if he were the most content man in the world. It made sense since she was flying high herself.

"What will you do when you finish your dissertation?"

She snapped her head to the side to catch his gaze. Not what she'd expected.

"I figured I'd continue on the road to professorship at the University of Ghana. Ever since I was young, people considered me to be strange because I understood so many languages. When I went to the university, I stood out in an impressive way, and it suited me. Things got even better when I started working as a teaching assistant. I loved it.

"The combination of teaching, researching, and being around like-minded people who live, not just speak, languages as much as me is my ideal job. It would allow me to travel and encounter other cultures and languages, as well."

His refined nose crinkled, and she raised herself onto her elbow to see him better in the semi darkness.

"What?"

The shoulder closest to her shrugged. "Speaking as one of your students, you're a fantastic teacher, and I can see you imparting your knowledge in the classroom."

"And doing research," she added.

"Okay."

"But …" she filled in for him.

"You're so gifted with languages that I can see you doing a lot more."

The follicles on her head tingled in recognition of the concept. Hearing something voiced that she had thought herself renewed the longing she'd once had about travelling the world. Maybe writing a book. Helping people in some way.

"Like what?"

His gaze held hers. "Working for the UN or something along those lines. Going international rather than being local. Doing something where your ability will be appreciated and praised."

"You don't think that will happen if I teach at Legon?"

He stroked a hand down her arm, sending sparks of heat along the limb. "With the title of doctor, you'll be respected anywhere in Ghana, but will your talents be fully utilized?"

Lamisi followed her impulse to brush her nose against his cheek and inhaled his spicy, musky scent.

"Thank you," she whispered against the hair on his cheek.

"For what?" His voice came out on a husky groan.

"Seeing so much in me."

Blaise elevated himself onto his elbow, separating them for a moment until he cupped her cheek. "I like everything I've discovered about you. I'm sure that the more I find out about you, the more amazed I'll be come."

She leaned in with a brush of lips that transitioned into a sweet encounter of love making.

This time, when he left her satiated body, the loss caused a crushing in her chest, representing more than just their physical separation.

CHAPTER TWENTY-EIGHT

An insistent vibration and pinging woke Lamisi from sleep. The morning sun streamed through a crack in the curtains when she opened her eyes. The heft of Blaise's arm blanketing her kept her in place. It had been the best night of her life. No regrets lingered.

The buzzing of her phone demanded that she leave their cocoon. When she shifted, he groaned and pulled her closer. The annoying vibration on the dresser wouldn't allow her to snuggle in. By the frequency of the dinging, someone urgently needed her.

Her heart picked up its pace as a number of nasty scenarios rampaged into her mind of the people she cared about being injured.

The phone shook with more incoming messages even as she picked it up. Lamisi slid her finger across the numbers which would unlock her screen.

Thirty-four messages. And more coming in. Did she want to open them? The prickly sensation and goose bumps on her arms said no.

"What's going on?"

She let out a screech. Whirling, she placed a hand against her chest as she gulped in air.

"Sorry. I didn't mean to frighten you."

Blaise's raspy voice reminded her of the first time they'd spoken, and her stomach flipped.

"It's okay."

He pointed at the still vibrating phone. "Is there a problem?"

A glance down at the device indicated that she now had a total of forty-five messages. "It's blowing up with messages. I think it's Deola."

The muscle in his jaw clenched. "I should've called her last night to tell her to cut it out."

Her core pulsed at the memory of what they'd shared. Nothing had ever made her feel so alive and connected with another person. For the rest of her life, she'd cherish having been with him.

Lamisi focused on her phone and tapped on her message button. She gasped as she noticed that the messages were from different numbers. TrueCaller had identified none of them. What had the insane woman done?

Swallowing her fear, she looked through the titles of the messages without having to open a single one. Each message held one word as she scanned down. The total message repeated until the phone came to its fill.

'Leave. Him. Alone. Otherwise. Next. Time.'

Hands shaking, she drew on her courage. Daring to open one text revealed the same singular word which had been in the title. When she opened the next six, they all held one word.

The next set of phone numbers were different. So were the next. And the next. Just like the guy who had sprayed her, Deola had gotten people to do her dirty work for her.

Eyes glued to the screen, she shook her head in disbelief. "She's certifiable!"

"I'm calling her right now." Blaise's tone held a level of rage that sent a chill down her spine. "This will stop."

A snort ripped out of her. "What good will that do? The woman wants you, and nothing will stop her."

Certain defeat hit her where only moments ago she'd held hope. She'd known it last night. Wasn't that why she'd made love to him? To experience being with him for one night. Their first and last time together.

'Next time…'

Would Deola attack her family? Friends?

Lamisi couldn't risk it, no matter how much she cared about Blaise. She had too much to live for to let another woman destroy her or anyone she loved.

"Once I talk to Deola—" Blaise broke into her thoughts, "—she'll understand that she and I aren't and never will be a couple. Ever."

Lamisi swallowed the lump in her throat. They had met less than a month ago. Why should letting him go hurt so much?

"She'll keep coming after me until I'm out of the picture so she can have you for herself."

Blaise tapped his chest. "She can't have me. Once I let her know definitively, she'll back off."

"Right. Just like she did the times you told her before."

"This will be differ—"

She flung up a hand. "Yes, it will. I won't be in her way. Blaise, I can't do this. It would be stupid for me to think I can ever escape her. She has too much money and influence, and knows how to use it to get what she wants."

"No, Lamisi. You are not breaking up with me. Not over this. We're good together, and you know it. I'm not just talking about in bed."

Boy, did she know. Unable to look into his earnest eyes, she spun and paced to the window. Commuters on their way to wherever they needed to be greeted her blurred vision.

Hands on her shoulders seeped a warmth into her that she couldn't resist. Lamisi rested her back against him. Making her choose between herself and Blaise was cruel.

He wound his arms around her and rested his chin against her shoulder. Their cheeks pressed, and she closed her eyes, breathing him in. This was where she belonged. In a perfect world, she would be able to stay.

She jumped as the shrill sound of her phone broke into her longing. Would her cell going off be a perpetual cause for fear? It would if she stayed with Blaise. Always looking over her shoulder wasn't the way she wanted to live. Not the way anyone should have to live.

"My alarm." She tore herself away from him to turn it off. "We need to get ready to leave so we don't miss our flight."

"Lamisi, we can work this out. Trust me. Deola will back off."

She tilted her head and took in his stunning features. Dark eyes stared back with a softness that spoke of the pleading that hadn't come from his mouth.

"When I was ten, I almost died. Typhoid fever created a hole in my gut. I had an emergency operation." She rubbed her arms to ward off the chill that came over her. "After the surgery, my wound got infected. I spent weeks in the hospital being poked, prodded, and in so much pain that I'm sure nothing could come close to it."

He blinked at her as if wondering the purpose of the story.

"I hate hospitals. I don't use that word for anything else but hospitals. Passing by them freaks me out. It takes an impossible amount of coaxing for me to go into one."

"You went in with me when I sprained my ankle."

"Yes."

"You liked me even back then."

Yes. But that wasn't the point.

"Whatever Deola has in store for me will not end well. You're a good man, and I've enjoyed getting to know you, but I have to think of myself first. Life is too valuable."

The sentiment she'd spewed came nowhere near what she truly felt, but if he knew that he possessed her heart, he'd become vigilant in his attempt to persuade her to stay with him. She was barely hanging on to her decision as it stood. No matter what convincing argument he came up with, she knew that walking out of this hotel in any kind of relationship with him would put her in danger. Her life mattered too much.

"I care about you, Lamisi. Give us a chance. We'll get through this and come out stronger for it."

Such a romantic. She'd miss that about him.

Rather than reject his offer, she took the couple of steps separating them, cupped his face, and raised herself to kiss his lips. Just like when they'd made love, she took in all of him, understanding, even if he didn't, that it would be their last time together.

CHAPTER TWENTY-NINE

"Your French has improved tremendously," Armand told Blaise as they walked to the front door after their tutorial.

Blaise had noticed that the man no longer looked pained after his pupil had spoken.

"*Merci*."

He didn't bother to explain about his journey to Côte d'Ivoire or how Lamisi had forced him to speak the language with everyone they'd encountered during the trip. The weekend had been a blast. Until it no longer had been.

They'd gone from having a slow relationship to taking off on a rocket. Being with her had been mind-blowing. Soul-shaking. Incredible.

His attempts to contact Deola had yielded three days of beeping in his ear with a computerized female voice stating that the phone had been switched off. He'd even had Alima try from her phone. Nothing.

Either Deola was ignoring him, or the oil rig she was supposedly on had no reception. Yet, she'd been able to contact him, organize an assault and an army of texters to harass Lamisi. His money was on her avoiding him.

He had spoken to Lamisi for a few short minutes each day. He could understand her perspective. He would've flipped out if someone had made him the target of their vengeance.

It had been a long time since he'd met a woman who matched and challenged him. He'd fight for her. Since it meant taking on Deola, then that's what he'd do. And he'd win.

Frustrated, he called the strongest woman he knew for advice.

"Hello, my son," his mother said in Hausa, the only language she spoke with her children even though she was also fluent in English and Twi.

An involuntary smile spread across his face. There wasn't a woman he'd ever loved more. "Hi, Mama."

In many ways, he considered her to be his best friend. He wouldn't take the step and talk about sex with her, but the topic of women was another issue. And she tended to share wise advice about them.

"The trip to Côte d'Ivoire was successful. I'm more fluent in speaking French."

"Anything you set your mind to, you achieve. You are my and your father's son, so it is must be so."

The woman knew how to encourage. Just like Lamisi. He stood and paced the room. May as well get everything out in the open.

"I've found a woman that I like."

"I knew I'd heard a change in your voice. More melodic. Who is she? I'm sure she's a good Muslim girl, if you're telling me about her."

"Lamisi Imoro. Yes, she's a Muslim." He'd leave out the fact that she wasn't as devoted as his mother would like her to be. "She's studying for her PhD in linguistics at the University of Ghana. She's the one who helped me translate my lyrics into French."

"She's going to be a doctor?" Her words came out breathy with excitement. "*And* she's Muslim. Praise be to Allah for answering this mother's prayers for her child. Allah is ever faithful. You have just made me the happiest mother in all of Ghana. When are you bringing her here to introduce her? What tribe is she? Is she educated? What work do her parents do?"

He tapped a hand against his chest to ensure that he'd survived the rapid fire of questions. "Mama, I only met her a month ago, and we're getting to know each other."

"You don't have the answers?"

"She speaks eight languages. One of them is Hausa."

His mother gasped. "Is she Hausa like us?"

"No, Mama. Her mother is Dagomba, she works for the Ministry of Agriculture, and her father is Ga. He owns his own business."

He chuckled at her squeals and claps.

"She's a Northerner *and* a Muslim. You have delighted my heart this day. I must meet her. Put her on the screen right now so we can talk. I'm hanging up."

"Wait, Mama." He caught her before she could disconnect the call.

"Yes."

"She's not here."

"Well, go get her. Call me back when you have."

Sometimes, there was nothing as frustrating as speaking to the queen aspect of his mother.

"I have a problem I need your help with." The words would capture her.

"What is it, son?"

"Deola."

Was that a growl on her end?

"I told you to stay away from her. She may be Muslim, but from her pictures, I could sense her evil heart."

He would've doubted it before, but after what she did to Lamisi, he knew it to be a fact. He told the story of Deola's treachery.

"I know why she doesn't want to release you. You're talented, rich, popular, and come from a royal and influential home. If that wasn't enough, you are loyal, kind-hearted, and generous. More than you should be at times. No woman would ever want to let that go."

Except Lamisi. Extenuating circumstances in a new relationship didn't count.

"What do I do?"

"First of all, be patient with Lamisi. She has every right to protect herself. As for Deola, keep trying to get in contact with her and let her know where you stand." His mother paused. "What makes you sure that she'll stop disturbing Lamisi once you've spoken to her?"

His mother wouldn't appreciate that he'd threaten her with information he knew she wouldn't want to get out to the public.

"I'll appeal to her better judgment," he answered.

"She has none, but do what you feel is best. As for Lamisi, give her time. Maybe invite her to the music awards. We're proud of you for all your nominations, especially Artiste of the Year."

His bowed his head even though she couldn't see. He always wanted to bring honour to the family. "Thank you, Mama. It's been a long, challenging journey. Lamisi is a private woman. This wouldn't be the best time to introduce her to the world. And until I clear things up with Deola, I feel as if Lamisi will stay away from me."

"It's what I would do," she said. "In the meantime, stay in contact with her. And if you can, keep her safe."

"Thank you for the advice."

"I hope you take it this time. Now tell me more about Lamisi."

He spent the rest of the conversation talking about his new favourite topic. By the end of the conversation, he felt like he knew more about Lamisi than he'd initially thought. He'd pulled out facts he hadn't realized he'd known. Perhaps he shouldn't have shared it all with his mother, but his tongue had been too loose to rein in.

He grinned at the fact that he was hung up enough over a woman to share the news with his mother. Now if he could get Lamisi to feel the same about him.

Lamisi had spent the past week and a half in a pseudo-state of boredom while transcribing the musicians' interview responses. Thoughts of Blaise creeping in led to the work being even more tedious, because she'd lose track of what the artists had said and would have to rewind the recording so she could type it in on her computer.

At least being in the house didn't cause her to tremble like the few times she'd had to venture out. By the time she returned to the safety of her home, she'd collapse onto the couch. Her muscles had protested the tension she'd suffered while paying such close attention to her surroundings. Yet, she refused to let anything, even being terrified that Deola would stage another attack, limit her life.

Her family had wanted to call the police and find every way to contact Deola once she'd told them what had happened. She'd reasoned them out of it, but warned them to be careful. It didn't feel like enough.

Lamisi sent up prayers that the heiress would understand that she no longer had any intention of seeing Blaise and back off.

The impulse to drive to his house because she missed him so fiercely was almost more than she could stand at times. She'd lunge onto the phone when the ringtone she'd assigned him pierced the air. Hearing his voice, even for the few moments she allowed so she could wean herself from him, gave her respite.

Her parents had taught her how to face her fears from a very young age, and here she was cowering in her own life. It wasn't like her to hide from anything but a hospital.

Giving up what she desired most wasn't like her, either, and it hurt to go against her natural instinct to cling to the man who'd filled her heart. Soon, she'd have to sever all ties with Blaise. Give it an official end so she could start to heal and move on.

As if that would ever happen.

CHAPTER THIRTY

Lamisi hadn't warmed up to him after their return from Côte d'Ivoire. In fact, she was drawing farther away every day. Not even the offer of a drive on his motorcycle had gotten him closer to seeing her.

Along with their daily phone calls, he'd sent her several poetic text messages, hoping she'd read them. That his smooth words would melt the ice she'd built around her. So far, they hadn't. At least, she hadn't cut him off completely.

His phone rang as he paced the pathway in his garden.

"Hello, Bizzy."

Deola's face filled the screen, as beautiful as ever. Only now did he see the tinge of ugliness within her.

"Hello, Deola." He kept his tone dull and looked her in the eyes. No further formalities needed, he dove right in. "I know you were the one who had Lamisi Imoro attacked in Abidjan and have been harassing her."

Red, glossy lips rounded as her extended lashes fluttered with each blink. "I have no idea what you're talking about. I've been on that oil rig, remember. It wasn't as bad as I thought it would be. Aside from a lack of consistent network connection, it had all the comforts of home. The food—"

"Stop lying. We all know you're responsible."

Deola's eyes narrowed. "According to whom? The woman who is after you for your money and fame? What do you even see in her, Bizzy? She's a local lowlife who isn't destined for any type of greatness. She can't help you rise to the top or be the best in the business. Not like I can."

And there it was. His fist flexed into a fist that needed to make contact with a solid surface. Other than a clenched jaw, he kept his expression neutral and his mouth shut so she could dig herself in deeper.

She raked multicolour-painted acrylic nails through the hair of her wig.

"I don't ever want you to say that I didn't warn you. She can't do anything for you but put you into debt with her poverty-driven spending." Her voice rose with her temper. "I realized it from the first time I saw footage of her at your house. Wearing cheap clothes and hugging you as if she were a whore."

"What are you talking about?"

"She's a gold digger. Before you know it, your money will be gone and your career destroyed," she said with bared upper teeth in a vicious snarl.

She was delusional if she thought he'd let go of what she'd let slip. He squinted, staring into her the eyes. "What did you mean by footage, Deola?"

She flipped down a hand in dismissal.

"Nothing. Something I said in annoyance," she said in a higher pitched voice with a smile meant to distract. "But can you please take my advice to heart? I care about you."

He replayed the sentence and the words *at your house* hit him. Would she have had the gall to do it? After what Deola had put Lamisi through, nothing should surprise him about the lengths she was willing to go to get what she wanted.

He clicked off the phone and sprinted out of his backyard until he reached the front of his house.

Turning, he scanned his roof. Nothing.

The gate gave a slight creak as he opened it. He ignored his ringing phone while perusing the roofs of the homes across the street.

The camera on the house two plots down caught his eye. When had they put up a security camera? The couple who owned the place had travelled to the States a few months ago, informing him that they'd left their son alone while he attended university. They hadn't mentioned anything about installing a security camera.

Jogging across the street, he assessed the home for more cameras. None.

Rather than bang his fist against the metal, he poked his finger into the doorbell. A young man opened the gate, wearing a wide smile.

"Yo, Bizzy. How's it going, man?"

He held out a hand that Blaise grasped and slid his palm across his before they ended the connection with a snap.

"I'm great, Felix. How're you doing?"

"Living the life. Catching up on sleep now that exams are done."

"*Abeg*. Did your parents have a security system put in?"

Felix tapped his chest with his thumb and chuckled. "I'm their security. They like doing things the old-fashioned way. Why?"

Blaise pointed to the roof. "What's that?"

Felix rotated, took a look, and then stepped closer to the camera. "What the hell is that?"

"You've never seen it before?"

"Nope. Never. Look how it's tucked under the roof's edge."

Blaise nodded. "If you didn't look up, you wouldn't see it. Who looks up at the roof unless it's leaking?"

"How did you find it?"

His nostrils flared as he glared at the offensive technology. He'd never experienced such a violation of his privacy. Not even the paparazzi had the tenacity to have him watched. She had no right. "I was looking."

Felix pointed from the camera along its trajectory.

"Damn, *Chale*." He used the local slang for friend. "It looks like someone's been watching your house."

Blaise tried to play it cool, even though his head was seconds away from exploding. "Yeah, seems that way."

The young man grinned. "Too bad they don't know how quiet you like to live for a hiplife artist. No off-the-chain parties for you."

Blaise shrugged. "It's not my scene, especially in my home."

"I get it."

He doubted it. People held a certain expectation of musicians. He didn't fit it.

"Listen, Felix, I'll make a couple of calls to get the camera taken down."

"No *wahala*. I'm around for the afternoon."

"Thanks, *Chale*."

Blaise stormed back to his home and contacted the guys who'd installed his home security system. They'd be there within the hour to investigate.

Stripping down to his boxer briefs in his backyard, he dove into the pool. The cool water didn't invigorate like it normally did. The laps he raced through did a better job of tamping down his rage.

Lifting himself out of the pool, he went to his clothes and dried his head, face, and hands on his shirt before slipping it on and picking up his phone.

"Hi, Blaise. What happened? I've been trying to call."

The sweetness of her voice irritated him to the point of wanting to throw the cell against the side of his home.

"You set up a camera on the house across the street from me."

Her eyes rounded. "What are you talking about?"

"Don't play with me, Deola. I have my security team coming right now. They've assured me that they'll be able to trace the signal to where it's transmitting." They'd said nothing of the sort, and he had no idea if it could be done, but he doubted she did, either. "You had it installed to spy on me."

"Come on, Blaise. Spy is such a harsh word. I only wanted to ensure your security."

He swiped a hand down his face and dragged in a breath through the palm he left over his mouth. "You're incredible. Stay the hell away from me and Lamisi."

"You don't belong with anyone but me." The venom returned. "That bitch can go to Hell."

No wonder Lamisi had wanted to stay as far away from him as possible. Deola was demented. He wouldn't put it past her to murder anyone who got in her way.

If only Lamisi knew how much of an upper hand he had, she would've had more faith in him.

Time to put an end to it.

"All I know is that you'd better leave her alone. If I find out that you've done anything to her, I'll be the one you have to answer to. Do you understand?"

Her laughter came out high and piercing. "Your kindness and innocence are two of the things I've always adored about you. You think you're going anywhere because you've found a side chick? Soon, you'll be begging me to restore your fame when your stupid French album tanks. And it will. Nigerians won't buy it, and they're all that matter in West Africa. English is the way to go. We tolerate your Ghanaian local languages because your beats are so catchy."

"Enough!" he barked out.

Her head snapped back. No one dared to speak to the heiress in such a manner.

"Do you remember the time you insisted that I spend the weekend in one of your guest rooms instead of a hotel?" Blaise asked.

"Yes. My dad was out of town. It was the night you kissed me."

Funny how he remembered her throwing herself at him.

"I had difficulty sleeping on Saturday night and went exploring through your massive home in search of the kitchen."

An ashiness replaced the make-up induced glow of her skin.

"I heard muffled screams and the sound of slaps coming from the room tucked around the corner of the first-floor hallway. Not knowing if you were in danger, I opened the door." He shook his head. "I always wondered why you hadn't locked it. Were you too excited about your activities, or did you want me to discover you?" He raised a brow. "Maybe join you? And your, um, friends."

She wiggled in her seat. "I ... I ... don't know what you're talking about."

"S&M isn't my thing."

He ignored her gasp.

"When I saw that you were safe and rather happy wearing your leather while wielding a whip on your poor, um, friends, I closed the door and left. Scarred with the image of the supposed virgin heiress partaking in—"

"You're lying. That never happened. I would never do such a thing."

"No?"

Strands of hair flew into her face with her vehement head shake.

"You want to degrade my name. It won't work, Blaise. Everyone knows I don't involve myself in scandalous behaviour. Especially not what you described." She let out a grunt of derision. "You'd better keep your fantasies to yourself. They don't reflect well on your wholesome brand."

He sat in the pool chair and anchored his free hand behind. "So the pictures I took won't stand as proof of your sadistic activities? Huh. Let's see what the public thinks about my evidence if you ever try to get in contact with or hurt Lamisi again. Don't think I won't bring you down in order to keep her safe."

"You're lying," she squeaked out. "What you're describing never happened."

He held her gaze. "You're known for your fashion sense, but bright pink leather doesn't look as good on you as you think. I give you props for the matching whip. Along with the spiked dog collar and leash you had on your other, um, friend."

The image on the screen flipped over and then went black as her phone landed face down. And then, the line went dead.

Blaise luxuriated in the knowledge that he'd won. Only a fool would challenge him. Several minutes ticked by as he lounged in the sun, waiting. When his phone rang, he turned on the recorder—he didn't doubt she'd done the same—before answering.

Deola tossed her hair over her shoulder, looking more in control than when he'd delivered the news.

"I have no idea what you're talking about, Blaise Zemar Ayoma." Deola enunciated his full name. He half expected her to add son of, throwing in his parents' names as proof to anyone who might listen to the recording in the future.

"About any of it," she continued. "I've been busy learning the family business and have been out of communication on an oil rig."

If he didn't know better, he would've believed her.

She released a deep sigh. "It's a pity your friend was attacked. The world is not the same as it once was."

"No, it isn't."

"Please give her my regards. I'll provide the poor dear with what you requested."

He dipped his head towards her in a sign of understanding. "With a reassurance that any such trauma will never come to her again would be helpful. You know how people look up to you and trust your word. If you say it won't ever happen again, then she'll believe that it never will."

Her contracted shoulders shortened her elegant neck. "I agree."

Lamisi would believe Deola's direct promise of leaving her alone.

"Thank you. There are certain things that will never come into public view because they're too painful."

"They should be deleted from all sources, never to be spoken of again."

"Yes. Just as some friendships should end, but cordiality maintained when running in the same circles."

She giggled, but her eyes remained cold. "Burning bridges serves no one. As always, it was lovely speaking with you, Bizzy. Take care of yourself."

"You, too, Deola."

When her face disappeared, his body went limp and the back of his head slammed into the wood of the chair. The relief of being rid of Deola outweighed the sting of pain.

Time to figure out how to convince Lamisi that they belonged together.

CHAPTER THIRTY-ONE

What had gotten into Blaise to make him send such romantic texts over the past few days? Every time she went to press the delete button, her finger spasmed in protest. She'd sighed with longing after rereading them at least twenty times each.

His words were too beautiful, reminding her more of poetry than messages.

One in particular had her heart racing.

'I am not worthy of such a blessing as her.
The woman of faith had me longing for more.
Light in her eyes, laughter from her mouth, kindness from her soul
Bring me to a state of need too great to contain.
My world has been thrown off course and a new path set.
It is with her that I see the future flow.'

She slid her finger across the screen to clear it. Time to stop moping about him and get on with life. His texts weren't enough to make her change her mind.

What would? her heart taunted.

Deola had contacted her and told her in a covert manner that she would back off. It didn't mean that she belonged with Blaise. If they got together, wouldn't some other woman who thought she deserved him more than Lamisi come and try to bump her off one day?

But then again, maybe she could be enough.

She'd never know unless she gave them a chance. Did she trust him enough with her heart to do that? Did she believe in herself?

She sank into her bed, ending the question and answer period in her overactive mind. Picking up the remote control, she turned on her television and switched to the station showing the music awards. They were still ushering people onto the red carpet, so she kept it on mute while watching the glamour pass by on her screen.

How many of the artists she'd interviewed would be at the ceremony?

Who was she kidding? She didn't care. She watched for one reason only. To catch a glimpse of the man who had shaken her world and caused her to question so many things about who she knew herself to be.

Whatever happened between them, she hoped Blaise won all the categories he'd been nominated for, especially Artiste of the Year. He deserved it. His competition consisted of some great musicians, but Blaise was the absolute best.

You only think that because you're in love with him.

She bounded out of bed, slapping a palm against her forehead. "Oh my goodness."

Dropping onto the edge of the mattress, she supported herself with braced arms so she wouldn't slide off.

Was she in love with him?

She wiggled her fingers, and prickles of numbness woke them. How long had she been contemplating her feelings about the man she'd tossed away out of fear and self-preservation?

Yes, she loved him. Unexpected and scary, but true.

What would she do about it? Love wasn't something that came into her life often. Precious would tell her to go for it. Should she, or was it too late? His texts didn't indicate it. Those treasurable words spoke of the opposite.

For the first time since she'd tried ghosting herself out of his life, she thought of Blaise and smiled. Her heart still hammered with uncertainty, but at least, she was willing to give them a chance.

A banging on her door jarred her out of her musings. "Come in."

Amadu burst in, glanced at the silent screen, and then grabbed the remote control. "You've got to see this."

Her breath caught as Blaise filled her screen.

Amadu turned the volume up. "He's singing a new song. In French, Twi, and English. Is it one of the ones you two were working on?"

As she listened, the lyrics sounded familiar, but the song hadn't been one she'd translated for him. She would definitely recall a tune that made her wind her hips while still seated. The music was slower than his previously released songs. Smoother.

After a few minutes, the impact of the words hit her, and she gravitated to the television.

"Damn!"

The lyrics were the same as the texts he'd sent her. Only instead of them being in English, he sang the chorus in impeccable French.

Amadu tugged her out of the way. "Yeah, he sounds amazing. I don't understand half of what he's saying, but the beat is killer."

The crowd seemed to think so, too, as they danced. Rotating their hips, showing off the strength of their thighs and asses. At least the ladies did. She expected at least one of them to injure herself with the extent of their movements. The men in the crowd didn't seem to mind as they watched with smiling appreciation.

Was she the only one who knew he was pouring his heart out? Did anyone else care that the lyrics could bring tears to their eyes if fully understood? Or was it just her?

She blinked away the burn.

And then, the camera focused on a woman with hair flowing over bare shoulders. An emerald green dress cascaded over her curvaceous body. Deola smiled wide with one hand against her chest as she blew a kiss to Blaise.

Lamisi's skin went cold with dread. She couldn't believe what she'd just witnessed. The two were together. They had to be. Why else was she at the event gazing at him like a woman enamoured? It had to be the reason why Deola had contacted her, because she'd won.

Like a scared sheep, Lamisi had walked out on him. Leaving him to fall in love with whoever his heart chose. It obviously wasn't her. She didn't blame him, either. The easy way out of a situation wasn't always the best. Now that she'd come to terms with her feelings for him, she wished she could've handled things differently. Trusted that he would take care of Deola like he said he would.

"Are you okay?" Amadu asked.

She forced a smile. "I'm fine. The song just got to me. It's a masterpiece."

"I'm sure the radio's going to be playing it on the constant when it comes out."

She nodded her agreement as she watched his performance come to an end.

Blaise looked at the cheering crowd and gave them a broad smile. "*Sealed with a Kiss* is dedicated to my mountain woman."

Had she heard him correctly?

If she hadn't, the camera panning to view Deola with her lips pressed into a tight line confirmed it.

Lamisi stared at the screen. Breathing didn't come easy as her chest tightened. The song had been for her. He'd created and sung it just for her.

The floor developed trampoline-like properties as she did high-knee jogs while squealing. She ignored her brother's look of incredulity as she jumped side to side and waved her hands high.

Breathing heavy and grinning so hard that her cheeks were starting to hurt, she flung her arms around herself and squeezed.

"What's gotten into you? One minute you look ready to cry, the next you're all manic. Do I need to call Mom and Dad to take you to the hospital?"

"For a case of extreme happiness? No." When his drawn brows didn't relax, she added, "I'm mountain woman. We first met on Mt. Afadjato."

Nodding, Amadu joined her with the grinning. "Now you can stop being so crabby."

"Hey, I wasn't—" Why bother to deny it? Being without Blaise had turned her into a grouch.

"Sorry," she said. It would've been a better apology without the ear-to-ear smile she still sported.

"No problem. It's good to see you happy. So, what happened between you and Blaise to get you down?"

"I was dumb."

He stumbled backwards and gasped three times in a row. "Are you admitting that women can be the cause of relationship breakdowns? I'm sure you can't tell, but I'm shocked."

The giggles wouldn't stop bubbling out of her.

Her phone pinged, indicating a text. She picked it up. Blaise.

'Did you watch my performance?'

She flicked a gaze to her brother.

"Thanks for informing about Blaise's performance."

Amadu chuckled. "Tell him he hit it hard. He's got a for sure number one on his hands."

"Just get out."

As soon as the door clicked shut, she tapped into her phone.

'Yes.'

Blaise: *And...*

Lamisi: *Amadu told me to tell you that you've got a #1 hit on your hands*

Blaise: *Tell him I said thanks. What did you think?*

Should she play with him or get to the point? How fragile was his ego about his music? May as well find out.

Lamisi: *I didn't cover my ears when you sang in French*

Blaise: ☺ *All thanks to you. What about the lyrics?*

The moment of truth.

Lamisi: *Even though you plagiarized yourself from the texts, they were beautiful. I thought so when they were words on my phone, but you singing them brought them new meaning. I loved the song, Blaise. You're an amazing musician*

When a response didn't come after a couple of minutes, she settled in to watch the award show while keeping a strict eye out for Blaise. She wished she could be seated next to him.

She didn't care if the world knew they were together as long as she could spend time with him. Appreciate his considerate and seemingly carefree nature. Laugh with and adore him until ... Hopefully, neither would get tired of the other.

Her phone played her favourite song of Blaise's. She'd have to get a hold of his new one and swap the ringtone.

Biting down on the inside of her cheek while her heart did dangerous things in her chest, she put the TV on mute and answered. "Hello?"

"I'm glad my number one fan liked the song."

Applause and people hooting filtered through the phone, corresponding with the activity on her television.

"It's always important to keep a mountain woman happy. You never know the consequences."

Their laughter merged.

"I'd like to see you tonight, but the awards ceremony seems like it's going to last forever."

Last year, it took five hours. "You have to stay and grab your award for Artiste of the Year."

"There's no guarantee I'll win. The competition is intense."

Such a humble man. Something she hadn't expected him to be before they'd first met, and it increased her respect for him.

"Yeah, but you're the best out of all of them. That award is yours. Make sure you have your speech ready. No bumbling around on the stage so that they cut to the adverts on you."

He chuckled. "I wish you were here."

"Me, too." She twirled a strand of her hair around her finger. "We both know I would've declined the invitation if you'd asked earlier."

"True. We need to talk, Lamisi."

They sure did. "Okay."

"How about if I pick you up tomorrow at around one and we'll have lunch."

"Sounds good. I have a couple of things to take care of in the morning."

He didn't need to know that she would've skipped out on washing her clothes to see him again. She had some apologizing and explaining to do.

"I take it," she continued. "You'll be partying for the rest of the night and will sleep the morning away."

An aspect of his life her introverted personality would have to get used to.

"Huh. Everyone calls me the old man, and that's when they're being nice. I'm a homebody. It's why my house is filled with so many expensive toys. I attend parties to show my face and meet the key players. Once that's done, I'm out."

She could handle that. "Try to enjoy yourself a little, old man."

He did a combination groan and chuckle. "I probably shouldn't have shared."

Things on his end started getting loud as music blasted through the air. "Nope."

"I've got to go," he shouted into the phone. "Text me your address."

"Okay. Have fun." *But not too much.*

"Thanks. Have a good night, mountain woman."

The unromantic nickname made her ecstatic. "You, too, King of Francohip."

His laughter tickled her ear as he hung up.

Thing between them had gone from miserable to getting so good. Love was pure power.

CHAPTER THIRTY-TWO

If Blaise didn't settle down, he'd crash his car before reaching Lamisi. He wrapped his fingers around the steering wheel to stop the repetitive cracking of his knuckles. Willing himself to keep his backside still, his leg no longer propelled the vehicle faster than he intended.

The computerized voice told him to take a right. Another turn had him on a wide dirt path where the road had yet to be paved. She'd mentioned that she still lived at home with her parents and two of her siblings. Would he get to meet any of them?

He wanted to be with her. If he had to chat up every member of her family to make it happen, then he would.

The app told him he'd reached his destination. Instead of calling to tell her he'd arrived, he opened the door, climbed out of his Volvo SUV, and strode to the gate. After pressing the bell, mouth dry and hands moist, he waited.

Lamisi bounded out of the house a minute later. She looked through the open slats of the large gate and waved at him.

Grinning, he returned the gesture as she let herself out.

Not even writing and recording his own songs had ever been as thrilling as this moment of finally being with Lamisi. Such a deep longing to see someone astounded him. Maybe he'd never been in love. Until now.

"Hi." She flounced towards him wearing a light blue floral dress that reached her knees.

"Hey," was all he could get out.

"Congratulations, Mr. Best Music Video of the Year, Hiplife Artiste of the Year, Record of the Year, and Artiste of the Year. A clean sweep. I told you you'd win."

He dove into the arms she held open. Their embrace was much too short as his head swelled at the pride her voice carried.

"You certainly did. Thank you for believing in me."

"It's easy to have faith in apparent talent." As if his winning the awards was an everyday event, she changed the subject. "Instead of going out, I cooked lunch. The house is all ours."

She broke eye contact and kicked at a stone. Was she worried that he'd say no? Being alone with her was his dream.

"That's if you don't mind. My food isn't as delicious as Aunty Vida's, but people have asked for another serving on occasion."

He chuckled. "I'd thought about inviting you over to try some of my home cooking."

She let him into the compound. "Next time."

Sounded like a promise. Although she seemed relaxed and happy to see him, playing it cool got harder with each moment in her presence.

He diverted his attention to the massive home. Nothing flashy, but solid. A place where five children could have their own space to explore. The interior was simply decorated and comfortable.

"I'll be right back with some water," she offered once he was seated.

He stiffened his muscles to stop himself from following her into the kitchen. Taking in a deep breath, he reminded himself that she had allowed him to see her. A positive sign.

She returned before he could study all of the pictures filling the room. He'd spotted Lamisi right away and grinned at the child missing two front teeth in her wide smile while standing in front of a cake.

He removed the bottle of chilled water from the tray, opened it, and took a sip.

"Are you hungry? The omotuo and groundnut soup are ready."

Mashed rice formed into a ball was one of his favourites. "I'm looking forward to eating your food, but I think we should talk first."

Why couldn't he let them continue on the path of renewing what self-preservation had set her to destroy? She appreciated his directness and willingness to communicate, but there was no need to dive into the main topic.

"How did you produce the song you sang last night so fast?"

"Would the fact that I was motivated be an adequate answer?" he asked in a deep, smooth tone. His voice of seduction.

Heat crept up her neck and into her face. Goodness, she wished she was better at flirting. "No, it wouldn't. First tell me what motivated you and then how you got it done so quickly."

His eyes lured her into their depths. Could he see that she loved him? She didn't care if he never answered the question, as long as she could stay near him.

"You inspired me to write and record the song. I needed you to hear it so you'd understand just how serious I am about us. How much I enjoy getting to know you. You're an incredible woman, Lamisi. Genuine, beautiful, supportive, kind, and playful. I'm a better man when I'm with you."

The sentiment must've punctured a lung because the air whooshed out of her.

She sucked in a deep breath through her nose. "Deola sent a sequence of texts saying that she was backing off. Thank you."

"I told you I'd take care of her. I promise that she'll never bother you again."

Curious, she hinged forward at the hips to get the dirt. "What did you say to her?"

His casual shrug let her know she wouldn't get the complete answer.

"We established an understanding."

Sounded rather gangster, but she wouldn't press it. Not fearing for her or her family's lives every time they opened the front door had dissipated.

Her body sang a song dedicated to him when he placed a hand on her cheek.

"Now that your life isn't at risk, are we okay? Can we get back on the dating track?"

She became weightless as everything in world clicked in place. "Yes."

Not wasting any more time, he captured her mouth in a kiss that she responded to with all the passion which flared up in her. A homecoming that made her forget why she'd ever tried to leave him. She knew for certain she wouldn't again.

Gripping the front of his shirt, she tugged him closer, opening to him. Giving and taking. Ravenous hands roamed over his shoulders. She took in his unique scent and minty taste as she absorbed his essence and gave hers freely.

She moaned, letting the perfection of the moment permeate into her.

He ended the kiss with a light brush to her lips. Pulling away, his soulful eyes gazed into hers with a concentration she adored having directed only at her.

"Lamisi, will you be my girlfriend?"

The proposal set off fireworks in her body. "Yes, Blaise."

He kissed her forehead.

"My mountain woman."

Her smile was wide with pleasure and teasing. "My old man."

"I'll never live that down, will I?"

"Nope."

Because he would always be hers.

EPILOGUE

Their section of the crowd went ballistic with cheering and hooting when Lamisi's name was announced to collect her PhD. Blaise couldn't be any prouder of her. His yells as she walked across the stage carried over the shouts of the other people who loved her.

When they'd first started dating, her family had invited him into their lives with open arms. It'd been much easier for them to accept him than it had been for Lamisi. His family, his mother especially, had loved her.

The past year had been a fast-paced whirlwind of incredible shared experiences.

They'd done their traditional Islamic wedding last month and registered at the courts to finalize it.

His career had shot off like a missile into the stratosphere.

Not only had the Francophone countries loved his French mixed music, it had caught fire everywhere. He'd approved collaboration requests from top musicians he'd only admired from afar.

Would any of it have happened if Lamisi hadn't been by his side? Yes, but it had been so much better with her in his life.

Blaise looked forward to the concert tour he had lined up. Lamisi would join him for the full three months on the road. When they got back, they'd take a couple of weeks to relax before she started her job as a lecturer at the university. She'd also spoken to a few embassies about doing translation work for them when they needed it.

At the close of the ceremony, her entourage of supporters went to meet her at the designated area.

As soon as she spotted him, her black gown billowed as she ran into his arms. He lifted her and spun her around, never wanting to let his wife go. Her clinging arms around his shoulders indicated the same.

He placed her on her feet. “I’m so proud of you, Lamisi. I love you so much.”

“I love you, too, Blaise.”

They gazed into each other’s eyes, promises of the intimacies they’d share later raging. Their families must’ve decided that they’d had more than enough time to themselves and surrounded Lamisi to get in their congratulations.

Blaise had no problem sharing her. In the end, his mountain woman would go home with him.

THE END

Thank you for reading Love and Hiplife by Nana Prah. If you enjoyed this story, please leave a review on the site of purchase.

Books in the series
Love and Hiplife
Love and Handicrafts

Nana Prah is a published author of contemporary, multicultural romances. Her books are sweet with a touch of spice that will leave you satisfied with that much deserved happily-ever-after. When she's not writing she's reading, over-indulging in chocolate, and enjoying life with friends and family.
Website: https://www.nanaprah.com
Newsletter: https://www.nanaprah.com/newsletter-sign-up

Instagram: https://www.instagram.com/nanaprahauthor/
Bookbub: https://www.bookbub.com/authors/nana-prah

MOST ELIGIBLE BACHELOR

This is a work of fiction. All names, characters, and places are fictitious. Any resemblance to actual events, locales, organisations, or persons, living or dead, is entirely coincidental.

Editor:
Zee Monodee

Cover Design:
Love Bites and Silk

Reach Empi:
empibaryeh.com

Dear Reader,

Most Eligible Bachelor was originally released in February 2012. Lord McKenzie is still one of my favourite heroes to write about. I know some of you didn't get to read the story, since it wasn't available on platforms and formats accessible to you. So when I got the rights back, I thought it would be a good idea to re-release it, first to give a chance to those who didn't get to read it. Secondly, I wanted to give more 'story' to fans of the book.

The basic story remains the same, but I've added brand-new scenes. Notably, one that introduces the heroes of the of the series.

Most Eligible Bachelor won "Book of the Year" in the 2017 Ufere Awards and got an honourable mention in Bookriot's article 28 Steamy Billionaire Romance Books.

As nervous as I always am, whenever I release a new book, I'm also thrilled for the opportunity to share Lord and Chantelle with you once again. I hope you enjoy reading about them as much as I enjoyed writing about them.

Thank you for reading!

DEDICATION

To everyone who has played a role in making this story come to be.

To all my readers. You make this job worth it.

BLURB

A one-night-stand with a billionaire bachelor leaves a happily single writer wanting more...

Magazine columnist, Chantelle Sah doesn't celebrate Valentine's Day—not since her fiancé's betrayal four years ago. She's thrown herself into her career, but after a botched assignment as a feature writer, she will do everything for a scoop this Valentine's Day. Even if it means breaking her rule and going on a date with gorgeous construction Tycoon, Lord McKenzie... opening herself to an onslaught of all things love.

When Lord—his given name, not a title—sets his sights on Chantelle, he has more than work on his mind. Yet, even the infamous playboy couldn't have predicted the magnetic attraction from the moment they met, nor the evening ending with more than just an interview. But now he has to convince Chantelle that their one-night stand wasn't a mistake... and that not all bachelors are heartbreakers.

CHAPTER 1

ALL IS FAIR IN *love and war.*

Sitting at her desk in the spacious office she shared with twelve others, Chantelle Sah typed out those words, the perfect title to her article for the April edition of *Odopa* magazine. The cursor blinked on the laptop screen as if in celebration of another job well done, well within her submission deadline.

A good thing, since she still had the feature story for April on her plate—an interview with construction tycoon and notorious playboy, Lord McKenzie. She snickered at the oddity of the name. What kind of parents named their kid Lord?

None of her business. Her job consisted of conducting the interview and writing her piece. God knew she couldn't afford to have her feature swiped from under her feet. Again.

After two years of building a solid reputation with her lifestyle column, she'd pestered her editor for a chance to do a feature. He'd given her that opportunity a few months ago, and she'd blown it. Somehow, her story had leaked out to their number one competitor, *Celeb* magazine, leaving her scrambling for a back-up. For the first time ever, *Celeb* had sold more copies than *Odopa*. And it had been her fault.

"Hey." The voice of her colleague, Dufie Swaniker, reeled her back from her momentary drift. "Busy?"

Chantelle sat back with a sigh. "I'm about to call his Lordship."

Dufie clutched her chest in a dramatic fashion. "Oh, I can just feel your pain."

"I swear. Randy's doing this just to punish me for the *Celeb* incident."

"Aw, come on. He's doing you a favour. Do you know how many writers would kill for an interview with Ghana's most eligible bachelor?"

A snort of laughter slipped past her lips. "Most eligible bachelor, my ass."

She winced. Maybe that was harsh. After all, she hadn't even met the guy. Not exactly his fault he looked like God's best work of creation, or that women didn't let him forget it, even if by some miracle he wanted to. She humphed. *As if.*

"He's probably as shallow as he is good-looking." Add that to his ego-boosting name, and she had one pain-in-the-ass interview on her hands.

"You really have it in for this guy, don't you?" Dufie chuckled. "Listen, a group of us single ladies are going out for drinks tonight. Do you want to go?"

She became quiet. Her gaze flickered over the cupid spin-danglers hanging from the ceiling and the floral bouquets and greeting cards adorning the rich mahogany workspaces. All around them, the office hummed with Valentine's Day buzz and animated banter about romantic dates later in the evening. They all reminded her she'd been happy once, hopelessly in love. How had it all gone wrong?

She shoved those thoughts aside, focusing her attention on her friend. "No, I think I'll just go home and have a quiet evening."

Dufie folded her arms, perching herself at the edge of the desk. "Chantelle, he's been gone four years."

She didn't answer, and the ensuing silence stretched between them for a beat.

"I'm sorry for bringing it up. I know what you went through losing Martin so tragically, and then to find out—" She stopped, as if realising she'd gone off on a tangent.

"It's all right, Dufie. You can say it." The part that had cut her deepest. "He was with another woman."

She released a jagged breath, stunned to discover those words hadn't been as hard to utter as she'd expected. The pain and anger still simmered somewhere inside, but, for the first time, she didn't feel their weight crashing down on her. Maybe time *did* heal all wounds—or perhaps, she'd finally perfected her ability to numb her heart.

"Martin was a jerk for breaking your heart, but you can't hole up at home every Valentine's Day because of what happened."

"That's not what I'm doing. I'm exhausted, and it's only Wednesday. I need to unwind."

Liar.

Truth be told, she didn't want to go out tonight, didn't want to hear love songs or see happy couples. It would fill her with longing for the warm embrace of a lover, the intimacy a woman shared with a man, the heated you're-the-only-one-for-me look. Going out on Valentine's Day would expose her to an overdose of things she couldn't allow herself to have, because she didn't know if she'd ever be ready to risk her heart again.

She gave herself a mental shake, bringing her mind back to the present in time to catch Dufie's response.

"Well, you have three whole hours until close of day to reconsider. Let me know if you do."

She nodded, even though she didn't intend to change her mind. "I will. Thanks."

With a shrug, her colleague stood and sashayed off to her own desk. Alone again, she decided to make the call to Lord McKenzie. *But not here*, she thought, watching two other colleagues gushing about an e-card one had received. Aside from a desire for privacy, she needed to escape before she got any more unsolicited invitations to go out tonight.

Grabbing a pencil and notepad, she headed out and found one of their small meeting rooms. Just as she sat at the round table, the door opened, and her editor peered in.

"Ah, there you are." He entered and shut the door. "How are we doing with McKenzie's story?"

She frowned. Randy didn't usually hound his writers, especially when they weren't at risk of missing the submission deadline.

"I'm about to call him. That's why I slipped in here." She noted the somewhat anxious look on Randy's face. "Is everything all right?"

"I just heard *Celeb* is also after him."

The words hit her like a kick in the belly, and a band of tension wound tight around her chest. *Celeb* had started a teaser campaign for their tenth anniversary celebrations, which they were kicking off in June. No details had yet been released. It seemed they were keeping a tight lid on it … which could only imply one thing. They didn't have the green light from McKenzie, or they would have started advance publicity for the issue.

Meaning her interview just became number one priority.

"The good news is we want him for April."

Despite her attempt at putting a positive spin on things, tension continued to coil around her insides. *Celeb*, known for their guerrilla tactics, would move theirs up in a heartbeat if they caught wind of her piece.

"Do I have to remind you why you need to get to him before *Celeb* does?"

She swallowed, shaking her head.

"Good."

And then he left.

She took in a deep breath to calm her nerves. That was a threat if she'd ever heard one. With her annual appraisal coming up in a few months, she couldn't afford to lose this story. Especially not to *Celeb*. That would be just too embarrassing, not to mention how it would affect her prospects for a promotion in the future. Hopefully, Lord McKenzie wouldn't make her jump through hoops before granting her the interview.

She retrieved the sticky note she'd received from Randy and unfolded it to reveal a cell phone number which she punched into her phone and hit send. While it rang, she idly wondered about Lord McKenzie's middle name, and what on Earth his girlfriend called him. *Correction, girlfriends.*

"Hello."

His voice boomed through the line, deep and husky, and an answering zing shot through her stomach.

She sat up. *Okay, count that under weird.*

"Hi." She grimaced, and then amended her greeting. "Good afternoon. Am I speaking with Lord McKenzie?"

"The one and only, sweetheart."

She frowned. *Sweetheart?* Oh, she'd be hating this guy after the phone call itself, never mind the interview.

"Hi, Lord, uh, Mr. McKenzie, my name is Chantelle Sah. I'm—"

"Hello, Chantelle. What can I do you for?"

His voice possessed a rich timbre, which coupled with his choice of words, evoked images of two bodies intertwined in passionate encounters. An unexpected thrill galloped up her spine.

Whoa, what the hell was that? Clearly, her self-imposed celibacy could use some reinforcement. She forced a smile, taking a second to compose herself.

"You could grant me an interview." *Good girl. Keep your mind on business.*

"Did I win something?"

"Well, you were voted Most Eligible Bachelor by readers of *Odopa* magazine."

He gave a soft melodious laugh. "I hate that."

She frowned, taken aback. "You—pardon?"

"Do you know how much trouble you put me in by naming me Most Eligible Bachelor?"

If by 'trouble' he meant more girls than he could bed, then yes, she knew. Well, she could only guess.

"Maybe you can clarify things in the interview."

Silence followed as if he were contemplating her offer. "Tell me, Chantelle Sah, are you single?"

"Yes, but I don't—"

Why on Earth would she say yes? An embarrassing warmth crept over her cheeks. Thank goodness this conversation wasn't face-to-face. A flustered image wouldn't make a good first impression. She should have rehearsed this call. Now she'd given him an upper hand, no matter how remote.

"Great. Why don't you escort me to *Afrodite* tonight?"

She frowned. "The nightclub?"

He chuckled. "Yes, the nightclub. I'm having a Valentine's party there. Surely, you must have heard."

Yes, she'd heard. For weeks now, Lord McKenzie's VIP party had dominated both traditional and social media. While technically open to the public, the venue—one of the most exclusive nightclubs in the city—and the ticket price restricted the party to the *crème de la crème*.

"Well ..."

She didn't want a date. Particularly not tonight. However, if he was willing to grant her an audience, what choice did she have? She couldn't let the opportunity slip through her fingers.

"Do you want the interview?" His matter-of-fact tone made it clear she occupied the beggar's seat in this discussion.

"Of course I do."

"Excellent." She could hear a smile in his voice. "Bring a recorder, and you can have your interview after the party. I hope you like to dance."

"No, I don't dance."

"Don't worry. I'll teach you."

She bit back a curse. She'd lost complete control of this conversation. Mechanically, she found herself agreeing to meet him at the party, anxious to secure her interview before *Celeb* beat her to it. Randy wouldn't forgive her for it. She wouldn't forgive herself, either.

"Oh, by the way, if you're available and looking, wear red. Otherwise, the dress code is white."

With those parting words, he ended the call.

She stared at her phone screen, unable to believe she'd allowed him to dominate the conversation. Now she'd talked herself into the Valentine's Day pit of Hell. She couldn't decide who to blame more: Dufie, for upsetting her by digging up the past, or Randy, for rattling her with his thinly veiled threat. Usually, she could muster enough resolve to sidestep emotional traps like those. However, today being Valentine's Day, emotionally, she was at her weakest.

Drat.

LORD MCKENZIE HAD a knack for reading people, detecting subtle hints others might miss. He could even pick up signals over a phone line, like the slight catching of Chantelle Sah's breath when he'd answered the call. It had been all he'd needed to know his plan would work. Now, if he just played his cards right, he could kill two birds with one stone.

As he placed the mobile phone on his desk, his gaze caught the latest copy of *Odopa* magazine, which lay next to the metallic letter tray where he'd laid it two weeks before. He still hadn't found time to read it.

Picking it up, he paused on 'Contents' long enough to find the page number for Chantelle's piece. He flipped over to it. Her photo caught his interest, as it always did. Thick shoulder-length hair framing a heart-shaped face and a smile that could steal a person's breath. She stared straight into the camera with confidence shining through mischievous hazel eyes. Her composed expression made you want to hear what she had to say whether on paper or in the sultry voice he'd have the pleasure of hearing again tonight.

He'd always wanted to meet her since first reading an article of hers a couple of years back. He had bought every copy of *Odopa* for two years running because of her. When Randy Brobbey, the editor, his old schoolmate, had approached him about an exclusive, he'd readily agreed.

Plus, Chantelle was the only reporter he trusted to write an article which would begin to rectify the general impression of him perpetuated by the tabloids. A perception which, to be fair, he hadn't done a thing to dissuade. Frankly, he'd thought it funny, bordering on ridiculous, the first time he'd earned the label of playboy tycoon. Granted, he didn't go out on more than a few dates with any woman, and he'd never left any of them under the illusion of their liaison being anything more than temporary.

However, he didn't play women. Something had to be fundamentally wrong with a man who pursued multiple women simultaneously. He treated his women well, and their break-ups were amicable.

Until one of his exes—he wasn't even sure he could call her that, considering they'd only been together two weeks—had done an exposé for *Celeb* magazine, based mostly on twisted truths and partly on falsehoods. Initially, he'd been pissed. He had even considered his lawyer's advice to take legal action, but he couldn't possibly sue every single paper for any untruths they printed about him. He'd eventually decided not to dignify any of them with a response.

He'd also refused to let those stories dictate his actions, so he'd maintained his social calendar, fully expecting it to blow over. Instead, the story had domino-ed out of control with more women coming forward with their own stories, and the labelling had continued: *heartbreaker, lady killer, lover and leaver, Lothario McKenzie*.

It wasn't his first experience of being called names, though. In secondary school, he'd been a lanky boy. Being the younger brother of the most popular guy in school had just made him more visible. As the butt of jokes for anything from his name to his physique, many of which had been instigated by his own brother, he'd had to develop a thick skin.

So the labels didn't bother him, but he drew the line when the public opinion of him threatened his company's chances at winning what would be their biggest project ever.

Enter Chantelle.

He should have been thinking about their upcoming meeting in a purely professional sense.

He wasn't.

Staring once again at her picture, he thought about her voice. It sounded the way he'd imagined, a little breathy and way too sexy for her own good. From the tone of her articles, he knew she was a strong-minded, passionate woman with a healthy dose of wit. Most men would be intimidated by that combination, but he wasn't most men.

And he wanted her.

He checked the time. Fifteen minutes until his next engagement. Good.

He'd barely settled to read the article when his phone rang. Reluctantly, he set down the magazine. At this rate, he'd never get to it, and for some reason, he wanted to read it before meeting Chantelle tonight.

He hit the answer button without checking the caller ID, intending to get rid of the caller quickly.

"Hello."

"Hey, lover boy. Guess who's returning to town in time for the Golden Stool Awards."

Lord grimaced. *Deconte*. Another perception he needed to fix.

"You?"

Her claim-to-fame girlish laughter carried over surprisingly clearly for an international call. "Turns out we're wrapping up earlier than planned, so I can make it. Are we still on?"

"I'm a man of my word, Deconte."

"Yes, you are." A brief silence followed. "You realise, though, that'll take us to ten weeks, right?"

"About that—"

She didn't let him complete the sentence. "You want to end things."

One thing he loved about Deconte: like him, she didn't mince words.

"This has gone on long enough, don't you think?" A short silence followed his question. "Deconte?"

"You're right." She tried to sound upbeat, but he caught the reluctance in her voice.

"It was never supposed to go on for this long. If the truth comes out—"

"I know, but I'm hoping to avoid any negative publicity before the release of my upcoming movie, and being in a stable relationship helps." She hesitated. "If I'm correct, you need it, too."

She had a point. If McKenzie Contractors hoped to win the pitch they were participating in, he couldn't afford a scandal, either; particularly since the papers only seemed interested in his love life. Much to his father's dismay. His jaw clenched as he remembered the many conversations he'd had with his old man on the issue.

"Just another two weeks until my movie comes out?"

He released a breath, weighing the options.

"Wait," Deconte said. "Have you met someone?"

His gaze darted to Chantelle's headshot, and he smiled. "I'm about to."

CHAPTER 2

STARS TWINKLED IN THE dark evening sky as Chantelle made her way to the club, Afrodite, in her Honda Civic. Grateful to Lord for letting her use the VIP entrance, she drove past the line-up of cars struggling to find a parking space. An attendant directed her to park.

After shooting Lord a text message about her arrival, she waited a minute, then got out. She drew in a deep breath to stem the nerves jangling in her stomach. Wherever Lord McKenzie went, cameras tended to follow. The only difference was she would be his trophy girlfriend in *Graphic Showbiz* tomorrow. Sadly, being slender and a shade over five-nine, she probably looked the part, too.

To her discredit, she hadn't been able to stop thinking about him after her fumbling mess of a phone conversation earlier. While putting together an exhaustive Q&A, rehearsing the interview, and reviewing old articles about him, she'd made lengthy pauses on his photos. The memory of his deep voice still played havoc on her usually composed demeanour.

Just as she reached the door, he walked out, six-feet-two-inches of shameless masculine beauty and sex appeal, all hard planes, chiselled grooves, and brushstrokes of perfection. The pictures failed to do him justice. He extended his hand and flashed a hundred-watter, rendering her momentarily speechless. Thank goodness he didn't wait for her to speak first.

"Hi, Chantelle Sah. Thanks for coming." He gave her a once-over, not bothering to be discreet.

Instead of taking offense, her heartbeat faltered under his appreciative scrutiny.

"Thank you for inviting me, Mr. McKenzie." She congratulated herself when her voice came out completely in-control and professional.

When she took his hand, though, the control seemed to surrender to his magnetic pull. The pictures *really* didn't do him justice. Lord McKenzie wasn't just handsome—he also had a certain intangible quality which drew a person in like a spell.

Loud music hit them as soon as they entered. Though he never released her hand, he stopped every few seconds to say "hello," to people, hugging many of them and introducing her as if he wanted everyone to know they were together.

She shook away the thought. *Absurd.* Why did he bother, anyway? They weren't friends or anything. In fact, aside from a thank-you note she intended to send the next day, they wouldn't as much as run into each other again.

So why did it bother her to note how the females he hugged clung to him for as long as they could? A few went to the extent of asking if she was his new girlfriend, with pointed looks in her direction suggesting how disappointed they'd be if she were indeed his new squeeze. She snorted. *Hardly.*

He took her straight to the dance floor and fell in step with the beat. Seeing no other option, she followed suit. He was an amazing dancer, his movements fluid, almost magical. She forced herself not to stop and admire.

After a while, he leaned in. "I thought you didn't know how to dance."

So he'd been testing her?

"I said I didn't dance, not that I didn't know how."

"What's the story?"

"None. I'm too busy."

He looked doubtful, and for a second, she feared he'd probe. Instead, he laughed. "What a shame. You're a good dancer."

His compliment shouldn't have made an impression, but, against reason, her insides turned to mush, affected by his generous flow of laughter. Easy to see how a woman could be charmed by all the attention, what with the way he trained his entire focus on her. As they danced, she decided he had to be the most handsome man she'd ever met.

She'd barely registered the thought when the music turned to salsa, the latest fad in town, and Lord proved a pro. In his arms, she felt she could have won any competition. Though concerns for when she could start the interview lingered, she found herself connecting with the music. Her insides bubbled with the exhilaration of memory. She'd forgotten how recklessly free dancing made her feel. A laugh tumbled out as he led her through a double spin.

Realisation hit her. She was actually having fun. Something she hadn't done in so long. Who'd have thought?

A few songs later, he asked, "Want to sit down for a moment?"

She nodded through a smile, trying to catch her breath. Amazing how she could hear him clearly over the music even though he didn't seem to be shouting.

He led her off the dance floor to an upstairs lounge. A burly man in all black acknowledged them with a nod and opened the door. She'd never enjoyed night life and had limited experience with clubs. The couple of times she'd visited one in her school days, she'd been put off by the loud music and the smoke. Thankfully, *Afrodite* offered a smoking-free environment for its clientele, the owner being a strong advocate against lung cancer.

Servers dressed in dark trousers and white shirts secured with ties or scarves and silk vests manoeuvred seamlessly around designer wood and steel tables, serving patrons seated on the expensive leather chairs. The guests looked every bit the part of people possessing ample means to reward themselves with the best life had to offer.

His hold on her hand tightened. "I want you to meet my friends first."

They approached a set of seats occupied by two men. As they got closer, she recognised them. She shouldn't have been surprised by the company he kept. After all, they were cut from the same ilk—handsome, wealthy, powerful men at the helm of some of the country's most successful companies. All had stature to catapult oestrogen into overdrive, and to the pleasure of many single ladies, all were unmarried.

When they stopped at the table, the three men exchanged handshakes and pleasantries before he pulled her in and extended a hand at the one closest to them.

"Chantelle, meet Don."

As in, Adonis Aggrey-Finn, CEO of Aggrey-Finn Group, a luxury transportation empire including a charter airline. Unlike Lord, Adonis hardly offered up his image for purposes other than official occasions like press conferences, earning himself the tag of reclusive bachelor. His dark suit and white shirt, with the top button unfastened, gave the impression he'd come straight from the office and had simply ripped off his tie. At about six feet, with shoulder-length dreadlocks secured at the back, he had presence.

He took her hand in a firm handshake. "Pleasure to meet you, Chantelle."

"Likewise."

Lord moved to the other guy. "And of course, Alpha."

As in, Alpha Mensah-Woode, owner of a chain of high-end fitness centres, restaurants, and nightclubs, including *Afrodite*. He appeared in the papers as often as Lord, but, given his occupation, not to mention his advocacy work to enforce laws banning smoking in public areas, publicity came with the territory. He sported a bald head with a thin moustache and goatee, with gold studs in both ears.

Both men were undoubtedly attractive, but she experienced no zing when their hands touched.

"Nice to meet you," Alpha said.

"A pleasure to meet you, as well."

"Did you already scare away your dates?" Lord asked with a grin.

Adonis scoffed. "Not a chance. They're just powdering their noses."

He said "powdering their noses" as if he thought the expression was code for something else. She wanted to tell him women really did excuse themselves to ensure their T-zones weren't glowing like neon signs. With the high levels of humidity in Ghana, keeping make-up flawless ought to be considered a small feat. For this reason, she often kept her make-up to a minimum—just enough for effect. Or maybe she just didn't fancy expending the time needed to clean off a full mask of cosmetics at the end of the day.

Alpha laughed. "Don't count your chickens before they're hatched, Lothario."

Lord shrugged. "The night's still young."

She looked from one to the other, a part of her prickling with curiosity. Did they have a bet going on? If so, how high were the stakes? Or perhaps she should be wondering what silly games young, entitled rich men played.

"Where's JQ?" Lord asked.

"Right here."

They all turned in the direction of the voice. She didn't readily recognise him, but with broad shoulders, a well-toned body, and a confident swagger, he looked every bit as striking as his friends. Naturally, an attractive woman accompanied him.

"You're late," Lord said.

"Fashionably so," came the reply. "Nothing says lame louder than arriving at a party early."

"Chantelle, meet the final member of the pack."

The new arrival extended his hand. "Jackson Quaye."

Of course. As COO of Quaye Cosmetics & Skincare, he didn't appear in the media as often as his sister, the CEO and the public face of the company.

"Pleased to meet you." She shook his hand. "I'm a big fan of your products."

"Very nice to meet you, Chantelle. Thank you for patronising QCS products."

"And here come our dates," Alpha said, nodding towards their right.

Their collective attention drew to two attractively dressed women, chatting and laughing as they approached. Clearly, they were acquainted. Discomfort inexplicably knotted in Chantelle's belly in anticipation of being the odd one out. It made no sense that it bothered her. She'd come here to do a job, not to get chummy with anyone.

The girls reached them, each slipping an arm around her date. Quick introductions were made before they sat.

"Are you joining us?" Don asked.

Lord looked at her. "Do you mind?"

She shook her head, now seeing the silver lining in being an outsider among this group of friends. She'd enjoyed their dancing far more than expected. Spending time with him in a group setting would help shake off whatever craziness came over her on the dancefloor. Besides, it might be nice to rub shoulders with Lord's crowd for a few minutes. Who knew—if she played her cards right, she could convince the other three to grant her all access interviews, too.

They took their seats in the U-shaped booth.

"What would you like to drink?" Lord asked.

"Amarula, if they have it. If not—"

"Of course they do." Before she decided whether to ask how he could be so sure, he added, "It's my party."

"This is *Afrodite*." Alpha made a show of being slighted. "Of course we have Amarula."

She fought an urge to chuckle. "I apologise."

Wearing a self-satisfied grin, Lord signalled a server who came to take their orders. Her Amarula and his Scotch arrived moments later. The ice clinked against the glass with the cream liqueur when she received it.

The next twenty minutes flew by as easy conversation flowed. She'd expected to be left out of the chatter, but Lord found a way to involve her by throwing questions at her or asking her to weigh in. He did it with such ease, a passer-by would never have guessed this to be her first time meeting every member of the group.

Don's date, a pretty, petite woman, suggested they head to the dance floor. An offer Lord, thankfully, declined. As much fun as the evening had turned out to be so far, she needed to get things back on track.

After the others departed, he placed his glass on the table before resuming his seat next to her.

"Red," he noted with an obvious glance at her top.

She shrugged. "I didn't want to be a party pooper."

Amusement glinted in his eyes as he sipped his drink. "So, you're not available and looking?"

In other words, dateless and desperate? She shifted in her seat. Why should his question make her uncomfortable? So what if she was single? It didn't amount to 'looking.' After all, her white trousers balanced out the dress code requirement. In any case, her personal life didn't concern him.

A chuckle rumbled out of him. "I'll let it slide, but tell me this. You say you don't dance, but not only are you good at it, you clearly love it. What—" His eyes narrowed. "Or who made you stop?"

Despite the smile, his eyes looked serious. Did he expect an answer? She couldn't give one, because she didn't want to talk about Martin. She'd enjoyed herself too much on the dancefloor to tarnish it with thoughts of her past.

"I'm supposed to be interviewing you, not the other way around."

He chuckled. "It's too loud in here for an interview, isn't it?"

You're not getting off so easily. Melodious laughter or not, she wouldn't leave without what she came for. "I can hear you just fine."

"Tell you what. Let's finish the drinks, dance some more, and I promise to give you my full attention. Alpha's office is upstairs, and it's much less noisy there. In the meantime, let's talk." He edged closer.

Too close.

She made a discreet shift backwards. Even so, she couldn't escape the heat radiating from his body. It sent a shiver snaking down her spine. His intoxicating essence filled her senses. Of their own volition, it seemed, her eyes dropped to his juicy-looking lips. She'd bet they could kiss a woman until she cried out his name. She didn't expect him to be stupid enough to kiss her, but with a playboy, one could never tell. A yearning lodged within her. When had she last been kissed?

She snapped her head up, blinking. She was not going there. When Lord smiled, her heart jumped into her throat. Had he caught her looking? God help her, but his pleased expression clearly indicated he had.

"Tell me about you."

He possessed one of those voices, deep and rich, that wrapped around you like a warm blanket on a cold evening.

Thanks to the hot and dry mid-February weather, however, she didn't need blankets, warm or otherwise. "Lord, this is strictly business."

"So this beautiful woman wants me to bare my soul to her, but I can't learn a little bit about her?"

She swallowed. The way he called her beautiful, you'd think he'd never said it to another woman. The guilt trip would get him nowhere, but the charm had begun to sneak under her skin.

"I'm not asking you to bare your soul." She smiled sweetly. "Just your life. What makes you tick?"

His easy laughter filled her ears.

"What makes me tick? You get right to the point, don't you?" He considered the question, his eyes looking pointedly into hers. "Women like you."

Oh, puleez. She resisted the urge to roll her eyes. After the pause, she'd expected something profound, not some uninspired, beaten-to-death line, which made her want to puke. Women like her. What did that even mean?

He studied her awhile, his expression soft and intense at the same time, and her insides trembled.

"I like a woman who's smart, strong, independent, knows what she wants … beautiful." He spoke quietly, reflectively.

She'd been gearing up to object to whatever he had to say, but she couldn't exactly argue with smart and beautiful, even if she knew such compliments came naturally to playboy types. How many women had he used the same lines on?

He furrowed his brows. "I don't often meet people, men and woman alike, who are genuine. Most people would do or say anything if they think it's what I want to hear."

"Translation, you like your women to play hard to get."

"No, but I want them to act like they have a mind of their own." He gave a little smile as if he had an ace up his sleeve. "Like you."

"You hardly know me."

"Ah, but I know *about* you. Your articles seem to be about love, relationships, and lifestyle on the surface, but are double-entendres. Every one of them."

"You're familiar with my work?"

She couldn't hide it; she was surprised he read her articles at all and impressed he'd discovered the dual meaning of her pieces. The freedom Randy gave her to play with words was one of the reasons she loved her job.

"I wouldn't let just anybody interview me." His stare dropped to his drink as he placed it on the side table, then it returned to watching her. "I'm curious to discover what you'll do with my interview."

"Oh, a profile story is quite standard. I ask questions, and you answer. A typical interview."

"I doubt it." His confidence was palpable and oddly attractive. "Typical isn't your style. You're not afraid to tell it like it is. I respect that. Actually, I like it."

The honesty and insightfulness took her off guard. This guy might not be as shallow as she'd expected.

Whoa. Had she just thought something nice about Lord McKenzie? She must be losing it. She took a gulp of her drink, hoping to shake off the temporary bout of insanity.

She cast a wide gaze around, half expecting paparazzi to pop out any second. The striking lack of flashlights when she'd first arrived had surprised her.

"Why the frown?"

"Oh." She shook her head. "I'm wondering where the cameras are."

"I pegged you for the private type, but I suppose looks can be deceiving."

Undisguised mockery laced his words, and stupidly, her cheeks flared with warmth. "I'm just surprised you came out without your usual entourage."

His satisfied look hardened. “Attendance was by invitation or vetting for those who bought tickets; the media wasn’t invited or allowed. Those who showed up were sent away, though I’d bet some brave ones are still lurking outside, waiting for their next victim.”

His voice turned humourless, giving a harsh edge to the word “victim.” Could it be possible he didn’t relish the attention? Or could this be a reverse-psychology ploy to make his party the most prestigious event of the night? No doubt, a public relations executive lurked in the background, providing the scoop to selected media. No way would Lord McKenzie throw a party and not have it hit the newsstands.

Before she could comment, he said, “Let’s dance.”

“Will it get me my interview faster?”

He gave her a one-sided smile, the hot, teasing kind. “Do I scare you that much?”

She released a snort. “You don’t scare me at all.”

Unless he meant the uncharacteristic lilt in her heartbeat each time he laughed, or the warmth coursing through her veins when he smiled—both of which indicated her defences were useless against him. Nothing terrified her more.

“If you aren’t scared, why are you so eager to run?”

She bit back a retort. No sense in handing the interview over to *Celeb* on a silver platter, which was exactly what would happen if she gave Lord a reason to back out. He didn’t grant too many interviews to start with. Already, he’d allegedly sent the media packing. You’d think with those looks, he’d be happy to pose for the cameras any day. Although, considering the way the media reported on him, he didn’t need to grant interviews in order to get publicity. As the sinfully handsome, openly single CEO of McKenzie Contractors, the largest locally-owned construction company in the country, both his personal and professional life made news.

He seemed amused by her lack of a response as he took her hand and led her to an open area in the lounge where a few couples already danced. The music turned slow. She hesitated. Slow music meant being in his arms, their bodies touching. She shouldn't do this. Yet, for some ridiculous reason, she wanted—*needed*, even—the closeness, to feel like a woman again. Just for a moment. Even if she must be certifiably insane for wanting all this in the arms of Lord McKenzie.

He pulled her gently, bringing her body flush against his. A tremor rushed through her. His warm breath on her face sent tiny tingles running over her skin. Heat radiated to her from each part of his body touching hers—his powerful thighs, lean hips, and firm abdomen, his hand pressed firmly on the small of her back.

When was the last time she'd been this close to a man? Her breath quickened as raw need surged through her. *Far too long.* Not since Martin.

Tears stung her eyes as the familiar loneliness accompanying Valentine's Day closed in. Old love songs always got to her. She turned away from his watchful gaze, focusing on other couples huddled close together on the dance floor. Yearning pierced her heart.

She gave herself a mental shake. She couldn't entertain such thoughts. Once she did, there would be no salvation.

As if sensing her distress, he pulled her closer, his hold tightening around her. Every thought flittered out of her mind as soon as their gazes locked, and she began to drown in the deep pools of his dark eyes.

"Happy Valentine's Day, Chantelle."

Was she stupid for liking the way he said her name? She opened her mouth to say something—about how Valentine's Day had been commercialised to the point of triviality, an occasion for errant lovers to feel better about neglecting their significant others, a day to buy enough emotional credit for another year, one day to make the unloved feel even less loved—anything to hide the strain of hearing those words.

But nothing came out.

His face hovered just inches away. Her heart stutter-stepped; her breath snagged. Without explanation, she wanted to know the taste of his lips. She wanted to erase it all from her mind. Her pain, his reputation. She wanted to believe he really was just the most eligible bachelor in town, and he had her in his arms.

He smiled, really smiled, not the movie star grins he'd been flashing earlier. His gaze emitted pure heat wrapped around a hint of gravity. What in the world could make a man with his looks and popularity melancholic? Surely, Lord McKenzie didn't have the same kinds of problems as mere mortals.

His fingers feathered her cheek, sending another wave of tremors through her. When his hand reached her chin, he lifted her face. Her mind barely registered what was happening before the space between them vanished. His searing kiss scorched her, inside and out. Nothing in her repertoire came close. A soft moan escaped her throat before she could stop it. She melted into him, curling her fingers around his nape.

When he pulled away, her breath came in fast, shallow bursts. In stunned reflex, her fingers came to her lips, which felt swollen, having not been used for this purpose in a while. Weak-kneed and aroused, she sensed she only remained standing because of his strong arms around her.

One of the couples dancing bumped into them, jerking her back to reality.

Shoot. This evening would be more difficult than she could have guessed. How was she supposed to conduct a professional interview when she'd just kissed the interviewee, and now that her mind insisted on dancing around words like ravished?

Suddenly, too exhausted from four years of keeping up her guard, she allowed him to stare into her eyes, burning her with his smouldering gaze, allowing her a glimpse into his own soul.

"Are you happy, Lord?"

She had no idea where the question came from but couldn't resist asking.

He stilled. She sensed him withdrawing mentally until his expression closed off completely. He pulled away.

"How about that interview?" Without waiting for a yea or nay, he led her off the dance floor.

At the back of her mind, she wondered if he had a middle name.

CHAPTER 3

"AFTER YOU."

He held the door open for her. A natural courtesy, or a game of him playing gentleman for her benefit? If he hoped to impress her so she wouldn't put a negative spin on his article, he'd soon learn she couldn't be bought.

She stepped into the office and was immediately drawn in by the modern décor themed in varying shades of blue.

Lord waved a hand towards one side of the room. "Make yourself comfortable."

She took in the richness of the leather finishing as she assessed her seating options, then bypassing the sofa and loveseat, decided on the safest choice—the one-seater. No need to invite a re-enactment of the scene from downstairs. From her vantage point, she noted how the accents of flowers and artwork on the walls complemented the blue tones to create a friendly-yet-sophisticated look.

She pulled out her digital recorder and a notepad, placing them on the glass-top centre table. "Alpha has good taste. It's no wonder *Afrodite* is one of the top clubs in Accra."

"I'll remember to tell him you said so, but I'll leave out the 'in Accra' bit. He believes his clubs are the best in the country."

She smiled as he grabbed the air-conditioner remote and pressed the 'ON' button. The appliance whispered out a current of cool air.

He stationed himself on the manager's desk, between the two comfortable-looking, barstool-inspired visitors' seats in front. Behind him, a cupboard with a glass door displayed various ornamental figurines, Valentine cards, and awards. *Afrodite* had garnered an impressive list of accolades.

"I'm all yours." He folded his arms and gave her a winning smile. "Unravel me."

A dozen comebacks popped into her mind, but she let it slide, knowing any one of them would send the direction of this interview east, west, or God-forbid, south. She flashed a smile of her own. Lord McKenzie in living colour, all hers to tear apart. *In a manner of speaking*. She allowed a few seconds to elapse, a good mechanism to soften tough interviewees and make them let down their guard.

Lord, however, merely sat there, ever confident and sinfully tempting, propped on one arm. Her gaze lingered on the flex of his biceps. He returned her stare, sending a shiver down her spine.

A little unnerved, she blurted out the first thing that came to mind, which was the general theme for the story and not meant to be a question. "Who's the real Lord McKenzie?"

A rumble sounded from him. She couldn't quite classify it as a laugh.

"The real me." His gaze darted elsewhere for a second. When he looked back at her, she could have sworn the room got warmer. "That's for you to figure out."

So he didn't intend to make it easy. Well, if he wanted to play hardball, fine by her.

"You've been called many things." She consulted her notepad, referring to non-existent notes. "Like real-life poster boy. How do you feel about it?"

"First, what makes me tick, and now you want to know my feelings. Are you sure this interview is for work?"

"Believe me, work is the only reason I'm here."

"It's Valentine's Day. I find it hard to believe you'd do interviews just because your boss insisted. Plus, you could have chosen someone else if you didn't want to do me."

With the cocky smile conspicuously missing, she assumed the pun hadn't been intentional, and let it slide. Again.

"Yet I'm here." She regarded him with a stern look, which evidently didn't achieve the intended effect as he responded with a lopsided smile. "Do you think you're a real-life poster boy?"

"What exactly *is* a real-life poster boy?"

She shrugged.

"You're rich and successful. Popular. In a recent poll, over eighty percent of Ghanaian women thought you were good-looking and wouldn't mind waking up next to you." *God, I sound like a groupi*e. "All this, and you're not a figment of someone's imagination."

He raised his arms in mock surrender. "Well, if that's the definition, then I guess I am. Tell me, where do you fall?"

"What do you mean?"

"Do you think I'm good-looking?"

Obliged by the question, and perhaps just an inherent desire, she gave him a look-over. From his designer dancing shoes, her gaze trailed up his athletic body to his trim black hair, which looked freshly cut. His disarming smile put a hop in her heartbeat and brought heat to her loins. She supposed it constituted finding him attractive.

"No," she said.

His expression suggested he thought otherwise, but he didn't push it.

"Doesn't the implication of such labels bother you?" she pressed.

He shrugged, picking up a paper clip from the stationary tray on the desk and unfurling it. Her sister shared the same habit, which drove her nuts.

"Stop it," she blurted out before she could restrain herself.

He frowned. "What?"

"The paper clip," she answered.

He appeared genuinely perplexed she should care about such a small thing.

"Just because it's inexpensive doesn't mean you can destroy it without cause."

He stared at the stationery in his palm, looking somewhat contrite, then folded it back. Of course, it didn't return to its original glory.

"To answer your question, I don't let it," he said simply. "I have more important things to do with my time, and everyone is entitled to an opinion, whatever it may be."

"But your reputation, good or bad, can affect the decision of a prospective business partner."

"If people make judgments on my character based on what the papers say about me, it's likely I won't want to do business with them in the first place."

"Then why are you always in the public eye?"

He leaned forward. "I'm an architect. I design and erect buildings. I don't solicit publicity, but I guess I'm a likeable guy."

He sat back with a pleased expression.

Something about his self-assured manner, perhaps its seeming effortlessness, commanded her admiration, despite being offensive in its arrogance.

"Just because cameras chase you around all day doesn't mean everyone likes you."

As soon as the words left her lips, she wished she could suck them back. But she maintained an even expression, since she didn't intend letting him see remorse on her face. No need to stroke his ego any more than he was already doing.

"Then why are you here, Chantelle?"

Work. Why being alone with him triggered a subtle rush of excitement was another issue altogether, one she refused to dignify with further contemplation.

"Maybe you're just a good story."

Something swept across his features. Irritation? Anger? It disappeared so quickly, she wondered if she'd imagined it.

"Next question."

His stern tone of voice took her by surprise, making her pause for just a second. Had she hit a nerve? Should she pursue this line of questioning? This was the most serious he'd been all evening, save for the time he'd kissed her. Perhaps it was worth a shot.

"Do you believe in capital punishment?"

His face drew into an unreadable mask. "What's this, a beauty pageant?"

"Are you saying you don't have an opinion?"

He snickered. "You'd like that, wouldn't you?"

"Pardon me?"

"I mean, you'd love to report how insensitive I am to important issues like capital punishment." He grinned. "And World Peace."

"Are you insensitive to them?"

His grin widened, and she inferred she'd just stepped into a trap. He left his place at the table and came to sit on the loveseat. Too close for comfort, but she squared her shoulders, determined to veil his effect on her. The kiss didn't mean anything.

"Oh, I'm sensitive." His voice deepened. "I'm very sensitive. If you let me, I'll show you exactly how sensitive I can be."

Sensitive? Puleez. He was probably a selfish lover. "What's my name?" and "Who's your daddy?" came to mind. Images of him *sans* his clothes assaulted her, and suddenly, it felt as if someone had lit a flame under her seat. Oh, man. She shifted, viciously kicking out the fantasies forming in her mind.

She cleared her throat. "I'm not looking for a turn-on, Mr. McKenzie."

He winced. "Please, Mr. McKenzie is my father. Call me Lord."

She fought to keep from rolling her eyes. "Are we skipping the question, then?"

"I'll give you a scenario from Friday's papers. A man breaks into a home; he rapes the woman and kills the man while their children watch." Anger flashed in his eyes, his jaw flexed. "If anyone, never mind the state, accosts and kills him, should that person be condemned?"

She swallowed, remembering the story. One of those things that made you wonder where the sanity of the world was headed. As much as such situations challenged her opinion of capital punishment, she believed the preservation of life mattered above all else.

"You think the solution to murder is yet another killing? Everyone has a right to life." She made sure to maintain eye contact. "Everyone. And no one, not even the state, should take a life. Two wrongs don't make a right, don't you think?"

He shrugged. "Someone once said, and I agree, the right to live is a human right no one owes to another. The thing is, a man who willingly takes away another's life automatically gives up the right to claim his own."

She didn't respond. His words made a lot of sense. Her twin sister had two adorable daughters. If anyone harmed them, Chantelle would be devastated, and she'd want to see the person pay, but could her grief lead her to kill? She hoped to never find out.

She flipped a page of her notepad, regrouping.

"You seem disappointed," he said.

"This isn't about me. Besides, few things disappoint me."

"Why is that?"

The question took her aback, which was the only reason she answered. "Unlike most people, I don't look at life through rose-coloured glasses. I rely on myself rather than others."

He nodded. "I see."

"What do you see?"

"You're one of those 'I stand alone' people who refuse to let anything or anyone affect them enough to risk hurting them."

No, she was the woman who'd let someone in, only for him to betray her in the worst possible way. No matter how many times she told herself to shrug it off, because bad relationships happen to everyone, she couldn't seem to get past the pain and the betrayal, and the lies he'd told her. Then he'd died, leaving her with questions.

Had he been unhappy? Had it been her fault he'd sought solace in another woman's arms? Had there been signs she'd failed to see? What could be so wrong with her that she hadn't been enough?

She looked away, hoping her eyes betrayed none of her thoughts. Lord was the last person she wanted to air her dirty laundry in front of. Who did he think he was, anyway? Considering his short-lived relationships, couldn't he be accused of the same? *Remove thou the plank in your eye before you try to take out the toothpick in mine.*

Feeling suitably back in control of her emotions, she returned her gaze to him. "You hardly know me."

"Oh, I know your type. You've been hurt once, and you're afraid to get hurt again, so—"

"What?" In reflex, she sat up, her back ramrod straight. "I've built a wall around me? Is that what you're about to say?"

"Not you, Chantelle," he said, his voice infuriatingly calm. "You've built a pedestal where you can stand on top of the world and look down on everyone." His tone dared her to deny it. "You do it so well through your articles, yet you give no one the right to judge you in return."

Now she was offended. "I don't judge people."

He made her blood boil and her body prickle with emotions refusing to remain buried. She tried to stay calm, but this guy irritated her with his answers and the smirk on his face. He thought he had her all figured out, did he? Well, he didn't. Whatever distance she kept, she did it to protect her heart. It didn't mean she thought herself better than everyone else.

"What is it about a confident woman that makes men like you feel small?"

A grin steadily crept to his lips, making her realise she'd probably said the wrong thing again. He took hold of her hand, effectively chasing out every thought from her mind.

"Believe me, I'm not small."

She swallowed, trying to prevent her jaw from dropping. *Breathe in, breathe out*. Oh, heck. Even the breathing exercise took her mind to other in-and-out motions involving him and the part of his anatomy he felt the need to brag about.

His gaze caught hers, refusing to let go, burning holes into her skull with its intensity. His eyes offered an invitation, a tempting offer. Her lips twitched in memory of his lips on them. If his kiss was anything to go by, then making love with him could be—

She shook herself mentally, blinking to break the connection. She withdrew her hand, but her heart continued to throb as her mind shamelessly lusted after images of his naked form stretched alongside hers, his long fingers finding her feminine folds, her body wrapped around him. Flames of passion licked her skin as her body temperature became unbearably hot.

This was insane. She'd never struggled so hard to keep her focus on work. Her body reacted to him in ways she'd never responded to a man before.

She crossed her legs. It seemed to help stave off the sensations purling between her thighs and making her want to slow dance with him again. She decided to ease the tension by switching to safer questions: background, family, school. When those were exhausted, she progressed to how he got into the construction company, set up by his father and now a *Ghana Club 100* company. Reluctantly, she moved to the reason why most of their readers bought the magazine in the first place. *Gossip.*

"You've been associated with actress Deconte Aggrey-Finn. You escorted her to this year's G.A.G Awards and the premiere of her last movie. Is she your girlfriend?"

The lord and the countess, as one tabloid dubbed them.

He smiled in the manner he'd been doing the entire evening, easy, yet sexy, relaxing against the chair.

He tugged his red designer T-shirt. "Single and available."

No surprises there. At least, his female fans would be happy to know their idol had become single again. Considering his record, it wouldn't be for long.

"Do you like children?"

"Yes." He laughed. "When they belong to someone else."

Clearly, being funny wasn't one of his strong fortes. A minor blot in his portfolio of attributes, for sure. She went through the personal information and moved to his opinion of the state of the economy and politics. Even with the serious topics, he found a way to disrupt at every turn, detecting double meanings in her questions, answering them as such. It irked her that he wouldn't just give her straight answers so she could get this interview over and done with.

The more disturbing thing, however, was the way his gaze heated her blood and how her heart expanded every time he laughed. Worse, she suspected he knew he was getting to her. Hopefully, his powers of discernment weren't strong enough to alert him to the extent of his effect on her. Because if he did, he might kiss her again knowing she'd let him.

When he crossed his legs, she noticed the slight bulge in his trousers. Shocked at where her eyes and mind had drifted, her gaze shot back up and collided with his. Had there really been a swell, or was her mind overworking itself? The cold flow from the air-conditioner didn't seem to be doing anything to cool her down. She shifted to a more comfortable position as she tried not to think about the spasms of awareness happening in the south of her anatomy.

An interview, which would have taken forty to forty-five minutes with another person, took an hour and a half, because Lord McKenzie didn't make it easy. She admitted, though, interrogating him brought exhilaration. Two months ago, she'd interviewed a government minister whose enthusiasm quotient could have bored a monk to death.

When they were done, and not a moment too soon, she flipped the notepad closed and switched off the recorder, happy to be on her way out. The experience had been less painful than she'd imagined, although having spent so much time with him, she'd started developing problems of a sensual nature. She blamed the kiss.

"One more thing," she said. "Do you have a middle name?"

Girl, you can't be serious.

His brows shot up questioningly. Truth be told, she didn't know herself why she'd asked, but once the idea occurred, she'd wanted to know.

"Yes," he said.

When she realised he didn't intend to elaborate, curiosity got the better of her. "What is it?"

A twitch on the corner of his lips and a gleam in his eyes told her he planned to stretch her before answering. "What, Lord McKenzie isn't enough?"

Of course, who wants to give out his middle name when he's named after a deity? "*Odopa* Magazine tells the whole story. Every bit of information is relevant, ergo—"

"Ergo?"

"Yes, ergo. It means—"

He waved a hand, cutting her off. "I know what it means. I'm merely surprised it's part of your working vocabulary."

"There's a lot more in my working vocabulary than you know about."

"Would you like to teach me?" A few moments elapsed as he stared into her eyes, and the air between them began to sizzle with tension. "You intrigue me, Chantelle."

He reached out and held her hand, emitting shock waves through his fingers. She pulled her hand from his grasp. *Focus*, she thought, in relation to both him and her wandering emotions. Feelings like those were reserved for special people, and Lord McKenzie didn't fall into that category.

She grasped through her mind for where they'd left off in the conversation. "I suppose after all the things you've revealed about yourself, you're entitled to some mystery."

"No mystery about it." He winked, flashing a devilish grin. "I'll show you mine if you show me yours."

Words stuck in her throat as an image of 'his' projected onto her mind's eye. Of course, imagination, without prior visual aid, couldn't fully fathom any part of such masculine perfection. She wasn't going there, though. The only thing she would be showing him was her backside as she walked out the door.

He chuckled as if he knew precisely where her mind had gone, and warmth instantly flushed her face. What were they talking about again? *Right*. His middle name.

"I could find out, you know." She crossed her arms and met his gaze in a clear standoff position.

"You could try, but I'm afraid it would be a wasted effort."

Not one to back out of a challenge, she pushed. "You forget I'm a reporter. It means I find people with the information I need, and I can be persuasive."

"Trust me, you couldn't pay them enough."

"Everyone has a price."

He started to say something but paused. She could almost see his mind shifting gears, his eyes twinkling with interest.

"Do you have a price?"

Sucker.

"Of course I do," she answered in the sweetest tone she could muster and relished the raised eyebrow he gave her, predictably assuming she'd defend her pricelessness. "You just can't afford me."

He smiled, visibly impressed. "You'd be surprised what I can afford, Chantelle. I'm a very wealthy man. Besides, they say the best things in life are free."

Her stomach did flips, with an s, which felt suspiciously like butterflies. They couldn't be. She knew the sensation of butterflies in the stomach, and it didn't feel this giddy. For a moment, she stared back, unable to tear her gaze away. Something in his eyes—a deep yearning and a genuineness—surprised her. It held her captive.

Her heart skipped a beat and swelled as if she'd just caught a glimpse of his true self, and that true self had connected with something in her.

Wait a minute. That couldn't be right. She and Lord McKenzie had nothing in common. Besides this interview, which put them in the same room at the same time, she and he didn't move in the same circles.

As she replaced the recorder in its case, he picked up her bag, took a step closer, invading her personal space. He touched her elbow and ran his fingers lightly over her arm, tormenting her body with desire until he slung the handbag on her shoulder.

"You can torture it out of me." His voice had turned raspy.

A thrilling sensation blazed through her, causing her to shiver. He seemed to suck the air from the room, making it impossible to breathe properly.

Robbed of oxygen supply, she couldn't think of an appropriate retort. "Be careful what you wish for, Lord. You might actually get it."

Instead of stepping back, he brought a knuckle to her chin, lifting her face as if readying her for a kiss. She swallowed. Chemistry, thick and magnetic, vibrated between them, trapped them in a sensual vortex. For the first time, she noticed something in his eyes. A reflection of the same confusion she experienced.

It all became clear. He felt it, too, and his nonchalance had been a cover-up. She was convinced of it. He blinked, appearing to rethink his actions, and then dropped his hands back to his sides.

Disappointment sliced through her.

He cleared his throat. “I’ll walk you out.”

She released a shaky breath, hoping he hadn’t noticed. Her mind continued to dwell on what making love with him might be like as she tried to bring her breathing under control. God, it had been so long …

Stop it. She needed to get out of there before another kiss ensued. That would be bad, because if it did, she didn’t know whether she’d be able to resist.

CHAPTER 4

LORD KNEW HE WAS in trouble the moment he reached for the door and found Chantelle's hand instead. She swirled around, her almond-shaped eyes widening. Their hazel intensity met his gaze, and he was done for. Energy passed between them, zapping his will to hold back.

"Chantelle." His voice came out heavy, having forced its way out of the vise gripping his throat.

He pulled her, intending to have one more taste of her luscious full lips. She offered no resistance as she stepped towards him. Her bag dropped to the floor just before her body slammed against his, every soft curve fitting perfectly into him as he laid claim on her lips. There was a moment of stillness, of surprise, and of recognition. A brief satisfaction of a craving sparked the second their hands first connected.

She kissed him back with the same hunger with which he devoured her. Fire ignited, took over. She gripped his T-shirt, tugging it out of his trousers in the process. He became instantly hard. When her hands grazed his skin, he lost hold of any control he tried to maintain. A kiss wouldn't be enough to douse the inferno of desire consuming them. Something it seemed she'd already realised, because she pushed the T-shirt up his torso.

Their breathing and moans mingled as they attended to the multiple tasks of kissing, shedding their clothes, and finding a place to settle. Chantelle's top came off first, followed by his, then her jeans and his. Stumbling urgently to the loveseat, they continued their kissing and frantic groping.

With one snap, her bra came off, making him pause. He needed to take in the sight before him. In nothing but a flimsy pair of lacy white panties, she was a vision of perfection, her body a work of art. Her tall frame ordinarily projected an impression of slimness, but underneath her clothes were curves, lush and feminine, ample hips narrowing into a small waist and firm breasts proudly pouting at him, all wrapped in flawless milk-chocolate skin.

"You're stunning," he whispered.

He couldn't wait to taste her. But first, he needed to touch. Reverently, he cupped her breasts and kneaded them, drawing a soft moan from her. He worked his way up to their beaded peaks and watched her lips part with the breath she sucked in and the whimper she released. She broke the stare, arching up as her gaze dropped to his lips.

He took one eager nipple in his mouth, rolled his tongue over it a few times, felt her tremble beneath him. He groaned, moving to the next and latching on as one famished. A soft cry left her lips as her hands cupped his head.

Pulling back, he trailed his hands down her flat stomach to her hips, enjoying the feel of her curves. His mouth followed with kisses, along the same path to her navel. He dipped his tongue in the hollow. With heavy breaths trembling out of her, she parted her legs, pressing her pelvis against him. Did it mean what he hoped?

Reaching for the hem of her panties, he paused, raising his eyes to meet her gaze. She watched him with sultry eyes, her pupils dilated. Seeing the desire in their depths caused several ounces of restraint to slip from his grip, but he needed to know they were on the same page. He wouldn't go any further if she harboured doubts.

"Tell me to take this off, Chantelle."

She gave a slight nod. "Make me feel like a woman."

With pleasure. He began to rid her of the panties, kissing every newly exposed part of her as the underwear slowly came off. When it reached her calves, he released it, concentrating his efforts on places between her legs. He caressed her inner thigh, and she sucked in a breath. She parted her legs further. She was wet, her sensitive bud swollen. Responding to her invitation, he stroked her gently while his mouth traced kisses back to her breasts. She moaned, reaching down to cuddle his head again as his tongue pleasured the dark peaks of her breasts. Her tender touch stoked the fire of his desire.

He groaned against a hard nipple as he slipped a finger into her slick heat. God, she felt so good. His erection throbbed, wanting—no, *needing*—to be surrounded in the same way as his digit. However, he needed to take it slow, to give her multiple releases before he extracted his own.

His thumb fondled her pleasure spot as his finger continued its invasion. He took his time, working her desire until he had her whimpering and breathing hard. Her hands dropped to her sides, clutching the foam beneath her palms. She stiffened. A whimper sounded in her throat, but her lips were pressed together. It seemed she suppressed her moans, releasing them only when the pleasure became unbearable. Why? Was she not used to relinquishing control, or just not accustomed to getting this amount of stimulation? Either way, he needed to get her to relax.

"Let yourself go, Chantelle." He spoke against her skin, tasting the salty sheen of sweat as his lips moved down her stomach. He dipped his tongue in her navel, mimicking the movements of his finger.

She responded with a sharp cry, and then a long moan as her body moved in rhythm with his strokes. She gripped his shoulders, her nails digging into his flesh. They were going to leave evidence of their moment of passion. It wasn't needed; he'd remember this night.

He pushed a second finger into her, drawing out another cry from her lips. Her thighs locked around his waist.

"That's it," he said, as her body tensed up. He traced his tongue along her skin to her ribs where he nipped her side lightly with his teeth, followed by an open-mouthed kiss.

Her body shuddered. "Oh!"

He loved hearing her moan. "That's it, Chantelle."

She'd reached the edge. He could tell from the sharp, shallow breaths and the trembling of her body. Yet, she held on, fuelling his determination to ensure this night didn't end with him almost getting her there. He moved over her until their eyes were level. Hers were closed.

"Chantelle, let go," he gritted out in a determined whisper.

Her eyes flew open, and he glimpsed the storm raging within them before they rolled back. She came quickly, with a gasp and a shudder, as if she hadn't wanted to or expected it.

Withdrawing his fingers, he licked them, loving the taste of her. When he lowered his lips onto hers again, the tenderness in her response stunned him, made him want her more. Her hands caressed their way down his body, wrenching a groan from deep within him. He burnt, his desire intensified at her touch. Urgently, he pulled away, wanting to give her as much pleasure as he could before connecting his body with hers.

He dropped to his knees, spread her legs. The scent of her arousal sent a sharp jolt through his groin. He wanted another taste of her, right from the source this time. Not losing another second, his mouth found her centre. He drank in her pleasure juices, making love to her with his tongue. He let his hands rise over her until they encountered and cupped her breasts. He rubbed the tip of her nipples with his thumb, felt them harden.

She writhed, her hands covering his as he worshipped her breasts. Her feet rubbed him, converging at the junction of his thighs. Her toes found his erect member, drew the length of it. He nearly imploded at the impact. A harsh groan rushed out of him.

She didn't relent. It seemed she was done holding back. Her moans flowed out uninhibited, her gestures bold. She intertwined their fingers. Finally, the sound of her moans escalated, the tone telling him her lips were parted. She twisted his fingers as she began to tremble again.

The urge to bury himself in her heat overwhelmed him. He reached for his jeans, extracted a condom, and slipped it on. He needed to experience her climax more intimately. Propping her against the edge of the chair, he gave in to the power of his desire, filling her slowly, allowing her body to adjust to his size. As he entered her paradise, she released a long, drawn-out moan, and her body began to spasm around his shaft.

Her release came again, delicious, unrestrained, satisfied.

As her body squeezed around him, he shuddered, shutting his eyes, fighting to prevent himself from coming before he'd even started. Bringing her further down, he lifted her so she half sat on him with her back against the edge of the chair, her legs wrapped around him. No longer the innocent bystander, she met him with equal passion, meting out as much pleasure as he gave. Moving inside her, he cradled her back in his hands. Opening his mouth over her breast, he kissed, licked, and sucked.

"I can't get enough of you," he mumbled.

She kissed the top of his head. She might as well have reached into him and touched his heart. For, without a doubt, he'd never be the same after tonight.

She cupped his cheeks, urging him to raise his head. Then, she rained kisses on his face, making him shudder with each one until he couldn't deny himself the pleasure of tasting her mouth. She met him halfway. Their tongues mated, sparred; hands skimmed over skin, moans blended in mutual fulfilment.

As he approached the edge of ecstasy, he slowed his pace, not wanting to get there before her, but she continued to move against him, tormenting him with bliss. Powerless to prevent the inevitable, a groan erupted from deep within him as his release rushed to the fore. He'd never left a woman behind, and the thought of this being the first time bothered him. He suspected, when it came to Chantelle Sah, he should prepare for a series of firsts.

"Aah, fuck," he groaned as he gave her one last deliberate push, which sent her tumbling over the edge again, this time with him in tow. He almost cried with relief as he heard her whimper against his skin and felt her internal muscles grip him. He shuddered with the remnants of his release.

Though she trembled, she attempted to stand up.

"No," he whispered. "Let me hold you."

Her intimate hug felt so right, he was reluctant to part from her. They remained like that for a moment while he basked in the joy of her wrapped in his arms.

Silence took over with neither of them speaking, as if talking might taint the moment.

Finally, he released her, then finding her panties, he helped her put them on. With reverence, he assisted her to dress. Once she was done and seated, he proceeded to put on his clothes. Lastly, he picked up her bag and handed it to her.

She took it without meeting his gaze. Her warm glow tempted him to reach for her again.

"Chantelle."

At the mention of her name, she looked at him. Everything in him stilled. The air around them remained thick. None of the tension and chemistry had dissolved. If anything, now that they'd shared the ultimate act of intimacy, it seemed even more tangible.

"Are you okay with this?" he finally asked.

She nodded and, without a word, turned towards the door—a sure sign of being anything but.

CHANTELLE'S BODY CONTINUED to buzz as she stepped out of the office. Fighting the urge to run and put the past few minutes out of her mind, she waited for Lord to lock the door. Her heart lilted as he smiled down at her before leading the way. Despite her satiation, she felt stiffness in her movement as pleasure metamorphosed into shock. Thankfully, an empty lobby greeted them. As if sensing her need for privacy, Lord led the way back to her car through an unmanned side exit.

She deactivated the alarm on her car before reaching it. He reached around her. She stiffened briefly, relaxing when his hands closed around the door to open it for her. Just as she turned to sit in, he held her hand, crouching so they were at eye level. She avoided his gaze, wishing he wouldn't speak, wouldn't remind her of what they'd just done. She wanted to forget it, and words would only substantiate their actions. If he said thank you, she'd pummel him until she drew blood.

"I'd like to see you again."

From any other man, it would have sounded like begging, but from Lord, it sounded like a proposal. It proved altogether too enticing.

She finally met his stare. The need in his eyes nearly knocked her off her feet.

She looked away. "I don't think it's a good idea."

"And it took you all of two seconds to decide?"

His harsh voice snapped her attention back to him. Desire he didn't bother to mask stared back at her.

She didn't want to get sucked in, didn't want to believe he actually wanted her. It would be an illusion leading to pain. She couldn't do pain again. Not this kind, anyway.

"Look, this was a—" *Mistake. Say it.* She couldn't bring herself to utter the word. "This was strictly business."

"Bullshit," he spat out between clenched teeth. "Do you sleep with everyone you interview? Tell me this wasn't the best damned sex you ever had."

His words cut her to the core. Her only defence was retaliation.

"I beg your pardon, Lord McKenzie. Don't let your high and mighty ego get in the way of reason." The parking lot appeared empty, but she kept her voice down just in case they weren't alone. "Thank you for the interview."

"Chantelle, wait."

The pleading in his voice threatened to weaken her. God, please don't let him say he's sorry. An apology would be far worse than a thank you.

She didn't give him a chance to speak. "Don't you have a party to return to?"

"Screw the party. We should talk about what just happened."

"No, we shouldn't."

Without waiting for a counteraction, she slipped into the car and shut the door. Turning on the ignition, she reversed, and as she shifted into first gear, called out, "Happy Valentine's Day, Lord."

◆◆◆

THE MIND COULD be a cruel thing. A moment ago, consumed with passion. Now, it only spoke one word: dirty. A mixture of shame, anger, and regret played havoc on Chantelle's mind as she entered her house. Shaking from the kaleidoscope of unwanted emotions competing for her attention, she collapsed against the door. For a while, she remained still, the only movement being the heaving of her chest as she tried to format her memory.

It didn't happen, one voice in her head said.

About time, another tossed back.

Nothing she could tell herself would make her feel better about what had occurred between her and—she didn't want to think his name—even if it had been four years since her last time. Of all the people she could have chosen, Lord McKenzie with his cheesy lines straight out of the Womaniser's Handbook.

It had been more than his words, though. He'd handled her as though he'd known exactly where to touch. No. Beneath his fingertips, everything in her had blossomed, turning her entire being into one giant pleasure spot. Even when he'd paused to give her a chance to back out, she'd given him permission to unravel her.

Her awareness of him had begun the moment they'd spoken on the phone. Had it been this morning?

She took in a deep breath, mentally shoving it to the back burner. Pretend it never happened. But she could smell him, taste him. Her skin simmered where his hands had touched her. *Everywhere*.

With that realisation, the anger broke loose, pushing past everything else. She dropped her bag, ripped off her clothes, and made a dash for the bathroom, determined to wash away every last bit of him.

With frantic fingers, she turned the faucet, not stopping until both hot and cold were on full blast. She allowed the water to soak her skin, the warmth working its way through to her bones like a massage. A pitiful moan lodged itself in her throat, refusing to come out. Still shaking, she squirted bath gel into her palms and lathered it over herself, rubbing away the feel of his touch, replacing each one with hers.

Shampoo followed. The foam soon covered her face, and she closed her eyes, working out the soap. Some of the lather found its way into her eyes. She placed her face directly under the shower's flow. Without warning, the veil of water seemed to cut off her air supply, making her gasp. The steam filling the bathroom became suffocating. She dropped to her knees, still taking in deep breaths. When a sob escaped from her lips, she realised she wasn't choking. She was crying.

How could she feel sated and cheap all at the same time? Why did her body still remember his kisses and caresses? She wept for this, and all the other times she'd made a fool of herself where a man was concerned, but also because she'd never come undone quite like she had tonight. She'd certainly never climaxed multiple times in one session. Lord McKenzie had touched her, and for a moment, all the colours of the rainbow had come alive in her. And she resented him for it.

CHAPTER 5

WAKING UP THE NEXT morning to her radio alarm, Chantelle continued to lie in bed reluctant, for the first time in years, to start the day. She shook herself mentally and forced her body out of the sheets. Even though she didn't have to be at the office at eight, she wanted to get there early and immerse herself in work. She knew where to channel the remnants of last night's anger. It should make for some pretty interesting reading in April.

That thought brightened her disposition, and she found herself looking forward to the day, after all. Although a photo shoot had to be done to accompany the interview, it didn't dampen her mood. She would just send one of the photographers, and they should be all set. In fact, she decided to make the call before getting ready for the day.

Remembering she'd left her phone in her handbag, which lay at her front door where she'd left it last night, she made her way out of the room. When she took a step, the tenderness between her legs caused her to grimace. *Sweet pain*—her twin sister Danielle's term for it. The words popped into her mind along with memories of being in Lord's arms last night, of blooming and flying, of shattering and healing. Heat pooled in her belly, need in her centre.

"Better archive it," she told that part of her body. "You aren't going to be exercising again anytime soon."

She was raising defences as strong and as wide as the Great Wall of China. No one would be getting through.

She detoured to the kitchen to get a glass of juice before coming to retrieve her bag. Taking out her phone, she saw three missed calls. She'd only dialled it once yesterday, yet she recognised the number instantly. Lord McKenzie. Temptation to return the call gripped her, but she didn't need any more of that deep voice giving her body erotic ideas.

Pushing the thought out of her head, she punched in her favourite photographer's number and waited.

"Hi, Joe," she greeted when he answered. "What's your schedule like tomorrow?"

"What do you need?"

"We're doing an exclusive on Lord McKenzie. I did the interview yesterday, and I need you to take pictures of him at work, on site, at home. You know the drill."

"No problem," Joe said. "Does he know we're coming?"

"He knows it's part of the deal, but you need to schedule an appointment. He said he had a busy week coming up, but tomorrow should be open. Otherwise, we'd have to wait until next Friday."

"Next week isn't good for me, but I can do tomorrow. I'll call right away to book a time. You have his number?"

"Yes." She checked her 'missed calls' log and gave it to him. "Thanks, Joe."

"See you tomorrow?"

"No." She shook her head as if he could see her and made up an excuse. "I have things to do which I can't push forward any longer."

"No problem," he said. "So what did you do last night aside from the interview? Get drunk? Get laid?"

Get laid. She flushed at the memory. Joe didn't have to know. "Just the interview."

"Chantelle, Chantelle, Chantelle." He gave her a tsk-tsk. "You really need to get out there and meet people. Increase your visibility. Get a boyfriend."

She shook her head. A boyfriend was definitely not what she needed. "Joe, I have to run. Let me know how it goes."

She hung up, satisfied she'd left the shoot in good hands. Being the lead on the story, she'd normally have been there at least to ensure it began without a hitch. But Joe was the best photographer on staff, and she'd worked with him on enough occasions to trust him with this.

He knew his stuff, which saved her from facing Mr. You-can-torture-it-out-of-me.

WHEN CHANTELLE ENTERED the office, Dufie and another colleague, Eyram, were huddled over a newspaper. Saying a cheery "good morning," she passed them and went to her desk, catching just a bit of their conversation.

"Who do you suppose she is?" Eyram asked.

"It must be one of those new models." Dufie gave a snort. "Look at how slim she is."

Chantelle tapped her nails against her desk as her computer took its sweet time booting. Tuning out the gossip, she clicked on Outlook and opened an Internet browser.

Dufie and Eyram approached her. They poised themselves by her desk, arms folded, and just stared at her.

Chantelle eyed them with suspicion. "What?"

"'Good morning'? That's all we get?"

"Yeah, are you okay?" Eyram, who looked absolutely cute in her second trimester of pregnancy, asked.

"What are you talking about?"

"Don't play innocent," Dufie said. "What's the top reason why two gorgeous and intelligent career women would be having so much fun reading newspapers?"

"One, you work for a magazine, and it's part of your job—"

"I said we're having fun doing it."

"Okay." She sat back, folding her arms. "Gossip. You have too much time on your hands."

Dufie slammed a copy of *Graphic Showbiz* in front of her. The sudden movement and the noise caused Chantelle to jump.

"Girlfriend, don't pretend you aren't interested in the chitchat."

"Yeah, you're always at the forefront when it comes to this particular alpha dog," Eyram said. "How did you put it the other day? Too rich, too handsome—"

Too gifted in the sex department. "Too much of any good thing is bad."

Dufie waved away their discussion. "Anyway, we were having a little fun before the boring work starts."

"For some of us, this is the highlight of our sex lives," Eyram said, patting her stomach. "Sefa still won't make love with me because of the nightmare about crushing the baby."

Her eyes lingered on Eyram's stomach and the loving gesture she'd just made. Her colleague positively glowed, as she should. The love in her voice and eyes when she talked about her family were enviable. A pang of longing crashed into Chantelle's heart at the memories, painful memories of shattered dreams which had once almost destroyed her.

"I told you what to do about that, didn't I?" Dufie said. "Just wait until he's asleep and sit on his—"

"Let's keep the conversation corporate, shall we?" Eyram raised a cautionary hand. "I tried it, but he sleeps like a soldier…with one eye open."

They all burst out laughing.

"I was luckier than you, thank you very much." Dufie batted her eyelashes, removing her hand from the paper to fan herself. "Happy Valentine to me."

The image on the front page caught Chantelle's attention, and she froze. A picture of Lord McKenzie outside *Afrodite* stared at her. He leaned over a woman. Her. *Oh, crap!* The headline read: *LORD'S SECRET VALENTINE?*

She wished the floor would open up and swallow her whole. Then, with relief, she noticed her face wasn't visible. Luckily, the picture had been taken when he'd opened the door, so his arm covered her face. She made a conscious effort to start breathing again, remembering she had company.

"Maybe it's Dufie in the picture, considering she got lucky last night," Eyram said.

"I got lucky, but not *that* lucky." Dufie shrugged. "I wonder who it is, though. Just out of curiosity."

Chantelle kept a straight face. "Maybe it's Deconte Aggrey-Finn. You know, his lady of the moment."

"Can't be. She's filming a movie in Nigeria." Dufie seemed to always know these things. "I'll hand it to him. The man knows how to have fun. The countess travels for a few days, and here he is with a stand-in."

The comment hit Chantelle like a slap on the face.

"Maybe they're already over," she said, remembering Lord's words.

It didn't change anything. Instead of a stand-in, she'd been a place-warmer until his next conquest.

Dufie snatched the paper back.

"Come here, you Adonis you." She sighed dreamily at the picture before turning to Chantelle. "You should learn from him."

Eyram giggled, before assuming a pious expression. "Yeah, she was probably at home watching TV."

If only.

"Working," she corrected, hoping the guilt deluging her didn't manifest all over her face.

"I heard it was a nice party," Dufie said, walking away, and Eyram followed.

Alone at last, her mind returned to the picture of her and Lord. Thank God whoever took it didn't get a good angle. Hopefully, no one else did. Still, it looked like he was leaning in for a kiss, when, in fact, he'd only been saying he'd like to see her again. Would she have let him if he'd tried to kiss her?

She chided her wayward thoughts. *If you have to ask.*

THE CONDOM BROKE.

Nine hours after being with Chantelle, and it was all Lord could think about—that and her refusal to pick up his calls. Rising from his chair, he walked to the window and gazed outside his

He disconnected the call. Before getting back to the blueprints on his desk, he buzzed his secretary and booked a call. A moment later, the call came through, and he ordered a bouquet of flowers to be delivered to *Odopa* magazine.

◆◆◆

DURING HER LUNCH break, Chantelle passed by the newsstand near her office to check for any other photos of her night with Lord. Luckily, she found none. Returning to the office, her disposition became much lighter, happier. With no further reminders of last night, she could finally put it behind her. She'd wanted to feel like a woman again, and she had. Nothing wrong with it, she told herself, but try as she might, her mind kept throwing words like 'unprofessional' and 'place-warmer' at her.

Last night was undoubtedly a common occurrence for him, but not for her. She'd never done something like that before—certainly not on a first date. It hadn't even been a date. But, God, the sex had been epic. It stung to think it was nothing more than another 'Day in the Life of' event for him. She decided to focus on the positive. He'd helped her move past the fear of putting herself out there again.

From a distance, she saw Eyram seated on her chair and Dufie standing in front of the desk. She frowned. Had she missed a meeting? Eyram said something which made Dufie turn. Chantelle saw their pleased expressions before noticing the … flowers?

Her step faltered as she continued her approach. She prayed they were from anyone, *anyone*, but Lord. However, her lack of a social life narrowed the possibilities. She didn't need undue attention from the media and her colleagues for one night's mistake, a mistake he wouldn't leave alone.

"Well, well, well," Dufie said when Chantelle came within earshot. "Someone lied about last night. Working?"

"I *was* working."

"Really?" Eyram asked. "That's not what these flowers look like."

Dufie handed the unopened card to Chantelle. "You, girlfriend, are withholding juicy information."

"I'm not lying."

Half the truth didn't constitute a lie, did it? Taking the card, she tried not to let them see the trembling of her fingers as she opened it. '*What's the price for seeing you again?*' She laughed, relieved to discover he hadn't signed his name, mad at the same time that he was obviously trying to hide.

Eyram beamed like a child about to open a present. "What does it say?"

She read the message out loud.

"Ooh."

"Aw, poor guy," Dufie cooed. "You're stretching some innocent soul."

She snorted. "Believe me, he's anything but innocent."

Dufie's eyes filled with glee, and Chantelle wanted to grimace. "So there is a someone. Do tell."

"There's nothing to tell."

Eyram pouted. "Who is it?"

"No one. Get back to work."

"Fine. Be like that." Dufie feigned offense. "I'm watching you."

Chantelle chuckled, returning her attention to the bouquet. Flowers weren't her thing, so she couldn't identify all the different blossoms. At least there were no roses. *Talk about cheesy*. Her lack of knowledge about flora didn't prevent her from admiring the beautiful arrangement, a stunning combination of deep reds, violets, and yellows against the green leaves.

Apart from its beauty, the bunch exuded a sense of warmth, the type you got from knowing someone had been thinking about you. Did she want Lord McKenzie thinking about her? Was he, though? Delivery of these flowers could have been arranged by his personal assistant.

She sighed. It appeared she'd been doing so a lot today. After the shock of Martin's death and the news of his infidelity, she had refused to entertain the notion of even a simple date with any man. When it came to men, 'dating' and 'simple' didn't go together. Case in point, Valentine's Day with the man who obviously thought himself to be God's gift to women.

It unnerved her, the way he'd seemed to read her. *Tell me that wasn't the best damned sex you ever had.* He really was a piece of work. Who said things like that? So what if he'd blown all previous experiences out of the water? She certainly wouldn't admit it to anyone. Least of all Lord McKenzie.

She read the card again. The memory of the conversation which had inspired it coaxed a smile out of her. He had a neat cursive handwriting, unlike her childish carved lettering.

Enough of this, Chantie! She shoved the card into her drawer. She wouldn't acknowledge the flowers, just as she didn't intend to answer his calls. Sooner or later, he'd get the message. She looked at her cell phone half-dreading, and half-hoping, he'd call again. Only so she could ignore it.

◆◆◆

BY FIVE-THIRTY, CHANTELLE'S mind needed a reset. She lifted her gaze from her workstation. A few others were still at their desks burning the after-hours oil. Channelling her jumbled emotions to work had resulted in a highly productive day, but now she craved a bath and her bed. She'd just finished packing up when her desk phone rang.

She answered it immediately.

"Good. You're still here," Randy said, not waiting for a greeting. "My office. Now."

She grimaced. "Okay, boss."

She tried to sound cheerful despite knowing she was about to be given an assignment. Meaning she could forget about a nice bath and her bed. She grabbed a pen and notepad and headed to Randy's office.

As she approached the door, the sound of laughter reached her. After being graced with it so often yesterday, she recognised it immediately. Refusing to pick his calls had obviously failed to communicate her intent. She sucked in her belly, refusing to acknowledge the flutter passing through it. She grimaced at the prospect of seeing him again.

Releasing an exasperated breath, she knocked and waited for an answer before entering. Her gaze sought Lord. The flutter in her stomach became a full invasion of butterflies. To say he looked good in a suit would be an understatement. The navy-blue ensemble adored his gorgeous body as though he was the reason business suits were made.

Randy stood. "Come in, Chantelle. You've met Lord McKenzie."

She nodded. "Good evening, Mr. McKenzie."

"Hello, Chantelle."

His deep voice washed over her like a cool shower on a hot day, and his lips curved up. The intensity of his gaze compelled her mind to rustle up memories of last night. She squelched the image.

"Randy, could you give us the room?" Lord said as if he owned the place.

"I need to step out for a ciggy, anyway," her boss replied, checking his pockets.

Wait, what? "You're leaving us in your office?"

"I trust both of you," came the reply as he pulled out a cigarette and a metallic lighter.

Lord shook his head. "This habit is going to kill you, man."

Randy shrugged. "None of us is getting out of here alive, right?"

Lord shook his head. She got the suspicion this was a conversation they'd had before. She frowned. Were Lord and Randy friends? Despite working with the man for two years now, she realised she knew little about him.

She waited until her boss had exited the office. "What are you doing here?"

"You've been ignoring my calls."

"So you decided to invade my workplace?"

"There's something we need to discuss, and it can't wait."

Worry weaved through her. "Is it about the interview?"

"No."

Concern became irritation. "Then it can wait."

She turned towards the door.

"Chantelle," he growled out. "Would you stop being stubborn for a damn minute!"

Gravity and desperation filled his voice, stopping her cold. The one reason she could think of seeped into her mind. *Oh, God.* Was there something in the papers, after all? It had to be bad if he'd deemed it necessary to warn her in person.

"There's something you should know about last night."

She faced him, bracing for the worst. The grave look in his eyes heightened her anxiety. "Okay."

He stared at her for several seconds before speaking. "The condom broke."

His words were like iced water injected into her veins. "What?"

"I didn't notice it immediately," he explained.

Her mind crowded, barely registering his explanation. Something about wrapping it in his handkerchief since the office had no adjoining washroom. She shook her head, trying to clear the fog clouding her mind.

He stepped towards her, but she retreated, and he stopped.

"I'm clean, if that's what you're worried about."

Good to know, but it still left her with another concern.

"We're within twenty-four hours." *Enough time to take an emergency contraceptive pill.* "I have to go."

"I'll come with you."

"No!" she snapped, giving him a look only an idiot would ignore. "You've done enough."

Several charged seconds followed. For a moment, she feared he might turn a deaf ear and drag her out of there in his determination to have his way. What else could be expected of him?

He released a breath and nodded. "I'm sorry about this."

"So am I."

Regret drenched her as she turned and headed out.

CHAPTER 6

CALL IT INTUITION. Chantelle sensed something amiss the moment she picked up Joe's call on Friday morning, but she kept her voice cheery. "Hi, Joe. What's up?"

"He's refusing to do the shoot."

He's what? Why wasn't she surprised? No, it did shock her. Lord didn't strike her as a man who would agree to something and then back out. Not without a good reason. Even his invasion of her workplace yesterday hadn't been a random act, and she'd been grateful he'd taken the pains to track her down. At least, he wasn't a total lost cause. It didn't explain why he'd back out now. She gritted her teeth and took in a deep breath to ensure her voice remained steady. Even though her fingers itched to do him some painful physical damage.

"Why?"

The sigh she got in response didn't bring comfort.

"He won't do it unless you're here."

Oh, come on!

"Are you serious?" She grimaced. The man had a problem. Obviously, he'd grown accustomed to making demands and having them followed. What nerve. She should have seen this coming. "Did you tell him how busy I am?"

"Yes. I even tried negotiating for him to do today's shoot without you, and we'd bring you over tomorrow for the home and on-site shoots," Joe said. "No go. He's adamant about having you here. We've been at it for thirty minutes. I'm afraid if you don't show up, he might refuse to do this altogether."

"Did he actually say that?"

"No, but he runs a *Ghana Club 100* company. He can't possibly have a lot of free time on his hands."

"You're right." She inhaled deeply, her aggravation with Lord sending a sharp pain to a point right above her left eyebrow. She didn't want to see him. Having to spend the next couple of weeks writing about him and staring at his photos made her nervous enough. "I'm on my way."

Her heart skipped a beat in anticipation of seeing him again. She swallowed. Would he bring up Valentine's Day?

WITH A SENSE OF pride and accomplishment, Lord appended his signature to McKenzie Contractors' proposal document for the Kumasi International Airport pitch. Instinct made him optimistic about their chances, but he exercised a practical amount of caution. They were competing against huge international corporations from Europe and China as well as one from South Africa.

A contract of this magnitude had never been awarded to a local company, mainly because the last time something this big came along, no Ghanaian company had possessed the capacity to handle it. The situation had since changed. There were now three local companies capable of handling the job. Added to the drive by the government to promote locally owned businesses, they were at an advantage. Still, the international competition would be stiff.

This contract meant a great deal to McKenzie Contractors, but also to him personally, since it would represent a huge milestone in his career. Many of the company's ground-breaking achievements had been under the leadership of his father. Though Lord had grown the family business into a prestigious *Ghana Club 100* company, proving himself beyond reasonable doubt, his past career in entertainment still created an amount of scepticism. He saw it in his father's eyes every time a picture or article about him appeared in the tabloids.

His father had given him the same look when Lord had put aside his MBA to work as a radio show host. It didn't seem to matter that he owned part of the radio station, or that he'd turned the station's *Breakfast Drive*, the show he'd hosted, into the number one radio programme in the country. Even now, his legacy lived on. According to the last *All Media Survey*, *Breakfast Drive* still held the number one spot in radio listenership and remained among the top five advertising revenue earners across media.

As he watched the photographer's frantic movements through the open glass door, he knew his odds with this pitch didn't account for the upswing in his mood. No. He'd attribute that to the prospect of seeing Chantelle again, even if it was to be in the presence of Joe and his assistant. Images of her flashed through his memory. How exquisite she'd looked in person, both with and without her clothes on.

Desire surfaced as he remembered her moans and her soft lips branding his skin with hot kisses. The way she smelled, a mixture of scents, something understated and feminine, not quite flowery, but intoxicating, nonetheless. He shuddered at the recollection of being surrounded by her heat. He'd imagined being inside her would be bliss, but nothing could have prepared him for the mind-shattering realm of ecstasy it had taken him to, an experience he desired more of. His very independent member exerted pressure against the fabric confining it, showing its eagerness for a do-over.

She could avoid his calls to her heart's content. She'd soon realise Lord McKenzie knew how to get what he wanted. And he wanted to explore this thing which started two nights ago. He wasn't about to quit.

CHANTELLE WALKED INTO McKenzie Towers, the polished marble floors making a clickity-clackity melody when meeting with the heels of her shoes. The plush main foyer on the ground floor sported several islands of stylish seating places, but she didn't have time to pause and admire the elegant décor. She stopped by the reception desk and was directed to a building plan on the wall next to the elevators. It took seconds to locate McKenzie Contractors on the map. *Top Floor.*

She rolled her eyes. "Of course."

She stepped into the lift, with two others. A couple, from the looks of it. She tried to clear her mind and gather her wits about her. Yesterday had been harder than she'd anticipated. Leaving Lord in Randy's office, she'd driven to a pharmacy to buy the medicine and a bottle of water. Returning to her car, she hadn't waited to get home. When she'd had the pill in her palm, however, she'd frozen. Suppressed memories over the past four years had come crashing in. The implication of her action had numbed her.

She'd have given anything to not have to take it, yet she'd forced herself to push past the sudden pain piercing her chest and had done what needed to be done. Then she'd spent the next thirty minutes sobbing, enveloped by a familiar feeling of aloneness.

Today, she pledged to move forward, to put the memories back where they belonged. In the past. It would be important for Lord to know what happened between them should never be mentioned. Ever. Especially not in the presence of other people.

The last thought put a nervous kick in her pulse. Discomfort lodged in her chest. Did anything embarrass him? She remembered him commandeering Randy's office as if he owned the building, sparing her the shame of her boss finding out what had transpired during the interview. Maybe he did have some redeeming qualities. Did he realise that while having sex with her may have been an added trophy to his collection, it represented a major event in her life? The prospect of sharing the same space with him again had all her nerve endings on full alert.

"Lovely outfit," the lady said with a nod at Chantelle.

She'd worn a Ghanaian print, faux-wrap blouse over a pair of brown stretch trousers which tapered into a slight boot cut. Her necklace and earrings combined colours from the top. Subtle make-up and hair loosely tied with a scarf-ribbon finished the look. She shifted on her elegant-but-practical two-inch pumps and murmured a "thank you."

The woman's companion, a forty-something-looking man, gave her a once-over. She returned his smile with a perfunctory one and faced away. Over time, she'd become wary of stares from men. While she appreciated their confidence-boosting capabilities, she tried to avoid the inevitable come-ons that followed.

"The beads go well with the top," the woman continued. "Is it custom-made? I own a boutique, and I'm always on the lookout for suppliers of quality African jewellery."

"The lady who makes it is a friend. I'll be happy to link the two of you up."

"Wonderful." She dug through her bag and fished out a business card. "Please give her my contact, and you can also check out my Facebook page for some of my current stock. You might find something you like."

She received the card. "Thank you."

"Oh, this is us," the woman said when the car dinged on one floor. She followed the man out, waving a cheerful "Goodbye."

Chantelle offered a polite smile before the doors closed again. Left alone, she made the rest of the journey like a sheep headed for the slaughterhouse. Gripping her handbag and the pack of non-alcoholic Malt drinks she'd bought on the way, she stepped onto the carpeted lobby of McKenzie Contractors.

The wall facing the elevators displayed the company's name boldly embossed in gold lettering. The space had an elegant décor in earth tones with stunning accents and expensive furniture pieces. Despite the luxury, the surroundings exuded warmth, which put her at ease.

She approached the woman at the main desk and introduced herself. Not knowing how things worked around here, she chose to be formal.

"Good day. My name is Chantelle Sah. I'm here to see Mr. McKenzie. He's expecting me."

The woman, who looked to be in her late twenties to early thirties, smiled. "Mr. McKenzie? Pop McKenzie or Lord?"

"Lord."

The receptionist nodded and made a call. "Chantelle Sah, here to see Lord." She paused for a few seconds and hung up with a "Right away." She turned to Chantelle. "Do you know where his office is?"

"No."

The lady stepped out from behind the desk, revealing her chic dress made from wax print fabric, and pointed to the corridor on their left. "Through there. It's the last door on your right."

"Thanks."

It came as a surprise to meet an older lady, easily in her late forties, at the front office. She would have guessed Lord's personal secretary to be a young, attractive woman who came with 'added value.' This lady looked matronly, with the air of someone who had been with the company for a long time. She squashed the hare-brained feeling of delight at the discovery. So he didn't mix business and pleasure. It didn't mean a damn thing. Smoke didn't exist without fire; he got his playboy reputation from somewhere.

Joe and his assistant waited in the outer office. She greeted them as Joe rose from his seat.

"Oh, good." Relief washed over the photographer's chubby round face. "I'm so glad you're here. You're lucky my next project is in the evening, or I'd have had to cancel."

"I'm sorry about this." She held out her peace offering. "I brought you some drinks."

They each picked one, leaving two.

Joe took a long sip of his. "This is why I like doing jobs for you. You're such a sweet girl. Why are you single? If I wasn't married—"

"Joe." She shot him a warning glance, despite the smile playing around her lips. He came from a different generation when men opened the doors and gave their whole hearts to one woman. In his time, men didn't just up and leave. Today, they said "I do," with one foot out of the door.

The secretary announced them before ushering them in. As Chantelle entered, an aeroplane taking off in the distance behind Lord caught her attention. The building must be sound-proof, because she couldn't hear the noise from the plane. Its smooth rise right above him made it look as though it glided over his head. Her intake of breath followed the aircraft's motion, her smile fading at the sight.

She'd always loved take-offs, even as a child. The grace with which they soared never failed to take her breath away. As a little girl, she'd watched the planes whenever they'd gone to see someone off at the airport, imagining all the exciting places the travellers might be visiting.

The 'wow' factor of Lord in a business suit, rather than the take-off, had her staring. Today's outfit might be a classic black with a red silk tie, but there was nothing classic about him. *Oh, Lord.* It wasn't the beauty of the take-off or the butterflies-in-the-pit-of-your-stomach sexiness of him that took her breath away, though. It was the way he smiled at her, with warmth in his eyes, as if it genuinely pleased him to see her.

He met her halfway into the room and extended his hand. "Hi."

"Hello."

She took his hand and steeled herself against the lightning bolt that zinged up her arm.

"How are you?"

"Fine."

Why wasn't she telling him off for dragging her here?

Because you're happy to see him.

She shoved the contrary thought out of her mind.

"Good." His eyes assessed her unashamedly.

He smiled with appreciation, nodding as though in approval. He seemed to like doing that. Would he have sent her home to change if he hadn't liked her outfit?

"I brought you a drink."

He quirked an eyebrow. "You got me a drink?"

Another thing he liked doing—throwing back her statements as questions. A personal quirk, or an excuse to think up the most appropriate thing to say?

"It's just a drink." She didn't want him ascribing any special meaning to it. "Joe and Kofi already took theirs."

He gave a soft chuckle.

"Keep it for me." He whipped around, slapping his hands together. "Okay, let's do this."

That was it? No complaints about why she hadn't arrived with the crew in the first place? Could he really just have wanted to see her? Of course not. He'd, no doubt, become accustomed to snapping his fingers and having things his way. This was one of such moments.

For the next few minutes, she watched him pose for Joe. Being in front of the camera came easy to him. No surprises there. From the pleased look on Joe's face, she knew the shots were going to be excellent.

After about fifteen minutes, Joe finally looked up from the camera. "Do you want to take a look?"

"Sure."

He switched to the display view and ran her through the pictures of Lord at his desk, working on his computer, and other poses: sitting, standing, leaning over the desk as if presiding over a meeting.

They were better than good. No denying the fact. Corporate had never looked this sexy.

The latest thought caught her off guard. She whipped her head up, afraid she might have said it out loud. Their gazes caught. His lips edged up in a lopsided smile.

"What do you think?" Joe asked.

She cleared her throat.

"They're good." Her attention remained on Lord. "Do you want to take a look?"

"No." He shook his head, his stare never wavering. "I trust you."

She reminded herself she didn't care about him. This was strictly business. Tearing her eyes away, she turned to Joe. "You're going in the right direction. Let's do more postures."

As Joe proceeded to coach Lord on new poses, Chantelle moved around the room, satisfied they would get some brilliant shots. The office wasn't ostentatious, the apparent theme being 'less is more.' His desk, a carefully designed structure with a combination of wood on one part and a curved glass top over steel legs, had both class and masculinity.

On one side of the office stood a wooden cabinet with glass slide-doors. It appeared he kept only the necessary things in his office. Being in here exposed a side of him the tabloids never mentioned, a more serious side. How would he feel about her talking to some of the staff? Before today, she'd have expected him to gladly grant her permission to do so, but now, she wondered.

Engrossed in her thoughts, she didn't realise they'd taken a break and he'd come to stand by her side.

"A penny for your thoughts."

The closeness of his voice startled her.

"Do you make it a habit to creep up on people?"

"No, I reserve that for those who want to expose me to the world."

If you asked her, he'd already done a good job of baring himself to the world. Frankly, in the literal sense, she'd do the opposite. If he were hers, she'd want to shield him from the world. Since he didn't belong to her, however, such imaginings proved fruitless.

"You make it sound like I'm forcing you to do this."

He moved from behind her so they were face-to-face. "Do I sound like I feel forced?"

This conversation was beginning to sound too much like déjà vu, and she had no interest in repeating the events of Valentine's Day. *Thank you very much*. Even if she wanted to, the translucent glass wall would make it impractical. Realising where her mind had inevitably wandered, she grappled to find something mundane to say.

He didn't give her a chance to do so.

"Are you okay?" Concern drew his brows together. "Last night, were you able to—"

"Yes," she said before he could complete his question, and to ensure he didn't lead her down that path, she went on the defensive. "Why did you ask me to be here today? I had to drop everything else on my plate to come."

He quirked a brow. "This is *your* story, isn't it?"

"Yes, but I assure you Joe is excellent and doesn't need supervision."

"I don't doubt his skill. I'd expect nothing less from you. However, I didn't agree to this interview because of him. If I'm going to invest my time in it, then so are you."

A smile softened the tone of his words. Still, she knew she'd just had another glimpse into a more serious side of him, perhaps the part of him only his business colleagues got to see. It struck a curious nerve, enticed her to prod until she found the person within. Why, though? She didn't know, so she refocused on something that would rid her of the urge.

"I received your flowers."

"Did you like them?"

She shrugged. "They were nice."

"I was going for exquisite, but just this once, I'll take nice." He leaned forward. "Don't tell anyone, or you'll ruin my reputation."

Despite herself, she laughed. A few seconds elapsed as she attempted to find something else to say.

"You're still not picking up my calls," he said, effectively cutting off her avoidance tactics.

Tension returned. Big time.

"You need to stop calling."

His eyes twinkled as if it were a game to him. "I'm serious about seeing you again."

"It's not a good idea."

"Why not?"

She gave him an exasperated look without answering the question. She hated that he looked so blasé while the timbre of his voice stroked her libido like an intimate caress, leaving her flustered.

He regarded her with stern determination. "I'm not going to stop."

"Well, I'm not going to pick up."

Unfortunately, he took it as a challenge. She saw it in the resolute look he gave her.

"I can be persistent."

"So can I."

A chuckle softened his features. Was he mocking her? That he wasn't taking her seriously infuriated her, but more disturbing were the butterflies in her stomach. Something about this man filled her with warmth and longing as much as aggravation. After Valentine's Day, she'd expected her attraction to him to dwindle, but it seemed to increase with each meeting. She knew of the dangers of allowing her heart to be captured, though, and firmly told herself the fluttering in her chest was all in her imagination. *Not real.*

Yet, when his eyes dropped to her lips, she realised it hadn't gone anywhere, the sizzling tension. Suddenly, it didn't matter what material the walls were made of or who else happened to be in the room. Right now, she existed exclusively in his eyes. She found herself battling with whether she'd let him kiss her if he tried, and "no" was gradually losing.

He lowered his voice to a shade just above a whisper. "Do you regret having sex with me?"

Shocked to reality by the unexpected question, she shot an anxious glance over her shoulder. Relief filled her upon encountering an empty room. Slowly returning her attention to him, she noticed just how close he stood.

"After what happened, do you have to ask?"

"The condom issue was unfortunate, but we've taken the necessary action. Crisis averted. Can we move on?"

The force of his gaze told her he wouldn't let it slide. He wanted an answer, which yesterday or the night before would have been an indisputable "Yes, we can move on in opposite directions." Now, her wayward mind wavered.

"I don't know."

"I do."

"Look." Her gaze darted around, making sure they were still alone. "It was Valentine's Day, and it had been a while since…" She let it hang, certain he knew what she meant. Having to admit it was disconcerting enough. "For just one night, I needed to feel like a woman again, and you gave me that, but I'm not interested in being your next fling."

He opened his mouth to say something, but just then, they heard the voices of Joe and Kofi as they returned to the room.

Lord pulled away from her without another glance, giving his full concentration to Joe as the photographer discussed a few more shots he wanted to take.

In the first sitting, he'd been watching her while taking the photos, but now, he didn't spare her a glance. Though his demeanour remained playful with Joe and Kofi, his eyes betrayed no emotions. For the first time, he seemed to have finally left her alone. She could have walked out, and he probably wouldn't have noticed. Why didn't the thought bring any joy? How in the world could losing his attention make her want it?

An hour later, they were done and packing.

"The site is out of town, so I suggest we start off at six tomorrow," Lord said as they made to leave. Finally, he turned to her. "I'll see you in the morning, Chantelle. Now, about that drink, you may leave it with my secretary. Oh, and—" He leaned forward speaking into her ear. "I'm not looking for a fling."

Without another word, he turned and walked back to his desk, his attention now focused on his computer screen.

She blinked. Words stuck in her throat as she stared at his seeming disinterest. How did he manage to do that? He always looked at her as if she were the only one in the room, and when he didn't, she felt like she didn't exist to him. If he wasn't looking for a fling, then what did he want? Surely, he didn't mean—

She shook her head. *Don't do this to yourself, Chantie.* She'd kept her heart safe for four years now. She couldn't let six little words derail her efforts despite the tiny part of her which wanted to believe in second chances.

CHAPTER 7

TWO HOURS HAD PASSED since Lord's secretary had popped in to say "Good night." Left alone, he finished up everything he'd set out to do today. The whole time, Chantelle had been on his mind.

Turning off his computer, he sat back, smiling at the memory of her breezing into his office, looking all sexy in a top which wrapped around her slender waist like two arms holding her from behind. With subtle make-up bringing out every striking feature on her face and her hair loosely tied with a scarf ribbon, he'd needed to catch his breath before speaking. Then she'd turned an intense don't-mess-with-me look on him. He'd wanted to kiss her.

Now sitting here alone with his thoughts, he still wanted to kiss her. Really kiss her. Not the frantic, adrenaline-driven type they'd shared while ripping each other's clothes off. Though excellent in its own right, he wanted to savour the experience, allow his tongue to slow-dance with hers, explore the depths of her mouth. He wanted to run his fingers through her hair and have her melt into him, moaning against his lips. He wanted to kiss her as if they had all the time in the world to kiss.

The sound of the computer shutting down snapped him out of his sensual reverie. He grimaced. What the hell was he doing thinking about her as if he had feelings for her? But it boiled down to that. He *had* feelings. He didn't know what they signified, but it felt so good, he wanted to find out where it led. Not that it made any sense. He'd never met a woman so determined to restrict their relationship to business.

At least, she didn't regret being with him. Okay, so she hadn't said those exact words. However, in this case, "I don't know," trumped outright rejection. It gave him hope that he could persuade her to give him a chance.

Zipping up the laptop, he exited the office. As he shut the door, he noticed the lights in his father's office. He frowned and checked his time. *Seven-thirty*. His father never stayed beyond six.

"Papa?" He knocked and entered. "Are you okay? It's seven-thirty."

"Son, come on in." His father smiled, looking up from a journal in his hands.

At sixty-five, his old man showed no signs of slowing down. Bearing the same good looks he'd passed on to his two sons, he didn't look a day over fifty. With his distinguished greying hair, he looked more like an older brother of Lord's.

"Your mother is playing grandma at your brother's while Ohene and his wife enjoy themselves, for a change."

Lord chuckled.

"That's what got them those adorable children in the first place." He came to sit down at the desk. "What are you doing?"

"Just reading." Mr. McKenzie adjusted his glasses. "With your mother not at home, there isn't much for me to do in that big house."

Lord smiled. After forty years of marriage, his parents still had stars in their eyes. He'd grown up having them as a standard for love and relationships. It turned out his parents had a rare kind of love. Until Chantelle, he'd never met a woman who made him feel remotely like what he'd seen of his parents while growing up. They were two peas in a pod. Two people who loved, trusted, and depended on each other.

"Speaking of your mother," his father added. "She says she hasn't heard from you in over a week."

Whenever his mother started complaining, the next thing was to show up at his house, unannounced, and pretend she saw skin and bones instead of muscle. She'd cook up a storm, trying to fatten him up in one day. He couldn't afford to have his mother turn up tomorrow and ruin his time with Chantelle.

He gave his father a determined look. "I'll call her tonight."

"What's this I hear about a photo shoot in your office today?"

He scowled. He'd known it would come up soon. "What about it?"

"You know how I feel about all the publicity."

The disapproving glare from the older man gave echo to the unspoken 'negative' in front of publicity. In his father's opinion, anything in a non-business magazine didn't bode well for the business he'd toiled to build.

"Papa, you know I don't intentionally pose for the reporters. They just follow my every move."

"Because you give them reason to keep coming after you, son." He thrust a paper in front of Lord. "Look at this."

He stared at yesterday's copy of *Graphic Showbiz* with a picture of him and Chantelle, when she'd told him she didn't want to see him again. The image of her in the body-shaping red top brought back memories of that night crashing like waves against a rock. He steeled himself against the effects of those thoughts, returning his gaze to meet his father's.

"Papa—"

"You know the pitch for the Kumasi airport is important to this company." His father pinned him with a disapproving glare while speaking in his trademark calm voice. "While our competition is being talked about in *Business in Africa* and *The Economist*, the CEO of McKenzie Contractors is out finding a new valentine."

If you put it that way. Chantelle had made a similar comment during the interview.

"The photographers here today were from *Odopa* magazine. I agreed to do an exclusive for them, because you're right. The media will keep coming after me, so I need to control what they say."

"But *Odopa* Magazine isn't a—"

"No, it's not a business journal. It's a lifestyle magazine, but that doesn't mean it's not a serious publication." When his father continued to look sceptical, he added, "Trust me, Papa. This company is my life as much as it is yours."

FOR A LONG TIME, Friday nights had been salsa night, but Chantelle had stopped four years ago. Initially, it had hurt too much to do something she used to share with Martin. Later, she had difficulty finding a partner whose style flowed with hers. Three years ago, she'd landed the job with *Odopa* magazine and thrown herself into work. In the end, she'd stopped needing a reason not to go. Now, her normal Friday routine consisted of a bottle of Amarula to go with a home-cooked dinner.

But dancing with Lord had awakened a long-buried piece of her heart, a part of her she'd allowed to die with Martin. The number of salsa joints had increased considerably since her dancing days, but the most popular on Fridays were the *Aviation Social Centre*, *Coconut Grove Hotel*, and *Boomerang* nightclub. *Aviation* pulled the biggest crowd, and, she guessed, would likely be where someone like Lord would go, so she settled on *Coconut Grove*.

She parked her car in the main lot and made her way to the reception. In a few minutes, she'd registered for membership. Anticipation bubbled inside her as she entered the dance hall. The main lights were off, leaving the room illuminated by the reflection from disco balls. The music gingered her into motion right from the door. They were doing a group routine, which symbolised the conclusion of the beginner classes, thus freeing the floor for all. She didn't hesitate to join the dance, since she knew the steps. When the song ended, the moves fizzled into freestyle.

Her lack of a partner didn't bother her. She didn't need one to relish the freedom and joy she derived from dancing. Besides, there were several other singles on the floor she could invite to dance with her. She revelled in the rush of moving to the beat, letting go of her thoughts and allowing the music to take over and imbue her with *joie de vivre*.

In the middle of a full basic turn, a pair of hands captured hers. She held on in order not to miss her step, one which brought her face-to-face with the owner of the strong arms. *Lord McKenzie*.

Her heart skipped a beat, her smile faltering. He'd changed into a jeans and polo shirt combo that worshipped his body. Once again, she noticed how well they moved together. He commanded the dance with skill, his sturdy arms powerful enough to catch her in various moves, yet his touch remained gentle. Giving herself over to the music and his lead, she succumbed to the exhilaration of dancing with an ideal partner.

"What are you doing here?" she asked loud enough for him to hear over the music.

"Dancing."

"I can see," she said, earning a grin from him. "Why here?"

"This is my salsa hangout. Why are you here?"

He stepped forward, reducing the space between them to a mere breath, effectively cutting off her response before sidestepping to the right and leading her through a series of twists and spins. Then she came flush against hard planes she'd explored intimately only a couple of nights ago. The memory sent tingling sensations through her. It should have been her cue to stop dancing and walk away right then.

"Someone recently reminded me of how much I enjoyed dancing."

"Smart guy."

His teasing tone made her chuckle. Unexpectedly, she found herself wishing the music wouldn't end.

"I never thanked you for doing the interview."

"No work talk, Chantelle. Dance."

Some men, when dancing with a woman who knew her steps, relied on the competence of the woman, allowing her to follow without guidance. But the really good dancers still actively maintained control. They were the ones who made you look sexy. And Lord had unparalleled skill. He favoured turns, constantly switching hands, which allowed him to wrap his arms around her, a lot. The way he handled her made her feel safe, bolder, sexier.

He executed a spin, dropping her hand on his shoulder as he turned. She traced a line down his strong back to his other hand waiting at his waist to recapture hers, realising she liked the feel of his taut muscles against her fingertips. Even though salsa was in itself a sexy dance, she enjoyed the sensuality of his movements.

"Are you up for a death drop?" he asked.

The move consisted of him twirling her around and her dropping backwards, his hand at the nape of her neck being her sole support; then he'd raise her again with that one hand—one of several manoeuvres they called death moves.

"What?" She didn't bother to mask her alarm. "No."

"I won't let you fall. Trust me," he said. "Can you do that?"

"I don't know."

Did it count if she wanted to trust him?

Grinning, he led her in a series of twirls, an uncomplicated dip, and a less daring version of what he'd asked.

He pulled her closer. "Not bad at all, scaredy-cat. Do you believe I can catch you?"

She hesitated. He had the skill, no doubt.

"Yes," she finally admitted. "But—"

"Don't think, Chantelle. Just do."

He whirled her around again, this time initiating a move to dip her between his legs and back. Having lost some of her concentration, she wasn't prepared for it. Instead of a smooth in-and-out motion, she lost her footing, dragging him down. He held himself steady, firming his grip, and managing to just prevent her from hitting the floor. He pulled her up.

"Are you all right?" he asked, concern evident in his dark brown eyes.

Too shocked to speak, she stared at him agape.

"Why did you panic?" Instead of an apology, he scolded. "I wouldn't have dropped you."

"Are you crazy?" she shouted, seething. Tears stung her eyes for fear of what could have happened. She threw her arms up and walked out.

"Chantelle, wait!" Catching up to her outside, he grabbed her by the arm. "I'm sorry. You're an excellent dancer. I didn't expect you to hesitate."

"Really? What part of 'no' don't you understand?"

"I wouldn't have dropped you."

"You wouldn't have dropped me?" she repeated incredulously. "This is not about you, Lord."

"No, it's not. It's about you." He pointed a finger at her, emphasising his point. "It's not a move you can't do. You just got scared."

And for good reason. "That was a death move. You could have injured me."

She'd never been a big fan of the more daring manoeuvres. In fact, the number of times she'd done them could be counted on her one hand. She wouldn't have tried this particular move even with Martin whom she'd dated for years, let alone this foolhardy nutcase on a vanity trip. It didn't matter that his skill far exceeded her ex's.

"Again, I'm sorry."

"Sorry isn't good enough."

"God, what does it take to impress you?"

She blinked. He wanted to impress her? Why? Despite the urge to probe, she decided it didn't matter. Getting personal with Lord meant flirting with danger.

"Showing off won't do it."

"Then what will?" he asked. "You won't even pick up my calls."

Her body trembled from her near-encounter with the floor, and here he stood making light of the situation. His eyes betrayed some amount of earnestness, but she'd do well to stay away from any man who did what he wanted regardless of other people's feelings.

"It looks like I'm doing everything wrong, so tell me what it's going to take."

"Look, don't make this awkward. We met to do an interview—"

"Oh, I take it that comes with sex."

Momentarily, she found herself speechless, but steeled anger soon broke through. She whipped round, and again, left him standing.

He caught up with her once more, just as she was getting into her car. "Chantelle, dammit. What is wrong with you? Why won't you give me a chance?"

"You have to ask?"

"Go out with me."

"No!" She sat in the car.

"One date. It's all I'm asking."

Without bothering with an answer, she sped off, leaving him staring after her.

◆◆◆

LORD BIT BACK an oath as he watched her taillights disappear around the corner for the second time this week. *One date*. What self-respecting man begged for a date? And shouting at the top of his lungs. This was exactly the sort of behaviour which invited negative press.

"Shit." He kicked the invisible forces acting against him, furious he couldn't just let go.

He stood with his hands on his hips, his frustration mounting. He'd never been in this position before, wanting a woman so much it hurt, as if someone had stuck a knife in his heart and twisted it. Admittedly, his ego hadn't been tested before, not like this. Not by a woman. Particularly not one he'd already been intimate with.

Turning back, he didn't feel like dancing anymore, so he headed for the bar. There, he ordered a drink, pondering his plight. She was right. He'd been showing off. And, yes, given the circumstances, he could have injured her.

Why did the need to prove himself suddenly plague him? Did he truly not deserve to be with a woman like Chantelle? He took a gulp of his drink, unable to banish her from his thoughts. A few times, he'd seen hunger in her eyes when she looked at him. Those looks kept him pressing on. There was, of course, no guarantee it had anything to do with him, but he chose to hope.

He gave an angry snort, remembering an occasion when a woman he'd broken up with had accused him of loving like a whore. He'd been unsure what she'd meant, but he hadn't cared. Love had nothing to do with it, though. That wasn't the case here. *Damn it all to Hell.*

A woman came to sit on the stool next to him. "Tough night?"

He turned to face her. She was pretty, her hair short and curled. Baby curls. He took in her long lashes and the curves of her lips. She wore a generous amount of make-up—not too much, just more than Chantelle wore. She adjusted herself, showing off her bare back.

"Something like that," he said, neither inviting nor discouraging conversation.

She reached out and laid a hand on his. "Do you want to talk about it? I'm a good listener."

He gave a snort of laughter. She wasn't interested in listening. The way she leaned forward, giving him an ample view of her cleavage, said it all. He could have her, and he wouldn't even have to work for it. Could she be a blessing in disguise?

Perhaps mindless sex would help him forget the woman he really wanted. Except, it wouldn't satisfy him. Not after being with Chantelle. It was like being handed out roasted groundnuts when he craved a double helping of *emutuo* and spicy groundnut soup with bush meat. He tried to shake it off, but the feeling of defeat persisted, weaving itself through every fibre of his body. Truth be told, he wanted it to persist, for now, anyway. He had no other link to Chantelle.

"I saw you dancing," Baby Curls said. "You're good. Like gold medal good. Do you give lessons?"

How many times had he given lessons which led to more? Most of his students, much like this woman, were more than willing to show their appreciation in kind. He'd always preferred it that way; no entanglements, no disappointments.

He pulled his hand away, having at the back of his mind how pissed off he would be if a picture of him and this woman showed up in the papers. It would upset his father further and give Chantelle another reason to avoid him. As if she didn't have enough reasons, judging from the way she kept running. He finished the rest of his drink in one gulp and paid for it. As he left, he sincerely hoped he'd done it soon enough.

Time to go home and think of how to approach the matter of Chantelle and her persistent rejections. He knew the usual tactics wouldn't work, but the alternative, opening up to her, was unthinkable. It exposed him to a level of vulnerability he'd never allowed himself, like going into the unknown with his heart on a platter. The thought alone sent trepidation down his spine. He wanted her, but could he trust her with his heart?

CHAPTER 8

CHANTELLE WOKE UP WITH a smile. Dancing last night had everything to do with it. Even though Lord had shown up and ruined her evening. The coincidence of it baffled her. Of all the places she could have picked to spend Friday night, she'd chosen his salsa hangout. Thank goodness after today, she'd be done with him. He aggravated her. So much so that, even after leaving him, he remained in her thoughts.

How could he be at the helm of a *Ghana Club 100* company and yet remain so risqué in his ways? She supposed his sort of personality had its merits. She doubted a man like him could feel heartbroken, not for very long, anyway. Especially not with those looks. He'd most likely laugh in your face if you tried to break up with him and then proceed to dump you.

She slid out of bed, took a quick shower and ate, then slipped into a pair of jeans and a tank top, accessorising with a string of beads around her neck and a matching bracelet. Since they were going to be outdoors for a bit, she picked a cap to go with her bag and loafers. Though satisfied with the way she looked, she wondered what Lord would think. Not because she needed or wanted his approval, she insisted firmly, but because he was pig-headed enough to ask her to go and change.

By a quarter to six, she was ready and getting into her car. She'd packed two boxes of juice and some sandwiches. Her mother constantly said, "People always get hungry." Somehow, the habit had stayed with her.

Humming a tune to herself, she turned the key. The engine coughed and sputtered before dying. You've got to be joking. She tried again and got the same response.

"Oh, man. Not now." She pulled the lever to open the bonnet and got out to check for anything amiss. Everything seemed okay, so she went in and tried to start the car again. Nothing. She glanced at her watch. She'd already lost ten minutes. There was no point in hanging around here. The car wouldn't fix itself, and she was no mechanic. She decided to call Joe.

"Where are you?" he asked when he picked up. "We're all here."

"My car won't start." She winced, imagining Lord blowing his top for her not being there. With her car giving up on her, she certainly didn't need any more drama today.

"Is it the battery?"

"I don't know. Maybe. It's not even kicking."

"Hold on." She heard him repeat her side of the conversation to someone. Some discussion ensued in the background. "Where are you?"

"Still at home."

Another break followed while he related the information to his companions.

Lord spoke next. "What's the address?"

The surprise of hearing his voice gave her heart an unexpected jump. He sounded confident and in-control, as a CEO should. Somehow, he also managed to make her feel calm despite her racing heartbeat.

Still, she resisted the idea of him coming over. "I can just get a taxi."

"I'll come and pick you up," he stated, his tone firm and uncompromising.

"What about Joe's car?"

After last night, she had even less interest in spending more time than necessary with him. A ride in his car would be one such thing to be avoided.

"I won't bite." She heard the smile in his voice, which aggravated her even more. "Now, where do you live?"

Giving him the directions, she felt as if she'd shared something intimate. *Oh, don't be silly*, she thought, flushing at the memory of having sex with him. She'd been a lot more intimate with him than sharing her address. This shouldn't have been a big deal, yet it was.

"I'll be there in twenty minutes."

The line went dead. While waiting, she called her mechanic, who arrived within ten minutes. After checking the car, he mentioned something about the alternator belt snapping.

"How long will it take to fix it?"

"Not long, but I don't have the right size with me," he said apologetically. "I'll have to take the car away. I can return it in less than two hours."

"Don't worry. I'm going out, so just call when you're done. I'll let you know when I get back home, so you can return it."

She handed him the key. He hooked her car to his and drove off. She was still a little mad at her car for pulling such a stunt today. Would one more day have killed it?

Lord pulled up shortly in a Toyota Hilux that gleamed as new cars did. Complete with a front guard rail and off-road tires, it looked as imposing as its owner, dwarfing Joe's saloon car behind him. He exited his truck, adjusting his designer shades. She averted her gaze from his form-fitting jeans, but the rest of him still sent her mind on a salacious excursion. His light blue shirt, tucked in with sleeves rolled up, had two unfastened buttons revealing a white T-shirt that stretched over his torso. Was there anything he didn't look good in?

"Is it the car or the man?" he asked, smile firmly in place.

Oh. Warmth crept up her face and ears as blood congregated there. Still, if her tongue were lapping at how delicious he looked, she didn't seem to possess enough resolve to stop staring. Just when she'd about given up on her girl-power showing up with some wit, it emerged and saved the day, for the moment, anyway.

"My favourite colour is navy-blue, so it's not the man."

He chuckled as if to say, "likely story."

She shook her head. How could he take her victory for himself? "You're in high spirits."

"I am." He grinned. "You look lovely."

She knew she'd gone officially insane when the butterflies now residing in her stomach started doing the hula. *Resistance, where art thou?*

"Why, thank you." She'd recovered enough to mock-curtsy.

"See? I can be nice."

That made her laugh, and she assumed it was as good an apology as she'd get for last night. She waved at Joe and Kofi as Lord opened the back door for her to put the snack bag in.

"What's that?" he asked.

"Juice and sandwiches."

He cocked an eyebrow without commenting. Instead, he closed the back door and opened the passenger side of the car for her to climb in. Going around the front, he slipped into the driver's side and clicked on his seat belt. The stereo came on as soon as he started the car, the volume set at a comfortable level, which allowed for conversation. She instantly liked the song—a ballad—but didn't recognise it.

"What's playing?" she asked.

"Michael Learns to Rock," he said. "They're a group from Denmark."

"They sound great."

"One of my favourites," he said. "You might recognise some of their more popular songs. This is their latest album."

His easy-going air wasn't odd, but the lack of tacky lines didn't go unnoticed. For now, she thought, knowing this 'normal' Lord wouldn't last. She stole a glance at him, admiring his control of the car, noticing details like his fingers tapping the steering wheel to the beat of the song. On one occasion, he mouthed the lyrics, seemingly forgetting he had company. For a moment, she was just a girl, riding in a car with a sexy guy.

As if sensing her attention, he glanced at her. "It can't be the car this time."

Her lips twitched with the beginning of a smile, which she held back. "I'm wondering why you're driving. Don't you have a chauffeur?"

"I enjoy driving, so after-hours and weekends I drive myself unless I have an event." He shrugged. "It keeps me grounded."

She snorted and rolled her eyes. He laughed.

"Where are we going?"

"Do you like surprises?"

Question for question. *Here we go again.*

"Not really."

She didn't elaborate, and he didn't say anything for a while. Martin's betrayal had killed her affinity for surprises. A week before his accident, they had been talking marriage. All the while, he'd been plotting the lies he meant to tell her in order to go off on a Valentine's Day getaway with another woman. No, surprises weren't her thing. She preferred the cold, hard truth.

"I have a secret project in Dodowa." Another few seconds elapsed while she waited for him to continue. "It's going to be an academy of performing arts. The auditoriums will be actual movie theatres, with special additions to inspire the students and facilitate some of the projects they'll have to undertake."

She noticed how serious he looked and the passion with which he spoke, a rarity as far as she knew. "You're still keeping in touch with the entertainment side of you."

"You could say that." He glanced at her. "I've added a few features to accommodate some of the latest equipment in film-making and music."

"Why is it a secret project?"

After all, it wasn't a strip club he didn't want the press to get wind of. There were hardly any institutions in the country equipped to produce world-class filmmakers and actors. His academy would be one of a kind. She wondered what it would be called. The Lord's Academy, maybe. The thought made her smile.

"What's funny?"

"Nothing," she said with haste. "I asked why it's a secret."

He shrugged.

"If I told you, I'd have to kill you." He gave her a wicked grin. "You're far too beautiful to suffer such a fate. Even now." He sounded mockingly grave. "I'm afraid I'll have to kidnap you."

Her efforts at remaining unperturbed failed, and she shot him a glare, which made him laugh again. *Oh, he makes me so mad.* For a few minutes there, he'd sounded ready to carry out a normal conversation, but then Mr. Comic had reared his head. It reinforced her suspicion that he used the jovial side of him as a cover-up. When people were busy laughing, they didn't probe or pry. It was a way of protecting himself. But from what? What could he possibly have to hide? Aside from a potential secret harem, that is.

"Do you always go about bearing gifts?"

She frowned in incomprehension. "Gifts?"

He pointed behind her seat. "The snacks."

"Oh, it's a habit I picked up from my mother." She smiled, thoughts of questioning him about the secret project shifting to the back burner. There would be time to probe later. "Whenever we went out, even to a party, she would pack food and drinks in case my sister and I got hungry before the meal was served."

"So you like your food, huh?"

"It's more for the people I'm with than myself."

"Ah, you like to fatten others up while you keep a trim figure."

She smiled. "The people will have to exercise restraint in their eating habits, won't they?"

He had nothing to worry about, though. His abundant muscles would weed out any fat finding itself in his lean body.

"My sister is worse. She takes napkins, toilet rolls, a potty, and lotion in her car."

She frowned. Why was she revealing such personal things to someone she wouldn't be seeing again after today? A man she couldn't stand, for that matter. When her eyes darted his way, their gazes collided. The corners of his lips tipped upward, and for the first time, his eyes smiled more, making hers falter. Emotions squeezed at her heart, her mind filling with what ifs.

"Are you and your sister close?"

"We're twins."

It didn't mean they were close, of course. After all, they weren't even identical. While Chantelle had a slim and tall frame, Danielle was shorter with rounder features. Their colouring also differed, with Danielle, the older twin, being fairer than Chantelle's milk-chocolate complexion. But they were close. As children, they'd fought a lot, but their fierce rivalry had transformed into an even stronger sibling love as grown-ups.

"That's not an answer," he said. "This is how people fail exams."

"I'm merely leading into the answer." Her sheepish reply came immediately.

His laughter caused her heart to dance to its melody. It strummed her newly awakened libido with promises of intense pleasure. It made it too easy to forget the brewing emotions were supposed to be nipped in the bud.

"To answer your question, there's nothing we won't do for each other. If she's in a fight, I'd step in with her no questions asked. She'd do the same for me."

He nodded, a look she couldn't decipher crossing his eyes, stirring her curiosity, but she refused to engage. Instead, she ventured into safe territory.

"How did I do, Professor McKenzie?"

He bellowed one of his contagious laughs. "Excellent answer. A hundred points."

Her insides vibrated with happiness. She should have squashed it, but for some reason, she couldn't. This feeling had been brewing since Valentine's Day, unlocked by a man who exasperated and yet excited her. After tasting joy again, the inclination to block it no longer appealed. She'd missed being happy with a man. It appeared she'd inadvertently crossed a line in the sand. Guarding her emotions had suddenly become her past.

"Are you and your brother close?" she asked.

His fame meant a lot about him was public knowledge. She knew he had an older brother who hadn't gone into the family business. Lord may be the tabloids' darling boy, but his brother also made headlines a few times as one of the leading cardiologists in the country.

"You can say that. Growing up, we had a typical big brother small brother relationship. Him being mostly annoying, but protective when he needed to be. Luckily, these days, I can kick his butt."

The comment made her chuckle. “Why does everything always come down to brute strength with guys? No one asked about kicking anyone’s backside.”

He didn’t respond. Instead, he pointed ahead. “There it is.”

CHAPTER 9

A BIG, CIRCULAR BUILDING loomed ahead. Chantelle could only make out the grey-white colour of the plastered walls and scaffolding. As they approached, it appeared more clearly. Two arc-shaped structures stood adjacent to the first building, their designs visibly artistic. She couldn't see what lay in the middle, but she guessed an open space. When the truck came to a stop, she discovered more land lay beyond the buildings.

"It's huge," she said, as they got out of the car.

"In terms of a school, it isn't."

"How large is it?"

"Fifteen plots," he answered as they joined Joe and Kofi.

She marvelled at how effortlessly he said fifteen plots. That was a little over twenty-five acres, or five soccer fields. In her mind, it sounded huge. And expensive. A little aide-memoire that he was out of her league—discounting all the other reasons why they shouldn't be together—even if she were interested.

"Wait here. I'll get some protective headgear and make sure it's safe for us to go in." He disappeared around the round building.

"What's this place?" Kofi asked.

"A school." She remembered Lord had called it a secret project. "That's all I can tell you right now."

"We should be safe without headgear at this distance," Joe said. "I'll take some shots while we wait."

She shielded her eyes as she did a visual tour of the place. Her gaze finally landed on the board showing an artist's impression of the finished campus. She walked over to it and read the information. No mention of McKenzie Contractors, she noted. Instead, it listed a third-party contractor.

A sound to her right drew her attention. She turned to find Lord walking towards her, wearing a construction helmet and holding a spare. Another man accompanied him. When they reached her, he introduced the new guy as Mr. Nti, the site manager.

"Nice to meet you," she said, offering her hand.

Mr. Nti shook it. "My pleasure. Lord tells me you're from *Odopa* Magazine."

"Yes. We're doing a story on him and wanted to cover some of his projects."

The two men looked at each other. There seemed to be some non-verbal communication going on. She sensed disapproval from the site manager, but since Lord had invited her, she chose to ignore it. She turned her attention to the board again and tuned out their conversation.

Moments later, a hand touched her shoulder. Fingertips brushed her bare skin, sending a ripple of sensations through her. Only one person had such an effect on her.

"Are you ready for a tour?" he asked.

She nodded. Affected by the heat radiating from his touch, she didn't trust herself enough to talk. She stilled while he placed a helmet on her head and adjusted it to fit. She'd effectively stopped breathing in anticipation of his hands inadvertently touching her face.

"There you go, my construction woman." He flicked her chin.

Neither his actions nor his words should have delighted her, but her body stirred with thrilling sensations. She forced to project an aloofness she didn't feel as they joined Joe and Kofi who'd also donned protective headgear.

"Mr. Nti doesn't look happy we're here," she commented.

"We've been having some trouble with stolen property lately, which has slowed down the work."

Understanding dawned on her. "And it doesn't help that his crew needs to stop working while we're visiting."

"Only in the places we'll visit. You're right, though. He isn't pleased." He winked. "But I'm the boss, and this tour is important. Besides, we're still within schedule."

As they walked through the uncompleted building, he shared his vision for the school—the perfect host, exhibiting thorough knowledge of his project. She couldn't help admiring him for what she knew he could achieve. She tried to imagine the future history to be created within these walls.

The tour of the grounds and one of the arced buildings took a little over twenty minutes.

"There'll be several other blocks as the school expands," Lord explained before leading them towards the big round building. "This one will have auditoriums of varying sizes. The largest will have a nine-hundred-person seating capacity, which is huge for the intended size of the school."

His eyes often drifted to her as he spoke, and though he didn't do anything specific to draw her attention, he held her interest.

"The students will write and perform plays and musicals. The idea is to encourage them to showcase their talents to the public," he said. "It will also serve as a cinema for those studying film."

In her mind's eye, she could see those walls painted and decorated, and students milling about, each one creative in his or her own right.

"Will there be film weeks and such?" Kofi asked.

"Absolutely."

His enthusiasm, while he expounded, reflected in the others' faces. Her attention came back to him. He appeared imposing in comparison with the other three men. For one, he stood more than a head taller than any of them. His stately gait distinguished him as he took them through the building that was his in every sense of the word. And he'd chosen to share it with her. How could she have avoided the admiration welling up inside?

On their way out, Joe and Mr. Nti led the way, followed closely by her and Kofi. Lord remained a step behind. Was he checking her out?

They were descending a flight of stairs when Kofi slipped. On his way down, his hand struck her leg, sending her toppling backwards. She let out a scream. In a flash, Lord caught her, supporting her back with his hands. Without hesitation, she wrapped her arms around his neck.

Shaken, she allowed him to sit her down on the stairs. He squatted before her, deep grooves of concern etched between his brows.

"Are you all right?"

She nodded. "Yes, I think so."

He turned to Kofi. "And you?"

The young man nodded while rubbing his thigh. "I'll be okay. I'm sorry, Chantelle. I hope I didn't hurt you."

Finding her voice again, she assured him she was all right. "Are you okay?"

"Yes. I think I need to go and sit in the car now, though."

When she tried to stand, Lord restrained her. "You should sit here a minute. We need to make sure nothing's broken."

She nodded.

"Go ahead. We'll be there shortly," he said to the others. When they were gone, he took her left foot in his hands. "Does anything hurt?"

She shook her head. *Just my pride.*

Slipping off her shoes, he gently turned her ankle. "Nothing?"

"Nothing." Except the shivers running down her spine.

He tested her right foot, and when he'd convinced himself she was indeed not hurt, he replaced the shoes. He didn't release her legs immediately. Instead, he slipped his hands beneath her jeans, massaging her as far up as her calves. Though her breath had returned to normal, the feel of his hands on her skin began to escalate her pulse, and she struggled not to show it.

He looked up at her, unbridled desire sneaking into his eyes, and her mind went straight to Valentine's Day. Would a second time be just as explosive? Would he be able to make her come multiple times again? She supposed he could. He'd done a pretty good job of planting ideas in her head with just the look in his eyes. She swallowed, calling up every ounce of resolve she had to tear her eyes away.

Finally, he released her leg and came to sit right next to her. Too close for comfort.

When he reached out and turned her face to look at him, she gulped. She didn't move, afraid any exertion on her racing heart would cause it to explode. Their eyes met before his dropped to her lips. Slowly, he raised her chin and leaned forward, resting his weight on one hand. First, he gave her a feather-light, chaste kiss. Every thought flittered out of her mind. Her lips parted, wanting to taste more of him.

At her open invitation, he tipped her head further and deepened the kiss, his tongue probing and searching, shaking her to the core by the extent of the pleasure he gave with his mouth alone. His hand closed around her waist, his touch so gentle, it made her shudder inside. She moaned, gripping his thigh and leaning in, begging for more. Then his fingers grazed her nipple, sending her into another realm of bliss.

After what seemed like only seconds, he pulled away, leaving her weak-kneed. She stared into his eyes trying to catch her breath, too stunned to speak. He shook his head in wonderment before his tongue snuck out to lick his lower lip. She swallowed, catching the tempting act.

He reached for her tank top, and she held her breath, barely stopping herself from closing her eyes when his fingers brushed against her skin. She swallowed her disappointment when he only straightened the garment. The friction of the soft fabric against her sensitive nipples caused a groan to lock in her throat. Her breasts felt heavy, aching for his caress, but it would be too dangerous to ask. *Get a grip.*

"Thanks." She managed to get that out with a steady voice, then realising what it sounded like, she added, "For catching me."

"You're welcome. The important thing is that you weren't hurt." Desire permeated his voice.

Picking up a nearby stone, he threw it at an undefined target.

"I know, but usually, it's the thought of what could have happened that frightens me."

"There's no need for fear when the danger has passed. You could have been hurt, but you weren't." He took in a deep breath.

She often struggled to see the glass half full in all situations. Something he probably had no problem with. As he exhaled, his sombre look dissolved into a cheerful one.

"As I said before, I'd never let you fall."

She laughed. "You're impossible."

They'd literally done a death drop. And he'd saved her. *Permission to be smug, granted.* Right now, he wasn't just Lord McKenzie. He looked more like a knight, *sans* the shining armour and white stallion, but maybe modern-day heroes came in jeans and navy-blue trucks.

LORD HAD NEVER built any walls around his heart. He'd never needed it. Love had, so far, remained an abstract concept. The women he'd dated posed no risk to his heart. So in a sense, he never really did stand a chance with Chantelle.

On their way out, his hand wandered to her back as though to guide her. Truth be told, touching her was more for his pleasure and sanity. Being here with her, sharing this project, made him happy. He refused to analyse how one could feel content just by the presence of another.

He tried to come to terms with the mixture of feelings raging like a storm within him. His heart swelled with these emotions until he feared it would burst, then tightened again as if it had been bear-hugged. Whatever the case, he didn't feel passive for the first time in his life.

He was falling in love with her. How could it be after knowing a person for only three days? He didn't believe in love in a few days any more than he did in love at first sight. Then again, he'd never been in love, so he supposed he couldn't argue against the possibility of falling for her after such a short period.

Maybe his feelings didn't start on Valentine's Day. Perhaps it began with his love affair with her writing.

As a businessman, he knew the correlation between risk and reward. The risk of feeling anything for this woman was the abiding knowledge that today marked the end of their professional relationship, the last day he could dictate her presence with him. Starting tomorrow, seeing her again depended on her. Pure and simple. Unless he gave her a reason to see him as more than just a good story.

That was why it had been important to share this project, rather than one of the company's, with her. She needed to make an assessment based on the truth, and not what the media wrote about him. Though his insides had developed a new pastime of bubbling over around her, there remained a tinge of dread at the possibility that she truly didn't want him.

He didn't dwell on the unpleasant thought. Instead, he focused on the other truth. She found him attractive; that much he knew. Was his allure potent enough for her to want him long-term? He stole a glance at her, noted her composure. He still reeled from their kiss, yet she appeared calm and collected. Her soft sounds had egged him on, but now with his heart crawling steadily up his sleeve, he realised he shouldn't have kissed her.

He was about to be the first person in history to suffer heartbreak without an actual relationship, and like a deer standing transfixed in the beam of a car's headlights, he couldn't do anything about it.

They exited the building and found Joe and Kofi at the parking area. Kofi sat in the car while Joe stood by the door as they chatted.

"Are you okay? No broken bones?" Chantelle asked.

"He's a man." Joe patted Kofi on the back. "He can take it."

They spent the next couple of minutes laughing about the whole incident. He wished he were man enough to walk away from his growing need to have Chantelle on a permanent basis.

"Did you get some good images?" he asked Joe.

"Yes, but none with you inside."

"Do you need me in these ones, too?"

"The story is about you, not the building," Chantelle said, poking him lightly in the chest.

The impulsive gesture caused another onslaught of the swelling-and-tightening thing in his heart. It was the most unrestrained thing she'd done in his presence since Valentine's Day. Her smile went right from her lips to wrap itself around his insides.

"I have to talk with Mr. Nti, and then I'll pose for you."

His gaze remained on her as he spoke. He had to talk with the site manager, but he needed more to distance himself from her for a moment. Otherwise, it wouldn't matter whether they were in the presence of others—people equipped to immortalise his actions on film—he'd kiss her again.

He found Mr. Nti waiting at the entrance of one of the buildings. As the site manager updated him on the progress of work, Lord's attention kept drifting to Chantelle. She stood with her back to him, and he had a good view of her fine butt. His hands itched to cup them. He fantasised about his fingers licking the little tease of skin between the jeans and her tank top.

He half listened to Mr. Nti, while the rest of his mind focused on more pressing things, like whether Chantelle was ticklish, what she wore to bed, if she brushed her teeth before or after breakfast, whether she squeezed the toothpaste from the bottom or the middle. Did she think about him outside of things concerning the article? What would she say if he told her how much space she'd occupied in his mind over the past three days?

After the site manager left, Lord remained where he stood, watching her. Her conversation with Joe and Kofi had her laughing, which resulted in a smile on his own lips. She looked fetching in her jeans and that slinky top. Too bad what he wanted to do was take them off and feel her soft skin against his again, tickle her until she begged him to stop, to make love with her.

On impulse, he pulled out his cell phone and dialled her number. It rang twice before she began to check her pockets. She looked at the screen and paused, then turned to look at him. Even from afar, he saw her frown. He pointed for her to answer, half expecting her to ignore it.

Suddenly, he could hear the two men talking behind her. She'd picked up! A sudden intake of air made him realise he'd been holding his breath. He couldn't be more grateful to be standing at a distance. No doubt he looked like a lost puppy that had just been found. He certainly felt like it.

"Hello," she said in a sexy, breathy voice, just like the first time she had called to set up the interview.

A happy sigh left his lips upon hearing her voice over the phone. Even better that he could see her. Although there was a unique joy to imagining what people were doing—in her case, without her clothes on, to make the fantasy steamier—when he couldn't see them.

"I thought you said you'd never answer my call."

She uttered an indignant sound. Visually, it looked like a gasp. "This doesn't count."

"Why not?"

"You're right here. I can see you." She pointed in his direction. "You could have walked right over."

He could hear the aggravation in her voice and the distress of realising he'd somewhat won. The outrage in her tone rather than the pseudo-triumph made him laugh. Still, he expected her to disconnect the call, but she remained online without talking, righteous anger building.

"I'm afraid it's not about what you think, Chantelle Sah," he said. "In my book, it counts. I called, and you picked up. That constitutes a breach of contract." A contract he hadn't agreed to, by the way.

"Why, you sneaky—" She pulled the phone from her ear, held it out to him, and disconnected as if she were detonating a bomb.

Her eyes flashed daggers at him when he made his way back to her and the crew. Her studied effort not to smile at him or his jokes didn't go unnoticed. Did she know how adorable she looked? He kept his hands to himself, though. If he intended to win her over, he had to show her he wanted her beyond her body.

"Where shall I pose for your camera, Joe?"

"We're good. I took some shots while you were talking to Mr. Nti," Joe said. "I think they work much better than if you posed. They look more natural."

He reached for Chantelle. "Then why don't you take one of me and the lady to commemorate this occasion?"

"Okay." Joe adjusted the lens of his camera.

Lord placed his hand over Chantelle's shoulder, noting how well her curves fit into him. He smiled for the camera, taking pleasure in the joy of simply having her in his arms.

CHAPTER 10

OKAY, SO SHE WAS attracted to him. Big deal. Attraction was a scientific reaction like throwing an object into the air; it had to come back down. Put a gorgeous man in the same confines as a sex-starved, red-blooded female, and sparks were bound to fly. A case of action and reaction.

That totally explained why her knees had morphed from bone to cartilage and her lips still tingled from his kiss. Why else would she relish the feel of his hand resting upon her shoulder as if she belonged to him? A completely inane idea, because she wasn't his woman by any stretch. Something she'd do well to remember.

On the journey to his house, she observed his subdued demeanour. He seemed so intent on the driving, she didn't want to intrude.

His restrained manner afforded her a private moment to observe him, to drink in the powerful arcs of his brows, the proud slant of his nose, the slight pout of his lips that looked equal parts alluring and arrogant, and as she remembered, a hundred percent sensual. Yet, his pull on her transcended his good looks. He'd exposed her to the astute businessman and the guy who wanted to give back to the entertainment industry which had given him his fame.

Her heart twisted in knots. In a matter of hours, there would be no need to see him again, no reason to come running because he beckoned, and zero chances of her heart lilting to the cadence of his voice, of his laughter. He'd move on, and she'd be a blip on his radar. No denying it. Lord McKenzie, playboy tycoon, had impacted her heart. She hated to admit it, but she'd miss him.

"What are you thinking about?"

She frowned. That sounded personal, not at all like an interview question. Why probe when it would all end today?

A sharp intake of air told her he'd indeed been deep in thought. He glanced at her, his look lugubrious.

"What am I thinking about?" From the expression in his eyes, there could have been a million answers to the question. His problem seemed to be which one to give. Finally, he broke into a series of smiles. "I'm thinking about what makes me tick."

Here we go again. Just when she thought he wasn't quite as insufferable as she'd first imagined, he proved her wrong. She'd discovered more to him than met the eye, though.

"And what makes you tick?"

"I already told you, remember?"

Right. *Women like me*. The first time he'd said it, she'd wanted to gag. Now, the idea of being a woman who made him tick held a lot of appeal. Secretly, it delighted her the answer remained the same. *What is it about me*, she wanted to ask, even though her head knew his words had to be only for show. How pathetic could she be?

"A man of your calibre must have more than one thing that makes him tick."

"No. I'm a simple guy. What you see is what you get."

She snorted. What an understatement. There was nothing uncomplicated about him. What she saw, no matter how explicitly sexy, was definitely not the only thing she got.

"I'll bet you stopped being simple the moment you learnt how to tie your shoelaces."

He chuckled. "I *was* a handful at that age."

His easy laughter did its bit to melt a portion of her heart, and she found herself wondering what he must have been like as a child. Cute and smart, she'd bet. The mischievous ones always were. From nowhere, imaginings of what his kids would look like surfaced. A host of motherly emotions rushed at her, rousing bittersweet thoughts of her baby …

She gave herself a mental shake, her mind reaching for something to say. "Tell me about your childhood. Were you a happy kid?"

She barely stopped herself from wincing. Why was she doing this to herself? She shouldn't be talking about babies, but it seemed her mouth hadn't received the memo yet. With any luck, he'd change the subject and save her from the emotional black hole she'd begun digging for herself.

"Childhood holds many fond memories. I grew up in a loving home with parents who never missed a chance to show my brother and me they love us." He glanced at her, his eyes twinkling. "It wasn't all fun and games, though. Despite always having a house staff, my parents ensured we had chores, and my brother made it his mission to make my life miserable."

Chantelle chuckled. "I can relate. My sister, Danielle, who's my elder by two minutes, seized every opportunity to remind me of the fact."

He laughed. "Ah, a kindred spirit."

"I'm afraid so."

A few minutes elapsed. "I'd definitely not do secondary school twice; I can tell you that."

His confession came as a surprise. "I've never heard of a popular kid who wouldn't want to relive secondary school."

"Who said I was a popular kid?"

She blinked. "You weren't?"

He smiled at her shock. "Don't look so surprised. Meet the lanky guy who got teased because he didn't know what to do with his height."

"I can't imagine you being teased." She caught the sight of his shirt sleeves tightening around his biceps as he negotiated a turn. "Or lanky."

"Oh, believe me, it happened. Being related to the coolest guy in school made my un-coolness more conspicuous. They even had a special version of the Lord's prayer just for me."

Unable to stop herself, she laughed harder. "Can I hear it?"

"No," he said, even though his voice rang with laughter. "I shouldn't have told you."

"I'm sorry for laughing. I didn't expect that."

"Well, it's not something I broadcast."

The conversation continued in like manner as they made their way to his home in the upmarket East Airport Residential area, a house hidden within a gated compound. He activated the remote-controlled entry, and it glided open to reveal a well-manicured lawn and a long driveway, leading to a closed two-car garage. He parked in front of the closed garage door as Joe's car also came to a stop behind them.

The house itself was stunning, merging traditional stoned walls of pre-colonial Ghanaian architecture with Victorian-inspired elements of steep pitched roofs and porches with turned posts. Large, double-pane windows and a section made of glass, overlooking the flower garden in front, gave it a trendy, modern look.

As soon as they got out, Joe took a few pictures of the exterior, before shaking his head. "The sun is too bright. I'll have to do the outside shots when it starts to set."

"Nice house, Mr. McKenzie," Kofi said in awed admiration.

"Thanks, but don't look so impressed. It's just a house."

Yeah, one straight from a magazine.

"How many bedrooms does it have?" Kofi asked.

It wasn't a large house in terms of what he could afford, but it wasn't particularly small, either. She guessed there would be at least three bedrooms, perhaps a study and a gym, considering his amazing physique.

"Three bedrooms including the master."

Chantelle smiled privately, wondering what else she got right.

"Did you bring any food?" Joe asked her. "Maybe I can get something into my stomach before we start."

"How could I resist when I know you enjoy my food so much?" Chantelle said, retrieving the snack bag from the car.

As she did this, Lord leaned forward, saying, "It appears your mother was right."

"Where Joe's concerned, absolutely."

"Let's get inside." Lord fanned himself with his hands. "It's getting hot out here."

Once in, he switched on the air-conditioner.

After snack time, Joe and Kofi set up their equipment. Chantelle found herself relegated to the position of observer. The shoot started with Lord in his large, fully equipped kitchen. They had him slice a couple of oranges to get pictures that appeared domestic. What female could resist a man who knew his way around the kitchen?

They moved to the sitting room, which had a cosy bar area where they took several shots of him preparing cocktails. Then they captured him relaxing and watching football on his large screen TV.

"Let's take a break," Joe said after a while. "I want to download these before we move to any other parts of the house."

"Are we going to do any bedroom shots?" Lord asked.

She thought she heard a suggestiveness in his voice, like he wasn't talking about bedroom 'shots.' Must be her mind playing tricks on her, luring her into imaginings about his room. How big was his bed? How would it feel to be in it with him?

Whoa, time out.

"No." She injected firmness into her voice for herself. "I think the rest of the world has done enough stories about you and your bedroom-related prowess."

Was that a look of gratitude he gave her? Not likely. Mockery, maybe. If he hadn't wanted bedroom pictures, he wouldn't have asked.

"I think we're good," Joe said, bringing her attention back to the group.

They all congregated around his laptop, viewing the pictures. The only problem they'd face was which ones to eliminate.

After the indoor pictures were done, they all moved outside. The setting sun provided the perfect backdrop for the exterior shots. By four o'clock, Joe was ready to leave.

"The pictures will be ready sometime tomorrow," he informed her. "I'll drop a pen drive on your desk by Monday morning."

"Thanks so much, Joe."

"Not a problem. I'd give you a ride home if there were extra space in the car."

"Don't worry, I'll take her home," Lord said, as if on cue.

Joe didn't appear to have a problem with the offer. In fact, he seemed delighted to leave her with Lord. He winked at her before driving off with Kofi, confirming her suspicions. She and Lord remained standing there for a moment.

"Well," she said. "It's been interesting. Thanks for letting us into your life. I'll try to do justice to your story."

He fixed his attention on her. "I have no doubts about it."

An awkward silence settled upon them. They were alone together for the first time since Wednesday. Looking into his eyes, she could tell the same thought had occurred to him. She began to prickle all over with increased awareness.

"I'll get my things."

She turned and hurried into the house. Once there, she busied herself packing the unopened box of juice, along with the two uneaten sandwiches. Then she picked up her handbag. Straightening up, she turned to find Lord standing right behind her. He seemed so imposing, so close, and so incredibly delicious. Her heart began thumping against her ribcage, her body overcome with tingling heat despite the air-conditioner.

"Stay."

His rough voice filled her with cosy warmth.

"I can't," she said, terrified of giving in to the force of her own desires. If she did, she might not be able to avoid a replay of what happened on Valentine's Day. She was only human, for goodness' sake.

His eyes narrowed. "Are you afraid of being alone with me, Chantelle?"

He didn't scare her. It was herself she feared, and the completely out-of-character desire to be unravelled again by his expert hands and lips.

"You don't frighten me." Her voice managed to sound indignant, but inside, she shivered at his nearness.

"Great," he said. "I don't want you to be uncomfortable in my presence."

Discomfort had many definitions, and though she wasn't discomfited in the way he meant, she did feel some amount of distress at being so close to him without being touched.

Eventually, he did touch her when he slipped the bag off her shoulder and dropped it on the marble coffee table. Then, if it were possible, he moved in closer, spellbinding her. His closeness robbed her of any more words of protest.

Studying her face for a bit, he brushed his fingertips against her cheeks before holding her firm by both shoulders. Her lips parted to release a shuddering breath.

"I promise not to kiss you." His voice was almost a whisper.

Despite the declaration, his gaze lingered on her lips, glazed with desire. Tension mounted. If he kissed her, she wouldn't want him to stop, but if he asked, she'd have to say no. She barely stopped herself from cringing at the thought. *Ugh.* The definition of blowing hot and cold. Could he read her mind? Did he know how hard she fought to keep her hands by her sides rather than wrap them around his neck and beg him to reconsider?

"Can I play some music?" The corners of his lips lifted in a slight smile. "I won't ask you to dance, either."

She released a short, shaky laugh, and some of the tension eased. With his back turned, she took the blessed moment to inject herself with some spine, though what she really needed was to escape. However, as an oldie highlife tune filled the room, she found herself taking a seat in one of his comfy leather armchairs.

"Do you want something to drink? Juice, tea, wine?" he asked.

"Do you have lemon?"

"I expect so. My housekeeper did my monthly shopping this morning."

"Can I have warm water and lemon?"

He made a curious face. "Doesn't sound like lemonade."

"It isn't." She gave him a sweet smile.

"Okay," he answered sceptically before heading to the kitchen to prepare her drink.

He returned a few minutes later with her glass of warm water and a bottle of concentrated lemon juice, and iced tea for himself.

"Let's sit at the dining table," he suggested.

Even better. A table between them would be a good thing at this material moment. He handed her the glasses and brought two coasters from the kitchen, placing them on one corner of the dining table. He pulled out a chair for her and then sat adjacent to her at the head.

She squirted some of the lemon juice into the water, trying not to think about being alone with Lord in his house. At least, he'd promised not to kiss her. That was good, right?

"Why did you agree to do this interview?" she asked, keeping it professional.

He shrugged. "Two reasons. First, I thought it high time I started controlling what people read about me."

"Didn't you say you didn't care what the papers wrote about you? You lied."

He fixed her with a steady gaze. "I don't lie. After all, the truth is far more intriguing."

"Then why bother controlling what people read?"

"It's not people I care about." He looked away from her for a split second. "But my father isn't people."

"You're doing this for your father?"

"In part. He doesn't approve of the attention I get."

The information didn't surprise her. Mr. McKenzie had a reputation of being extremely private. Too bad he hadn't imparted some of his camera-shyness to Lord.

"You've been getting attention for years. Why now?"

"The right opportunity hadn't come along."

"What makes this the right opportunity?"

"McKenzie Contractors is pitching for the Kumasi International Airport project. If we win, it's going to be the biggest contract we've ever handled, so until a winner is announced, everything said about me and the company should, in some way, contribute towards the pitch."

"After all this time of letting the media have free rein, you think that will work?"

"My PR people think so." He held her hands, playing with her fingers, then met her gaze. "And if you're as good as I believe you are, then I'd say yes."

With her knees growing weak, she started to remind him, "You said—"

"I said I wouldn't kiss, not that I wouldn't touch you." He traced a line up her arm. "Do you like it when I touch you?"

Her throat went dry. She swallowed, pulling her hands away from his to get her drink. She wished she'd asked for a cold one, because now her body was on fire.

"You said there were two reasons." She found her voice surprisingly steady. "What's the other?"

He sipped his drink. "I wanted to meet you."

Her eyebrows shot up in surprise, and she gave an embarrassed laugh.

"Yeah, right." Had he forgotten who the celebrity was? "There were no guarantees I'd be the one assigned to this project."

"Randy didn't tell you, then."

"Tell me what?" she asked, even though the answer had already occurred to her.

Initially, she'd tried to get out of this assignment, but Randy had informed her Lord had requested her. She'd assumed it was his way of making her work to regain his trust.

"I had only one condition for doing this interview. You."

She released a breath, letting his words sink in. Randy had been telling the truth. Her insides did a little dance as a thought occurred. If Lord had requested her, did it mean *Celeb* magazine didn't pose a threat? That they hadn't been a threat right from the start? The relief spreading through her made her realise how anxious she'd been about the prospect of botching this assignment. Another thought boggled her mind, though. Why on earth would the CEO of McKenzie Contractors want to meet her?

Suddenly, he stood.

"Come." He held out a hand. "I want to show you something."

Curiosity got the better of her, and she gave him her hand. He led her out of the dining room through a corridor. Her heartbeat escalated as she realised they were likely headed for a bedroom. She chided herself. Nothing would happen that she didn't want. The problem was, her head seemed to be dictating less and less of what she desired.

She breathed relief when she found no bed in the room they entered. The study—complete with a large desk and rows of books lining two walls. He led her straight to a cabinet and opened it to reveal more books, newspapers, and magazines. He handed her one of the papers.

She recognised it straightaway. "I have an article in this."

"I know," Lord said. "It's your first work I read, and I was so impressed by the depth of your thoughts, I started looking out for you." He picked another one, showing it to her. "Then I found this one."

As she took it from him, a stack of *Odopa* magazines caught her attention. Curious, she picked up the first one. Their January edition. A closer look at the spines of the stack revealed they were in chronological order dating back three years. He had every copy of the magazine since she had started working there. Stunned, she finally turned to face him.

He was leaning against the door of the closet, locking her in, both physically and with the deep browns of his eyes. Moving out meant arching her back to pass under his arm. If she did, her breasts would graze his solid chest. Thinking about it filled her with yearning.

"I'm a big fan." His voice had turned husky.

He could boast of more than a big 'fan-ship.' She knew it for a fact. In effect, that was one of the reasons why her knees began to weaken as she held his unflinching gaze. His free hand rose to her face, but she suspected her face had met him halfway. She allowed him to caress her cheeks, and her eyes began to close as she sucked in a breath.

"You do things to me, Chantelle …" His gruff voice trailed off.

"Like what?"

Who said that? Was that her voice? It sounded too breathy and inviting. Why the hell hadn't she hightailed it out of there?

"Everything about you drives me crazy." He shook his head, and his Adam's apple bobbed when he swallowed. "I can't stop thinking about you."

His hand curved against her throat, his thumb drawing a line on her jaw. The playfulness disappeared from his eyes, leaving full-blown, unbridled desire. His gaze skimmed over her face, settling on her mouth. Her breath snagged, her lips parting slightly.

"I'm not going to kiss you, because I promised not to," he said. "That's a promise I'll never make again."

Before she could beg him to reconsider, his hands came to rest on her shoulders. "Come on. I'll take you home."

She couldn't decide whether it was relief or disappointment fuelling her veins after he said those words.

IF LORD WERE TO list everything Chantelle did to him, their conversation would have been lengthier, and it wouldn't have ended with him taking her home. Not in this state. His rigid member threatened to burst out of his trousers. His body trembled discreetly from the extent of his need. Talking made it worse, so he remained silent.

Besides, she didn't appear to be in a conversational mood, either. She'd set the radio to *Atlantis FM* as soon as she sat in the car and reclined the seat. Now, she had her eyes closed, but the occasional humming of the song playing conveyed her wakefulness.

She had to be tired. He didn't blame her. It had been a long day. Fatigue would have had him yawning, but his arousal kept him awake and on edge. He'd have to forget about sleep tonight.

Glancing over at her, he noticed her eyes were still closed, her breathing a little heavy. She looked so peaceful, oblivious to the desire raging inside him. He fought the urge to reach over and touch her.

"Are you asleep?"

"Hm?" She cleared her throat, sitting up. "Are we there?"

Her sleepy voice went straight to his groin. God, she was sexy. What would it be like to rouse her with kisses and have that voice, so riddled with sleep, in his ears? How would it feel to have all night to explore the treasures of her body? To bring her to a point where she begged him to ease her need?

He blew air out of his mouth. "No. Just another ten minutes, though."

She sat up. "I'm sorry I fell asleep on you."

She could sleep *on* him anytime. Too bad his body couldn't fall asleep. "It's been a long day for you."

"For you, as well." She tried to stifle a yawn and giggled when her attempt failed.

In turn, he lost the battle to keep both hands on the wheel and reached out to ruffle her hair. "Go back to sleep. I'll wake you when we get there."

By the time they arrived at her home, she was fully awake although she'd had to suppress a series of yawns. He walked her to her door, and waited until she opened it. He didn't linger.

"Goodnight," he said, shoving his hands into his pockets to prevent them from acting of their own accord and holding her. "Dream well."

She gave him a tired smile. "Goodnight."

He watched her until the door closed. Linking his fingers, he draped his hands around his nape as he walked away. Back in his car, he released another heavy breath from his mouth. With one last look at the house, he drove off to a cold shower and a sleepless night.

CHAPTER 11

CHANTELLE HAD BEEN TOO wired to have much sleep. Every time she'd dozed off, sexy images of Lord had invaded her dreams. Before her eyes had flown open, he'd been poised, waiting to be guided inside her. Threads of girly excitement snaked through her abdomen. She allowed the emotions to take their course and subside naturally, since she'd concluded Lord wasn't odious, after all.

Getting out of bed, she slipped on a robe and headed straight for the kitchen. Rummaging through the fridge, she pulled out a tub of plain yogurt, which she preferred to the flavoured type, and sat in front of the TV. Under the pretext of planning her article, she thought about Lord and his performing arts academy. His words last night about his father's disapproval of his publicity had remained with her, and the need to redeem him in his father's eyes consumed her.

She saw the older man's point, although being in the public eye had intrinsic worth. After all, entertainment celebrities always planted stories and leaked 'secrets' just to appear in the papers. Lord didn't have that problem. He just needed to carefully manage the narrative of reportage about him.

As she flipped through channels trying to decide what to watch, her cell phone rang. She checked the caller ID before answering.

"Hi, Ben," she said. "The prodigal friend finally calls. How long has it been this time? Two months?"

Ben's soft laughter drifted across the line. "I know. I'm sorry."

She chuckled. "No, you're not. Everyone knows your job is your first love."

As a senior reporter for the largest private newspaper, Ben often went undercover, which resulted in a tendency to drop off the radar for months at a time.

"I promise to do better," he said.

"You always say that."

"I mean it this time."

A smile formed on her lips. Many of their conversations started this way. Due to the demands of their jobs, they couldn't get together often, even though Ben counted as one of a select number of people she called friends. But, hey, it made for a good conversation opener.

"All right," she said. "I'll let you off the hook. Again."

She could hear the smile in his voice when he spoke. "I have two tickets to the Golden Stool Awards."

"Are you passing on the info, or is it an invitation?"

Ben chortled. "It's an invitation if you're interested. Unless you're working."

"I'm not, but are they guest tickets or press passes, because you know the magazine can get me passes."

He tut-tutted. "Chantelle, you disappoint me."

"Real tickets!" She squealed, excited. "I thought those were sold out months ago."

The Golden Stool Awards, so named after the Golden Stool of Ashanti, and with a nod at the American Golden Globe Awards, was one of the most prestigious events on the country's entertainment calendar. She'd planned on attending the event on a guest ticket, which signified a good seat, and best of all, no name tags. Unfortunately, by the time she'd gone to buy one, there had been no tickets left.

"I have my ways," Ben said solemnly.

She laughed. "Yes, you do."

"I take it you want me to reserve one for you?"

"Absolutely."

"Great. See you on Saturday."

"Okay, bye."

Her smile lingered several moments after hanging up. Hearing from Ben always cheered her up. Such a sweet guy, and yet considered one of the most notorious journalists in the country, responsible for exposing corruption in the highest echelons of society and government. A fact you'd never guess from talking to him. How he managed to sneak into some places remained a mystery to her. Being on the chubby side and soft-spoken helped, she supposed. No one ever thought him to be harmful.

As she resumed the task of surfing channels, a beep sounded on her phone. A message from Lord. She bit her lips as she opened it to read: *'Good morning, Chantelle. Thanks for spending time with me last night. Hope you slept well. LM'*

A smile spread across her face, and she hugged the phone to herself. She sighed, refusing to question the elation his text message brought. What were his plans this morning? Having visited his house, she could imagine him there. And imagine, she did.

She started replying several times, struggling to find a response which was both polite and not too eager. Unable to settle on something appropriate, she decided to chew on it a little. Hopefully, a good answer would occur to her soon.

Finding nothing worth watching on TV, she got back on her laptop to do some writing. The computer had just booted when her doorbell rang, and she went to answer it, welcoming the distraction.

Peeping through the window, her gaze encountered her sister, Danielle, with her two daughters. She opened the door.

"Good morning, Auntie Chantie," her nieces screamed, rushing past her into the house.

Danielle smiled. At five months pregnant, her glow neared blinding proportions. "Hi, sis."

"Hi." They hugged. "What are you three doing out here this early on a Sunday morning?"

"It's already nine, Chantie. We went to check on the house we're building in Adenta. You know I like to do that early," Danielle said. "Where's your car?"

"With the mechanic. It refused to start yesterday," Chantelle said. "I can't believe you woke up the kids just to take them to the site."

"Oh, that. David says he's exhausted, so I thought I'd take the girls with me and give him a chance to rest. They love visiting construction sites like you did when we were young." Her sister waddled straight to the kitchen and did her bit of rummaging through the fridge. "We decided to have breakfast here."

"Is that right?" Chantelle laughed. Her sister had an open invitation, but a heads-up would have been nice. "What if you didn't find me home?"

"Please, sis. This early on a Sunday?" Danielle laughed. "You're one person I can guarantee would always be either at home or at work."

She didn't feel positively about this dose of truth. "I could have spent the night out. How about that?"

Danielle raised her eyebrows and crossed her arms over her stomach. "Something you want to tell me?"

"Nothing. I'm just saying."

"Girls, come help your auntie make breakfast," Danielle yelled to her nine and seven-year-old daughters who could be heard laughing and screaming somewhere in the house. They came running to the kitchen.

Araba, the younger one, did a victory dance. "I won, I won."

"You cheated," Kukua said, though both of them were laughing.

Danielle patted her stomach. "I hope this one's a boy. Maybe fate crossed my children's personalities, and the boy will be calmer than the girls."

"I don't think David will be pleased to have a timid son and two rowdy daughters."

Danielle waved a casual hand. "He'll just be happy to have a healthy baby and his wife back in shape."

"Girls, you didn't hug me when you arrived," Chantelle said to them.

They did a blame game about her accusation, before rushing and slamming into her as if it were a competition.

"Whoa, girls. It's too early for rough hugs." She patted them on the head. "What should we eat?"

A list was chanted out: pancakes, toast, eggs, sausage, tea, oats, cornflakes. Eventually, they settled on a bit of everything. With all four of them chipping in, breakfast got done in record time. The girls insisted on eating in the sitting room where they could watch cartoons while Chantelle and Danielle sat at the dining table.

"Is your article for March done?" Danielle asked.

"Approved and submitted last month."

"Can I read it?"

"We go through this every month, Dani; the answer is no." She laughed. "You're going to have to wait like everybody else."

"I'm aiming at wearing you down," her sister said between bites. "What are you doing for April?"

"An article about women who cheat on their husbands and a profile story. That's all I'm revealing."

"Killjoy."

She rolled her eyes. Just then, Araba and Kukua started fighting over something.

"Girls, what is it this time?" their mother asked.

"She doesn't want me to have the remote," Araba said.

"Who used it last?"

"I did," came the guilty reply.

"Then give it to your sister. What have I told you about sharing?"

"Sharing is caring," the little girls sing-songed before quieting down again.

Danielle looked at her. "Do you want to keep them?"

"And deprive you of your motherly duties? I wouldn't dream of it. Besides, as soon as you get home, you're going to start missing them." She reached over, rubbing a reassuring hand on her sister's arm.

"I know." Danielle leaned back, sipping her tea.

They talked a few more minutes before the girls started laughing and fighting over something again. Danielle rolled her eyes and sighed. The girls raced to the dining table, Kukua hiding something in her palms. She released it to her mother's custody, sticking her tongue out at her sister. The girls' eyes met, and they screamed, hurrying back to the sofa.

"Your phone," her sister said, lifting it. Turning it around, she pressed a button, and the lights came on. Something on it caught her attention, and Chantelle realised, as her sister raised her brows, that she must have left the message screen active.

"'Good morning, Chantelle. Thanks for spending time with me last night,'" Danielle read with mounting interest. "'Hope you slept well.' Ooh, who is LM?"

"No one." She snatched the phone.

"Is this why you said you could have slept somewhere last night?" Danielle gasped. "You have a boyfriend?"

"I don't have a boyfriend."

"Auntie Chantie has a boyfriend!" the girls began to sing.

She glared at Danielle who looked even more convinced of her suspicion.

"Your eyes are dancing. You definitely have a new boyfriend. About time, too."

Just then, her phone rang. With relief, she noticed it wasn't Lord. Danielle would have had a field day. The call lasted less than a minute.

"Is that him?" her sister asked.

"It's the mechanic returning my car."

Danielle continued to stare at her with a pleased expression.

"I don't have a new boyfriend," Chantelle repeated before going to get her purse.

As she walked out the front door, her nieces rushed past her, racing until they'd each touched her car and ran back inside, oblivious to their mother's caution to slow down.

"I didn't know you had children," the mechanic commented, smiling after the girls. "They have a lot of energy."

"My nieces," she said.

The mechanic opened the bonnet of the car and showed her the work he'd done.

"Everything is fixed." He handed her the key and the bill.

She gave him the money. "Thanks for washing it for me."

After watching him leave, she went back inside. The girls seemed to have finally found something on the TV they could both watch. Her sister stood at Chantelle's laptop, beaming.

"Are you doing a story on Lord McKenzie?" she asked, innocently. Too innocently.

"Why?" She didn't remember opening the document, but it would have been in her Quick Access file, and she'd titled it Most Eligible Bachelor. *Dumb move.* Knowing her sister, she'd opened something.

"Question for question," Danielle said. "That says guilty."

"He's my profile story for April, if you must know."

She prayed her sister wouldn't link it to the message.

"LM!" Danielle gasped, her eyes brightening up by the nano-second. "Lord McKenzie."

An even more dramatic gasp followed.

"No, it's not."

"Then who's LM?"

"Lester—" She struggled to find an 'M' name when her gaze locked on the snack bowl on her table. "Mint."

"Mint?" Danielle laughed. "C'mon, Chantie, you can do better. There's no one called Lester Mint."

"What makes you so sure?" She went to retrieve her laptop.

"Because you have 'guilty' written all over you." She sat down, putting on a mock-analytical face. "Is he Mister Lord McKenzie or just Lord McKenzie?"

"Stop it."

"Because the mister takes the oomph out of the name." The teasing continued. "So what happened between you and Lord last night?"

"Nothing."

"Guilty face again." Danielle beamed brighter than the morning sunlight pouring in through the large sliding windows. "Did you kiss? Please, tell me you did."

"No, we didn't." At least, not last *night.* So it didn't constitute a lie.

"You spent time with Lord McKenzie, and you didn't let him smooch you?"

Her mind inevitably journeyed down Memory Lane to last night, to his words and how much she'd wanted to lock lips with him again. It wasn't she who hadn't allowed him to kiss her, as Danielle supposed.

"No, he promised not to, and he honoured his words like a true gentleman."

Her sister grinned. "You talked about kissing. You like him."

"I don't like him."

"Yes, you do. Oh, my Lord," Danielle said. "Or should I say *your* Lord?"

She glowered at her sister. "I'm going to spank you, Dani, and I don't care that you're pregnant."

The threat didn't work. They never did.

"He's definitely a step up from Martin the lying cheat."

"He is?" she asked, even though she agreed completely. Then again, after what he did, almost anyone would be an improvement over Martin.

"Of course, he is. Several steps, actually. He's smart, handsome, wealthy—"

"And a playboy."

"Oh, puleez. Playboys turn around all the time when they meet the right woman."

"Oh, yeah? Name one playboy who settled down."

Danielle shrugged. "Boris Kodjoe."

"He wasn't a player. Besides, I meant someone we know."

"Details. The important question is," Danielle said. "Does he like you?"

"Well, he did say he wanted to see me again."

"And?"

"Of course, I said no."

Her sister threw her hands up in exasperation. "You said what? Sis, the mourning period is long over. It's time to stop being afraid of relationships. There's a gorgeous guy who wants to see you again. Live a little."

She rolled her eyes, having every intention of doing the exact opposite. Living meant risking her heart, and she'd done that already. Once was enough.

"Does the house seem quiet to you?" Danielle, forever attuned to her daughters' shenanigans, easily shifted from sister to mother mode. "Where are they?"

They found them asleep in the couch. Her heart twisted with emotion at their angelic faces. She should have been a mother by now, trading stories with her sister.

She pushed away the thought and draped an arm around Danielle's shoulders. "They are adorable."

"They are, aren't they?" Danielle sighed. "But thank God they're sleeping. They can wear a person out."

A solemn silence settled over them as they continued to watch the girls.

Her sister gave her an affectionate squeeze. "You know, one day, you'll have children of your own, and they'll be just as cute."

She preferred not to entertain fruitless wishes. To have children, she needed a man, and to have that meant risking getting hurt again. She didn't share her thoughts with Danielle. It would only earn her a speech about Mr. Right being out there somewhere, so she nodded and let her sister think they were on the same page.

They spent more time talking until around two o'clock, when Danielle and the girls left, allowing her to return to her work. The rest of the day passed quietly as it returned to a normal Sunday afternoon. However, at night, before going to bed, she received another text message from Lord.

'Dream well. LM'

THE WEEK FLEW by at an alarming rate. Friday found Chantelle still on a high. Since last Sunday, she'd woken up every morning to receive a message from Lord and another at night. The night messages were always the same: *'Dream well.'* Just that. Not 'Goodnight,' not 'Sleep well,' but 'Dream well,' as if he knew he'd been starring in her dreams lately.

He'd wooed her, steadily chipped away at her resistance, and despite her efforts not to be affected, she'd started falling for him.

Even in her wakeful hours, she thought about him, often with a smile, sometimes with a question she hadn't asked. She and Eyram, the art director working on her pages, devoted their lunch hour browsing through his pictures. Dufie gladly joined them.

"This guy is so sexy," she said. "It shouldn't be legal."

"There has to be some international law against looking this good," Eyram said. "Can you imagine how cute his children would be?"

"Ladies, let's be gentle with the man, okay," Chantelle said. "And stop swooning, both of you."

"Gentle?" Dufie viciously latched on to that. "You're *defending* the guy? Are you all right?"

"I'm fine. I'm just saying—"

"Give her a few days," Eyram said. "I think she caught the Lord McKenzie bug. You would, too, if you spent two days with such sexiness."

Three days. She wasn't about to give them any more ammunition to suspect her feelings for Lord had changed in any way. After all, their time together had ended. Even though he'd been religious about sending her a text message each morning and night, he'd soon tire.

"Does he have a little black book?"

"In his case, a custom-made iPhone?"

Discomfort assaulted Chantelle as she listened to her colleagues lambaste Lord. To think she'd championed such conversations in the past shamed her. A new picture of Lord talking to Mr. Nti at the site loaded up.

"Look at that," Dufie said, dreamily. "What's he like, up close and personal?"

"Dufie, it was an interview, nothing more." *Liar, liar.*

But her colleague didn't appear to be listening. She stared at the computer monitor. "Ooh, you look good together."

A picture of her and Lord at the construction site filled the screen. She looked at the image and caught her breath. He looked great, and they did look good together. The joy in her own eyes stunned her. She looked as though she'd been exactly where she'd wanted to be in that moment. A smile crept to her lips before she could stop it.

"You'd make a stunning couple," Eyram agreed.

"We would?" Again, her response was purely reflex.

Her two colleagues eyed each other and said, "Yup. She caught the bug."

"I did not." She couldn't extinguish her smile. "I think we're done here, ladies." She extracted the thumb drive and handed it to Eyram. "When can I check on the layouts?"

"Hm, it's Friday. Let's look at it on Monday."

"Okay, good."

"Snap out of it, Chantelle," Dufie said. "I like you better when you trash handsome men."

She shook her head, rolling her eyes. As Dufie and Eyram left, Danielle called.

"Hi, Dani."

"I have a question."

"Shoot."

"I think it's going to be best for the girls to call him Uncle Lordy instead of Uncle Lord. I don't want it to interfere with their faith." She giggled. "What do you think? After all, he's your boyfriend."

She lowered her voice to speak. "Stop it. He's not my boyfriend."

"Then why are you defending him?"

"I'm not." She pursed her lips. "You're not going to let it rest, are you?"

Danielle laughed. "No, I'm enjoying this too much. Besides, I'm home alone and bored."

"I'm at work. Stop calling if you have nothing important to say."

"Okay, just one more thing. Have you responded to his texts?"

"Goodbye, Dani. I'm hanging up."

She heard her sister's laughter before disconnecting the call. Sitting back in her chair, she heaved a sigh. Her mind dawdled with the issue of whether to reply the messages, still unsure what she'd say if she did.

CHAPTER 12

CHANTELLE HADN'T CONSIDERED THE possibility of seeing Lord again until this moment when she stood in front of her full-length mirror. The Golden Stool Awards was the kind of event he would attend. He'd be in every journal for the coming week, wearing a designer tux and looking like God's gift to women.

She'd settled on an elegant off-white dress, which accentuated her clear milk-chocolate complexion, accessorising it with a silver necklace with a heart-shaped pendant and matching earrings. Not much for sophisticated hairdos, she opted to leave her shoulder-length hair flowing in gentle waves. Assessing the image looking back at her, she nodded her approval. But would he?

Though she took in a deep breath to calm her nerves, her heartbeat surged. It was one thing to be alone with him, but today was a public event. Would he even acknowledge her when they set eyes on each other? *If* they set eyes on each other. *Okay, stop obsessing*. With great effort, she shook off the scepticism. She looked great. It didn't matter whether Lord noticed. She tried not to concentrate on how ecstatic it would feel if he did notice.

At six-thirty, she set out from her house, since she'd agreed to meet Ben there. With him, you never knew when some 'inside info' would drop and he had to go. She operated by a better safe than sorry policy, and not just with Ben.

Arriving at the National Theatre forty minutes later, she found a bit of traffic leading to the entrance. This was the guest entrance, of course, and not the main entrance reserved for celebrities. *Guest entrance, my foot*. She tapped her fingers on the steering wheel while waiting in line. Without a press pass, she couldn't use the side gate.

"Thank you," she murmured to the powers that be when she made it through. She found a parking spot and headed for one of the side doors where she and Ben had agreed to meet. She found him already waiting when she got there.

"Wow!" he said, taking in her outfit. "I'm excited to be your date tonight."

He opened his arms for a hug.

Being taller than he, even without the two-inch boost her shoes provided, she had to bend forward to hug him. "Thanks, Ben. You look fetching yourself."

"Please, I look short and fat."

"I'd say cuddly and huggable." She linked her hand through the arm he offered. "There's a difference."

"Always kind and gentle. That's why I keep you as a friend," he said as they entered.

She laughed.

"Chantelle," Dufie's animated voice greeted her when she and Ben entered the main foyer. "Wow, you're all dressed up. I didn't know you were coming. Why aren't you wearing a tag?"

"I'm not working tonight, and I'm not using a press pass."

"You look gorgeous." Dufie pouted. "I'm jealous."

"You, too, Dee, but you know it already."

Dufie wore a black sheath dress with modest heels and make-up. She looked chic, as any self-respecting fashion writer should, even with the press tag around her neck.

"Can I get you ladies a drink?" Ben asked.

"A glass of water for now," she said. "Thanks."

Dufie raised a bottle of mineral water. "I already have something."

When Ben left, Dufie gave her friend a look. "Water? You aren't working. Have a real drink."

"I might, but not right now, though. I just got here."

Dufie checked her time. "I love you, but I have to go and scout for fashion wows and oopses. See you after the show."

Chantelle laughed and waved her off. Alone now, she wandered towards the middle where she could mingle, but not too far so Ben could still find her. She looked around searching for familiar faces, one in particular. Every now and then, cheers erupted outside, signalling the arrival of some famous person. She checked her time. They still had about forty minutes until the main event.

Ben returned with two bottles of water and handed her one. "Here you go."

"Thanks, Ben."

"Do you want to go in now or wait a little?"

"Now." In the next fifteen minutes, there would be a crowd of last-minute entrants, which would create traffic at the door leading into the theatre. At the entrance, Ben showed their tickets to the ushers who let them in.

It didn't take long to find their seats somewhere in the mid-section of the auditorium. She picked up the programme brochure tucked in the corner of her seat. As she lifted her gaze, her body froze as reality came checking in with the force of a typhoon, bringing her jittery expectations to a crashing halt.

The man she'd been hoping to see all night stood in the aisle looking even more dashing than she remembered. He walked with Deconte Aggrey-Finn, the woman he was supposedly no longer dating. She had her arm linked through his as they acknowledged guests' greetings, looking every bit like a couple.

An unexpected stab of jealousy and anger pierced her heart. Stunned, she forgot to breathe until the pounding of her heart forced her to gasp for air. A series of deep breaths didn't assuage her shock. It was a miracle she continued standing, since she couldn't feel her legs anymore. Anger and disappointment were feelings she'd known before—even pain—but not to the extent of it taking her breath away.

She'd stupidly thought she could keep it all under control, even after giving in to the powerful attraction between them the night they'd met. How had she believed refusing to engage him via text messaging would insulate her against his allure? Despite all her efforts at remaining unaffected, Lord had proven to be a master player. While admonishing herself not to fall for him, it appeared she had.

What an idiot she'd been. Somehow, she called up enough strength to prevent the onslaught of tears threatening to surface. She wouldn't cry. Not here, not now.

He looked up, and their eyes met. She saw a moment's pause in his step, a raise of his eyebrows and the beginning of a smile. Deconte tugged at his arm, drawing his attention away. She whispered something in his ear, and they laughed.

Jerk. The word materialised without warning, but it felt good.

She sank onto the seat, considering an early exit. How could she have been so foolish? Falling for his charms like all the women she'd ridiculed so many times before. Believing that what she'd seen in a few days held truer than the playboy reputation he'd spent years cultivating. How could she have been so naïve? She'd allowed herself to be played again, trusting he'd told the truth when he said he and Deconte weren't dating.

Anger triumphed over every other emotion, and she decided she wouldn't run just because he chose to parade his girlfriend in front of her. She'd been a fool one time too many, and it ended here.

"Are you okay?"

Ben's voice broke through her train of thought.

"Yes, I'm fine," she said, paying close attention to her brochure.

Just then, the overhead lights dimmed, and the host walked onto the stage. Despite the breath-taking décor and programming, her concentration often drifted to the couple sitting several rows ahead of her.

Every time Lord leaned sideways to whisper something in Deconte's ear, she caught the movement. She had to keep reminding herself she didn't care. Not even when Deconte won the Best Actress award, and Lord placed his hand on her back to let her pass. Her skin tingled in memory of the sweet warmth of his hands the few times he'd touched her in the same manner.

Two-timing SOB. Although the actress was one of her favourites, and obviously also a victim in this whole situation, some of her anger towards Lord spilt over to his date.

At ten o'clock when the awards ceremony ended, she considered leaving, but Ben wanted to attend the after-party, so she agreed to stay awhile. There were at least a couple thousand people here. No chance of bumping into Lord. They moved to the banquet hall, going through the main foyer where the award winners were giving interviews and having their pictures taken.

Deconte, in her elegant black evening gown, produced smiles on demand while answering questions from a group of reporters who had surrounded her. Lord stood firmly by her side, smiling. *Idiot.*

Luckily, she and Ben were passing behind them, so chances of Lord spotting her were slim. She needed a drink now.

Entering the banquet hall, she turned to Ben. "I'm going for a drink. Do you want one?"

"Let me get it," he offered. "What would you like?"

"A glass of champ— oh, here comes a waiter."

She grabbed a glass while Ben excused himself. "I'm going to get myself a malt," he said.

"Okay." While downing the contents of her glass, she spotted Dufie moving towards her.

"How did you find the show?"

Since she hadn't been paying much attention, she shrugged. "Same old thing."

"You're right, but the fashion this year is impressive," Dufie said. "Look at Nana Yaa Brown." She pointed. "She finally got it right."

Chantelle took the opportunity to scan the room. Lord and Deconte weren't there yet. Good. She didn't want to have to face him, or she'd have a murder on her hands. As Dufie talked, Chantelle picked up a second serving of champagne from a waitress passing by and placed the empty glass on the tray. She checked her time. Ben seemed to be taking long getting a drink. She hoped he hadn't gone off to chase a new story without letting her know.

Dufie fell quiet all of a sudden, her eyes widening, and she knew Lord had to be standing behind her even before turning. He'd appeared out of nowhere, making it too late to run.

"Hi," he had the guts to say.

Dufie raised her eyebrows and glanced at Chantelle.

"Hi." She gave him her most winning smile and extended her hand. "My name is Dufie."

He shook her hand, his eyes still fixed on Chantelle, who maintained a straight face.

"Nice to meet you, Dufie." He flashed a smile of his own. "May I borrow your friend for a minute?"

Chantelle tried to communicate a "don't leave me alone with him" warning with her eyes to Dufie, but her plea fell on deaf ears. Not a surprise since her colleague never looked away long enough to notice anyone other than the man standing in front of them.

"Sure. I have to go and pretend I'm working."

Dufie giggled at her lame joke and left her to face Lord alone. Though he smiled, she still regarded him with a straight face, exercising great restraint in keeping her hands from harming him.

"I'm surprised to see you here," he said.

I bet you are. There were a lot of names running through her mind, but she kept quiet. She didn't want a stream of foul language to be her debut into the tabloids.

"You look ... wow."

He had such a nerve to come up and talk to her. Had he no shame? At all? Well, she did, and spending any more time in his presence embarrassed her. Determined to be the bigger man—yes, the bigger *man*—she turned around to leave with her head held high.

"Whoa." He caught her by the arm. "Wait. What's going on?"

She glanced down at his firm hold on her arm and then back at him, cock-eyed, lips pursed, glaring at him with pure venom. He did not want to go there. *Unhand me, you vile man.*

As though sensing his action had infuriated her, he released her.

"What do you want?" she said through clenched teeth, unmoved by the fact that he seemed taken aback by her coldness. She should have been doing a lot worse to him. Again, she reminded herself she didn't give a hoot about him or his snake-charm.

"I got your text messages." His expression began to brighten at her words, making it all the more pleasurable to see it turn to shock when she said, "Stop harassing me."

"Hold on a minute. What's going on? I thought after this past week, we—"

Chantelle didn't let him finish.

"There's 'me' and there's 'you,' but there's no 'we.'" She said it methodically, as if talking to a little child.

His frown deepened. "What the hell is going on?"

She had to hand it to him; he could act. From his perplexed look, anyone could be fooled into believing in his innocence. Maybe the Best Actor trophy should have been given to him.

"What do you want from me?" she asked.

"Just trying to talk to you."

"Why, Lord? You're here with Deconte—"

"And so bloody what? Why should that be a problem?"

She blinked. If his previous attitude puzzled her, his last response topped it. A player who didn't care when he'd been caught red-handed. Without a doubt, Lord stood in a league of his own. She looked at him with disgust, unable to believe she'd even thought, at some point, that he had any redeeming qualities. She didn't care about Ben's whereabouts; she couldn't stay here another minute. Again, he grabbed her arm, turning her around.

"Would you stop doing that?" she said between clenched teeth.

"Would you give me a chance to talk?"

"You want to bury yourself? Fine. You have thirty seconds. Speak."

He seemed thrown off, uncharacteristically out of his element.

"I can't believe this. Are you jealous?"

"Of course not. Why should I be?" She forced herself to shrug. "You're here with your girlfriend. It's perfectly normal."

Unbelievably, he chuckled. She started to turn around again, but he held her put by the shoulders, forcing her to stay, to look into his eyes, to hurt, because even now, stranded in his gaze, he could make her feel like no one mattered except her. But she knew better.

"I told you before, she's not my girlfriend," he said.

Yeah, and the sky isn't blue. Did she have 'stupid' written on her forehead or something? Seriously. What would the poor woman say if she knew her boyfriend had renounced her? Twice.

He heaved a despondent sigh. "I might as well tell you now. Deconte is my cousin."

◆◆◆

THE SHOCK ON Chantelle's face confirmed Lord's suspicion about her being jealous. Though surprised, the discovery pleased him. Not that he liked making a woman jealous, but it meant she cared enough about him to feel such a strong emotion. Armed with this new knowledge, his determination to clear up the mess once and for all became a driving force. He wanted Chantelle in his life, and nothing would stand in his way.

"C-cousin?"

From her expression, he could tell she didn't quite believe what she'd heard.

"Yes. Not my girlfriend."

"If you're related, why hasn't either of you mentioned this?"

"We've never claimed to be an item. People have just assumed we were." As they presumed he'd slept with every woman he'd ever been seen with.

"But you let them. Why would you want people to think your cousin was your girlfriend?"

It sounded awful when she put it that way. "We thought it would be funny to see how presumptuous people can be."

It was a stupid agreement he and Deconte had made when they'd first discovered they were related about a year ago. They'd known each other for years, but she'd always been Adonis' off-limits half-sister. Last year, at his grandmother's funeral, they'd discovered their grandmothers had been sisters. Despite their relation being several steps removed, matrilineal bonds were considered deeper in the Akan tradition.

They'd had a good laugh, because people kept commenting they'd make an attractive couple. They'd had a few drinks, so when they agreed not to reveal their real connection except to close friends and family, it had seemed like a good joke. In retrospect, it had been a terrible idea. Now, it could have cost him Chantelle's trust.

"I don't know what to believe."

Believe me. The words popped into his mind, but he had a feeling "I don't lie" wouldn't work this time. Instead, he threw her a challenge. "Don't believe me. Ask her."

"But—"

"I'll introduce you." This time, when he closed his hands around her upper arm, he didn't flinch when she tried to rip out of his grip.

Her eyes darted left and right. "We're going to attract attention."

"I don't care."

"What about your father?"

Touché, but he couldn't care less. His father had seen many unflattering pictures and stories about him in the papers. One more wouldn't destroy him. On the other hand, if this moment with Chantelle went wrong, he might never get it back.

"Don't worry," he said. "The press is more interested in the winners tonight, but I'll release you if you promise not to run."

"Fine!"

"Fine, what?"

"I promise not to run."

He released her and led the way to where the actress stood.

"Deconte, there's someone I'd like you to meet. Chantelle Sah from *Odopa* magazine." He turned to her. "Chantelle, my cousin, Deconte."

Deconte raised her eyebrows in surprise. Shaking Chantelle's hand, she said, "Well, if you revealed our little secret to her, then she must be special. How come I'm only meeting her now?"

"You've been gallivanting all over the continent lately."

"True." She laughed. "I suppose I'm going to my movie premiere alone."

"After winning Best Actress for both the Actors' Guild and Golden Stool, you can do anything you want," Lord said.

"Ah, but there's still the Academy of Film and Theatre Awards to conquer."

Just then, an announcement came on the public address system asking all award winners to take a group photograph. Deconte rolled her eyes, though her expression remained pleased.

"Remind me not to wish so hard for a win next year. I'll be all out of smiles by the time the night is over." She turned to her. "I'm happy to meet you, Chantelle."

"Likewise, and congratulations. I'm rooting for you to take home the Academy Award, too."

"Oh, thanks."

His cousin gracefully excused herself and left.

"Are we now clear on the issue of my girlfriend, or do I need to take a lie detector test?"

To his relief and delight, she smiled. A hint of mystery about her grin put all sorts of ideas into his head.

"A lie detector test won't be necessary at this time."

"I'm sorry for causing you any distress over my relationship with Deconte." He managed to keep his tone light, although what he wanted to do was jump and yell, "Yes, yes, woohoo."

In response to his apology, she giggled, then laughed, really laughed, as in, head thrown back, makes-you-want-to-laugh-too. He doubted he could have achieved the same reaction with his best joke. God knew he was no comedian. Her sweet laughter flowed out uninhibited. He was smitten with it and with her.

Now that she'd stopped throwing daggers at him with her eyes, it seemed comical, what he'd been thinking of doing a moment ago. He'd been on the verge of begging her to tell him what he'd done wrong. He'd have gone down on his knees if it would have given him the answer he sought.

"There you are." A voice spoke from behind.

He turned to find the guy who'd been sitting next to her during the ceremony. Primal behaviour had never been his style, but all night long, he'd wanted to punch him in the face, because he got to call her his date.

"Ben! Sorry. I moved from where you left me," she replied, trying to force the laughter away. When she succeeded, a smile remained, which, though meant for her friend, made Lord's heart swell with emotion. She went on to make the necessary introductions.

He quirked a brow. "*The* Ben Annan?"

"Yes," Chantelle said.

At the same time, Ben shook his head. "I'm hardly famous enough to be referred to as the Ben Annan."

The understatement of the decade. The man had to be the most feared journalist in the country. He had a way of getting to the most privileged news. He'd been instrumental in exposing a huge drug trafficking scandal involving people in high political offices. He was once reported to have entered a high security off-the-record interview with a hidden recorder. It had taken the government months to clean up the mess. Anyone with anything to hide needed to fear this guy.

"I'm sorry, I guess I expected Ben Annan to be …" His voice trailed off as he searched for the appropriate word.

"More formidable?" Chantelle said helpfully. "That's the word I used when we first met."

"I get that a lot," Ben said, then turned to Chantelle. "Listen, I'm sorry, but I got a call—"

Alarm shot through him. Was she leaving? They hadn't even had a chance to talk. Once again, he experienced a visceral urge to hurt the guy before he could take Chantelle away.

"You have to go," she said. "Aren't you glad I came in my own car?"

Her own car? Did it mean she wasn't going with Ben?

"Are you sure you don't mind me leaving you here?"

"Go." Chantelle shooed him.

Lord had an idea. "Don't worry, man. I'll make sure she gets home safely."

"It won't be necessary," Chantelle began to protest.

"No, I insist. The guy is concerned," he said to her and then to Ben. "Don't worry about her."

She relented, though he sensed it wouldn't be for long. The warm hug she gave Ben made him yearn for one, too. Would throwing a tantrum get him a hug like that?

The moment Ben went out of earshot, he launched into the next phase of the conversation. He'd never been one to beat about the bush, so he went for the jugular.

"Are you two together?"

He tried to keep the edge out of his voice, but some of it seeped out. Apparently, he wasn't immune to the effects of the green-eyed monster.

"Yes. I mean, not together *together*. I accompanied him here today."

Her answer brought relief, to say the least. The competition didn't bother him, but the fellow seemed like a nice guy, and it would have been sad to sidestep him to get Chantelle. The way she affected him … the way he suspected she felt about him told him they were meant to be more. He'd stop at nothing to find out where this led.

"I'm back," Deconte announced her return.

He bit back a curse. Evidently, a few minutes alone with Chantelle was too much to ask. He needed to think of something fast.

Deconte stifled a yawn. "I'm tired. I think I'll skip the after-party."

"Let's go home, then." He turned to Chantelle. "Ready to leave?" When she nodded, he offered, "Come on. We'll drop you off at your car."

She readily agreed, and the three proceeded to exit the building.

In the parking lot, the driver came to a stop next to Chantelle's car. Lord exited first and held the door open for her. Deconte, who seemed to have taken to Chantelle in that short period, hugged her, whispering something in her ear. Chantelle slid out of the car, the corners of her lips twitching with a smile she tried to hold in. *What's that about?*

Closing the door for her, he leaned into his car. "I promised to get her safely home, so you go on, and the driver can come pick me up from her place after he drops you off."

Not surprisingly, Chantelle objected. "I'm fine. Really."

He knew she'd be okay. She was a big girl, and she'd done fine all by herself without him. The problem was, *he* might not do so well without her. He'd made an important discovery tonight and wanted to explore it. Maybe he could now be open about his feelings for her, or find a tangible reason to let go.

"I'm a man of my word, Chantelle," he said. "I promised to get you home, which is what I plan on doing."

After giving directions to the driver, he hopped into her car. He had no doubt they'd crossed a line in the sand. Whatever happened at her place tonight would determine the future of their relationship.

CHAPTER 13

I*'M TAKING LORD MCKENZIE home.*

No matter how many times Chantelle repeated those words in her head, she couldn't wrap her mind around them. She chanced him a glance. He rested against the seat, his eyes open, staring straight ahead. Despite the seemingly relaxed posture, she sensed a deliberateness about him that told of restrained tension. Nonetheless, his profile made a formidable impression against the backdrop of high-rise commercial buildings illuminated by the streetlights in the city's central business district.

Her mind crowded with questions, like what taking him home meant.

Forget the rumours. He's a good guy, Deconte had whispered to her, but being a good guy didn't make him any less dangerous to her heart, did it?

She sighed, knowing she needed to make a decision about him by the time they parted today. Easier said than done, since her heart and head held differing views.

As though sensing her attention, he turned to meet her gaze, and her heart did a flip. The ever-present thread of awareness between them heated into something profounder. It cut her breath in half, forcing her to break the visual connection and return her focus to the open road ahead.

"You do look stunning," he said, filling the silence.

The low rumble of his voice sent torrents of shivers up her spine and down again. Amazing how the same compliment had hurt and angered her a few moments ago.

"Thanks. So do you." A smile formed on her lips in self-realisation. "Handsome, I mean."

His hand covered hers on the gear stick. It seemed like the most natural thing when she splayed her fingers and he linked his through. It was such a 'couple' thing. He squeezed her hand, sending more tremors through her.

Couple. The term had her stomach in knots. She'd invested so much into her relationship with Martin. After three years, she'd thought she had known everything about him. As an investigative reporter, his long hours and unscheduled meetings had raised no suspicions. Maybe she should have taken a cue from the many female friends he'd had, but she'd trusted him completely. Fool that she was.

Even when he'd called on the eve of Valentine's Day telling her he'd been sent on an impromptu assignment, she'd believed him. Then again, she'd been preoccupied, after discovering they were going to have a baby. It had taken every ounce of her willpower to keep from blurting it over the phone, but she'd wanted to do it in person, so she'd decided to postpone it until his return.

Instead, she'd received the call which had shattered her whole world, and in the ensuing turmoil, she'd lost everything. She didn't know if she could handle being hurt like that again. However, if her reaction to seeing Lord and Deconte tonight were any indication, she was also not ready to swear off men. Was this particular guy the right one for her, though?

He was out of her league—and it wasn't insecurity talking. She could only fathom his life of privilege, the extent of his power, his influence. He could have any woman he wanted, and for some reason, he'd chosen her. For the first time in years, the thought of being with a man didn't set off an alarm warning her to flee. God help her, but she wanted to stand firm and let her heart take the hit.

When she pulled up in front of her house, neither of them attempted to get out of the car. The side of her face warmed, and she knew he must be staring at her. She turned.

"We need to talk," he said.

"I know. Do you want to come in?"

"Yes." It sounded both like a desire and a promise.

Her pulse raced, each heartbeat bouncing off her ribcage and reverberating through the rest of her body all the way from the car to her front door.

She hesitated a second when they reached it. "This isn't an invitation to—"

"I know."

She nodded and opened the door, then held out her hand. He took it. The contact was pure electricity, but she didn't withdraw from the current. Instead, she firmed her grip—a show of determination to herself—and led the way into the house. Breaking their hold, she locked the door and turned to face him. The walls seemed to close in, making her sitting room feel so much smaller.

He made no attempt to touch her. Instead, he watched her as if waiting for her to make a move. A mixture of excitement and anxiety drew her hands into fists by her sides. If she didn't control herself, she might rush into his arms. They both knew how that had ended the last time.

She pushed out the thought, because it bred temptation rather than caution.

"I'm sorry," she found herself saying.

He frowned. "For what?"

"All the names I called you earlier today … before … you know."

He raised an eyebrow. "Names like what?"

"Like jerk and idiot."

She bit her lip and winced. Why tell him this? A demonstration of trust, or an attempt to push him away by some part of her still obsessed with self-preservation? She wouldn't let that portion of her lead. Not anymore.

"Strong words." He seemed more amused than anything. "What else?"

"That's all I'll confess."

He appeared contemplative for an instant. "I'll forgive you if you answer four simple questions."

Uh-oh. She eyed him suspiciously. "Okay."

"A yes or no will suffice, but you have to promise you'll answer them." He grinned. "Don't worry, none of them will be inappropriate."

Define inappropriate.

"All right." She owed him that much.

"Do you like me?"

She blinked at the swift shift from jovial to earnest. Her face must have shown surprise, but she quickly composed herself. A week ago, she wouldn't have hesitated to say no, but now, she didn't want to be left wondering what could have been. Besides, she did like him.

"Yes," she answered.

She'd expected a self-satisfied grin, but he only took in a deep breath and nodded. Had he expected her to say no? Did he not see through her exterior as easily as he'd managed to tear down her defences?

"Did you like receiving my text messages?"

Calm down, my heart. "Yes."

Even though she'd started responding to several of them, she'd ended up never hitting 'send.'

This time, a brief smile touched his lips. "Did you enjoy the time you spent with me?"

"Yes."

"Do you … dream about me?"

Images of some of her raunchy dreams flashed through her mind, and heat pooled in her lower belly.

She inhaled deeply. "I do."

Presently, he took a step forward. "Do you take advantage of me in your dreams?"

Warmth flushed her face. "That's five questions."

He chuckled, closing the space between them. He reached for her hand and held it between them, linking their fingers.

"I like you very much, Chantelle. I'd like to receive responses to my text messages. I've enjoyed every minute spent with you." His lips curved in a wicked grin. "And I definitely dream about you."

If her dreams were anything to go by, then she knew exactly what they'd been doing in his. Why didn't the thought scare her? Why did it make her blood simmer with anticipation?

"I can't stop thinking about you." Smug was gone; serious was in. "I've never met anyone like you. I'm reduced to keeping a copy of your magazine on my desk just so I can look at your picture. I think you feel something, too."

She nodded.

"So what are we going to do about it?"

Nervous tension gripped her. There hadn't been many times she'd been rendered speechless, but right now, she couldn't think of anything to say except, "I don't know."

A beat passed.

"Would you like me to leave?"

She shook her head. "No."

The moment the word made it out of her mouth, he tugged her closer, wrapping his arms around her waist. Her hands rose to settle on his broad shoulders. As she met his gaze, nervous tension gave way to a different type of tension, the electrifying kind.

Instead of kissing her, he paused, taking in her features. "You're exquisite, and I've known many beautiful women."

Her heart tumbled, and she stiffened. What was she doing? Nothing he'd said, nothing she felt, changed who he was. He offered paradise for a while, and then left you in Hell.

Pulling out of his arms, she looked up at him, trying to read him.

"Must be a long list."

He didn't attempt to pull her back. Emotions darkened his eyes.

"I know what I've been painted as, and frankly, until now, I didn't give a hoot what they said about me. Until you." He lifted his hand to the back of his neck and rubbed it. She'd never have pictured anxiety on him, and yet, nothing else better described the look he gave her. "I'm not going to pretend to be a saint or a monk, but I haven't slept with as many women as people think."

There he went again with reference to numbers, of which she was just a part, another bullet point in the list.

"You're the only woman I've been with in over a year."

"Please, I don't need a blow by blow account of your sex life and how many broken hearts you have under your belt."

"Is that what you think I'm going to do? Break your heart?" Anger flashed in his eyes, and he clenched his jaw. "I want to get to know you better. I've never felt this way about anyone."

He took a step backwards.

"If you don't feel anything for me, tell me, and I'll walk out of here, but please don't make assumptions about who I am. Spend time with me, get to know me, and decide for yourself." He came forward again, placing both hands on her shoulders like he'd done before. "We can take it as slow as you want. Deal?"

Tears. She blinked rapidly to prevent the waters from breaking loose. Why did the prospect of walking away from him sadden her when indecision still wracked her mind? Would she risk her heart based on his words? On the other hand, would she forgo the chance of being happy with him? Could the joy she experienced in his arms, even now, be much more? The answers to all those questions pointed to one thing. It was worth a shot.

"Deal," she said.

He released a heavy breath. A mixture of emotions clouded his eyes before he crushed her against him. Air rushed out of her at the impact.

"Chantelle," he murmured just before his lips descended on hers.

Her mind blanked, and her body filled with a dizzying sense of joy at being in his arms like this again. The taste of his tongue and his masculine scent engulfed her senses, and she was lost. When he licked the seam on her lips, she didn't hesitate to open up, to receive and to give back. She'd thought their previous kisses had been epic, but this surpassed them all. With each possessive stroke of his tongue, he revealed himself to her, and everything he told her sent electricity to her toes and desire to her centre.

"I've been wanting this."

Her whispered confession drew out a grunt from him.

"Me, too," he mumbled against her lips.

The kiss intensified, the urgency of their unified desires racing through them. His hands swept down her body to cup her butt. Instinctively, she curved her arms around his nape rendering support as he lifted her, bringing her feminine mound up to meet the thick length of his arousal. She moaned, shivered. The mermaid cut of her evening gown halted her attempt to wrap her legs around his waist. With a whimper of frustration, she pulled back.

"Stupid dress," she mumbled.

The sound of his deep chuckle did nothing to lessen the sexual energy gripping them.

"If we were dancing right now, would you let me lead you through a death drop?" he asked, still holding her against his arousal and not releasing her from his gaze. "Without hesitation?"

She quirked her brows, but his earnest expression made her realise his question wasn't about an obsession with the dance move. He wanted to know if she trusted him.

"Yes," she answered.

"Do you believe I won't let anything happen tonight that you're not ready for?"

She nodded.

He eased her back to her feet.

"Lift up your dress."

The sexy command sent a rush of excitement through her. She kicked off her shoes and bunched the gown up until the fabric pooled around her waist. He raised her again, and she wrapped her legs around him. He moved a few steps and pinned her between himself and a wall, pressing his hardness against her centre. A shuddering breath rolled out of her lips.

She touched his face, staring into his eyes. "I do that to you."

Her voice echoed with some amount of wonderment.

He nodded. "You do a whole lot more to me."

His words were like gasoline over the flame his kiss had ignited. When their lips met again, an explosion of fireworks occurred. He continued the sensual dance of his pelvis against her centre, and she rocked her hips, meeting each thrust. Need pulsed in her core, reminding her how good it had been to be filled with him, how it had never been so intense with anyone else. Even now, with the barrier of fabric between them, the connection became euphoric, turning need into ache.

"Oh, God," she groaned, throwing her head back as she continued to grind against him.

Her breath had become pants, her cries desperate as pressure built in her core. If they kept this up, she'd climax.

As though he'd heard her thoughts, his movements slowed.

She whimpered. "Don't stop."

"Chantelle—"

Caution laced the desire in his voice, a reminder of his promise in respect of their agreement to take things slow. Her body buzzed, wanting to blaze to the finish line, but her head knew he was right. As their breathing slowed closer to normal, she swallowed down her frustration and released her legs.

"I'm sorry." She licked her lips, eyeing the bulge in his trousers with both yearning and regret. "I shouldn't have let it go so far."

"Don't be." He shook his head. "I can never regret kissing you."

His voice had turned gruff, which didn't help the agenda of regaining composure.

"May I use your washroom?"

She nodded, pointing at the door to the bathroom serving both guests and the second room of her two-bedroom flat. When he left, she took advantage of the alone time to calm herself. She took in a deep breath, letting it out with a self-deprecating laugh. For someone bent on not rushing things, her body seemed determined to do the exact opposite. How could it not, when one look from him, one touch, filled her with enough passion to charge an entire city?

He emerged from the bathroom, and her gaze dropped to his crotch. Whatever he'd done in there had helped partially. Realising where her eyes and mind were, she rushed her focus back up to his eyes. She'd expected a cocky smile. Instead, she saw only a reflection of the desire rolling like a whirlwind within her.

"Let's sit," he suggested.

"Okay."

She followed him to the couch where he took off his shoes and sat, one leg on the chair, then settled her in the crook of his thighs. She leaned against him, angling her head until their gazes met. Slowly, the space between them disappeared as their lips fused together.

This time, he controlled the kiss with measured brushes and strokes, as if in no hurry to end the other-worldly bliss that left her exhilarated and wonderfully light. She released a contented sigh into his mouth. His hands did an unhurried exploration of her body, travelling down from her face to her neck, and then her shoulders. She held her breath as his fingertips brushed the top curve of her strapless gown and lingered.

His body trembled beneath her touch as if he held himself together by a thread, physically restraining himself from letting his passion overtake him. She arched up, fitting her breast in his palm. He made a guttural noise that sounded like her name and cupped her fully, traced her nipple through the fabric, triggering a sharp intake of breath.

She slipped her hands inside his jacket, feeling his taut muscles and the warmth of his skin through the shirt. When she rubbed his nipple, he groaned, holding her hand, then pulled back. She looked at him askance.

"You don't want to do that," he said in a low, raspy voice, his breath short and ragged.

She blinked.

"I'm very sensitive there."

He gave her a sheepish grin, which she returned. This would be harder than she'd thought. Blowing air out of her mouth, she leaned against him with one hand behind him and the other lying on his stomach while he sat back, wrapping his arms around her.

"What did Deconte whisper to you in the car?"

"If I tell you, I'd have to kill you," she mumbled.

His chest rose and fell with a silent laugh accompanied by a lilt in his heartbeat. She hugged him closer. They remained in this position without talking as he caressed her arm. She sighed, listening to his heartbeat, enjoying his warm embrace. She'd never known a man like him, a man who would rein in his desire in order to let her know, ironically, how much he cared. It proved her trust had been placed in safe hands.

With that thought swirling in her mind, she closed her eyes.

LISTENING TO THE chirps of crickets and the incessant ticking of the wall clock he hadn't noticed until now, Lord's heart continued to race, his arousal still straining painfully against his trousers. He didn't mind. The joy of having her in his arms like this made up for the discomfort.

He took in the surroundings. Her sitting room was a tad bigger than his master bedroom closet, the decor tasteful but minimalistic. The only pieces of furniture in sight were the L-shaped sectional they were on and the sideboard where she kept some family photos. Above it, her TV had been mounted. A climbing plant on one wall and an impressive painting gracing the opposite side complimented the large rug covering a greater part of the floorspace.

Everything about this room was complex in its simplicity. Just like the woman who owned it. You could tell a lot about a person by studying their personal space, and this place gave him one important insight about Chantelle. She didn't like complications, which might explain why she'd wavered in her decision to be with him.

Tonight, she'd finally let down her guard, and he'd somehow managed to get past the wall she'd raised against him. She'd allowed him in. He'd do everything in his power to shield her from any complications of his celebrity status. He'd make himself deserving of her trust.

He pushed those thoughts out of his mind and focused on the present. "You have a nice home."

She mumbled a response, wiggling herself into a more comfortable position, which gave him problems of a sensual nature. He looked down and found her asleep. He smiled, tightening his arms around her. His mind drifted to a conversation with his mother a few days back when he'd asked how she'd known his father was 'the one.' It turned out his dad had been the one to know from Day One.

Thirty minutes after their first meeting, his father had told his mother he'd marry her, a statement she'd laughed off as the imaginings of an arrogant and entitled man. Of course, her disbelief had only spurred his father on to win her heart.

He laughed picturing it. He'd often been told his confidence, sometimes labelled arrogance, had been inherited from his father, but even he didn't have the guts to make such a declaration to a woman he'd just met. Although he'd always held a long-term view when it came to his future with Chantelle.

His smartwatch beeped, interrupting his thoughts. He checked it and released a regretful sigh while reading the message alert about his chauffeur's arrival.

"Chantelle?"

He gave her a mild nudge. When she sighed and snuggled closer, he tapped her with a little more insistence. She woke up with a start, tossing a wide gaze around before looking up at him. Her lips stretched into a smile, and his chest expanded to breaking point.

"My car's here," he whispered.

She nodded, disappointment pouring into her eyes. He wanted more than anything to stay longer, but he couldn't trust himself to take it slow like he'd promised.

At the door, he faced her. She yawned, then covered her mouth halfway through like an afterthought, and giggled. He'd never heard a cuter sound.

"I'm sorry, I'm still half asleep."

"It's late. You need to get some rest." He leaned forward and kissed her. "Talk to you tomorrow?"

Why did a part of him still fear she might wake up in the morning and push him away? He wouldn't let her, though. Not after today. He hadn't lied. Every moment spent with her had been special, but having her in his arms tonight? Willing? That meant everything.

“Goodnight,” she whispered, when they pulled apart. “I’m happy it’s not goodbye.”

“Ditto.” He tugged her closer and kissed her one final time. “Dream well.”

He waited until she’d stepped back inside and locked the door before turning and walking towards the limo.

CHAPTER 14

'GOOD MORNING, GORGEOUS. What are you doing?'

The beep from Chantelle's cell phone woke her up to Lord's text message. Memories of their toe-curling kisses came rushing back, filling her with fuzzy warmth.

She sent a reply. *'Good morning, handsome. Just woke up'*

'Me too'

She chewed on her lip, tickled to bits to know she'd been his first thought. *'Did you sleep well?'*

'Yes. You?'

'Ditto'

As soon as she'd sent it, the phone rang, and she answered. "Hi."

"Hi."

Lord's voice over the phone at seven o'clock in the morning brought on a smile. Her heart fluttered. She liked this, waking up to his voice. He did sound like he'd just woken up. What she wouldn't give to see what he looked like this early in the morning. The anticipation of finding out sent her heart dancing.

"You sound very sexy when you've just woken up," he said.

"Don't make it a habit." She yawned for good measure, even though she'd willingly condone this habit. "I like my beauty sleep."

"I can tell." He chuckled. "I suppose I'll have to think of going back to text messages. Alternatively, I could make you crave my voice every morning."

Her brows shot up. How did he plan on making her crave his voice each morning? She hoped it didn't involve starving her of it.

"You're a confident man."

"What can I say? I like to capitalise on my strengths."

"Is that right?"

"That's right."

"Any more strengths you'd like to share?"

"No. I like to reveal my dexterity in little doses," he teased. "I wouldn't want to overwhelm you and leave you breathless."

His easy, just-woken-up drawl made her think of him slowly undressing her with his teeth, his warm breath sending heat to her bones. He sounded very much like he wanted nothing more than to leave her breathless. She inhaled sharply, licking her suddenly dry lips.

"What are you doing today?" he asked as if he hadn't just triggered her imagination.

"Regular Sunday." She forced normal back into her voice. "A bit of writing and generally lazing about. You?"

"Visiting my parents. My family gets together once a month for lunch at their place."

"Oh." She couldn't keep the disappointment out of her voice. After last night, she realised she wanted to spend time with him, get to know him better. Like he'd said, she needed to draw her own conclusions about him. When she spoke again, she made a conscious effort to sound cheerful. "That's great. I hope you have fun."

"Why don't you come with me?"

Taken off guard, uncertainty gripped her. "I don't think it's a good—"

"You really need to learn how to stop saying that."

She heard a note of frustration in his voice, but she resisted its persuasion. How would the McKenzies feel about a stranger showing up at a family lunch?

"I want to spend time with you," she said. "It's just, this is a family thing."

Wasn't that moving too fast?

"And you're my guest. Look at it as part of your article. My father is the chairman of the company, and he's going to be there."

"I thought your father didn't like publicity."

"He doesn't, but this article is about me. His part in it would be minimal," he said. "Besides, it will be an informal setting, and he'll be less guarded."

As tempting as the offer sounded, it didn't feel right. "I don't like the idea of getting information for my article without his consent."

"We'll get his approval," he said. "If not, just see it as a lunch date."

She considered this awhile. It would be great to see how he interacted with his family. She could take a few pictures. They wouldn't be as good as Joe's, but they should pass.

"I promise to be on my best behaviour," he said with a teasing lilt in his voice that suggested he'd make good use of any opportunities to do the exact opposite. "Say yes."

"Okay, I'll go."

"Excellent. I'll pick you up at twelve."

"I'll be ready."

"See you." As if he sensed a fragment of doubt remained in her mind, he added, "Don't worry. My family is nice."

After hanging up, she pushed all apprehension aside. Her mind had other things to think about, like the image of him taking her clothes off with his teeth. She had an urge to run around the house screaming "lunch date, lunch date," in a manner that would have put her nieces to shame.

He picked her up at noon in a BMW 5-series, the same navy-blue colour as the Hilux. *Must be his favourite colour, too.* And she'd previously thought they couldn't possibly have anything in common. Apparently, they did. *How about that?*

Despite her misgivings about meeting his parents, getting to spend time with him brought excitement. After all, it wasn't a *date* date. It would be nice to not spend a weekend alone, for a change. Plus, like he rightly said, it could provide some good detail for her article. You could tell a lot about a person by the way they related with the people closest to them.

"Tell me about your family. What should I expect?"

It was common knowledge Lord's older brother had married his university sweetheart and they had three children. She didn't know much else about him. His mother who had a background in event planning supported various charities and threw some of the best parties in town.

"My father turned sixty-five last month, though he has enough energy to put forty-year-old men to shame. When it comes to showing affection to each other, sometimes, both my parents behave like teenagers." She didn't miss the fondness in his voice. "My mum is a very motherly sort of woman. We often tease her about having too much time on her hands because she hasn't worked in an office since I turned four."

"Wow. I can't imagine not having to work." In fact, given the option, she'd choose to have a career even if she didn't need one. "Doesn't she mind?"

"Mind? She says her job is to take care of her family, and she's one of the lucky few who can do it without having to spend forty hours or more a week slaving for someone else."

"That's one way of looking at it."

She'd never thought of it that way. Perhaps if, in fact, she did have all the money in the world, she'd want to use her time differently. *Who knows?*

"By taking care of the family, she means meddling and feeding." He laughed softly as he continued. "My brother, Ohene, is a doctor with his own practice, which you might already know. He has three lovely kids with his equally lovely wife, Jane. As for what to expect: noise from the children, really good food, good conversation, no dirty jokes." He gave her a smile. "And perhaps a really good story. Are you nervous?"

"No," she lied.

Rich and famous, she could deal with, but the McKenzies were wealthy and powerful. They had the kind of money and clout many only dreamt of. What if they thought she wasn't good enough for their son?

"They'll like you." He reached out and gave her hand a reassuring squeeze. "Oh, by the way, my mother might try to get you to take some food home. You don't have to accept it if you feel uncomfortable."

She'd stopped listening. Her mind had gotten stuck on "they'll like you." He shouldn't have said that, because now, it felt like they were on a real date. If it had been a work meeting, she would have been in her element, fully in control. Though she'd been lured by the promise of a few minutes with his father, the real reason she'd agreed had nothing to do with work. Curiosity had gotten a hold of her. She wanted to know him—the man. Getting some more detail for her story was purely a bonus at this point.

"You aren't what I expected," she said.

"What would that be?"

She hesitated a fraction, since all her previous expectations had been very, with a capital V, negative. But she'd already started and figured she might as well finish. "I expected you to be self-absorbed and obnoxious."

"Whoa. Talk about preconceived notions," he said. "Thank goodness it's a short list."

"Actually ..." she began to say, making an apologetic face.

"You had a longer list?" He raised his brows in mock-wonder. "You didn't like me much, did you?"

Heat flushed her face. "I didn't know you."

"And now?" He looked a tad concerned.

"I have a clean sheet."

"What if I really am self-absorbed and obnoxious, and I'm just great at hiding it?" He grinned. "Unless, of course, that turns you on."

"Seriously, anyone who spends enough time with you will know there's more to you than what the papers say, but you keep allowing your image to be smudged. Why?"

He shrugged.

"It's easier for the masses to believe a lie than the truth. I just got tired of trying to convince people to like me." He paused. "Even for those who know me, many only bother spending time with me because of what I can offer them."

He had a point. Sometimes, the more you tried to convince people of something, the more they held fast to the opposite.

"Maybe it's because if you believe the worst of people, then they can't disappoint you," she said.

If she'd applied that philosophy with Martin, she wouldn't have had her heart ripped out and trampled upon. She'd lost her very soul to him because she'd trusted him so much. Never again.

"But if you decide all people are inherently evil, then you make the good ones have to fight too hard for your love. That can't be fair."

Love? The way he said it tempted her to believe in happily-ever-afters, but those were western notions. Fairy-tales. Not grounded in reality—her reality, anyway. None of it mattered, though. She knew first-hand if you believed in the good of all people, *you* got hurt, and *that* wasn't fair.

FRANKLY, LORD THOUGHT his parents' house was too big. A ten-bedroom house in itself wasn't large. However, they'd been living alone for many years now, and they didn't need the space. His mother always said the extra rooms came in handy when the children, namely he and his brother with his wife and three kids, came to visit. Even if each of them got assigned to a room, there'd be a few left over. She could explain away the bedrooms, but not the three kitchens or two dining rooms.

He had to admit, though, it made hide-and-seek so much fun. Maybe he could find somewhere to hide with Chantelle. The idea held a lot of appeal, and he found himself taking a mental tour of the house. He'd need to seriously consider the option, since spending the whole afternoon without kissing her seemed like an arduous task.

They arrived a little after one o'clock, and the security guard at the gate let them in. He entered the large compound and parked beside his brother's Lexus LX. Looking over at Chantelle, he noted the tense, squared shoulders. A definite sign of nerves. He supposed the idea of meeting his parents, in their house no less, would be a little intimidating. Although he had no doubt once she got used to the surroundings and met everyone, she'd feel right at home.

"I'll open the door for you," he said, getting out of the car.

He held her hand, helping her out. Not wanting to make her uncomfortable, he settled for putting his hand on the small of her back rather than looped around her shoulders like he wanted. Although touching her at all might not be a good idea. He'd brought her here as his guest, not his date. If his family suspected he liked her that way, they wouldn't let it rest. He pressed the doorbell, but didn't wait for an answer before opening the door.

The three musketeers, his nephew and two nieces, came running towards them as he and Chantelle walked in.

"Hey, guys," he said.

They came to bear-hug him.

"Uncle Fee, who's this?" the middle one, six-year-old Gladys, asked.

"This is my friend, Auntie Chantelle. Say hello."

They chorused their hellos, the older two extending their hands in a most grown-up manner. It pleased him to see how comfortable she appeared, shaking the children's hands and asking how they were doing, what school they attended.

"The kid is here."

He heard his brother's voice before Ohene and his wife, Jane, emerged in the main hallway leading to one of the three sitting rooms.

He used to hate it when his brother referred to him as the kid, but the more he'd shown it, the more Ohene had persisted. As children, one of his brother's favourite past-times had been to tease Lord, because he always got a reaction. Through the years, he had learned to ignore the jabs. Having his own personal tormentor since childhood had given him a level of immunity against the articles about him in the papers. They didn't bother him as much as they should have.

"Sorry, he's a typical older brother," he said against her ear, then out loud, "Good one, Ohene. Embarrass yourself in front of my guest." He hugged Jane. "You look good, no credit to the doctor."

"Thanks, dear." Jane laughed.

Looking curiously at Chantelle, his brother asked, "And who is your lady friend?"

"Can you be a little less subtle?" He looked apologetically at her. "My brother spends so much time with patients, he's forgotten normal etiquette with healthy people."

They laughed as he introduced them. They exchanged handshakes and greetings.

"Maame and Papa are in the back," Ohene said.

Allowing his brother and Jane to lead the way, he held Chantelle's waist as they went. Just when they were about to step out of the door, he saw a window of opportunity and took it. Without warning, he pulled her back in. With the element of surprise on his side, she didn't have time to protest or resist as he lowered his lips on hers for one precious moment.

"I've been dying to do that all day."

Her eyes gleamed with excitement. "We're going to get caught."

"Where's your sense of adventure, woman?" He earned himself a good-natured swat and stole another kiss, anyway. "Okay, let's go."

They found Mr. and Mrs. McKenzie in the back. His father stood at the grill cooking kebabs while his mother manned the lunch table. As soon as he'd introduced Chantelle, the women whisked her away.

"Don't look so worried," Ohene said, handing him a beer.

"I'm not."

"Liar. I remember how I felt when I first brought Jane home and Maame asked her to help her in the kitchen," his brother said. "I've since discovered they would only do that when they like the woman."

"Are you sure?" He didn't like the idea of the women testing Chantelle when he hadn't prepared her for it.

"Look, you know Maame. If she doesn't like someone, she wouldn't trust her near her kitchen."

True enough, though it didn't do much to assuage his concern.

"She's pretty and seems nice." Ohene took a swig of his beer. "So what's the story? Are you going out with her?"

After last night, he didn't know whether they were dating. He wouldn't discuss it with his brother until he knew for sure where he stood with her. "There's no story."

"Come on, there has to be," Ohene persisted. "You don't look at other girls the way you were looking at her, and you certainly don't bring girls home."

"I haven't brought her home. She's doing a story on me, nothing more."

"Hmm." Ohene nodded, though his cock-eyed expression indicated he didn't buy the explanation. "If it makes you feel better, I'll go check on them."

Lord nodded, grateful.

"If there is something between you and her," Ohene said, before walking off. "I'm not saying there is, I think it's good."

As his brother left, Lord moved on to his father. "How's the kebab doing?"

"It shouldn't be long now," his father said.

"Need help?"

"You can get a plate ready."

While retrieving a plate from a small table near the grill, Lord decided to venture into the reason he wanted a one-on-one with his father.

"Papa, remember the profile story I told you *Odopa* Magazine is doing on me?"

"Yes." His father didn't take his focus off the grill.

"Chantelle is the one writing the story," he said. "I thought it would be a good idea for you to talk to her, as well. After all, you started the company."

Mr. McKenzie paused to face his son, his look not quite disapproving, but not pleased, either. "Have you already told her I'm going to grant her an interview?"

"I promised to ask you and that if you said no, at least the food would be good."

His father remained silent for a moment. "Is she done with you?"

He wouldn't say she was finished with him. In fact, she'd just started with him, in the way that mattered. His father didn't need to know that yet. "Yes, she is, but she agrees a section on my family will be good."

"This is important to you?" his father asked.

Right now, nothing mattered more. *She* was the most important thing.

"Yes. It's time I cleared up the misconceptions about me, and—" His father liked figures. "*Odopa* sells five times over *Business in Africa*."

"I'll think about it."

His father hardly ever made any decisions without thinking about it. Even when it appeared he'd made a spur-of-the-moment decision, it usually meant he'd anticipated the situation and done his homework before it came up.

"Thanks, Papa."

A beat passed.

"She seems like a nice girl. Smart and grounded," his father said.

His heart swelled with a sense of pride. While he didn't plan on discussing Chantelle with his father, it pleased him to know the older man approved. "She's here for work, Papa."

His father grunted, giving him a wizened version of Ohene's unconvinced look.

Lord shook his head. Noting some of the kebabs were done, he filled a plate. "I'll take these to the table."

His attention moved to the table where Ohene and the women were setting places. His mother had started dishing out. His focus went straight to Chantelle. She'd worn a dress—as if she wasn't feminine enough—white with large orange flowers and a stylish big belt around her slim waist. She didn't appear nervous at all. Rather, she seemed to fit in perfectly, like she was meant to be here, with him and his family.

As he approached them, he noticed the younger two of the three musketeers, Gladys and Ato, had come to stand next to her. The three-year-old boy handed her a paper. Being in the middle of his artistic stage of development, he guessed it to be a drawing.

The gesture tugged at his heart. Ato didn't readily take to strangers. It showed the kind of person Chantelle was, one of those few people who were meant to be loved, who made you want to love them. He watched her smile and take the paper from the boy. Whatever she said had him beaming in his three-year-old unbidden innocence. It brought a smile to his lips.

"Kebabs are ready," he said when he got within earshot.

No one appeared to be listening to him. Jane and Ohene were busy with the girls on one side while Ato still held Chantelle's attention, and his mother counted something on the table.

"I like her," she said.

It took him a moment to realise she was talking to him. Her eyes sparkled with curiosity.

"There's nothing going on between us, so don't give her a hard time," he said.

His mother feigned shock. "Why would I give her a hard time?"

"Because you might be under the impression that I'm—"

"Interested in her?" She finished off the sentence for him, with a beaming smile. "Aren't you?"

She had him cornered. He couldn't say no; neither could he say yes. He grimaced when his mother gave him a triumphant look.

"Why don't you go and rescue her?"

He looked up and discovered Gladys and Baaba, the eldest of the three, were now playing tag around Chantelle. Instead of being flustered, she seemed to enjoy their company. Jane, however, didn't look pleased as she tried to get them under control. *Mother knows best.* Placing the kebabs with the rest of the food, he went to her rescue.

He lifted Gladys up, whirled her around before landing her back on the ground. While she squealed in delight, the others begged him to carry them, too, and he obliged.

After three rounds each, they abandoned him for a new interest.

"Are you okay?" he asked Chantelle when he'd had a moment to catch his breath.

"Yes," she said. "You really do like other people's children."

"That was supposed to be a joke, you know."

"You're good with them."

"So are you."

"I have two active nieces around the same age." She smiled, though her eyes appeared sorrowful. The look disappeared within seconds, replaced by a cheerful expression which seemed a little forced. "Did you ask your father?"

"He says he's going to think about it."

She made a doubtful face. "That's a good thing, right?"

"It is."

In a few minutes, his old man brought the rest of the kebabs, and they sat down to eat. Lunch was a rowdy affair with the children excited as they always were when they visited their grandparents, while the adults asked Chantelle about her work. A discussion on the state of the economy and youth unemployment ensued. The topic somehow moved to traditional versus western weddings.

Out of the blue, Baaba asked, "Uncle Fee, are you going to marry Auntie Chantelle?"

The unexpected question threw him off, and he choked on the water he was drinking.

CHAPTER 15

MARRY HER? NOT LIKELY, Chantelle thought. They hardly knew each other. True, they'd had mind-blowing sex and unrivalled kisses, but that was hardly a recipe for marriage. Besides, even when men made wedding plans with you, they could disappear the next week. And his reaction said it all. The concept of forever with her didn't appear to be on his wish list. Good thing she wasn't nursing any delusions of happily-ever-after. Once bitten, twice shy.

Despite the pep talk, sadness clung to her like second skin. Was she unmarriageable? She had to force a smile when Jane, sitting next to Lord, patted him on the back as he released the last remnants of cough.

"Baaba, where are your manners? Auntie Chantelle and your uncle are just friends." Jane turned to Chantelle. "I'm sorry."

"Don't worry about it."

She didn't have to force her smile, though, when after the coughing had subsided, Ohene started teasing Lord. Being a good sport, he told his brother to laugh it up now.

"You'll soon be laughing from the wrong side of your mouth," he said.

"Brave words," Ohene said. "What are you going to do, design me a killer house?"

More laughter followed, and this time, Lord joined in. God, he looked so handsome, jesting so freely with his brother. His eyes connected with hers at a point and paused for several seconds. Her breath caught, and she couldn't look away. Energy surged within her, between them. Just like the first day when he'd shaken her hand. Finally, he released her from his gaze, focusing a little too intently on his plate. She noticed Jane look from her to Lord, a curious frown knitting her brows together. The commotion encouraged the children to get loud and start a food fight that was promptly terminated by Mrs. McKenzie. She wasn't going to have any of her good cooking used as ammunition.

"Sorry, Chantelle," Mrs. McKenzie said. "My children and grandchildren seem to have lost their manners."

Though she forced some amount of firmness into her voice, the affection was unmistakable.

Jane shushed the children. They stopped throwing food, but their game continued with easy-going barbs and quiet giggling. The fun was infectious, however. Try as she might, Jane couldn't suppress her own wry smile at her children. Chantelle's heart filled with warmth as they reminded her of her nieces. Her heart ached, too. Had things turned out differently, she would have had a son or daughter about the same age as Lord's nephew. She forced the thought out of her mind. This was hardly the time for regrets or wishful thinking.

When things were relatively calm again, Mr. McKenzie said, "Chantelle, my son says you'd like a few minutes of my time for an interview."

She shot a surprised look at Lord, trying not to appear overly excited—a difficult undertaking when he winked at her. "Yes, sir."

"How about after lunch?"

"That would be excellent. Thank you." She mouthed a "thanks" to Lord, as well, which he acknowledged with a nod. Her heart fluttered. She enjoyed those private moments when his attention seemed focused on her alone. Even when addressing someone else, his eyes often wavered to her.

She hoped the sensations causing sweet havoc on her insides didn't translate into some goofy look for all to see. In Jane's words, she and Lord were just friends. Only, her emotions were beginning to feel way stronger than friendship. Right now, she really wanted to kiss him senseless.

Something brushed against her leg, causing her to jump. All eyes were on her, all looking concerned. All except Lord, that is. He sat back with a pleased expression as he played footsy with her leg. His toes traced circles on her knees, moving upwards. She glared at him to stop it as she tried not to show any emotion.

Her body refused to cooperate, evidenced by the quickening pace of her heartbeat. She shifted her position, but his foot seemed to gain greater access to her thighs. Expertly, his toes slid under her dress, sending a ripple of desire through her. He had incredible footsying skills. Need surfaced in her lower abdomen. Her lips and throat became dry. She grabbed her drink and took a long sip.

"Are you all right, dear?" Mrs. McKenzie asked.

"Yeah, Chantelle, are you okay?" Lord asked with exaggerated concern.

"Yes." She managed to get that out in a strained voice. She needed to pay him back for it. A brilliant idea occurred as she remembered her left hand on her thigh. She grabbed his toe and pinched him.

"Ow!" His exclamation, though low, sounded genuine, and remorse replaced her momentary delight.

"Are you okay?" Jane asked him.

"I'm fine."

Maybe she'd applied too much force. She squelched the urge to mouth an apology when he scowled at her. Her annoyance at his daring foot moves hadn't subsided. What if someone had found out? How embarrassing would that be? She wanted to stick out her tongue at him even though she preferred the pleased look to the slighted one.

Seeing him with his family brought up all sorts of tender emotions within her. The way his brother seemed to take pleasure in pulling his leg brought on a silent laugh. They behaved like teenagers—much like when she and Danielle got together.

After lunch, she got to spend fifteen minutes with Mr. McKenzie for a short interview. As he talked about how he established the company, she noted that his eyes and nose were the same as Lord's. Father and son didn't look particularly alike, but both were exceptionally good-looking, a trait all the McKenzies seemed to share.

She had to admire the man's sheer will and determination as he explained how he established McKenzie Contractors with one truck and no office. When he talked about his family, he spoke with open devotion. Amazing how her admiration of Mr. McKenzie's work translated into mushy feelings for his son. By the time she'd completed the interview, she just wanted to run into Lord's arms.

Instead, she thanked Mr. McKenzie and strolled over to where Lord sat with Ohene and Jane. As she approached, she sensed his eyes lasered on her, making her feel giddy and special. She had to force herself from grinning like a fool and skipping the rest of the way. When she reached them, she discovered there were no extra chairs.

He stood. "Take my seat. I'll get another."

"No, take mine," Jane said, standing up. "I can use the opportunity to sit on my favourite seat." She crossed over to sit on Ohene's lap.

Something tugged her heart when the couple kissed. Longing? Envy? Her gaze sought Lord's before dropping to his lips. He pouted in a kissing gesture. She almost giggled, but remembered her surroundings and composed herself. Her blood simmered, a reaction he seemed to have no trouble extracting from her. Something else brewed underneath, something comfortable, something she could get used to. The thought gave her pause. It excited and scared her at the same time. She liked him. She really liked him. What had she gotten herself into?

A few meters away, his parents sat together, talking and playing with Ohene's children. Every gesture they made told of love and devotion. She watched them with longing. It made her think about her parents, who lived in Cape Coast. They weren't as touchy feely. Even so, there was never a doubt about their affection for each other.

"It's enviable, isn't it?" Lord's voice broke through her thoughts. The longing swirling in her chest reflected in his voice. "My parents behave like they are still seventeen."

She smiled. Yes, it was enviable. Finding someone you could be completely open with. Being free to love the person because you knew they'd love you right back. People didn't love that way anymore. She'd never experienced it before. Or at least, she'd discovered the love she had once trusted had been something less than love.

"They wake up early each morning to drink tea and talk," he said.

"Sounds nice."

"We've started that tradition, too," Jane said, apparently now part of their conversation.

She could see why they would want to adopt such a habit. Her mind conjured up an image of her and Lord sharing a quiet morning together drinking tea and planning their day. It wouldn't happen, of course. He could dispute his playboy reputation all he wanted, but he couldn't argue about the fact that he hadn't had a long-term girlfriend in as long as she could remember.

Deconte, the only woman anyone had seen him with for more than five outings, had turned out to be his cousin. Why hadn't the thought occurred to her yesterday, before she'd agreed to get to know him? Had she set herself up for a fall?

"It's not as easy as it seems. We've restricted it to the weekend when the kids sleep in," Ohene said. "And Jane loves her sleep."

"Maame and Papa are a hard act to follow," Lord said, his tone suggesting a determination to do just that.

It dawned on her. He wanted what his parents had. The reason he couldn't hold a relationship or didn't bother trying, whichever applied, lay right in front of them. He wanted perfection. But she wasn't perfect. Not like her sister.

Danielle had met David in her final year of university, and they were married soon after her graduation. Eight years of marriage, and David still looked at Danielle like the first day they met. She hadn't been so lucky. She was the woman a guy wanted to date for three years while cheating on her for half of that time. How could she be surrounded by love, and yet fail so miserably at it?

Feeling unexpectedly sapped, she turned to Lord. "Can we go now? I just remembered something I have to do."

"Are you leaving already?" Jane asked, alarmed. She checked her time. "Wow, it's almost four."

"We should get going, too," Ohene said. "The children have school tomorrow."

They got up together and walked to Mr. and Mrs. McKenzie to bid their goodbyes. She thanked Mr. McKenzie for the interview and his wife for the lovely meal.

The compliment earned her a smile from Mrs. McKenzie. "Let me pack some for you to take home."

"Don't say I didn't warn you," Lord said in low tones. She started to decline when he whispered into her ear, albeit jokingly, "She'll be gutted if you don't take some home."

"I'm packing some for both my boys. Adding one more for you won't be a problem," Mrs. McKenzie said. "Besides, my husband and I can't finish all this leftover food in enough time. We'll end up throwing some away."

"Then I'd be happy to have a pack, too. Thank you."

"Why don't you come with me? You can choose exactly what you want," the older woman offered. "There's no sense in giving you food you're not going to eat."

Her heartbeat quickened. This sounded like a trap. She wracked her brains for an excuse to escape the unknown danger her mind seemed to be warning her about. Nothing presented itself.

"Uhm, okay," she found herself replying.

Seeing no other choice, she followed Mrs. McKenzie into the kitchen. Wow. Even though she'd been in there once already, she took a moment to appreciate the stunning white cabinets and ultramodern chef-grade appliances. Pendant lights hung from the pitched ceiling above the large centre island whose dark grey worktop created a stunning contrast against the white. What could be seen of it, anyway. An array of food covered most of its surface.

Mrs. McKenzie waved her hands over the display. "What would you like, dear?"

The question yanked her back, and she managed to reel in her wonder just as the other woman turned. She noticed they weren't alone. A middle-aged woman in a blue dress and a pristine white apron approached the centre island with a plastic storage bowl.

Swallowing her discomfort, she selected a combination of dishes she'd enjoyed the most during lunch.

"Do you live with someone?" Mrs. McKenzie asked. "Akos can pack extra."

She shook her head. "I live alone."

Lord's mother nodded while the other woman, who had to be the cook, finished dishing out the selection of food into two containers and packed them in a paper bag instead of polythene. She tried not to look too impressed about the bag. Many, including herself, had advocated for reduction of plastic waste in the city. It pleased her to see someone making an effort.

After placing the packed food on the countertop, the other woman left. Mrs. McKenzie took the bag and handed it to Chantelle. As she received it, their gazes met.

"Don't hurt my son," she said.

Chantelle blinked. What? Her lips moved without words coming out. She braced herself for the warning to leave her rich son alone.

"I can see he's crazy about you, and you seem to feel the same way."

She swallowed, forcing her voice to work. "I would never hurt him."

If anything, he had the capacity to break her heart. Not the other way around.

"I sense uncertainty from you," the older woman said. "Take my advice and work out whatever it is you need to sort out. Otherwise, your doubt will eventually hurt him, and I can't have that. Do you understand what I'm saying?"

Before she could think of a response, Jane popped her head in. "Am I interrupting?"

"No, Jane. Come in." Mrs. McKenzie's smooth switch from scary to sweet left Chantelle both stunned and fascinated. "Your packs are ready."

Jane gave Chantelle an understanding smile as she walked past her to pick four other bags. Had she survived a version of her mother-in-law's warning?

The older woman thrust the pack in her hand in Chantelle's direction. "Here you are, dear."

Mrs. McKenzie smiled as if she hadn't just ambushed her. She may not have expressly threatened her to stay away from her son, but the caveat lay in words she didn't have to say.

The two Mrs. McKenzies led the way out of the kitchen. When they joined the others, Jane handed one of her take-away bags to Lord, and they all headed out. At the car, the children all came to hug their uncle. When Ato finished hugging Lord, he turned around and wrapped his little arms around her, too.

"Bye-bye, Auntie Chantelle," he said.

A lump grew in her throat as she squatted to be on the same level with him. "Bye, Ato. Thanks for the picture you drew for me."

Without another word, the boy ran back to his mother, appearing to be shy. He hid behind Jane, peeping at them from that safe point. Getting into the car, she waved at them as they drove off.

CHAPTER 16

LORD COULDN'T HELP NOTICING how quiet Chantelle was on their return trip. Back at the house when she said she'd remembered something she needed to do, it had felt like a sudden decision. He'd sensed something amiss. Now, in the car, she sat stiff-backed with her arms crossed, looking outside. They'd had short, inconsequential conversations, punctuated by long silences. What went through her mind?

"You're quiet," he said.

She turned to face him. "Am I?"

She's buying time. He recognised the signs. Question for question, pretending she hadn't realised the obvious.

"What's on your mind?"

She shook her head. "Just thinking."

"Do you want to talk about it?"

"Not really." Her smile lessened the sting of words.

His heart swelled. She looked stunning when she smiled. She looked gorgeous even when she didn't. He slipped his right hand behind her neck and began to rub gently. She closed her eyes, letting out a big sigh.

"You're tense."

He found it hard to believe Chantelle sat in his car, allowing him to massage her neck. Especially after running away from him on Valentine's Day and avoiding his calls afterwards. Above all, because he'd worshipped her through her articles for so long, it felt unreal to have her so close.

"Feels nice." She moaned. "You've got talented hands."

"I have many skills you don't know about." He assumed the voice of a Chinese sage, as they were portrayed in movies.

She chuckled, then sighed. "Like playing footsy?"

He grinned. "And there I was thinking you didn't appreciate my efforts."

She gave a soft snort of laughter.

Another period of silence followed. When he pulled his hand away, she stretched, covering her face with both hands, then bent forward and rested her elbows on her lap. He laid a hand on her back. She had to be tired. After the awards event last night, he should have let her rest today instead of dragging her out for an afternoon with his family.

That didn't account for the worry weaving through every sinew of his being. Something was wrong. He knew it. While thinking this, he felt her body shake. Alarm shot through him as he realised she was crying. He parked by the side of the road.

"What's wrong?" he asked.

When she didn't answer, he got out of the car, walked over to her side and opened her door.

"Hey." He prodded lightly, trying to get her to raise her head. He wanted her in his arms. "Come here."

When he tugged her hand, she came out of the car, falling into his embrace, still crying.

He tightened his hold, wishing he could take away whatever had caused her tears. He didn't think he'd said anything to upset her, but he'd been accused of such a thing before. After a short while, she pulled back. The tear-stained face filled him with a strong desire to protect her. But from what?

"Wait, did my mother say something to you in the kitchen?"

She shook her head. "I'm sorry. I don't know what's wrong with me. I guess I'm just a little overwhelmed."

Overwhelmed was a good thing, right?

"Your family is nice. Your brother's children are cute, and I had a good time."

"So these are happy tears?" he asked, hopeful.

Her one-sided smile pacified him to some extent. She leaned back, resting against the car. The gentle breeze blew some tendrils of hair onto her cheek. He brushed them away before framing her face with his hands.

"I don't want to overwhelm you."

The tenderness in his voice caught him unawares. What about this woman made him go weak in the knees? His lips brushed hers. The contact left a desire to surrender.

Her tongue skimmed over his lower lip, knocking the breath out of him. He sought a deeper taste of her mouth. Closing his eyes, he drank her in, taking his air supply from her, because he'd stopped breathing on his own. Why in the world had he thought he could resist?

He groaned, reluctantly pulling away. For a moment, he tried to come up with something witty, or even corny, to cover the effect of the kiss, but words eluded him.

Her palms rested flat against his stomach as she tortured him with the tender motion of her fingers, her lips puckered. So tempting.

"I want to make love with you," she said.

Forget resisting. If they were somewhere private, much more private, he'd be ripping her clothes off. Those words coming from Chantelle felt like a huge victory, just like yesterday when she'd uttered the word deal. He wanted nothing more than to make sweet love with her, but he needed her to want him until it hurt. Despite her words, he sensed making love with her too soon would be a mistake.

"Don't worry, we will," he said. "When the time is right."

Words he'd never uttered before. In the past, if a woman said she wanted sex, he didn't ask questions. Now, dear God, he was willing to wait. Whatever she'd done to him, she'd done it well.

She took in a deep breath. "I smell the ocean."

"Do you want to take a stroll? The beach is just beyond the curve."

She nodded.

A few minutes later, they were at the beach. Stepping off the road, they walked between coconut trees interspersed between the road and the beach. This part of the seashore was practically untouched, with debris from the ocean washed up on the golden sand. They took off their shoes, and he folded his jeans up to his knees.

"It's easier to walk close to the edge of the water, where the sand is wet," he said.

They began their stroll with the light wind caressing their faces.

"I like the sea," she said. "The breeze, the salty air. We grew up in Cape Coast, and our house was a ten-minute walk from the coastline. Sometimes, I'd stroll over there and sit at the beach just watching and listening to the waves."

"I like the beach, too. Unfortunately, I don't get enough free time to come here. Except for stolen moments like this, I don't get to see the ocean at all."

"You must be a very busy man."

"I am," he said. "I work hard, and I party hard."

"Does partying hard include women?"

"In the past, it did," he said candidly. "You have to understand, Chantelle, women usually date me for my money or my looks … or both. It's a fact I've come to accept and even expect."

He glanced down at her, gauging her reaction, but her expression gave nothing away. At least she wasn't running off. He counted it as a win.

"Are you saying women objectify you?"

He smiled. "Would it surprise you?"

"A little." She cast her gaze seaward. "You've gone out with a lot of women, never dating any of them for a significant length of time."

"Would you feel better if they dumped me instead of the other way around?"

She obviously missed the teasing tone of his statement, as she turned to face him with curious eyes. "They dumped you?"

He chuckled. "I asked hypothetically, but the answer is yes. A few times, I've been dumped. Otherwise, parting ways is by mutual understanding." After a moment, he added, "Besides, I could be a dull guy who can stay interesting only for short periods of time."

"You're not boring, and if anyone thinks you are, then you didn't let them see the real you."

"Believe me, they aren't interested. Not even enough to despise me like you apparently did."

She fidgeted in his arms. "I didn't despise you."

"Fine, but before now, you didn't like me much."

"I didn't know you enough."

They walked in silence for a little while. He sucked in a deep breath of the crisp ocean air, watching her. She wore a pensive look. He could almost see the wheels of her mind turning. Once again, he found himself relegated to the position of an outsider wanting to get inside her head.

"How do you do it?" she asked. "How do you date someone you don't care about or vice versa?"

He didn't need a neon sign to tell him there were no correct answers to the question. Truth be told, dating was much easier without the entanglements of emotions. None of his previous relationships had ever given him the slightest inclination to do everything in his power to make things last. With Chantelle, he resolved to do just that and then some.

As he faced her, about to take his best shot at the question, he realised he had something more important to say. "I care about you, Chantelle."

The smile she gave him made his heartbeat stall.

"I know what you're looking for," she said out of the blue. "You want what your parents have, and you won't settle for anything less."

He smiled, putting an arm over her shoulders, pulling her close. "Do you read minds now?"

As he'd hoped, she chuckled. It saved him from having to admit settling for less was exactly what he'd have had to do if they hadn't met. No other woman made him want to wake up for tea at six in the morning.

"What about you?" he asked. "What's your love life been like?"

"Nothing to tell, really."

"Nothing, as in you don't want to talk about it, or you just don't date?"

"I don't have time to date."

"Nobody has time, Chantelle. You make time for the people who matter."

"Some people think I'm picky."

"Are you?"

She considered the question. "Maybe. I mean, if you're going to share your life with someone, you have to be particular. It's like going to the supermarket to buy an orange. You don't select just any orange. You take the juiciest-looking one."

The analogy made him chuckle. "I think somebody hurt you. Whatever happened scared you off relationships. That's not being picky. You're afraid of getting hurt again."

She started to say something but stopped and just kept walking.

"Am I close?"

She gave him a quick glance. "Yeah, too close."

"What did he do?"

For several moments, he thought she wouldn't answer the question. He didn't intend to give in without a little push, though. If he had to pay for another man's sins, he needed to know what they were.

She sighed.

"We were engaged. I thought I knew everything about him. I mean, we'd been together three years." She paused in her stride, casting a wide gaze over the Atlantic Ocean. "It was almost Valentine's Day, and we'd planned a weekend getaway. The day before we were supposed to have gone, he called from work to tell me he'd been sent on an impromptu assignment. He died in an accident on his way back."

Deep sorrow filled her eyes as she turned to look at him. Something dark and unfamiliar twisted in his chest. He wanted to be able to turn back the hands of time and spare her the vicious hand Fate had dealt her, except it would mean never having the chance to be with her.

"At the funeral, I discovered there had been no assignment. He'd gone with another woman on the vacation we were supposed to have taken."

Cruel bastard. Who the hell walked away from a woman like Chantelle? Anger pulsed through his veins. He wished he could reach into her heart and take out the pain she obviously still felt.

Tears glistened in her eyes, but she held them back. The desire to take away her pain intensified, crippling his senses. He gathered her into his arms.

"I'd have, at least, liked to know what I did to send him into another woman's arms."

"You did nothing." His voice grated against his throat. "He was an idiot for doing that to you."

She sniffed against his chest, and he held her closer, letting her wet his shirt with her tears. After several moments, she withdrew from his embrace, raising damp brown eyes to meet his.

"I'm not going to break your heart," he promised.

"Funny. Your mum thinks I'm going to hurt you."

He bit back a curse. "So she did say something."

"You can't blame her for looking out for her son."

"I don't need protecting, and I mean what I said."

She nodded. He couldn't tell whether she believed him, but it had been important for him to confess it. Silence prevailed for a couple of minutes. Had anything he'd said, particularly about women, been taken in the wrong context? The issue might need revisiting at a future date. Right now, he felt she'd had enough emotional drain for one day.

She folded her arms around herself, rubbing gently.

"Are you cold?" She had to be, wearing that sleeveless dress. "It's getting chilly."

"Let's head back."

"Why do Ohene's children call you Uncle Fee?" she asked after a moment.

"My brother made it up." Coined it from Lord's middle name. "You may have noticed he likes goofing around at my expense. I guess he thought I'd hate it, but the first time the kids called me, it sounded so adorable, I couldn't ask them to stop."

She chuckled. "You're sweet."

He smiled without responding. Instead, he wrapped his arms around her to keep her warm as they made their way back to the car.

CHAPTER 17

"IS IT TRUE? ARE YOU dating Lord McKenzie?"

Chantelle's heart tripped over a beat. "Mum, how did you …"

The question died away as the obvious reason her mother—who lived in another city—would know about her and Lord occurred. She'd somehow made it to the front page of some tabloid. She thought they'd been careful.

Over the past two weeks, they'd seen each other every evening but had kept their outings low-key. He'd even resorted to using a rental to pick her up instead of his regular cars, which all had personalised licence plates. Where had they slipped up?

"Danielle mentioned it," her mother said, assuaging her momentary worry about the media circus bound to happen when the world found out about her and Lord.

Right now, though, she had something else on her mind. Ways to kill her twin when they next met.

"Don't blame your sister. It was either revealing your secret or finally introducing you to some of David's single friends."

She could just imagine. After all, she'd heard enough lectures from her mother about moving on, and the older woman's many attempts at recruiting Danielle's help in getting Chantelle to meet new men, which her sister had dutifully deflected. It seemed their mum's persistence had finally won out.

She released a resigned sigh. Maybe she'd let Danielle off the hook this time.

"Yes, we're seeing each other."

She bit on her lower lip to stop the squeal building up in her throat. She'd admitted it out loud. To her mother, no less. Her mind settled firmly on the subject of her happiness. She could just imagine the cocky grin on his face when she told him. Of course she'd tell him. She didn't know how to keep secrets from the people she loved.

She sucked in a breath. *Love*. She loved Lord.

Her chest expanded with the desire to gush about her feelings, about how happy he made her, but she squelched the urge. Her mother didn't do sentiment.

"Chantelle, do you think it's a good idea?" her mum asked with a note of disappointment.

She blinked, her excitement deflating with the same grace as a balloon pricked with a toothpick. Her mother had been a young girl in the sixties when many schools in Ghana still had British teachers and principals. Coupled with working as a nurse in the UK for a few years in the eighties, she still had a hint of an accent and a proper headmistress-y way of talking. You did not contradict her when she got that way. Which was how she'd asked the question.

"Aren't you the one who's been telling me it's time to open my heart again? I thought you'd be happy for me."

"I'm glad you're finally ready to date again, yes, but you're not moving on unless it's with the right person."

"What does that mean? What's wrong with Lord?"

"I don't deny he looks like prince charming and he probably makes you feel like a princess now, but all you need to do is read the papers to know he's never had a long-term relationship. Do you think a man like him is going to offer you marriage?"

Her mother's words made her flinch. She sidestepped the verbal darts.

"Mum, he's nothing like what the media says about him."

"I see he's managed to pull the wool over my usually smart daughter's eyes. You need to tread carefully. He's young, rich, entitled, and probably thinks he has all the time in the world to settle down."

The words pierced her. More than ever, it pained her to know she'd said similar things about him in the past. She realised how unfair she'd been, and though she wouldn't disrespect the woman who'd given birth to her with a rude remark, she wouldn't listen to her mother's unjustified tirade against the man she loved.

"Mum, I'm not a child. I can take care of myself."

She hated the edge in her voice but refused to feel bad about it or apologise. Lord made her happy. She'd stopped questioning and decided to enjoy it.

"Chantelle, I know you're a grown woman, but a man like Lord McKenzie can easily charm his way past your better judgement."

She loved her mother. The woman could always be counted on to tell it like it is, but sometimes, she didn't seem to realise the bluntness could be hurtful.

"I'm sorry if I sound harsh, but I'm only trying to protect you from making another mistake. You've already wasted four years after Martin."

Time she wouldn't get back, but she'd needed it to heal.

"And I'm finally ready for the next chapter of my love life."

"Love?" The sigh drifting across the line was equal parts resignation and frustration. "Does he at least make you happy?"

"Yes, Mum. More than I've ever been."

"And he makes you laugh?"

Her lips effortlessly stretched upwards. She couldn't dim it if she tried. "He cracks some unfunny jokes, but, yes. He makes me laugh."

"Then I hope I'm wrong about him. Just be careful, okay?"

"Yes, Mum." Despite the conciliatory turn of the conversation, she decided to change the topic. "How's Daddy?"

"He had to attend the funeral of a former colleague in Sekondi. You'd know if you called more often."

Uh oh.

She said the only thing she could to avoid another lecture. "I will, Mum."

"He should be back by six."

Call him. Her mother didn't add those words, but Chantelle heard them distinctively. She intended to do just that. If anyone could convince her mother to give Lord a chance, it was her father. But not tonight.

"I'll call him tomorrow. I can't today."

Silence followed, thick with the question her mother didn't ask. The older woman's ability to convey complete thoughts, emotions, and questions with a look or deliberate silence was uncanny, sometimes even scary.

"I have a date."

A sleepover, actually, but her mother didn't need to know the details.

"So he gets to see you when he pleases, and we don't even get regular phone calls."

"Mum—"

"I'm not complaining." But she was. "I get updates from Danielle. As long as I know you're doing well, I'm happy."

She hated when her mother got that way.

"You're right, I'll call more often," she promised.

"And you'll come for Easter."

Not a question.

"Yes, Mum."

"Good. Invite him."

As soon as the words reached her ear, she realised she'd been played. From the moment her mother had called, the conversation had been heading this way. *Smooth, Mum.* If she hadn't been so preoccupied with her emotions, she might have had enough presence of mind to sidestep it.

"Is there a problem, Chantelle?"

"No, Mum. Of course, I'll ask him."

What else could she say? Any attempt to deflect would cement her mother's negative opinion of Lord and make their first meeting more of an interrogation.

"Good. Now don't forget to call your father. We have joint service tomorrow, so we'll only return home from church after twelve."

After the call ended, she sighed, leaning against the back rest of the sofa and crossing her legs beneath her. Mentally, she kicked herself for letting her emotions distract her from what she should have known. Now she might have committed Lord to an Easter date with her parents. She'd worry about it later, though. Easter was a few weeks away, meaning she had time to think up an excuse to get out of her mother's invitation or at least prepare Lord for it.

Instead, she thought about their date tonight, and anticipation built, winding tight the chords of desire that had remained unfulfilled. Though they'd seen each other daily over the past two weeks, it had always been for a couple of hours after work. Most times, they just drove around the city catching up on each other's day before he dropped her at home. There'd been a lot of kissing and making out, but they hadn't made love again.

A couple of times, she'd not so subtly asked him to send the driver away for a few hours. He'd declined, citing early morning conference calls with business partners in Asia. It made sense, of course, but she sensed he'd deliberately kept a certain emotional distance.

Their conversation after lunch with his family often came back to her. She'd told him she wanted to make love again, and he'd said they would "when the time was right." Did that mean tonight? He'd asked her to pack an overnight bag. Surely, he didn't plan on spending the night together without making love. If his plan had been to stoke her desire until she couldn't think about anything else, then he'd succeeded.

****

"I CAN'T BELIEVE you went through all this trouble for me."

Chantelle's heart swelled as she gawked at the luxury yacht in front of them.

"It was no trouble at all," Lord said with a lopsided smile.

Right. What was a few thousand cedis when you had billions? Or maybe he'd just asked his buddy, Adonis Aggrey-Finn, and obtained the keys. The emblazoned A-F logo announced it to be part of the Aggrey-Finn cruise line. Besides, he most certainly had people handling the details of chartering this beautiful boat for two days. A man like Lord just commanded, and things got done. Still, her gratitude rose in response.

"Thank you," she said, meaning it.

"You're welcome."

She'd been sceptical about going out with him in public like this where anyone could snap a photo and splash it in the papers with an untoward headline. He might not mind the exposure, but she preferred to maintain her privacy. She didn't know how he managed to be so charitable, always smiling for the camera even when captured in situations where other celebrities would throw fits.

She'd once heard him say he did it because a reporter could be just one photo or story away from their big break. At the time, she'd thought it pompous of him to presume his photo would make someone's career. Now, she believed his intentions to be honourable, having seen the man who always wanted to do something for others. As he'd done for her now. Why else would he take steps to avoid the potential hype of a public date?

Ada Foah, a town about a hundred-and-ten-kilometres East of Accra, provided the perfect setting. Wedged at the Gulf of Guinea where the Volta River emptied into the Atlantic Ocean, it was out-of-town enough to escape watchful eyes in the capital city, but also cosmopolitan due to its tourist attractions.

"When you said dinner at the beach, I didn't realise it would be on a boat."

"Yacht," he corrected.

"What's the difference?"

"It's bigger."

She laughed, shaking her head. Though nowhere near as huge as those Caribbean cruise liners she'd seen in photos, it looked no less impressive. Sporting the general shape of a motorboat, it stretched at least thirteen metres. There were several other yachts, alongside motorboats, kayaks, locally crafted canoes, but this one stood out. With its graceful sloping lines and refined finishing, it gleamed in the late afternoon sunlight.

"You wanted privacy," he said.

His matter-of-fact tone made her laugh, a reflection of her disposition. She returned her gaze to him, and a fluttering in her heart made her briefly hold her breath. He was gorgeous, no denying it, but the intangibles, like his thoughtfulness, served to enhance those superior physical qualities. He could still be cocky, but even that had started growing on her.

He offered his arm. "Shall we?"

They'd taken off their shoes for the short walk from the clubhouse to the beach, so they each held their footwear in one hand, and she looped her free arm through his. Shaking off the sand wedged between their toes, they stepped off the wooden platform onto the yacht.

A man in a pilot's uniform met them. "Welcome on board, Mr. McKenzie. Welcome, Madam. I'm Philemon Adjei, and I'll be your captain during your stay. You'll have a steward attending to you. Your luggage has been deposited in the master cabin. Dinner will be served in a moment. Would you like to rest or freshen up before?"

Lord looked at her. "What will it be?"

Since breakfast, she'd snacked on bananas and roasted groundnuts in the afternoon. Though filling, it had been more than four hours ago, and she was starved.

Besides, neither of them appeared any worse for wear after their two-and-a-half-hour journey from Accra in a chauffeur-driven car. Lord looked handsome in charcoal grey trousers with a lavender-coloured shirt and a blazer. Since he didn't seem to be able to take his eyes off her red cross-over dress, she took it to mean she looked as good as intended. The flared bottom undulated in the breeze, showing him glimpses of her thighs. *Perfect*.

"Let's eat first," she said.

"Right this way," the captain said, leading the way.

As they crossed the distance from the stern towards a lounge on the main deck where a formal dinner had been set up, she paused at a large sun bed. It tempted her to lay on it and enjoy the breeze and what remained of the late-afternoon sun, but a tiny growl in her stomach made it clear where her priorities should be.

A sudden gust of wind whipped up her dress. With a gasp, she released Lord's arm to hold the skirt down. While she secured the front, he moved behind her, placing his hand on her bottom.

At his touch, sexual energy zapped her. Arousal surged so intense and immediate, she moaned. He didn't release her even after the wind had died down. Electricity continued to crackle between them. His breath against her ear matched the escalating pace of hers. They remained unmoving, both caught up in the maelstrom of desire. Pressure on her ass jerked her back.

"Did you just squeeze my butt?" she asked in low tones to avoid being overheard by the captain.

"No," he whispered. "I was protecting your virtue."

A short, husky laugh trembled out of her lips. "By stealing a squeeze?"

"Are you saying you don't like me touching your butt?"

He caressed the curve of her ass before moving upwards to the small of her back.

She swallowed, taking a second to contain the wanton pleasure his touch evoked. "You're playing with fire."

"It's a good thing I don't mind getting singed."

Heat invaded her body, and her breath hitched in her throat. "Do you really, Lord?"

"What does that mean?" He closed his hands around her shoulders and turned her to face him.

"Do you want to make love with me?"

His look of surprise multiplied severalfold. "Are you joking right now?"

"Two weeks ago, I told you I wanted to make love again, and you said, 'when the time is right.' Yet, somehow, it feels like you're holding back, and I don't know why. Touching me like this makes it hard."

She knew how she sounded. Desperate. Deprived. God, she hated it. She'd been the one who'd wanted to take things slow. Wasn't that the point, though? She had needed time to be certain about him, while he'd always seemed sure. Why would he hold back now?

He brought his hands up to frame her face.

"Do you truly think I don't want to make love with you? Do you know how hard it's been to maintain a pace I feel you're comfortable with?" He gave a snort. "It's taking everything in me to hang on to the reins of my control."

"And I'm saying you don't have to."

"Are you sure?" Shaking his head, he laughed. It sounded strained. Nothing like his usual carefree ones. "The first time we made love, I asked if you wanted to, and you said yes. Do you remember?"

"Of course I do."

"Then you ran from me."

Emotions were raw in his voice. Hearing it stung, knowing she'd hurt him without realising it. His carefree nature and larger-than-life confidence may have fooled her into thinking nothing affected him. She hadn't paused to consider his feelings that night. She'd been the definition of selfish.

"I'm sorry. I didn't realise—"

He didn't let her complete the sentence. "You don't have to be. I should have done things differently. I wanted you, and when you said yes, being a gentleman went out the window. I'm taking my time now because I should have done it then."

Silence followed his words, and in those seconds, unmasked remorse filled his eyes. God, how had she never seen how much she'd hurt him?

"I don't want you to have regrets, which is why I need you to want me so much that running won't be an option."

"Oh, Lord. I had no idea. You must believe me. My actions had nothing to do with you. I'd spent years being closed to the option of dating. Then you waltzed in and rendered my efforts null and void. You got to me in a way no one has, and it scared me." Silence met her confession. "I'm not afraid anymore, and I won't run again, because I don't want to."

His expression became intense, and for a moment, she thought he'd carry her down to the lower deck. Part of her wished he would.

"Are you sure?"

"I am. I want you tonight."

"Then you shall have me." He brought their lips together for a short, but deep, kiss. "You know you've just ensured I won't taste any of the food, right?"

Clearing things up sparked joy and awakened her flirtatious side.

"Poor you," she cooed.

When she resumed walking towards the dinner table, she put an extra sway in her hips.

"Now who's playing with fire?" he muttered, and she laughed.

CHAPTER 18

LORD MIGHT AS WELL have had parchment paper in his mouth for all the enjoyment he got from the meal. It had nothing to do with the food. A-F Cruises had top-notch catering services. Chantelle's words kept echoing in his mind, distracting him. 'I want you tonight.'

He'd wanted to skip dinner altogether, but she'd only eaten a snack in the afternoon, which meant she must've been hungry, so he'd crushed the urge to whisk her to the cabin and had instead followed her to the table.

Besides, if he was to fulfil her request, then they both needed sustenance. However, dinner couldn't have gone any slower if someone had flipped a switch to put the world in slow motion. All through the three-course meal, he struggled to keep his attention on the conversation while forcing to take his mind off the insistence of his arousal.

With dinner almost over, his control began to crack under the pressure of his eagerness. He held on, however. If he had his way, tonight would be as different from their first time as night from day. He needed to be patient and not let the enthusiasm lead.

"I never dreamt of being a princess, you know," she said, drawing his attention.

Shit. He'd drifted off again. He didn't know what he'd missed. At least, it wasn't a question, so he didn't have to grapple with his mind for a response.

"For as long as I can remember, I've wanted to be a journalist," she continued, saving him the need to answer.

She stared ahead at the passing coastline. Once they'd started eating, the captain had begun a leisurely sail. Now that the sun had set, spots of light decked the coastline, punctuated by several patches of darkness, which he suspected marked undeveloped beach.

"Other girls wanted to be Cinderella or Snow White, but I wanted to be Lois Lane. I have to admit, though, tonight, I see the princess appeal."

For several seconds, he took her in. He'd thought her to be beautiful from the first time he'd seen her picture. That opinion had grown with each of her articles he'd read over the last couple of years. Tonight, she looked stunning in a red cross-over dress which flared from her waist. She could compete with any princess, and in his eyes, she'd always win. He realised how sappy those thoughts were, so he kept them to himself.

"There's no law preventing you from being both," he said.

She turned to look at him, her lips parted, but she only sucked in a breath. *'I want you tonight.'* Dammit, he needed to stop thinking about that.

"I guess not." Her voice had turned husky. "What about you? What did you want to be when you were a kid?"

A little laugh flowed out of him, the question saving him from his lustful thoughts. "A fire truck."

Her eyes widened. "You mean a fireman?"

He shook his head. "I used to watch this cartoon about everyday heroes. The fire truck and ambulance were the resident heroes, but the ambulance was a girl."

She laughed. The sound of it arrested him for several seconds. She scooped some ice-cream into her mouth. Damn. The way her soft lips moulded around the tiny spoon sent blood rushing to his groin. He swallowed.

She'd opted for dessert, which she now ate with relish as if she didn't often allow herself the pleasure of indulging her sweet tooth. The way she licked the spoon had his mind drifting to thoughts he'd better hold at bay for the time being. Did she want him to burst at the seams? He shifted his mind from the rock in his pants back to the conversation.

"So you've always wanted to help people."

"As a child, I just wanted to be a hero, but now, I also want to support others to achieve their dreams."

"Like with the academy?"

He nodded. "Me, Don, Alpha, and Jackson also started an agency which provides grants or start-up capital for promising business ideas. In exchange, the agency gets a small percentage of the company."

Her brows hooked up, and her lips curved up in a warm smile. "What a great idea. I know a few people who dream of starting their own businesses but don't have the money."

"I'll put you in touch with the woman who runs the agency. Maybe we can help."

"Tell me about Don, Alpha, and Jackson. How did you become friends?"

"Al and I went to secondary school together, so we arranged to share a room when we got admission into the same university. Don and JQ had the next room. One day, a girl on the floor below us was beaten by her boyfriend because she didn't cook for him or some other outrageous excuse."

As he'd expected, she appeared indignant. "What?"

"She reported it, but his family had connections. They pulled strings, and the case got nowhere. The four of us vowed to teach the guy a lesson."

"Don't tell me you beat him up."

"Let's just say, he stuck to the straight and narrow afterwards."

He'd expected her to tell him off for taking matters into their hands instead of using their influence to push the legal system. Those words never came out. In fact, the look in her eyes told of admiration. Pride swelled in his chest.

A moment of silence ensued while she studied him. "You're a regular prince charming, aren't you?"

A look crossed her face, which he couldn't read in the shadows cast on her face by the limited lighting.

"Hey." He tugged her hand. "What's wrong?"

"It's nothing. Just something my mother said."

"About?"

"You."

He quirked a brow. "You've talked to your mother about me?"

"My sister," she corrected. "My mother called to ask."

"What did she say?"

"It's not important."

"Come on. You drifted off while we were talking. It can't be something trivial."

She sighed. "She thinks you're leading me on."

His first reaction was to go on the defensive. However, something else occurred to him, something far more important than her mother's opinion of him.

"What about you? Do you believe I'm leading you on?"

She stared into his eyes, her answer immediate. "No."

"That's what's important to me."

Silence stretched between them. She continued to search his face, uncertainty engraved in her expression.

"There's more. She's invited us for Easter."

"She has?"

"Don't worry. I'm going to find an excuse to give her."

"No, don't. I'd love to meet your mother."

"Are you sure? You know she's going to give you the third degree, right?"

"I expect nothing less. She's looking out for her daughter, which already makes her one of my favourite people. Besides, how else can I convince her I'm the best guy for you?"

"Best guy for me, huh? What if she still doesn't like you?"

He grinned. "Are you kidding? After I flash her this smile and tell her how much I care about you, she'll love me."

She rolled her eyes, giving in to a short laugh. "Most men would worry a little about meeting the parents of their—"

Her eyes widened before she focused too eagerly on her ice-cream. He'd bet if the lighting were better, he'd see her cheeks colour.

"Their what?" He didn't conceal his smile, suspecting why she'd stopped. "What are you to me?"

Her chest heaved with a breath she inhaled. "I don't know. We talked about getting to know each other better, but—"

"What do you want us to be?"

She swallowed. Passion, hope, longing, and a hint of panic fused together and burst into a myriad of emotions over her face.

"Say it, Chantelle," he urged. "Make us official."

"I want to be your girlfriend. Your only girlfriend, for as long as this will last."

The past two weeks with her had assured him of her commitment to seeing where their feelings led, so on some level, he'd expected the declaration. Hearing her say it, though—claim him with her words—set off a chain of sensations he couldn't control.

"I wanted you to be my girlfriend even before we met," he said. "As far as being the only, it goes without saying."

He recognised the same shock in her eyes as he'd experienced seconds earlier. Knowing and yet being taken by surprise.

"Naturally, you can expect the same from me," she said.

In that moment, he conceded defeat. His control had shattered.

◆◆◆

CHANTELLE TRIED NOT to look too impressed when they descended the stairs into the elegant lounge in the lower deck. It had enough standing room for ten to twelve people, but mirrored surfaces gave the impression of a larger space. Luxury permeated every inch of varnished mahogany and lacquered woods interplaying with crisp leather sheathing of the seating areas.

Everything about this place, this night, highlighted the vast gap between them. Could she really live up to the expectation of being his girlfriend? They should be incompatible. His money, cockiness, and sense of entitlement alone should have sent her running for the hills, yet he also calmed and excited her. No other man had managed to make her heart and body come alive quite the way he could.

"Would you like a tour?" he asked.

She returned her attention to him. He stood a metre away, one hand in his pocket, appearing nonchalant, but the stiff lines of his body gave away the reined-in passion. The intensity of his gaze told her he wanted to pounce and devour. She swallowed. Anticipation charged both her heart and nerves as the reality of the moment hit. Their first time had been frenzied, driven by adrenaline. What if the pleasure had been in the rush? What if tonight didn't measure up?

Her heart immediately countered her insecurity. From their first conversation, it had been clear she'd never experienced anything—anyone—like him. With just a look or the most innocent of touches, he engraved himself a little more on her heart. Tonight would obliterate Valentine's Day. She inhaled, letting the reassurance wash through her, then exhaled through parted lips.

"You can give me a tour in the morning," she said. "Right now, I'm interested in the master cabin."

His nose flared, and his chest expanded as he sucked in a breath. His eyes narrowed with predatory intent. She expected him to swoop down on her, but there was nothing rushed about his calculated approach. He looked every bit like a lion on the prowl.

He extended his arm, then cocked his head in the direction of the rear. "This way."

Hand-in-hand, they crossed the short space to the door, and he opened it. When they reached the master cabin, he pulled her into his arms. His heated gaze raked over her face. With mounting anticipation, her heart hammered an exuberant beat.

"Would you kiss me already?" she said.

Without waiting for him to react, she wrapped her arms around his neck, rising on tiptoes. The joining of their lips brought both fulfilment and need. His tongue probed the seam of her lips, and she opened up, sucking on it. Best tasting tongue ever. The pleasure it wielded drew a moan from her, compelling her to press into him, needing to feel the rigidity of his arousal, the only part of him that could fully satisfy the mounting hunger in her core.

With a grunt, he pulled back, leaving her lips plump and tingling. Her whimpered protest turned into another moan when his lips grazed her neck, kissing the dip below her jaw and downward to the open V of her dress. She arched her back, giving him ample access. While his mouth branded her skin, his hands sought her zip tab at the nape of her neck and eased it down. The soft fabric nearly hurt her sensitised skin as it flowed down to pool at her feet. She grunted at the relief of being free of it.

Without wasting a second, he unhooked her bra and released her breasts from their lacy confinement. He paused and stared at them for a few seconds, and her nipples tightened, ached. With an impatient whimper, she thrust her chest forward. He took in one hardened peak, alternating between teasing it with his tongue and nipping it with his teeth, then deep suckling to soothe the sting of his bite. She grabbed his hand and guided it to her other breast. He worked both, sucking each one in turn while kneading and tweaking the other with his hand.

How had she imagined tonight wouldn't compare to their first time? *Laughable.*

He released her breast and looked up at her.

"What's funny?"

"Nothing." Her breath rushed out in pants. "Just don't stop."

The corners of his lips edged up a little before he lowered his lips on hers in a ravaging kiss. Tension wound in her belly as his hands slipped between her thighs and he swept aside the damp seat of her panties to find her slick heat.

"You're so wet," he murmured against her lips.

She cupped his head, kissed him deeper. Her body trembled as he pushed two digits into her heat. A long moan staggered out of her. His responding groan hummed through her body in delicious waves.

"Oh God," she cried out, parting her thighs, offering him more.

He broke the kiss again to meet her gaze while continuing his sweet assault between her thighs, charging her desire until she thought she might explode. She closed her eyes, trying to absorb every sensation swirling within, consuming her. With trembling legs threatening to give out, she clutched him for support, digging her nails into his shoulders in the process.

"Oh, God," she cried again, riding his fingers harder. It didn't take long before her muscles began to clench, winding tight, coaxing her to embrace the tidal wave of her approaching climax.

"I love the sounds you make when you're coming," he said.

She'd meant to hang on a little, extend the bliss for just a moment longer, but hearing his voice pushed her over the edge. She let herself go as her release swept through her. He didn't relent until the last remnants of her climax shuddered out of her system.

Finally, he withdrew his hand and held her tight against him. She held on to him, waiting for her breath to return to normal. She couldn't resist taking in a drag of his intoxicating scent and letting it fill her. Renewed need blossomed in her core, and she had to stifle a moan.

She pulled back to look at him. "How do you do it? You make me come apart like that, and I still want more."

His eyes softened as he brought his hand up and traced the edge of her lower lip with his thumb. She caught a whiff of her erotic fragrance on his fingers. A shiver skittered up her spine. This time, she couldn't suppress the guttural sound emanating from her throat.

"You're easy to please, Chantelle. All I have to do is touch you, and you light up."

She sank against him, feeling his rigid arousal. She sucked in a shaky breath. He brought their lips together in a lingering kiss which left her breathing hard.

"Did I ever tell you you're full of yourself?"

He quirked his brows and laughed. "We have to fix that, then. You need to be full of me."

She gasped, unable to mask her shock. "I can't believe you just said that."

He wiggled his brows. "I did, and in a moment, you'll be saying it, too."

"I will not!"

He didn't offer a rebuttal, but his confident grin didn't need the reinforcement of words. He back-walked her until they reached the bed. She sank onto the welcoming soft sheets. While he began unbuttoning his shirt, she slipped off her panties and grimaced at how soaked it was. If she ever tried to deny his effect on her, her body would betray her in an instant. She tossed it on the bedside unit closer to her. When she returned her gaze to Lord, he'd rid himself of the shirt. She stared as one transfixed while he unbuckled his belt and unzipped the trousers.

His arousal sprang free when he yanked it down with his briefs, and she stared. Sure, she'd seen him naked before, but not like this. She didn't try to mask her appreciation as her gaze lingered on his erect manhood. Muscles quivered in her lower belly while her centre heated and wept with need. She forced her eyes to rove upwards, taking in the impressive ridges of his midsection, his massive chest and broad shoulders before settling on his face.

"Where do you want me?" he asked.

Her gaze dropped to his erection which he now stroked gently.

As much as she wanted to taste him, the insistent ache in her core superseded every other need. She parted her legs with an unmistakable invitation.

"Any special positions you prefer?" he asked as he got on the bed.

"I know it sounds boring, but right now, I want to feel your weight on top of me and look into your eyes."

He climbed above her, lowering himself onto her so his face hovered just inches above hers and his hard length rested against her core.

"Like this?"

She released a breath. It didn't make sense to feel protected and loved while crushed between him and the bed, but nothing else came close to describing the emotions swirling around her insides.

"Exactly like this."

"By the way, I don't do boring."

He moved his hips, dragging his hard length against her hot wet centre.

"Oh, yes," she moaned, matching his movements.

Their lips found each other as they performed the mock dance of love in silence broken by their heavy breathing and groans of tortured pleasure. For a moment, her need was appeased, but the pleasure mounted until she wanted more.

She widened her legs, needing to feel him closer, hoping to catch his crown and have him sink into her hot depths. But he kept slipping.

"I need more," she groaned.

He pulled back, scorching her with his hot gaze. "You want to be full of me?"

A whimper left her lips. He was not going to make her say it.

She nodded instead of a verbal response.

"I want to hear it."

"No."

He cocked his brows and groaned. "Say it, or face the consequences."

His laboured breathing told her he wanted to be inside her just as badly. He couldn't afford to play this game too long.

"You're not going to stop," she teased.

"Refuse to say it," he threatened, "and I'll make you come like this."

He increased his pace, creating friction against her clit, then angled himself to reach between them to knead her breasts. Intense pleasure assaulted her.

"No," she cried, forcing her pelvis to disengage.

It didn't work. Her body wanted this too much. Needed him too much.

"What will it be, Chantelle?"

She swore. Infuriatingly, he gave a soft laugh, already savouring his victory.

"I want to be full of you," she said.

He stilled at once, rolling off her to reach one of the drawer units next to the bed. He took out a condom and ripped it open. While he sheathed himself, she took the moment to dial her desire back a notch. She wanted to enjoy an extended ride.

He resumed his position on top of her, and she guided him inside her. The fusion of their bodies surpassed what she remembered, and from the harsh sound emanating from him, he felt it, too. Without breaking eye contact, he began to move with a steady rhythm.

"Chantelle," he grunted.

He rotated his hips as he drove in and out of her, stimulating her sensitive bud in the process. Intermittently, he dipped his head to sip from her lips.

"Oh, Lord," she mewled.

A deep throbbing in her stomach signalled the start of her climax.

"This feels incredible," he said. "Your body is …"

He shook his head.

Pure Heaven, her mind completed the thought. She sobbed as the contractions began in her core. She grabbed his ass, urging him deeper and faster while her other hand curved around his head, seeking for something to hold.

With a frustrated whimper, she swore and reached up to grab a tuft of her own hair. His hand covered hers, and she released her hair to grip his fingers. Her heart filled and expanded with trust and love and other emotions she couldn't find words for, but she knew what they meant. She'd fallen in love with Lord McKenzie.

CHAPTER 19

"WHAT'S MAKING HIM SO happy?"

Lord jerked out of his thoughts and encountered Jackson's questioning gaze.

"What's the only reason a grown man would sport a stupid smile like that?" Don responded.

A knowing grin spread on Alpha's face. "The almighty pus—"

"Shut up," Lord snapped.

Three pairs of eyes stared back at him with varying degrees of 'what-the-fuck?' expressions. Understandable. Of the four, he prided himself in being the laidback one, never letting anything get to him. Objecting to what they'd deem to be normal banter was out of character. However, this conversation concerned Chantelle. Though he considered the three men his closest friends, he never wanted to hear them speak about her in any unsavoury manner. He absolutely didn't want them referring to her intimate body parts.

"Don't worry, man. You'll be back in Accra tomorrow," Don said with a tilt at the corners of his lips. "At least, you're not pretending to be Deconte's boyfriend anymore."

Lord grimaced while Al and Jackson laughed, returning the mood to what it had been before he'd drifted off thinking about Chantelle. He hadn't seen her since Sunday when they'd returned from Ada. She'd had a late-night assignment on Monday, so they hadn't been able to meet in the evening as he'd hoped.

He'd flown to Kumasi the following day in preparation for a courtesy call on the Asantehene with some of the company executives on Wednesday. Although the Kumasi International Airport was a government project, anyone who wanted to do business on such a scale in the Garden City knew getting the blessing of the Ashanti king was imperative.

He'd stayed an extra day to support Alpha who was opening a new club in Kumasi today. Naturally, Jackson and Don had also flown in this morning to support their friend. Four full days of not seeing Chantelle affected his concentration. Their daily video chats didn't have the same impact. The problem with being at this launch party was that he couldn't help thinking about her and the night they'd met—at a nightclub like this one.

The snapping of fingers yanked him back to the present.

"Again?" Jackson said.

"Did you hear anything I just said?" Don asked at the same time.

He swore. "Sorry, guys. It's been a long couple of days."

Alpha snorted, giving him a 'yeah, right' look.

Jackson chuckled. "Who is she, anyway?"

He gave a resigned sigh. He might as well let the cat out of the bag. "Her name is Chantelle Sah. She works for *Odopa* Magazine."

"Wait a second. You mean Val's Day girl?" Alpha asked.

"She has a name."

Thankfully, he managed to keep the edge out of his voice. His friends had no clue how he felt about her, so it wouldn't help to act like a caveman whenever her name arose. Then again, when it came to Chantelle, he had little control over his emotions because everything became personal.

"*Chale*, you know we agreed we don't have to keep the ladies' names unless they last more than a few dates."

"Yeah, man," the other two chimed in.

The four of them were considered playboys, and despite his many denials, the title wasn't entirely undeserved. For various valid reasons, none of them had had a serious girlfriend in a long while. Since their liaisons were often just hook-ups, it had become easier to remember each other's dates by the events or some other aspect of the outing rather than their names. He hadn't realised how obnoxious it sounded until it applied to someone he cared about.

"Yes, she's the lady you met on Valentine's day. Her name is Chantelle Sah." He divided a glare between the three. "Learn it."

"*Chale*, don't bundle me with them. I know her name," Don said.

Alpha quirked his brows. "How does this chap know about her and we don't? JQ, back me up here."

He chuckled, making an effort to lighten up. "I needed a yacht."

"So it's serious?" Jackson asked. "You have a woman, and you're keeping her under the radar?"

"She doesn't like the publicity, and frankly, it's nice to have her all to myself."

It wouldn't last, of course. If he wanted to get the media off his back, the best strategy would be to make the news public and do something he'd never bothered with—task his PR agency to keep her out of the news as much as possible. It might cost him, because they'd most likely have to buy some of the photos to keep them out of the media. For Chantelle, it would all be worth it.

"She's special," he found himself saying. "I've never met anyone more genuine. She's not blinded by the fame or the money, you know."

Alpha sniggered. "Yea, we get it. The sex is that good."

Lord levelled his friend with a glare.

"Don't be a dick, Al," Don intervened, despite his lips curving up.

Alpha put up his hands in mock-surrender.

"Now you got that off your chest, can we enjoy the party?" Jackson said.

As if on cue, a group of women dressed for the occasion were ushered into the VIP lounge where they sat. While his friends played a game of which-of-them-are-you-taking-home-tonight, he sat back and sipped his drink while thinking about Chantelle. He couldn't wait to have her back in his arms tomorrow night.

"OH MY GOD, this can't be happening."

Another involuntary series of spasms overtook Chantelle. Her stomach lurched, and she retched, gasping for air. Only saliva came out—a lot of it, sapping her energy. After the release, her stomach settled, leaving a pit in her belly. Raising her head from the sink, she stood, shaking, staring disbelievingly at her reflection in the mirror. She backed away until she bumped into the wall, her mind in turmoil.

She couldn't be pregnant. If she was, the only time it could have happened was Valentine's Day. The condom broke. Lord's dire news the following day echoed in her head. But she'd taken the morning-after pill as directed. Granted, no contraceptive provided a hundred percent protection, but could she really have fallen within the margin of error? Twice?

No. Her mind rejected the notion. It had to be something else, something she might have eaten. Or maybe just the fact that she hadn't seen Lord for this entire week, as he'd been in Kumasi since Tuesday. Besides, wasn't it too early to show any symptoms?

"I'm not pregnant," she mumbled. "I refuse to be pregnant."

Even as she repeated the words like a mantra, she couldn't ignore the signs: tender and sensitive breasts; the uncharacteristic crying in Lord's car after spending a wonderful afternoon with his family; the cramps she'd experienced the past two mornings; the unusual craving for corn flakes and plain yogurt yesterday.

She sucked in a breath which didn't calm her racing heartbeat. Despite the evidence, she decided to take a test before she'd believe herself to be carrying Lord McKenzie's baby.

Lord!

Oh, God. What would he say? He'd be returning from Kumasi today. She couldn't hide this from him, yet the thought of telling him … unthinkable.

Her phone rang. She checked the screen and held her breath when she saw his photo flashing. With her mind in turmoil, talking to him would be the worst idea right now. One look at her image, one word from her, and he'd know something was wrong.

She cut the call with an auto "I'll call you back" text message. To compose herself, she thought, because she really wanted to hear his voice, to see his smile. She wanted him to assure her this was the best news he'd ever received.

She'd be a fool to believe that lie. He wanted perfection, and a pregnant girlfriend didn't qualify. She'd have to do this alone. A throbbing materialised in her head as panic gripped her.

Was this history repeating itself? She couldn't help drawing parallels between now and the past. Finding out about being pregnant while the man responsible was away supposedly on business. Had Lord truly gone to Kumasi for business? He'd attended a party last night. Had he been with another woman? She couldn't handle that. *Please, God.*

She shut her eyes, shoving the thought out of her mind, forcing away the accompanying tears. No. She wouldn't do this to herself. She trusted Lord with every fibre of her being. She'd seen him with his family, witnessed the way his brother's kids adored him, and children didn't lie.

Fool. Was once not enough? She couldn't let it happen again.

Somehow, she managed to call up enough resolve to shed her nightie and step into the shower. She couldn't let her internal turmoil affect her day, because work was the only thing in her life that made sense right now.

Her day was, nonetheless, cast in a shadow. Every instinct begged her to hide somewhere and have a good cry. Yet, she carried on with a constant fix of determination, thinking, not only about Lord, but also about Martin and her first pregnancy. She'd been elated, eagerly awaiting his return, so they could celebrate the new life they'd created. They had discussed marriage weeks before, so naturally, she'd spent hours online looking at rings and bridal gowns. Little had she known how quickly it would all fall apart.

At least, with Lord, she had no illusions of eternal bliss no matter how great their time together had been. He might be interested now, but once he found out about the baby, she wouldn't need to ask him to stop calling. A child out of wedlock was hardly an ideal situation for anybody, let alone someone searching for perfection, something she couldn't offer him if she were indeed pregnant.

Speaking of his calls, it seemed the more she avoided them, the more persistent he became. By three o'clock, he'd already called five times. Already, fatigue had set in. Since she'd completed her tasks for the day, she decided to take the rest of the afternoon off. Time to face what she'd been avoiding all day.

Dufie stopped her as she passed by her desk. "Chantelle, are you okay?"

She shook her head. "Yes, just feeling a little under the weather."

"Have you taken anything for it?"

"I'll pass by the pharmacy on my way home."

Luckily, she wouldn't have to go far, as there was a big pharmacy just opposite their building.

"Good plan. Enjoy your weekend."

Moments later, she sat in her car manoeuvring into the traffic on the main road. She drove a few metres to a set of traffic lights, then U-turned onto the other side of the dual carriageway. Exiting into the parking lot in front of the small shopping centre housing a pharmacy and several boutiques, she found a parking space. Slowly, she got out and walked towards the entrance as if doomsday awaited her on the other side.

Inside, she dilly-dallied until she'd gone through every aisle but the one she needed. After ten minutes, she finally ventured in, stopping in front of the shelf. Several brands stared back at her. She picked two different ones, compared the claims on the packaging, and eventually decided to take both.

"You're avoiding my calls again."

She stifled a scream. For a few seconds, she couldn't feel her pulse, until she sucked in a breath which seemed to jumpstart her heart. Death would have been a more welcome choice than facing Lord, but her heart had never beaten with more enthusiasm.

In reflex, she swiped her hand behind her, hiding the evidence as she turned to face him. Her jaw nearly dropped as she took in his clean-shaven look and the grey suit that gloved over his broad shoulders and athletic body.

"What are you doing here?" she asked, her voice a shade above a whisper.

"I followed you from your office. I got there as you drove off, but then I noticed you parking here and decided to come after you." He studied her face. "I wanted to make sure you were okay. Obviously, you're not."

When he looked like he'd just walked off the cover of a magazine and talked with concern, it messed with her mind. She couldn't allow that.

"You shouldn't have followed me," she said.

He paused. Must have been the steel in her voice. His expression turned to something unreadable, and he seemed to, now, notice where they stood. The look in his eyes shifted to dawning as he stared from the shelf to her.

His eyes narrowed with a hard expression. Was it anger? Hate? Something else?

"Are you pregnant?"

"No." Her voice quivered.

"Do you think you are?"

"I'm not pregnant."

"Then why are you standing here?"

"That's not what I'm buying."

"I saw what you picked." He held her gaze.

Her heart raced, waiting for him to turn and walk away. Surely, he'd want to maintain a clear conscience by not knowing for certain. Instead, he took a step forward, and then another. He stood so close, she could feel the heat emanating from his sexy body. He seemed taller, more imposing, his six-two frame dwarfing her.

He brought his arms around her, tempting her to melt into him and savour the joy of being enfolded in his arms. She wanted to sigh happily and nuzzle up against him. She realised her mistake in allowing him to come close when he swiped the packets out of her hand and stepped back.

He took one look at them. "Let's go."

"I can do this myself." *You big bully.*

"I'm not letting you do it alone, Chantelle."

Determined not to be pushed around, she stood her ground. "I'm not going anywhere with you."

"If you don't, I'll carry you out of here on my shoulder."

"You wouldn't dare."

He narrowed his eyes, his stance intimidating. "Do you really want to test me?"

One look at him, and she decided not to call his bluff. "Don't you have a meeting or something this afternoon?"

She snatched the packs from him and started walking towards the counter with confidence she didn't feel.

"That can easily be taken care of," he said, and she heard the beeping sounds of his phone as he dialled a number. "Mrs. Bonsu, please cancel my meeting this afternoon. Give the minister my apologies and tell him I'll personally call to reschedule. Thank you."

After hanging up, he said, "See? No meeting."

Arrogant. Who did he think he was cancelling meetings and ordering her about? She chose to ignore him as she placed the packs on the counter. He handed his card to the teller before she could retrieve money from her purse.

"How are you?" he asked the teller.

She watched with disgust as he smiled charmingly at the woman, basking in the attention from all the feminine eyes around. He certainly enjoyed being centre stage. Not that she cared. Why should she?

The teller ripped the receipt from the machine and slipped it into a small plastic bag with their purchase. She smiled sweetly at Lord and handed the bag over to him. *Hello, it's for me, not Don Juan*.

"Thank you," Lord said, turning to her with the same fake smile. "Shall we?"

She glared at him but followed him until they were outside. "Can I have that, please?"

"Did you think I was joking?" he asked. "I want to be there when you take the test."

"I'm not going to do it now. I have somewhere to go." She hadn't expected him to buy it, but a girl could hope, couldn't she?

"Fine, I'll go wherever it is with you."

Her shoulders slumped. "You're a stubborn man, Lord McKenzie."

He shrugged. "Persistent; not stubborn."

With an infuriating smile, he deactivated his car alarm. "We're taking my car."

His tone left no room for argument. He opened the door and tossed the bag onto the back seat, then quirked his eyebrows as if to ask, "Are you coming?"

She harrumphed and got in. Since he'd confiscated the test pack, she had little choice. Folding her arms, she sat straight and focused her eyes ahead of her. She wasn't going to talk to him.

The journey to his house proceeded in silence. Evidently, he didn't want to talk, either, which took the wind out of her sails and made her blood boil hotter. When they arrived, she made no attempt to get out of the car. By this time, nervousness about taking the dreaded test had overpowered the anger. He opened the door for her. Getting out, her gaze dropped to the bag in his hands. She snatched it, glaring at him for good measure before making her way to the door.

Inside, she took out the two packs. Putting one down, she started opening the other.

Lord picked the one she'd left on the table. "So what do we do with it?"

"You don't know?"

"How would I know?"

"I just thought—"

"I must have done this many times?" He threw his hands up in aggravation. "God, Chantelle."

He looked like he wanted to grab her by the shoulders and shake her. If the situation hadn't been a precarious one, he probably would have done so.

"I hate to break it to you, but you're the only woman I've impregnated. I hope that makes you happy."

Why was he talking as if he believed her to be carrying his child? He was supposed to wish the opposite. God knew some part of her did, as insensitive as it may have sounded. With a contrite sigh, she opened the box in her hand and took out the stick.

"You need to put urine on the tip and wait for five minutes. If it shows one line there," she indicated the result window, "then it's negative."

"What if it's positive?"

"There'll be two lines." She hesitated.

They proceeded to the guest bathroom. Concentrating on the task at hand, she didn't give more than a cursory glance at the plush marble floor or the Jacuzzi or the soft fluffy linen. She peed on the stick and placed it on the cistern, covering it with a piece of toilet paper, then washed her hands and exited the bathroom.

She found Lord leaning against the wall just outside. The noise of the door shutting made him turn. He'd taken off his coat and tie and unbuttoned his shirt. She tried not to stare at the exposed skin or remember how his taut chest had felt under her touch.

"What now?" he asked.

"We wait."

She led the way back to the sitting room.

The five-minute wait stretched for an eternity. She alternated between sitting and pacing. Countless thoughts raced through her mind, both present concerns and past worries, and she couldn't focus on any one of them. She glanced at Lord. How could he be so calm? She'd expected him to panic. Be angry. Something! From his composure, he could have been waiting to enter a meeting, and you wouldn't have known the difference. Truth be told, she appreciated his presence. If nothing else, his calmness steadied her nerves.

"It's been five minutes," he said.

She stopped pacing. Her reluctance must have shown, because he suggested they go together.

Opening the door, they entered the bathroom. She looked at him, silently imploring him to lift the tissue. He did, and she stared in horror at the two, clear pink lines confirming what she'd known all along. The room started spinning, and she became lightheaded. Her legs gave way, and she began to go down. He caught her, holding her steady.

"I don't understand." Though she had all the signs, she'd still hoped for one of the many other reasons for pregnancy-like symptoms.

She looked at him in confusion. For the first time all afternoon, she saw signs of worry in his eyes. Had they been there before? He ran a hand over his hair, stopping at the nape of his neck.

"You said you took the pill." His quiet voice didn't veil the accusation.

She recoiled from him as though he had a contagious disease. "What are you accusing me of?"

"You refused to let me go with you, and I accepted your word when you said you'd taken care of it."

"I did!"

"Then what happened?"

"I don't know. It didn't work."

He rubbed the top of his close-cropped hair. She'd never seen him ruffled, and the sight increased her own anxiety. So much for hoping he'd be happy about it.

"I shouldn't have let you go alone. I should have been there."

"To do what? Make sure I can read the instructions?" she replied. "You think I planned this?"

"You couldn't have, obviously with the condom breaking. However, given my position, it isn't inconceivable that a woman would take advantage of it."

"What?"

His words hit her like a tidal wave of destruction, but the mistrust in his eyes cut her deeper.

"I'm not like your other women, Lord, and I thought you knew that."

"All I'm saying is—"

"Save it."

Unwilling to hear further accusations, she walked past him back into the sitting room and sat down on the couch, her heart racing from an emotion stronger than anger. Pain sliced through her chest begging for release, but she refused to cry. *Not here, not now*. From the corner of her eye, she saw his shadow darken the coffee table. He came to squat by her side, reaching for her.

"Don't touch me." She snatched her hand away.

His big shoulders slumped, and he withdrew his hand. "Chantelle, I'm sorry."

"While we're throwing about accusations, why don't you answer for your part in this?" she said. "Did you put the condom on correctly? How long had it been in your wallet, huh? Or maybe despite all your wealth, you're too cheap to buy quality products."

He winced. His pained look silenced the rest of her tirade. For several seconds, they glared at each other, the gravity of her words humming between them. Her lips twitched with the need to soothe him with an apology, but old scars on her heart ripped open and began to sting, reminding her she needed to look out for her wellbeing first.

She stood. "Take me back to my car."

"Can we, please, talk about this?"

She shook her head. "I don't feel like talking to you."

She'd thought they had something special, that their time together had shown her the kind of man he was. She'd defended him when her mother had warned her against falling for his charms, yet at the first sign of adversity, his first instinct had been to doubt her.

"Please, just—"

"Take me to my car, Lord, or I'm calling a taxi." She grabbed her bag and the unused test packet to show her seriousness.

"I'll drop you off." As one defeated, he grabbed his car keys.

Feeling more crushed than he looked, she followed him back into the car.

"I'm sorry for what I said, but you have to see it from my point of view," he started.

She stared at him as though seeing him for the first time. "Your point of view? What about mine? I'm just as shocked as you are, so I don't need your insinuations about me trying to trap you."

He started to say something, but she wasn't listening. Her mind highlighted her foolishness and the cruelty of Fate. Fear gripped her. She couldn't do it over again. She couldn't survive if she lost another baby. Her head felt stuffy and began to ache from all the pressure of holding in the tears. Finally, the waters broke loose, and she wept.

He stopped the car to rub her back. "I'm here, Chantelle. We'll get through it, okay?"

She didn't have the energy to push his hand away, so he continued to comfort her. Soon, crying turned to sniffs, and she wiped her eyes. She sat back, quietly, as he restarted the car.

Back in front of the pharmacy, he parked. "I'm sorry. I should never have said those things."

"You're right. You shouldn't have, but I'm glad you did. Now I know where I stand with you."

Her flat tone managed to conceal the turmoil of emotions within her. He cupped her cheek, and her heart shuddered even in the midst of breaking. She stiffened, steeled herself against the effect of his touch.

"I didn't mean to hurt you," he whispered.

"And yet, you did."

His mother had thought she would hurt him, having no idea how much more vulnerable she was. The irony of it.

"I can't tell you how sorry I am."

As his hand left her face, she released the breath she'd been holding, then squared her shoulders in an effort to pull herself together and do what had to be done.

"I'm sorry, too," she said. "Please don't call me. Don't text, and don't look for me."

"Chantelle, we're having a baby. You can't just—"

"I'll take care of the baby."

"Take care of the—are you thinking of having an abortion?"

She continued as if he hadn't interjected. "This is a less than ideal situation, for you, I know. Don't worry. I'm not going to create any negative publicity."

"I don't care about publicity. I care about you—"

She shook her head. "You don't have to say that. After all, we made each other no promise of love or marriage, so parting ways shouldn't be hard, right?"

Except that it was.

"We need to talk about this."

She met his gaze, wishing her heart would stop aching so much. "There's nothing to talk about."

"What are you saying?"

"Goodbye, Lord."

She got out of his car and made her way to hers. Without a backward glance, she sparked the engine and drove off.

She didn't go home, lest he follow her there. It hurt too much to look at him, yet she might not be able to resist if he showed up. His presence would make her want to be in his arms.

How could she be angry with him and want him at the same time? She needed to stop thinking about him. The less he stayed on her mind, the easier it would be to move on. If she didn't do this now, she'd be holding her breath waiting for him to leave. A man like Lord didn't take anything less than the best. And this situation was far from ideal.

Slipping on her Bluetooth headset, she called the one person who could make her feel better.

"Dani, I'm coming over," she said, when her sister picked up.

"Is everything okay?"

"No." Chantelle blinked away tears.

"Sis, what's wrong?"

"I can't talk over the phone."

"Okay, drive carefully," Danielle said.

Hanging up, she put the phone on 'silent.'

CHAPTER 20

THE SISTERS HUGGED AS soon as Chantelle stepped out of her car. Neither spoke until they'd entered the house. A sense of calm settled on her. Danielle's home always had that effect even though it couldn't be more different from hers. While she kept her décor tasteful but simple, her sister had gone all out with a full suite of sitting room furniture, throw pillows matching the curtains and complementing her full floor carpeting, strategically placed potted plants, family photos adorning the walls—the whole nine yards.

Danielle had quit her job as an event planner to be a stay-at-home-mum after having her children. It didn't stop her from using her organisational skills in her home. The result was a welcoming space which conveyed the assurance of safety and love. A sanctuary—precisely what Chantelle needed right now.

Leading her to a comfortable armchair, Danielle muted the TV, which was on a children's channel although the girls were in school.

"Do you want a drink?" her sister asked.

She shook her head, watching Danielle pack away some documents on her centre table. Most likely her family's meal plan and the kids' activity schedule for the month. The woman was more organised than some CEOs.

Danielle finally came to sit beside her. "What's wrong, Chantie?"

"I messed up," she said. "Big time."

"Is it work?" Danielle asked, concern written all over her face. "Did your story leak again?"

"No."

She found herself fidgeting with the remote and flipping channels on the TV. Some irrational part of her wanted to keep quiet, as if withholding the information would somehow nullify the whole thing.

"Is it Lord?"

At the mention of his name, her heart pitter-pattered shamelessly. She missed him already. Why did this have to happen now? Why couldn't Fate give them a chance to get to know each other better before delivering a blow like this? Why hadn't the pill done its job? How could he accuse her of not taking it in the first place? How could he expect her to trust him when he couldn't extend her the same courtesy?

Fat tears dropped from her eyes as her lips quivered. Without another word, Danielle hugged her. They remained like that for several seconds before pulling apart.

"What happened?"

She fished a handkerchief from her pocket and dried her face. "I'm pregnant."

Danielle's jaw dropped. "What? With whom?"

"With Lord, of course."

"What do you mean by of course? You just started dating him."

"Yes, but last weekend wasn't the first time."

Danielle's lips moved, but no sound came out. She saw the unasked question in her sister's eyes. When?

"Valentine's Day."

"Didn't you meet on Valentine's Day?" She raised her hands immediately. "I'm not judging, but it doesn't sound like you at all. Didn't you insist on protection?"

"The condom split, and the Plan B pill I took didn't work."

"Does he know?"

A dry laugh escaped from her. "Oh, he knows, and he thinks I lied about taking the pill."

"What?" As expected, her sister looked outraged.

"You should have seen the aversion in his eyes when he said it. Like I'm some gold-digging woman trying to trap him." She blinked away another onslaught of tears threatening to form.

"Mum was right. He made me feel like a princess, and I let my guard down. I gave him the power to hurt me. What was I thinking?"

"You were thinking he makes you happy, and you deserve some joy."

She had been content those moments spent in his presence, and especially in his arms. Her mind drifted back to their weekend away. They'd docked the next morning in a small fishing village in the Volta Region, where they'd taken a walk on the beach and eaten coconut for breakfast. They'd gone local for lunch, eating *akple* with okra soup and dry fish in a chop bar. It had been great to be out with him without worrying about their photos making it to the papers or social media. They'd returned to the yacht and made love again while sailing back to Ada Foah.

She shook off the memory, bringing her thoughts back to the present.

Danielle sought her eyes. "The day I came over with the girls, you were glowing. I've never seen you like that."

"I was?"

"Yes, and if he can make you glow like that, there must be something there."

"Not anymore. After what he said, I lashed out, too, and told him I never wanted to see him again."

"You're having his child. Do you really think he'll let you shut him out?"

Her heart thudded. She'd broken up with him, but she couldn't keep him away from his child if he truly wanted to be involved.

"You're assuming he wants this baby."

"Of course he does. After all, he's going to need an heir for all those billions."

She huffed, even though a small part of her lit up with imaginings of being a family with him and watching him play with their child as he'd done with his brother's kids. She gave herself a mental shake. No point in dwelling on impossible things. Instead, she changed the subject.

"Do you have any food?"

Her sister's quirked brows suggested she knew exactly what Chantelle was doing though she didn't call her out. "I made some soup today. It's really spicy."

Her mouth watered. While worrying about the test, she hadn't had much of an appetite for lunch, but now, with the uncertainty over, her desire for food had returned full force.

"Spicy soup sounds perfect."

"I'll get you some." Danielle stood. "In the meantime, I have an exercise for you."

She disappeared into an adjoining room she used as a study and returned after a moment with a magazine. She opened to a full-page picture of Lord.

"Do you want to draw warts on his face or stick pins into him?"

She heaved a sigh, looking longingly at the image. He was gorgeous in the picture, but it still diminished him somehow, because it told nothing of his charm or his searing kisses.

An involuntary smile began to tease the corners of her lips as she stared sadly at the picture. If only she could reverse the condom breaking, because then, she wouldn't be pregnant, and he wouldn't have had to mistrust her. She wanted him.

"Oh my God," Danielle said. "You're in love with him."

"I'm not."

Even in her ears, it sounded too defensive. Yes, she'd thought herself to be in love with him, but she'd only known him what, four weeks? Five? Though, admittedly, her feelings for him, be it anger or passion or jealousy, surpassed anything she'd felt for anyone else. It was still an extremely short period to truly fall in love. Life didn't work that way.

"Prove it." Danielle placed a pen and a box of pins on the table. "Stick it to him where it matters."

"Fine." She took out a pin. Hesitating for a moment, she pushed it into his forehead, feeling sorry she had to destroy the photo.

"I meant his family jewels," Danielle said, folding her arms.

"You're being mean."

"It's just a picture, Chantie." Danielle selected a pin, her look conveying her determination to demonstrate what she meant.

"Dani, stop it." She snatched the magazine from the table. "The new baby must be a boy. You weren't this vicious while pregnant with either of the girls."

Her sister scoffed. "I rest my case."

She waddled off to the kitchen, returning a couple of minutes later with a bowl of soup on a small tray. "Here you go."

She received the platter from Danielle. The smell of the dry shrimp and smoked fish reached her nose first, making her stomach growl. She brought the bowl to her nose and took in a long whiff of its aroma before dipping the spoon in for her first sip. The spiciness hit her in just the right places, killing any evidence of nausea.

"Hmm, this is so good." Her eyes watered as the soup traced a peppery path down to her stomach. "It's just what I need." She noticed her sister's expectant gaze. "What?"

Danielle swatted her on the arm. "I can't believe you slept with him, and you didn't tell me. How many times have we spoken and seen each other since Valentine's Day?"

She put the bowl of soup to her mouth and drank directly from it, trying her best to ignore her sister's eager look.

"So ..." Danielle urged. "Day One? How did he wheedle his way around your self-imposed vow of celibacy?"

Though her emotions ran helter-skelter, a smile broke free. "I'm not talking about it, Dani."

"Avoidance tactics." Danielle made an exaggerated show of shaking her head. "So mature."

She rolled her eyes. "The truth is I don't know. He just did."

"Whatever it is, I think this is a blessing in disguise."

"How? I'm having a baby with a man I just broke up with who thinks I'm after his money."

"This baby defied all odds to exist," Danielle said. "Some might say it's a miracle."

Her sister always had a way of looking at the bright side of things. Something she had in common with Lord.

Hold it right there. What would possess her to compare her sister to him?

"I'm going to say something. Don't bite my head off." A beat passed. "Is it possible you overreacted?"

"I can't believe you're supporting him."

"I'm not. It's just … well. If it hadn't been about you, would it really be unreasonable for him to think a woman had taken advantage of the situation?"

"The point is, it *was* me, and it's not just about what he said. It's how he said it. How he looked at me as if I'd betrayed him."

"Which makes me think he has feelings for you. What matters is whether you two can be happy together."

"I doubt that very much. If his reaction to this was my trying to trick him, doesn't it say what he really thinks of me?" She picked up her phone and accessed her call log. "Look at this. Nothing from him. Lord doesn't do silent. If he really had feelings and he wanted me back, he'd have called or sent a text by now."

"Maybe he's working up the courage to call you."

"Somehow, I find it hard to believe he would feel intimidated by anyone, least of all me."

"Never underestimate the power of a woman."

She shook her head. "You're such a romantic."

She didn't want to confront the longing in her heart. Doing so would tempt her to return and beg him to take her back. That wasn't an option. If losing him after being together for such a short period could make her heart feel as if it were being ripped out of her chest, then what would happen if he broke her heart after they'd dated for a longer period? She didn't want to know.

LORD SLAPPED HIS hands together and regarded all twelve pairs of management eyes focused on him.

"I'm happy to announce we've been short-listed for the Kumasi International Airport project, making McKenzie Contractors the only Ghanaian company left in the running."

As murmurs of congratulations filled the boardroom, he forced himself to smile. At least, he couldn't complain about work, which was more than could be said about his love life.

"This is good news," one of the department heads said.

"Indeed, it is." He paused for the murmurs to die down. "Congratulations to all of you and your staff for the work and the hours you put into the proposal development stage. That was the easy part. The competition will get tougher, but I have confidence in this team."

A few "thank you, sirs" were mumbled before he went on. "If there's nothing else, I'd like to conclude this meeting. Don't forget; we're closing at four today for a small party downstairs."

While the department heads spent a few minutes interacting with each other, he headed for his office. He checked his watch. *Two o'clock.* Taking mental stock of his schedule, he realised he had little to do between now and four o'clock. More than enough time to dash to *Odopa* Magazine, or wherever Chantelle was, and back. But he'd stay put for the same reason he hadn't called since they'd taken the test.

He was CEO of a *Ghana Club 100* company, arguably one of the most influential people in the country, dammit. Why did the idea of facing her again scare him? How many times, over the past week, hadn't he wished he could take back his accusation? In the time he'd known her, she'd given him no reason to doubt her integrity. He'd allowed past events to cloud his judgement, leading him to hurt her—exactly what he'd promised not to do.

"I don't want to be disturbed for the next hour," he said to his secretary when he returned to his office.

"Yes, sir."

Mrs. Bonsu insisted on addressing him formally, which bugged him, but he'd come to accept it. Being on the verge of turning fifty, she was set in her ways.

"Mr. McKenzie," she called as he opened his door.

He turned.

"Is everything okay?" She studied him with motherly concern, bringing the number of times Mrs. Bonsu had got personal to a handful. The last time was when his grandmother had passed away last year.

"It will be," he replied. As soon as he saw Chantelle again. "Thanks for asking."

Shutting the door, he walked straight to the window and gazed out. Now he knew why some people avoided the entanglement of love. They were saving themselves from this place he found himself. He wasn't sure how he was still standing. Everything ached. He'd never known being responsible for someone's pain could actually hurt you more. Thoughts of Chantelle and how she fared kept him awake at night, yet he couldn't shut her out of his mind.

He missed her voice, her laughter, the way she glared at him when he teased. He missed the way it felt to hold her in his arms, to make love with her. Most of all, he missed the way he felt around her—happy without explanation. He didn't know how much longer he could stand not seeing her, but he had to be careful about their next meeting, or he might never see her again.

The finality of her words, the look in her eyes when she'd said goodbye, haunted him. As if for a moment, she'd traded living for simply existing. And it was all his doing.

Had that really only been a week ago? It felt like forever. He returned to his desk, where his copy of *Odopa* magazine now constantly lay open to her page. He couldn't believe he'd doodled around her picture. His friends should see him now.

His eyes misted over. His body had never played host to so many emotions raging violently for dominance. The sheer intensity of it crippled his senses. Burying his face in his hands, he blew air out of his mouth to ease the burning in his eyes.

He heard his door open and lifted his head in time to see his father enter.

"I've been meaning to talk to you," the older man said, coming to sit down. "Is there something going on I don't know about?"

"No. Everything's fine."

Concern etched in his father's features. "Are you sure? You haven't been yourself the past couple of days, and today, you seem stressed and somewhat distracted."

"Don't worry. It's not going to affect my work. It hasn't so far."

"That's not what I'm concerned about, son. Your mother and I are worried about you."

"I'm fine." He forced a smile and made the quick decision to sidestep any further inquiry into his emotional state. "Actually, Papa, it's good you're here. I've been thinking about the pitch for the Kumasi Airport."

"What about it?"

"The ministry will be releasing the short-listed companies tomorrow. I think we should call a press conference to share our plans with the media. Just the business papers, if you like."

His father thought about it. "How much of the plans are we sharing?"

"We'll give them a general overview of what we propose for the airport, highlighting a few of the standard requirements from the brief, so we won't be divulging any of our unique propositions. Basically, we assure them of our commitment to use our knowledge of the local market in finalising our design."

Not for the first time, he was grateful he had a company to run and a few thousand people relying on his leadership. It was the only thing keeping him focused.

"Hmm," the older man nodded. "Have we checked with the ministry if we are allowed to hold a press conference?"

"Yes, I spoke to the minister this morning."

"Let's do it, then," his father said.

"Great. I'll schedule it for Monday afternoon. That gives us three days to prepare. Mrs. Bonsu and the PR Manager will make the necessary arrangements."

His father stood. "How's Chantelle?"

For a second, words failed him. His father had never enquired about any of his girlfriends. Well, he had never introduced anyone else to his parents, but neither had he ever kept any girlfriend a secret.

"She's fine," he said, hoping that was the truth.

Worry had worked his insides into knots, and yet, it wasn't his body going through changes.

His father nodded. "I'm going to tell your mother she shouldn't worry about you."

As the older man made to leave, Lord called him back. "Papa, there's something else."

His father turned around.

"How do you feel about having a new grandchild?"

"Jane's pregnant?"

"No." He braced himself for the disappointment the older man would regard him with once he broke the news. "Chantelle is."

His father's eyebrows shot up, but the displeasure he expected wasn't there. "How long have you known?"

"A few days."

A moment of silence followed.

"I didn't know you were dating her."

"It's complicated, Papa."

Given a second chance, he'd do things differently. Chantelle carrying his baby was the most wonderful thing to ever happen to him. He'd just have liked to marry her first. In that moment, he made his decision.

"I'm going to ask her to be my wife."

Brave words, considering she'd walked out of his life. At least, that was what she thought, but he intended to convince her to take him back.

His father came to sit down again. "It's the right thing to do."

"I'm not doing it because it's the right thing." Confessing his feelings seemed to take a load off his shoulders. He wanted to rush out and yell it to the world, but for now, he'd have to settle for an audience of one. "I love her."

"She's a lovely young woman," came the cautious reply. "But are you sure about this?"

"I've never been more certain about anything in my life, Papa."

"Son, marriage and babies are miles apart from bachelorhood. Your life isn't going to be yours anymore. Your family has to come before you every time."

Great. Thirty-three years old, and he was getting 'the talk.'

"I know, Papa. It didn't happen the way I would've hoped, but I want her in my life." He picked up a pen and fiddled with it absent-mindedly. "When we received the news about making it to the next stage of the pitch, she was the first person I wanted to tell."

His father nodded, a knowing smile playing on the corners of his lips. "Your mother and I liked her when you brought her over. So did Ohene and his family."

Lord smiled, remembering the drawing Ato had made for her. He'd known for sure, then, he was in love with her. The length of time he'd known her didn't matter. Only the way he felt. The past week without her had been Hell. Somehow, talking to his father seemed to have lifted some of the heaviness.

"There's only one problem," he said. "She's not talking to me."

His father smiled. "If you love her, I'm sure you'll find a way to get her to listen."

CHAPTER 21

THE WEEKEND COULDN'T HAVE arrived sooner. Chantelle had just finished her new morning routine: throw up, brush her teeth and wash her face. Back in her room, she performed her next 'new routine' task—stand naked in front of the mirror to study her body for any changes. Other than her tender breasts, there didn't seem to be anything different. Yet, she felt extraordinary, connected to the new life growing inside her.

She brought her hand to her lower abdomen. A week ago, she'd been in a huge panic, but now, she believed she'd been blessed with a second chance. Where the baby was concerned, not the father. Danielle had been wrong about Lord. He hadn't called or sent a text since they'd last seen each other. And it had been seven days.

"It just goes to show, doesn't it?" she said to the baby. "Don't worry. I love you, which is all that matters."

She smiled. How could she already love the baby so fiercely? Was it even possible to love someone she'd never met? But she did. No question about it. Just as she loved Lord. He'd crept into her heart without warning and snuggled up in there. But she didn't want to think about him. It hurt too much.

She'd rather concentrate on the baby. This pregnancy felt different. The mother-child connection had been present the first time, too, but thinking back, there'd never been a time when she'd said or thought the words "I love you." Instead, her emotions had been wasted on Martin—initially missing him, and then being angry at him for what he'd done to her, even wishing she'd been in the stead of the woman who'd perished with him.

She hadn't taken proper care of herself, and she'd lost the baby as a result. Now, having learnt her lesson, she refused to dwell on Lord no matter how much she missed him.

Saying goodbye had been easy. She'd been angry enough to do it. However, she hadn't counted on it hurting this much or on missing him unbearably, his corny lines included. Most of all, she missed the way, even amid people, he gazed at her as though she were the most important person in the world.

The sound of her phone ringing snapped her out of her thoughts. She slipped the dressing gown back on and shuffled off to get it.

"Hi, Dani."

"Hi, sis. How are you?"

"Good," she said, smiling. "Just pregnant." She liked saying that.

She was rewarded with a chuckle from Danielle. "I'm more pregnant than you, girlfriend."

They both laughed.

"Has he called?"

"No. Stop asking. He's not going to call."

"It's only been a few days. Maybe he's been busy, or he's afraid to call."

"Trust me, the word 'afraid' isn't found in his dictionary. And in his own words, 'you make time for those who matter.' Evidently, I don't count."

"Of course you do. Don't even think that way."

"Don't worry. I'm not wallowing in self-pity. I'm just saying."

"I don't understand. How come he used to send you text messages every morning and every night?" Danielle said. "Maybe he's gathering ammunition to come guns blazing."

"He's not gathering ammunition. Those text messages just confirm he was after one thing." Memories of that 'one thing' they'd shared momentarily broke her concentration. Longing filled her, seeping to her most secret parts.

"Do you want to see him again?"

Her sister's voice broke through her reverie.

More than anything. She sighed, sitting on the bed. "It would be nice."

"If the horse won't go to the water …"

"And what would I say to him?"

"Tell him how you feel and find out if he loves you, too."

Or if he's already moved on.

"I'll think about it," she said, although at the back of her mind, she wondered how stupid she would feel if he told her to get lost.

After hanging up, she mulled over her sister's words. She'd tried but failed to convince herself that everything she'd come to believe of Lord had been a lie. She wanted to know for sure and somehow come to terms with whatever the truth turned out to be. She needed what she hadn't had with Martin. Closure.

WHEN LORD WALKED into his office on Monday morning, he felt a rush, which had nothing to do with the press conference. He had a plan. He'd spent the weekend thinking about Chantelle, going over their conversations. It had hit him as he sipped a less-than-palatable concoction of warm water and lemon juice, her drink of choice when she'd visited him. He needed to convince her she was the only one for him, his perfect orange in the supermarket, and he'd never take her for granted or hurt her. Most of all, he'd never doubt her again. All he needed was to get her here.

"Good morning, Mrs. Bonsu," he said to his secretary when he got in. "Is everything set for the press conference?"

"Yes, sir. The hall is ready, the press kits, too." She tapped on a stack of McKenzie Contractors official folders on her desk. "Unless you made some edits to your speech. Did you go over it?"

"Yes, and I made changes."

She followed him into his office.

He handed over his revised speech to her. "How many people are we expecting?"

"There'll be about thirty in all from thirteen media houses," the secretary said. "Three TV, four Radio, and six Print."

"Did you send the special invitation to *Odopa* magazine?"

"Yes, sir."

"Excellent."

He considered calling Randy and insisting he send Chantelle, but this time, he didn't want to have to force her to come to him. He'd sent an invitation. If she loved him, she'd come.

"If there's nothing else, Mr. McKenzie, I'll be at my desk."

"Very well," he said, and his secretary left the office.

Two o'clock found him on his way to the conference room where members of the press awaited him. There'd been no time to check the media log for Chantelle's name. Entering the hall, he could only hope she'd come. He whispered an order to the public relations manager to find out if she'd arrived, before taking his place at the podium.

Under the pretext of composing himself, he took a few seconds to scan the room. She hadn't come. Or he just couldn't see her. Had their time apart fogged his memory? He doubted it. If anything, the amount of time he'd spent thinking about her had etched her face on his mind's eye. He should have spotted her right away. Perhaps she was intentionally concealing herself.

"Good afternoon, ladies and gentlemen of the media. Thank you for coming," he began. "As many of you are aware, McKenzie Contractors has been short-listed for the Kumasi International Airport project, making us the only local company in the running. This is an important milestone, not just for our organisation, but for private enterprise in the country."

His address took ten minutes, during which he expounded the importance of this news for McKenzie Contractors. He went into some detail on their commitment to making the project something all Ghanaians would be proud of. Finally, he commended the government body overseeing the project for its objectivity in giving a fair chance to local businesses.

"I'll take your questions now."

Several hands went up, and he pointed at a young guy in a chequered shirt.

"Peter Konadu, *Business and Financial Times*," the journalist said. "How do you rate your chances of winning the contract?"

Lord emphasised the mix of expertise the company had and their commitment to developing something they knew to be the best. He answered several more questions. Still, he didn't see her. Turning to the public relations manager, he saw the man shake his head. His hopes of using this opportunity to talk to her came to a crashing end.

He realised now he hadn't really given her a reason to come. She must have taken his silence these past few days as a second betrayal. When he'd wanted to see her again after Valentine's Day, he'd called incessantly, yet when it mattered most, he'd remained quiet, thinking she needed time. Now he saw his error.

He looked at the people in front of him. Two hands went up. He took one.

"No more questions," he said afterwards. "There's one more announcement."

Shit. His father would have his head, but what other choice did he have? He'd intended on talking to Chantelle in private after the press conference, but it wasn't to be. The more he considered what he planned to do, the more convinced he became that he needed to do it. He'd deal with the consequences later.

"Many of you have gone through a great deal of effort to speculate about my love life. This is my first and final word on it." He took in a deep breath. "This goes to Chantelle."

Silence met his announcement.

"I'm in love with you." If it were possible, a deeper hush settled on the room as the people watched him with shock and rapt attention. "I miss you. I can't help it, or I would. You asked me to stay away, but I can't do it anymore. These past few days without you have been miserable. So if you can forgive me, then allow me to love you and take care of you."

He paused, realising he had nothing more to say. Worse, his eyes were watering. "That's it. Thank you."

As he stepped off the podium, someone shouted after him, "Who is Chantelle?" but he didn't pause to answer. Instead, he made his way to his father's office. He needed to break the news to him before it came on the seven o'clock news. If the old man hadn't already watched the live transmission.

WAS IT JUST HER, or were people staring? For the past five minutes, it had seemed traffic around her desk had been heavier than usual. She could have sworn some people giggled as they passed by. Had they found out her secret? It was getting hard to hide the frequent trips to the ladies' room. She saw Dufie approaching. There was no mistaking the 'Eureka!' look on her face. Hopefully, it had to do with a potential scoop. She could use some work-related excitement.

"I thought you said there was nothing going on between you and McKenzie," Dufie said, stopping in front of the desk.

Her stomach turned at the mention of Lord's name and the bold accusation. What did Dufie know? Had she heard her throw up in the washroom? She shook her head. Even if she had, there was no reason to think it had anything to do with Lord.

"There isn't," she said.

Dufie folded her arms and perched a hip against the desk. "Then why did he just announce to the whole world that he loves you?"

Chantelle gasped. "He did what?"

"Oh, yeah. Whatever he did, give the guy a break. How can you even look at his handsome face and stay angry? You should have seen him. He actually looked like he was going to cry."

"He did?"

"And it made him look so adorable."

She doubted Lord would like to be associated with the word 'adorable.' Babies were adorable. Lord was handsome, charming, sexy, a lot hotter than adorable.

"You're not making this up, are you?"

Before Dufie could respond, Chantelle's phone rang.

Danielle's name flashing on the screen alone confirmed the news. "It's true, isn't it?"

"You didn't watch it?" Danielle squealed on the other side of the line.

The mere thought of viewing him on TV had been painful because she missed him so much. Plus, with pregnancy hormones making her extra emotional, who knew what might have happened while watching? In fact, she should have attended the press conference. Although the print run for April's edition of the magazine had been scheduled to start this week, the editor had put a hold on it and given her the go-ahead to add a few lines from the conference to the feature story. She'd asked Randy to send someone else. Between the press kit and the pictures, she'd get enough additional material for the article.

"Oh, this is so romantic," Danielle said. "You don't have a choice now. You have to go and see him."

"Don't worry. I've already planned to go and give him a piece of my mind tomorrow."

"A piece of your mind? He just declared his feelings for you on national television, Chantie. What more do you want?"

"I don't know, sis. If he really said he loves me on TV, then he's put me on the spot." She tried to ignore the pouty look Dufie gave her, on behalf of Lord, no doubt. "Everybody now expects me to forgive him, because he's *Lord McKenzie*, and any woman would be crazy to turn him down after this."

Which was perhaps why he'd done it in the first place.

"Do you love him?"

Her heart's skittish beat escalated. "Yes."

"Watch him at seven o'clock."

"Believe me. You don't need to ask twice."

They said goodbye, and she hung up.

Dufie sighed. "I hope the piece of your mind you'll be giving him is along the lines of 'I love you, and I've been an idiot.'"

Chantelle smiled. Missing him weighed on her. Had he truly said he loved her? On TV? She should be mad at him for putting her on the spot as she'd told her sister. She wasn't, though. She'd made the error of not considering his feelings before and didn't intend to repeat her mistake. This time, she knew enough to appreciate what such a move had cost him.

What would his father think?

It didn't matter. He'd taken a stand for her, and she'd defend him before Mr. McKenzie if need be.

With her spirits lifted, the rest of the afternoon went by fast. Before she knew it, the time was five o'clock. She had to prevent herself from running to her car and speeding home.

FIVE O'CLOCK FOUND Lord hiding in his office nursing the wounds on his ego and his heart. His mother had called while he'd been speaking with his father. Ohene and Jane had called just when he returned to his office. But not Chantelle.

He swore as anger at himself boiled. What the hell had he expected? That she'd call as soon as she heard him? Or come running because he'd given a pitiful confession to the whole country? *Shameful.* Though at the time, it had seemed like the right thing to do.

Thankfully, his father hadn't been angry. But he would be when the seven o'clock news gave more airtime to his confession than the real reason for calling the press conference. Knowing his history with the media, the declaration would take precedence. Sadly, despite this knowledge, he'd do it again. What's the worst that could happen? He'd already lost her.

If anyone had told him it was possible to feel this alone, he'd have laughed in their face. He swore again.

At six-thirty, he decided it was safe to leave the office. At least, he wouldn't have to ward off any pitying stares from his staff. Unwilling to go home to watch the news, he chose to pass by the gym first. By the time he arrived home, it would be after eight. He'd take a shower and go to bed. If he exercised strenuously enough to deplete his energy, he might sleep through the night.

AT SEVEN O'CLOCK, Chantelle sat in front of the TV for the 'show,' complete with a bowl of honey-toasted cornflakes in plain yoghurt. In theory, it sounded gross but tasted divine. When the news started, she thought she'd burst with excitement. She had to wait fifteen long minutes before the newscaster got to the McKenzie press conference.

Her breath caught when Lord's handsome face appeared on the screen. Her heart did flips, and butterflies flitted in her stomach. Then she saw his eyes and nearly gasped. They bore no trace of their usual sparkle. It cut her like a stab in the heart.

When he started to speak, he smiled, but it didn't reach his eyes. She listened to excerpts of his speech and questions he answered. Then the picture returned to the newsroom. Disappointment filled her every pore. Had he called back the famous confession?

"That wonderful news isn't what everyone's talking about, however," the newscaster was saying. "The question on everyone's lips is, 'Who is Chantelle?' as the handsome tycoon confessed his love for her right before he left the stage."

And he was back on. Her heart danced.

"This goes to Chantelle," he said. "I'm in love with you."

She gasped. By the end, she sat transfixed. Tears streamed down her face. She yearned to see him and be in his arms. She grabbed her cell phone lying on the table next to her and dialled his number. It went straight to voicemail. She tried a couple of times more and got the same result. Her heart sank. She checked her time. *Eight-fifteen*. He didn't sleep early, judging from the timings of his nightly messages.

With the urgency of someone on a mission, she rushed to her room. Tomorrow was too far away. She slipped into a pair of jeans and a shirt. Her frantic fingers zipped up her denims and buttoned her top. Her pulse raced as if she meant to save the world, not just her heart.

She picked up her bag and headed out of the door. Her car roared to life when she turned the key. It jerked into motion as she stepped too forcefully on the accelerator after shifting into gear. She laughed and cried at the same time.

By the time she stopped in front of his gate, she was a ball of ecstasy and nerves. What would she say to him? She got out and pressed down the bell, fidgeting as she waited. She pressed it again. What was taking him so long? She pressed it a third time and waited. With increasing disappointment, she conceded he might not be home.

The fresh tears making rivulets down her cheeks weren't those of joy. Just as she turned, however, the gate began to slide open. Even before her mind could register the fact, headlights drenched her in their beam. As one hypnotised, she watched the BMW come to a halt right behind her car. Excitement built up. Taking in a deep breath, she waited.

The lights flashed, and she assumed he was asking her to go in. She got back into her car and drove inside. With trembling fingers, she turned off the engine, stepped out, and waited for him to get out of his car.

When he did, he just stared at her, his manner cautious, as if he didn't want to do or say anything to chase her away. He wore workout clothes and held his gym bag. She stared back, melting under his gaze. If she didn't sit down soon, her legs would give out.

"Your phone is off," she said, although she just wanted to jump into his arms.

His stance didn't change much, though now that her eyes had adjusted to the dim lighting, she saw the yearning in his gaze.

"I didn't think you'd call," he said quietly. "I'm glad you came."

She ventured a smile, itching to touch his face, but caution restrained her.

"Let's go in." He led the way.

He opened the door and held it open for her to enter, then followed her in. Standing in the middle of his sitting room, he continued to stare at her with a look akin to disbelief. A small smile finally crept to his lips.

She touched his face, and he closed his eyes. Her heart turned into a puddle.

In a swift motion, his hand covered hers. He pressed his face into her palm, then he planted a kiss in her hand. Searing heat rushed down through her middle to her toes. Yet, she trembled.

As though he'd just realised he was holding her, he continued to kiss the length of her hand, pausing at her neck before capturing her lips. He gave her a long, hard kiss before releasing her.

He let out a heavy breath. "If I'm dreaming, I don't want to wake up."

His voice, a soft whisper filled with myriad emotions, gave so much more weight to his words.

Moisture brimmed in her eyes. "Don't worry about waking up, because I'll be right here when you do."

He touched her face reverently. "I love you, Chantelle. I'm lost without you."

Every emotion swirling through her had a visual interpretation in his eyes and in the gentleness of his touch.

"Lord, I'm sorry for walking out on you the other day."

"You have nothing to apologise for. I should never have doubted you, and I promise to never do it again."

She released a breath, melted against him as his hands moved to rest on the small of her back. He applied pressure to his touch, bringing her abdomen flush against his body. She trembled with anticipation, but she needed to come clean to him before she could give herself over to the passion brewing between them.

"I need to tell you something."

"Okay," he said, though his hands didn't stop their exploration of her back.

She swallowed. "Can we sit?"

"Okay."

They sat on the sofa. Silence fell between them as she gathered up courage to reveal a past she'd spent the last four years trying to bury.

"I've been pregnant before," she said. "Four years ago. I found out on the eve of Valentine's Day, the same day my fiancé called to say he'd been sent on an assignment. I wanted to tell him in person, so I decided to wait until he returned."

Her throat tightened, and she swallowed. He took her hands, giving her a squeeze of encouragement.

"Of course, he never returned." She paused, trying to bring her emotions under control. "I got caught up in my grief, and when I found out about the other woman, I became so angry. I wasn't eating well or sleeping more than a couple of hours each night. I didn't take good care of myself."

A lonely tear escaped, trickling down from the corner of her eye. "One night, I cried so hard, wishing I'd never got pregnant. I guess the baby thought I didn't want it. A couple of days later, I woke up bleeding. By the time I reached the hospital, it was too late."

She sniffed, searching his eyes. Seeing love shining in their brown depths, she realised she shouldn't have feared rejection or blame from him.

"When I found out about this pregnancy, all those past feelings came rushing back."

"I'm so sorry you had to go through that." He wiped the tear, leaning in and kissing the corner of her eye. "There had to be more to it than you realised. I know you'd have loved that baby with all your heart, because it's how you love."

He pulled her into his arms, enfolding her in a snug embrace. She'd never felt safer or more loved.

"I love you," he said. "I've been going crazy without you."

"I love you, too, Lord," she said against his taut chest.

He pressed a kiss in her hair, and she held him tighter. They remained in each other's arms for what seemed like ages, before finally parting.

He placed his hand on her stomach, and a sensation swirled in her womb as if even the baby had felt the touch of its father's hands.

"You'll be a great mother, and this baby will know how much we both love him or her."

"You'll be a wonderful father, too."

Smiling, she pushed his head down and found his lips. The kiss was deep yet unhurried, as if they were rediscovering each other. His hands slipped underneath her shirt, igniting her passion like hot embers burning through a chilly night. She moved to sit astride him. Despite their clothes, she wanted to feel his hardness against the heat of her arousal. He groaned, finding one lace-clad breast. His fingertips grazed her nipple, and she sucked in a breath. Her hands reached for the elastic band of his gym trousers.

He pulled away, leaving her a little disoriented. She could see the desire in his eyes, feel his arousal against her core. She frowned, questioningly.

"I have to take a shower," he said.

What? Now? Too turned on to form a coherent word in protest, she watched him seat her back on the chair.

"Don't go anywhere."

She could have sworn she heard teasing in his voice, but he didn't invite her along as he disappeared around the corner. She swallowed, blinking. Like hell she wasn't going anywhere.

Consumed by need and mental images of him naked, she ventured into the corridor he'd taken and soon came to a door at the end of the hallway. It stood ajar, ushering out the sound of running water. With her heart pounding, she walked in.

The bedroom was bigger than her sitting and dining rooms combined. The large king-sized bed looked inviting, but she didn't allow it to distract her. What was a huge bed without a hunk?

She entered the bathroom and stopped in her tracks, taking in the sight before her. Water from the shower streamed down his body, pooling in the grooves of his strong back and sliding down the honed muscles of his powerful thighs as if paying homage to some Greek god of perfection. Her tongue skimmed over her dry lips. Was she jealous of water?

Just then, he turned. Her gaze dropped to his impressive member, which went from zero to practically ninety degrees before her eyes. Her gaze shot back up to meet his. Her breath came in quick short gasps as she imagined being filled by him. He stretched his hand, beckoning her.

Forgetting she was still in her clothes, she went over to join him, allowing him to pull her into the constant spray of water.

CHAPTER 22

CHANTELLE WRAPPED HER ARMS around Lord's neck, melting under his hot gaze. She'd never been happier or had such a profound sense of completion. Now she realised she hadn't truly known what it meant to love someone with her whole heart.

"I told you not to go anywhere," he said, the corners of his lips lifting in a teasing smile.

Fully drenched, she gently cupped his handsome face with one hand. "Didn't anyone warn you not to starve a pregnant woman?"

He laughed softly as he pushed away a film of hair the shower had swept across her face. Then he kissed her, deep and insistent like a man who'd gone days without food. Yet, the strokes of his tongue were unrushed, as if he didn't want to miss any part of the feast.

She pressed against him, enjoying the feel of his hard member rubbing against her stomach, drawing out a groan from him.

"Is that what you're hungry for, my darling?" he mumbled against her lips.

"Yes." The word tumbled out of her mouth, the need in her voice palpable.

Her body was on fire, both from his kisses and the pulsing of warm water soaking her to the skin.

"I promise you'll have it soon."

She whimpered her impatience as he caressed her through the glued-on shirt, pulling her into him with a firm hold of her waist. He then nudged her shirt up and touched her skin.

The contact burnt and soothed. She moaned, leaning further into him, deepening the kiss. Her hands explored his body with sensual adoration as her lips captured his tongue. She nibbled and circled and sucked while he unbuttoned her shirt with the same deliberate urgency of his kisses.

He unhooked her bra and removed it along with her shirt in one fluid motion. They embraced, skin touching skin. She sucked in a breath.

"God, I've missed this."

He groaned. "You have no idea."

His expert lips traced a path down from her mouth, capturing her earlobe with a gentle nip. Her breath caught when his lips grazed her neck and his hands began to unzip her jeans. She stretched forward, willing him to get to her breasts already. When he seized one eager nipple in his mouth, she cried out.

A deep, guttural sound erupted from him as he sucked and played her nipple with his tongue and teeth, sending messages of anticipation to her centre. She arched her back, wanting more of what he gave. As one hand kneaded the other breast, the other slipped into her jeans, seeking her hot feminine wetness. Her legs trembled, and she wondered how much longer she'd be able to stand. She whimpered when he left her breasts, though it could have been from the pressure of his fingers exploring her private places.

"I want to taste you," he groaned urgently as he traced wet kisses down towards the part of her that hurt for attention.

Going on his knees, he tugged down her jeans, kissing her inner thigh. When the trousers were pooled around her ankles, she forced her feet out of them. Leaning against the wall, she parted her legs, allowing him access as he kissed a trail up her thigh. With her knees wobbly, she gripped his shoulders to steady herself. As he got closer to her core, she held her breath, anticipating the moment his tongue would make the contact she craved.

He lifted one of her legs onto his shoulder and then the other, propping her against the wall and steadying her with his hands firmly cupping her butt. He teased her, just enough to make her want even more. Then his tongue touched her swollen bud, and she thought she'd died and gone to Heaven.

Her moans filled the room as he kissed her thoroughly, licking, flicking, circling, stroking with his tongue. Lost in the pleasure of the moment, she didn't attempt to hold on and prolong the intense pleasure. She felt her release coming as her body began to tighten. Closing her eyes, she embraced the tide. Rapture consumed her, lifting her in ecstasy, and as she tumbled back to Earth with her final release, she cried out, "Oh, Lord."

He helped her down from her pedestal. Not trusting her legs to keep her up, she sank to her knees, wrapping her arms around his shoulders. As the last shivers left her body, she pulled back to look into his face. The despair had dissipated, leaving desire. She pushed back some hairs plastered over her face. For the first time tonight, he smiled at her, really smiled, with pure and absolute love. And melted her all over again. She smiled back, embracing her completion.

Leaning over, he flicked his tongue over her earlobe. "I've missed you."

The sensation made her giggle. "Me, too."

He tickled her ear with his tongue, surprising her with the erotic sensation it created. Pulling back, she continued grinning.

"What day were you born?" She injected her voice with innocence, maybe too much innocence.

He narrowed his eyes at her, though his hands never stopped their loving motions on her body. "Why?"

"Just wondering," she said sweetly, although something must have given her away, for he chuckled in response.

"I'm not telling you my day name." Giving her a full-mouthed kiss, he said in a deep whisper close to her ear, "You can torture it out of me."

Her heart raced with glee. "What sort of torture are we talking about?"

She lowered her lips on one of his nipples, passing her tongue over it and sucking, drawing a deep moan from him.

"Something like that," he said in a raspy voice.

She nipped it with her teeth, and he groaned.

"Do it again."

She did. "Are you going to tell me now?"

Kissing her way to the other nipple, she gave it the same treatment. She revelled in the tightening of his muscles, his deep moans, and the heightened pace of his breathing.

"You're killing me."

"That's the idea," she said, blowing air against his skin, running her lips over his strong torso to his neck.

Touch turned to caress as he cupped her breasts with promise. She arched her hips towards him, bringing her lower belly in contact with his erection. Her earlier release was quickly forgotten as renewed need surfaced. She wanted him inside her. Reaching forth, she captured him in her hands and gave him tender strokes.

He groaned, finding her lips. His fingers slipped between her legs, where he served her the same torturous pleasure she fed him. It didn't take long before they found themselves panting again.

"Lord?"

"Hmm?" he mumbled against her lips.

"I want to be full of you."

Impatiently, he lifted her up, seeking paradise. She straddled him, guiding him into her, and held on tight. Their lovemaking was tender and passionate as the shower continued to rain with tepid water. Though she'd already surrendered her heart to him, somewhere amidst panting and his voice calling out her name, she lost herself in love again.

Her intimate muscles began to contract once more. She writhed and let out a cry as her body blossomed. With renewed vigour, she rode him, meeting his swift thrusts with equal ardour. His arms tightened around her. With one final thrust, he released a harsh groan and came apart in her arms.

After they had towelled down, they made their way to the king-sized bed, which was every bit as cosy as it had promised to be.

"Hmm, nice bed," she said. "Very comfy."

He lay on his side, his head propped up on one hand so he could look down at her with unbridled love. His free hand ran lightly over her skin.

"It's not half as comfortable without you in it."

She smiled, snuggling closer. Her hands did their own exploration. "I'd planned on visiting your office tomorrow, but after seeing how dejected you looked on TV, I knew I had to come now."

He chuckled. "So it had nothing to do with my confession?"

"Well, that, too. Plus, you looked as miserable as I felt."

"And you came to my rescue." He grew serious. "I'm sorry for not getting in touch. I thought you needed space."

"I did," she said. "I didn't realise it at the time."

"Still. I shouldn't have let you go more than a couple of days without trying to talk to you again. I'm sorry."

Somehow as they spoke, the distance between their lips had decreased to an inch. He gave her a hot, lingering kiss. No teasing. He meant business. Pulling back, he returned to his initial propped up position. He gave her one of those I-still-can't-believe-you're-here smiles. His hand paused on her stomach.

"How's our baby?"

Our baby. It sounded so good to hear him say it. She wasn't alone anymore. "What makes you think there's just one?"

His jaw dropped, his eyes widening with amazement. It was priceless. She almost felt sorry to have been teasing.

She laughed. "It's too early to tell, but I'm a twin, remember?"

He regarded her with awe, as if she'd just solved one of the world's biggest mysteries. "How are you?"

"I'm fine and happy," she said. "You make me happy."

A moment of silence elapsed. As the charged atmosphere lightened, a smile crept on his lips. Their petting had become more playful now. She heaved a contented sigh.

"I'm hungry. For food this time. I left my dinner to come here." If cornflakes and yogurt could be considered dinner.

"You didn't eat?" The alarm in his voice reflected in his eyes. "What would you like?"

"Pancakes, scrambled eggs, yogurt, cereal or porridge, baked beans …" She giggled at the look of increasing surprise he gave her. "I'm too hungry to be picky."

"Let's go." He pulled her out of bed, tossed her a bathrobe, and wrapped a towel around his waist.

In the kitchen, he took out a tray of eggs and other ingredients from the fridge. "Have you eaten eggs with garlic before?"

"No, but I like garlic." With a teasing grin, she added, "As long as we both have garlic breath, I won't mind kissing you."

He returned her grin.

"Do you really want pancakes?"

"No, the eggs will be fine. Do you have bread?"

"Fridge," he said.

As she took out the loaf of sliced wheat bread, she spotted something of interest. "You like plain yogurt."

"I like it better than the fruity stuff."

She nodded with approval, picking up a yogurt. "Do you want one?"

"No, but a glass of juice would be nice."

She took that out, placing them on the worktop. "Glasses?"

He pointed to a cupboard where she retrieved a tumbler and a mug for tea. She flipped the switch on the kettle to heat water. She watched him slice the onion and tomato. He was indeed a very sexy man, she observed, finding him even more tempting as a towel-clad chef.

"Watch and learn." He carefully chopped the garlic into tiny pieces. He then cracked four eggs into a bowl, beat the veggies into it, and poured the concoction into a pan on the stove.

"Cooking suits you."

He gave her a smile and came to hold her. "Does it turn you on?"

"Mildly."

"I'll have to change that," he said, frowning. "I don't do anything halfway, sweetheart."

His lips teased hers, his tongue delving in when her lips parted. Next thing to part was her robe when he undid the belt.

"Are we moving up from mild?" his husky voice spoke into her mouth.

"Definitely getting hotter, but you need to watch the eggs."

"Right," he said. "The eggs."

He hurried back to the stove, turning to her with an apology. "Looks like we're having an omelette."

"An omelette is good, too." She cleared her throat, resisting the temptation to strip and let him have his way with her right away. Forget the food.

Fastening the robe, she concentrated on making herself a cup of tea and pouring juice for him. Her stomach growled as the aroma of the eggs reached her. However, a different kind of hunger stirred as her gaze settled on his muscles flexing with the movement of his arms. He dished out onto a plate. Opening a drawer, he retrieved a fork and knife and cut a small piece of egg. He blew on the piece until it had cooled.

"Taste," he said, feeding it to her.

Using her tongue and lips, she drew the egg off the fork and chewed. She made a soft moaning sound as she tasted the subtle flavour of garlic with the onions, tomatoes, and egg.

"It's really good," she said. "How come I never thought of it?"

He gave her one of those disarming smiles, his eyes twinkling with satisfaction. He handed her the fork, then took a sip of his juice. Without any formal plan, they began to eat, leaning against the counter. Images of doing this every night filled her mind. Her heart fluttered at the thought.

"Yes," she said.

He frowned as he finished off his second glass of juice. "Yes, what?"

"I think you're good-looking, and I'd love to wake up in your arms." A question he'd asked the first day they met.

He gave her a pleased smile.

"Then you don't have anything to worry about." He leaned in for another kiss. "Henceforth, you'll be waking up next to me."

"Really?" she said. "And how do you know this?"

"Because you're going to be my wife."

She had to laugh. Only Lord McKenzie could get away with such a proposal. "Is that so?"

"It is."

He caressed her through the robe before tugging her belt again. The garment fell open, giving him free access to her bare skin. The pressure of his touch increased as he concentrated his efforts on a particularly sensitive spot around her groin.

"Do you have any objections?"

His lips hovered so close, she could touch them with a pout.

"No." She managed to get that out before he stole her words away in a kiss.

EPILOGUE

WEDDINGS WERE SUPPOSED TO be the woman's territory, but for Lord McKenzie, it was the happiest day of his life. Well, it came toe-to-toe with the day about two months ago, when Chantelle had walked back into his life and told him not to worry about waking up because she'd still be there.

Not only had she rescued his heart that day, but it seemed she'd also brought good luck with her. Just two weeks ago, McKenzie Contractors had won the bid for the Kumasi International Airport. And Chantelle had been the first person he'd called.

Staring into the faces of the most important people to him and his wife-to-be, he waited in his blue-black suit with his brother and three best friends standing behind him. He and Chantelle had both wanted a small wedding, just family and close friends, and had agreed the compound of his parents' house was the ideal venue.

On one side, Chantelle's sister, Danielle, sat between her husband and their mother. His mother-in-law, considering they'd already done the customary ceremony that morning. A seat had been reserved next to them for Chantelle's father. On the second row sat a colleague of hers with her husband. Both her sister and colleague were heavily pregnant. It brought on images of what Chantelle would soon look like. Already, her waistline had increased slightly, though it was only apparent when she was naked. Then there was her friend Ben Annan.

They'd agreed *Odopa* magazine would do an exclusive on their wedding. Joe, their official photographer, with his assistant, Kofi, were there to immortalise their big day.

His parents, sitting on the groom's side, looked into each other's eyes as though they'd only just met. His father whispered something into his mother's ear. Her smile widened, and she nodded. Deconte and Jane sat next to his parents. The kids were in the bridal train.

There were ten others, important friends of their parents who'd had to be invited.

"If you keep staring at the couples in love, you're going to get emotional, kid," Ohene whispered to him. "Believe me, you don't want to cry before you see the bride."

"I'm not going to cry. Period." He was too happy for tears.

"Wait until she comes out," Ohene said. "My wife looks so beautiful, I want to marry her again."

Lord's gaze darted to Jane in her elegant blue *Kente*, before travelling to the end of the aisle as music began to play. Kukua, Chantelle's niece, came into view as she began a processional to the front. Ohene's first daughter, Baaba, followed. They'd been arranged in order of age, so next came Araba, Chantelle's other niece, followed by Gladys, and finally, Ato, a little man in a three-piece suit, bearing the rings.

With mounting anticipation, he watched Chantelle's friend, Dufie, the maid of honour, walk up to her place in front. The music changed to Bach's famous 'Jesus, Joy of Man's Desiring,' Chantelle's favourite wedding procession song. He had, himself, always been partial to it.

She emerged, a vision in ice-blue, her hand looped through her father's arm. His gut tightened as if he'd been hit by a tidal wave. She looked stunning as always, but the significance of the day, and the outfit, gave her an added splendour.

The gown covered her shoes, making her movement appear as though she were gliding. His throat grew suspiciously tight. *Damn.* Ohene hadn't lied. He blew air out of his mouth. There was no way he'd let tears form.

It had seemed a short distance when the others came through, but it took forever for her to float to his side. Finally, when they got to the front, her father embraced her and went to his seat.

He extended a hand, and Chantelle placed hers in it, taking her place beside him where she belonged, and the music gradually came to an end.

Pastor Annor, the minister from his parents' church, cleared his throat and beamed at them.

"Dearly beloved, we are gathered here in the sight of God and in the presence of these witnesses, to join this man and this woman in holy matrimony."

The preacher began solemnly, and Lord wished he could put the ceremony on fast forward.

He forced himself to remain patient, using the time to focus on his beautiful bride.

"If any person can show just cause why they may not be joined together, let them speak now or forever hold their peace," Pastor Annor continued as if he had all the time in the world.

If this hadn't been his wedding, he would have fired the man for taking his sweet time. But how could he when his bride listened to each word with rapt attention, as if there had never been greater words spoken?

"Who gives this woman to be wedded to this man?"

Mr. Sah stood. "I do."

Pastor Annor nodded. "Let's pray."

He forced himself to close his eyes. He would have forever to gaze at Chantelle. Thankfully, the prayer, which centred on love and marriage, was short. The minister continued the ceremony in the same unhurried way.

"And now the vows," he finally said.

His heart raced. Chantelle's grip grew firmer, and her smile brightened further.

"Do you, Lord Festus McKenzie, take this woman, Chantelle Ohemaa Sah, to be your lawful wife? Do you promise to love her, comfort and keep her, and forsaking all others, remain true to her as long as you both shall live?"

"I do," he said.

The twinkle in her eyes, while she gave her promise, told him he was done for now that she knew his middle name. But he had his whole life to get even with her. Starting with this kiss.

THE END

Thank you for reading Most Eligible Bachelor. If you enjoyed this story, please take a moment to write a review to let other readers know so they can also enjoy it. Thank you!

MEN OF DISTINCTION ALERT

Did you enjoy Most Eligible Bachelor? Would you like to be notified when new books in the series release? If yes, click below.

Sign up to receive an email

OTHER BOOKS BY EMPI BARYEH

Men of Distinction series

Dinner and a Kiss

From Ghana With Love series

Chancing Faith

Expecting Ty's Baby

Royal House of Saene series

His Inherited Princess

The Illegitimate Prince

Standalones

Forest Girl

Be My Valentine Anthology: Volume One

Unwrapping Hanie

CONNECT WITH EMPI

Receive new release alerts, sneak peeks, exclusive freebies and more:

Join her mailing list.

Join the conversation:

You're invited to the Empire where you can discuss MOST ELIGIBLE BACHELOR and other books by Empi.

Join her Facebook Reader Group

Link up:

Instagram: @EmpiBaryeh

Twitter: @EmpiBaryeh

Tiktok: @empibaryehauthor

Facebook

ABOUT THE AUTHOR

Empi Baryeh is the award-winning author of Most Eligible Bachelor (Book of the year, 2017 Ufere Awards). She works fulltime as a university administrator and spends her spare time writing sweet and sensual African, multicultural and interracial romance, and women's fiction.

Her interest in writing started around the age of thirteen after she stumbled upon a YA story her sister had started and abandoned. The story fascinated her so much that, when she discovered it was unfinished, she set out to complete it. Somehow the rest of the story began to take shape in her mind, and she's been writing ever since.

She lives in Accra, Ghana, with her husband and their two lovely kids.

www.empibaryeh.com

The One That Got Away

island girls: 3 sisters in mauritius

zee monodee

First Published in Great Britain in 2022 by
LOVE AFRICA PRESS
103 Reaver House, 12 East Street, Epsom KT17 1HX
www.loveafricapress.com

Available as eBook and paperback

ISLAND GIRLS: 3 SISTERS IN MAURITIUS

BLURB

Eldest sister of the Hemant sibling trio, Lara Reddy, returns to Mauritius as a divorcee and must contend with Indo-Mauritian society's outdated views about marriage and the modern woman. In the middle of this dumpster fire, she comes across Eric Marivaux, the white French-Mauritian man she loved as a teenager and gave up because their interracial, mixed cultural relationship would not stand a chance on this island. But here comes a second chance: Eric wants her back in his life, and he will stop at nothing to win her back. Will Lara be her own worst enemy and thus end up unhappy ever after?

CHAPTER ONE

Come on, Lara. You can do it.

It's only your mother.

Thirty-two-year-old Lara Reddy gripped the steering wheel tighter as the thoughts raced in her mind. Her left foot itched to slam onto the clutch so she could reverse out of here before her mother realised she'd made it close to the family home in Curepipe, one of the biggest towns on the island of Mauritius.

But she'd simply be delaying the inevitable.

Why, oh why, hadn't she thought of this before she'd left London? True, the lure of the job had been immense. The possibility of running her own state-of-the-art international conventions centre on the island. It had been nowhere close to her position as Events Manager at a renowned business hotel in London. For someone in her early thirties, life didn't get much better than this, career-wise. If she'd stayed in the UK, she'd probably wave menopause goodbye without making it any higher up the corporate ladder.

A once-in-a-lifetime opportunity. Not to mention that the company had head-hunted her.

She'd jumped … without giving due thought that she'd be plunging into the deep end of the local pool where the sharks dwelled.

No child of Mauritian origin who'd grown up in England or elsewhere in the world would choose to come back there to live. Too much gossip and drama. People poking and prodding into personal lives. Mauritius and its Indian-origin society reminded her of a fishbowl, where any foreigner was a goldfish. The locals ranged from piranhas to barracudas, in between which swam killer whales and every kind of shark. Proof of the pudding—her mother was one of the worst social predators ever.

She gulped and tried to unclench her hands from the steering wheel.

The urge to smoke hit her from nowhere. She'd given up cigarettes exactly three years, two months, one week, and five days earlier. Ever since that God-awful argument with Roy—

Lara closed her eyes tight. No, she wouldn't think of him. She'd ponder anything else.

Like a smoke?

She slapped the thought away and forced in a deep breath. Damn it, she hadn't thought of smoking in weeks.

Not true, sing-sang that little intruder again.

She'd thought of it just that morning. In the no-smoking international airport, when she'd lifted her head because there'd been a prickling along her nape. Then, she'd seen him. The tall, big white man with the long, shaggy blond locks and shoulders that seemed wide enough to take on all the concerns of a woman's world.

A gasp escaped her once more.

Eric.

The boy she'd loved as a teenager, when she didn't even know what the word love entailed.

The one that got away.

He left, remember? Without a word.

Rooted on the spot, the air had hitched in her throat. She'd sent furtive glances around, looking for an equally blond and even more beautiful woman in his vicinity. His French wife. Pain had ripped her heart when she'd wondered if she'd also have to see their child—probably children, by now—as well.

Her gaze had landed on the board announcing all the flights. The only other arrival besides her London Gatwick one had come from Johannesburg.

Eric Marivaux lived in France—why would he return to Mauritius from South Africa?

Her panic had alleviated then.

It wasn't him. Couldn't be him. The Eric she'd known had been tall but not as imposing or brawny. He'd also hated having his hair longer than an inch. This man had locks any shampoo company would kill to feature in one of their adverts. Must be an Afrikaner who bore a striking resemblance to him.

Still, with her hands clamped tight on the handle of her luggage trolley, she'd crept backwards until she'd tumbled out of the air-conditioned lobby through an automatic sliding door. The cloying, humid heat of the January summer had wrapped around her, crushing the breath inside her chest and further addling her brain.

It wasn't him, she told herself again now as she eased the car into first gear and crawled along the street she'd called home during the two and a half years she'd spent on the island.

The air from the vehicle's fan turned cooler. For once, rain wasn't falling in a steady drizzle over Curepipe. When they'd first moved there, she and her sisters had marvelled at how much the climate in this spot at one of the highest altitudes on the island resembled British weather. Minus snow in winter, Curepipe was a perfect contender for dark, gloomy, and wet climes. Except on days when the sun shone, when everything looked sharp and crisp, bathed in a clear glow while the temperature soared to a pleasant, tolerable heat—like today.

Massive houses with well-tended lawns and front gardens dotted both sides of the mile-long road into the quiet and affluent residential area. She remembered what the family home looked like, but she took her cue from the sight of the low, pruned tea bushes rounding Lees Street into a cul-de-sac. When the dark-green plantations came into view, she slowed the car before turning left into the open driveway of the Hemant residence.

Gravel crunched under the tyres, the sound of chirping birds in the big, leafy maple tree in the front yard contributing to the blissful peace.

Not for much longer.

A whiff of hot cooking oil touched her nostrils. Her stomach rumbled upon registering the scent of frying bhadias, those little cakes made from a batter of gram flour and herbs. The distinctive blend of coriander and chillies floated on the edges of the aroma. She glanced at her watch. Three o'clock, meaning teatime, and why her mother was frying savoury cakes. And that also meant—

She winced as she cut the engine and heard the strident sounds of feminine chatter coming from the opened kitchen window. Damn. Company.

Please let it not be a cluster of aunties.

A horse-like chortle screeched through the air. Lara closed her eyes in despair and let her forehead touch the steering wheel. Neighbourhood gossip and busybody Auntie Ruby was here. She'd bet her life the other member of the Terrible Three—as she and her sisters had dubbed their mother and her two best friends—would be here, too. Auntie Zubeida from next door. Of course, her mother would have her two besties around. Didn't Gayatri Hemant suffer from obsessive-compulsive talking disorder and the need for a permanent audience around her?

She shouldn't have come. The sound of her mother's high-pitched voice crept over the din, asking if someone had heard a car stop in the driveway. They'd come out in the next minute.

Picking up her courage and wishing it were the Dutch kind despite not being a drinker, she tore her fingers and head from the wheel and threw the door open. She then peeled herself out of the vehicle as a chorus of gasps resounded in the garden.

All three older women were suddenly on her like a bad rash. Hugging her and kissing her cheeks, holding her face in their hands while they exclaimed how beautiful she had become. All of which were simply tactics to lull her into complacency before they'd really pounce on the meaty topic—her recent divorce.

With their deceptively frail-looking hands on her shoulders, they pushed her towards the back door to the kitchen. A memory assaulted her—of being pushed towards the altar on her wedding day, a glittery gold and red veil over her eyes.

She stopped in her tracks, the forgotten pain returning to slice through her heart. Because she'd believed in Roy, had offered him her heart on a platter that day. He'd thrown it back in her face ten years later ...

The biddies must not have noticed her stilling. They simply continued to steer her inside until she was seated at the table. A plate of towering hot bhadias appeared in front of her, along with a bowl of satini cotomili—the coriander, tomato, and chilli paste-like dip Mauritians ate with all their fried foods.

Auntie Ruby, the resident gossipmonger, lived up to her reputation. She was the first to mention Lara's failed marriage before they made it back into the house.

The sound of the grating voice droned on. Lara chose to ignore it before her mother gave her a slight slap on her shoulder.

"You wicked girl. You said you were coming on Monday, and here you are surprising us now."

A sigh escaped Lara. This was code for "how could you have kept this a secret and made me lose face in front of everyone when I told them you are coming on Monday?" Her mother lived for hearsay, and the general idea of "what will people say?" like most people in Mauritius. Whoever said the ton and its silly rules had died in the Regency era had not taken a trip to Mauritius in the year two-thousand-something.

"But my poor little girl," Auntie Ruby said in a cajoling tone, bringing nothing but danger to mind. "Of course, you wanted to come home earlier. Who wouldn't? Look what that awful, awful man has done to you."

Translation: "And here's your cue to air out the laundry, from the sheets to the knickers, you silly goose."

Other than saying they'd had irreconcilable differences—the same reason listed on their divorce papers—she'd kept mum about the whole business. Roy's family had had a field day dirtying her name, but she hadn't fallen to that level.

The same couldn't be said about her relatives, though.

"Our hearts went out to you, dearest girl, you who are like a daughter to us," Auntie Zubeida chimed in. "We never saw this coming. How could you not have told a soul you and that scoundrel were having problems? We would've spoken to him, set him right, showed him this is not how he is supposed to treat our daughter."

"Tsk-tsk. And what a beautiful couple you two made. How could anyone have thought you would break up?" Auntie Ruby added.

Beautiful. She huffed. She and Roy had been pretty faces. Young, sexy, rich, with prosperous careers in London and a flat right next to Tower Bridge. No wonder they'd been the envy of everyone here. Maybe said envy had cast the Evil Eye on the couple they'd made.

Lara shook her head. Silly of her to heed such notions as the Evil Eye. People made their own futures, and she and Roy had made their beds. She might not be at fault, but she'd had her hand in these irreconcilable differences. Maybe if she'd made an effort, if she'd changed. If Roy had given her time—

"Tell us what happened, Lara beti. You cannot keep shouldering that burden alone!"

Lara forced a small smile. As if they really cared about her, calling her the tender affectionate moniker for 'daughter' in Indian tongues.

"I'm doing fine, Auntie," she said. "That's what matters."

All three women watched her with narrowed eyes. No way was she doing away with the Inquisition. She should've thought of that before coming.

She should've ensconced herself in her newly-bought semi-detached in a gated community in Grand-Baie, the farthest northern tip of the island, content to while the days staring at the brilliant blue sea from the upstairs veranda.

"How can you be fine?" Auntie Ruby screeched. "We have been so preoccupied with your plight. How on earth are you going to get along? How will your parents bear all this? To think they still have an unmarried daughter on their hands. Now, they are ending up with two daughters. Oh, what fate God has dealt them."

Lara bit her lip to keep from answering back. Right, the ton must've been more solicitous than this. The aunts were simply nosing for gossip. But then, that's what Jane Austen wrote in her subtext, too. The concern was merely a polite way of enquiring about tattle in their society.

When the coppery taste of blood registered on her taste buds, she took deep, calming breaths to keep her temper in check. The urge to suck on a lit cigarette gnawed at her insides. While smoking was not the answer, one inhale would be terrific stress relief right now.

The relentless rambles picked up crescendo around her. Growing physically sick, she jumped to her feet.

"For God's sake, Auntie! We only got divorced. It's not the end of the world."

Silence blanketed the room. The women stared back at her with eyes like saucers and utter disbelief etched on their features.

At the transformation, laughter welled up in her throat. The three faces appeared so pinched that face-lifts couldn't have stretched their skins so well. She choked down the chuckles before they erupted since she'd merely throw oil on the fire if she burst out laughing.

However, her mother seemed to be choking on another emotion as her fair, wrinkle-free face went all red.

Lara squirmed around from one foot to the other as a sinking feeling settled in her gut. She had asked for trouble with her outburst. However much she'd told herself she wouldn't give in, she'd done it. Let her mouth run off. If there was one thing her mother disliked more than anything, it was being spoken back at, especially by her own children. When they'd been little, such behaviour had earned them a sharp backslap to the mouth.

"What are you giggling about?" her mother asked as she stood and brought a hand onto her heart. "We are trying to make good lives for all of you. But our struggles and worries are not your concern, are they? How can they affect you so little? You just lost a husband."

Lara shut her eyes. Inwardly, she also closed her hearing. For goodness' sake, it had been three years ago! Roy had even moved on—getting remarried, his wife expecting their first already. His mother, the sick witch, had proudly shown Lara all this back when she had still lived in London, in the family house she'd won in the proceedings.

She'd lived on top of a gunpowder keg in the past few years with a fuse just waiting to be lit.

Her mother had just lit said fuse.

Lara'd had enough. Enough of the woman's outdated views about marriage and the Indo-Mauritian woman. How much longer did she have to stay to avoid being impolite?

She'd like to meet her sisters and her father, but her mother had her wanting to run for the hills before she'd seen anyone else.

"Mum, please," she said softly as she glanced at her parent. "Not now."

Her mother had the grace to appear contrite and shut up.

"Of course. You must still love him, and—"

"I don't love Roy anymore."

Not after he'd betrayed her. No, he hadn't cheated, but he'd done worse. He'd wanted a bride with Indian origins yet a modern take on life and career. She'd been all that … until the day it became everything wrong with her.

The women blinked.

"Well, I say, if my husband had run off with another woman who doesn't even have the decency to be fairer-skinned than I am, then I, too, wouldn't love the dog anymore," Auntie Zubeida said.

And here we go again. It always had to come down to fairer looks in the Indian world.

Auntie Ruby gasped. "That home-wrecker is darker than Lara? How could he? Men really have no taste, do they?"

"Haven't you heard?" Auntie Zubeida asked in a hushed tone. "She's the niece of Mrs Morea, the woman with the shop across from Spar. Her sister's daughter. And we all know everyone from their family has skin as dark as burnt halwa."

"Shame on him. You poor thing, Lara. You must be seething. How could he have fallen so low?"

Anyone listening would think Lara had skin as white as snow. Of course, she didn't, having inherited her father's nut-brown, olive-toned colour. But she'd been considered a good prospect, thanks to her family name and their fortune. Exactly like in the ton, with the added bonus of her perfect scores at school and the subsequent formidable career outlook.

"He didn't cheat on me, Auntie. We separated, and that's when he met the girl he married."

When his mother paraded that girl in front of him. Once, she'd paraded Lara in front of him that same way.

Her mother huffed. "It's what he wants you to believe. How do you know he wasn't doing the dirty with her behind your back?"

She'd asked herself the same question, only to slam into a brick wall. Never a masochist, she had dropped the query. What would it change if he'd cheated? He'd hurt her way more by attacking her very soul.

"You're not even a woman, Lara. You're a damn robot!"

Although those words had stuck, they hadn't been the worst slur.

"You stink like a chimney sweep!"

Considering Roy had lit her cigarettes in the past, those words had been bull's eye.

She'd quit her addiction the same day, cold turkey. To be fair, she'd become a robot, throwing everything into her job and working her way up from simple hotel event planner to event manager within a year.

"But now you're here, and we'll take care of you. Good thing I got your room readied in advance."

Lara winced as another realization crashed in. She had yet to inform her family she would not be staying with them. "About that ..."

"How have you crammed all your suitcases in such a tiny car?" her mother asked. "I've never known you to travel light. Your shoes alone come in a trunk."

The trunk would arrive by cargo along with most of her stuff from London.

How would she worm out of this revelation alive?

If only she hadn't been so eager to escape Roy and his pregnant missus. Yes, the sight had hurt because she had loved him. Not a mad, crazy passionate love, but she had agreed to commit her life to him. How much more steadfast could someone get?

She'd thought they were in this together.

How wrong she'd been. One day, he'd said he wanted a child, and it was high time she got her priorities sorted so they could have a family. No discussion, no compromise. A shock, considering he had always been easy-going and malleable. Headstrong, she'd said no, and that had been the end of them. He'd left their flat the same night to go to his parents' and never returned. A week later, a legal clerk had served her the divorce papers at work, in the hotel's busy lobby.

She wasn't cut out to be a mother. He'd known and appreciated that she'd never had any hang-ups about it. The sight of babies scared her the way other people had clown phobias. While she could get on with little kids, she'd seen herself as the slightly batty old hag auntie every family had. She didn't trust herself around babies, not even with the prospect of her own. Maternal instincts must've passed her genetic makeup, and she'd always gone after the things she was good at. Motherhood not being one of them, she'd scrapped it. Roy had also never said he wanted children. His career as a hot-shot actuary had been his sole focus.

So how could they have gone so wrong all of a sudden? She still had no clue.

A piercing wail sliced through the air. The roar of a kitten, thinking it was a fierce lion, came on the coattails of the screech, along with loud sobbing.

The kitchen door flew open, the sole of the little kid who'd kicked it still in the air. Lara gazed over the mini-man with the Mohawk before sliding to the side onto the pigtailed little girl with tear-stained cheeks. A stretch of dull grey stood behind the children. Seriously, this couldn't be …

Her mother tore out of her seat to march towards the door. "Bon dié o, Neha. What have you done to this poor baby to get him to scream so?"

Lara blinked. What happened to beautiful Neha who looked like the muse for a serene Renaissance painting? This was not the woman she had met four years ago during her last visit!

Their mother deftly ripped the swaddled lump from Neha's arms. With a rocking motion, she got the baby to stop screaming.

"This is how you do it, Neha. I would believe you'd know by now."

Neha bit her lip before she nodded.

She still allows herself to be bossed around.

Her poor sister … Maybe with her being here now, she could help? Provide a shield against their mother. She and Neha had never really been close, but maybe—

Hold on, was she imagining this, or did Neha just give her a false smile?

"Lara. We weren't expecting you before Monday," Neha said.

"It was a surprise," she replied.

Another forced smile. What was wrong with her?

A loud kick resounded from the kitchen door. Lara leaned to the side to catch sight of the little boy practising karate chops on the wood panel. "That's Kunal, innit?"

She turned to the still-sobbing girl. "And you must be Suzanne. Look how you've grown."

Terrors, the lot of them. She shivered when she imagined this could've been her fate if she'd given in with Roy.

"And why is she crying now?" Auntie Ruby asked. "Anyone would think you terrorize the poor child, Neha."

Neha lowered her eyelids, and a faint blush crept over her pale cheeks. "I can't get her to stop," she said in a low voice. "Since her father left for Madagascar this morning, she hasn't let up."

Feeling sorry for her sister at the defeated tone, Lara had an idea. "Wait. I know exactly what will cheer her up."

She dashed out to the car, pulling out the large shopping bag full of gifts. And with her head stuck inside the potpourri-scented vehicle, she took a deep breath and gathered her thoughts.

Hopefully, Neha's arrival with the children would be distracting enough for the aunties, and they'd leave her alone.

Fat chance, but she could hope. Hope is what idiots live on, as the French saying went.

With the handle in her grip, she traipsed back to the kitchen, rummaged into the bag and pulled out a wide, flat case which she handed to her niece. "This is for you."

The sobs stopped, and the little girl gingerly reached for the offering. She blinked once she closed her hands on the box, then let out a screech loud enough to burst an adult's eardrum.

"It's got all the Disney princesses, even Elsa and Anna! Thank you, Auntie Lara."

Lara had to smile at the unbridled enthusiasm. At the corner of her vision, she saw the little boy stealthily approaching. Reaching into the bag again, she extracted a large carton of Avengers action figures. "And this is yours."

His eyes grew wide, and he jumped up and down. Lara didn't know when he wrapped his bony arms around her neck. In his eagerness, he nearly snapped her neck in two as he pulled her to his level. Then, just as abruptly, he released her and plopped himself down on the rug in front of the dining-room door, where Suzanne was tearing out the contents of her gift.

Finally, Lara handed a blanket wrapped in a package to her sister. "This for the baby."

"His name is Rishi," Neha said in a clipped voice.

"For Rishi, then."

Another squeal ripped through the kitchen as the back door slammed open. Lara glanced up only long enough to brace herself for the energy bolt heading straight for her.

"I can't believe you're here already!" her youngest sister, Diya, shouted as she hugged Lara and made them both hop like bunnies on steroids.

Lara reeled to get her balance back when the girl released her. How could such a petite woman who could pass for a life-size doll pack so much energy and zest into her tiny body? She became drained simply from listening to the teenager talk a mile a minute.

"Oooh, is this the goodie bag?" Diya asked. "Please, please, please tell me you got the game I asked you for. I wasn't sure you got my last email—"

"I got it," she said, simply to make the girl shut up.

"And the Body Shop basket? And the Boots hand cream? Oh, and tell me you made the Boxing Day sales and got me those killer sandals from NEXT—"

"Yes, yes, and yes." She pulled out the latest Assassin's Creed PC game case from the bag. "Here you go. The rest is coming by cargo."

"Oooh, you're the best!" Diya grabbed the thin plastic box before she hugged Lara again. "Okay, gotta be off. Everyone will kill to be in my shoes when they see I got this."

"And where do you think you are going, young lady?" their mother asked.

"Meeting with some friends at KFC. Be back for dinner, or ask Daddy to pick me up when he gets home from work. Oooh, look what Suzanne got. No, sweetie, wait. That's not how you apply blusher."

Neha gasped. "You got her makeup?"

"It's kid-friendly. I double-checked after the salesgirl at the Disney shop assured me it was safe."

"She's eight years old. Much too young for all this."

"Oh, don't be such a ninny, Neha. I started wearing makeup when I was her age, and I'm none the worse for wear, am I?" Diya asked with a roll of her dark eyes.

"That's what has me worried," Neha said under her breath, but loud enough for Lara to hear. "And I can't believe you got Kunal dolls."

"They're action figures, sis," Diya said as she breezed past them to the door. "Take a chill pill, will you? Tata, ye all!"

The quiet in Diya's wake felt strangely anticlimactic as if all the air in the room had been sucked out. Neha kept her reproachful glare on Lara, who, to escape the malevolent scrutiny—after all, what was her sister's problem?—turned towards their mother and the aunties.

Bad move.

"We better get you settled. Not yet one hour since your return, and you three are already back to bickering like children."

"We aren't bickering—" both Lara and Neha said simultaneously.

"Are, too," their mother said with finality in her tone. "Now, go get your suitcases, and let's get you upstairs, Lara."

Here it is. The moment of truth.

"About that," she said again. "I won't be staying, Mum."

"I beg your pardon?"

"My stuff's at my place in Grand-Baie. Didn't I tell you? I bought a house there."

She kept her voice nonchalant and averted her eyes from her mother's unnerving stare.

The numb shock reverberating in the still kitchen told her she had another think coming. The silence lasted, but unfortunately, was short-lived.

"You mean you're going to be living alone?" her mother asked in a burst of righteous indignation. "But it is just not done. Absolutely not proper. What will people say? You are a single woman, Lara. It is not right for you to stay alone. And you've still got us, your family. People will say we don't want you at our place, that we're ashamed of your divorce, which couldn't be further from the truth. There'll be so much talk. It'll undermine all your future prospects."

The voice seemed to carry concern and care, but all she heard were recriminations and barely-concealed disbelief. Nothing more than an attempt by her mother to save face because, all her life, her mother had always made appearances and conventions come first. There was no concern for her there, for the daughter she and the aunties claimed to love and support.

Everything was about them, and them alone. Exactly like Roy had done with her. Nobody cared about her.

Her mother opened her mouth again.

Lara sighed. She didn't want another fight. Thinking of Roy always made her feel low, and no one could argue with Gayatri Hemant when feeling low, for she'd run the person down like a bulldozer. Nonetheless, steely resolve filled her. She'd come here for a purpose, a job. Anything else was negotiable.

She wasn't putting up with her parents again. She'd left home at nineteen and wouldn't return at thirty-two. After thirteen years of living on her own, she wouldn't give her mother the pleasure of monitoring her movement with detention-centre rigour. Living under the family roof would mean just that.

And, she could win this with logic. Hadn't she thought the pitch out? She took a deep breath. "Mum, I'm a Managing Director now."

The older woman brightened, pride glowing on her face. Lara gained confidence.

"As such, I need to be present and available at very short notice."

Her mother slowly nodded.

"I need to be close to work. This place is more than an hour away from the centre. I cannot be available and be so far, right?"

Her mother continued nodding.

"So it's better if I live at this new house in Grand-Baie."

With a sudden jerk that made her worry about the possibility of whiplash, her mother stopped nodding. The dark, almost black, gaze—made more striking by the kohl liner contrasting with perfectly smooth, milky skin—stared Lara straight in the eye.

"You'll be living alone, and that's not done."

Reproach dripped from the words.

She sighed to conceal a snort. She was losing the calm and the battle. Worse, she didn't want to hold on to patience any longer. She wanted out ASAP. For goodness' sake, she would have scores of people working under her authority. Surely, she could reason with her mother.

Couldn't she?

"Mother, it's my final word. I'm going to live there, whether you like it or not. You forget I lived alone in England."

"Yes, but that was the Western world. This is just not done here. Also, you're all alone. Single."

The aunties nodded and echoed the sentiment. Even Neha looked at her with concerned eyes.

If she hadn't been on the brink of a mental breakdown when her husband had left her, then today, the urge to crash would have caught up with her. How would she survive here?

By staying as far away from her society-proper family as much as possible. By finding another temporary addiction to help cope with them. Her new boss was gonna love her.

Though this was Mauritius, where one could travel from one tip to another in two hours. She'd never be far enough, truth be told.

All for the job, she told herself. She deserved this.

She'd committed her life to Mauritius but had forgotten to check her sanity when she'd crossed into this backward society. A mistake she hoped to never make again, but from here on, she was doomed.

Highway to Hell, we meet again.

CHAPTER TWO

Eric Marivaux closed his eyes and let the back of his head touch the fluffy cushion on the sofa on his family home's veranda. Crickets chirped in the garden, the sound coming through on a gentle breeze belying the oppressive island summer. On the hillsides of Floreal, an affluent neighbourhood next to Curepipe, summer was definitely the best season, with none of the scorching heat and humidity of the coastal areas. Where he lived, in the north, the air-conditioner stayed on constantly.

This felt like bliss, and he sighed. If he let himself go, he could easily fall asleep and wake up with a crick in his neck. Those sofas were decorative more than functional.

He didn't have to ponder long over this—a backhand slap landed on his shoulder. The cushion next to him seemed to groan with an exaggerated huff when someone plopped on it.

He forced an eye open, smiling when he saw his younger sister, Angélique. She always made him smile, but tonight, even more so as she positively glowed with happiness.

"It's your fault," he grumbled. "You just couldn't wait, could you?"

She back-slapped him again. "Cut it out, Eric. Do you know how long I've been sitting on this?"

"Three weeks. That's how long I've been in South Africa. It can't be more than that."

"*Ayo*, you're no fun! *Maman* was adamant we had to wait for you to be here before I could bring Patrice home."

He tore both eyes open to stare at the young man and his father sitting at the patio table and sharing a glass of Perrier. Good choice—the guy would be driving back to his home in Bel-Ombre, the farthest southern tip of the island, later tonight.

"Thanks for the consideration, Ange," he quipped. "You were ready to bring him home with me out of the country."

She poked her tongue out at him. "At least that way, you wouldn't have been able to find fault with him."

He winced—he had been a bit uncompromising regarding his baby sister's boyfriends. She'd never brought one home until today, which made him scrutinise the man who had won his sibling's heart. Big and brawny, Patrice Laroche looked like the rugby front-row prop he was for the national team. The baby face belied the savage air, though. Eric hoped the man had the mental fortitude of a full-back, as well, because he'd need it to deal with wilful Angélique.

"Seriously, Ange. A deer breeder?" he jest.

She poked him with an elbow in his ribs. "He's not a deer breeder, silly. His family owns the biggest *chassé* on the island, which happens to have the biggest deer population of the whole place."

He laughed as he pulled her to him. "I know. I was just having fun at your expense."

"Hmmph," she snorted into his side.

"You're happy?" he whispered close to her ear.

She nodded. "Yes."

"Then that's all that matters."

His sister pulled away to stare at him with big grey, wide-open eyes. "You mean that?"

He ruffled her dark hair, which prompted her to evade his touch. "Of course I do. He makes you glow, *ma puce*. As long as he keeps doing that, he's okay in my books."

She threw her arms around him to hug him, then got up and left to go back to the table, where she plopped down on Patrice's lap. The poor guy seemed to lose his breath.

Eric smothered a laugh and relaxed against the sofa again, closing his eyes. However, two seconds later, the cushion dipped next to him, in a more dignified manner this time.

He opened his eyes to find an older version of brunette Angélique sitting next to him.

"So that's why you couldn't have me miss dinner tonight, even though I just got home after a twelve-hour delayed flight," he told his mother.

She smiled, threading his arm with hers and resting her head against the back of the sofa. "She has been driving us crazy, you would not believe."

"I can imagine." He winced.

"So, what do you think?"

He raised an eyebrow. "What do I think? I thought I didn't have a say in these things, seeing how the elders always weighed in on those matters."

"Oh, you're insufferable," she said with a slight slap to his shoulder. "I mean it, Eric."

He sighed. "Can you ask me that when I'm not jet-lagged and carrying the weight of three weeks of intensive training and surgery on me?"

She rubbed his shoulder. "I'm sorry, *poussin*. Jet lag doesn't bother you usually."

He groaned at the endearment. Seriously, being called 'baby chicken' stopped being cute after he turned thirteen, over a good twenty years ago.

"But this was too good an opportunity to miss," she continued. "To learn besides one of the best paediatric surgeons in the world. I knew you'd be perfect for it."

A niggling doubt insinuated itself in his mind, and he frowned as he sat straighter. He'd always wondered how he had gotten the traineeship. True, he was one of the few paediatricians on the island who also specialised in paediatric surgery, but still …

"Did you have anything to do with me getting that placement?" he asked.

His mother rolled her eyes. "Of course not. Your credentials spoke for themselves."

But how had said credentials gotten in front of Dr Bekker's eyes? He tried to put two and two together.

"Hold on. You are good friends with Pastor Van Ryk, no?"

She shrugged. "So?"

"And he also happens to be good friends with Dr Bekker."

This was starting to look more and more like a setup. He hated setups.

His mother huffed. "What do you want me to say? Yes, Pastor Van Ryk enquired if you were a paediatric surgeon, to which I replied yes. What wrong was there in that?"

Nothing per se, and if there had been, she wouldn't see it as such, either. His mother lived by her very own code of conduct.

But he had to admit the traineeship had improved his position as an authority in paediatric surgery on the island and in the Indian Ocean region. Was he looking a gift horse in the mouth here? Things tended to have a price tag with his mother involved, one he might not be willing to pay.

"Look at her, Eric."

He turned towards the table, where Angélique had thrown her head back in laughter.

"She's happy," he said softly.

His mother nodded. "And such a good match, too. I really couldn't believe it. The Laroche family is one of the oldest blood on the island."

He tightened his jaw. She'd always paid heed to these notions about family lines, pedigree and whatnot. It had driven him crazy in his youth. Still did, in fact.

If she hadn't been so inclined, would he have considered—

No, he couldn't think of it, of her. He'd vowed to stop seeing her everywhere.

Sometimes, it happened, slipping under his guard, like this morning at the airport. There'd been the tell-tale prickle along his nape, and he'd glanced around. So many brunettes around Customs and Baggage Claim, but the only young woman with straight jet-black hair had been Chinese.

Not Lara Hemant.

"The official engagement party will be in two weeks," his mother continued. "Your grandmother is coming from France."

He turned back to her. "Seems you've been busy during my absence."

"Your sister sprang this on us. Believe me, to make a half-good engagement party, you need to get started months in advance. *Dieu merci*, Patrice's father has offered us the lodge at their Bel-Ombre *chassé* as the venue. I don't know how we would've gotten a decent club or hotel booked on such short notice."

Ange and Patrice should elope. Seriously. If he ever tied the knot one day, that's what he would do.

That's what he'd thought to do with Lara. They would've flown to Vegas, why not, or even just gotten married on the neighbouring Reunion Island, where his French passport made him a national. Anything to get away from stifling family stuff.

But things hadn't worked out.

"And speaking of your grandmother, Eric." She paused, taking a breath. "Sophie might be coming with her."

A nerve ticked and hurt his cheek as he clenched his jaw. He didn't want to hear that name, hadn't wanted to since he'd left her begging and crying back at Château Armont, his mother's family estate in France. Sophie de Maivière was the goddaughter of the matriarch of the aristocratic Armont clan. Of course, she'd worm her way in.

"She's coming with husband number what? Three now?" he asked through gritted teeth.

"Don't be so harsh, Eric. You know her husband died last month."

Her third husband. The Italian count had been so old, his dentures always fell into his soup bowl at formal meals.

"You two were good together," his mother added in a light tone.

Sophie had thought so, and she had made his family believe it. She was a simpering fraud who'd used him as a conduit into the prestigious Armont family through his grandmother's favour.

She'd never turned his heart because the organ had belonged to Lara. But she'd sucked his time, and he'd lost a year in her stifling clutches, consequently losing Lara.

The hurt squeezed his chest, and he tightened his fist on the fluffy fur ruffle on one of the decorative cushions.

"*Maman*, please. Don't talk about Sophie to me," he said as he stood. "If she comes to Ange's engagement party, you can count me off the guest list."

She grabbed his hand and stood, too.

"I'm sorry. It's a sore spot. I shouldn't have." She paused and squeezed his hand. "I just want you to be happy."

He glanced at his sister and her fiancé, then turned to his parent. "Correction, you want to see me settled down, especially now that your youngest child is tying the knot, and this makes it even more obvious that the eldest is still entirely unattached."

She sighed. "Eric, *mon chéri*. You're thirty-three. Isn't it time you settled down, though?"

No, it wasn't. Not yet. And it wouldn't be the right time until he could settle down with the one and only woman he'd loved.

Lara.

The one that got away.

But she was happily married in London, and here he was, thousands of kilometres away, still pining for her. He couldn't fault her for what she'd done. He was the one who hadn't given proof of life for close to a year after leaving for France.

Maybe seeing his sister so happy with a lovesick idiot Patrice brought home Eric's loss more viscerally. Was a little bit of such happiness in his life so out of reach?

He'd never have a whole heart—the ship had sailed, but he could have something …

For the first time in fourteen years, he wilfully pushed the thought of Lara Hemant—now Reddy—aside and turned to his mother.

"Okay," he said. "I'll think about it."

CHAPTER THREE

Sometimes, you have to hit rock bottom before climbing back up.

True in Lara's case.

She'd hit the abyss floor more than once recently, but the mini-breakdown one week after her arrival had helped her spring back into top shape. True to form, her mother had strong-armed her into attending a family wedding. That day, Lara had been bulldozed by her parent, had received a very cold shoulder from Neha when she'd asked for help to tie a sari—because Western clothing was just not 'done' at family gatherings—all before walking into the lion's den.

Well, make that whole pride of lions, in an arena similar to the Coliseum. Her divorce had still been the talk of the town, and everyone, from the aunties she'd never met to the cousins she didn't know existed, had taken their turn to make her feel like a pile of poop.

Running home hadn't been an option so she'd borne it all, and she'd been sorely tempted to hand in her resignation letter and book the first flight out of this viper's nest as soon as she'd stepped foot home.

Reason had finally prevailed, after a pint of Haagen-Dasz had disappeared into her stomach and the condensation had ruined Neha's prized silk sari. She'd come to work the next morning and had thanked the heavens when Markus Hendrickson, the head honcho, had officially handed her the reins to the conference center that morning.

Since then, work piled up on her. For the first time, she didn't bemoan her boss acting like a borderline slave driver because she needed the exertion to forget about the other aspects of her life.

The packed schedule also gave her a perfect excuse to avoid going to her parents' place. In the past three weeks, she'd deftly fielded calls from her mother, avoiding numerous invitations for lunch or dinner.

One month down—so many more to go.

The hectic career made time fly. Perhaps she could sail through her existence here.

Lara tore her eyes from yet another incomprehensible report and reclined in her chair. Their first conference loomed ahead, less than a fortnight away. What she'd handled in England was nothing compared to her new responsibilities. A handful of corporate portfolios, at best, there while here, the enormity of pulling off a weeklong conference rested solely on her capacity and direction. She, and the centre, would be toast if she failed at this baptism by fire.

A loud knock resounded in the office. Please let it not be another manager needing a meeting with me. She usually loved being the social butterfly at work, but her position in the hierarchy worked against her. She sighed. They saw her as a foreigner, and worse, since she was of Mauritian origins, she should've been one of them … but she wasn't. She was 'other', even more so than their fully expat boss.

Everyone dealt with her with formal reserve, the legendary Mauritian welcome and good-naturedness there, but again, slightly held back. She tried to befriend them and find out more about their personal lives to strike a rapport. Apart from her personal assistant, she wanted to believe she was eroding their aloof manner chip by chip, but she'd be kidding herself. She needed a popularity coup to end up on the staff's good books.

Not right now. Not with her first conference looming like a behemoth about to crash into her and the centre.

Stop the defeatist thoughts!

Seconds later, Doris Li, her PA—a middle-aged Mauritian woman of Chinese origin—strolled in with a steaming black mug in her right hand.

"Here's your coffee, and there are four messages, all from your mother," Doris said.

At the mention of her mother, weariness gripped her, and all the energy drained from her body. Despair overwhelmed her, sapping her muscle control, and her head fell onto the desk's surface.

A soft bump resounded when her forehead hit the cold glass. As heat formed on her skin where it lay against the cool surface, a thought crossed her mind. The glass is very solid. She'd already bumped her head at least a dozen times on it through the past month. Each time because of her mother.

She lifted her head to stare into Doris' doughy face. Lara never failed to be amazed how the other woman could appear so soft and serene all the time. But that was a tricky assumption, she'd realized after less than an hour in the woman's presence. Doris was as tough and unyielding as she looked gentle and precisely the right person to handle Lara's mother.

Lara was lucky to have such a hardworking force of nature as her second in command. She straightened and rubbed the sore spot on her forehead with her left hand. With the other, she grabbed and took a sip of the scalding hot brew.

"What does she want now?" she asked as she put the heavy porcelain mug down.

"Oh, the usual." Doris shrugged. "For you to call her back ASAP as it's urgent."

"God, she's gonna run me dead." She moaned with a shake of her head. "But forget it. Just please continue to stave her off for me. Oh, by the way, has your daughter reached Melbourne safely?"

"Yes. She got there right in time for the new semester."

Her cell phone rang, interrupting their chat. When Lara saw the caller ID, she let her head drop onto the desk again in despair.

Does she ever let up?

Puffing a breath, she swiped the screen and brought the phone to her ear without bothering to lift her neck from its tricky angle. She didn't know if she'd be able to, anyway.

"Hey, Mum." She tried to keep her voice flat. Hopefully, her mother would take the hint and not linger for hours.

"Hello, darling." The shrill voice almost sang. "That awful secretary of yours keeps saying you're in meetings every time I call."

The effervescence tone turned to a whine during the diatribe, eradicating her patience.

"It's because I am in meetings all the time, Mother. It's my job."

"Oh, never mind. You'll never guess. Kamini's just had a baby, and it's a boy," her mother said in an excited rush. "She had an emergency C-section when her labour just wouldn't progress this morning after the whole night she spent at the clinic. She's done good, that girl. A male heir for her first born."

What on Earth was her mother talking about?

"Kamini? Isn't she the one who just got married? She sure didn't look ready to pop at the wedding."

Wrong thing to say, she realised too late. Her mother did not have a sense of humour.

"Oh, Lara, don't be silly. How dare you say something so shameful? Pregnant on her wedding day." Gayatri Hemant huffed. "Anyway, I'm not talking of that Kamini. I'm talking of the other Kamini, Lalita's daughter."

There was only one Lalita in their family, and she'd met the woman's son at the wedding. Vishal, as he was called. The only person who hadn't thrown a stone at her. He'd reminded her of an eager puppy, but she'd clung to his kindness like a life raft that evening.

"Your father is busy as always, and visiting hours at the clinic start at three o'clock. I know you're finishing at one o'clock today since it's Saturday, so you can come pick me up and take me to visit her."

Lara groaned and tried her best to keep her mother from hearing it. "Mum, the poor girl's just had a baby. She must be tired. Let her rest. You'll go see her tomorrow."

She winced and held the phone at a distance from her ear with the ensuing outburst.

"But that is just not proper. What will Lalita say? That I'm not concerned at all about her first grandchild. No, we have to go today."

Lara closed her eyes. She didn't trust herself to reply and took deep, calming breaths to steady her nerves. But air wasn't what she needed. She craved a cigarette. Bad. If things remained constant, she'd never be rid of the debilitating urge as long as she let her mother get to her.

"Lara, are you still there? Never mind, I'll wait for you this afternoon. Don't be late."

The beeping of the cut call resounded in her ear, and she itched to slam the phone down to ease some of the pent-up frustration gathering in stormy spirals inside her. But she kept herself in check. It wouldn't do for the Managing Director to be caught vandalising her own office. Her mother wasn't worth that kind of career self-destruction.

As she took in the wide expanse of her office, or her domain, as she called it, the calm refused to come.

"Damn," she said with a sigh. The desire for a burning drag on a cigarette welled up, making her wish she'd broken something. At least then, some of the fury would've vented off and not flared through her like fire attacked defenceless paper.

I need a smoke. No way around this certainty. One wouldn't hurt, right?

However, to keep herself in check, she went into the adjoining bathroom, locking the door behind her. There, in the privacy of the white-marbled loo, she removed her shoes and kicked the punching bag she'd stealthily installed in the middle of the cold space.

Blessed relief filled her as her shins took the brunt of the onslaughts, and dull pain radiated in her bones. As she'd found out, work plus kickboxing had proven to be the best antidote against cigarette cravings and encounters with her mother lately.

From the spot where she stood next to her car in the clinic parking lot, Lara was awed by the grandeur of the imposing structure of solid concrete.

Once inside, however, she had to admit the cosy interior made one forget that medicine and life-and-death decisions occurred within the premises. The whole place pulled off a light green and yellow palette, with touches of contrasting colour added by the many painting replicas hung on the walls. Overstuffed and comfortable-looking furniture made up strategic corners, with glossy marble underfoot. On the whole, the tasteful, understated elegance of the place could pass for a hotel.

She could not hope to remain in the car waiting for her mum's return, so she cut her losses and put up no fight to follow her parent around the rambling corridors. Her mother barged into the halls of the maternity ward as if she owned the place while Lara trudged behind. At the nurses' station, they learned Kamini's room number, and after a short walk down a narrow hallway, they found the location. The door lay wide open, and relatives overflowed from there.

Amidst all the bodies and faces, she caught a glimpse of the new mother, whom her mum embraced with exuberance. Kamini's weary gaze travelled around, meeting with Lara's. Lara nodded at this cousin she didn't recall ever meeting. Yet, the washed-out girl returned a genuine, albeit faint, smile.

Sympathy overwhelmed her heart. The poor creature seemed absolutely knackered as if she wanted nothing but to sleep. Kamini probably longed for the support of her husband, who'd been relegated to a corner. And she could've done without her mother and mother-in-law fussing and clucking like geese on crack around her.

A fresh wave of empathy gripped Lara. She could so easily relate to her cousin. Both of them were prisoners of their society and its way of life.

She approached the bed and reached out to clasp the hand to which an I.V. line was attached. The girl, who couldn't be a day older than twenty, returned the gesture with a squeeze, and a bond formed between them. For how long, she didn't know. But at that moment, it existed, and both women shared it with a touch.

A fresh wave of relatives arrived, making her itch to leave the stuffy room. Disgust and revulsion filled her like a rush of burning bile up her throat when she had to fight her way out of the maze of people. Nausea kicked in, her head going light. The air conditioning was barely adequate with so many people around. Despite the lingering tinge of disinfectant and the sickly smell of hospitals, she was grateful for the cleaner air in the corridor outside.

Every step she took away from the room toned down her feelings of revolt. Yet, she couldn't keep the injustice and the insensitivity out of her head. How could all these people be so obtuse and narrow-minded? Didn't they see their presence was awkward at such a time and in such a cramped space?

Lost in her thoughts, she rounded a corner of the hall, slamming into someone's side. Disoriented and dizzy with confusion at the jolting oomph of impact against a solid form, she stumbled, losing control of her legs. The walls moved up rapidly, but a strong pair of hands grabbed her arms before the back of her head hit the floor.

"Bon sang, mademoiselle! Où courez-vous comme ça?" a rich, deep masculine voice asked in the sharp yet lilting accent of white French-Mauritian natives.

Where are you running to, miss? she figured out from her rusty French.

Away from you. Something inside her acknowledged the danger before she could process his words. She knew that voice. Her head spun again, yet her mind remained so very alert.

Could it be …? No, it couldn't.

Her brain had to be playing tricks on her. The sound with its particular accent belonged to the very distant past. How was she hearing it at this moment? Had she fainted?

That's it. She wasn't conscious, and since she'd probably worked herself to exhaustion, the condition had triggered all sorts of switches in her muddled consciousness.

The image of the man from the airport burned itself into her mind, and she gasped. No!

"Is everything okay?" The chuckle had gone from the tone, replaced by worry.

Solid strength still held her ribcage, the back of the hands warm and smooth where they touched her arms. Their heat went to her head, churning all coherent thought into a jumble.

Your eyes won't betray you. They'll see the truth.

She risked a glance up beneath her lashes. She had to be certain. To know if this was all a trick of her imagination ...

A tall form with broad shoulders outlined in a short-sleeved shirt filled Lara's vision. The lapels of the opened collar framed a strong jaw, and a wide mouth was set in a worried line above a square chin. A fine, straight nose sat above those sensual lips.

She had to gulp back the ominous lump wedged in her throat. Her heart hammered in her chest, and her mouth went dry. Her suspicions looked dangerously close to being confirmed, and the nagging notion played havoc with her thoughts. She closed her eyes.

When she opened them, she found herself staring into a pair of blue irises. A blinding flash went through her head, plunging her heart to her knees. She'd recognize those irises anywhere. Deep-set, bright, and laughing eyes the colour of the deepest ocean. The heavy, golden locks brushing his forehead accentuated the frown knitting his eyebrows.

Locks that had somehow broken free from the thick, brushed-back hair. She itched to sweep them back, to run the tips of her fingers along his smooth skin, like she used to in the past, onto the soft buzz of hair he used to keep so short.

Her mind went into a crazy spin, and all her senses reeled as everything became a vivid kaleidoscope of colours. Her stomach heaved, and her knees went weak as her body became limp.

But the man's firm grip was still on her, and he kept her steady on her feet.

"Are you okay? I think you better sit down here," he said.

The voice made its way into her perception, and she couldn't suppress the relief that flooded her. His voice had always had such power over her.

He still hasn't recognised me.

She'd changed a lot in the past decade, and with her head still bent forward, her hair shielded her face. She wanted to escape. To close her eyes and then open them to find it had all been a dream. Or a nightmare.

But this was real, and how long could she remain incognito? Lara swallowed with difficulty. Of all the people from her past, Fate had had to choose that precise person to shove along her path.

She allowed him to lead her to a sofa. Her saviour lowered her into her seat with extreme care and gentleness and sat next to her, turning to her. The smell of his aftershave—fresh, spicy, and very elusive—filled her nostrils and made its way into her foggy mind.

He still smells the same. Like a cool sea breeze wafting through the unique musk of a man's warm skin.

Lara took a deep breath and gathered her courage. There'd always been a risk of coming across him on the island. She'd preferred to hide from the probability, but she couldn't run anymore.

So, she lifted her head.

A frown marred the broad forehead. As devastatingly handsome as ever. Or maybe, even more than ever. His features were arresting, masculine, adult. No longer those of a teenager.

Her mouth went dry again, and her heart beat faster when the straight line of his lips broke into a large smile a few seconds later. His eyes lit up and widened.

"I'll be damned! Lara? Is it really you?" he asked, switching effortlessly to English.

She forced a smile and took a deep breath. "Hello, Eric. How are you?"

She couldn't have sounded more like a cold, distant bitch if she'd tried.

He stared at her for long seconds. Would he brush her off, get up, and leave her stranded again? After her stilted greeting, he'd be well within his rights to do so.

"Well, isn't this a surprise," he said.

His low tone and the lack of sarcasm or irony comforted her. He wasn't angry, thank goodness.

"Yes, it is," she replied before biting her tongue.

"I'm good. How about you? It's been a long time ..."

The way he paused, she didn't dare peer up to witness the emotion playing on his face in those too-beautiful eyes.

Yes, it has been. She didn't say the words, knowing they'd open a can of worms best left untouched. No point in rehashing the past. They were where they were. Since she couldn't stand up and run away, she should switch topics.

"What are you doing here?" When you're supposed to be in France, married, and already a father.

Before he could respond, a nurse approached them. "Excuse me, Doctor Marivaux. There's a call for you."

"Thank you. I'll be right there." He nodded at the woman before turning his attention to her again.

The exchange made its way into her hazy mind. "You became a doctor, after all."

He smiled in reply. His mouth had retained the easy manner of breaking into a sunny smile.

Her insides melted to jelly as she allowed her gaze to travel over him, to notice the casual ease that had replaced the stiffness in his body.

Dangerous. Comfortable territory with him would mean her doom.

"I'm a paediatrician."

"Oh."

The words didn't pierce through the internal bashing she subjected herself. She simply couldn't allow Eric Marivaux to see how his actions fourteen years earlier had completely altered her life. That a part of her still cared for him. He'd been her first love, after all.

He smiled again, and amusement danced in his eyes. The unconcealed joy on his face wrapped her in a trance. Could he be happy to see her?

Damn idiot—he's married!

She threw a glance at his left hand. No ring. But something glinted on his right, and her heart sank at the sight of the thick silver band on the third finger. She couldn't kid herself because, sometimes, European men wore their wedding bands on their right hands.

"Are you sure you're okay?" he asked.

"Huh?"

She blinked out of her stunned state. Eric was not for her. He'd never been and never would be. She wanted to shake herself out of her crestfallen spirits, but couldn't, which infuriated her.

"Back there," he said with a nod. "You didn't seem too well. Is something wrong?"

"Oh, that." What could she tell him? That she'd been bowled over by seeing him again? "Heatstroke, nothing worse."

A warm blush spread into her cheeks, and she averted her face from his view. Out of the corner of her eye, she noticed her mother pacing the corridor's far end. Now that would be trouble.

She shot to her feet in a lightning-quick move, and her head spun. She swayed, and Eric caught her with his arm on her waist.

"Lara, what's wrong?" His tone was low, concern heavy in the words.

Yet, what registered more in her desperate, love-starved brain was his touch on her back, on the flimsy silk blouse. Tingles shot up her skin from the point of contact, and heat spread throughout her muscles in the surrounding area.

She made the mistake of glancing up then. His head was a few inches from hers. If he lowered it any more, he could kiss her.

She parted her lips, a puff of hot air escaping her mouth. She couldn't miss how his eyes darkened, and he tensed his strong jaw. How they must appear to the world, like a couple in a sensual embrace.

And how far from the truth such an assumption would be. Nevertheless, Lara would be in trouble if her mother saw them like this. She rolled her shoulders and tried to shrug away his touch.

Except he wouldn't let her. He tugged her closer, and she had half a mind to offer no resistance so she'd land against his solid chest. Would it feel as hard as it looked?

Get a grip on yourself! Eric dumped you.

She averted her face once more.

"I'm fine, Eric. It's just, uh, the sun and the heat. You know how bad it gets here in summer, even in Curepipe ..."

Humiliation flooded her as soon as the words blurted out of her mouth. She had to get away, by any means. Still, the burn of shame trickled inside her at her idiocy. What was she chiding herself for? Her stupid reply, or her sillier reaction to him?

She pulled out of his arms when he loosened his grip. Head down, hair shielding her face, she vowed not to look at him again if that's what it took to hang on to what little remained of her sanity.

"I'm sorry, Eric. I have to go. But it's been nice to see you."

Better leave it at this. She didn't intend to meet him again.

"It's been nice to see you too, Lara. You ... You're on vacation here?"

Better not let him know she was here for good.

"Something like that," she mumbled.

He nodded. "Take care, okay?"

She'd already taken a step away from him when something in his voice stopped her. Was it regret? Sadness?

Probably wishful thinking on her part, she reasoned, dismissing the notion. Why would Eric be sad when he was the one who'd done the leaving all those years before?

She gave him a small smile. "I will. You take care, too."

"Bye, Lara."

"Bye, Eric," she added softly.

She hadn't been able to resist saying his name aloud again.

Lara allowed her still-yearning-for-Eric gaze to linger on him for a second longer before turning on her heel and walking away. He moved, too. She sensed his movement even though he wasn't in her eyesight, that tiny prickle niggling at the back of her neck.

Exactly like in the past. And exactly like at the airport. She couldn't kid herself anymore—it had been him that day …

She reached her mother right before the older woman turned the corner to the spot where Eric's and her paths had collided, glad her mum hadn't noticed him. Or his touching her. God knew how many questions would arise then. She would never live it down. Eric was not an Indian man. He was white—his status thus way above what anyone from her family could aspire to. Akin to breaking into the aristocracy, or a commoner snagging a prince. She was no Kate Middleton or Crown Princess Mary of Denmark.Things like that happened to one girl in a billion every decade. She wasn't so lucky.

Hadn't that been one of the reasons she'd never allowed herself to dream of a future with him back in the day because she'd known already 'they' could never exist? Kids got away with it. Adults? A whole other kettle of fish she hadn't been prepared to touch.

For once, she welcomed her mother's incessant babbling. Gayatri Hemant, as usual, launched into an endless flow of talking as soon as she had a pair of ears in range. The senseless ramble took Lara's focus away from fruitless memories.

"What a snob Lalita is. I cannot believe it. This clinic charges a fortune, and she had to have her daughter admitted into this very one. She doesn't know what to do to show off her money."

Pointless to remind her mother how Neha had given birth to all three of her children in the same clinic. It hadn't been showing off then but affording the best care.

"Now, Vishal. What a pleasant young man. Such a fair complexion, so handsome. And I also heard he makes a lot of money. He's got a very good job, apparently ..."

Half an hour later, she was glad to be rid of her mother when she dropped her off at the family house. Not feeling fit enough to bear her parent's ramblings for longer, she declined the invitation to stay for dinner.

Instead, she burned the asphalt as she sped towards Grand-Baie. She craved the quiet and peace of her own home to be able to force a semblance of order and resignation into her muddled brain.

Not an easy task since she had the meeting with Eric on her mind.

Eric, the man she had loved like no other.

◆◆◆

Eric stood in his private practice office, staring out of the window at nothing. The Grand-Baie summer sun beat down on the pane and licked at his skin, burning him, but he paid the physical sensations no heed. All his focus lay on his memories, especially his earlier encounter with Lara.

How did meeting her again make him feel? He didn't know, and this uncertainty rattled him. A part of him didn't dare browse his feelings.

He'd made such great progress only a week earlier, when he'd gone on a date with Annabelle de Castelban. At his sister's engagement party, his mother had invited every eligible young woman in their circle, it had seemed, and there'd been a spark with the pretty brunette. A lot of people brushed her off, her reputation as a wild party animal during her university days still sticking to her years later, but he'd seen something in her smile. Guileless. Not someone trying to stick to him to finagle a connection to the illustrious Marivaux and Armont names.

And now, Lara had landed in his life again, after fourteen years … Was Fate really such a cruel bitch?

He didn't want her back. Not in his proximity, not in the same place, not on the same soil. The more distance between them, the better. He'd had to work so hard to finally accept such a reality, so why had the universe chosen that moment to put her back onto his path?

He ran a hand in his hair, letting his fingers work at untangling the knots. He should cut the long locks, but damn if he found the time.

Why now? He'd just started to get over the idea none of his relationships would work out because she was the only woman he'd ever loved. If he hoped to settle down someday, he'd do so for convenience and companionship, but never for love. Annabelle had let on she wasn't looking for roses and romance, either. They would be perfect together.

But just one face-to-face meeting with Lara and his certitude spun away like a crazy top.

No, she shouldn't be here. He'd wanted to run when he'd recognized her earlier. Run as fast as his legs could carry him. Run from the hurt and anger that inevitably crept into his whole being and consumed him completely whenever he thought of her.

Yet, he hadn't been able to resist. One glance at her, and he'd been a goner. Again. So, he'd given in, not fighting the joy of being around her again. He'd revelled in those short but sweet moments they'd shared. She'd felt so good in his arms.

He sighed and ran his hand over his face again in a gesture fraught with weariness and frustration. Lara. He'd stumbled aback when he recognized her. She'd changed in the past decade and a half since the last time he'd seen her.

She was a woman and not a skinny eighteen-year-old anymore, though she still boasted a very slim figure. The long hair had also tricked him. The straight brown locks with the chestnut highlights framed the sides of her face now and covered her forehead in a thick fringe. In the past, she drew it back into a high ponytail that bounced with every step. He'd loved to tug on her long hair, which would annoy her so much, and when she'd frown and narrow her gaze at him, he would swoop in and steal a kiss. After which, she would smile. Reluctantly, but she'd smile, nevertheless.

Why was she back? He had returned to Mauritius because she wouldn't be there. Her life was in London. What was she doing here? Though she had said she was on vacation.

He closed his eyes and let his head touch the surface of the window. The glass was hot against his forehead. As drained as he felt, he couldn't bother with a possible burn to his sun-sensitive skin. Meeting her again had shaken him up. More so because he couldn't bear to see her and know she belonged to another man now. To that tall, dark, and handsome husband of hers, who, he'd been loath to admit, resembled a Bollywood movie star. The guy also had brains since he was some hotshot actuary or something, working in investment. And Lara had seemed happy with him. He remembered the joyous expression on her face when he'd seen them once at Piccadilly Circus in London.

That day, he'd known for good she was lost to him, stupid fool that he was. He'd been an idiot for leaving abruptly for France years before while his relationship with her had been unfinished business.

But it had all been a long time ago. A different lifetime, even.

He forced his eyes open and rubbed his nape as he peeled himself from the window and stepped closer to his desk. No use pondering the past. He actually had a future to look forward to now.

Eric steeled himself with resolve. In a swift move, he pulled his executive chair and settled behind his desk, eyeing the pile of letters on the table with weariness. The time spent in South Africa meant he still dealt with a backlog. With a resigned sigh, he attacked the stack of envelopes. The sooner he got the task out of the way, the better.

The last letter was an invitation to a medical conference at Le Sirius Hotel and Conventions Centre. He disliked such events, preferring the hands-on side of medicine, where he could take care of his patients.

However, one of the seminars was about microsurgery techniques, which would prove efficient in paediatric care and benefit his patients.

He reached for the phone and spoke to his secretary via the intercom. "Claire, book me a place for day five of that conference, will you?"

CHAPTER FOUR

Will that bloody phone stop ringing?

Lara was tired of picking it up. However, since she was stuck alone during Doris' lunch hour, she couldn't rely on anyone else. She hated fielding calls. It didn't help when the clients wanted to interact with her rather than the staff. And she'd already dealt with a nightmare barely thirty minutes ago, when that guy she hardly knew, Vishal, had called to ask her out on a date. She didn't have it in her to field another crisis today.

She ruffled through a sheaf of papers with exasperation, exhaled a calming breath as she punched the button with a steady hand and laid her elbows on her desk to answer the call. "Lara Reddy."

"Hey, babe. How you doing?"

Sam. Bless her. Relieved, she let out the breath she hadn't known she'd been holding. She'd expected to hear her mother at the other end or some nagging client. Her best friend couldn't have chosen a better time to call, and she was grateful for the respite a short conversation with her would provide.

"Hey, babe. What a pleasant surprise. How's it going in Casablanca?"

Sam chuckled. "Oh, I wouldn't know ... seeing how I was in Dubai last night ... and am now heading to my beachfront property in Grand-Baie for a much-needed break."

"Oh my God! You're back!" Lara squealed.

"Finally. That hotel room had even started to look like home, know what I mean?"

She nodded. "That's the worst."

Sam sighed. "Okay, you sound rattled. What's up?"

Lara laughed. Sam knew how to lighten up her mood.

"You'll never believe this. I'm here just a month, and my sister is already trying to fix me up with someone." Diya needed a stern talking-to!

Sam burst into laughter, her voice bubbly with amusement. "Well, good for you. Finally, the family's out with it. I wondered how long it would take them to start arranging potential matches."

"Very funny," Lara said, her tone dripping with sarcasm. Nothing funny there—only more problems created by her entourage.

"Yes, it is," Sam replied as her voice lowered to the normal, slightly breathless tone. "Anyway, I need to drop by the office before heading to the bungalow. Let's meet up at six?"

"Of course. Should I order sushi?"

"Perfect. After a month of rich Arabian spices, I so need soothing Asian flavours for my palate."

"Great. See you any time after six."

She cut the call with a smile. Finally, something to look forward to. She'd have to run by the store on the way home to nab some Haagen-Dazs tubs. Only then would the evening with Sam be a hit.

Sam arrived at her place at precisely six-thirty and flopped down on the sofa as soon as she reached the living room. Lara took a minute to study her, then shook her head in disbelief.

In her dark-burgundy tailored suit, Sam could pass for a model. Actually, Sam would resemble a model in a potato sack. The A-line skirt touched her knees, but even what lay exposed could be contenders for the longest legs on earth. With her pale skin and reddish hair, most people mistook her for Caucasian rather than Indian.

Bloody cow. Sam didn't pay attention to her appearance other than to seem put together. Yet, it eluded Lara how a woman could look sexy and beautiful without any conscious effort. Her own five-foot-eight figure could rival any model's, but Sam had a special something that turned heads everywhere she went. “You look like such a bitch, you know?”

Sam stretched wine-coloured lips into a very bitchy smile. “Thank you, darling. It’s the exact effect I wanted to achieve.”

The corporate world expected nothing less from the women who dared to ‘infringe’ into its circle. More the case in Sam’s cutthroat strategic business development world.

The atmosphere lay still for a minute before they burst into laughter.

“So, what are you doing around this area in the middle of the week?” Lara asked as she bumped the freezer door closed with her hip, tubs of ice cream in her hands. She’d called for the sushi delivery, which was supposed to come around seven.

In the living room, she handed Sam a carton and a spoon while she hogged the other. Flopping onto a seat across from her best friend, she popped the lid and dunked her spoon into what she called orgasm in a tub.

Sam sighed. “Long overdue for a break, sweets. I’m starting my weekend already here.”

The words hid something, and the feeling deepened when she noticed Sam hadn’t opened her ice cream. There was definitely something wrong because Sam was more of an ice cream fiend than she was.

Narrowing her eyes, she studied her friend.

Hollow cheeks, high cheekbones, and the shadowed circles camouflaged by skilful concealer application under the tired eyes.

Sam was an expert at hiding her feelings, but Lara knew her. Something was bothering her friend.

“Babe, what’s the matter?” She then gasped and sat up straighter. “Something happened between you and Salim?”

Goodness, no. Her two best friends in the whole world couldn’t be breaking up! She hadn’t seen him at all next door in all the time she’d been here, come to think of it. Was Sam getting the bungalow in their divorce settlement?

No, that couldn’t be. No couple was as glued to each other as this one. Or, actually, no husband was glued to his wife as Salim was to Sam.

Sam closed her eyes, and a veil of sadness settled on her face as she let the corners of her mouth droop. "I got my period. Again."

A flood of relief coursed through her. So they weren't breaking up.

Then, the implications of Sam's words filtered in.

"Oh, babe. I'm sorry." She reached out and clasped the perfectly manicured hand resting in Sam's lap.

"This is a curse. I just can't get pregnant. And all the travelling isn't helping. I swear I am just about ready to take a full year off and park myself next door doing absolutely nothing in hopes it will make me relax."

The vehemence in the tone hit her hard. She'd never known Sam to be so down and angry. And Sam, relax? Those two words did not go together in any situation. Still, she had to try to calm her friend.

"All hope isn't lost. You've only been trying for a few months—"

"A year!"

"Twelve months, then. It's not something you can just wish for and have it fall into your lap."

Sam managed a faint smile. "I know that, silly. I thought the injections the last doctor prescribed would do the trick, but I've got this thing again."

Lara threw her hands up. *And here we go again.* "Sam, if you keep changing doctors every other month, you're bound to be on a hectic road with all their different treatments. How can you expect anything to work, then?"

Silence greeted her words before Sam burst into tears.

Great. She'd bumped herself off the list of nominations for *Best Friend of the Year* with her comment. But she and Sam had vowed to be perfectly honest with each other, come what may. At least she wasn't faltering in her role. Yet, she wanted to kick herself. She'd never been good with words, and she'd probably made it worse. Sam would take a hug as pity, so she remained where she sat, lost about how to change the gloomy mood.

An idea popped up.

"You'll never guess who I met the other day," she said.

Sam stopped crying and dried her tears with a delicate stroke of her finger.

Lara couldn't resist a frown at how the perfect face was not marred by crying. Trust her perfectionist BFF to use only waterproof makeup.

Blinking, she remembered the topic. Her throat closed for a second, refusing to allow her vocal cords to utter the sound of his name because saying it aloud would change everything.

But she was doing this for Sam. So, she leaned forward and dropped her voice to a low, conspiratorial tone. "I saw Eric."

Sam's eyes grew wide as she bolted upright in her seat. "Get out of here! You met him? And is it the same person I'm thinking of?"

Lara smiled, happy to see the mood back to friendly chatter. She nodded. Sam was one of the few people who knew of her past with Eric.

"Well, are you just gonna sport such a dumb smile? Come on, out with it. I want all the details." Sam's voice thrummed with excitement.

Lara laughed and recounted the meeting at the clinic.

"Okay, the real question I want you to answer. Was he wearing a wedding ring?" Sam asked as Lara finished her tale.

The elation of sharing the confidence crashed, the shards wrapping around her like tendrils of choking agony. "He had a ring on his right hand."

"So he's not married."

"You've forgotten how European, especially French, men wear wedding rings on the right hand."

"No, but this convention means squat in Mauritius. If it's not on the left hand, the ring means nothing."

Could there be hope? Could Eric be unattached after everything that had happened?

And where on Earth would such confirmation get her? Eric was out of her league, always had been.

"Come on, Lara. So this means he could be free, and what you saw could've been a misunderstanding—"

She shot to her feet. "I know what I saw, Sam. The photo didn't lie, and the paper said he and his French floozy named Sophie de-whatever-bollocks were expecting their first child."

"Still, it doesn't sound like Eric," Sam said in a soft tone.

Lara whirled around to stare at her friend. "Excuse me? I remember thinking you're the one who wanted to lead a mob to rip the skin off his spine when you found out."

Sam rolled her eyes. "Don't I recall that."

"Then what the heck are you talking about today, giving him the benefit of the doubt?"

"Because life is short, you idiot. And we're all older and wiser today." Sam paused. "Tell me, sincerely, would you refuse if you were given a second chance?"

The slow burn of anger, combined with the bite of disappointment and the sharp rips of crushed dreams, slashed their way through her. "You know what? If that happened, I definitely wouldn't care."

"The more fool you, then," Sam said.

"Oh, bugger off, you sanctimonious cow."

Sam snorted. "Trust me, we are so not done with this topic."

And that's exactly what has me worried.

A part of her remained on tenterhooks for the next hour. The food delivery came, they settled to eat, and she'd opened a bottle of that non-alcoholic pear cider that was only made in Mauritius.

"So," Sam started as she leaned back on the overstuffed rattan sofas on the upstairs veranda. "Eric, huh?"

Lara turned her head the other way. She couldn't bear for Sam to see how a senseless part of her would grab onto the hope of another chance with Eric if one ever came within a hundred miles.

"Heartbreak, Sam." Lara blinked. What had she let slip? Had she grabbed the wrong bottle at the shop, the boozy kind? How to recover now? "I mean, Roy—"

Sam grabbed the glass from her hand and slammed it on the table. The anger in the gesture stunned her.

"I thought we'd agreed you'd forget about that good-for-nothing arsehole."

She blinked. "Huh?"

"Oh, don't play dumb with me. You're just evading my questioning."

Lara sighed. "I can't help it, Sam. Sometimes, I do think about us—"

"There is no 'us' any longer, don't you get it?" Sam reached for her hand. "You are now single and free and ready to step forward into a wonderful life. Stop wallowing in the past and what might have been. You know that's no good."

"I know."

"And there's so much you can look forward to," her friend continued. "Like Eric."

She pulled her hand back. "Excuse me?"

Sam waved the question away with a wide gesture. "Stop being such a nincompoop. When will you figure out his path crossed yours for a reason?"

"Atonement for him, punishment for me. That's why we met again."

Sam sighed. "You are such an idiot."

"So you keep saying. May I remind you he could very well be married?"

"The ring was not on his left hand, for God's sake."

"Still, I'm not taking chances. I'm not a homewrecker."

"Won't you always wonder what could happen if he isn't married?"

"And what if he is? How would you feel if I pushed you into the arms of a married man? Would an affair making you the other woman satisfy you?"

"I wouldn't be the other woman, Lara, because I'm a Muslim. Muslim men are allowed to marry four times, so I'd be wife number something in his life."

"That is not the point!"

"Then what is the real problem?"

She sagged in her seat. "Eric is white, Sam. I'm brown. Where does that leave us?"

"Exactly where you two left off fourteen years ago. The difference in skin colour was never an issue before, was it? What's changed now?"

Everything. Sam didn't know that, for Lara, their cultural and ethnic differences *had* been an issue. A big deal, even, because such diversity could be a double-edged sword. Would they have had a future? Would they have fought? Could they have done it back then, and could they do it now if needs be?

She had no answers to these questions and wouldn't search for answers. To do so would bring too much pain by opening a wound she'd thought healed a long time ago.

Except she hadn't healed. She'd patched an Elastoplast on and gotten on with her life. Seeing Eric again had ripped the sticky strip off the festering cut.

"I'm starting to get a headache. I'd forgotten this cider doesn't agree with me." She blurted the excuse, not daring to glance up at her best friend.

"Fine. Let's call it a night."

They went downstairs to the front door. On the porch, Sam stopped and turned around. "Promise you'll at least give it some thought."

Lara bit her lip and nodded. Sam might plead all she wanted, but there'd never be anything between her and Eric again. Highly improbable that they'd bump into each other once more, and if they did, she knew how she was supposed to act.

She'd never had any place in Eric Marivaux's life—something she should never forget.

CHAPTER FIVE

"Seen today's papers yet?" Doris asked as she popped into the office.

Lara smiled without lifting her focus from the reports on her desk. "Yes, good reviews again."

"It's no mean feat, you know, especially since the conference is not yet over."

She glanced up at her PA. "As you say, it's not yet over. I'll bask in the glory tomorrow when everything's concluded, and I'll know nothing untoward happened."

"Oh, well. Suit yourself."

The words carried on a heavy sigh, and she caught the exaggerated shrug before the other woman walked out of the office.

She couldn't help but smile. Doris, and most of her staff, thought she was hard on herself. Somehow, she had broken through their reserve and established a positive team spirit on all the floors of the conventions centre. They'd dubbed her as "the MD's own slave driver," given how she never let up in her own perfectionism. She laughed them off, but she couldn't slacken the reins just because she'd been doing a good job until now. One moment of inattention and everything could crumble—the centre was too young to stand on its own feet. She'd been given a job and had vowed to do it to the best of her capabilities.

The clock on her desk read eleven-thirty. She'd promised to attend a talk, the last one of the morning, set to end at noon. She would then have to mingle with the guests during the one-hour lunch break.

She also had a few phone calls before leaving her office and attended to them before going down to the main conference floor.

A quick pass through the main lobby assured her the catering manager had again pulled off a spectacular spread on the white-draped trestle tables. She'd been observing him since he'd seemed a bit out of it during the conference lead-up. She knew his wife had just had a baby. The poor bloke had to sleep over at his in-laws' place rather than his own home, as most young mothers on the island chose to spend the first forty days after birth at their own mothers' house. The tradition always gave her the heebie-jeebies. She'd cut the man some slack as he'd seemed to feel the same way. Still, he hadn't let her down, nor had the IT guy. Highlights of every talk played continuously over the many screens and interactive terminals dotting the area.

All seemed set. She prayed no mishap would happen today, and they'd all emerge from this maiden voyage unscathed and actually flying high.

Pausing at the closed door of a soundproof room, she hoped she would be able to slip in quietly without disrupting the exposé going on inside. Inconspicuous—that's how she should be around here. And so far, she had managed to be just that.

Would he constantly be reminded of Lara everywhere he went?

Eric sat at the back of the conference room, his attention on Lara's father behind the podium. Prem Hemant, one of the leading cardiac surgeons in the Indian Ocean region, presented the talk on developments in cardiac surgery. Professor Hemant was known as a very busy man, so how had the organizers managed to get him to host the session?

As he cut his gaze from the man, a door to his left opened, and Lara made a discreet entry.

He sat up straighter and blinked. Once. Twice. The image refused to change. He couldn't be hallucinating, could he? And what was she doing there? Just his luck, she'd accompanied her father. He'd come to the conference to get his mind off her, and there she was. Was Fate taunting him yet again?

From where she stood near the front of the room, she had eyes only for the man on the stage. At the same moment, her father beamed a smile her way. Her face softened when she smiled back.

A spear of pain pierced through his heart. There'd been a time when she had peered at *him* like that. Adoring love had drifted out of her every glance, her every smile. The whole world had seen no one else but him in her heart.

How wrong he'd been because the same certitude had shone on her face the day he had seen her with the man she had married. The day he'd known for sure, he'd lost her forever.

How had he been so stupid to let her go? Lara could raise Hell when she wanted, but his relationship with her had been the best thing for him. He'd always felt a little reserve on her part, a slice of her trust she'd never given entirely, but he'd thought he'd have time to conquer her defences and get her to trust him completely.

Then, France had happened. He'd scrambled to get there in time and settle into a medical student's life. Sophie had seen the opening to get into his life.

He'd lost touch with Lara as a result. She had turned her back on him and fallen into the arms of that other guy.

Eric blanked out his mind and let his gaze roam over her.

She wore a crimson tailored suit which accentuated her tall, slim figure. The rich colour brought a glow to her olive skin, and the subtle light in the room played on her features to highlight her cheekbones and the soft line of her jaw. Her dark eyes were hooded as she watched her father as if she understood every intricacy of triple-bypass surgery. A strand of hair fell across her cheek, and she reached up to tuck the silky brown lock behind her ear.

His gaze travelled to the back of her slender neck, left bare by her swept-up hair. Delicate strands resembling spun wisps brushed the matte skin, and he itched to touch her to see if she'd still feel tingles from his fingertips there …

Eric snapped out of his reverie and shook his head to dissolve the sensual picture in his mind. He closed his eyes and took a deep breath. *Merde*, but he shouldn't lose his control over the mere sight of her. He forced his eyelids open once he'd driven the message into his brain, but he couldn't refrain from staring at her again.

So much for control. He might as well indulge, right? A masochistic tendency, but what could he do?

He drank in every detail of her body, going over her delicate profile, softly rounded shoulders, and the lean line of her arms crossed in front of her. Her left hand lay over the sleeve on her right arm, and her golden skin made a startling contrast against the dark fabric.

Bells rang in his head, and he sat ramrod-straight in his seat as the realization struck him.

No ring on her third finger.

Which meant …? Had she broken up with her husband? He couldn't conceive of any other reason for her not to wear her wedding ring. Lara had a thing for showing her commitment. She'd worn the charm bracelet he had gifted her on her seventeenth birthday every single day.

A thought of Annabelle crossed his mind. They'd spoken over the phone a few times, and though he had found an easy camaraderie with her, something remained missing.

Because she wasn't Lara.

He'd thought he'd lost her for good, but maybe not … Trying to get over her had always been like swimming upstream when the water just wanted to carry him downward and away. He was tired of the constant battle, and maybe he should give up arms and stop fighting. What point was there trying to beat the inevitable?

Hope swelled in his heart. Could this mean he could try to win her back? He had no scruples about wooing her if she were free. He'd realized long ago his happiness lay with her, try as much as he had to bury that thought, and he'd be damned if he let her get away again.

Movement erupted around him, and he realized the talk was over. His attention fastened on Lara, watching her every move as she made her way to the front of the room with a slow, languid pace that set his blood to boil. Was that how she'd move in a bedroom? One of his greatest regrets remained that he and Lara had never made love. She'd been a virgin, and he'd wanted to wait for the right time, the perfect time. But then, the university's acceptance letter came, and all his projects crashed.

Today can be a new beginning.

He got up and moved to where she stood, chatting with her father and Markus Hendrickson.

Markus, a friend of his father's, called him into their midst.

"Eric, what a surprise. Didn't think you'd attend, seeing how you once said such symposiums weren't your thing." Markus laughed. "How are you, dear boy?"

"Fine, thank you," he replied with a smile and clasped the outstretched hand.

Out of the corner of his eye, he noticed Lara lower her gaze and avert her face. But not before he caught the deep blush staining her cheeks.

"Eric, allow me to introduce Professor Prem Hemant and Lara Reddy, his daughter, who also happens to be this centre's Managing Director," Markus said before turning to the other two people. "This is Dr Eric Marivaux, one of the country's leading paediatricians."

If he hadn't been standing stock-still, he would've lost his footing.

Lara *worked* here?

His mind went into overdrive, scrambling for all the implications the statement carried for him. Surely, they wouldn't appoint a temp to such an important position.

Which meant she could be here permanently. And alone, too? Come to think of it, had she actually confirmed she was here on vacation back at the clinic?

He recovered in time to shake Prem Hemant's hand, forcing his mind to clear. "It's an honour to meet you, sir. I have studied a lot of your work at the faculty in France."

The cardiologist's face broke into a significant smile. "Really, young man? Where did you pursue your medical career?"

"The faculty is now known as Bordeaux Segalen," he replied before turning to Markus. "Thank you for introducing us. But I already know Lara. Our acquaintance goes back to our high school days."

"Good Lord, ain't that a surprise." Markus turned his startled face to Lara.

Prem Hemant also turned to her. "I thought I knew all your friends from your high school days. How come we never saw this young man at home?"

"It was a long time ago, Daddy," she said in a small voice, not lifting her gaze.

A movement caught his eye. She clutched her hands so hard, knuckles white. Yet, she refused to acknowledge him with a glance.

She's searching for an escape.

Why did Lara want to run? He meant her no harm. In fact, he wanted only the best for her. He wouldn't presume he was that, but he'd try to be, if she ever gave him a chance.

Their paths hadn't crossed again for no reason. He had to take his shot.

With a step, he moved to her side and dipped his head so he could speak in her ear.

"How about having a drink with me later, when you're finished here?"

She froze before she snapped her head up, fire blazing in the depths of her gaze. He'd bet she was about to open her mouth to give him a verbal lashing.

But after a second, she blinked and settled her features into a mask of calm, detached composure.

Her mouth betrayed her, though. Set in a tight line, the lips opened only to say, "No."

He wouldn't disrespect her consent. Ever. But a part of him wanted—needed—closure if a second chance wasn't on the cards. For that reason, he'd push.

The sound of a throat clearing cut through the tension-filled air, and they turned towards the two men who were still in their midst. Prem Hemant and Markus Hendrickson both wore quizzical expressions.

Eric bent his head slightly, his lips mere centimetres from her ear.

"Please," he said in a whisper. "And also, it would be rude of you to turn me down now."

She jerked her head away in a swift move, and he caught the smell of her perfume. Light and sweet, with headier notes of some flower, maybe ylang-ylang. He'd smelled the essence at a plantation on nearby Reunion Island once.

The delicate scent belied her ferocious nature, though. Anger flashed in her eyes, which she'd drawn to slits, and fury turned her mouth into a tight, white line.

He had her cornered. Far from him to be jubilant, but they needed to have that—possibly—last conversation.

He needed to say sorry, at the very least.

"Five-thirty, lounge bar," he added.

Through no mean feat on her part, the hours flew by. She'd wanted to lose herself in work, lose track of time, but she reckoned the precise moment when five o'clock struck on the clock. Her focus trained out the window onto the sprawling garden bathed in late afternoon sun, Lara bit her lip.

She should've said no. The thought had bugged her the whole afternoon, gnawing at her insides while she cursed her weak resolve. Eric had no right to affect her so much, not now, not after having dropped her out of his life like a hot potato he didn't want to handle. She should despise him, be on extreme alert in his presence, especially so she would notice when she turned into an idiot who fell under his spell after a mere four-five seconds of staring. How had she not realized he had all but compelled her into accepting the date at the lounge?

It's not a date!

She couldn't afford to go. It wasn't simply a matter of being in close proximity with him, but also pertinent to the little sanity she had left, snatches of equilibrium Roy had not robbed her of. Eric played havoc with her senses, and she hated the loss of control more than the treacherous feelings blooming inside her whenever she thought of him. As if a door had opened and everything that could overwhelm her was trying its damnedest best to squeeze in at the same time.

Yet, in not saying no, she'd agreed to meet him, so she couldn't go back on her word.

Damn him. He still knew her so well. Her demise had come from the penetrating, intense look he had sent her when she'd been about to decline his invitation.

That same long, pointed glance had been her downfall in the past, because it could conquer all her defences and lay her bare. Somehow, it had always spoken to her about the formidable, demanding man Eric could be beneath the easy-going attitude. Shivers used to course through her when he'd stared at her like that, when she'd imagined him undressing her with more than his gaze and setting his warm hands all over her body.

When Eric trained that kind of attention on her, she'd agree to whatever he'd ask of her.

Hence her inability to say no to his invitation.

Damn it. Why did he have to have that very effect on her? She still reeled from a painful divorce with a man she'd grown to love. So, she shouldn't be pining after another man, no matter if he happened to be her first love, the one that got away.

But she'd caught her breath and felt her heart go all pitter-patter when she'd taken full notice of Dr Eric Marivaux in the conference room. He wore a dark olive-green suit over a beige shirt, with a green and gold silk tie. The outfit had brought out his light golden tan and made his thick hair gleam with the rich colour of a wheat field basking under the sun. His deep-blue eyes had struck her as darker than she remembered, as if offset in contrast to the golden aura of him. Mind-boggling gorgeous would be an understatement, something she hadn't thought possible. How could he appear even more handsome than all those years before?

True, a nineteen-year-old teenager couldn't compare to a thirty-three-year-old man. Age had defined and sharpened his features, and those mesmerizing irises still holding so much laughter had acquired unfathomable depths brought on by life experience. From a lanky lad, he'd grown into a well-built man, and his shoulders had filled, thus giving him the breadth to carry his height of well over six feet.

Lara sighed and closed her eyes. Like a kaleidoscope of images and sensations, in her mind, she flashed back to the memory of her first kiss. Under the gentle heat of miraculous winter sun in Curepipe, feelings had wrapped around her, imprinting themselves into her whole being for a lifetime. The first time a man's warmth had wrapped around her, and she'd given in to the heady, intoxicating feel of being alive in the embrace of someone who pressed light, fleeting kisses onto her lips while she basked in the protective hold of his arms.

Of Eric's arms.

A tear trickled down her cheek, and she blinked hard, her gaze unfocused, to stop the moisture and return to the present.

Quarter past five. She should go down.

At the edge of the lounge, she stopped in the doorway to give the interior a quick scan.

There he was, seated near one of the windows facing west, towards the sunset. Rays of sunlight merrily danced in his hair, lighting them time and again with a soft, golden glow.

How handsome he is.

She pursed her lips and gave herself a mental slap. She was here to honour her word. Full stop.

Eric had deserted her and broken her heart. She wouldn't hand him a second chance to toy with her again.

Eric felt Lara's presence before he saw her. A sudden tension bristled along his spine.

He turned to face the doorway in case she thought of fleeing.

She met his gaze, distrust pinching her face. The beautiful, lush mouth was again in a thin, flat line.

Any sane person would duck for cover right away. He refused to give in to her formidable stance, though. If she thought he'd flinch from the accusation in her eyes, she'd be wrong.

She had every right to hold a grudge against him. But he would stand his ground because this was a new beginning.

She slowly made her way to his table, and he stood while she seated herself. Manners drilled into him from childhood about etiquette and propriety might bring good dispositions. Not that Lara appeared ready to cut him any slack, though.

"Should I order a 7-Up for you?" he asked once he returned to his chair.

"I prefer Pepsi."

Since when? She used to hate any kind of cola. From the tight expression on her face, she might've contradicted him just for the fun of it. Seems she'd make him sweat.

He tensed and nodded, signalling the waiter. After he ordered, silence descended even after the server brought her drink and set the glass before her.

Eric watched her. *Merde*, but she was more beautiful than in his memories. Teenage Lara had nothing on the grown woman. She'd matured into an alluringly sophisticated creature.

However, beneath the façade, had she really changed? He still seemed capable of rattling her, same as long ago. She was not over him, possibly, just like he'd never gotten over her.

Where did that leave them?

Her left hand lay on the table, and he darted a quick glance at her fingers.

She pulled her arm back and placed it under the table as soon as she noticed his perusal.

Not enough time to spot if a paler band of skin rested on her third finger where her ring should've been.

The seconds ticked by, and she neither spoke nor did she reach for her drink. He'd been right. She'd ordered Pepsi to contradict him.

Lara. He wanted to sigh. *This is me you're trying to kid.*

"You know," he said. "When I asked you for a drink, I didn't mean it just literally. I planned on some conversation, as well."

She shrugged. "What do you want to talk about?"

"Everything and nothing." He paused. "How's life? And how's your husband?"

She lowered her eyelids at the mention of the other man. The silence stretched, and he wondered if she would answer him or tell him to get lost.

Lara took a deep, audible breath and brought her gaze up to meet his.

"He's doing okay, I guess," she said softly.

Trouble in paradise? A part of him wanted to jump with joy. Callous of him, but the only thing he registered was that she could be free. The urge to find out burned through him like wildfire, but he wouldn't press, at least not yet. So he raised an eyebrow.

She squirmed under his scrutiny before squaring her shoulders. "How's your wife?"

He clamped his jaw, and a muscle started ticking in his cheek after a few seconds.

So that's what happened. Lara thought he'd married Sophie. So much for Lara having faith in them.

But what was done was done, and they had to look forward, not back. Could they have a second chance today? Or in the future?

He wanted Lara. If there was a chance she wanted him, too, he would fight to make them happen.

So, he shook his head and gave her a slow, lazy smile. She'd never been able to resist that one back in the day.

"I'm not married, Lara. Never have been."

She widened those almond-shaped eyes, and her lower lip trembled when she opened her mouth. Different emotions played on her features. Surprise, doubt, insecurity, and finally, anger. She bit her lip as if to refrain from saying something aloud. A blank mask settled over her face in the second that followed. Yet, as before, she couldn't mask her gaze.

Her pupils were dilated by some strong emotion, and the dark irises darted back and forth.

"What happened with your husband?" he asked gently.

She stared back for what seemed like ages. Had he pushed her too far?

"We divorced three years ago. I'm back here now."

Words died on his lips at her whispered statement. He'd hoped to hear she was single and had prayed for it. Hurt crashed through him that she'd had to face something as terrible as a divorce. She'd had her share of struggles in the past, enough for a lifetime.

Lara must've suffered through her breakup. The agony on her face spelled the trauma all too well. She deserved careful, gentle handling. He'd have to go slow with her.

She shot to her feet. "I'm sorry. I have to go now."

No—he wouldn't let her run away. Not when he'd found her again.

Eric caught her wrist as she passed by his chair. She slowly turned and faced him.

"Have dinner with me one night."

The words spilled from his lips before he could think them through. What happened to careful and gentle handling? If he spooked her, she'd run. Not good.

Training his gaze on her, he pleaded for her acceptance with his eyes.

She pursed her lips and withdrew her hand, running the tips of her fingers along his when she pulled back.

Don't do this, please.

"I have to go," she said softly before turning and leaving the room at a hurried pace.

CHAPTER SIX

Lara slumped on the sofa in her living room when she returned to her house.

She had no clue how she'd gotten home. She remembered hyperventilating while walking to the car and then trying to regulate her breathing once inside the vehicle. She'd switched on the engine, and the next thing she knew, she sat on her sofa. How on earth had she survived driving back with no conscious thought? She hadn't even made it back into her office. Of course, it wasn't like her to cut and run like this, but there had been extenuating circumstances, right?

Thank goodness she was still in one piece and hadn't hurt anybody during the drive.

Why is everything getting so complicated? Why now?

She closed her eyes for a second and clutched her hand, which he'd grasped as she'd been leaving. Her skin still tingled where he'd grazed it.

No man had ever left such an impression on her. Not even Roy.

She threw her head back, staring at the ceiling. Why was she getting all worked up over Eric? She had no place in her life for a man. And he had betrayed her. Getting thrown once, shame on him. Getting thrown twice, shame on *her* for allowing such a thing to happen when she should've learned her lesson.

"Have dinner with me one night."

The words, spoken in a husky, seductive tone, had flowed over her like a caress. His deep blue irises had pierced through her heart to her soul in the way only he could.

Roy had dimmed memories of Eric when he'd walked into her life. Now her husband was gone, and her first love seemed hell-bent on stepping back in.

What should she do? Barricade the door, or open it wide?

Wanting an anchor, she had the good sense to ditch her clothes, wrap her knuckles, and put on the ankle supports. Then she started attacking the tethered punching bag in a room at the back of her house.

An hour later, she was half-naked, glistening with sweat, exhausted both physically and mentally. Still nowhere close to finding an answer, let alone a solution, to her dilemma.

She should be ashamed for wanting to welcome a man who had discarded her after stomping all over her heart.

The loud ring of her phone zapped her out of her thoughts. A quick glance at the screen, and she sighed. In the wake of the meeting with Eric, she'd completely forgotten she had to go out that evening.

"Hi, Sam." Would her friend pick up on the weariness in her tone?

"Where the hell are you? The function is about to start, and you were supposed to be here ages ago."

Lara sighed again. No way out of the whole affair. Sam's sister-in-law, and incidentally Auntie Zubeida's daughter—one just couldn't escape neighbours who morphed into relatives of some sort here—was getting married. If she didn't go, she'd have the whole Majeed clan and her own mother all on her back. In other words, Hell would look like R&R.

"I'll be there shortly. Some unexpected stuff cropped up at the centre in the afternoon."

"All right, we're waiting for you. Hurry up."

The pain in Lara's heart came back. Another wedding, she sighed.

She remembered her wedding. She'd been radiant, according to Roy.

"If I wasn't already smitten with you, I would have lost my heart when I saw you walking towards me in your bridal outfit."

Until the moment before the ceremony, she'd thought she'd been dreaming, and reality would poke its head in soon dissolving the arranged marriage.

Lara had never thought she'd marry someone like Roy. A man like Eric had seemed more likely. Born and raised in England, where she'd spent her first sixteen years, a proper Indian husband hadn't fit into her plans. Instead, she would move out of the family house and become one of the many young, single and carefree of a new generation living in cosmopolitan London.

First, her father landed the once-in-a-lifetime position to manage Mauritius's newly established cardiac surgery hospital. Then, with patriotism as an excuse, her mother had utilised the perfect opportunity. She'd brought her daughters back into a culture-driven world where she could make them lead proper lives away from the loose morals of Western culture.

The marriage proposal from Roy Reddy, a British subject born to an Indian father and a Mauritian mother, had come one month after her eighteenth birthday. Roy's mother had been an acquaintance in London, and Gayatri Hemant had kept in touch with her. When it became time for Sarita Reddy to search for a bride for her son, she'd naturally thought of Lara.

Under normal circumstances, she would have refused the proposal, like the half dozen 'proper' matches her mother had pushed her way since she'd turned eighteen.

However, this proposal had come seven months after Eric's departure to France. And a few days after she'd stumbled upon a picture of him with a beautiful blonde socialite in the glossy pages of a French society rag.

With a heavy heart, she'd agreed to marry Roy, knowing she needed to confine Eric to her past. Her mother had ascribed her acceptance to her being homesick for London and Roy being a way for her to go back there.

In a sense, her mother had been correct. Lara had wanted to put distance between her and Mauritius, which had brought her nothing but shattered illusions and a broken heart.

Tears gathered in her eyes as she thought back to that harrowing episode of her life, and she quickly blinked them away when her phone rang again. Sam.

"You're thinking of your wedding, innit?" her friend said in greeting.

Spot on, but she couldn't admit to that. "I was thinking of your own wedding and how Salim crashed through the door to have a forbidden glimpse at you before the function."

Sam burst out laughing. "Yeah, and all the old biddies nearly had heart attacks."

After a pause, she added, "Lara, I know you must be thinking of Roy today. Don't lie. I know he's on your mind."

Lara remained silent and lowered her gaze to her lap. Was she so transparent? Did everyone know she was tortured by the memory of her failed marriage?

Sam sighed. "I have to go now. Try to forget him, and come over and enjoy yourself."

She nodded in reply, then added a small yes. What else could she do? Happiness seemed to thrive around her, but the feeling didn't appear like it wanted to knock on her door.

Are you sure? What about Eric?

Where had *that* come from? She was alone but not unhappy. Twice, she'd made the mistake of putting all her trust in a man, and twice, it had been thrown back into her face. First with Eric himself, then with Roy.

A third time would be one time too many.

What if he's thinking of you?

She shook herself inwardly. *Get a grip, Lara.*

Eric had his life, probably filled with his work and a woman who hung on to his every word. Gorgeous, rich, and eligible men like him didn't remain single for more than a day. So why would he pine for Lara, the one he'd dumped?

She should heed Sam's words and try to enjoy herself tonight. Granted, it would be no mean feat, but she could definitely try.

Well, at least if she stopped thinking of Eric.

"Penny for your thoughts," a soft, throaty voice said.

Eric forced his wandering mind back to the present and focused on the woman who sat opposite him at the restaurant table. The slight smile on her beautiful face took the edge off the sharp question.

"I'm not lost in my thoughts," he replied with a chuckle.

"You haven't listened to a word I've said all through dinner," Annabelle said with a pout.

He closed his eyes for a second. She spoke the truth. He'd been miles away, thinking of Lara and how she'd run from him earlier.

He sighed. He'd go after her. But would she allow him back into her life? By the look of things, he had his work cut out.

"Eric." Annabelle sighed. "You're zoning out on me again."

He blinked out of his worries. "Sorry. I have a lot on my mind today."

She skewered him with a narrowed gaze over the flicker of the candles lighting the table. In the soft glow, she was stunning and elegant in her navy blue dress. However, her piercing grey eyes drew his attention, the silver irises fixed on him.

The waiter arrived, cleared the dishes and left.

Eric leaned across the table and gave her his full attention.

"I know I haven't been good company tonight, and I'm really sorry."

Truth be told, he didn't want to be here.

Annabelle watched him over the rim of her coffee cup. Then she shook her head, put the cup down, and trained that frank gaze once more onto him.

"This is not going to work," she stated.

He agreed, but he wouldn't be a *connard* and say so aloud.

"I'm sorry," he simply said.

She shook her head again, sending long dark tresses flying every way. The waiter had a very narrow escape from the lashing locks.

"We both know why we're here. We both thought we were having dinner with your mother."

His turn to sigh. The woman had set them up, something he hated.

"And when your mother calls," Annabelle continued. "You drop everything and say yes. Trust me, she might not have a job title, but everyone on the island knows of her. Her formidable reputation precedes her, and her influence makes things happen."

Yes, something like that. As if by magic, too. He'd never underestimated his mother, and he wouldn't start now. Still, he'd fallen into that trap, as well. Easier to acquiesce than fight back, though he would where it really mattered.

Like Lara.

He took in a sharp breath at the thought of her. He shouldn't have her on his mind, not while he was here with Annabelle. Not fair on his dinner partner, even if they had been coerced into this date. They'd reported to the maître d' pulpit of this French restaurant in Pamplemousses, a small village twenty minutes from either Grand-Baie or Port-Louis, the capital city where Annabelle worked … only to find that Agnes Armont-Marivaux had had to excuse herself, but her booking still standing, the two of them could have dinner together.

"Okay, something's really on your mind. Dish," she said. "I'm a good listener."

Really? She wanted him to talk to her of the woman who held his heart in her grip?

"Fine, I'll go first," she stated. "I have a confession to make."

He raised an eyebrow at this.

She rolled her eyes before fixing them on him again. "Remember how I told you I didn't want romance and love and all that hoopla?"

He nodded.

Her turn to raise her eyebrows. "Well, I lied. I do want all of it." She paused to take a deep breath. "And I know that's not going to happen with you."

Her words made him reel. Here she was giving him the perfect out—he should jump on it.

But he couldn't. She was too much a precious, beautiful soul for him to hurt her that way. "I'm sorry."

She shrugged. "It's okay. I like to tell myself I can do that, marry for convenience and not love, but I can't. I just have to take one look at—"

Was she going to confess her secret crush? Silence settled between them, making him yearn to know.

"Who?" he couldn't resist asking.

Annabelle sighed. "My cousin, Simmi, and her fiancé."

The name rang a bell. "Your cousin? Do I know her?"

She nodded. "Of course you do. Simmi Moyer. Bernard Moyer's daughter."

He remembered now, mainly because Simmi's mother had been of Indian origin. That wedding had created rifts and havoc in their French-Mauritian community when it had taken place so many decades earlier. It had been held over all their heads as something to *not* do ...

And sadly enough, Simmi, being the product of that frowned-upon union, had borne the brunt of the social exclusion directed her mother's way.

He'd thought of that when wanting to pursue Lara. A part of him had hoped things would be different in their time for their children ...

"How is she?" he asked. He'd lost touch with Simmi. They'd been around the same age, friends when they'd been kids. Maybe he should reach out to her once more.

Annabelle gave a long-suffering sigh. "Like I said, engaged. To this guy, Lars."

Something wasn't adding up here. "And you ... like him, too?"

She blinked. "Wait, what? No! Actually, I'm the one who set them up on a blind date. I didn't know him back then. He is a friend of Magnus, my ex. No, they're just so ... mushy and in love! It's a pain to watch. I just wish I could find someone like that, too, you know," she finished.

He hesitated to reach out and grab her hand. Not that he thought it would be misconstrued, but he didn't want to rub salt in her wounds.

"You deserve someone who worships the ground you walk on, too," he said.

At this, she laughed. Then, as she sobered and peered at him again, she grew serious. "You have someone like that, don't you?"

He frowned. He'd never said anything to her.

She rolled her eyes once more. "Come on, it's written all over you. Not to mention that you are who you are—son of Agnes Armont-Marivaux, successful paediatrician also with a reputation that precedes him all over the island. You've got height and good looks, and you're still unattached in your thirties? Hello? I'm not that much of an idiot to not be able to put two and two together."

He debated whether to tell her anything. In the end, she made the decision for him.

"Tell me. What's her name?"

What point was there in fighting? He wouldn't be hurting Annabelle by telling her about the woman he loved.

"Her name is Lara."

"Hmm. Full name?"

"Reddy."

She squinted, then her eyes grew wide. "Wait a second. Isn't that the new MD of the conference centre at *Le Sirius*?"

Surprised, he stared at her. "How do you know that?"

"*Mon chou*, I work in PR. I know everything there is to know about anything or anyone worth their salt on this island."

Okay, she'd firmly put him in the friend zone with that chummy endearment. His shoulders relaxed, though his spine still bristled. If she really knew that much, could he glean some info about Lara through her?

"Okay, I get it. You're too much of a gentleman to ask. I'll tell you what I know."

"I didn't say anything!"

"You didn't have to. PR, remember? I also know how to read people." She leaned forward and propped her cheek onto one palm. "Your girl is the buzz of the place. They say Markus Hendrickson personally recruited her after he had top head-hunters find her and pinch her from the corporate business hotel she worked for in London. Her first conference was a stellar hit, and there are rumours that, with her expertise and drive behind the centre, they are going to bid to host the next Commonwealth Nations' conference should Mauritius be hosting it.

"Now, her personal life. It's all a bit hush-hush. Reports say she is divorced. Already was when she rose up the ranks in the English capital. Comes from a very well-known family from Curepipe, her father almost a celebrity thanks to being renowned for his pioneering of cardiac treatments locally. Personality-wise, they say she's a bit of an ice queen, but I'm reserving judgement on that until I meet her myself. They also call Simmi an ice queen, yet I know her as one of the warmest human beings to have ever existed." She finally paused for breath. "Question is, now—where do *you* fit in amidst all that?"

Should he tell her? Strangely, a part of him told him he could trust her. And *merde*, he so wanted—no, needed—to finally get his thoughts and feeling about Lara out in the open.

"She spent about two years here as a teen, for her A-Levels. We ..." he paused. "We dated back then."

Annabelle's eyes grew even wider. "No way!"

"Way," he said with a chuckle. Being with her felt like being young and carefree again. He'd missed that kind of lightness in his life.

"So now ..." She tilted her head as she studied him. "She is single, from what I've heard, and so are you. What next?"

He sighed and ran a hand in his hair as he leaned back in his chair. "Next? I have no clue."

"It was serious between you, wasn't it?" she asked softly.

He nodded.

"Then you just have to win her back."

"As if it's that simple."

She made a grimace. "That's true. Especially considering who you are and all that."

He grimaced, too. She didn't need to spell it out—they were speaking of his mother now. Formidable Agnes Armont-Marivaux was one obstacle he would totally crash into in his quest to get Lara accepted as his partner. Lara would never fit the bill.

She was of Indian origin, divorced, and not from a 'good society' family.

But this was his life, and no one could or would choose for him. One way or the other, he would have her.

Even if Lara didn't appear to want him back, he'd win her over in the end.

"Any help you need, I'm here," Annabelle told him.

Eric smiled at her as he did reach out to clasp her hand this time.

"Thank you."

CHAPTER SEVEN

Emerging from deep sleep, Lara turned onto her side.

How come the edge of the pillow felt cold and wet? She frowned without opening her eyes. She wasn't at home, so where had she slept? Sliding farther, she bumped her cheek against something soft and slightly threadbare. When she opened her eyes, the sight of Sarah, her childhood rag doll, greeted her from the edge of the mattress. Across the room, she found Ronan Keating front and centre on the Boyzone poster staring at her from the life-size image tacked onto the wall.

She was home. Well, no longer 'home' for her. Her parents' place and her former bedroom.

The function had lasted until the wee hours of the morning, and her father had refused to let her drive without getting some shut-eye first. Hence, she'd crashed in this room which looked like she had stepped out as an eighteen-year-old yesterday. Her mother hadn't altered a single detail. Wistfully, Lara recalled the many mornings she had awoken in this same squishy bed that never remained warm enough in the cold temperatures of Curepipe. Interior heating had been an alien concept in Mauritius back in the day and still was today.

This morning felt no different than the ones she'd experienced over a decade before. The birds sang outside the window, heralding the promise of a sunny day, even if the temps wouldn't hit much above twenty-seven degrees Celsius—a veritable heatwave for Curepipe natives—in the thick of summer. The sound of her mother exuberantly chatting on the phone drifted upstairs, along with the clutter of breakfast dishes. And she lay snuggled in her single bed, wrapped in the too-thin, faded blue quilt, the sight of Eric's handsome face floating before her eyes.

Lara sat up with a start. Cold air washed over her where she'd dropped the quilt, but she dismissed the shivery sensation.

Eric's face didn't belong to the here and now. He should be firmly confined to her past, to the two secondary school years she'd spent in Mauritius. He had no place in her life anymore.

Wait, it must be the poster playing tricks on her mind. Strange how she'd never reckoned how much Eric had ended up resembling Ronan Keating. Especially with the long hair now, they could be doppelgangers.

She blew at the strand of hair that had fallen across her face and tucked it behind her ear. She'd undone the braid before going to sleep. Her hair had still been damp, an invitation to catch a cold or worse if she'd kept the not-dry hair tied up in the cold weather.

A grimace tugged at her lips when she saw the kinks in her locks. Great. When she actively wanted waves, her hair never complied. Disgusted, she glanced at the display on the Minnie Mouse clock on the bedside table. Ten past seven.

Damn. She had to be in her office at nine. If she was lucky enough to evade any traffic jam while going through Port Louis, the trip alone would take an hour. And no, she would not be testing the very steep slopes of the new mountain motorway, not when she had a tendency to lose track of speed in her brand-newMercedes. She didn't have a death wish, thank you very much. Still, how the hell had she not thought to set on an alarm to wake up at five-thirty?

She scrambled out of bed and dashed into the bathroom. She'd slept in an old T-shirt of her dad's, and on her way out after a quick shower, she searched for her discarded *kurta* suit. She groaned when the realization struck. Her mother had already spirited the outfit away for laundry. What would she wear?

Still clad in her towel, she dashed into her sister's room adjoining hers. "Dee, I need some clothes. Can I borrow your stuff?"

A muffled response came from the mound obliterated by a fluffy pink quilt.

Teenagers, she thought with a shake of her head. How come she'd never been plagued by the sleep bug when she'd been of

Diya's age? She'd always gotten up with the sun, trusting the muezzin's call from a nearby mosque for the Muslim Morning Prayer as her wake up alarm.

Piles of discarded clothing dotted the carpet, and she rummaged through in hopes of finding something wearable. Petite Diya hardly topped five feet, whereas Lara had a tall, lean body. All the clothes resembled dolls' outfits.

Finally, she grabbed a stretch top and a wraparound skirt and quickly dressed. The top clung to her like a second skin and squashed her chest like a sports bra, and the skirt barely covered her arse, but she could manage in them. She'd do without underwear for a few hours, though. Diya's stuff would be like children's clothing, and though her mother and she wore pretty much the same size, she wasn't about to ask *her* for underwear. Oh, what shame. She'd have to hope she wouldn't flash anyone before she managed to get home to grab a change.

On her way down, she passed her mother, who stood on the landing with her ear glued to the phone receiver. Probably a very interesting gossip session, never mind that it was still so early in the day. Gossip knew no social schedule in Mauritius. Her mother appeared transfixed as she bobbed her head in agreement with whatever the other person was saying and didn't notice her.

With a shrug, Lara ignored her and went into the kitchen. She paused only long enough to hug her father, who sat at the kitchen table with the morning paper and a huge pot of tea in front of him, then dashed to the stove to grab hot water for a cup of coffee.

Diya stomped into the room as she was grabbing her first sip. How anyone could stomp with their feet in fluffy Minnie Mouse booties eluded her, but trust Diya to be ever the drama queen.

"Lara!" the girl whined. "Did you really have to make so much noise in my room? I can't go back to sleep now."

"It'll do you good to wake up like normal people sometimes." Their father chuckled before exchanging a conspiratorial wink with his eldest daughter.

Just like old times. She smiled back and settled down at the table with her cup of coffee. She loved to take the time to savour her wake-me-up drink, the only time in the day when she didn't feel bombarded from all sides by issues she had to resolve. So, she took her time. The minute she emptied the mug, she'd be out of there.

She'd hardly taken another mouthful when her mother stalked into the room. A cold, disturbing feeling swept over her as she took in the older woman's jubilant expression and wide smile. Trouble brewed as certainly as the witches turned the cauldron to bubbling in the opening scene of *Macbeth*.

As soon as her mother stepped into the room, both her father and her sister made a go for the door. Lara belatedly realised they'd both had the wisdom to leave before being snapped up by Gayatri Hemant's overflowing tongue. The caffeine hadn't hit her bloodstream yet. Otherwise, she'd never have been caught out. Alone with her mother in the deserted kitchen? Not good. How would she escape? She'd burn her mouth and throat if she tipped back the remaining scalding coffee.

She forced down a sip and another. Half the mug to go. She could finish the contents on the way to the sink. So, she stood and started away from the table before something in her mother's diatribe stopped her in her tracks.

"Excuse me?" She turned to face the woman who'd given birth to her and blinked. She had to have heard wrong.

"You silly girl. I knew you wouldn't realize what good fortune has befallen us. Nirmala just called. She has got such a good proposal for you. You'll never believe it."

"Proposal? As in 'marriage'?" Her voice came out in a croak.

"Pfft. But of course. What else could it be?"

Her mother added some derogatory Indian word calling her an airhead somewhere in the statement, but she let the remark pass. More life-threatening matters to tackle first.

A bloody proposal? For an arranged marriage? Never again, not on her life. While a part of her had always known her mother would try to fix up another marriage for her, she'd never taken the threat seriously. Or fathomed that the relatives would get in on it, as well. Stupid of her not to have anticipated such a coup. She was the talk of the island, wasn't she? The only way to wipe off her divorce scandal would be to shack her up with someone else ASAP.

Still, she couldn't blow her top and scream as she wanted to. A tantrum would only be ammunition for her mother's plough-Lara-down campaign. So, she settled for cool logic and detachment.

"Mum, what are you talking about?"

"Nirmala has this wonderful relative. The woman is so concerned about the plight of unmarried girls. Anyway, she has found someone for you, and like I said, you couldn't think of a better offer."

Her mother yapped like a happy puppy, unable to keep to one spot in her excitement. "He's a very good prospect. Rich, of course. Apparently, he has three houses, four cars, and a beachfront villa in Pereybère. Works in a very good position in the Ministry of Foreign Affairs. Must have some good contacts there. Probably even knows the Prime Minister."

Lara sighed. She could at least try to get her opinion forward, but knowing her mother, her words would only fall through. She should simply ride the tide out, except she didn't have time. The sooner she hit the road, the better her chances to make it to the office at nine. And by the look of things, she would be late because she absolutely had to get changed beforehand.

She had to put a stop to this drivel once and for all.

"Mum, I don't plan on getting married again."

Gayatri Hemant's eyes grew big. "What nonsense, Lara. Every woman needs a husband. You're getting such a good proposal. Don't be stupid and refuse this opportunity. You already let one good man go."

She blinked. "Excuse me? So now Roy is no longer a bastard but a *good man*? Since when?"

She should've known, though. This kind of reasoning coming from her mother? Nothing unusual or unexpected. Her mother twisted everything to suit her purposes all the time. Lara had no hope of emerging the victor in such a setup.

So, she blanked out the shrill voice and slurped her coffee, getting closer to freedom as she emptied the mug.

Then her mother stopped talking.

Bad sign.

Lara lent half an ear to the ramblings when the talking started again.

"Only problem is he has two children. They're already into university, but they could fight you for the share of his wealth you'll be due."

Lara didn't know which part of the statement angered her the most. That they were shipping her off to a man old enough to have twenty-year-old kids. Or how they'd already distributed the poor man's wealth between his heirs and his potential new wife before he'd even gotten remarried?

The fury built, rising up right along with incredulity. The pounding throb in her head picked up again, and her lungs burned with the need to drag a full cigarette to ashes in one pull.

Try as she might to calm down, she couldn't, and the words bubbled out of her.

"You mean you are saddling me with a man old enough to be my father, and on top of it, you want me to turn into a gold digger?"

Her mother only shook her head and tsk-tsked reproachfully. "Look at you getting on your high horse." She snorted. "He's a widower. Perfect for you."

At that point, Lara wanted to know only one thing. "How old is he, Mum?"

"If you really have to know, he's in his prime. Nirmala said fifty-nine years old," her mother replied with a dismissive wave of her hand.

"Damn it, Mum. This makes him twenty-seven years older than me. I could be his daughter."

What could she possibly have in common with a man so much older than she? While perfectly possible to meet someone so much older and hit it off, such a relationship seldom happened in an arranged match.

"Would you consider this unfortunate situation you dug yourself into?" her mother asked. "How do you think you'll cope if we're not here to lend you a helping hand? If we'd been by your side, I'm sure none of those idiotic fights between you and your husband would've happened. I mean, look at you—"

"Oh, shut up, will you?" Lara screeched the command, unable to contain herself any longer. "Stop trying to control my life. You've always done this. Why can you never let go?"

Yes, she was screaming, but she needed to win her calm back. She felt entirely capable of murdering both her mother and that Nirmala.

"Lay off, Mother. I'm not getting married again. Full stop."

What had sounded more deadly? The screams or the cold calm in her last statement?

Better yet—had either of her tactics worked on her mother?

No such luck. The older woman stood with legs braced and her hands on her hips. Battle stance.

Alerted by the noise, her father and sister returned to the kitchen. Neither Lara nor her mother bothered with them. Engaged in fight mode, neither ready to be the first to give in.

But the fight wouldn't be bring anything other than making her blow her top. Throwing one last glare at her mother, she headed out and paused as she went past her parent.

Gayatri Hemant's stricken expression conveyed she hovered on the verge of a heart attack. She clenched her hand to her bosom and heaved in big gulps of air.

"What am I going to tell your aunt? She has managed to get you such a good match. How will I tell her you're refusing? Think about it, my girl. You'll be well provided for. You won't need to work another day of your life. And he's not going to bother if you cannot give him children—"

Those last words cut through her with the agony of a red-hot sword tip plunging into her back. So even her mother thought her to be barren? Her husband had kicked her out of his life. His family spoke of her as an evil witch. Society had a thousand and one theories about what failings she must possess for her marriage to have crumbled. But she'd clung to the belief she had her family on her side all along.

Turned out she'd been wrong.

The pain of this realisation flared to obliterate every other hurt inflicted on her in the past few years.

Lara grew aware of a heavy weight dragging her hand down. She still clutched her empty coffee mug. Under her tense, forceful grip containing all her anger and disappointment, her knuckles had gone white around the handle.

The reality of her situation dawned on her then. She was an ex-wife. Getting a divorce had made her cross onto the other side, where people were no longer considered living, breathing creatures with a heart and feelings. More than a pariah, she also had the label of 'discarded property' slapped onto her back like a scarlet letter she should be ashamed of.

Sounds blanked, sights blurred, and nothing but the whoosh of blood at her temples hit home in her perception. Anger shrouded her, wrapped its ice-cold yet burning tentacles around her, scorching her insides like the creeping sting of frostbite.

What had she been thinking when she'd returned to this God-awful place?

In an impulsive fit, she hurled the mug across the room. The ceramic hit the far wall and clattered in pieces onto the hard tiled floor.

Silence rang while all eyes turned onto her. Emotional displays were so not her thing usually. No wonder they were all stunned.

But she wasn't done, far from it. She might be neck-deep in the most bottomless bog of social hell, but damn if she'd give up the fight. High time she put a stop to the marriage bollocks. They weren't in the goddamn Regency era, for goodness' sake. She also had to hold on to the little sanity she still had left, which wouldn't be possible until she'd dotted the i's and crossed the t's with her mother.

She stalked towards the woman and stopped a few inches before their chests bumped.

Only five feet tall, her mother's diminutive stature allowed Lara to tower over her. Using the advantage to the best of her ability, she narrowed her gaze. Her mum took a step back, only to bump into the kitchen counter, nowhere to run.

"Let me clear a few things with you, Mother, and please go repeat it to all those old cronies of yours."

Ice dripped from her tone, and her mother flinched as if burned by acid.

"First, I don't want children, which is why I don't have any. Not because I'm barren. Second, Roy gave me a generous settlement to leave with the least fuss, so I am well provided for financially and don't *need* a job to take me from paycheck to paycheck. Third, my job is my life, and sod you all if you think it's a waste." She paused to inhale. "Fourth and last, tell that old cow to get lost with her proposal and mind her own business for a change."

Not a breath could be heard in the stillness. She bent to stare straight into her mother's eyes.

"Have I made myself clear?"

She turned around and marched out of the kitchen without waiting for an answer. However, with every step she took, her bravado failed, replaced by the dull, sawing cut of betrayal in every cell of her body.

As she passed her father, he placed a hand on her shoulder. She stopped only long enough to peer into his stricken, concerned face.

"I'm sorry," he mouthed.

A heavy lump formed in her throat as she clutched his hand and trained her gaze on her younger sister. Tears shimmered in Diya's eyes, wet stains on her soft cheeks.

She shouldn't have to suffer like this, Lara thought. She was still too young and innocent.

Carefree youth. Had any girl of Indian origin ever experienced some? People directed every moment of their lives, and they lost even the prospect of hope.

Not anymore, though. At least, not for her.

She'd also give her damnedest best to ensure her little sister got a chance at living her life the way Diya wanted to.

She reached out and touched the girl's delicate jaw. "Don't cry, Dee. It's not worth it."

She brushed past them and made her way to the first floor so she could grab her things from the bedroom. Halfway down the stairs on her way out, her cell phone rang, and she wearily answered without glancing at the screen.

"Hi Lara, it's me, Vishal. I was wondering if you'd like to go out for a drink later today."

The pounding inside her skull increased. She didn't need this, of all things. Not now, and probably not ever, she reflected. How did she get rid of him without being rude, though?

But she was overwrought, unable to be gentle and courteous right then. At one point, she would have to deliver the message that she wasn't interested.

"Vishal, I'm sorry. Today's not a good day. I have to go. Bye."

Reaching the last step, she paused when her feet touched the floor. Lara forced in a deep breath and lifted her foot to move away when a vicious grip closed around her arm.

She whirled around to find her mother right behind her.

"That boy, he's been calling you often, hasn't he?"

She peered into the eyes ablaze with reproach, eyes so like the ones she saw whenever she looked into a mirror. Except hers had never carried so much spite and misplaced righteousness. The recrimination in the tone washed over her. She bristled with the disgust and outrage welling up in response to the position her mother had made her take today.

Yet, she chose not to reply and reached up to loosen her mother's grip on her arm before stepping away on her way out.

Her mother followed her. "He's not very proper for you, you know."

And just when she'd thought nothing could get any worse ...

Lara stopped in her tracks and turned around to face the older woman. She was sure daggers of rage and loathing shot from the glare she directed at her mother. For a second or two, she revelled in the satisfying pleasure of watching her mum squirm. Fuelled by a wave of contempt, she wouldn't mince her words when she opened her mouth. Truth be told, she didn't wish to spare any hurt her comments could inflict.

"Now, what is this supposed to mean, Mother?" she asked in a cold, detached voice. She cocked her head to the side and crossed her arms in front of her. "I suppose you're saying I'm not virgin enough to attract a young man who's never been married? Never mind if a total trollop hooked up with a guy like him. As long as she still had her hymen intact or had never gotten divorced, she'd be a 'proper' girl, now, wouldn't she?"

Her mother paled and flinched. Lara gulped when tears threatened to blur her vision and a lump settled in her throat.

"Don't you think I know I'm tainted from my divorce?" she whispered. She forced a smile onto her face. "How could I not when every one of you people here have done more than her fair share to remind me?"

Spent with her final question, her shoulders threatened to sag. But she wouldn't give anyone the satisfaction of knowing their poisoned arrows had hit home.

Lara didn't bother to see what theatrical display her mother was bound to make.

She passed by her father, Diya, and Neha, who must've come in at some point, on the way to her car. No one tried to stop her.

Just as well.

No one would've managed to, anyway. She slid into her Mercedes and slammed the door shut. Switching the engine on, she jammed her foot onto the accelerator and sped out of the courtyard in a cloud of dust and spitting gravel.

She thought she smelled burned rubber, but the only thing she fully registered were the tears finally coursing down her cheeks.

CHAPTER EIGHT

Eric breathed in the salty sea air, letting it sting his nose and fill his lungs as he strolled along the edges of the Caudan Waterfront esplanade in Port-Louis. He'd had a tough morning at the practice, where he'd been called for an emergency after dealing with a premature birth at the clinic. He frowned and kicked a small rock into the harbour's murky green waters.

A little girl with a congenital heart malformation. Not yet two years old—what had she known of life already? He'd been unable to do anything other than put her on the waiting list for a transplant. *Merde.* As a physician, he was meant to care for his patients and make them better. Yet, sometimes, he had difficulty keeping his personal feelings aside and not taking on his patients' suffering and pain. Whatever had possessed him to go into medicine? A doctor couldn't save all sick people. He was only human, after all.

The helplessness had brewed in him all day long, not helped by the turmoil Lara had already stirred.

He'd come here to unwind. To witness healthy, lively children playing and enjoying carefree childhood. That's the way things should be. Children weren't meant to suffer.

He ran a heavy hand over his face as something in the distance caught his attention.

Lara. Did he have to think of her, and she'd appear out of thin air? First, at the conference yesterday and today, she was at the waterfront.

Would he bump into her every time he sought to escape her? Maybe he couldn't avoid her. Was it Fate's way of telling him to deal with the matter?

He slanted his gaze back towards her. She sat at a table in a far corner of a terrace, seemingly engrossed in conversation with an insipid-looking youth opposite her.

However, she'd clamped her arms to her chest. If he remembered correctly, she usually did that when she was cornered and wanted an escape. He studied her face, which grew more flustered with every passing minute.

Was she in some trouble with this man?

But she'd say it was none of his business. She lived her life. He lived his. She'd made that clear the day before when she'd run away from him.

She definitely seemed to be in some sort of trouble, though, as she shook her head while speaking.

Drawn by the furtive glances she sent around her, he couldn't help but venture nearer. She must not have seen him approach because she didn't acknowledge his presence. She pressed her spine in her chair and threw her head back, eyes closed, lips in a tight, white line.

Something was wrong. Something to do with the guy. But one glance at him, and Eric wasn't sure if he was so at fault here, for the youth looked on the brink of crying.

As he swerved around the table right behind them, he caught the sound of her voice.

"Vishal, I'm already seeing someone."

His step faltered, and his heart started to race as he reached out to grasp the back of a nearby chair to steady himself.

Is it true? Is she with some other man? Maybe back with her husband …

But then, he caught her peering up as if asking for divine help.

He chuckled softly as a smile spread across his face. He pretty much had an idea what she'd gotten herself into. Another poor hopeful needed to be driven away. She used to attract boys like moths to a flame. Seemed that hadn't changed. He'd run to her rescue on more than one occasion in such sticky situations.

And today, he couldn't possibly ignore her plea for help, could he? Granted, she hadn't addressed it to him, but maybe he was God's answer to her. He had no way out of any predicament in which she starred, so he might as well turn any scenario to his advantage.

The fun's about to start.

Lara cursed softly under her breath. What would she do with this kid? She'd called him to gently inform him no future existed for them. Yet, her strategy appeared to have fallen through because Vishal just sat there. She'd just resorted to inventing a boyfriend in a last-ditch effort to get him to back off. But he just gaped, and tears filled his eyes again.

Disgust at his overblown reaction churned her stomach. He reminded her of a spoiled child who'd been denied a ride on the merry-go-round. She hoped he wouldn't prove her right and throw a tantrum in front of everyone. How would she get him to leave, then?

Suddenly, a warm, strong hand settled on her shoulder as the brush of a fleeting kiss caressed her cheek.

What the heck?

She swivelled, paying little heed to the possibility of smacking her skull against the head of whoever had kissed her. But she shouldn't have worried since he'd drawn up to his full height, which left her to stare at the jeans waistband of a virile man with narrow hips and an absolutely flat stomach.

Her mouth grew dry at this snapshot of male perfection. *Who ...?* Her gaze travelled upwards. A close-fitting white T-shirt hugged a well-defined chest and broad shoulders. A face with clear-cut features and sparkling blue eyes that winked at her.

Her mouth grew drier, and she struggled to swallow the lump wedged in her throat.

Of all the people in the world ... Of course, Fate would choose only Eric. She closed her eyes, only to have her traitorous hormones urge her to glance up again and drink her fill of the beefcake goodness.

She didn't want to see him—didn't *need* to—and certainly not when he looked as delectable as now. She couldn't tear her attention from him as she finally understood the allure of blue jeans and a white T-shirt on a man. She'd constantly harped on the need for a suit and tie for any man to make it on her sweet dream list. Roy had been an elegant dresser and hadn't possessed the casual streak to wear jeans.

Yet, on Eric, the very simplicity was a compliment to his masculinity and virility. Who knew casual could be more lethal than classy?

Had she ordered a drink? She needed something, anything, to soothe her parched mouth and throat.

Damn. She hated losing control, especially over her emotions, and Eric made her lose it every time.

As if on cue, he smiled, and she was a goner again. Her little pep talk to get over him? Vanished in a lust-blazed smoke.

"Hello, sweetheart," he said in a husky tone. "Sorry, I'm a little early. I finished with my last patient earlier than planned, so I thought I'd come meet you."

He spoke the words to her as if she were the only living creature within a mile. His face drew level with hers, his bright gaze plunging into hers, into her soul, laying her bare.

I'm glad you're here.

Bewildered, she shook her head. What was wrong with her? She had other issues to deal with, too.

What is Eric doing here, and what game is he playing?

But all conscious thought evaporated as he trailed a hand along her nape, where he stopped to play with little tendrils of her hair. He touched the delicate spot along her hairline, sending shivers down her spine.

She fluttered her eyelids, and a soft moan escaped her lips. Was it really so hot on the terrace? Her tension-filled body grew light under his touch, making her wonder if she'd end up floating up to the sky if he kept doing that to her.

A strangled yelp brought her back to the present.

She'd all but forgotten Vishal sat at her table.

She blinked as if coming out of a dream. Her eyelids were heavy, as were her lips. What was wrong with her? And worse, where was she stuck?

She allowed her gaze to take in the man—okay, the kid—opposite her, then she turned towards Eric at her side. His hand still lay tangled in her hair, and his face hovered near hers. She jumped involuntarily, which made her forearm brush against the soft fabric of his T-shirt to register the warmth from his skin permeating the garment.

Lara tried to speak, but no word could escape her lips. Not even a croak.

Her mind couldn't form a coherent thought. Like in slow motion, she watched as Eric tilted his head, and his lips grazed her temple in a fleeting butterfly kiss.

"Play the part," he said in her ear.

His low, rumbling voice washed over her like a caress. The smoothness of his tone, the huskiness in his whisper, wrapped around her. She slowly blinked up at him as she parted her lips. His eyes darkened.

Lara suddenly realised they made an intimate picture in this pose.

As intimate as two lovers.

The lovers we never got to become.

They'd never become lovers because Eric had left. Had left her for someone else.

But she dismissed the hurt. She'd had enough time already to dwell on that particular betrayal. More pressing matters were at hand, like the wreck of a man—child—she needed to be rid of. So she'd go along with this farce for now.

She peered up at Eric and pasted an adoring smile on her face, hoping it lit her features with the glow of a woman in love. At least, Sam said a woman in love glowed. She had no way of knowing, never having seen that elusive radiance in the mirror.

"There you are, darling. I was just telling Vishal about us," she said. "Oh, how silly of me, you two haven't been introduced. Baby, this is Vishal, my cousin. Vishal, meet Eric, my boyfriend."

Her voice trickled as sweet as syrup when she addressed him with an equally sickening smile, and Vishal gulped a few times as if trying not to throw up.

Eric drew a chair up and sat beside her.

"I sure hope I'm not disturbing you," he said, staring straight at Vishal. He turned to her, then. "I didn't know I'd be barging in. Forgive me?"

Lara smiled back. "There's nothing to forgive, darling, and Vishal was leaving, anyway." She turned to face the other man. "Weren't you, Vishal?"

She dreaded a teary episode, but fortunately, Vishal seemed to have found his composure. With the appearance of a forlorn, beaten dog, he quickly said goodbye and left.

As soon as he was out of sight, she heaved a huge sigh of relief and let her body sag in her chair. She brought her hands to her pounding temples, hoping to avoid a migraine. A couple of paracetamol pills to kill the pain and the comfort of her bedroom with all the curtains closed would do the trick.

The sound of a throat clearing startled her from her reverie, and she blinked to find Eric still sitting next to her.

He'd draped his broad frame in his seat, one arm casually on the back of her chair. His eyes were on her, and a smile lifted the corners of his mouth.

Damn it, he really is gorgeous.

But he's not for you.

She had to keep reminding herself of this. Her life without a man in it was complicated enough. He'd also let her down in the past, and he would probably do it again if she gave him a chance.

But what if he doesn't?

She dismissed the thought as soon as it struck her mind. *Dead end.* She had sworn off men, hadn't she? Look what trouble she'd gotten into with Vishal, and she hadn't even done anything there.

Still, she owed Eric her thanks. Had it not been for him and his timely intervention, she'd still be stuck dealing with Vishal.

"Thanks for the help," she said, forcing the words out. "I really appreciate it."

Eric's smile widened. His eyes were still on her, though—deep, intense, making her squirm. He wouldn't let her off the hook.

"Care to tell me what all this was about?" he asked in a slow drawl.

He'd always spoken English with a lilting accent, only the edges of his words sounding slightly sharp. Probably something he carried over from his Mauritian French native tongue.

His voice hit her as low and full of concern. The tone invited secrets and promised to offer support and caring.

Lara breathed in, filling her lungs. Unfortunately, the sea air didn't unscramble her mind or change her situation as an emotional wreck, a disadvantage when dealing with Eric and his concern and attention.

She fought the part of her wanting to confide and ease the load on her heart. However, the heavy burden threatened to crush her, considering what had happened earlier with her mother.

She needed a sympathetic ear, and Eric had played the role so many years ago. Did it matter if he paid attention to her woes now? She certainly had no intention of meeting him purposefully again, so she might as well make the most of this opportunity.

So, she straightened and stared at him. Then, with a shrug, she started her story.

"Vishal is a cousin of mine who's got a crush on me, and the family doesn't see it with a good eye. So I called him here to set things straight with him."

Eric certainly was a good audience. He didn't interrupt her, simply gave her all his attention.

Relieved that he allowed her to vent, Lara was drawn into the depths of his eyes, the gentleness of his gaze, the encouraging curve of his mouth when he smiled.

"Then, this morning, my mother butted in again, and I gotta say, she's only made things worse," she ended on a sigh.

Eric laughed at the mention of her mother—a rich, deep bellow, full of insouciance and amusement. Its echo tingled its way into her, and she remembered the many laughs they'd shared in the past.

"How *is* your mother?" he asked, bringing her back to the here and now. "She used to be tough."

Don't go there—don't go thinking of the past.

"Well, let's just say she's not getting any better with time." She chuckled. "Probably the onset of menopause."

Eric watched as the smile broke upon her face.

How beautiful she is.

He was pretty sure she hadn't laughed in a long time, though. Her face appeared weary, her features drawn, with a greyish tinge to her skin. She used to glow with a golden light, like women in those advertisements for Arabian bronze blush beads his sister had been pestering him to buy for her for months.

He'd noticed the fatigue on Lara the day before, but today, the strain looked more pronounced. She'd also lost weight. She hadn't been so thin when he'd seen her at the clinic.

"I have a feeling you need a break," he said. "You're probably working too hard."

She glanced back at him for a while, seemingly lost in her thoughts.

There used to be a sparkle in her eyes. Now, I can't see it.

Had life really been so hard on her?

After a little while, she gave him a weary smile in reply, and she shrugged, like in the past.

Just like his girl used to.

That girl still lived in her. He'd glimpsed her, even if only for a fleeting second.

His girl. Eric vowed to bring her back. Come Hell or high water, he'd make her return and give her all the love and care she deserved.

All the love and care he hadn't been able to give her during those years they'd lost.

He had to tread carefully, though, especially with a control freak like her. He doubted the years had made her any mellower.

So only careful planning and organized steps to woo her again, bring her back to life as the cheerful, carefree young woman he'd known. He would take his time to court her because he would rest only when he and Lara became man and wife. He'd also put his desires aside for the moment and show her she could count on him. Hopefully, she would realise it soon, but he'd wait. He could be a patient man when the need arose.

Small steps, one at a time.

A light wind started to blow around them, signalling the approach of dusk. Lara peeked at her watch.

“Eric, I really have to go. There’s this wedding I need to go to this evening, a friend of mine.”

“It’s okay. I’ll walk you to your car.”

She darted a quick glance over her shoulder as she bit her lip.

“Only if you don’t mind,” he said.

She smiled back after a few seconds, and they both made their way to the parking lot. Walking side by side, with less than a foot between them, negotiating the pressing crowds. But the distance could’ve been as vast as an ocean while she kept to herself during the five-minute trek to the marina parking area.

“Which one is yours?” he asked as he surveyed the overflowing lot.

“The blue one near the docks.”

He caught a glimpse of the brand-new Mercedes coupé and whistled softly.

She laughed again—the soft, husky sound could drive him over the edge. At the car, he held the door while she got in. He shut the door, and she lowered the glass, turning towards him.

“Thanks for everything, Eric. I really appreciate what you did for me today.”

Bending by the window, he brought his face level with hers. “At least if nothing else, we’re friends, Lara. Don’t forget it.”

Her right hand lay on the steering wheel, and he reached out and clasped it with his own. He brought it to his lips and pressed a kiss onto the back.

“Bye, Lara.”

“Bye,” she whispered.

Lara sat in her car for a long moment. The warm imprint of Eric’s lips still tingled on her hand.

His parting words had rubbed a soothing balm on her heart. They had undoubtedly been friends before being anything else. Could they build on that again?

Or was this very foundation too weak? The structure hadn't held in the past.

When his head had levelled with hers, she'd wanted to see his face and eyes for the truth. Yet, with the setting sun behind him, shadows had played upon his features, cloaking him with a thin mask of darkness, enough to conceal anything his expression might've revealed.

What she would have seen in his too-beautiful, haunting face? Hope? Love?

Would you have liked all this coming from him?

Silly notion. Her future had no place for a man. But a part of her was desperate for attention, consideration, love, and affection.

All of which she could get from Eric.

A jolt of adrenaline went through her, along with extreme unease and discomfited. Her first instinct was to search around for an escape.

Is there one?

Weariness rushed over her, making her slump like a limp noodle onto her seat. The high spirits Eric had put her in crashed like a thousand shards of crystal, leaving her spent.

She had to get over this, over him, because there was no future for them.

Shaking her head, she switched the engine, eased the car out of its parking space, and made her way back to her house.

Cut your losses and gear up for the most vital battle.

She still had a tough evening ahead of her, where she'd be facing her mother again.

CHAPTER NINE

The late afternoon sun filtered through Sam's lace curtains hanging in the house. Lara had sighed and simply let her best friend get her kicks out of decorating both sides of the semi-detached. Lord knew she'd never have time or the inclination to hang up frilly window accessories around any place she lived in.

She glanced at the sky before closing the front door. Sun rays pierced through the thick canopy of rain-laden grey clouds, making twilight hover over the island at five-thirty. The air hung thick and stifling, not a hint of breeze to alleviate the high humidity.

March in Mauritius. They'd be putting away their thickest coats in England in anticipation of spring. But on the tropical coast, only two weather conditions prevailed—humid and more humid.

She stepped out of her high-heeled stilettos in the hallway and welcomed the cool touch of the glossy marble under the heated soles of her feet. She then dropped her handbag on the sofa and headed upstairs to the bathroom. Thanks to the suffocating heaviness shrouding everything, her clothes stuck to her skin.

Once in the bathroom, she rid herself of the cotton blouse and linen skirt and removed the pins in her bun before turning the shower on to full spray. After stepping under the cool jet, she allowed the water needles to drum on her exhausted body, washing the remnants of the cloying heat from her skin and hair.

Ten minutes later, she stepped out of the cubicle, wrapped herself in a thick towel, and walked into her bedroom. Her wet hair loose, and in a pair of shorts and strappy cotton jersey top, she picked up her cell phone, intent on calling Sam's mobile as she went downstairs. Her friend hadn't visited her side of the house this weekend.

She'd barely woken the screen up when the phone rang in her hand.

"Hello, Mum," she said with a sigh.

"Is this the way to greet your mother? You haven't called me in a week, and that secretary of yours never puts me through to you."

"It's because I'm busy, Mum. I'd call you if anything happened."

"Never mind. When are you coming by Curepipe? It's been so long since we last saw you."

Lara sighed again and rolled her eyes.

"For God's sake, we met four days ago at the groom's reception for Yazmin's wedding." Trust her mother to turn a challenging day into an even harder time. She sorely lacked the energy or the patience to deal with her. "Mum, sorry, but I have to go now, okay? Bye."

She sure has guts.

Ever since the whole proposal incident, she'd kept a low profile with her mother. But Gayatri Hemant was back to her overwhelming self again, as if nothing has happened between them, and Lara knew no respite from her.

The halfway landing was dark and gloomy when she reached it. Grappling for the light switch on the wall, she pressed the button to turn the wall sconces on.

A few steps from reaching the ground floor, the lights went out on her. At the same time, a brilliant flash lit up the house, followed seconds later by an ear-splitting, crunching sound that boomed over the whole area.

A thunderstorm.

Her mind froze, and she stood rooted to the spot, as it always happened when thunder raged. One of her first memories was two-year-old her waking up in a strange bed after hearing thunder during her first visit to Mauritius.

She'd been lucky so far not to have run into any thunderstorm on the island. With summer being nearly over, she'd believed herself spared the trauma of the sickening roar when it hit the island.

Some part of her brain that still functioned told her she had to get a grip and light some candles so she could see where she was going. But panic clamped down and anchored her solidly on the step as cold sweat broke on her back and the icy numbness wrapped around her.

A sound like a chime filtered through her consciousness. Startling, she glanced down. The phone was ringing in her palm and she forced herself to answer.

"Hello?"

"Lara, it's Eric. Where are you? Are you alone?"

Eric?

"Lara? Hello?"

"I'm … I'm here … at home … alone … it's dark … power out," she said, hanging on to the sound of his voice.

"Where do you live?"

A blinding streak of light and another horrendous growl resounded, and she nearly dropped the phone.

"Lara, where's your house?" he again asked.

She gulped in a deep breath and forced a coherent thought to form in her numb mind. "Number twenty-six, Seaview estate, near the hotel in Grand-Baie—" *Beep, beep, beep.*

The line went dead. The phone screen had also gone blank. Damn, the battery was out. No electricity meant she couldn't recharge it right away.

Bloody phone and her own lack of vigilance over the battery. No way was she going out to try the travel charger that plugged into the car.

The storm gathered momentum outside, winds picking up and lashing rain onto the windows. Every successive thunderbolt sounded louder than the previous one.

Lara sank into a motionless heap on the stairs. Her limbs had frozen solid, and her heart thrashed frantically rush in her chest. Cold sweat broke on her forehead and on the palms of her hands. The cell phone dropped onto the marble floor. Beyond caring about the damage, she didn't check if the device had exploded into pieces.

She couldn't recall how long she stayed thus, arms wrapped around knees she had brought up to her chest. Mere minutes could've been hours for all she knew in her fear-induced daze.

Loud pounding resonated in the still air between two claps of thunder.

At first, it seemed the storm had started to pelt hail outside, but this was Mauritius, not England. No hail here.

And when the noise didn't stop, she reckoned it had to come from the door.

But she didn't dare to move. She lay ensconced in her little world where the thunder couldn't get her, and no way would she break from it. Perhaps the visitor would leave if he didn't get any response.

When the pounding didn't stop, she forced herself to the door with a dragging step and opened the panel, blinking in surprise.

Eric stood on her front porch, and he pushed into the hall as soon as she opened the door wide enough for him to enter.

Eric is here, and everything will be fine.

A deep sense of relief washed over her as he shrugged out of his wet jacket. His solid presence filled the small space, and his aftershave's fresh, tangy fragrance soothed her ragged mind. Her heart stopped beating its frantic roll and settled at a somewhat normal pace.

Until another loud crack of thunder bolted, and she jumped in panic.

◆◆◆

One minute she'd been standing before him, and the next, she'd pressed the length of her feminine perfection flush against his body.

For a split second, Eric didn't know how to react.

As she gripped his shirt in tight fists, she shivered, as much from the cold sheen of moisture on her skin as from the violent emotion.

She was scared.

He was here to make sure she had no reason to be scared.

So he placed his arms around her and pulled her to him. She sighed against his shirt, her breath warming the humid fabric and making it cling to his pecs. Then, wrapping her arms around his neck, she burrowed her face into his shoulder while pressing her whole body to his frame. The fruity fragrance of her damp hair made its way into his mind, and he once again noted how cold she was as the skin of her arm brushed the back of his neck.

A wave of tenderness and an irresistible urge to protect her overwhelmed him.

This was his girl, today his woman.

With his hand on her back, he cradled her softly. He caressed her hair with his other hand and murmured soothing words to calm her. If he paused long enough, he could make out the rapid beat of her heart slowing against his chest.

"It's okay. I'm here now. Nothing wrong's gonna happen to you," he whispered in her ear.

Little by little, the tension drained from her body, and she snuggled into his embrace. Lara felt firm, yet soft, against him. She had the luscious body of a woman, so different from the thin girl she'd been and yet so similar in the feelings she brought to his mind.

Tenderness, love, affection, and desire as hot and intense as raging flames. The latent fire burst from every fibre of his being. The heat gradually returning to her body seeped into his, and he grew rigid and tense, like a coiled spring.

Slow and easy. He had to remind himself of it. No point in frightening her away with the rash demands of his body. But *merde* if that wasn't hard when she fuelled the very blaze with her tantalizing presence.

And here she stood in his arms. With hardly a thing on to cover herself.

How long would he be able to keep himself in check before lust won over and he ravished her right there in her front hallway?

◆◆◆

Had she been drugged? Or had she fallen and hit her head?

Everything inside her mind drifted in a hazy rhythm while her senses remained numb in contented inertia. Wherever she was, the place felt comfortable, oh so comfortable, with just enough warmth to blank out the chill, yet not hot enough to burn.

Peaceful.

Whatever she leaned against moved fleetingly under her, but she noticed the shift.

Where was she? She forced her mind into battle with her foggy consciousness. She remembered the lightning bolt and the subsequent thunder strike that had gone "ka-boom" while she'd had the door open... Why had she opened the door in the first place?

The 'thing' against her moved again. Finally, she forced her mind into focus. Little by little, messages started to travel up her synapses to form a picture in her head.

Her arms were wrapped tight around something deceptively hard because she could also feel a soft give under her grasp, like the sinuous play of muscles. Whatever she was pressed against stood firm and warm. Deliciously warm, but not scorching hot.

And it felt ... Lara shifted, which made her cheek brush against something resembling smooth cotton covering a shallow hollow. When she tried to tear herself away, a strong yet gentle grip kept her anchored. A light, gentle caress smoothed her hair, going down in long, calming movements.

A touch on her hair and firm muscle holding her in place? Bells rang. She was in a man's arms.

She gasped. *Eric.*

She stiffened and jerked her head up. True enough, there he stood. Or, she should state that as there *she* stood, wrapped all around him. *Shame on you.* She had her arms around his big shoulders and every inch of her front pressed against his body.

Shame, shame, shame. What a hussy.

How could she ever face him again? She hadn't ever let herself go with a man. Not even her husband. Theirs had never been a cuddly or affectionate marriage. Was that why she craved such hands-on contact? She'd been as limp as a rag doll against Eric, pliant and awaiting his next order so she could be ravished.

Embarrassment filled her and burned her cheeks.

As he gently released her, she disentangled herself from his grip with care. He opened his arms, allowing her to leave his embrace.

His embrace. Goodness, how long had it been since he'd last held her?

Don't. Go. There.

Breaking free from his hold, she took a step back and lowered her head. Wringing her hands, she lowered her gaze as her face, and her pride, burned with indignity. How could she have let herself go so much? The thunderstorm was not an excuse. She should've been made of sterner stuff.

His steady gaze burned onto her, and then he reached out and tucked a strand of hair behind her ear. The tips of his fingers brushed her cheek in a fleeting caress, and she closed her eyes for a second.

"Feeling better?" he asked.

Barefoot, she suddenly felt tiny in front of his mighty height of six-foot-three. Never before had she felt so delicate and vulnerable.

"I knew you'd be scared with the storm," he said. "That's why I came around to check on you."

He'd remembered she was afraid of thunder. What did it say about him, about their friendship? And possibly, about more between them?

The warmth in his tone and the caring in his words touched her heart, and gentle, soothing warmth flooded through her, radiating from where he'd touched her cheek only seconds before. The pleasant heat filled her with courage, and she lifted her eyes to stare into his.

His irises were an intense shade of turquoise, the shade deeper thanks to the twilight darkness in the hallway, and she lost herself in their depths. His warm smile mimicked sunshine and could melt ice.

And she smiled back, all notion of awkwardness brushed aside under the pull of his guileless grin. She stood rooted to the spot again, though from a different feeling this time.

When did he get so handsome? He'd always been a nice guy, too.

How had she managed to lose him?

Eric took her arm, snapping her out of her reflective musings, and drew her into the living room.

"I think we better light some candles. It's awfully dark here," he said. "Also, I love to stand, but right now, I could do with a seat."

He winked at her, and she smothered a giggle. Yes, she was pathetic, as pitiable as a fan in the throes of boy-band mania, but what could she do? No matter how idiotic it painted her, this feeling remained preferable to the distress caused by her family and their society. Eric was solid and reliable. He'd never shift and morph on her. If she allowed him, he'd become her anchor again, her safe harbour from all the storms. He'd give her the bubble she needed to thrive.

Nothing looked better right now. She needed him in her life.

So Lara gave in to the warmth in her chest as he tugged her to the living room. She leaned onto the doorway as he made his way around the ground floor, lighting the lavender-scented candles she'd placed all over only the day before. The soothing aroma drifted into the air. Perfect for her overwrought nerves, not helped by his presence.

He settled his broad, well-built body onto the sofa when he finished the task and patted the cushion next to him. "Come join me."

Don't tempt me. An open-ended invitation like that, and she'd jump all over him again. Jump his bones, literally.

Heat stung her cheeks, and she lowered her head to let her hair cover the flaming features.

She made her way into the room but sat at the far end of the three-place sofa. She didn't trust herself to be too close to him and thus left an enormous space between them as she huddled into her seat, drawing her legs under her.

She however couldn't escape his intent scrutiny and glanced at him. He smiled and then shook his head.

"You're still the same, especially where thunder is concerned."

She returned the grin. Amazing how she, a grown woman past thirty years of age, could still be afraid of thunder. Some things couldn't be explained. She chuckled softly.

The atmosphere around her shifted, and tension filled the room, making the hairs on her nape stand up and sending her heart into a frantic beat. She met his eyes. There burned a different emotion in them. The blue depths were dark, hooded, and fire smouldered in them.

Lara swallowed hard. Eric used to look at her like that whenever they'd been alone ...

"Some things don't change," she said in a hushed tone.

She didn't know how the comment came out of her mouth. Speaking of the past was dangerous, because those memories constituted uncharted territory, a minefield of unfulfilled dreams and longings.

He studied her for a long moment. "Yes, it's true."

Silence settled between them as she pondered his reply. It sounded like a confession. Was it wishful thinking, though? Was she reading unspoken things into his every word? She didn't know.

She only knew that the soft, candlelit atmosphere drifted around them conducive to exchanging secrets and confessions. And she craved to know his secrets, to hear his confessions. Anything to fortify her certitude that she hadn't made a hasty decision fourteen years earlier, that she'd been right in taking a new direction.

"Didn't you get married in the past decade?" she asked.

He didn't answer her immediately. Instead, his eyes took a faraway glint, and a veil of sadness settled over his face.

He shook his head in reply a few seconds later.

A tug nipped at her heart when she took in his forlorn expression. She'd better drop the subject, yet, irrepressible curiosity grappled for hold all through her. "Why not?"

Eric remained silent for ages, his deep, sad gaze on her face.

"I didn't find the woman I wanted. The right one was already taken."

She drew in a sharp breath. Could he be talking about her?

"You got married shortly after I left," he said.

She nodded, and the words, heavy with meaning, hung in mid-air between them. A sizzling tension bristled in the confines of the living room, and she wanted to beat herself. Her mouth had won over again, and once more, she'd stuck her foot in it. Why had she ventured onto that path? She'd never wanted to bring up that particular subject between them. Then, she'd have to face the truth—maybe she'd been hasty in deciding Eric no longer had a place in her life.

"My marriage was arranged," she said.

But you've always had the choice to refuse.

Where did *that* come from? Her conscience had it in for her lately.

"Were you happy?" he asked.

She blinked. She'd expected recriminations after her last comment. Not concern, or caring.

He asked about Roy. She'd read between his every word in the past, and right now, she flashed back over a decade. "Does it matter?"

"If you were happy, then no."

A dilemma raged inside her. Tell Eric the truth, or pretend things were all right?

Sam's words rang in her mind. How long could she continue to exist in denial?

On a deep breath, she started her very own confession. "I thought I was happy. I thought Roy was happy. I thought ours was a happy marriage."

Eric didn't say a word. But his raised eyebrows queried her.

To say so little already hurt so much, and she wasn't sure she had it in her to face more truths and half-truths tonight. Better leave it there, and let him construe what he wanted from her words.

She shrugged and gave him a small, sad smile. "In the end, we found out we didn't want the same things in life."

He didn't prompt her for further explanation. She'd assumed he would, though. But he was just being his caring and attentive self. Tears unexpectedly stung her eyes, and she swallowed the lump forming in her throat.

No more of this melodrama. She needed to get herself back on track again. She couldn't allow herself to break down even more in front of Eric, of all people.

"Anyway, to cut it short, Roy wanted children, but I wasn't ready. So we divorced, and now he's remarried, and his new wife was expecting their first, last I'd heard."

The play of emotion on Lara's face gave her away. She'd started to let her hair down with him. But minutes later, the impersonal façade of the strong career woman had shuttered back down.

She still hadn't lost her knack for control.

As stubborn and uncompromising as ever. Granted, that Roy fellow must've been a swine to treat her thus, but was the man really so much at fault here? Lara drove a hard bargain. Always had, and probably always would.

So, was it foolish of him to believe he could make this whole business bear fruit? Or would he be trampled again? Patience was his virtue, but he didn't have a never-ending supply of it.

He heaved in a long breath.

No, he wouldn't falter this time. Everything would work out fine because he'd see to it personally. He loved Lara, and she still felt something for him. Today was of proof enough she wasn't immune to him. She could still have feelings for him buried under that hard shell of hers. But he'd bring down the walls of her fortress and conquer her every defence one by one.

He trained his gaze on her, and she returned a bold stare. Their eyes remained locked for a long moment, and spoke their own language. Neither would give in nor bow out first.

Where would such pig-headed tenacity leave them?

Brilliant light flooded the room, making them both blink in surprise. The power had returned. He should tell Lara to have a word with her estate manager since the emergency generators had failed to kick in when the electricity had gone out earlier.

Eric glanced at his watch. Two hours had elapsed in the time they'd been together. How could it have been two hours already? They'd talked for only a few moments.

Lara bolted from the sofa and stood in the middle of the living room, wringing her hands together, hopping from foot to foot.

Et puis, merde, alors. Those short shorts and her skimpy top did *not* constitute clothing. He'd never seen her look so sexy, so tantalising. The late hour meant dinnertime. But he grew hungry for another kind of sustenance, which could earn him a kick in the groin if he pressed his intention.

He better leave quickly. He didn't trust himself to behave in a gentlemanly fashion when she appeared so delicious.

So, he stood and faced her. "The power is back, and the storm is over. You're safe now, so I'll leave."

He didn't hope she'd ask him to stay back. Knowing Lara, he still had a long way to go before winning her trust again. He made his way into the hall, and she followed in his footsteps.

On the threshold, he stopped.

"I live not far from here, in Cap Malheureux. Call me if you ever need anything."

She had his number since he'd called her from his cell earlier, and the call log must've recorded the contact info. Thank goodness he'd snagged one of her business cards from Markus back at the conference. She wouldn't have given him her contact information so freely.

Lara nodded but didn't say a word.

She made this hard on him. He snickered softly. When had he ever had anything easy with her?

"Come around one day and take a look at my house," he said, unable to resist the temptation to throw the invite out.

"I … I'll think about it," she replied after a few seconds.

"Okay." He should be content with that. At least, she hadn't given a flat-out no. "Take care of yourself, Lara."

She nodded. “Look after yourself, too,” she said, barely above a whisper.

◆◆◆

Lara closed the door softly behind Eric. Shaken to the core, she leant onto the hall wall for support. Her eyes drifted closed as weariness crashed over her.

Damn if she hadn’t crossed a line in her relationship with Eric, whatever this *relationship* happened to be at the moment. Their friendship, or what had remained of it, had taken a turn into deeper territories. However, she didn’t know if that was for the better. Or for the worse.

She only knew she felt torn. On the one hand, she had the security of her single status, her independence, and a fulfilling and successful career. Mistress of her destiny, captain of the path she charted for her life’s path.

On the other hand, she’d been asking herself more often if being at the boat's helm gave back enough. She longed for a relationship and the warmth and comfort such a connection brought. Her heart constantly asked for love to fill its emptiness. She lived a lonely existence, with no one to share her joys, sorrows, or pain. Not to mention that an empty bed consisted of everything except a woman’s fulfilment. Even when Roy had ditched her and she’d been smarting with indignation, she’d sometimes yearned for companionship and love.

Today, was Eric the answer for her? Had he been the answer all along?

Lara winced as the questions slammed into her like a haywire tennis ball machine.

Did she have the guts and determination to go after a relationship that had once seemed impossible?

How did anyone make the impossible possible? In Mauritius, of all places?

CHAPTER TEN

Back from the weekly directorial meeting, Lara stopped by her PA's desk. "The directors approved all pending decisions. You can send the newsletter around and update all the staff."

Fifteen minutes later, Doris popped into the office. "Just been on the coffee break. You've worked a coup. They're all talking of the upcoming film shoot."

She smiled. "So you'd say the mood is good among the staff?"

Doris rolled her eyes. "Good? They're ecstatic. They're all wondering how you've managed to get such an important film crew to shoot on our premises."

"I didn't do much, Doris. They contacted me first."

"You've sure worked wonders. They all revere you now," the older woman said with a wink before she walked out of the office.

A soft laugh escaped Lara's throat. She leaned back in her chair and gazed out the windowed wall of her office. The view opened to a lushly vibrant garden. Huge, colourful hibiscus blooms dotted the intense green of thick bushes and the lawn, and strategically placed palm trees offered shade from the burning tropical sun.

No wonder a Bollywood film crew wanted to shoot here. The very architecture of the centre made it stand apart from any other building on the island. Its modern design of steel and glass tended toward futuristic in some places. Under the Mauritian sun, the dome sparkled like a jewel. She'd been told the production team consisted of one of the biggest names in the Mumbai cinema industry. Not that she'd know, being clueless about Indian movies. Still, given the hype around the project, she'd been convinced the shooting would be for a blockbuster-type project.

The ringing of her cell phone broke through the silence. Her mind still lost on the garden's beauty, she picked it up.

"Lara Reddy."

"*Bonjour*, Lara. How's it going?"

Butterflies took flight in her stomach when she recognized the rich voice. "Fine, Eric. You?"

Damn, if she could form more than one-word responses suddenly. The sound of his lilting accent was enough to turn her brain to mush.

You're pathetic.

And frankly, I don't care anymore.

"Not too bad." He chuckled. "What's up?"

Her heart missed a beat. She didn't know what to say or do, so she threw out the first thing that popped into her head. "I just heard all my staff now revere me."

Stupid fool. Now he'll take you for an egomaniac. She closed her eyes in despair and cursed under her breath.

Eric laughed, and the rich, throaty sound wreaked more havoc among the butterflies in her stomach.

"How did you manage such a feat?" he asked.

Lara's eyes flew open, and she gave an inward sigh of relief. At least he wasn't taking her for an idiot. "Turns out part of the biggest Bollywood project for the year will be shot on the centre's premises."

"That explains it, then."

His laid-back tone prompted her to relax, and she rolled her shoulders as she slouched a little in her seat.

He'd always been easy to talk to. How could she have forgotten?

"Well, I figure they're more interested in rubbing shoulders with the actors, but still, I'm happy they like it. And the centre will get a lot of publicity as a result, so it's really killing two birds with one stone."

He chuckled again. "I'm glad for you."

Had his voice always been so husky, or was her mind playing tricks on her today?

She then realised he'd been talking. "Uh, sorry. Could you repeat that, please?"

"I said, how about going out with me tonight to celebrate?"

Her mind scrambled. Eric was asking her out on a date?

"Lara? Hello?"

"Oh, uh, I'm still there," she said, blurting the words. "I was just wondering—"

"About what?" he cut in with a gentle tone.

She had to stop this whole matter now before it got out of control. She had no time or energy for the complications of a relationship. She certainly didn't need to have her heart trampled again. She had to say no to Eric. No matter how much she hated being alone at times, better to be alone than unhappy.

So she took in a deep breath.

"What sort of celebration?" she heard herself asking.

What? That wasn't what was supposed to come out of her mouth!

"How about a movie? You still like popcorn action flicks?"

A soft gasp of surprise escaped her. He still remembered? How many little things about her *did* he recall? Roy hadn't even bothered to find out about her tastes, always assuming she'd go along with whatever he chose.

Eric cared.

"Um, what's showing?"

"They started projection of the latest Marvel at the waterfront. How does that sound?"

Back out, Lara, while there's still time.

"Sounds good."

"Great. I'll pick you up at seven."

◆◆◆

Over two hours of non-stop, adrenaline-filled thrills—Lara adored the film. The plot had been hilarious, and though she'd figured out what would happen right from the start, she'd been reeled in by the rest of the story. There'd been no time for self-consciousness about being with Eric and the physical proximity between them as they sat side by side and shared a tub of caramel popcorn.

Earlier, she'd been high-strung, but the movie relaxed her. When the credits appeared on the screen, it all returned to her with a vengeance. Eric's very presence, the smell of his aftershave, his warmth so close to her.

She was in deep trouble because she teetered on the verge of giving in to him. She needed to get out of there, fast. She was losing what little control she had over her life. Come to think of it, did she *have* any control over her emotions where Eric was concerned?

"How about getting something to eat?" he asked.

Eat? As in spending more time with him? Definitely not a good idea, her mind screamed. However, her stomach answered for her, as it gave a protesting grumble.

Eric stopped in his tracks, right in the middle of the esplanade, and turned around to face her. A severe expression marred his handsome face.

"Have you eaten anything today?"

"Of course," she replied quickly.

Maybe a little too quickly, she reckoned when he narrowed his eyes to slits as he fixed them on her. Not a good sign because he could make her quake in her shoes when he stared at her this way.

"Okay, I forgot to have lunch because I was busy," she said with a shrug.

Totally not a big deal. Why did he have to make an issue of it?

He sighed and shook his head. "Lara, it won't do you any good to starve yourself."

Oh, no, he wouldn't start with her. If he didn't want a fight, he'd drop that hot topic right this instant. Food and starving—not a path she wanted to venture upon. They reminded her of when she had failed miserably at everything, including living. She'd always hated having to confront her failings.

"Eric, let it go, will you?"

She started to turn in the opposite direction, towards the parking lot. This night was officially over, the comment about food throwing a dampener on her mood.

But he grabbed her shoulders with his strong hands and didn't allow her to move any farther.

"Lara, look at me. This is a serious matter."

She tried hard to blank out the concern in his voice. If she paid it any heed, she'd crumble. Neither the time nor the place to let *that* happen.

"Eric—"

"Don't you remember what happened the last time you said this to me?"

Anger permeated every word in his question.

Damn him for treating her like a child. How could she ever forget what had happened?

She tried to shrug out of his grip, but he wouldn't let go. All her fighting was in vain. He stood like a dog with a bone, one he wouldn't release.

Oh, but he could be stubborn, too, when he wanted. She'd conveniently forgotten that.

"Lara, stop acting like a kid. This can be dangerous."

She tried another attempt to shrug free from his hold without success.

Then, he relaxed his grasp, clenching her shoulders in a gentle embrace while he peered down into her face.

"I care for you," he said in a softened tone. "And I don't want to see you go through all that pain again."

Tears filled her eyes. Eric had been the only one who'd noticed her distress all those years back. He'd been the only one to care. Had it not been for him and his help, she would've probably succumbed to the eating disorders that had punctuated her late adolescence.

He still cares, while no one else does. Not her parents, not her sisters, not even Roy. No one had ever noticed her aversion to food had nothing to do with dieting.

Eric's soft voice interrupted her thoughts.

"How about some pizza? You used to love that."

She could only nod.

They settled at a table for two at the food court terrace on the edge of the Caudan esplanade. Still shaken by her emotions, she couldn't trust herself to sit in a booth with him. She didn't know what the proximity would entail, and she didn't feel emotionally fit enough to test those uncertain waters. Not when he'd brought up the ugliest episode from her past, which she tried to forget every day and had convinced herself she'd gotten over. The first time she'd picked up a cigarette had been to curb the urge to eat before throwing it all up. That's how she'd gotten hooked on the cigs. She'd found a less dangerous way to cope. Win-win, right? Her husband had thought it stress relief or some other manner to fit in socially.

No one had noticed except for Eric.

His presence threw a reassuring blanket over her, cutting out the chilling loneliness of being an island in the immensity of an empty ocean. Eric brought comfort, something she hadn't experienced in a long, long time.

He'd had the same effect on her in the past, and she hadn't found the same feeling elsewhere. Not even with Roy.

Could it be she was falling under Eric's spell all over again?

Or had she never fallen out of love?

Her self-induced psychotherapy drew to a slamming close when the café owner slid their food on the table. The tantalizing aroma of the tomato sauce and basil on the Margherita pizza and the sight of rich melted cheese had her forgetting all her inner dilemmas. The knot usually twisting her stomach had disappeared, and a screaming appetite had settled in its place.

She grabbed a slice and couldn't keep a moan from escaping once she took a bite of the deep-dish pizza. Eric laughed softly, and she grew aware of his gaze on her.

Lara dared glance up. He was smiling at her. All her movements froze solid, yet she could feel her insides melting like the mozzarella cheese she'd just bitten.

"It's good to see you eat," he said.

"Like a normal person, you mean?" The teasing question rolled from her lips out of the blue. She hadn't thought she'd have in her to strike for light and funny right then.

Another one of Eric's miracles—how he brought out the best in her.

He threw his head back and laughed heartily. The sound melted her insides even more, and she giggled. Then, the laughter died, and he peered at her with so much tenderness on his face, her heart pinched.

"You should laugh more often, Lara. It really suits you."

She wanted to agree, tell him she hadn't had many opportunities to laugh, tell him he made her laugh as no other person could.

But she couldn't. Not only because emotion choked her throat and moistened her eyes, but because she'd be in too deep if she confessed.

"I think it's time to go now," she said in a whisper.

He graciously acquiesced to her request they leave. Probably satisfied she'd eaten at least one slice of the pizza, he had the rest of the food packed for take-away.

They walked companionably to the parking lot in silence that felt comfortable and intimate. They didn't need empty words between them because a touch, a glance, could spell out so much. Walking side by side, with their hands close enough to touch but not touching, struck her as being in the place where she was meant to be all along.

Could the secret be to let go and live for the moment?

Once at his massive, silver Toyota Prado, he held the door open while she climbed into the SUV. A little more chivalry and she'd believe he would've held her hand daintily like a gentleman helped a lady into a high carriage. She stifled a giggle at the thought. Eric sure behaved like a gentleman, though. Somehow, she'd thought men were no longer gallant, and she'd been pleasurably surprised when he'd been so courteous ever since he'd picked her up at her place.

The drive back to Grand-Baie took place in hushed quiet. A comfortable silence again, but she grew aware of the tension mounting between them.

Soft music played in the car. She could make out Ronan Keating's distinctive voice crooning the lyrics to the *Notting Hill* soundtrack "When You Say Nothing At All." How fitting, because her and Eric's best communications happened when they spoke with their eyes and hands and let the silence around them develop full of meaning.

Where was she heading with him? It seemed apparent *he* wanted a relationship.

Or was she mistaking friendship for something else? Eric hadn't clearly stated his intentions, had he?

So lost in her thoughts, it took her a few seconds to grasp that the car had stopped. They were in front of her house, the light on the front porch sending a soft, faint glow into the interior of the SUV.

The night draws to a close, Cinderella. At least your ride didn't turn back into a pumpkin.

And what about her Prince Charming? Did he sit right there beside her in the vehicle?

Silly notions best suited to a teenager, not a grown woman. She shrugged them off. Yet, she couldn't discard the magic as easily as she wanted.

She'd spent a pleasant evening, and now, she reckoned the trip could turn into 'drab' as quickly as it could morph into 'fantastic.'

The moment of truth ... She turned to her right to face him.

"Thanks for a lovely evening."

"Pleasure's all mine," he said with a smile.

Silence fell heavy between them again, the chirp of crickets piping up from outside. But inside the car, their eyes locked as emotions and feelings wound up in turmoil.

The soft click of a seat belt unbuckling echoed in the stillness. Blood rushed in her ears.

She sat still as Eric drew nearer until his warm breath brushed her skin. Anticipation rocketed inside her, making the blood pound heavily along her temples.

She closed her eyes, and his lips touched hers in the next second. Softly, gently. His kiss lingered as he coaxed her into replying in kind, flooding her with sensations.

Past, present, future—the lines blurred. She gave in to the pull of this kiss, to the enchantment of this touch.

How could a single touch like this one make her feel so much? In a heartbeat, her mind transported her to another time when Eric had kissed her the same way. When things had been perfect. Before doom had befallen them ...

A part of her heart yelled at her to break the spell, but she was beyond hearing its call.

She couldn't draw away, *wouldn't* draw away.

Parting her lips, she returned his kiss and tilted her head so he'd get closer. The gentle touch deepened and roughened, and he grazed her lips with his tongue in a light, tentative, inviting caress.

This whole experienced carried her onto another plane. She gave up the consciousness of everything except the sensations triggered by Eric's kiss. Into some dark, pulsing, bottomless void where she willingly lost herself.

And then, the palm of his hand—smooth, warm, but strongly male—pressed against her cheek, all while he sought her mouth with his in a hungry frenzy.

As suddenly as it had started, the kiss ended.

Blood pounded and whooshed in her head, sounds morphing louder with a dull echo as she returned to Earth, back to the interior of the Prado.

Lara forced her eyes to remain shut. She couldn't take opening them to find out nothing was as she'd experienced. Who'd broken the kiss first? Surely not her because she wasn't so much of an idiot. Her senses reeled, figuring out why Eric's mouth no longer drank from hers.

Her lips tingled, and she could still feel his hand on her cheek. She opened her eyes, only to lose herself in his orbs that carried midnight in their depths. Darkness from the night or from something else? Some other, debilitating feeling … like the lust singeing through her still.

Hopefully, she wasn't the only one who'd had the world tilt on its axis in the past few seconds.

He should say something. But what if he'd only open his mouth to tell her they were making a huge mistake? She gasped. Yes, they *were* making a terrible blunder, but not giving in would be equally stupid. Either way, they'd burn.

Might as well go down in flames.

Did she dare say it aloud? She pulled in a deep breath.

"Eric," she said but paused when he cradled her jaw and rubbed the pad of his thumb along her cheekbone.

"The offer for dinner at my place still stands, you know," he said in a raspy voice.

No, not a mistake. If it was, it wouldn't be one-sided. She could live with that, surely. They were both responsible, consenting adults. If they met the end somewhere down the road, so be it. But this was Eric. Her rock. The one solid thing in her life. What he gave, he'd never take away.

And though she couldn't think straight, as his kiss and his touch had messed her up in a jumble, she couldn't get past how right this moment felt.

A part of her knew she shouldn't, and couldn't, trust herself to answer him. Slowly, she reached for the door latch.

But try as she wanted, she couldn't tear her eyes from his face.

"How does Saturday sound?" she heard herself asking.

CHAPTER ELEVEN

The rest of the week passed in a blur. Lara had no idea how she functioned, let alone got anything done. The centre hadn't sunk, so she'd done a good job even while phoning it in, it seemed. Thoughts of the date, and the subsequent kiss, with Eric kept drawing her to La-la-land, and Sam, that cow, hadn't been any help—amid a flurry of giggles unbecoming her, her bestie had told her to seek the sexual healing she so clearly craved. Lara had cursed her out before shaking her head. Sam had still been laughing when she'd cut the call.

Back at her house that fateful Saturday, Sam's words kept ringing in her head. *Sexual healing*. She did need it, but with Eric?

The eruption of a swarm of butterflies in her stomach gave her the answer. She had to admit she wanted him. And what about him? What did *he* expect of her visit?

With a sigh, she resigned herself to face the situation ahead of her. She'd take things as they came and would deal with them when, and *if*, certain things actually happened.

The decision anchored in her mind, she faced the daunting prospect of choosing her dress for the evening. She'd need to wear something light and comfortable, as summer still raged on the coasts. Yet, she also had to choose an outfit that wouldn't make Eric think she was coming on to him. At the same time, the clothes should convey she'd be interested in 'it' if ever the occasion arose.

Goodness, was *she* really thinking in those terms?

Lara giggled. The last time she'd been so nervous for a date had been ... Actually, she couldn't remember. It'd been way more than a decade since she'd prepared for a date with a new man, and she had to admit the thrill of attempted seduction got to her in a powerful, elated rush.

Her feet grew heavier with every successive trip she made between the wardrobe and the full-length mirror. Nothing looked appropriate. Most of her clothes were formal business suits or traditional Indian attires.

Half a dozen unfruitful trips later, she stood nowhere near a compromise. The soles of her feet grew hot as she paced the rug between the wardrobe and the bed. Exasperation won and she pulled all the clothes from the racks and threw them in a messy pile on the floor.

A peek of a tie-and-dye design caught her attention, and she pulled it from the mountain of fabric. The sleeveless cotton sundress hung light and breezy, perfect for a summer evening, with the knee-length skirt not too short and the non-plunging neckline. The deep, bottle-green colour made the same kind of statement as a bold red, but without the apparent seductive undertone.

Thirty minutes later, during which she'd ironed the dress without burning it and after having taken a shower, she was ready. Lara checked the image the mirror sent her. The dress draped over her figure and hinted at her curves. All right, at the bones of her hips, since she didn't have fleshy curves. But still, the illusion of femininity helped bolster her confidence. Lightweight, strappy wedge sandals encased her feet. She wore no jewellery or accessories since the humid heat would only make them cling to her skin and make her uncomfortable. A dab of tinted moisturizer had evened her skin tone. A touch of lip-gloss emphasised her full lips, and a few vigorous brush strokes in her thick hair left it shiny and full of bounce.

She looked exactly like she wanted—fresh, casual, with a hint of sophistication. She smiled at her reflection and couldn't help imagine Eric being bowled over when he saw her.

The elation remained with her as she left the house and got in her car. But once on the road, Lara realised she had no idea of the precise location of Eric's house. The only indication she had pointed towards Cap Malheureux, located a fifteen-minute drive northeast from Grand-Baie.

She pulled over to the side of the road and reached for her phone.

"Hi, Eric," she said when he picked up. "I'm on my way to your place, but I don't know exactly where to go."

"Hey, Lara. So you're not gonna stand me up, after all." He chuckled.

A hot blush crept onto her face, for the idea *had* crossed her mind a few times. She shrugged the mortification off, though. "I don't know the area very much, so I'd need concise directions. The roads seem to have changed since I was last here."

"You're right. They *have* changed, but Royal Road is still in place once you leave Grand-Baie," he said. "Do you know the red church on the beach in Cap Malheureux?"

"Yes." The church was a tourist landmark, and everyone knew its location.

"As soon as it leaves your rearview mirror, you'll notice a rocky wall on the left, about two hundred yards down the road. That's the property. The gate is at the far end, in dark wood. The code is five-seven-six-zero. Punch it in, and it'll open by itself."

"Fine, that should do. Thanks."

"Anytime."

A little while later, she eased her car along the driveway leading to Eric's property. She'd had no trouble finding the house, his directions perfect.

Tall bamboo hedges grew on both sides of the lane, giving it the feel of a narrow tunnel. The exterior setting already impressive, she lost her breath and braked a little stiffly when she emerged into the courtyard.

The house sprawled low in a Mexican hacienda style, with a single floor, whitewashed walls, and terracotta tiles on the roof. A profusion of colourful bougainvillaea grew on one side of the villa and shaded a large patio from prying eyes. A rolling, lushly green lawn occupied half of the property, and the sea appeared within reach beneath the sloping landscape.

She spotted an empty space in the garage at the side of the house. The setup was designed to accommodate three cars, but Eric's massive silver Prado occupied nearly two spots. She managed to fit her Mercedes in and walked to the front door.

With every step she took, anticipation grew in her, making her jittery and excited. She stopped before the heavy oak door and rang the real, old-fashioned bell.

A minute later, Eric answered the door.

"Hey."

"Hi."

The awkwardness melted the moment she took in his smile, which competed for attention with the big smiley face on the apron he wore, *Kiss the Cook* scribbled under the smiling circle.

Laughter bubbled in her throat, and she threw her head back and gave in to it. She'd also forgotten his quirky sense of humour. He could always brighten her day with a well-placed quip.

"So, are you gonna invite me in?" she asked.

"Sure." He winked.

"Well, move out of the way. You're blocking the path."

His smile widened, and he motioned towards the front of the apron before giving her a sly grin.

"Oh, heavens." She gave an exaggerated shake of her head yet drew closer and dropped a kiss on his cheek.

He sighed. "I'd been hoping for a real kiss to let you in, but this should do, for now."

He let the words hang between them, and the butterflies woke up in her stomach. A real kiss that could—*would*—lead to more?

Apparently oblivious to the turmoil he'd created, he took her arm and drew her into the hall before closing the door.

"I'm still busy in the kitchen," he said. "Get something to drink, then you can take a look around."

He led her into the kitchen, in a far corner of the house. Lara poured herself a glass of chilled white wine while she took in the spacious kitchen.

The golden glow of the afternoon sun bathed the room, the light filtered through wispy lace curtains at the windows and bouncing off the light yellow walls and pine wood furniture.

Eric stood at the centre island, busy arranging a platter of food.

She settled her gaze on him. The sun highlighted his thick, blond locks and paled the fine dusting of hairs on his bare forearms. Unabashedly checking him out all over, she wet her lips at how broad and well-defined his shoulders appeared under the casual, white cotton shirt. His long legs were encased in grey denim. The fabric shifted with every move he made, reminding her of the play of those solid and sinuous muscles under the clothing.

Heat started low in her belly and flamed through her within seconds. She craved to touch him, yearned to feel his bare skin, and find out if it was still as warm as she remembered. She about died with the urge to run her hands in his hair, let her fingers tangle in their thickness when all she'd known before with him had been short, buzz-cut locks.

She averted her face, so Eric wouldn't see the rush of colour stinging her cheeks from the debilitating, lustful thoughts she had of him. She had to get herself in check, or she could jump him right there and then.

"I'll take a peek around," she said. "It's quite hot here."

He smiled, and she turned on her heel, almost spilling the contents of her near-full glass in her rapid move. She ventured out a few steps into the corridor and, after a few deep breaths, turned into the living room.

Large, sliding glass doors occupied a whole wall, and the tangy, salty sea air wafted in on a warm breeze. Lara stopped at the view from the opened doors, which knocked the breath out of her.

The room opened onto the large patio she'd seen from outside. Beyond it, the endless horizon of sea and sky met in a stunning clash of cobalt and turquoise. The spectacular, peaked outline of the Coin De Mire Island cut through with its majestic, black stone solidity. The late sun played upon the jutting rock, mingling shadows and contrasts into its landscape and sending blinding flashes of light where its rays hit the water.

What an impressive house. To think he came home to this sight every day—she shook her head. Goodness, people would kill for such a view. All that had to be proof enough he'd made it, and made it big, on the island.

Which, in turn, made him more daunting. More inaccessible. More impossible for any 'them' to rise from the ashes.

So where the hell did it leave her?

◆◆◆

Eric watched the woman standing in front of the opened doors.

Lara's here. In his house.

He'd tortured himself with the idea of this date since their outing to the cinema, dreading she'd work her way out of it. He couldn't bear the thought of losing her again, not when he had her so close and the level playing field so wide open between them. Crazy as it might drive him to find all his efforts seemed to have had no effect on her, the kiss they'd shared *had* been amazing.

Yet, he also knew her, and she wasn't easy to convince.

She turned and met his stare. Her eyes held his, and he was certain she'd sensed his presence the minute he'd walked in. They'd been so finely attuned to each other before, too.

One more certainty he'd relied upon back in the day. When two people had such a connection, they could weather any storm.

Or not. Look at them about to head into the same tornado again. Would Lara grant them a happy ending?

Across from him, her lips parted, but no sound escaped.

She blinked and took a sip from her glass.

"You like it?" he asked.

"The view is magnificent."

"I agree."

The flustered expression came back on her face. Colour stung her golden cheeks with a delicious, crimson stain, and she lowered those thick, long lashes that had never needed makeup to lure any man.

She must know he hadn't been speaking of the view outside. How would she react to his unspoken message?

She stared up at him with steely resolve darkening the narrowed eyes. Everything in her glare, in the coiled stance of her body, stated she wouldn't allow herself to be caught off guard.

We'll see about that.

The duel lasted for a long moment before she broke the silence with a calm, detached question.

"Where's the pool?" she asked, lifting her eyebrows.

"Around the corner." He gave a slight nod. "You can't see it from here."

The discomfited guise came back.

"You must be making a lot of money to afford such a place."

"I get along okay."

Tension bristled in the air, and their eyes never left each other.

Pig-headed tenacity—he'd always known such stubbornness bristled between them. None would bow down first.

Except, she surprised him when she lowered her head a few seconds later.

"I'm sorry, Eric. I had no right to pry."

He smiled. She wasn't as harsh and rigid as she wanted him to believe. He could fly the flag of hope high, after all.

"It's okay. No offence taken." He stepped towards her. "Actually, I bought the place with the inheritance my grandfather left me. The house used to belong to a friend of mine. I fell in love with the property the first time I saw it and bought it before he even put it on the market."

She gave him a small smile in return.

"How about a tour of the place?" he said softly. "Dinner won't be ready for another twenty minutes."

***

Lara couldn't keep her awe from deepening the more she toured Eric's residence. The house was every bit as beautiful inside as its front suggested. The rooms sprawled, large, airy, and filled with natural light. The various shades of vivid orange and crisp white on the walls, and the dark wood furniture, mingled to create an inviting ambience, bathing the whole place in a warm, cosy feel.

This had to be the most beautiful house she'd ever seen. And more surprising, she felt entirely at ease within its walls, letting the tension go as the setting worked its soothing atmosphere over her.

"Did you do the decoration?" she asked.

"No," Eric replied with a laugh. "I'm not good with it at all. You remember my little sister, Angélique? She's the one who designed all this."

"Of course, I remember her. She's about the same age as my baby sister, Diya. What's she doing nowadays?"

"She just left for Florence, actually, to get her diploma in interior decoration."

The sun had set by the time they returned to the living room.

"Dinner's gonna be out there," he said as he led her to the patio, which occupied most of one side of the vast house. A comfortable-looking set of wicker sofas occupied two-thirds of the area, and a large, freeform pool rounded out the far end. In between, a candlelit dinner table set for two glowed.

She sighed softly and turned to face him. "You've gone for the whole works."

"The occasion was worth it."

A knot settled in her throat, and she had trouble swallowing. The desire she'd felt for him lingered in her, and her breath came out in ragged puffs whenever she allowed the sizzling emotions to surface.

What was she doing, getting involved so deeply with this man? Her mind screamed at her, but she chose to ignore its call. She'd see this through, if only for once in her life. Today, she'd listen to her heart for a change.

She allowed Eric to take her hand and lead her to the table, where he pulled out her chair. Once she was comfortably settled, he made his way into the house. The soft, romantic rhythms of Kenny G's sax filled the air, adding a seductive feel to the twilight atmosphere.

Lara let herself drift to a hazy mood as the music lulled her senses.

He came back a few minutes later and slid a plate in front of her. Her mouth watered at the sight of the appetising, picture-perfect lasagne portion. Once he settled himself opposite her, she picked up her fork and took a bite of the rich pasta.

Damn, he's even a good cook. The taste of the meat and rich, cheesy béchamel lingered on her taste buds to bring forth a delightful feeling of well-being. And no hint of garlic. Had he remembered she hated the flavouring?

Over the flickering light of the candles, she met his eyes with hers. "The food is delicious."

"Glad you like it," he said. "I'd be happier if you actually ate all of it."

She smiled. "I intend to."

And she did polish her plate between the casual chatter he kept up throughout the meal.

"Second serving?" he asked with a smile and a raised eyebrow.

She settled back into her chair. "Now that would be pushing your luck."

He laughed as he stood and took her hand to lead her to the outdoor living room. They sat on the plush, comfortable cushions of the wicker sofas for dessert. Eric went into the house and came out with a decadent chocolate cake covered in thick cocoa and cream icing.

"This one, I bought because I'm not good at cake making."

"At least your food is edible, hardly what I can say about my cuisine," she said between pleasure-filled forkfuls of the delicious cake.

At a biting sting on her leg, she slapped her ankle.

"I see the mosquitoes have come out," he said. "We better head inside."

While he went to drop the dishes in the kitchen, she found herself alone in the living room a few minutes later. Lost in her thoughts, lulled by the romantic sound of the music, she stopped in front of the sliding doors.

A cool breeze wafted around her, the scent of citronella essential oil from the mosquito-repellent candles tingeing the air.

She stood with her back to the interior doorway, but she could pinpoint the exact second when Eric stepped into the room. The nape of her neck started to tingle. All her senses picked up to rush forward in a kaleidoscope of stimuli to make sensual awareness shroud her like a fog. Her heart pounded in a frantic rhythm, and her pulse raced all through her body. At the chill running down her spine, every hair on her skin stood on end.

Even the air she dragged into her burning lungs struck her as still, heavier, denser.

Taking a deep breath, she forced her mind to focus. It wouldn't do her any good to lose all her marbles. To pass out before she even got to anything the least bit pleasurable? She'd make such a fool of herself then.

God, was this what sexual tension felt like?

She'd never before experienced such anticipation, such a rush of longing, or yearned for a man's touch, for him to take her body and do decadent, forbidden things to every part of her.

She made out when he started towards her because the fragrance of his aftershave intensified as he got closer. Her muscles tensed with every step he took as if anticipating the delivery of a much-longed-for promise.

Sam was right. Nearly fifteen years in the making, since their very first meeting, when the tension had sizzled between them from the very first glance across the room.

She could now smell the distinctive, heady musk of his skin. Her breath caught when he stopped inches behind her, her throat tight as his warmth radiated out to her. He remained motionless, so close they'd touch if she breathed in too deeply. She could only close her eyes as his warm breath brushed the nape of her neck. Shivers ran along her bare arms when he grazed her exposed shoulders with delicate strokes of his long fingers.

Lightly, he let his touch run along her skin. Teasing, tempting, making her want more, yet she begged him to stop the torture he made well up inside her.

He moved away, urging a moan of protest from her. The sound squelched into an incoherent plea when he splayed his hands flat on her waist, settling his fingers possessively over her.

Even through the fabric of her dress, her skin burned from the imprint of his heat. She'd have given anything to feel those strong, capable hands on her naked flesh.

His breath grew warmer on her neck, convincing her he'd dipped his head lower, closer. A strangled sigh escaped her when he dropped a fleeting kiss on the dip of her collarbone with his soft lips. And another. And another ...

She wanted him, no denying it. But, more than want, she *needed* him. The certainty thrummed in every cell of her body. She wouldn't fight this feeling. She was done fighting. Done with doing the right thing, with listening to what everyone deemed proper.

For once, she'd tune in to what *she* deemed essential. *Eric.*

Slowly, she turned around, and he wrapped those strong arms around her to bring her closer to him. To crush her against the rugged expanse of his chest.

Her mouth went dry, and everything inside her melted in his embrace. If he hadn't held her, she would've pooled to the floor in a mass of liquid, lust-molten goo.

So all she could do was blink up into his eyes, where she encountered tenderness and the darkness of passion.

Just the two of them, alone, together, and about to do the one thing they'd never gotten to experience before.

"I haven't done this in a long time," she said in a low voice.

His eyes darkened even more, and his grip strengthened.

"We have to make it worth it, then."

Wild butterflies took wing in her stomach. Their momentum carried her up and made her stretch onto the tips of her toes to press her lips against his. He'd kissed her every other time before. This time, she would take the reins.

The illusion of her control lasted only a second before he slanted his mouth over hers and took over the kiss. He nipped at her lips, and when she opened for him, he teased her with his hot tongue. How could the edges of one's lips be so sensitive? With every stroke of his tongue, he awakened a tingling need in her that welled up fast into a raging inferno of desire.

His hand cradling her head, he bent lower, deepening their kiss as she tilted to accommodate the ever-hungrier play of his mouth on hers.

Then, he bent his knees, and before she could shift her position, he'd swooped his free arm under her knees and had her in his hold. Lara yelped at the sudden sensation of losing the ground under her feet, but the sound lost itself in his mouth, as he hadn't stopped their kiss yet.

He tore his mouth from hers once he'd taken a few steps. The walls rushed past in a blur as he ate the distance with long strides towards the other end of the dwelling.

No one had ever carried her this way. Elated by the conquering display, a part of her couldn't stop thinking of the practicality of such a move.

"You should put me down. I'm not so light, you know," she said.

He chuckled. "You weigh hardly more than a feather."

They'd reached the bedroom, where he placed her back onto her feet.

He cradled her jaw in his warm palms. "A part of me is afraid of breaking you. *Merde*, Lara. When did you get so fragile?"

Not the time or place to talk about that.

I don't break easily.

She'd open a can of worms if she said the words aloud. Better she showed him and silenced his concern in the process. His lust, she craved. His prodding of her soul and way of life, she could do without.

So, she reached up and ran her hands over his shirt-covered chest. That, at least, had the intended effect, for he tightened his grip on her jaw and bent to place another scorching kiss on her mouth.

He released her face, pushed his hands into her hair, and she moaned. She'd always had a sensitive scalp—did he have any clue what his touch was doing to her? She had to do something, quick. With hands infused by desperate vigour, she pulled at the fastenings on the thin cotton of his shirt. Some buttons slipped through the buttonholes. Some pinged away somewhere onto the marble floor. Did she care? No. Not when the expanse of smooth, warm male skin revealed itself under the garment. Her palms flat on his pecs, she couldn't get enough of his warmth, of touching him.

He hissed in a breath. "*Merde*," he said against her mouth.

She smiled, only to have the elated feeling flare out in a blaze of fire as he pushed the straps of her dress down and divested her of the garment, her bra, and her knickers in one single stroke.

Damn him. How did he do it?

Did he have so much practice undressing women?

The stiff ridge of his jeans' waistband pressed into her belly. One more piece of clothing they didn't need between them. She attacked the metal button and the zipper, peeling the trousers and boxers from his hair-roughened legs.

Once he stepped out of the jeans, he grabbed hold of her shoulders and marched her towards the bed. When the back of her knees hit the mattress, she fell back in an undignified heap. She yelped again, only to have the cry stifled against his shoulder as he rolled her into his arms and cradled her close.

"I got you," he said into her ear.

Then, he made her peek up with his thumb under her chin, and he kissed her.

From that moment on, she surrendered. She only wanted to feel, to experience her first time with Eric and burn every nanosecond of their encounter into her memory.

She touched him where he touched her, kissed him where he kissed her, let her lips and tongue rove all over his delectable, hard-muscled body after he'd sampled every inch of her skin in the same way.

With his fingers first, then his mouth, he made her crash down into explosive release every single time he set his mind to the task of bringing her pleasure.

But Lara knew she waited for the ultimate prize, for the moment when he'd make her his ...

And then, finally, he hovered his big, manly body over her after rolling a condom onto his erection.

She parted her thighs, opened for him, and wrapped her arms around his shoulders before pulling him close to her.

Their mouths touched when he joined his body with hers, stretching her, taking her completely.

She moved when he moved, their rhythm instantly in sync as if they'd done this countless times before, yet still found something new and magical every time they came together.

Je t'aime.

She thought she heard the words, but right then, her orgasm soared and blanked out anything except the feeling of completion she achieved … for the first time in her life.

CHAPTER TWELVE

Eric awoke with a start and sat up in bed. The space next to him lay empty. Had he, again, only dreamed of Lara's presence?

He ran a hand over his face in weariness and confusion. If this had been a dream, how come everything, every touch and every kiss, had felt so vivid? He couldn't have imagined such an encounter.

Hadn't Lara spent the last evening with him?

His eyes adjusted to the dark, and he noticed the heap of clothes littering the bedroom floor. A soft breeze wafted in from the sliding doors, which were ajar. Turning in that direction, he made out the silhouette of a woman on the terrace.

Lara. She stood leaning on the railing of the balcony.

He heaved a deep sigh of relief as he closed his eyes and dropped onto the bed.

So she *had* spent the night with him. This time, his encounter with her hadn't been just another dream.

His whole body relaxed, and the tension left his stiff muscles as he swung his legs over the side of the bed. Sitting there, he contemplated her.

The wind lifted small strands from the hair she'd tucked onto her shoulder, and the moon's cool glow lit the highlights in the shiny locks to make them glisten like spun gold. His shirt hid most of her, and he let his focus travel to her long, bare, exposed legs.

This woman was different from the one he'd left over a decade earlier. More grown-up, mature, and confident.

She appeared lost in her thoughts, her features slightly drawn, her gaze settled on a distant point in the sky. Longing filled his heart to bursting as he watched her, and, unbidden, his mind went back to the last time he'd seen her before this year. On the eve of his departure for France.

She'd cried without words or sobs as they'd parted. His heart had broken upon seeing her tears, yet, he hadn't had it in him back then to work something out for them. He also hadn't had it in him to reassure her things would be all right or ask her to wait for him.

That had been his worst mistake. When he'd next tried to get in touch with her, he'd learned she'd left the country. Desperation and extreme loss had overwhelmed him. The news of her marriage, relayed by Rahul Kiran, her neighbour, when he'd finally deigned to answer Eric's frantic calls, had driven the nail in the coffin shortly after. That's all Rahul had told him—that Lara was married, that Eric should leave her alone.

He'd messed up big time back then.

But not today. Not anymore.

This time would be right for them. She was back in his life again, and he was going to keep her this time around, make sure she stayed, that she wouldn't ever wish to leave him again.

He would allow nothing to come between them.

The sound of doors sliding farther open startled her out of her thoughts and made her jump. Lara turned to find Eric standing in the doorway.

She gasped, a hand clutched upon her heart. "Goodness, you nearly scared the life out of me."

He didn't reply and just kept watching her intently. In the dark, his face loomed sombre, his jaw clenched. She frowned.

"Is something wrong? I didn't want to wake you, so I snuck out."

His heated, narrowed scrutiny kept her rooted to where she stood, and she could only watch as he crossed the space between them with two mighty steps. He stopped his powerful shape inches before her as he peered down, letting his intense eyes bore into her own.

She swallowed with much difficulty. Why did he ogle her like a big cat about to pounce on its prey? Her heart picked up an accelerated beat, and blood started to whoosh in her head.

He drew closer and brought his hands up to frame her face. Her mouth went dry, and the heat from his touch flowed into her bloodstream, igniting the latent fire smouldering in her. He slowly brushed her lower lip with his thumb, and a shiver coursed through her at the silent, sensual invitation in that stroke.

How could he do this to her with a simple touch? And how could she have allowed a man to have such power over her?

The question tortured her, but she chose to ignore it. His lips were now on hers, and he kissed her with a hunger and a passion more powerful than anything she'd ever dreamed existed.

Soon, he wrapped her in his arms and crushed her to him. She'd never relished feeling as feminine and delicate as she did when he held her this way. His heat enveloped her, overwhelming all coherent thought, and she gave in. Stopped fighting. Stopped thinking. Only allowing her body, her every sense, to feel, to experience him.

He tore his mouth from hers to trail hot, hungry kisses along her jaw.

"I don't ever want to lose you," he said in her ear. "I'll wait forever for you, Lara. But don't make me wait so long. Please."

Though she heard him, the certainty in the statements, the shameless begging in that last word, didn't fully register. Instead, all her thoughts converged on the gorgeous, sexy man intent on devouring her.

This time, she'd take the lead.

So, she stepped back and took his hand when he frowned at her sudden departure from his embrace. *Not for long*. Threading her fingers with his, she tugged him into the bedroom. Along the way to the bed, she let go long enough to discard the shirt.

He hitched in an audible breath when she stood stark naked in front of him. Her breathing came out laboured as she perused the length of his frame, catching sight of how ready and willing he was for her.

She bit her lip. "Where do you keep the condoms?"

He nodded at the bedside table. She reached for the drawer and retrieved a small foil packet. Removing the condom from the sealed envelope, she rolled the thin protection over his rigid length.

They exchanged no words during those moments. They didn't need to because their gestures, their need, spoke their own language.

She led him to the bed and gently pushed down on his shoulders. He fell back into a sitting position, and she straddled him before he could reach out for her. With her previously denied yearning for him flaring in engulfing flames, she didn't need any other touch or kiss to make her ready to welcome him. She sank her body onto his, holding him into her core with a drawn-out sigh carrying every hint of the rough, encompassing passion that engulfed her under his possession.

He snaked an arm against the small of her back to pull her flush to him. Her breasts flattened against his chest, and when she tipped her head back with pleasure, he placed his hot, wet mouth on her throat. He pushed his hips up, slammed into her, and she tightened the hold of her legs against his waist.

Over and over, they soared together. Then, somewhere in the moment, they kissed.

When she opened her eyes to stare into his passion-filled gaze, something inside her tilted. Suddenly, it no longer mattered who stayed in control. Chaos, when created together, held a devastating pull of attraction.

Wrapping her arms tightly around his neck, she threw herself back to land on the mattress with him on top of her.

His chuckle drowned in the kiss she stole from his lips.

He started moving against her, into her, and she gave herself to him.

◆◆◆

Eric awoke shortly after dawn, the early morning sun streaming through the thin curtains stirring him out of deep slumber. He never bothered to close the heavy drapes in the bedroom, preferring to awaken naturally with the sunshine. That is, unless his screeching phone tore him out of sleep to go take care of an emergency.

This morning, he awoke with a languid, heavy inertia in his muscles. That's when he remembered the past night. He smiled at the brush of soft, rounded buttocks against his groin.

He propped himself on an elbow and watched the sleeping woman in his bed. She looked content, peaceful almost. Her face was relaxed and smooth, her beautiful features bereft of their usual frowns. The morning sunshine played upon her skin, lighting her matte complexion with a honeyed glow.

He'd come across many beautiful women in his life, yet none had ever struck him as more beautiful than Lara. He chuckled at the thought. He'd fallen in love with her at first glance. Her answering glare had shot daggers at him, though, as he'd been her most tenacious opponent on the high school debate circuit, the only one who had dared go head to head against her in order to land the top spot in the competition. Everyone had written off the contenders from the other schools, Lara's English-speaking academy clearly the most probable winner with her at the helm of its team. He'd taken his French-speaking school's team, perfect outsiders, all the way to the final battle her side had relentlessly won. Fire had lit her dark eyes every time they had met, and he'd wondered if she burnt with the same ardour inside.

From what he'd gathered the previous night, she certainly did. She'd responded to his every touch with a passion and an abandon he could only cherish. She didn't give herself easily, yet, she'd been totally his when he'd made love to her.

A small smile appeared on her face. Tenderness overwhelmed him, and love burst in his heart. He'd devote his whole life to make her happy, if only she'd let him.

He sighed. No good to venture *there*, his mind chided. He'd promised to take things easy with her. So be it.

She stirred in her sleep. But she didn't wake up, and merely turned onto her stomach.

His body grew tense, already craving her again as he took in the sight of her graceful back and the thick brown hair lying on her pillow like a shiny river. She'd dyed it sometime in the past decade—her hair had been midnight black when they'd been younger.

He wouldn't wake her. Not yet. She probably needed the sleep. He hadn't forgotten the tiredness she'd carried around like a draining cloak these past few weeks. The rest would do her good, as would some food once she woke up.

He got up and threw on a pair of shorts before making his way into the kitchen. The clock on the wall showed six o'clock. He reviewed his plans for the day as he put croissants to heat in the oven.

Sunday. His parents surely wouldn't expect him for lunch, since he hadn't said anything about attending this week. Knowing his mother, though, she'd probably nag him into attending the family meal so he wouldn't be alone.

He chuckled. Little did Agnes Armont-Marivaux know her son wouldn't be on his own today, and hopefully, from now on.

Still, he'd give her a call and work his way out of the family commitment.

The air around her felt warm and snug, the strong sunshine bathing the place tickling her skin. The song of chirping birds, heralding a bright, beautiful summer day, filtered through her hazy, still-sleepy mind.

Lara emerged out of a soft, dreamy, cottony world as she opened her eyes. When she glanced at it, the room was unfamiliar, yet she felt at home in its surroundings. Could she be in a hotel on the coast? The sun's warm rays brushed her back, and the sheets wrapped around her provided delicate cool against her skin. She yawned and stretched out of slumber.

She couldn't remember when she had woken in such a peaceful way. Not for a very long time. She savoured the blissful feeling. Her body, limp and heavy, sank into the soft mattress.

Images of the previous night flashed into her mind, and she sat up with a start, drawing the sheet to her shoulders to cover herself. Her whole body grew tense, all notion of languor forgotten.

She was in Eric's house.

For God's sake, she was in Eric's *bed*.

After they'd made love all night long.

She closed her eyes and covered her face with her hands.

What had she been thinking? That was it, though. She *hadn't* been thinking. Her sex-starved body had shut her mind off and done as it pleased. She couldn't believe she'd given in to the heed of her body, and not once, but repeatedly. Thank God Eric wasn't here to witness the shame burning her cheeks as she remembered her lack of inhibition in the past twelve hours.

Eric. Where was he?

She sat up straighter and strained to pick up any sound in the house. After a few seconds, she made out his voice, talking to someone. Who, though?

It's none of your concern.

She needed to get out quickly. She didn't know how she'd face him. The only times she'd encountered a lover the morning after had been with her husband. The awkward feeling ate her alive.

Was that how people felt after the first time? If such was the case, then she totally wasn't cut out for a life of one-night stands.

She had no more time to ponder the question because Eric walked in, a heavy tray in front of him.

"*Bonjour, ma belle.* Slept well?" he said with a large smile.

The blush burned hotter on her face. How come she wasn't dead of embarrassment yet? And how could *he* be so casual and carefree? He simply took it in his stride unless he'd done this so many times.

Flames shot before her eyes as the heavy dagger of jealousy sliced her heart.

"Have you done this often?"

She wanted to bite her tongue the second the words were out. Too late. She'd let her motor mouth run once again.

He settled cross-legged on the bed and placed the tray between them before lifting his eyes to hers.

"You mean prepare breakfast for the woman I spent the night with? Let me think." He paused for a few seconds, his eyes never leaving hers. "No, I don't recall ever doing that."

She let out the breath she didn't know she'd been holding. Relief flooded through her, and she yearned to kick herself because his reply made her feel so good.

Then, another query slid in—he didn't make breakfast because he didn't bring women to his bed or because he always slunk away during the night?

Not something she should ponder. The women he'd taken to his bed before were none of her concern, and if he did a runaway act ...

"I figured you'd need some reinforcement after last night," he said with a wink.

Hot flames ate her cheeks again.

"Eric, don't tease, okay?"

She averted her eyes to stare down at her lap. Would she ever live through this? Highly unlikely. Shyness overwhelmed her, piling onto the embarrassment bubbling inside. Lara suddenly wished for the earth, or the bed, to open up and swallow her out of the situation.

His gentle fingers on her chin made her lift her face until her eyes peered into his.

"Last night was wonderful." His voice thrummed out low and husky. "I hope you don't feel bad about it."

She searched his eyes and her own heart. Did she regret last night?

No, she didn't.

"It was wonderful for me, too."

He drew closer and placed a gentle kiss on her lips.

"I'm glad you're happy," he said when he pulled away.

Happiness, warmth, and strange desperation wound up in turmoil inside her. The latter won the struggle, and her mind returned to the question that haunted her.

"Eric, what happens now?"

He remained silent for a few seconds, his face serious.

With a pang, she clamped down on the urge to touch him. How could he appear even more handsome, as if severity accentuated his features and brought out his virility with startling evidence?

Damn. What was she thinking? Her libido was getting the better of her again.

"I don't know, Lara." His low voice tore through her self-induced beating. "I guess we take things as they come. I don't want you to feel any pressure, but I want you with me."

She couldn't say anything in reply. He didn't ask, didn't order, didn't expect anything from her.

Her throat closed, and tears threatened to fall from her eyes. What was she to say? Eric didn't ask her for much. She could at least give him that, even if she didn't contemplate anything serious in the future. The two of them had no happy ending. She had to live for the moment. Seize the day, *carpe diem* or whatever other philosophy that would cushion her for a while before she slammed into the rocky wall of the cliff looming right ahead.

Nothing but the moment ...

So, she nodded and let a tremulous smile curve her lips.

He smiled back, and somehow, everything fell into place.

He nodded at the tray. "Eat your breakfast before it gets cold. There are croissants, and the coffee is as you like it. Black with two sugars."

She couldn't help but laugh. "How many more little things like this do you remember about me?"

He winked. "Just what's needed to win you over."

"You're a charmer, you know that?" She laughed as she picked up her coffee and took a sip.

A thought struck her, and she voiced it aloud. "Who were you talking to a few minutes ago?"

Great, Lara. Motor-mouth runs again.

"My mother," he said.

Something inside her froze. Family. She hadn't thought beyond the two of them. If their families got involved ...

"I needed to worm my way out of lunch today to be with you," he said.

At the mention of his family—the white people who looked down on anyone without their colonist blood—dread filled her to chill her insides. Dare she find out?

"Eric, what would your family say if they knew about us?"

He took a sip of his coffee.

"There's nothing to say, Lara. It's my life, and I choose how to live it."

His words and the conviction in them sounded final. Could she believe him? Would it be as easy as him taking a stand for them against the world?

"What would *your* mother say about all this?" he asked, eyebrows lifted, bringing her back to the moment.

She rolled her eyes, and despite her churning thoughts and uncertainty, a hearty laugh escaped her.

"My mum would surely go ballistic. Probably have a heart attack." She chuckled. "Good thing my father is a cardiologist."

Eric laughed, too.

They never got around to eating the croissants or finishing their coffee. Because they were kissing, the world around them and all its considerations stopped spinning.

CHAPTER THIRTEEN

Damn. Lara blew out another sigh as she peeked at the clock on her desk. Still another three hours before she could meet Eric again. She'd come to hate Saturdays when his private practice overflowed with patients. And because she had a whole afternoon to kill before they could get together at six.

Work no longer appealed to her, as she now lived only for the weekends, especially the Sunday mornings, when she'd wake up with Eric by her side. She smiled as the thought crossed her mind. She hovered in an alternate reality lately, a place that made her want to get out of the office quickly so she could be with him.

For how much longer, she didn't know. She'd stopped asking herself the question. Why rock a boat that looked like it would never capsize on the calm waters of their relationship?

Live for every moment.

Her cell phone rang, and she fumbled with the screen in her attempt to answer, hoping to hear Eric's rich voice at the other end.

"Hi, Lara. It's Dee."

Diya? Why, ever, would her sister call her? Diya existed in her own little bubble, and she only came down to Earth when she needed to wrangle something out of one of the adults in her entourage.

"Hi to you, too. To what do I owe this honour?"

"Come on," her sister said. "I know it's been ages since we last talked, but you gotta admit it's not like you've been around lately, either."

True. Since she'd started to see Eric, she'd lost touch with other parts of her life. A flurry of guilt erupted inside her, scorching like acid. She'd also neglected a lot of things, a lot of people.

"So, what can I do for you?" she asked. "Knowing you, I'm sure you're gonna ask me for something."

"Shoot, am I getting so predictable?" Diya gave a startled gasp. "But yes, I do have something to ask. Actually, I was wondering if I could spend the night at your place."

Meaning she wouldn't be able to meet Eric? *Hell no!*

But then, another feeling took hold of her, rushing in the wake of the guilt. As the older sister, she had a duty to look after Diya. And she had to admit she hadn't been very present for the girl throughout the years.

Something niggled at her, though. Diya had a fleet of friends, and she was always crashing at their place. So why did she want to come to her house? "Dee, is something wrong?"

Her sibling laughed at the other end. "No. It's just Mum being a pain, and I badly need to get out of here for the night. I figure she'll let me go if I come to you."

Lara smiled. That did make sense. Come to think of it, her mother hadn't nagged her for a long time. "So Mum's on your case, huh? Probably why I'm not her top priority right now."

"So, can I come?"

"Sure. What do you say to a chick night?"

"That'd be wicked. I'll get us some movies. Oh, and you do have a DVD player, right?"

"Yes, Dee." Her sister sometimes thought all adults lived in the Dark Ages.

"Wicked," Diya said. "See you later."

She pondered over what she'd say to Eric as she held the phone in her hand for a few minutes. She didn't want to cancel their evening, but she hadn't had the heart to refuse her sister. God knew their mother was tough to deal with, and she fully understood Diya's plight.

I'll owe him one now, and Eric'll never let me live through it.

She pressed the speed-dial for his number with a heavy heart.

"Couldn't you have picked something *not Magic Mike*-related?" she asked as she surveyed the pile of DVD cases her sister dumped on her bed.

"I did." Diya's eyes grew big as she defended herself. "There's *Love, Actually.* I am in *heaven* when I hear Hugh Grant's accent. Hugh Grant *and* Colin Firth in the same movie—what more can you ask for?"

"You're in heaven anytime a bloke opens his mouth and spins you some British accent."

"Hey, I'm much more discerning than that."

Lara raised her eyebrows.

Diya rolled her eyes. "Shoot. Fine. I admit it. Now, tell me you didn't let special things turn your head at eighteen?"

She'd already been married at eighteen. Grown up. Mature. A homeowner with a mortgage.

Had she had to grow up too fast?

Don't go there.

She shook her head as she surveyed her youngest sister. What a world of difference between them at this same age. Diya struck her as the typical teenage fashion victim, with well-cut jeans riding dangerously low on her hipbones, tighter-than-tight tank top baring her midriff, and pigtails. Innocence with growing sophistication.

"Are you trying to look like some anime character?" she asked with a dubious twist of her mouth.

Diya hit her with a cushion. "This is not your generation, and you won't get it. So drop the scrutiny."

"Thank God." She didn't want to appear scrambled together in what the youngsters considered 'cool' fashion. Whatever happened to notions like class and chic? A shiver ran through her as she contemplated being dressed like her sister. "Let's just hope you outgrow it when you're my age."

Diya poked her tongue at her in reply. "You got any food around? I'm starving."

Lara stared at the petite girl so unlike her elder siblings. Where she and Neha were tall, big-boned women, Diya looked like a strong breeze could break her in half. Deceptive, though, and she would be worried for the breeze in the confrontation, because her baby sister was nothing less than a phenomenon of Nature.

"You're always starving. God knows how you manage not to turn into an elephant with all the junk food you eat. Have you even heard of organic food?"

"I don't sit behind a desk all day, like *some* people."

"How dare you, you cheeky git?" Lara hit her with a pillow.

Diya burst out laughing. "You're just jealous that you look like a bag of bones while guys find me cute."

Immersed in the relaxed and carefree banter, she opened her mouth to retort how Eric found the bag of bones very satisfying. She caught herself before the words flew out. She had no intention of letting her family know about her and Eric. And to let Diya in on any secret meant the news would be plastered all over the place within the coming hour.

"I'll order some pizza. And don't you dare touch my cell phone," she said over her shoulder as she left the room. Diya was mad over the iPhone, the latest model that their parents had refused to get her. Knowing her sister, Lara was sure she'd be up to something forbidden, since the lure of danger always won Diya over.

She couldn't help but smile when she thought of her youngest sibling. Diya had been four years old when she'd married Roy, and the fourteen years apart in two different countries hadn't really helped their relationship, either. She was glad their friendship was picking up again. God knew the younger girl could do with some guidance.

They watched *Magic Mike* while eating their pizza. Halfway through *Dear John,* the doorbell rang. Lara made her way downstairs and opened the door.

She blinked, and surprise and astonishment battled inside her as she took in the sight on her doorstep.

"Eric? What are you doing here?"

What a sight, indeed. She gulped. Carefree and casual in jeans and a green linen shirt, he leaned against the opened doorway, smiling his gorgeous smile at her. Heavy golden locks fell over his forehead, and her knees went so weak with longing, she had to reach out and brace a hand onto the wall.

"I was missing you, so I thought I'd drop by for a minute," he said in a low, husky, and oh-so-sexy tone. "Aren't you gonna invite me in?"

He missed her? Her heart melted.

Then he reached out and wrapped his arms around her. With one big step, he entered the hallway, and the door closed with a tap from the heel of his shoe.

Fire ignited in her blood as he pulled her closer to him, and she eagerly returned his hungry kiss as she wrapped her arms around his neck, letting her fingers tangle in his thick hair.

"Laaaara? What's up?"

The call made its way into her heated mind, having the same effect as an icy shower.

She broke free from Eric's embrace just as Diya popped her head at the top of the stairs. The younger girl's eyes grew wide.

Diya grinned brightly, making Lara think of a shark about to sink its pointed teeth into some fleshy prey.

"Aren't you gonna introduce us?" the girl asked with a cheeky lift of her eyebrows.

No way out of introductions, not when these two had come face to face already.

Lara turned around. The heat of anger burnt her cheeks, and she narrowed her eyes to slits as she stared at her sister.

"Diya, this is Eric. Eric, meet my little sister, Diya."

"Hi, Diya. Pleasure to meet you," he said with a warm smile.

"Hi, Eric." Diya had all but drooled through the greeting. "Pleasure's all mine."

She needed the nosy git packing and leaving. A part of her was afraid Diya would really drool on Eric if she got any closer.

"Dee, aren't you missing the end of the movie, back in the bedroom?" she said through clenched teeth.

The message also implied, "stay there until further notice." Diya appeared to pick up the unspoken command because she turned around and headed upstairs.

For once, Diya had listened. Surprise, surprise.

Eric chuckled as soon as Diya went back up. Lara trained her eyes on him, and he seemed to choke back his laughter at the icy, pointed glare she sent him.

"She sounds sweet," he said.

"Don't let the appearance fool you. She's not the little doll she looks like." In fact, Diya was a barracuda in sheep's clothing. No, she had not gotten her metaphors confused because that's exactly what her baby sister was.

A sly smile appeared on Eric's face.

"Seems like that's the case with the Hemant family. I know for sure you're not the ice queen you let people think you are."

He took a step with every word he spoke, and soon, she found herself jammed between him and the wall. Her heart rate picked up as he lowered his face closer to hers.

"I still haven't finished with you," he said before settling his mouth over hers.

All notions of little sisters and propriety flew out the window as her blood flared into flames at his touch. He snaked a hand under her skirt, letting his light touch graze her thigh. Before she could understand what she was doing, she braced her back against the wall and wrapped her legs around his hips. Somehow, she'd ditched her knickers, and he'd undone his jeans.

He'd gone commando under the trousers and thus had no trouble sinking the rigid length of his arousal into her waiting body. Goodness, how she loved the rush of letting him take her when and where he wanted. A couple of weeks ago, they'd had 'the talk' and decided on unprotected sex since they were going steady. She had pregnancy covered with the pill.

A milestone in their relationship, one she refused to contemplate whenever the notion popped into her head. Because she and Eric, in the long term, spelled—

Pleasure crashed through her. She bit her lip so hard to squelch the noise and blood registered on her taste buds.

"Now see what you've gone and done," he said against her ear before he kissed her and gently sucked on her lower lip.

Despite everything they'd done so far, this last kiss hit her as the most intimate thing Eric had done to her. Were she not holding on to his shoulders with tense arms, she would've melted to the floor at the wave of emotion.

With her forehead pressed into the hollow of his collarbone, she closed her eyes and let her senses stop swimming. Little by little, he released her so she could slide her feet back onto the floor. As she slowly returned to the moment, she smoothed her skirt and then reached for his jeans.

"Sending me away after doing the naughty with me?" He chuckled.

Heat seared her cheeks. "It's not that. It's just—"

"You're babysitting tonight. I get it." He reached out and tucked a lock of hair behind her ear. "I missed you tonight, Lara."

"Me, too," she admitted in a breathless whisper.

He released her and took backward steps. Then, with a wink, he opened the front door and stepped out, leaving her to stare at the wood panel.

What had happened here? Something inside her told her that a vital part of her being had shifted on its axis, but damn if she wanted to acknowledge it. Whatever *it* happened to be.

So, she did what she did best—put the concern away for the moment, and made her way up the stairs. She shouldn't forget, like she had just before, that she had an impressionable teenager in her home. After a quick dash in the bathroom to rearrange her clothing and her hair, she walked out and marched into her bedroom, only to stop in her tracks.

Diya sat in front of her vanity, the polished wood surface littered with all the makeup Lara possessed. Even the new, unopened ones.

"What do you think you're doing?"

A clutter resounded as Diya dropped a blusher box onto the table.

"Darn, Lara. You frightened me. Don't you know you shouldn't creep up on people like that, especially when they're wielding a mascara brush? I nearly poked my eye with the wand." She shrugged. "I'm having a look at your makeup, duh. What else?"

Lara stared at her, mouth agape and with her hands on her hips. "Who gave you permission?"

"The fact I'm your little sister," the girl said with a dismissive roll of her eyes.

Not for much longer. She should've drowned the brat a long time ago.

Diya threw her arms out and huffed. "All your stuff is Chanel and Dior, yet you've got only dreary neutrals. How the heck you landed such a hunk with such a palette, I wonder."

She didn't know how she should react. Be piqued by the barely-veiled insult or be aghast that Diya had sunk her teeth into the notion of Eric's presence in her life. She didn't want to talk of Eric, and certainly not with the nosy git in her house.

"It's none of your business, Dee."

Silence hung heavy in the next seconds, and Diya, looking nonplussed, continued with her experimenting in front of the mirror.

"So," she said. "I gather he's a good shot, as well. How was it?"

"How was what?" Lara asked as she leaned against the wall.

"The steamy quickie you had downstairs."

Lara scrambled to her feet. "We didn't—"

"Oh, don't give me that," her sister said. "You're smirking wider than Sylvester when he manages to eat Tweety."

Goodness. No point in denying it. As appalled as she was to discuss her 'quickie' with her sibling, she couldn't hide her head in the sand. Diya might be her baby sister, but the girl had grown up. What was she to do in such a situation?

Lara took a deep breath to try to calm her nerves. If news of this encounter leaked out ...

"Dee, give me your word you won't tell this to anyone, least of all to Mum."

Diya threw the eye shadow palette down and turned to stare at her.

"Hello? You think me *loco* or what?" She twirled her index finger at her temple to highlight her point. "Does any of us really need Mum working more drama than she usually does?"

At least she held some good sense in that airhead skull. Lara blew out a sigh of relief.

Diya grabbed her hand and pulled her onto the bed. Startling how the tiny girl could pack such strength in her delicate limbs.

"Out with the details, though." Diya grinned the shark smile again. "How long have you two been together?"

No way out, again. So Lara sighed once more. "Little more than a month now."

She didn't elaborate. However much she loved the budding girlfriend relationship with her sister, that's all she was prepared to share. She needed to change the subject.

"You never got round to telling me why Mum is now on your back."

"Oh," Diya said with a shrug. "She's found out about my boyfriend, who is totally unproper, apparently." She made quote marks with her hands when she said the word 'unproper.' "So Mum, with nothing better to do, as usual, is going bonkers and driving me mad in the process."

A boyfriend who did not fit the bill? Unless he'd been handpicked by their mother, no man would be considered 'proper.'

At the same time, though, Lara knew rules of propriety and the like existed as a framework for guidance. And it seemed to her that following rules and paying heed to advice were not part of Diya's genetic makeup. As a big sister, she had to look out for the girl.

"Dee, be careful, okay? I don't want you to get hurt. If this guy is not worth it, drop him."

Diya engulfed her in a big hug. "Aww, sis. That's too sweet." She squealed before growing calmer again. "I know what I'm doing. I'm careful. I just wish Mum would let me live, though."

Lara laughed. "The day Mum lets us do that, we'll know for sure she's gone mad."

◆◆◆

Friday evening arrived, and Lara settled in her living room with a pile of documents in her lap. She spent more and more time away from the office and consequently brought a lot of work back home with her.

Tired of reading yet another report, with the graphs and figures of estimations and projections blurring before her vision, she closed her eyes and rested her head on the sofa. Home was *not* a favourable setting to dissect the financial reports of the different departments she had under her responsibility. Yet, she worked everything that way to share more time with Eric.

A smile lifted the corners of her mouth as she heard him puttering in her kitchen.

Intent on taking care of her, he usually prepared her dinner on the weekends. He stayed with her all the time he could, and they'd taken to arranging their schedules around each other. His presence brought the calm and comfort she'd longed for, and his attentive loving soothed her body, mind, and soul.

I could grow used to this life. She sighed. If only things could be so easy, with only Eric and her in their little world. But it was not possible. There existed a big, bad world out there, and she wasn't certain the society they lived in was ready for something like the two of them together.

And truth be told, she dared not find out, either. She refused to acknowledge anything that could burst the bubble she thrived in lately.

The telephone ringing cut through her thoughts, and she glanced around for the device. Fishing it from under a cushion of the sofa, she answered with a weary sigh.

"Good evening, darling."

"Good evening, Mum." Lara closed her eyes in despair. Just what she needed. "How are you?"

She heard a snort at the other end.

"As if you care. I haven't heard from you in so many days, yet you ask how I'm doing?"

"Sorry, Mum. I'm very busy lately."

The litany of excuses fell from her lips like a recorded, automated response. *For an excuse to ditch Mum, press one. For a plan to worm out of Saturday dinner, press two.* And so on ...

"Oh, never mind," her mother said.

This got Lara to pop her eyes open and sit up straighter. Since when did her mother let her off the hook that easily?

"Tell me, is that girl at your place yet again?"

She blinked. "What girl?"

"Diya, of course. She's never around anymore."

Lara sent out silent thanks. The radar had clocked in on her youngest sister, and for once, not on her. "She's not here, Mum. She's probably at some friend's place or still on campus. Isn't she doing exams right now? And why are you looking for her?"

"Oh, dear me. Didn't I tell you?" The tone dropped to a conspiratorial low at the other end. "She's gotten involved with some good-for-nothing, and she thinks she's in love with him. But that's not the worst, Lara. There are talks how that boy is a Muslim. Can you imagine?"

Here we go again. Not only had she eluded her mother's ramblings lately, she'd also had a respite from the social mores and double standards. Perfect to consider a Muslim or Christian neighbour as closer than family, but let one of 'their own' try to fall for someone from a different religion or culture, and the sword fell.

Lara tuned out of the conversation as her mother continued her discourse on Diya and the 'unproper' boyfriend. She added a "yes" or a noncommittal "uh-huh" along the way, but she doubted her mother noticed.

Her boredom must have come off her in waves, because Eric came to stand behind her, and he bent to drop kisses along her neck.

What a tease. She had to get him to stop. None of *that* when she was on the phone with her mother, of all people.

However, she couldn't conceal the giggle welling up in her throat.

Deathly silence fell on the line, and she wondered if the call had been cut.

But her mother's voice came back on a second later.

"What are you giggling about?" *Long, very long, pause.* "Lara, I sure hope there's not some strange man with you."

Oh, no, her mother would really drive the nail in now. She needed to get out of the conversation, by any means. "No, Mum. There isn't some *strange man* with me, as you say."

And that was the truth. Eric wasn't 'some strange man.'

Lara nearly laughed again, but she caught herself just in time. It wouldn't do to spill the beans after all her hard work.

"Sorry, Mum. I have to go now. I've still got loads of work to do. Talk to you soon. Bye."

She pressed the icon to end the call before her mother had any chance of following up on her question. If Gayatri Hemant came to know the whole truth about Eric ...

"What's the matter?" Eric asked as he settled in the seat opposite her.

She smiled at him and shook her head. As much as she reeled from the close encounter with her mother, she couldn't help but see the incongruity of the situation. "Nothing. Just my mother thinking I live a bad life because she suspects I have strange men in my house."

He chuckled. "I figure the strange man referred to is me."

She laughed along with him.

But moments later, the laughter died, and he grew serious.

Strong foreboding took hold of her, with an unexpected, biting chill. *Nothing good, that.* Her stomach churned, powering on empty. Bad sign, because an empty stomach and strong emotions did not go well together for her.

She tried to shake the feeling, but she couldn't. Somehow, the impossibility of breaking free from the disconcerting notion added to her discomfort.

"So your mum thinks you live a bad life."

He let the words hang between them. They reached out at her, heavy, powerful, to grip her heart with iron hands.

Chills descended along her spine, and her hands grew cold and clammy. She couldn't utter a word, though, as the silence closed around her throat and paralyzed her vocal chords.

"It can be easily remedied, you know."

He spoke the words slowly, softly. Yet, they resounded in her mind. She didn't know what he was getting at, but suddenly, she grew scared, apprehension battening down her every defence.

Lara somehow raised her eyebrows in question, and the gesture seemed like all the prompt he needed.

"Marry me, Lara."

CHAPTER FOURTEEN

Obliterated by the irrational fear taking her hostage, Lara's head spun. Fear clogged her airways, and she couldn't breathe. This had to be a nightmare. When would she wake up? She had to wake up to take a breath, since her lungs threatened to burst in her chest.

The terror gripping her proved more debilitating than anything she'd experienced before. Her heart pounded, the only muscle able to move in her whole body. Cold sweat broke on her skin, and she wanted to hug herself tight to keep the warmth from leaving her. She wanted Eric to appear by her side, to hold her close to his chest and tell her she was imagining things.

She awaited deliverance, but none came. Her stomach started to heave, but she contained the nausea. Marriage and a future together had never been in her plans. She'd settled for carpe diem, and she could do nothing to stop the cold running icy in her veins.

This can't go on. She attempted to move, but her body felt frozen solid while her oversensitive mind amplified everything around her. The hiss of her shallow breathing. The drum roll of her heart in her ears. The numbness slowly creeping its way up her hands and feet. The overwhelming sensation reached her neck as darkness descended before her eyes, and she fell into the black void calling out to her.

Lara awoke as soft heat radiated from her limbs. She stretched her leg, and her foot rubbed against the warm and slightly rough surface of a woollen blanket. Her neck lay propped on something soft and lolled back with weakness when she attempted to lift it.

"Don't try to move."

Eric's soft, calm voice filtered through to her mind.

She opened her eyes. He huddled on his knees beside her, his face level with hers where she lay on the sofa.

Confusion filled her mind. “What happened?”

He touched her cold forehead with his warm fingers.

“You fainted.”

“What?”

Disbelief flooded her, and she jerked up into a sitting position. Vivid colour erupted before her closed eyelids as her sense of gravity plummeted from the abrupt movement.

“I told you not to move,” he snapped.

She popped her eyes open. Why did he look so strained? His lips were white with anger, but his touch was full of concern and precision as he held the back of her neck. With his other hand, he took her wrist and pressed two fingers upon her pulse.

Lara blinked. Here before her wasn’t her lover, but the competent doctor in him. What on Earth had happened? She’d get no answers if she stayed this way, with no control over anything.

She tugged her wrist out of his hold with a gentle twist. “I’m okay now.”

He snorted. “You were unconscious less than a minute ago, and you expect me to believe that?”

She frowned as she took in his words. “I never faint, Eric.”

“You just did.”

“But, how can that be? I feel fine.”

He kept his eyes fixed on her. Was it her imagination, or did they turn to an icy, arctic blue? His jaw also appeared unusually clenched, a small nerve twitching along his cheek. Not a good sign.

“I guess you’ve had a shock.”

That wasn’t calm in his tone, but ice, and irony. She shook her head, which made her senses spin again. She blinked to let her balance settle once more.

Why was he so hard with her?

Cold, steely hands clutched her heart, and she gasped as the breath left her. The last words she’d heard before she’d lost it came back to her, and she clamped a hand to her mouth.

He’d asked her to marry him.

The scene played again in her memory as she stared at him, seeing the man she had spent the past two months with, yet, at the same time, a stranger.

He narrowed his eyes, eyebrows knit in a frown. Great—he'd probably seen the flash of recollection on her face.

"You don't think it's a good idea," he said, the words cutting the heavy silence like a knife.

She opened her mouth, but no sound escaped with her tongue and throat dry as sandpaper.

His face grew more sombre, his lips drawn to a tight line.

The lick of apprehension tickled all over her spine. She'd never seen Eric angry. A formidable temper lurked in him, one that could cause mayhem when provoked, and the furore seemed to be coming out of its dormant state. Still waters did run deep, after all.

"Why?"

Only one word, yet, she felt the full blow he dealt her with it. Hurt, anger, and confusion battled for space in the three letters.

Lara turned her face the other way. She'd never wanted to hurt him. But she should've known they'd face this situation someday. Time to set things straight with him, to stare reality in its face and wake up from the dream. No more living for the moment, because the bubble had burst. No further evading any issue.

She turned around and focused on him. It broke her heart to see him so distraught, but she had to do what she had to do.

"There's no hope for us, Eric. Everything is against us. Society, our families. No one will accept us. It's next to impossible. Your life is here, as is mine, but this leaves the two of us nowhere," she said in a careful tone.

She'd heard of mixed origins couples emigrating to live their lives away from the prying tentacles of Mauritian society. No such possibility for them.

He remained silent for a few seconds. "Don't you think it's up to us to decide that?"

The calmness of his reply angered her. How could he imagine there wasn't anything, like a condemning society, their formidable families, to face for them to exist? No matter how much she disliked facing it, people *did* talk and make life difficult for others. She shook her head and bit her lip to keep all her justifications within her.

"Why don't you answer me, Lara?"

His voice slammed in cold, detached, and millions of miles from the man she held in her affection. The shift in him came as a total surprise, and suddenly, she could make out the stubborn determination in his eyes as she peered at him. He raised his eyebrows, and the confidence and smugness in the gesture sent her temper over the edge.

Two can play this game. If he was so intent on an answer, she'd give him a very good one. "There's the real world out there, in which we have to live. How long can we hope to exist in denial?"

The outburst echoed in the room. Locked in a clash of will, both knew none would give up the first. Animosity filled the air as their eyes bore into each other's.

"You don't trust me."

Spoken on a whisper, the words carried upon the silence to her and sliced through her insides. Pain welled up and choked her throat.

"Don't say that," she said softly.

"You never trusted me, even back then ... Or else, we'd have worked everything out a long time ago."

The hint of recrimination in his tone hit her like a slap. How dare he accuse her? Fury erupted in her blood, and fire ignited her mind. "How could I, when you disappeared off the face of the Earth after leaving me stranded here?"

In a quick, lithe move, he stood up and faced her from his full height. From her position on the sofa, intimidating didn't start to describe how he appeared to her, repressed anger tensing his every muscle.

His eyes drew to slits, and hardened once more to pale, icy blue.

"Stranded? I left you *stranded*? Not the impression I got, since you were already in another man's arms barely a few months later."

This time, he'd crossed the line. As he'd thrown the first punch, she wouldn't sit around waiting for another blow. Oh, no. She'd reply, and in kind.

Lara threw the blanket off her and sprang up to face him with defiance.

But the movement had been too quick, and her head spun as all her blood drained down her body.

He reached out and clasped her arms as she fell. He held her up, and a previous similar situation flashed in her mind. When they'd met again at the clinic ...

He pulled her close, and she snuggled into his embrace.

How good it felt to be near him. She sighed and settled her hands on his broad back, where her fingers encountered the bunched muscles in his shoulders.

The reason for the tension grazed her thoughts, and she stiffened and shrugged out of his arms. After flattening her palms on his chest, she pushed him away.

"Our break-up was my entire fault, then? You don't mention the snob you got involved with. What was her name? Sophie? Your picture in that society magazine left no room for misunderstanding."

He remained where he stood, his arms limp by his sides.

"That's exactly what it was, a picture—"

"No, it sure wasn't. I saw you with her, and I read the caption, Eric. Like I said, no room for misunderstanding there."

His nostrils flared, and he crossed his arms in front of his chest. "Really? What did it say?"

She rolled her eyes. "We're really going to do this?"

"Yes, we are. Because you've got it all wrong."

He was convinced of that, wasn't he? She glared at him. "Fine. The caption read, and I quote, word for word, '*Éric Marivaux, étudiant en médecine et héritier de la famille Armont, accompagnant Sophie de Maivière, qui attend un heureux évènement.*'"

He remained silent, which doubled her anger. If he wouldn't defend himself, it only meant ... She bit her lip.

"How much did you score in French that year, Lara?"

She whipped her head up to glare at him. What did that have anything to do with their fight today? She quirked her eyebrows and crossed her arms.

He chuckled, but the sound came out devoid of any humour. "Lara, the way the caption was written, grammatically, meant Sophie was the one happily expecting." He paused. "Sophie alone."

What?

"But I saw you with her on there. There could be no doubt—"

"If you'd waited for me, I would've explained it all to you. Yes, Sophie wanted the world to believe she was expecting my baby, but this couldn't be the case as I'd never slept with her. *Merde*, I'd never even kissed her."

Oh, no. She'd had it all wrong all along?

"But you didn't wait, Lara, and you jumped on the first escape route that came your way."

Oh, the gall of the man. "How dare you—"

"Yes, I dare," he said through clenched teeth as he took two steps to stop right in front of her. "I dare because you always search for the easy way out. And, *ma belle*, I'm sorry to say there *is* no easy way out, not in a relationship where two people are equally involved."

His words hit her like a blow, and she stomached the implications hard.

Before she could comprehend what she was doing, she lashed out and slapped his cheek.

Her mouth dropped open when she realized what she'd done.

Horror, and disgust at herself, brought the foul taste of bile in her mouth.

"I'm sorry. I didn't mean to," she said in a whisper.

He closed his eyes and averted his face. When he opened them again, he peered down at her.

"My patience has limits, Lara. I told you that once. I better leave," he said as he turned on his heel and made his way to the front door.

Numb shock descended on her as she watched him move away from her, powerless to stop him, or call him back.

On the threshold, he stopped, his back still to her.

"You don't even trust yourself. That's probably why it never worked."

Upon those words, he walked out of the house, closing the door softly behind him.

Yet, the gentle click echoed with the full force of a slamming door in her head. His departure became the drop to make her overflow, and her weak legs gave way under her.

He had left. The immovable anchor had freed itself and moved away, abandoning her to be carried away in a sea of choppy waves ...

Lara sagged onto the floor, where she gave in to the sobs wracking her body. Tears flowed down her cheeks, but she had no power, no strength, and no desire to stop them.

In a crumpled heap, she cried the tears of a woman who may have made a very big mistake, and now had to pay the price for the rest of her life.

◆◆◆

The pounding on the door wouldn't stop, alternating between two chimes of the doorbell. Why could the caller not leave her alone? She'd been alone for the past … come to think of it, she had no clue how long she'd been holed up in her house. How many times had she phoned the office to let them know she was calling in a sick leave? Doris thought she had a bad cold. Not hard to deduce, since all the crying had rendered her throat scratchier than when she'd smoked three packets of cigarettes a day.

She'd also started to screen her calls, if ignoring the ringing cell could be construed as call screening. She couldn't be bothered. There were matters to think upon … or not. However much she knew she would have to face the truth—the one Eric had spelt out—she also knew she was a total chicken who would hide her head in the sand for as long as she could.

If only the bloody pounding at her door would stop.

With weary steps, she trudged to the front door and threw it open.

"What?" she snarled at whoever had the misfortune of standing on her doorstep.

The misfortune was hers, though, because in front of her stood her bratty little sister.

Diya pushed into the house and started towards the living room.

"Why the hell aren't you answering your calls? Is it to escape Mum's wrath? You won't, you know. She's coming for you right after she's done with me." Diya shivered. "And I have no plans to let her be done with me, so I suppose you're off the hook for now."

God, would that girl stop her incessant babbling? Her head already hurt, and she didn't need the chirpy little butterfly in her home. If Diya stood here, it meant she'd decided to spend the night at Lara's place.

Better to cut her losses while she could. So she slammed the door closed and brushed past her sister on the way to the kitchen. She still had half of a chocolate cream cake waiting for her.

"Good grief! What's happened to you?" Diya gasped. "When was the last time you brushed your hair? And you're wearing sweats and wool in this heat? Are you sick?"

Just had my heart ripped out and trampled on. Nothing major. *Second time, too. No. Third. Shame on me.*

She plonked herself on a stool at the counter and reached for a fork that she dug into the cake, then pushed a huge mound of Chantilly cream and chocolate *génoise* into her mouth.

Diya chattered around her. Her sister sounded hysterical. She shrugged. When was exuberant Diya *not* hysterical? She was the only child who'd had the misfortune of taking after their mother.

Lara reached the last forkful of cake. A pile of cream with glacé cherries lay inside the box. With a finger, she scooped up the buttery goodness and pushed it past her lips.

And all that butter on her tongue made her sick.

She blinked at the box, realising she'd put away a cake intended for twenty people.

Nausea burned up her throat. How could she have lost control so much?

But nothing was really lost, was it? She could still win over this lapse, recover the balance, wipe away her loss of discipline ...

She rushed into the bathroom and dropped to her knees in front of the toilet bowl. Reaching down her throat with two fingers, she made her gorge rise so she could throw up all the cake.

That would make things right. Erase the excess. Bring a semblance of order and control to things spinning out of her grip ...

Someone grabbed her shoulders and shook her. She blinked into her baby sister's face. Right. Diya had arrived a little while ago, hadn't she?

Why was the girl dragging her away? She wasn't done yet. She threw the strong grip off, and forced herself to throw up again.

Diya left her blissfully alone.

Lara didn't know how much time she remained there on her knees. Her throat burned, her eyes were all misty and blurred, her stomach churning on empty. She'd gotten rid of the cake. She should be feeling all right, shouldn't she? So why were tears coursing down her cheeks again, and the clang of despair grabbing hold of her heart?

"Oh, babe. Tell me you didn't do this."

She blinked. *Sam?* How had she gotten here?

Gentle hands settled on both her arms, and she glanced around as if coming out of a deep haze. Sam held one arm, Diya the other. The two of them led her away from the floor towards the sink, where Sam ran the tap and moistened a small towel. She then wiped Lara's face and softly pulled her into the living room.

She paused on the edge of the room. Greasy pizza boxes lay on the floor near the sofa. A stain like spilled cola darkened one of the cushions.

This couldn't be her place, surely. What had happened to her, to turn her into such a slob?

And then, she remembered, and the sobs rolled up.

She would've crumpled to the floor had the two women not been holding her.

"Eric," she said in a croak. "He's gone." She turned to her best friend. "He's gone, and I had it all wrong."

"Shh." Sam soothed her with a hug. "Come sit down, and tell me about it."

She shook her head. "I can't."

"Of course you can."

Sam made her sit on the sofa, at the opposite end of the cola stain, and took her hands as she squatted in front of her. "When did this happen, sweetie?"

She choked back a sob, and snorted loudly to stop her running nose. "Friday."

"Today is Tuesday," Diya said on a gasp.

"She's in bad shape, I'll grant you that," Sam replied.

Lara glanced up at them. "Hello? I'm still here, you know."

"Only just." Sam snorted. "Okay, Zombie Girl. Tell us everything, and then, we'll bring you back into the world of the living again."

***

Eric reached out from the halfway place between slumber and wakefulness. When his hand landed flat on the bed, onto the cold, empty space beside him, he tried to shake away the cloak of cold threatening to engulf him. The nightmare was back to plague him—he remained all alone, Lara no longer here with her warmth and softness.

Except this time, his brain triggered the memory. He wasn't in the throes of a nightmare.

One week, and the pain hadn't abated one whit.

Lara had really left.

Or, he'd left ... The succession of events blipped hazy in his mind, blurred by the warped veil anger and disillusion had woven over his perception.

He sat up and let his head fall into his hands. Cold and strangely empty. That's how he existed now. All because Lara wasn't there with him.

And probably wouldn't be again.

He sighed and ran a hand in his hair.

What had possessed him to pop the question? He'd vowed to take his time, hadn't he? Never one to let his temper get the better of him, he hadn't been able to contain himself.

She'd rejected him, though. He'd given her all he had, yet, it hadn't been enough for her. It had never been enough.

He wanted to kick himself. Why couldn't he have been satisfied with what she gave? He'd have coaxed more out of her with time.

But when the opportunity had presented itself, he hadn't been able to resist. He wanted her, as his wife. Nothing less.

Her reaction had thrown him off, and he'd never experienced the total loss of his wits as when she'd blacked out in front of him. Sheer reflex and training had kicked in when he'd checked on her vitals and stretched her limp body onto the sofa.

The fear of losing her had wrecked through his soul and torn his insides, and he'd prayed to never have to experience that feeling again.

He hadn't known worse waited further down the line. Because his life would stretch empty, as he'd lost her.

He stifled a curse as he let his body fall back against the pillow.

He and Lara as a couple—they could've worked.

Maybe if he'd given more. Maybe with time, she'd have seen what the future could hold for them.

But his patience had run out the minute he'd figured out she didn't trust him. Anger had taken over, burning logic and coherent thought, any notion of rationality, and had spelt the end.

Distress like he'd never thought existed had erupted inside him. Daggers of hurt and betrayal had slashed through him, and the pain had taken hold of his whole being.

What could he hope to build out of a relationship where the fundamental of trust wasn't even present? He knew Lara well, and he'd surely been in denial over the fact that she wouldn't commit in a situation where certain things escaped her control.

Et puis, merde! He threw the sheet off him in a fit. Damn the day when Lara had walked into his life again.

But he couldn't shake off the images of her crowding his mind, making him relive all the wonderful weeks they'd spent together.

He should've known he'd be trampled again. He hadn't heeded the call, and it was too late.

The ringing of his phone cut through his reflections.

"Eric Marivaux," he answered.

"Doctor, I'm sorry to disturb you, but we have an emergency. The Jeffries boy. His parents just brought him in, severe asthma attack with heavy coughing and wheezing."

He sighed. Not an emergency at four in the morning. Yet, he should've expected it. The seasons were changing from summer to winter, and the autumn-type period during the change spelt viruses and asthma attacks all over the island.

Weariness dropped like a heavy weight onto his shoulders, anchoring him to where he sat on the bed. He didn't want to leave his home. He didn't feel fit for anything other than a pity party. But such were the hazards of his job, and he couldn't escape his duty.

"Start the nebulizer with the regular dose I prescribe for him every time," he said. "I'm on my way."

Maybe if he threw himself in his work, he'd forget about Lara.

Fat chance. But he could still try.

With a heavy sigh, he got up and walked into the bathroom.

CHAPTER FIFTEEN

"Doris, get me another coffee before you leave, please." Lara sighed as she lifted her finger from the intercom button on the phone. She needed to get herself in gear, and coffee would surely do the trick. Again.

Seconds later, her PA walked in with a steaming mug in her hand.

"There you go. It's your seventh of the day, if I may remind you," the older woman said in a tone full of reproach.

She dismissed the comment with a wave of her hand as she sipped the hot brew. "You may leave, Doris. It's already one o'clock. I'm sure your family needs you."

"I'm leaving as soon as I finish some filing in the office. What about you, though?"

"I have a lot of backlog I need to work through, so I'll stay here for the moment."

Doris crossed her arms in front of her chest. Her whole stance spelt, *don't kid me, girl.*

She sighed. "Really. I do have backlog I'm carrying forward from the week I took off."

It pained her to admit she'd needed the time off, but thank goodness her colleagues, PA, and her boss had no clue why she had needed to stay away from the office. They were also clueless to the three-times-a-week evening visits she'd been paying to a psychiatrist, the same one who had worked with her during her first brush with eating disorders as a teenager.

Doris huffed, but left, nevertheless. Once alone, Lara eased herself into her seat with her mug in one hand and turned towards the windowpane. Sipping her coffee, she waited for the caffeine to kick in as she gazed at the beautiful gardens.

Not as beautiful as the garden at Eric's house.

She shook her head as the thought hit. Lately, she'd been having increasing trouble to work Eric and his memory out of her mind. Time had not dulled the feeling of loss at all. In fact, she'd say that with each passing day, she hurt a little bit more. Deader than the previous day, yet having to power on. She had no escape, easy or not. She chuckled without humour. Little things about their time together came back to haunt her at every occasion, and anything could trigger them off. She'd hardly slept in the past weeks, and combined with the desperation she threw into her work, fatigue and burnout were taking their toll on her.

"Aha. I knew I'd find you here."

The sound of the Slavic accent cut through her thoughts, and she turned her chair around to see her boss walking into her office.

Markus pulled up a chair and settled himself in front of her desk.

She gave him a welcome smile. "The mere fact you've bothered to come here implies there's more work coming. Am I right?"

"Lara, I love to work with you," he said with a wink. "You understand everything so easily."

"What is it this time?" She set her mug down and rested her elbows on the desk, bending slightly forward to give him her full attention.

He remained in his casual stance, but the way he wrung his hands together betrayed his excitement.

"Remember the bid we made the week after your first convention, for the Commonwealth conference?" He paused. "I just heard we've been short-listed."

She blinked in surprise. She'd winged the proposal together in a couple of days. "That's wonderful news, Markus. I wasn't sure they'd love our offer, but if they do ..."

Silence greeted her reply, and she frowned with worry as she stared at him. "I'm sure there's a problem, so what is it?"

"You," he said with a straight, solemn face.

She blinked. "Excuse me? I don't get it. I thought you said I was doing a good job here."

He sighed and shook his head. “Lara, it’s nothing to do with your job. Actually, I can’t think of a better director than you. But you’ve got me worried lately.”

Uh-oh. Would he get on her case, too?

“Why is that?”

“Listen, what I’ll say to you is off the record, simply from me to you, not from boss to employee.” He paused, as if carefully choosing his words. “These past weeks, you've practically lived out of here so much you don’t leave your office.”

She opened her mouth to protest, but he put his hand up and silenced her.

“Hear me out. Something is very wrong with you. I won’t pry and ask what, it’s none of my business. But you gotta know this contract will be tough to bag, and it’ll ask a lot from you.”

He drew his intense gaze onto her, making her squirm.

“Will you be able to take it all on?” he asked. “It’s the first time we’ll be handling something this big.”

More work? That’s exactly what she needed. “We’re more than ready for this, and the challenge will only make it better. Imagine how we could place the centre on the map if we bag this contract.”

“If this is what you say,” he replied with a quirked eyebrow. “I wanted to run the news past you. I’ll be off now.”

On the threshold, he stopped and turned to face her.

“Lara, my dear, try not to turn into the phantom of this place,” he said with a chuckle.

She found herself smiling at his comment, and she welcomed the lightness, for she didn’t have reason enough to smile lately. All because of Eric.

She’d always known she’d be in for pain in a relationship with him. Yet, why hadn’t she reasoned with herself before getting into the whole business?

She sighed. It would do no good to think of the past. Because what had happened had been inevitable. She shouldn’t let it have so much hold on her.

Lara forced her mind to focus on the information Markus had supplied. The Commonwealth Nations’ Conference represented a very big affair. If they landed the deal, it would indeed mean dedication and hard work.

Maybe that'd take her mind off Eric.

She wanted to kick herself as the thought crossed her mind. Why did everything have to come back to him?

Her phone rang, and she lashed out to pick it up, the receiver nearly falling out her hand in her haste.

"Yes?"

"Whoa, babe. Easy does it." The feminine voice at the other end chuckled.

"Sam, hi." Weariness crashed over her, and she let her body sag, limp, in her chair. "What's up?"

"I knew I'd find you in your damn office yet again."

She closed her eyes in annoyance. Everyone was saying that to her, lately. Couldn't they find another topic to talk about?

"I've got work to do, as opposed to some people who are on leave."

Sam laughed at her rebuke. "Speaking of leave, I'm at Caudan right now. Why don't you come join me?"

"Thanks, but I still got loads to do. Some other time, maybe."

God only knew what would've happened that fateful Tuesday if Diya hadn't called in the cavalry through Sam. The two of them had put her back on her feet, and she'd be eternally grateful. Not that what they did had changed her predicament. She'd returned to the world of the living, but it didn't mean she enjoyed life as a living being. Surviving suited her fine right now. And maybe forever, because that's how she'd have to live the rest of her days ...

The psychiatrist was doing his darnedest best to have her work through that, to no avail, it seemed, though. What did he know about heartbreak? She'd lived through it twice already, and if this third time was breaking her, then so be it. Who had that much in them to weather so much failure in love and relationships?

"Lara, I'm worried about you. You don't go out anymore, and this is not good."

She sighed. As if she wanted to enjoy herself right then. "Sam, don't start. I'm really busy, I swear."

"Okay, but how about dinner tonight? Don't tell me you work in the evenings, too, now," Sam said on a small laugh. "Come on, don't say no. And I know you don't have an appointment with Dr Tristan tonight."

"Fine," Lara replied after giving it some thought. "Let's meet at the Chinese restaurant on La Salette road in Grand-Baie at seven."

She put the receiver down and got up to take a few steps. Her legs had gone stiff from too much sitting, and her back hurt. Pins and needles erupted along her feet, forcing her to shed her pumps.

Maybe she should take a walk outside. The lawn under her soles would ease the tingling feelings, and the fresh air could do her some good.

Like erase any thought of Eric.

Damn, why was she thinking of him again?

***

The pretty girl with him tightened her arm around his waist and snuggled up to his side as they strolled along the waterfront.

Bad sign. She wanted something, and she wanted it like, yesterday.

"Can we have popcorn? And candyfloss? *S'il-te-plait? S'il-te-plait? S'il-te-plait?*"

If she hopped one more time, she'd smash his toes with the heel of her platform shoes.

Eric shook his head. "Bad for your teeth. You know you shouldn't have this stuff with your braces."

She stopped dead in the middle of the Caudan esplanade and punched him in the arm.

Merde, but since when did his younger sister's punches start hurting? Could those jujitsu classes she'd started taking in Italy be making her so much stronger? Even lethal?

"The orthodontist removed my braces last week, Eric," she said with a shake of her head. A long strand of dark brown hair whipped him in the face.

Right. He winced, because he'd had his head in the clouds lately. That's why she had returned to Mauritius for the two-week break.

"Sorry, Angélique." He pulled her into his arms and pressed a kiss to her temple. "Still, sugar is bad for you, so no."

She wormed out of his arms and pouted. "You're no fun."

He stared at her with raised eyebrows before lifting the hefty array of shopping bags in his hands. "Remind me again who footed the bill for all these?"

Angélique smiled. "You're not a bad sort." She grabbed his arm once more as they made their way to the food court. "So, tell me, am I still allowed to drink water?"

Cheeky little brat.

"I'll even let you have a milkshake," he said with a smile.

While he got up to go place their orders, he squirmed, registering the intense, pointed stare of someone watching him burn the nape of his neck. He turned around and blinked.

Strange.

The girl behind the counter handed over his order, and he took the drinks back to their table. All through the trek, he still felt the stare, but *merde* if he could place where the scrutiny was coming from.

Angélique fell on her milkshake as if she were starving. Anyone looking at them would think he hadn't fed her in the past twenty-four hours, the time she had spent at his house. His baby sister had picked up on his doldrums, but thankfully, hadn't asked outright what his problem was. Instead, she'd whisked him into endless games of Monopoly, reruns of *The Big Bang Theory*, and a whole day of shopping today. Trust young adults to have their priorities sorted in such simple ways.

Angélique squealed, and Eric winced. Only one person could turn the twenty-year-old girl into such a hysterical banshee, and he twisted around with a smile as his sister jumped up and threw her arms around the tall, sandy-haired man who approached their table.

Patrice nearly toppled over under the exuberant assault of his fiancée. The kiss Angélique planted on him would surely bring security in their surroundings, since such public displays of affection had to be illegal. In the nick of time, the girl released the poor man.

He stepped up and clasped his future brother-in-law's hand. Patrice had turned red—from embarrassment, or from the death grip Angélique still had on him with her arms around his neck?

"Ange, don't kill him just yet, will you?" Eric told her.

His sister huffed and slapped his arm.

Patrice laughed. "You don't mind if I take her off your hands?"

Eric smiled. "Be my guest."

As much as he loved his sibling, twenty-four hours with her would turn any sane man into a raving lunatic.

The lovebirds left, Patrice saddled with the bags Eric had been carrying until then. The two stopped in front of the popcorn stall, where Angélique got a carton of caramel popcorn and a big, fluffy mass of candyfloss.

Eric shook his head. Patrice was toast. Angélique could do whatever she wanted to the big man.

As he took a pull from his milkshake, the burning feeling on his nape returned. The scrutiny felt less intense, though. Sitting back casually in his chair, he threw a quick glance around the food court.

A woman sat a few tables from him, and he'd bet she'd been watching him ever since he'd settled there.

Remarkably beautiful, with the ethereal quality of supermodels on her well-defined features and in the shiny, chin-length red hair, he was certain he didn't know her, though a flicker of recognition did prick him fleetingly every time he returned his focus to her face.

She seemed to know who he was, though, gauging by the intense way she stared back at him.

Without taking her gaze off him, she stood up and walked towards his table to stop inches from him.

From up close, she looked even more ravishing, yet, her identity still eluded him.

"Eric?" she asked in a husky, slightly breathless tone.

Who was she? He nodded in reply.

"I'm Sam, Lara's friend."

Sameera. Lara's shadow in secondary school, her best friend. The one who'd told him he better forget Lara when he'd called her soon after the society magazine debacle.

No wonder she had appeared familiar. And no wonder she had stared at him so intensely when he'd been with Angélique, because no one would peg them as siblings at first glance. Sam must've thought he'd already replaced Lara in his life. She'd been out for blood last time he had spoken to her. Was this the case today again?

He was no chicken, and he'd hear what she had to say to him.

"Have a seat." He indicated with a nod. "You've changed. I didn't recognise you."

"You still remember me from back then?" she asked as she pulled a chair and sat down.

"How could I forget?" He gave a soft laugh. "You used to cover for Lara whenever we met."

A chuckle escaped her. "Yes, these were the good old days. Too bad it's changed now."

She let the statement dangle, obviously a challenge for him to pick up.

Questions lay heavy in her words, and he heard every one of them. If he recalled properly, Lara had mentioned Sam had become a business strategy consultant, and a very good one.

And if she was still the determined girl she'd been fourteen years before, he was in for some explaining.

He had nothing to explain, though, but he was certain Sam acted that way for her friend's sake. For Lara's sake, he would answer her.

"Nothing's changed, Sam."

She remained silent, but raised a perfectly arched eyebrow sceptically.

"I still love her exactly the same way."

"I find that hard to believe."

Her voice came out soft, but the tone held concrete hardness. He wouldn't want to be across any negotiation table with her opposite him. But he was done providing excuses, covering for Lara. High time he'd started thinking of his own happiness in the whole matter. His sanity, too.

"What's so hard to believe? How I may still care for her, even after all I went through for her sake?"

"Lara's hurting, a lot," she said. "Because of you."

A sigh escaped him, and he passed a hand over his face in a weary gesture. "Don't you think I know that?"

A flicker of surprise crossed her face, but she quickly concealed it. "Why did you leave her, then?"

"Because I was sick and tired of living only on her terms. I didn't ask for much, Sam. I swear I didn't. But Lara never thought of giving back, not a little bit."

Her face softened as she took in his outburst.

"Why don't you make her understand, then?"

He snorted, and her eyes grew wide.

"You know Lara as well as I do. Can you make her see sense when she's stuck in pig-headed corner?"

A small smile appeared on her face. "True enough."

"Sometimes," he started. "You have to step back and let others work things out for themselves. I can't do any more for Lara. She's got to tread the rest of the way."

"Will you be there, though?"

He hesitated before replying. What could he say? He noticed her eyes narrowed as she watched the emotion pass over his face.

"Can Lara count on you?" she asked.

Time for the truth, and nothing but. "Sam, no other woman can take Lara's place. I only hope she realizes it before it's too late, for her own sake."

Silence hung heavy between them, before she sighed.

"She's lucky to have a man like you."

He gave a small, ironic laugh. Tell that to Lara, who'd never trusted him ...

"I better go now," she said. "I'm meeting Lara for dinner. It's been nice talking to you."

"Same here."

She got up and started to leave, and he called her back.

"Make sure she eats, okay?"

***

"Lara, drop the chopsticks. The linen is eating more than you are."

Lara glanced up at her friend, worried Sam might've seen through her ploy not to eat. She'd toyed with the lacquered duck pancakes and managed not to eat any. No such luck with the rice, though, as Sam asked the dreaded question.

"Since when do you, of all people, eat with chopsticks? And rice, too?"

Sam snatched the bamboo chopsticks and thrust a metal fork into her hand.

No escape. She'd have to take a bite or two. Sam would kick her into the ground if she confessed she had no appetite. How could she, when her life no longer had any purpose? Every day, she rehashed the mistakes she had made, and every time, she dug herself into her grave a little further.

Maybe if she kept Sam talking, she could work her way around the dishes. Why had the woman ordered enough food to feed a regiment? So she could get the leftovers packed and not have to cook any dinner for a week?

"My stomach's not feeling too good. I must have caught some bug or something." The sickness excuse should work.

Sam dropped her fork and stared back at her. "This is what happens when you live on black coffee alone."

Damn it. No way out. Sam had always seen through her game. Why would that have conveniently stopped today?

"Okay, I'll eat. Pleased?"

The redhead smiled back and pushed the plate of Cantonese fried rice her way. "Very."

"How come you're having dinner with me today?" Lara asked. "Where's that husband of yours?"

"On a business trip to Cape Town. Good thing he's not here. He wears me out when he's around." Sam winked. "It's fun trying for a baby."

Goodness, no. Not marital bliss and sexual contentment. Not when she was in dire craving of both. "Have some concern for my new celibate existence, will you?"

Sam pointed at her with her fork. "And whose fault would that be?"

"Don't you start with this."

She didn't need her BFF to get on her back, too. Her conscience was enough, thank you very much.

"Come on, Lara. You could have all of it today, but the stupid git you are chose to throw it all away."

As if everything was so simple. A headache started to throb behind her forehead. The anger melted, to be replaced by the rational bent she forced into her perception anytime the void of loss threatened to engulf her.

"Why do I feel I have to explain myself to all of you? This never would've worked. We're too different, worlds apart in birth and upbringing, and we don't think the same."

"You still haven't given a valid reason," Sam said. "All that wasn't a problem when you were together."

Lara threw her fork down and pressed her back into her chair. "Come on, it was only a matter of time before our families got involved, and by then, the whole of society would be rubbing their salt in the gaping wound. We would never have weathered that."

Damn it. She'd agreed to this dinner to take her mind off all of these things, not to actually have to motivate her every action with a valid reason.

"How will you know if you never try?" Sam asked in a dead-serious tone.

She stared at her friend with her mouth gaping open. First Eric, then Sam. Why was everyone intent on pushing her beyond her limits?

"We'd only get hurt if we'd gone ahead with it," she replied coolly.

"As if you're not hurting now?"

What was the woman getting at? What more was there to consider?

"That's not the point. It wouldn't have worked, full stop."

Sam remained silent for a long moment, and Lara felt the full force of her friend's scrutiny on her, until the woman broke the silence.

"I think you're making the biggest mistake of your life."

She nearly choked on the sip of water she'd taken. Was she hearing right? Sam, resident relationship bliss killer whose motto had been 'love them, use them, leave them,' talking of abandoning a man as a mistake? When had such a one-eighty turn happened?

"Why are you being so insistent? It's not like you," she said.

Sam shook her head, and sadness played on her beautiful features. "You know why I fell for Salim?"

Lara shrugged. She'd stopped trying to figure out how, overnight while in Cape Town, Sam had agreed to marry Salim after he'd chased her for years without success.

"It's because I realized with utmost certainty that I'd never meet a man who'd love me like he does," Sam said.

She tried to swallow the lump suddenly forming in her throat. So love had happened.

"You and Salim have something special."

"I know. But I'd never have known if I hadn't given him a chance."

The lump grew bigger, and tears stung her eyes.

"What are you trying to say?"

"Just that, sometimes, you gotta give in a little to get a lot more in return."

She stared at her friend for a long time.

Had she been hasty in rejecting Eric? Somehow, she couldn't help but feel a nagging doubt take root inside her. Why did that notion have to come plague her now, when all hope was lost?

"You know, Sam," she said. "Sometimes, I wish Roy was back, and we'd pick up from where we left off. Life was so uncomplicated back then."

"You don't mean it. In your heart, you know there's only one man there."

"Still, I can't help it." She let the words trail off, and they dissolved into the air like thin wisps of smoke.

"Be careful what you wish for. You might get it."

Lara came back to present when she heard the longing and bitterness in Sam's voice.

Intent on her own problems, she hadn't noticed her friend might also need her. "Babe, is something wrong?"

"Not really," Sam replied with a tremulous smile. "Remember how I wished not to have kids when we were younger? Seems like my wish got fulfilled."

Her heart went out to Sam, and she clasped the other woman's hand in silent support.

"I'm sure you'll get pregnant. Didn't you tell me you went to a new doctor?"

"It's funny, you know. I desire the thing I can most certainly not get."

Don't we all.

The thought crossed her mind, and a sinking feeling of loss settled inside her.

Maybe she *had* made a mistake when she'd let Eric go.

But she'd never know for sure. Because Eric was done with her.

CHAPTER SIXTEEN

"As usual, your father is busy, Diya is God knows where, and Neha's baby is sick. So I have no one but you to take me shopping."

Lara had more than grown tired of her mother's gripes. As much as she wanted to not pick up the phone when she saw the Hemants' home number on the caller ID, she couldn't do that. As a daughter from an Indian-origin family, she had a duty to perform where her family was concerned. Still, said duty didn't mean she couldn't worm her way out of the incongruous situations as they happened.

She sighed. "Take a taxi, Mum. It's what they're here for."

Her mother had just crossed past fifty. Couldn't she learn how to drive? Her father could afford another car, if not more.

"I have a daughter who's single and has her own car, and you want me to take a taxi?"

Great. She'd forgotten 'single' meant 'at the family's disposal for every errands.' Truly, single people were not expected to have a life in Mauritius.

Her mother rambled on. "When I know my daughter is free to take me where I need to go? Shame on you, Lara."

The childish whining got on her nerves, and she had no idea how, by some feat, she managed to keep the lid down on her temper. No good would come from trying to fend off her mother, so she might as well give in.

Cut her losses—her new philosophy in life.

She snorted.

"Fine," she said. "I'll take you on your damn shopping."

"No need to swear, young lady." Her mother huffed the reprimand in a tone full of reproach.

Still, the lure of the trip must've obliterated the older woman's outrage. God, she switched through moods faster than a chameleon through its colours.

"I'll have your opinion on the curtains to choose. I'm so excited," Gayatri Hemant said. "Bye, darling."

She put the phone down with another sigh. Her mother could drive anyone to the asylum without realising the damage she could wreck on a person's sanity.

Four hours later, a splitting headache tore through her head as the two of them settled at the table of a café in a mall of the edges of the town of Quatre-Bornes, for the afternoon tea.

For the life her, she'd never, ever again, take her mother shopping for curtains. They'd spent ages in the stifling, cloying heat of the open-air Quatre-Bornes market to sort through hundreds of different fabric swatches.

Not one had been up to the mark, her mother always searching for something else, something more, whatever the heck that 'something' happened to be, since it seemed to Lara even her mother had no clue what she was looking for.

A thought nagged her. Had this whole trip been pretence for them to spend time together? Her mother defined 'shopaholic,' and the fact she hadn't spent a single rupee in more than an hour made Lara suspicious.

She glanced up at her mother, who was busy fanning herself with a napkin.

"Mum, why did you drag me along today?"

The older woman fluttered her hand in an evasive gesture. "You know, darling, two views are better than one when decorating. And you have such good taste, as well."

The voice dripped nice and sweet as syrup.

She frowned, feeling her eyebrows draw together as warning bells rang up a cacophony in her head.

"Mum, I've got awful taste for anything domestic, and you know it. Diya's the one with sound decorating taste."

Her mother sighed and dropped the napkin to the table. "Whatever," she said. "I need to talk to you."

A heavy weight sinking her heart, she closed her eyes. Only a matter of time before her family found out about Eric and her mother asked for the settlement of the gossip account. News travelled faster than the CIA's satellite information on the island. A miracle she'd escaped the radar for so long.

She'd have to face the facts today. Was she ready? Hell no. But did she have a choice?

"What about?"

She'd admit to the affair, tainting herself further in her parent's eye, but she needn't dwell on the matter for too long. The admission itself would compromise her. No need for the salacious details to mar her tattered-beyond-repair image even more.

Her mother sighed again and dropped the napkin. "It's about Diya."

Diya? Lara blinked a few times as the information made its way into her mind.

Tension left her body, and she let herself relax in the seat. However, knowing her mother, she'd need to be on her guard.

"What's the matter with her now?" she asked.

"Well, it's this boy she's involved with. He's more unproper than the last one. And it's been confirmed this one, too, is a Muslim. Can't you talk some sense into her? She won't listen to me."

Her mother never let her live it down that she was the older sister, and thus, like a second mother to her sisters.

She rolled her eyes. "Mum, she's young—"

"No, no, no!" Her mother shook her head. "She's living a dissolute life, and it'll just affect all her future prospects when it's time for her to marry."

Lara closed her eyes and pinched the bridge of her nose. They were back to it again. Marriage as the end of the road for the Indian woman. She'd heard the line ever since she'd turned thirteen, and nearly two decades later, the words still grated on her mind like nails on a blackboard.

Revolt gripped her when she realised her sister would also have to go through all that. Unable to contain the disgust, she forced her eyes open to stare at her mother.

"For God's sake, Mother. It's her life, let her live it," she burst out. "You've been trying to run all our lives since the day we were born. And it seems all you care about is getting rid of us through marriage. You did it with me and Neha when we turned eighteen, and now, it's Diya's turn?

"Stop it, you hear me? Stop running *our* lives like *you* want. Bad enough you uprooted us from the only life we'd known in England to shove us into this snake pit of conventions and gossip which did nothing but stifle us. You've been lucky with Neha and me, but why on Earth do you think Diya rebels so much?"

The silence blanketing their surroundings echoed louder in her head as she took in the startled expression on her mother's face.

She hadn't screamed, because all around them, people kept to their businesses. Yet, she'd never expected to deliver such an outburst in front of her mother. In blowing a fuse, she'd set the stage up for some mighty lecture, and she braced herself for the recriminations surely to come.

However, the woman in front of her remained silent, and after what seemed an eternity, her voice took on a previously unheard softness when she broke the stillness.

"Haven't I let you live, Lara?"

Stunned by the subdued tone even more than by the words themselves, Lara blinked as she took in the question. Her mother asking for feedback? Since when did *that* happen?

And what the hell could she reply?

Yes, she hadn't let her pursue her personal hopes, and had clad her in their sectarian, cultural life?

And what good would the accusation do?

"It's not the point, Mum, and you know it."

Guilt took hold of her, and her conscience started to impinge upon her thoughts.

Was that what she'd have done all those years before, given the choice? Would she have broken from the pack … for Eric?

The sound of her mother's voice cut through her thoughts.

"You know, I've always just wanted the best for you. A proper marriage, a husband who'd understand you, who'd provide for all you'd need. For society to acknowledge you for your worth, and to give you the status you deserved."

Lara snorted, and her mother grew quiet.

"Hasn't exactly turned out that way, has it now, Mum?"

Opposite her, the eyes with the faint lines at their corners lowered.

But after a few seconds, her mother brought back up the sharp gaze that rarely missed a thing, and Lara couldn't recognise the emotion in the dark irises or on the features suddenly looking older.

"What's wrong, Lara?"

The voice that could soothe her biggest worry as well as rouse up her worst nightmare softened to a level she had never heard before, and she swallowed, hard.

"It's not like you to lash out like this," her mother said.

Annoyed at the guilty pricking in her, she shrugged. "Forget it, Mum. It's nothing."

High time they got out of there, as the conversation taking a too-personal turn. She'd never been chummy with her mother. She wouldn't start today.

"Is it Roy?"

She shook her head in reply. Better leave it at that. She reached for her cup of now-cold coffee and drained the contents with one long gulp. Perfect, they could leave.

After a tense silence, her mother fidgeted in her seat and drew in a deep breath.

"Is it because of the man you're seeing?"

So her family did know about Eric.

Stunned, she didn't allow the emotion to show. Better to play it cool and detached. No one could get a hold on her, then.

"What do you know about him?"

"Nothing much, I admit." Her mother shrugged. "But look at you. You're miserable, and it shows. There's got to be a man behind it all."

A small smile tugged at her mouth at the despondent tone. For a second there, she'd wondered if the woman who had given birth to her wouldn't get up, pick a sword, and slay all the dragons that dared breathe fire onto her daughter's life.

Her heart swelled, because, for the first time in her life, she'd recognized genuine concern in her mother's tone, and the realization warmed her insides beyond what she'd expected. At the same time, the emotion prompted her to take stock of her own thoughts and beliefs, to face the truth.

Maybe she hadn't given her mother an opportunity to befriend her, and that was why they felt so awkward around each other.

But then, sadness cloaked her when she thought of the 'man' in question.

"It *is* because of him," she said with halting words. "But this episode of my life is over now, and I don't see it working out."

"Why, darling? What's wrong?"

She chuckled with irony. Conspiratorial concern from her usually hysterical parent. Who'd have thought?

"He's very unproper, Mum. He's white, from a very rich and old family, and he descends from French nobility on his mother's side. Society will have a rave about it."

Her mother watched her with a contemplative expression on her face. "Society's not all there is, you know," she said in a little voice. "Does he love you?"

"Yes."

"And you?"

She thought back a long time before answering. "I don't know."

Lara shrugged. In all her reflections lately, she hadn't asked herself the question, afraid of the answer she'd find. Not to know that she loved him, but in case she found out she'd never felt any love for him.

She shook out of the thought. "He's also a doctor. You always told us to stay clear of them and their crazy schedules."

Her mother smiled back. "Is he like your father?"

"No, he's a paediatrician."

"They're actually the best of the lot, you know," the older woman said with a laugh. "Well, after dermatologists. These never get called for emergencies in the middle of the night."

She laughed along with her mum. Something she'd never thought she'd do outside a forced social context.

"You know," her mother continued. "I always told you to avoid doctors because I know what it's like to be one's wife. When we were first married, your father worked all the time, as we had a house to support. And you came along less than a year after our marriage, and I was alone in a foreign country. I just wanted you to have someone who'd be there for you, so you wouldn't be lonely."

At the wistful tone, her heart went out to her mother—God knew she'd had her share of a tough existence. And her father didn't make matters any better, always running to and fro between conferences and surgeries.

With a guilty heart, she reckoned she'd never given her mother her due.

"Neha and her family are coming to dinner tonight. You sure you don't want to come?"

Her mother hadn't said 'home,' but she'd heard the word, nevertheless.

She smiled. "Okay, I'll come home with you."

Her mother smiled back, and she knew she'd carry the image forever in her mind.

Once they were in the car, she gave in to a sudden impulse and reached out and hugged her tight. After a few seconds, her mother returned the hug, and a strange peace descended over her.

"Lara, is there really no hope?"

"I don't think so, Mum."

◆◆◆

Dinner resembled an Indian feast fit for a royal. Her mother had outdone herself with the many different dishes she'd prepared. No wonder. Neha and her brood of kids had come, and so, their mother had cooked for an army.

Lara glanced around for a sighting of her younger sister as she settled on the sofa in the living room. She finally noticed her by the stairs. As usual, Neha appeared harried by her children. The baby in her arms cried without letting up, and her two eldest clung to her clothes while making a ruckus.

A smile grazed Lara's lips. She'd always thought her sister to be the worst-case scenario of post-marriage life, run over by domesticity and losing her identity in becoming nothing more than a mother.

Then, her smile died. Where was the children's father, Neha's husband? Was it a wonder Neha looked so harassed, reduced to being a single parent to three small kids?

She needed to have a word with Rahul, her brother-in-law. He'd been a good friend when they'd been younger. There'd even been talks of an arranged match between the two of them. But she'd seen him as a brother, exactly as she saw Salim—Auntie Zubeida's son who'd married Sam—and nothing but friendship had bloomed between them.

High time she clocked the so-called friend over the head, because he was being a total arse with his family. With her sister.

The cushion next to her gave as someone plopped down onto the seat.

She smiled at her father. "It's a wonder we caught you for dinner tonight."

Prem Hemant gave a hearty laugh. "Ah, the hazards of the job, sweetheart. So, how's my little girl doing? Haven't heard from you in a long time."

She chuckled softly. "Daddy, I'm thirty-two years old. Hardly a girl any longer."

"Oh, my, that old already?"

He laughed louder when she hit him with a cushion.

"You'll always be my little girl, though," he said as he drew her into a hug.

She hugged him back and let the contact soothe her, like it had so many times in the past. Her father and his steadfast love had been the only constant in her life, something she knew she couldn't do without.

"Daddy …" She pulled away. "Have I been a disappointment to you?"

He frowned as he held her at arm's length, his clear, light-brown gaze on her. "Never, sweetheart. Never."

"Even with the divorce?"

"Even then. So what if you've had some misfortune in life? It can happen to anyone. Is this why you look so sad?"

"A little," she lied.

"Oh, I thought it probably had to do with a man, but I was wrong." He smiled at her as if she were a small child.

Her cheeks burned, and she must have turned a bright shade of red. Was she so easy to read, that even her father had picked up on her turmoil? Astonishment cut her vocal cords, and she couldn't answer.

"Not a man, huh?" he continued. "Certainly not Roy. Maybe Doctor Marivaux ..."

She jerked her head up at the mention of the name. "How—?"

He laughed again, a hearty chuckle.

"Sweetheart, I saw the way he looked at you at the conference." He reached out and tucked a lock of her hair behind her ear. "And more important, I saw how you watched him back. I put two and two together. Simple."

Goodness, had she been that transparent?

"But I gather things are not so right, huh?"

He punctuated the question with bushy eyebrows raised, and she laughed at the mock-stern picture he presented.

But the laughter died seconds later, sadness clattering in her chest.

"Things went awfully wrong. And it might've been all my fault."

"How wrong? Bad wrong, or wrong a sorry could erase?"

"Not bad wrong, but I doubt a simple sorry would work here. We both have issues we need to deal with."

"You sure it's not just you who's got the issues?"

What did she answer to that?

When she remained silent, he added, "Think about it, sweetheart. It might be worth everything to ask that question."

His phone rang, and he got up.

"Duty calls, again," he said with a sigh.

He dropped a kiss on the top of her head and left.

Lara pondered over his words as he walked out of the room. She didn't want to acknowledge the potential truth in his advice, but maybe he was right.

Then, another thought passed through her mind, and she shrugged the whole idea off.

Though her parents looked like they'd accept him, Eric's family wouldn't welcome her with open arms.

The sound of bickering caught her attention, and she turned in the direction of her nephew and niece. But they sat quietly, for once, watching an animated film on the living room TV.

She got up and went in search of the noise, in hopes of distracting her from her gloomy thoughts. The rapid outbursts drew her to the staircase, where her mother and Diya were arguing over who would get the phone like teenagers.

Well, Diya *was* a teenager, but her mother? Laughter bubbled inside her, and she watched the two with fondness. Both turned in her direction with eager faces. They'd want to drag her into the fight, so she escaped and went upstairs, to the comfort of her old bedroom.

To her surprise, she found Neha there, breastfeeding her baby.

Her sister turned around.

"Oh. It's you. I thought—" Neha shook her head. "Never mind."

Lara could feel when she wasn't welcome, and Neha's attitude screamed at her to keep her distance. Her sister had always kept an ocean of ice between her and anyone else, and lately, Lara in particular. They'd always ascribed the somewhat antisocial behaviour to Neha's timid and reserved temperament.

On any other day, she would've turned tail and stormed away. But since she'd built a bridge with her mother earlier, she had to build a gateway of understanding with her sister.

So, she stepped into the room and went to sit down on the bed.

"Where's Rahul?" she asked.

Her younger sibling shrugged. "Madagascar. He was supposed to come home this morning, but there have been last-minute complications with an order or something, and he had to stay back."

Those few words from Neha could be construed as rambling, since the girl she'd been had never spelt out her thoughts or her concerns to those who should be close to her.

"Everything okay between you?"

"Of course. Why wouldn't it be?"

The answer sounded way too bright to hold water. Her sister's marriage was in trouble.

Yet, how could she go about helping them? High time she had a talk with Rahul, when she managed to get her hands on him.

Lara laughed softly. "You realize I've been here for nearly five months, and I haven't met him once? I swear we talked more when I was in England than now when we're on the same soil."

Her sister remained silent. Did she even get to talk to her husband any more than Lara did?

The baby started to wail, and Neha shushed him before she turned him around and gave him her other breast.

He latched on, and in the silence, his eyes grew increasingly heavy as sleep settled over him.

She glanced up at her sister. "Does it hurt?"

Neha frowned. "Breastfeeding? No, it doesn't. A little on the first few days, but then, you get used to it."

"On the third, you should know by now."

Neha gave her a rare smile, before she returned her attention to the now sleeping infant. In a gentle move, she slid her finger into the side of the baby's mouth and deftly unlatched him from her breast. Next, she settled him on her shoulder, where she slowly rubbed his back.

How could motherhood, and the ease of being around babies, come to some women and not others? To this day, she still hadn't held a baby in her arms, always afraid she'd let the bundle drop and hurt the kid beyond repair.

"Were you always this good at it?" Lara asked.

"Babies, you mean? No, but I learned."

"Neha, don't be offended, but didn't you ever want ..." She remained unable to find the right word.

"More?" Neha gently suggested.

She nodded.

Her sister shrugged, before her eyes took on a faraway glint. "You know, from the first time I saw Rahul, I knew I wanted to be with him. Look after him, have his children. I never desired anything else."

"Don't you ever find it limiting?"

Neha laughed. Lara couldn't remember when she'd last heard her laugh.

"Limiting? No. It's a job like any other. Just, I don't get paid for it."

A job like any other. Right. To thrive in any career, a person had to have an affinity for the profession.

What if she'd never had any affinity for motherhood?

She squirmed, and her sibling seemed to pick up her discomfort.

"Listen, Lara, I envy you and Diya for going after life like you're out to grab the best of it. I never felt like I had it in me to do so, that's all."

So Neha had always been certain of what she wanted, and how to get it. Maybe she would share her insight, if Lara asked.

"How did you know for Rahul?"

"If I loved him?" Neha prompted.

"Yes."

She shrugged again. "I never thought of it, really. I knew he made me feel better than anyone else did, and I went on that."

Eric makes me feel that way.

She shouldn't think of him.

"Weren't you afraid you'd lose the two of you in marriage and children? It's no longer the same, is it, once a child comes along?"

Neha finally smiled a genuine, warm smile transforming her face from the pinched expression to one that made her delicate features blossom with feminine grace.

“Marriage, and any relationship, is a give and take. If you're comfortable with it, it’ll all come to you. I know I’m no longer the only recipient of his love as when we courted. That love had been for his girlfriend. I share it with the children now. But Rahul also loves me in a deeper way, as his wife. As his partner. As the mother of his children. As a woman who’s trying her best to make a good life for him.”

“It all scares me, you know,” she said so softly, she barely heard the words.

Neha reached out and held her hand. “All of it doesn’t take anything from you, but instead, only gives more back.”

Wasn’t that what Sam had said? She and Neha seemed to have figured out the secret of a happy relationship.

Emotion choked Lara’s throat. Would the emotional day take its toll on her and make her burst out crying in front of her sister? She squelched the tears threatening to fall and choked back the sobs.

“Look at me here. I’m the older sister. I should be advising all of you,” she said in hopes of lightening up the heavy atmosphere.

“We all learn at our own pace, Lara. When you’re ready for something, you’ll know.”

CHAPTER SEVENTEEN

"Eric, will you tell me what the problem is?"

Eric sighed. Exactly what he didn't need, his mother asking questions. What had gotten into him to come to lunch today at the Marivaux household in Floréal? Angélique had asked, and he hadn't been able to say no. Then, his little sister had done a runner on him, when Patrice's mother invited her to their family home for the weekend.

Consequently, he had lunched alone with his mother, his father away on a business trip yet again.

He should've left as soon as he'd finished his food, but that would've been rude, and his parents had never tolerated any rudeness or slight to propriety.

As he sat in a wicker chair on the colonial dwelling's opened porch, he let his focus drift downhill to the houses on the slope. Rich-looking abodes and well-tended gardens populated this area, one of the wealthiest regions on the island, where most foreign dignitaries and ambassadors lived. The trappings of fortune and luxury were not lost on him, throwing his thoughts back on the notion of whether or not he belonged in this world. The people in it would not openly accept a mixed origins couple. He knew it. Didn't mean he had to choose to remain in such a universe, though.

"Eric?"

At the touch of a cool hand on his cheek, he glanced up at his mother and forced a smile. "Nothing's wrong. Nothing at all."

To say any more would open the floodgates, and he didn't need that to happen. Not right now. Not ever.

"Don't give me this."

Had she picked up on his lie?

"Something is very wrong," she said. "Yet, you refuse to talk about it."

He closed his eyes, and the weariness he'd been keeping at bay crashed over him. He ran a hand in his hair then peered at her once more.

Under the pointed stare, she gasped. Good. As long as she kept her distance.

"Work is hectic, *Maman*. I get called in almost every night for emergencies."

Only half the truth, and she probably knew he fibbed. So, he averted his gaze.

"Answer me." She cradled his face in her palms. "For weeks on end, we didn't hear from you unless we called. And now ..."

When he didn't reply her, she rubbed the pads of her thumbs against his cheekbones and knelt in front of him.

He frowned. She'd dirty the skirt of her white dress. His mother never allowed a speck of dust to touch her clothes. She must be really worried about him.

She sighed. "*Chéri*, what is it that's eating you alive like this?"

Try as he wished, he couldn't tell her. Not if he wanted to hang on to the little peace of mind he still possessed.

"*Maman*, forget it. I don't want to talk about it." He settled a palm over her hand and gave her fingers a reassuring squeeze.

She reached out and brushed a lock of hair from his forehead, then took a deep breath.

"The only time I've seen you like this was shortly after you left for France."

He remained silent, but the way he clenched his jaw must've betrayed him, letting her know she'd hit the mark.

"The same thing is happening again, isn't it?" she asked.

Seconds ticked by, before he finally nodded. He dragged her hands away from his face and stood.

"A woman?" she asked softly.

He nodded again.

"Someone I know?"

He shook his head.

"Who, then?"

Silence descended on them, a cool breeze wafting on the terrace. Winter hadn't fully hit the upper plateaus, and the air stung a bit.

He forced in a deep breath. He'd have to tell her about Lara if he wanted her to lay off with the Inquisition. Now? Not the best time, but when would it ever be the perfect moment?

His phone beeped. Saved by the event of an emergency. He glanced at the number, noting the text message had come from the nearby clinic. He could make it in less than ten minutes.

"I have to go. Sorry."

He started out of the house. But he hadn't counted on her tenacity, since she dogged his steps all the way to the drive outside where he'd parked his Prado.

As he opened the SUV's door, she grabbed his arm, hard.

"Answer me, Eric. Tell me what's wrong. Who is this woman?"

Her grey eyes battled with his blue ones. She wouldn't bow down. He recognized the same stubbornness that thrived inside him. Who was he kidding? He'd gotten the trait from her. No way out of a confession.

"Her name is Lara Reddy. She's the director of the new conference centre in Grand-Baie."

She opened her mouth, then closed it without making a sound.

Exactly the reaction he had expected.

"Do you love her?" she finally asked.

"Yes," he said. "But that's all there is to it."

She blinked. "She's from India, *n'est-ce pas*?"

Eric snorted softly. Lara had been right, it appeared. If she'd been an expat from India, a foreigner, their alliance could've gone down with only a little fuss.

What double standards. He loved his mother, worshipped his parents, but where *his* life was concerned, *he* decided. Not anyone else.

He reached up to her hand on his sleeve and worked her grip off. "No, *Maman*. She is not from India. She's from a Mauritian household whose ancestors came to work on plantations owned by the likes of *Papa*'s family."

She paled at the naked truth he hadn't bothered to hide in his reply.

"But how—?"

He chuckled, without amusement. "How is because I fell in love with her."

"But she's ..."

"Brown? Yes, I know."

She paled further.

"Though, I suppose it won't make any difference that she is a wonderful woman with not one ounce of evil inside her. A beautiful person." He paused. "All of it doesn't matter, *n'est-ce pas, Maman*?"

"How can you say so?" Her lower lip trembled as she asked the question.

He shrugged. "I'm stating the truth."

A truth Lara had warned him they'd have to face, and one he hadn't wanted to acknowledge.

He still believed they could've made it if they'd stuck together. If Lara had trusted him.

"No need to work your wits over this," he said. "It's over between me and her."

He pulled the SUV's door open and climbed into the vehicle.

His mother didn't hold him back. Just as well, because he didn't feel fit to battle with her anymore. She knew the truth, knew where he stood, and that was enough.

If it wasn't, tough. He was done living with secrets.

"Doris, please hold incoming calls. I don't want to be disturbed for the next hour."

Lara took a sip of her coffee before putting the mug down. Work kept creeping up on her, and she needed to delegate tasks on a daily basis. However, the bid for the Commonwealth conference rested solely on her shoulders—she didn't trust anyone with it before she'd ploughed through with a fine-toothed comb.

With a heavy sigh, she picked up the gigantic folder and opened it.

Soon, papers littered the desk, some strewn onto the floor. As she pulled back to survey the huge load before her, dull throbbing picked up along her temples. When had she last eaten? Taking paracetamol tablets on an empty stomach was a no-no, apparently. And the blister pack was empty—she'd forgotten to bring in a new one. Guess she'd have to power through. Story of her life.

The intercom buzzed, and she groaned.

"What now?"

"There's someone here to see you. She doesn't have an appointment, but she says you'll see her, anyway." Doris paused. "Her name is Agnes Armont-Marivaux."

Eric's mother?

Lara blinked, her heart sinking right along.

What was *she* doing there?

Blood pounded in her head, and the pain brought a film of black over her eyes. She wouldn't faint, she told herself as she gripped the sides of her chair to give herself an anchor into this spinning moment.

"What do I tell her?"

Her PA sounded awed. Was this woman really so formidable that tough Doris cowered before her? Intense fear settled in a lump, blocking her throat.

Somehow, she had to face the terror, if only to know why Agnes Armont-Marivaux had taken the trouble to come to her office unannounced. Which looked more petrifying—to face up to Eric's mother, or to find out why the woman had sought her out?

She licked her dry lips and took a deep breath. "Send her in."

With resolve seeping into her every muscle, she got up from the desk and made her way to the door. The wood panel opened silently before her, and Doris ushered a beautiful brunette in.

In her fifties, the woman could still pass for a model in an advert for *Vanity Fair*, everything about her, from her posture to her graceful walk, conveying elegance and high-class upbringing. The linen suit on her screamed understated class, and her perfectly styled dark mane brushed her shoulders in those sleek, flippant curls only a daily blow-dry from a professional could give.

Yet, her eyes were her most arresting feature. A deep grey, they held a piercing quality, and Lara squirmed under their cold, assessing scrutiny.

She however picked up her courage and put her hand out. "We haven't been introduced. I'm Lara Reddy."

The hand clasping hers felt soft and cool, and she couldn't mistake the iron strength in them.

"Agnes Armont-Marivaux," the woman said, her eyes never blinking once.

Eric's mother, the voice implied, and Lara heard the message. The cultured voice carried a pronounced French accent, though her English sounded fluent. She frowned. Eric's mother came, after all, from a French *duché*. Nobility might exist only in titles in modern France, but history counted for something. Of course she'd be fluent in English and other tongues.

Fear churned Lara's stomach, yet she didn't allow it to take hold of her.

"Please have a seat." She indicated the black leather sofa set occupying a corner of the office. "Would you like some coffee, or something to drink?"

"No, thank you."

She swallowed hard as she settled across from the older woman. Her mind screamed at her to proceed with caution. "What can I do for you?"

Icy eyes fixed her, yet, she caught a flick of the fire that burnt beneath the cold. *Not a woman to cross.* She could easily imagine what it would be like to be in Agnes Armont-Marivaux's bad books. God, why on Earth did she ever get involved with Eric?

"Paul Decaen had only good things to say about you," the woman said.

Lara didn't allow her surprise to show. So Agnes had gone to the president of the tourism and hotels' association—and her fellow white French-Mauritian—to get the dish on her. Why wasn't that surprising?

"Did he now?" she asked coolly. "Far from me to be rude, Madame Marivaux, but why are you here?"

"I came for the truth." Agnes Armont-Marivaux's words rang in the silence that followed.

Truth. *Right.*

"What truth do you want to hear?"

Courage fuelled her blood, and she vowed not to back down in front of this woman. She sat up straighter and accepted the challenge.

"About what is going on between you and my son."

"What has your son told you?"

Two perfect eyebrows drew together, and fine lines marred the smooth forehead. Agnes appeared to weigh her words in her head before she spoke.

"Apparently, he's in love with you," she said softly.

Lara gasped. He'd gone as far as telling his mother that? Not at all like him to expose his feelings. Unless push had come to shove. What else had he said?

Her heart told her the time had come to play all her cards. She didn't have anything more to lose.

"It's true," she said slowly.

"What are your intentions, though?"

"My intentions?" She gave a small laugh. "Madame Marivaux, I have no intentions at all. But I'm not surprised Eric didn't tell you we've broken up."

"He did mention it, in passing."

Surprise flooded her, and she frowned as she took the words in.

Curiosity grabbed her, and she couldn't quell it. "May I ask what you're doing here, then?"

The other woman lowered her gaze, and when she peeked back up, the ice had left the piercing irises.

"Far from me to pry into your personal life, but may I ask why things went wrong between you?"

"Eric asked me to marry him, and I refused," Lara said.

"Why?"

A sad smile lifted her mouth, as she recalled another similar question being asked to her.

"Why? We had no hope of existing, that's why."

"Enlighten me here." The frown on Agnes' forehead deepened. "How long have you been with Eric, for him to speak of marriage?"

"A few weeks, but our relationship goes back over a decade. We picked up from where we left off, I guess."

When only silence greeted her, she glanced across, and found herself being studied.

However, this time, the scrutiny didn't make her uncomfortable, just quizzical. "Is something wrong?"

Agnes took ages to reply. "The summer after Eric left for France, something happened, and you were involved. What took place back then?"

Lara couldn't brace herself for the shock. "I got married."

The whisper echoed in the stillness, turmoil brewing in her. The black veil returned in front of her eyes, and she drew in deep breaths, trying in vain to stop the room from spinning.

"*Vous vous sentez bien*?"

Concern lay heavy in the question asking her if she felt okay, but she couldn't acknowledge the worry as bile rose in her throat and made her nauseous.

A glass of water was thrust into her hand, and she gratefully took a few sips. When the room returned back to normal, she glanced around, astounded to find Agnes by her side.

"I'll be fine," she said.

Agnes returned to her seat, frowning.

Lara's turn now to know the truth.

"Did something happen to Eric back then?"

His mother gave a pained smile. "He threw all he had in his studies, became a shadow of his usual self. In short, he stopped living. It took a long time for him to regain some normalcy in his existence."

Pain welled up and gripped her heart as the image of a young, desolate Eric filled her mind. Tears threatened to spill from her eyes, and she tasted their bitter tang in her throat, where a huge lump had settled.

"How is he now?"

Agnes patted her hand before she got up and picked her handbag. "He's back to the same state, I'm afraid."

Lara closed her eyes, and a single tear rolled down her cheek. Through a hazy mist, she heard the words spoken to her.

"I'll leave now. I got what I came looking for."

She only listened as the footsteps retreated, stopping when they reached the door.

"You don't look any better, either," Agnes said. "And I just want you to know … I only want the life back in my son's eyes."

For days, those parting words echoed in her head. Lara replayed the scene countless times in her mind, and she always came to one conclusion.

Agnes Armont-Marivaux had given them her blessing.

However, she couldn't help but erase a doubt in her mind—that she wasn't being accepted for her worth, but only for what she brought Eric. Could she hope to be satisfied with so little? Her marriage to Roy had borne the complete approval of all involved, and that'd helped a lot in building their relationship, and their very existence.

The ringing of the phone interrupted her musings. She picked up and had to keep the receiver at a distance because of the outburst from the other end.

"Whoa, Sam, calm down. You're so delirious, I can't understand a word you're saying."

"I have great news. I went to the doctor today, and guess what?"

Lara gasped when she registered the happiness in her friend's voice. "You're pregnant?"

"Yes!"

"Oh, I'm so happy for you! I told you it would happen."

"I know. I couldn't believe it myself. You're the second person to know after Salim." She giggled with gleeful abandon.

"This is wonderful, Sam. I never once doubted it."

"Funny, you know. All those treatments I've had, yet, it's a simple thing that did the trick."

"What was it?"

"Well, this doctor gave me folic acid supplements. Nothing else. She said lots of women fail to conceive because they don't get enough folic acid. Amazing, isn't it?"

"Yes, it is. I'm so happy for you. I wish you were here so I could give you a big hug."

Sam laughed at the other end, and the merry sound seemed to come from the depths of her soul. "I'll take it on the line. I have to be off now, gotta call my family. Bye, sweetie."

"Bye, Sam."

She put the phone down with a heavy heart. The words echoed in her head, and she couldn't help it that her friend's happiness tinged her own misery darker.

As guilt assailed her, she shook out of the sombre thoughts. Sam deserved all the good coming her way, and Lara's loss was no reason for others to feel the same pain, as well.

She forced her mind to focus on the impending arrival, and as Sam's best friend, she wanted to celebrate the good news. A baby shower down the line, definitely. But what of the most immediate celebration? She reached for her cell, about to call Eric, but pulled her hand back as soon as she touched the phone.

Pointless to call him. What could she say that could take them across the rift she'd allowed to grow between them?

She shook her head, intent on chasing the gloomy thoughts away. She'd go out, and that would do the trick. She needed to gift Sam with something, anyway, so she might as well distract herself by hitting the shops.

However, more than an hour later, she still roamed the shopping centre at the entrance of Grand-Baie aimlessly, with no clue what to buy. She'd never had a pregnant woman in her entourage, not someone as close as she and Sam were, anyway. When her sister had been expecting, thousands of miles had spread between their two countries, and congratulations had happened over the phone. This left her completely oblivious about mom-to-be gifts and baby stuff.

She stopped in front of the bookstore and stepped in—the least she could do was get a 'congratulations' card.

The clerk on duty ignored her greeting, busy fussing over a white woman who stood before a magazine stand looking, for all intents and purposes, harassed by the constant, unwanted attention.

Lara took in the scene, and though highly annoyed by the clerk's behaviour, she shrugged her disgust off as she made her way to the card display stand.

Her mind wandered as she browsed around for a suitable card.

What a mighty example of the different worlds Eric and she lived in. When faced with the choice between service to a white person and any other racial group, the former usually won the upper hand. Only foreigners could hope to compete with them. She should open her mouth and spew out her BBC accent—that would surely send the clerk rushing, taking Lara for a tourist. She chuckled quietly.

"Lara?"

Her thoughts cleared, her spine stiffening. Though spoken in perfect English, the sound of her name still carried a slight tinge of a French accent, sharpening the 'r.' She slowly turned around and took a deep breath when her suspicions were confirmed.

Agnes stood a few feet from her and closed the gap shortly after.

"I thought it was you, but I wasn't sure," Eric's mother said. "How are you?"

"I'm fine," she blurted before catching herself. "I didn't expect to bump into you here."

"Neither did I, but it's a small world, *n'est-ce pas*?"

The accompanying smile beckoned warm and sincere, and the tension eased somewhat from her shoulders.

A flutter of activity materialized around them, the formerly busy clerk suddenly intent on helping them out.

Agnes turned her now cold stare upon the woman. "We'll call you if we need your help. I believe there are people waiting for you at the counter," she said with a slight flick of her chin.

Though spoken in French, Lara heard the full rebuttal the words carried, and she couldn't help but smile as the clerk hastily got back to her counter.

"Service is not exactly what it was," Agnes said with a sigh. "But forget it. What brings you here?"

"A friend of mine just found out she's pregnant, and I'm wracking my brain to find a proper gift for her."

"Have you tried a pregnancy book? They're very helpful."

"I hadn't thought of that, but it's a good idea."

A tall, bulky man entered the store, and Agnes asked to be excused.

As Lara reached the self-help-books aisle, the pair caught up with her.

"Lara, come here," Agnes said. "Let me introduce you. This is Mathieu Laroche, the owner of this bookstore, soon to be a family member. My daughter, Angélique, is betrothed to his son, Patrice."

Agnes turned towards the man as she added, "Mathieu, this is Lara Reddy, a friend of Eric's. She's the director of the new conference centre in Grand-Baie."

Mathieu Laroche put out a large paw and gripped her hand in his.

"I saw you and Eric a few times, and I wondered when I'd have the privilege of meeting you," he said with a large smile.

Lara couldn't help but smile back. "It's a pleasure to meet you, too. You have a very nice store here."

"Ah, we do what we can," he replied in heavily accented English. "Though I have to say, it isn't often I've seen Eric in such good company."

She felt herself blush, and Agnes came to the rescue.

"Mathieu, you're making her uncomfortable," she said with a small laugh. "I won't keep you any longer, though. I simply wanted you to meet this young woman here."

The man said his goodbyes, leaving the two women alone.

Awkwardness cloaked Lara, and she struggled to find the proper thing to say.

"Is something wrong?" Agnes asked.

She shook her head. "No, not really."

"Eric also says the same thing."

The woman let the words hang between them, and she heard the sadness in the voice.

"Madame Marivaux—"

"Please, call me Agnes."

She nodded. Was that an olive branch? She wouldn't know if she didn't ask, right?

"What do you think I should do?" she asked.

Agnes kept her eyes on her for what felt like ages. "I think you two should work your issues out."

Lara didn't reply her, and let her head hang to hide the pain flooding her. "How can I hope to do this?"

"Lara, it's your life, and Eric's, ultimately. He made me see that." Agnes reached for her hand. "It's you who'll have to live it." She paused, as if for emphasis. "I come from France, you know, and my husband spent all his life here on this island. It was very much a culture shock for me when I arrived here, and to think we'd both come from pretty much the same culture." Another pause ensued. "I didn't want my children to feel this kind of … off … for lack of a better word, when they decided to settle down."

Lara nodded. That made sense.

Agnes grabbed Lara's other hand and held on tight.

"But this I do know, my dear girl. If my son has singled you out for his love, it must mean you're worthy of it. I trust him, if that's what you need to know."

Lara made her way back home and dropped on the sofa, dumping her bags on the living room floor. The house lay in a state of chaos. Less than when she'd let herself go after Eric's departure, but filthy, nevertheless. Not that she cared.

All her focus congregated on the thoughts screaming around in her head. Her skull neared explosion, with hot, searing pain pounding all over her brain. She got up and wet a cloth in the sink. Once back on the sofa, she applied the cool compress on her forehead and breathed out with some relief when the heat receded from her skin.

How had Agnes Armont-Marivaux guessed her thoughts?

She couldn't imagine any other reason for the woman to add those last words at the bookstore. Confusion and understanding battled inside her, and every time she dared to work some comprehension out of it all, the pain increased double-fold to send piercing daggers along her cranium.

Food. The hurt must be amplified thanks to her empty stomach. She wouldn't be able to reason with herself unless she ate something.

With a heavy sigh, she recalled her freezer was empty, as she'd yet again delayed a much-needed trip to the supermarket.

An idea struck her. Blessed be home delivery. She fished around for the phone receiver, and five minutes later, threw it on the sofa after calling the nearby pizzeria.

She closed her eyes and let the cool cloth continue to work its magic on her.

From a faraway, misty place, she made out the sound of the doorbell ringing. Startled awake, she wearily got up to answer the door.

Would the poor delivery boy get a scare when she greeted him? She hardly looked her best. A hefty tip would compensate any fright she might induce, though.

She threw the door open, and the smile she had forced out died on her face when she noted who stood on her front porch.

He smiled. "Hello, Lara."

This couldn't be ...

"Roy?"

CHAPTER EIGHTEEN

Lara blinked a few times, trying to clear the image in front of her. But as much as she willed it, the sight didn't change.

Confusion boiled inside her, and shock dried her throat.

Roy stood there. Tall, dark, and handsome. In a tan-coloured Savile Row suit, even while on holiday in Mauritius, his broad shoulders and tall stature could easily be mistaken for that of a model. Rimless glasses framed his eyes, and small lines crinkled there when he smiled at her.

Smiled at her. The cheek of the man.

Still, as it always inevitably happened when she saw him, she lost her breath. Dashing didn't start to describe his allure. Any woman with blood coursing in her body would take a second peek at this man.

But she couldn't ignore the cocky lift of his mouth. She travelled her gaze over him and saw the slightly arrogant and overly confident man who'd turned her life upside down on a whim.

Sense returned, and she quelled her surprise.

"What are you doing here?" she asked.

"Won't you ask me in?"

He hadn't changed, still thinking everyone owed him everything.

Her eyes narrowed as she glared, but he didn't seem to feel any of the displeasure she directed at him.

Cut your losses, again. Nothing to be won with her slamming the door in his face, no matter how much she yearned to do just that.

So, she slowly nodded and moved aside to let him enter the hall.

In a few steps, he reached the living room and turned around to face her.

"May I?" he asked with a glance at the sofa.

"You might as well, since you're already here."

She stood in the doorway as he eased himself comfortably on the sofa where she'd been only minutes before.

He appeared out of place in the room. Too broad, tense, unfitting.

So unlike Eric.

She pushed the thought aside and focused her attention on the man before her. The man with whom she'd shared ten years of her life.

"What are you doing here, Roy?"

A slight tinge of anxiety invaded her as she watched him take in the disorder that reigned. But she didn't allow the sensation to linger. She was in her house. Not his, not theirs.

He startled a bit when he glanced at the bag on the floor. Clearly visible through the clear plastic lay the cover of the book inside—*Your Pregnancy and You*. A small frown marred his forehead as he turned around to face her.

"Is this for you?"

His intense dark eyes pierced her, and a quiver thrummed in her voice when she opened her mouth to answer.

But she snapped her lips shut. She had nothing to justify. If anything, he was the one who had things to explain.

She sighed and leaned against the doorway. "Roy, why are you here? And how did you find me?"

"You left this address with the lawyers."

"Not very professional of them," she muttered. "You still haven't answered me."

She lifted her chin and crossed her arms in front of her. With her shoulder braced against the doorframe, she hitched in a breath when she realised the tension that usually sizzled in her whenever she'd faced her ex-husband had left her.

In the time away from him, she had grown and shrugged off any influence he might've had on her existence, on her psyche.

Calm descended over her. Roy no longer had any hold on her. Closure, finally?

"I'm waiting," she said, tapping her foot lightly.

That gesture used to drive him to distraction. With a small smile of gloating satisfaction, she relished the movement, for the first time free from the need to pacify him.

A severe, sombre face stared back at her, and his deep eyes wrestled with hers.

She kept up with the challenge, didn't allow herself to back down, and lifted her eyebrows in question.

And just like that, the careful façade before her crumbled. He took his glasses off, and with his thumb and forefinger, pinched the bridge of his nose. Then, on an exhaled curse, he ran a hand through his hair.

Bells rang in her head at these exterior signs of his turmoil. Roy very rarely took off his glasses and never allowed himself to show any vulnerable expression. She frowned. What he was getting at? Could all this be a ploy of his?

"What's wrong, damn it?" She stiffened her spine and drew to her full height. "For more than three years, I don't hear from you, other than through lawyers, and now, you drop out of the sky, coming all the way from London, to flash me that dazzling smile of yours?"

He glanced up. "I haven't treated you right, have I?"

Fuelled by resentment and anger, she continued with her outburst. "Damn right you haven't. One day, you decided you wanted a child, when you never mentioned you'd ever want one, and expected me to do your bidding at the drop of a hat. And when I refused, telling you we'd never even cared for a cat, you asked what sort of woman was I for not wanting babies and you stormed out, and the next thing I saw of you was a sheaf of divorce papers. Served to me by a legal clerk in the lobby of the hotel I worked for, just past the clocking of lunch hour. Damn right you didn't treat me properly, Roy!"

"I'm sorry, Lara."

The words hit her like a bullet, and she had to sit down to let them sink in. She reached the sofa opposite him and dropped her weight in it.

He was sorry? After all this time? This confession had to be priceless.

Laughter bubbled inside her, and she gave in to the hysterical fit.

She laughed harder at his puzzled expression. However, she caught herself before the fit turned to tears.

"If I ever thought I'd see the day ..." But then, gloomy depression fell on her like a cloak, and she shook her head. "What do you expect this'll change now?"

He shrugged. "I don't know, Lara. I don't know anything any longer. I hoped, maybe if we talked again, we'd understand what happened to us."

A wave of surprise almost knocked her over at the uncertainty in his unusually soft tone. She'd always known him as a confident man whom certainty never eluded. This new side of him puzzled her, and intrigued her even more.

"Roy, what happened was that I wasn't ready for children, but you were. I'm afraid to say you didn't handle the situation in a very civilized way, but it's over and done with, and we have to live with the consequences now."

"Lara, I'm sorry."

She didn't want to smile, but she had to. She'd wanted—needed—to get those words out, and she suddenly realised that those facts, and to say them out loud, no longer hurt as much.

And here was Roy ...

"Roy, it's okay. It didn't work, that's all. *We* didn't work. I admit I was hurt, and angry, but these feelings won't do any of us good, so better for us to leave such things to the past."

A weight lifted from her shoulders, and she sighed.

The sensation filled her with peace, and calm finally soothed her ragged heart.

Sadness and a wistful affection gripped her heart at the uncertainty and confusion drawing his features, ageing him beyond his thirty-nine years.

He took a deep breath. "I know I hurt you, and I'm so sorry for having said all those things. They weren't true, you know."

She couldn't bear the sincerity in his hushed tone, and she averted her eyes. "Forget it. It's all in the past now."

"I can't, Lara." He threw his hands in the air. "I can't believe what a bastard I've been to tell you all those things."

And then, as suddenly as the outburst had caught hold of him, he hunched in his seat, and his voice came out all strangled when he next spoke. "You would've made a very good mother, you know that?"

The whispered words slammed into her stomach like an iron fist, knocking the breath out of her.

"What?"

Silence settled while they both simply stared across at each other, cocooned in another world. One where emotion ran rampant, and past deeds and actions vied for acknowledgement and a reason for their existence.

"You'll make a wonderful mum someday. I'm just sad it won't be for my children."

Lara didn't know if she needed to laugh, cry, or have her head checked for hallucinating tendencies. This was Roy spewing such words to her?

A nervous giggle escaped, and she quelled the laughter by pressing her hand to her mouth. A rush of emotions clogged her throat and tripled the size of her tongue, so she couldn't form a word, let alone utter a sound.

He must've seen the disbelief in her eyes, because he reached out and clasped her hand.

"It's true, Lara. I know you have what it takes to be a great mother, but it's you who's got to feel it first. My mistake for not having given you the time."

"Why are you telling me all this?" she asked when she'd shaken the stupor away.

Without taking his eyes off her, he smiled.

"Preety, my wife, is the perfect Indian daughter-in-law. A domestic household goddess." A small chuckle escaped him, before his voice grew sober again. “But there are days when even she is at her wits end with dealing with the baby.”

Lara shook her head. “It still doesn’t explain how I’d make a good mother.”

Roy smiled. “I’ve known what it’s like to be loved by you. When you love someone, you give him everything you have.” He squeezed her hand. “I didn’t realise it when I had it. But I hope this won’t keep you from loving someone again. To this man, you’d give everything, Lara, even children.”

The lump in her throat grew bigger, and she could do nothing to stop her tears from flowing. How had Roy pinned her down so well?

The doorbell rang. She blinked out of her thoughts and got up while drying her cheeks. Taking deep breaths along the way, she tried to blank all thought from the turmoil in her mind as she exited the living room.

The pizza delivery boy stood on her porch—she’d completely forgotten about her order.

Back in the living room, she dropped the box on a table in the corner and sat back down.

But Roy didn’t look up, his focus riveted on a picture he held in his hand.

She wondered what he was staring at, and was on the point of asking when he broke the silence.

“I’ve never seen you like this.”

“Like what?”

“So radiant. Full of life, of laughter. So beautiful,” he said as he glanced back at her.

Her cheeks flamed, not simply from the words he spoke, but also from the unconcealed longing in them.

She reached out and grabbed the picture from his hands.

After a quick glance, she tossed the glossy aside.

Past memories, better forgotten, her mind screamed.

“Oh, that,” she said with a small laugh. “A one-off happening.” Silence stretched between them. “My life isn’t that way most of the time.”

She could've kicked herself at the sadness in her voice. He must've also heard her dejection.

"What's been up in your life?" he asked.

"This and that. Nothing much. Terribly taken with work. We got short-listed for the next Commonwealth conference ..." A hot blush crept up her when she realised she was babbling. "Forget me, though. What's up with you?"

"Nothing, either." He shrugged. "My relatives here wanted to meet Preety and the baby, so we've come down to visit."

"Did you have a boy or a girl?"

Roy smiled, and fierce pride burned in his eyes. "A girl. We named her Rani."

Rani—*Queen*. Lara had no doubt the little girl would be the queen of Roy's life. She smiled, too, before tension bristled between them as they faced each other.

It suddenly dawned on her that, despite having shared each other's lives, neither of them had ever really been intimate in exchanging confidences. They'd merely lived next to the other, rather than with the other. This intimacy between them today seemed forced and too polite. She should lighten the atmosphere by any manner.

"You've put on weight," she said. "I gather your wife is a good cook."

Roy gave a small laugh. "She cooks very well. The house is also spick and span, and her laundry skills cannot be rivalled."

She couldn't stifle the small laugh that escaped her, and he glanced at her with surprise. But then he, too, joined in the laughter.

"It's what you wanted, after all," she said.

"True, but like the saying goes, be careful what you wish for."

"I'm sure she looks after you well." She paused. "Better than I did, certainly."

"Believe me, after knowing an independent and determined woman like you, she sometimes strikes me as so … passive."

She frowned at him. "You don't really mean it."

"No, not really." He gave her a sheepish smile. "I love her, but it feels … different."

Where had their *love gone?*

The question popped in her head, and from the intense expression on Roy's face, he must be asking himself the same thing.

"We were a good team, weren't we?" he asked.

"Yes. But we couldn't make it work."

"Yeah."

The word hung in the air.

He reached out and clasped her hand. "Please tell me I haven't ruined your existence."

Emotion choked her throat, and tears stung her eyes. "No, you haven't."

A link broke between them, but in the following second, another, deeper thread wove itself in the path—that of friendship.

As she squeezed his hand, he smiled. And she smiled back.

Roy stood, and she followed suit.

"I guess I'd better leave, then," he said.

"I guess you should."

He raised an eyebrow. "Are you throwing me out or what?"

She laughed at his teasing smile. "Far from me to do so. My door's always open to a friend."

He peered down, before training his eyes back upon her face. "Lara, don't get me wrong, okay?"

"What?"

"For what it's worth, I've never seen you look as happy as you do in that picture."

She swallowed hard as the lump returned in her throat.

"Have I made you happy, Lara?"

"Yes, you have," she said softly, before she reached out and hugged him.

After the initial second or two of surprise, he hugged her back, and she settled her cheek on his chest.

"Can I ask you something?"

"Uh-uh," she said against the soft fabric of his jacket.

"That man, he makes you happy?"

She jerked her head up and stared at him, eyes wide. "What are you talking about?"

"The picture. A man made you happy when it was taken. You shouldn't waste it."

His last words left a burning imprint on her heart, and she winced. When Roy squinted at her with concern on his face, she reached out and hugged him again.

"Take care, Lara."

"You, too."

A minute later, he left and got in his rental car. She stood on the porch until the vehicle had disappeared from sight, then she entered the house, closing the door behind her.

Darkness cloaked her, and she went around switching on the lights as she traipsed back into the living room, where she plopped down on the sofa. The headache came back with a vengeance, and her stomach gave a dull groan.

As she glanced around, her gaze landed on the pizza box in the corner, and she reached for it. The movement dragged at the surface of the coffee table, sending some papers onto the floor. She couldn't stop herself from glancing at the picture that landed face-up at her feet.

She reached down and turned the image over, then picked up a piece of pizza.

As she nibbled at the cheese, her attention kept straying back to the picture. With a groan, she threw the food back into the box and bent to pick the photo.

A radiant, sun-kissed woman stared back at her. The wind blew in her hair, and the strands shone like diamonds where sunshine hit them. Her face carried a delicate flush, and the broad, dazzling smile on her features shone, spelling out her happiness. The yellow colour of the strappy sundress matched the radiance of the bright tropical sun.

As she closed her eyes, Lara remembered how the sun had felt on her bare shoulders that day. Soft and warm, its rays had caressed her skin gently. The gust of wind had lifted her hair from the nape of her neck, and she could still feel the sting of the salty spray as it had hit her face every time she'd turned towards the sea.

Upon one such moment, Eric had snapped the picture. A totally unplanned, spontaneous image he'd managed to catch on his camera. As soon as he'd clicked the photo, she had lost her footing in the sand and had fallen. He'd been there to catch her, though he'd fallen down, too. They'd laughed when they'd hit the sand, and she'd grown serious again when, against the dazzling sun, he'd brought his face down for a kiss.

Eric always said she'd been so beautiful in the photo, he'd had to have it printed so he could carry it with him everywhere.

A tear rolled down her cheek as the memories replayed in her head, and she opened her eyes to blink away the flood menacing to unleash.

Her heart constricted, and every time she thought of him, she wished for the world to open up under her feet and swallow her whole. She'd never experienced the hurt that slashed through her when memories of him returned to plague her.

Memories of how good it had felt to be with him. Of how well they understood each other. Of how peaceful he made her feel when she lay in his arms, as if nothing in the world could ever reach her.

She longed for their world, and she longed for him.

The tears flowed down her face.

Images of their times together flashed in her head, and then other images, and words, took their place.

Words she'd heard all around her ...

Neha telling her she'd known Rahul was the man for her because he made her feel better than any other person did.

Agnes' voice telling her Eric cared for her.

Her father's voice, asking her to work her issues out.

And Roy's voice, telling her not to waste herself if love lay so near, saying she'd happily give the man she loved children ...

When Lara realised she could picture a blond miniature of Eric in her arms, she stood up with a start. With a hand on her mouth to stifle her gasp, her heart pounded so hard, the muscle threatened to break out of her ribcage.

Realisation had her rooted her to the spot.

She loved Eric. She'd always loved him.

How could she have been so stupid? Cold dread filled her when she realised she'd nearly thrown her life out of the window with her foolish issues and insecurities. Another thought jumped into her mind, and the blood ran icy in her veins.

Had she lost Eric? For good?

Her stupid behaviour could've ruined everything. She had to know.

Adrenaline fuelled her blood, and she glanced around for her car keys. Throwing herself on the sofa, she sent the cushions flying in trying to locate the keys. When she closed her fingers on the ring, she pulled out with all her might. As she turned towards the front door, the lights went out, and a blinding flash of lightning lit the room. The growl of thunder resounded seconds later.

A thunderstorm? In June, on the edge of winter? *You have to be joking!*

She stood petrified. Panic burst through her, the rapid beat of her heart echoing in her head, and she closed her eyes and clasped her hands against her ears.

Soon, another strike came in, and she again couldn't move. Cold sweat broke on her skin.

Eric.

His name flashed in her head, and a renewed surge of energy took hold of her.

With quickened steps, she forced her way out of the house and got into her car, hitting the road in a screech of tyres, her foot hard on the accelerator. Heavy rain fell in a downpour, and visibility neared zero with the lampposts barely emitting any light in the thunderstorm.

She ploughed on, grateful the road lay empty before her. Caution advised her to take her foot off the pedal, but a desperate need to reach the man she loved surged through her and urged her not to stop. She'd lose him if she did.

As she reached his property, she pulled the car up and rolled the window down. Twice, she punched in the wrong entry code. A voice warned her the alarm would go off if a wrong number were entered for the third time.

She forced herself to take a deep breath as she recalled the sequence of numbers she'd so often punched into that very keypad. With intense concentration, she entered the code, and the door opened in front of her. As soon as the Mercedes could pass though, she sped into the property and braked hard when she reached the house.

She got out in the torrential rain, and hope plummeted in her heart when she didn't see the Prado in the garage. Out of desperate hope, she made her way to the front door, where she rang the bell.

The sound of rainfall drowned the delicate tinkle. With the power out, the doorbell wouldn't ring, either.

Only one thing left to do. Lara threw all she had into pounding upon the massive wooden door.

◆◆◆

Eric had been sitting on a stool in the kitchen when the lights went out. Almost immediately, the low growl of thunder had rumbled through the air.

Lara! She'd be panicked by the storm.

He quickly stood, but turned back when he reached the kitchen door.

She wouldn't want him barging in on her.

With a heavy heart, he made his way into the living room, where he lit a few candles. Candles she'd left here and there, he thought with a sad smile. Heavy rain beat against the roof and drowned all the sound in the empty house.

Did he still have the heart and desire to remain in this dwelling any longer? While the place had been flooded with joy and happiness whenever she'd been here, without her, the empty structure appeared desolate and neglected.

He closed his eyes as he imagined the sound of her voice when she called his name. The lovely trill bounced upon the walls and filled the house with merriness. He remembered her way of walking around barefoot, and how she carried sand back in whenever she returned from the beach. He chuckled when he recalled the sound of the fridge door opening and closing at any time of the day, when she'd rummage in for something to eat.

She probably didn't eat any longer. Sorrow cloaked his heart, and he shrugged the memories off as he pried his eyes open. No good to ponder over all that, because a part of his heart would always bleed, no matter how long he gave the organ to heal.

He had finished lighting the last candle when a sound came from the hall. Venturing closer, he could make out someone was pounding on the door. From the urgency of the drumming, it surely had to be an emergency.

Numb shock overcame him when he opened up.

Lara stood before him, drenched from head to toe, a strange light burning in her eyes.

"What are you doing here?"

She stared at him for a few seconds, her eyes intense and fiery.

"Do you want children?" she finally asked.

He blinked. "What?"

Lara wanted to shake herself like a rag doll. What had she asked him?

Her near-hysterical nerves made her jittery, and she threw her weight from one foot to the other. A dash of practicality caught her. She might as well get an answer to the question, since she was so intent on working her issues out.

"Do you want children?" she again asked.

Eric stared at her with eyebrows drawn together. From the pointed stare he gave her, she was sure he must be weighing up if she'd be a likely candidate for a mental institution.

"Just answer me, please."

A puzzled expression settled upon his face as lines creased his broad forehead.

"Lara, first come inside, and then we'll talk. Okay?"

No! She needed to tell him what a fool she'd been all along. The thoughts and emotions screamed in her head, and it seemed her brain had cut all her control over her limbs as she stood there rooted to the spot.

When it must've dawned on him that she couldn't move, he reached out and gently tugged on her arm. He had her take a few steps until she stood in the hall, and he closed the door behind her.

In the dark, with only the muted glow of the candles shedding a semblance of light, she couldn't make out the expression on his face.

"Eric, we need to talk."

He remained silent for a long moment.

"I think so, too. What's the matter, Lara?" he asked, his voice dropping low and tinged with concern.

She wanted to throw her arms around him and tell him to hold her tight, but they had their issues to deal with.

"You do want children, right?"

"Yes ..." His answer sounded tentative.

"Anytime soon?"

"I beg your pardon?" He gasped. "You're not … pregnant … are you?"

Lara knew she played her whole life on how she'd answer him, and in the balance lay any hope of a future with Eric.

"No. But I'd like to be ... Having *your* baby …"

The frantic beating of her heart grew more rapid when instead of saying something, he took a sharp intake of breath.

"What happened, Lara?"

She'd prepared herself for the question. Her worst-case scenario, in fact.

But, in her nightmare, his voice had been filled with anger, not the hope and longing ringing clear in his breathless tone.

"Roy came, and we talked. I realised that what you said was true. I didn't trust myself enough. But now, I know that if I have your support, I can overcome everything, and I can then lay aside all the insecurities that have robbed me of living my life fully for all those years."

She paused for breath, before finally saying what she'd come all this way to tell him.

"I love you, Eric. And I know the trust you've always had in us will be enough for both of us. If I have you by my side, I can make it."

She stopped talking when her lungs threatened to burst. The sound of her shallow and ragged breathing echoed in the still of the dark lobby. With every second ticking by, her hopes plummeted, until she couldn't stand the wait any longer.

"Will you grant me a second chance?" she asked softly.

Eric sighed. Her mouth went dry when he came to stand right before her. The glow of a nearby candle lit his face, highlighting the tautness in his jaw, the small muscle twitching in his cheek.

"I have one condition, though."

His face didn't lose its sombre air, and she gulped back. "What is it?"

He stared at her for a long time, then a smile broke upon his handsome face.

"Only if you'll be my wife."

As the words sank in, Lara's smile grew, and her heart soared.

"The sooner, the better," she replied, before she tilted her face and allowed her lips to touch his.

They sealed the deal with a kiss.

EPILOGUE

One year later…

Breathe, Lara, breathe.

Could this be the longest two minutes in a woman's life? She glared at the small device in front of her, refusing to allow herself to think while watching the progress on the strip.

A second pink line slowly appeared, and her smile grew on her face along with it.

Elation filled her when the realisation sank in, and she jumped in her spot with joy. Reining her excitement, she opened the bathroom door and cast a glance over the room. The pale light of dawn slowly lit the bedroom up, chasing the gloom and the shadows.

Lara Marivaux gazed fondly at the man sleeping on the bed. Joy and love washed over her.

He'd chased the dark and the gloom from her life, leaving no stone unturned, and had given her the security and the peace she'd so long craved. His trust in her had made her overcome all her fears and the obstacles in their path, and she'd found a new lease on life by his side.

She went and sat down by his side. A part of her knew he deserved the sleep, having come in late from an emergency last night, but another part wanted to wake him right away.

But she couldn't bear it anymore, and sank between the sheets, angling closer to him.

She ran a hand along the lines of his face and trailed her fingers to his broad shoulders. When she reached his chest, he groaned and pulled her swiftly beside him. He hugged her close, yet didn't wake up.

As she nibbled his earlobe, he groaned again, and she smiled.

"Happy wedding anniversary, darling," she said in his ear.

He mumbled something in reply, and she could feel he was waking up.

"I've got something for you." She took his hand and placed it on her belly.

He opened sleep-filled eyes and stared at her with a confused expression on his face.

But then, his eyes grew wide, and he sat up straight. He returned his hand to her belly and stared her with astonishment, his gaze pleading with hers for an answer.

She laughed softly and nodded.

He brought his other hand up, ran his fingers in his hair as he took in her implication.

"A baby?" he asked in a hushed, reverent tone.

"Yes." She couldn't believe it herself—it all felt like a dream.

Laughter bubbled from her throat when he reached out and hugged her. He crushed her to his chest, and seconds later, loosened his grip.

"Did I hurt you?" Concern rang heavy in his voice.

Lara rolled her eyes. "Dear husband, I'm only pregnant, and it doesn't make me a fragile doll, you know."

Sinking into his embrace, she settled her head in the crook of his shoulder. As she closed her eyes, serenity washed over her.

She sighed. By his side, she'd found her place … on the other side.

Thank you for reading The One That Got Away by Zee Monodee. If you enjoyed this story, please leave a quick review on the site of purchase.

Island Girls: 3 sisters in Mauritius by Zee Monodee

The One That Got Away
How To Love An Ogre
Falling For Her Bad Boy Boss

Also by Zee Monodee

Be My Valentine Vol 2 Anthology
Unravelling His Mark (The Protectors #2)
The Torn Prince (Royal House of Saene #4)

From always sneaking a Mills&Boon romance under the desk at school, Zee went on to make a career out of writing the kind of emotional romances she adores.

Of Indian heritage & a breast cancer survivor, she lives in paradise (aka Mauritius!) with her long-suffering husband, their smart-mouth teenage son, and their diva-like tabby cat.

Fun facts about Zee:

Paws are her kryptonite.

Tarot & all that woo-woo stuff is her jam.

Cheese is a food group for her.

Would buy a new lipstick every time she goes out if she could.

In her day job, she is a book editor who loves helping authors make their stories shine.

Website: http://www.zeemonodee.com/
Email: zeemonodee@gmail.com
Instagram: https://www.instagram.com/zeemonodee/
Facebook: https://www.facebook.com/zee.monodee

LOVE'S BEGINNING BY NKEM AKIN

A Love Rekindled – Vol. 1

~~~~~~~~~~~~~
~~~~~~~~~~~~~

A Love Rekindled is a work of fiction. Names, characters, and all events and dialogue therein are products of the author's imagination. References to real people, places and organizations are used fictitiously.

Blurb

"Efe Sagay grew up and went to school in Nigeria. While attending school she met the love of her life, her soul mate, the person she wanted to spend the rest of her life with...Kevwe Mukoro. And the feelings were duplicated by Kevwe. As soon as Efe graduated, they would be married. This was the dream and this was the plan.

But real life doesn't always see things the way we do. The perfect future can always be destroyed by unforeseen circumstances."

Book Review by Martha A. Cheves, Author.

1

Benin City. July 15, 1999.

After posting the visa documents, Efe Sagay arrived at the lecture hall just in time because right behind her, strolled in the Business 102 lecturer. Dr. Eboche was a law unto himself, coming to class only when he liked. The only favor he did them was to give the course outline, a reading list and his lecture notes. Efe ran to sit where Nneka beckoned as the lecturer dropped his books and walked to the blackboard. The red coral beads around his wrist jangled as he wrote out the title of his course and the topic for the day.

"Entrepreneurship… the topic at the heart of business…" He turned back to the class. "How many of you have read ahead on this topic?" Dr. Eboche adjusted his black dashiki and wiped the sweat from his bald head, hairy arms and bearded chin. More coral swung around his neck. He was thickset, over six feet tall, and reminded Efe of a bear with his deep voice, an intimidating undertone in his every word.

Nobody spoke, so he went into a long tirade, calling the students lazy and foolish, and promising they would all fail his course with their unserious attitude. Efe felt a wave of tiredness wash over her and by the time he started on the real lecture, she had to fight to keep her eyes open. The bustle in the hall faded into the background.

"You! Tell me what I just said now," Dr. Eboche shouted.

Startled, Efe looked up, but she didn't understand his anger till Nneka pinched her. She turned to see Dr. Eboche staring at her under glowering brows.

"Young lady, what did I just say?" he repeated.

All sleep fled her eyes and Efe stood up, feeling like a dim-wit. "Ehm... Sir, ehm..."

"Yes?" The sarcasm in his voice made her wilt.

"You talked about a sole entrepreneur, sir, and you said..."

Before she could complete the sentence, a loud sneeze cut through the tension. The whole class erupted in wolf whistles and catcalls. Some of the boys shouted "rendered homeless" while others stamped their feet and slapped their desks.

"What's happening?" Dr. Eboche asked, with suspicion bold across his face.

At the rear of the class, a popular noise-maker stood, and several other students shouted his name. "O-jo, O-jo, O-jo..."

"Sir, millions of bacteria have just been rendered homeless," Ojo said. "We want to exterminate them before they contaminate us."

"You are all sick," Dr. Eboche declared with an air of irritation, and then he smirked, "Well... since I don't want to be infected too, I beg to take my leave."

This last statement was made with the air of someone who'd just had his request handed over on a platter of gold. Dr. Eboche packed up his books and left the class. Some of the backbenchers continued whistling, but Efe guessed it was in protest of the lecturer's exit. Since it was their last lecture, they joined the rest of the students in packing up their bags.

"That man is a truant," Nneka complained as they left the building. "Imagine; he left the class for such a silly thing."

"Please leave that side. Don't you realize I was just let off the hook? I have no power for Eboche's wahala." Efe wiped her nose. This was the first time she would fall asleep in class, and she was ashamed of herself. Was this how she would cope in America?

Nneka stopped walking. "But Efe, what happened?"

"You know I had to finish filling those visa forms last night?" Efe asked, and Nneka nodded, laughing when a wide yawn interrupted Efe. "When you left the library, Ovie persuaded me to read till daybreak. And while she fell asleep at midnight and didn't stir till morning, I couldn't fall asleep."

Nneka shook her head, "I don't think I can do TDB sha."

Efe shrugged; it had been worth a try. TDB was fine when one read through the night, but it had disadvantages too. She'd woken up late and also fallen asleep during a lecture, but at least she'd sent off the completed visa lottery forms to her parents. Now, when she got to her room, it was straight to bed for a long siesta. America dreaming…

Benin City. July 15, 1999. 5pm

Kevwe and his close pal, Wale, sat under the shade of an umbrella in front of Omega Café, one of the popular joints on campus, both cradling chilled bottles of beer. A sales girl wiped down the empty tabletops but a passing car raised more of the red dust that coated every surface in the vicinity.

The sun blazed and Kevwe wiped his face, taking a long sip from his drink. Everyone waited for the next rain, but it was July and the skies had also dried up from the heat.

"Who's that girl?" Kevwe nudged his friend with a foot under the table. Two laughing girls walking along the street had caught his attention.

"Which one?" Wale asked as they admired the two girls passing. "The light skinned, tall and beautiful one, yeah? Curved in all the right places, face like a goddess..."

"Easy now," Kevwe laughed. "I mean the slim milk chocolate one. Don't you think she's just right for me?"

"JJC like you, yeah?" Wale sneered.

Kevwe remained aloof at his friend's teasing. Wale often displayed a strange sense of humor, having been born in London. His parents moved back to Nigeria when he was thirteen, but he was yet to lose his British accent because he spent all his vacations in the United Kingdom. He added 'yeah' with an inflection into every other sentence he made, and said 'cull' instead of 'call'. Sometimes this got on Kevwe's nerves, but he would ignore it now, because he wanted information.

"What do you mean?" Kevwe asked, still following the girls with his gaze.

"They're hard to get," Wale said, "They're real ladies, yeah? Not like the many *ajebutter* for mouth, and back for ground in this Ugbowo."

They laughed uproariously and slapped each other's knees. Kevwe remembered why they were flat mates; Wale always cracked jokes and could be so down to earth too.

"Oh God, you kill me," Kevwe said holding his sides. "But fill me in, man, talk to me."

"That particular babe is in her first year," Wale replied, "The gist is that she still doesn't have a beau, though it hasn't been for lack of guys trying their luck. Come and see how guys rushed her when they were admitted in October last year. Let me tell you a story. You know we call them Jambites when they first get in, yeah? A good friend of mine tried his luck on your babe then, and do you know what she said?"

Kevwe gestured for him to continue.

Wale spoke in a high falsetto, "I am too young to have a boyfriend. I want to concentrate on my books and make my parents proud."

Kevwe smiled. That was a good attitude, but he could bet she was past that stage now. It was almost a year, and she'd be more used to the freedom of university now.

"And don't think guys have gone off on such a hot babe since then o." Wale said. "I know some friends of friends, and guess what the grapevine reported? She told one guy just a few weeks ago that she didn't want to raise his hopes or break his heart."

"She has already broken mine," Kevwe said, clutching his chest with a moan. He was attracted to the girl, and would give it a go.

"Yeah..." Wale said with a straight face, "you and half the guys on campus."

Kevwe laughed, sitting back to take a long swallow from his drink, which had become warm from the heat. "Mmm... I think I may have an edge, being a new face and all."

"Don't forget to mention a mysterious history too," Wale said, "Girls won't fail to fall for your bad boy charms, yeah? Rumor has it you're a cult guy, expelled from UniLag..."

"That's not true." Kevwe wasn't surprised at the question. He'd completed his transfer to the University of Benin just three weeks ago in June. He'd come to UniBen because he wanted to change departments, and he hadn't been able to do that in Lagos. However, the timing couldn't have been worse. Since the new president had been sworn in two months ago, the country had been abuzz with anti-cultism slogans. Students had been rusticated from several universities, and many more had been suspended.

"You see why I didn't go to that school?" Wale interrupted him with a sniff. "I hear the vice chancellor sponsors the cults to maintain an upper hand. Is that true?" He did not wait for Kevwe's reply, "I know someone was killed last year by cultists here in UniBen, but at least there's an anti-cult group here. You know five Student Union Government officials were recently hacked down in Ife, and nothing has been done? I hear they target people whose parents are loaded to harass, so I have to be careful. You have to be too; I hear your parents are one of those that own Benin..."

Kevwe shook his head. "Wale, I hear you."

2

Benin City. July 31, 1999. 11pm

Efe looked around the Hall Two common room and wondered if it was time she packed up her books. The people in the room were much less than when she arrived, and like most others, Nneka had left earlier. Efe stayed because a month to exams, she still lagged in the recommended reading. She was bored by their courses and daydreamed about America.

A frisson shook her, and she sneaked a glance over her shoulder. It felt like someone staring, and she guessed the guy she just started seeing was at it again. He did all he could to get her attention, following wherever she went. If she left and came back, he also left and returned, and then spent half that time just looking at her as if he had never seen a girl. Well, he'd succeeded in his devices, and she'd noticed him.

Many times, she had to force herself to stop dreaming about his handsome looks and concentrate on her books. Once, he almost caught her studying him, but she turned away just in time. Brushing him out of her mind, she decided to study further.

An hour later, as people continued to leave; the chair beside hers became vacant. Debating whether to pack up, she felt someone take the vacant seat. Goose bumps prickled over her skin when she looked at the newcomer. Golden brown eyes gazed back at her, and her heart began to cartwheel inside her chest.

"Hello," her new neighbor said. "Are you done?"

"No." Efe replied, surprised at the normalcy of her voice. Her breath had hitched as his rich baritone stroked her senses. Up close, he passed for beautiful. His skin glistened and the mark in the middle of his brows set off the flaring, well-sized nostrils and thin upper lip. She turned away from the temptingly full lower lip, biting her own lips. Pulling her bag into her lap, she dug through it, not searching for anything in particular. She wanted to avoid the eyes which felt as if they could see her thoughts.

Efe went back to her books but couldn't bear sitting beside him for long. Her heart pounded in her ears each time he turned towards her. After thirty minutes, she packed up, stacking the library books in the table corner.

"Oh, leaving?" he asked.

"Yes, it's getting late." Efe got to her feet and picked her tote.

"It ***is*** late," he corrected. "Let me walk you back to the hostel."

Efe wished he wouldn't, yet she hoped he would. She remained silent as he also stood up and followed her out of the study room.

"You didn't expect that I'd allow a beautiful young lady like you walk into the night alone?" he asked, as they walked out into the car park.

Her nose itched at the flattery, and she fought the urge to touch it. "But you...."

"No excuses. I am tired, and it's time I returned to my own room too." His smile lit up the night, "I am Kevwe Mukoro. Do you always read in that common room?"

"I read here with my friend sometimes, but she left early today. It's also nearer to my hostel than the library, so I can walk back alone." Efe avoided saying her name, finally wiping her nose. Too bad there was no such relief for her racing heart.

Silence stretched, as the kerosene lamps and candles filled the air with choking smoke. "Buy bread and moi moi here..." a couple of fast-food hawkers still loitering in the hostel car park chorused.

Some popcorn was pushed into their faces, but she refused his offer to buy a pack, finding herself tongue-tied for the first time in her life. It wasn't even as if he'd propositioned her, but her wariness of male students was high. She racked her brain for something safe to fill the silence. When he asked which hostel, she said Osasogie Estate, not wanting to tell him the specific hall where she lived.

"Ah, I'm also going that way to BDPA Estate." Kevwe asked. "Do you stay in Osasogie Hostel itself, the one in Jowitz and near the AP filling station?"

He obviously knew the area well. Efe nodded to his questions, and when he said he also often read in the common room, she couldn't stop another nod. She bit her tongue when his teeth flashed.

"You know?" he asked, "You always looked serious. I didn't think you noticed me."

She closed her eyes and pinched her nose. They strolled past the suya mallam, whose kebabs sizzled as he grilled them over a banked fire in the stone ring beside his kiosk. The smell of charcoal and roasted meat filled the air, soon joined by the noise from the patrons at the Dreams cafe. The revelers sang at the top of their voices, and she walked faster out of habit. That place had a terrible reputation for drunken fights that usually ended with someone in hospital. She slowed down when the tall figure beside her matched her step for step. Efe was glad of his presence, but a sigh of relief still escaped her when the Jowitz sign appeared.

"So what's your name?"

"E... fe... E... Ife..." she stammered, heart hammering in fear that he'd catch her lie.

"Ife?" He smiled at her, "that's pretty and suits you. What..."

"We're here," Efe cut in once they were in front of her hostel, leaving him with the false name. "Thanks for walking me back... goodnight."

"Goodnight, and sweet dreams," Kevwe replied.

Efe tried to hold on to the dregs of her composure as she walked away. He was still there when she turned to close the gate. Once inside, Efe ran up the stairs and all the way down the corridors to her room. She closed the door and leaned against it, letting out a sigh with her eyes closed. Her two roommates stared back at her when she opened her eyes, but she ignored them, and walked to her bed.

"Who is it, what's wrong?" asked Jane, the outspoken one.

"Nothing," Efe replied. "I'm just tired." When they went back to their books, she undressed and got into bed. Meeting Kevwe

Mukoro had shaken her, and something told her he would be a part of her life.

Benin City, August 9, 1999. 4pm

Kewve slammed the door of his mother's car and waved off the driver, he was glad to be back. The weekend at home started off well, but an extended church service and lunch were all he could take of the Sunday.

Avoiding a speeding *okada* as he trudged along, he soaked in the ambience, slinging his knapsack higher up his shoulder. Music blared from the shops lining the road, their wooden extensions sheltering mostly students. The difference between the campus and the quiet reserved area where his parents lived couldn't have been greater.

He stepped over a covered gutter and into Ochino's Restaurant, his favorite of the bars and food shops on BCPA Estate's main street. As he'd thought, Wale and Osas were already there. He smiled and walked to them. They both had a bottle of Star beer each, and while Osas drank his straight from the bottle, Wale sipped from a large glass.

"Kevwe, you look happy. How're you?"

"So-so," Kevwe replied, greeting them with their usual handshake. "Hey there, get me a Star too." He gestured to the bar girl to bring a glass with it as he sat.

Wale leaned as far back as he could on his chair, and asked about his parents. "Did you tell them of your new girlfriend?"

"What?" Osas shouted, "A girl in two months. That's fast, man."

"Don't mind Wale and his stories," Kevwe replied, laughing. "Do I look as if any babe is giving me sleepless nights? I'm concentrating on my studies."

Wale sat up, "Are my sources not correct then?"

Kevwe continued laughing, "What do they say, your radio stations without borders?"

Wale laughed too. "My sources are impeccable."

"Oh, so you mean this thing na true business?" Osas asked.

"Sure, but you won't know the girl," Wale replied, not bothering to look at Osas.

"Who be the girl?" Osas demanded.

Wale looked at Kevwe as if Osas was not there. "What do you think we should do tonight? Should we go and visit her?"

Kevwe glared at Wale, not liking this part of his friend much. Wale always tried to put Osas down whenever they were together, once calling him a sycophant to his face. On the other hand, Wale treated Kevwe with respect because he felt they belonged to the same social class.

"Who said I had a girlfriend? Even if I did, do you think I'd be visiting her with you?" Kevwe replied with irritation. Turning to Osas, he asked, "Do you want another bottle?"

"Yes o, make them bring am, abeg," Osas replied. "How I go turn down shayo?"

Kevwe ordered the drinks, pushing his bag under the table. He looked up at Wale's laughter, following the pointing arm.

"Prove me wrong, man. If that is not your babe, stay seated here with us, yeah?" Wale said.

Before he finished speaking, Kevwe was on his feet. Wale was right, two girls had just walked past, and the sight of the petite one set his heart racing. He'd thought about her a lot over the weeks since walking her home. Her innocence pulled strings in his heart, and he wished to feel more of that.

3

Benin City. August 9, 1999. 4.30pm

Students bustled about on the popular street as Efe and Nneka strolled back to the hostel after Sunday fellowship. Efe pulled at her scarf, and wished for something better to protect her from the ball of fire overhead. The sun was merciless, and gave her a headache.

"Hey Ife, Ife, wait."

Efe slung her handbag higher on her shoulder and glanced behind them. Someone had called out what sounded like her name, but she wasn't sure.

"Who is he? Did he call Efe or Ife?" Nneka asked.

"I didn't catch what he said." Efe wanted to ignore the caller, but Nneka had slowed then stopped. The person indeed gesticulated at them, so they waited at the side of the road.

Efe squinted against the blinding afternoon sun for a better view, and her heart jumped into her mouth. In the approaching figure, she recognized the guy from a few weeks ago. She'd thought of him often but they had not seen since then.

She flicked some hair away from her face, whispering behind her hand, "I think I recognize him." Just then the sun went behind the clouds, and she opened her eyes fully to see Kevwe Mukoro standing before them.

"Rest awhile strained eyes, cease squinting but just for awhile. Behind the clouds is the sun still shining," Kevwe said with a smile.

Efe recognized the Longfellow quote and had to stop herself from smiling back at his cheerful face. Nneka looked at her as if to ask, "Do you know this guy?" and she hesitated, thinking to deny him, but then she changed her mind.

"Nneka, this is Kevwe Mukoro, and this is Nneka...."

"Nneka, the pretty serpent?" Kevwe teased, extending his hand.

"Oh no!" Nneka laughed, returning the handshake.

Efe smiled, 'Nneka the pretty serpent' was the title of a Nigerian home video, and this was not the first tease her friend had got about the name.

"Ife," Kevwe began, turning to her. "I..."

"It's not Ife but Efe," Nneka corrected, "Efe Sagay."

Efe felt like sinking into the ground as Kevwe focused accusing brown eyes on her, but he didn't comment on the lie, as he continued, "Oh yes, Efe, I haven't seen you in Hall Two for some time. Are you all right?"

"Yes," Efe assured, "Nneka and I just prefer Hall One now."

"Oh, fine. I decided to find out when I saw you pass." He searched her face, and she looked away. She wanted it clear she wished to avoid him, even as she secretly admired his confidence.

"Thanks for your concern," she replied.

"Sure," Kevwe said, his smile unwavering. "See you soon."

As he walked off, she admired him from the back. Kevwe Mukoro was a nice specimen of masculinity. He was well-built and there was strength in his shoulders and arms which made her feel safe. He seemed just under six feet, but that was much taller than her five-five, and it didn't hurt that his face was so striking too. His eyes did funny things to her insides, but there was also an observant intelligence in them she liked.

As she turned away with Nneka, Efe scratched at her nostrils. This guy was surely one to watch out for.

Benin City. August 19, 1999. 1pm

Efe searched through the clothes on her overhead hanger while Nneka slouched on the bed, rifling through a HINTS magazine.

The shirt Efe had on was patchy with sweat, and they were back in her room so she could change before the next lecture. Efe picked out a print top and then put it back. She wanted something less ordinary would in case she met Kevwe. They'd seen often since the last time, and she looked forward to the day they could talk. As she passed through the clothes again, Nneka sat up and dropped the magazine.

"Efe, hurry up please. I don't want to be late and enter wahala with Eboche for this last lecture of the semester."

Efe opened her mouth to reply, and was interrupted by a shout.

"I SAY MAKE YOU NO JUST TRY AM AGAIN!"

Nneka jumped to her feet. "What's happening?"

"Sounds like the girls in Room 20…"

Jane ran inside, breathless. "Abosede and Nancy are at it again!" she shouted, referring to the occupants of the room next to theirs.

By the time they got outside, the girls from the other rooms in the hostel had gathered in the corridor. Efe, flanked by Nneka and Jane, joined the small crowd, craning their necks to see the fight. When it spilled out of the room, Efe found herself beside to the combatants.

"You're a wretched person!" Nancy screamed at Abosede.

"Don't you dare curse me," Abosede shouted right back. She approached the other girl and poked her in the chest. "Don't you just try me, or I will deal with you."

"You fit?" Nancy sneered, moving closer to Abosede. "You're nothing!" Abosede cut her off, with another poke to the forehead.

"I'm warning you, if you touch me…" Nancy did not finish because Abosede shoved her, hard, and she stumbled against Efe.

"Nancy, abeg watch it." Efe stopped snickering and tried to change position. She pushed back at Nancy to maintain her balance and immediately regretted standing so close. As she shifted away, she muttered under her breath, "I don't know why I'm here, more fool me…"

Nancy's shout rode over her words, and her glare scorched. "What! Efe! What did you just call me? So I won't hear again because of you, eh?" Nancy clapped her hands. "Everywhere I go, it is Efe this, Efe that. Make you no vex me, you hear?"

Efe couldn't believe her eyes. What had she done? Was it the one sentence she just said? She heard some people begin to gossip.

"Eh Efe," Nancy continued, "I'm talking to you or have you gone dumb? You no know your mate again, to call me a fool!" She added a jab to Efe's chest for emphasis.

Efe wanted to explain that Nancy must have misheard, but Abosede spoke first, calling Nancy's attention. Nancy ignored her and grabbed Efe's collar instead. "Efe, I say do your worst today."

Abosede and a few of the girls, including Nneka, tried to get her off, but Nancy maneuvered till she had Efe against the wall. Abosede finally forced Nancy's fingers off and pulled her away. Anger twisting her features, Nancy charged, but Abosede stopped her with heavy slaps on both cheeks.

Defeated, Nancy banged into Room 20 with the final words, "Don't worry. It's me and you. Efe, wait for me, you will see."

The girls who had gathered broke into groups. Efe thanked Abosede, and then went into her room with Nneka to change.

"Nancy is always so quarrelsome!" Jane said, walking in with them. "Only Abosede can manage her in the same room."

Nneka hissed. "But Efe, how did you get yourself into it?" Nneka sat down on one of the beds with a groan and wiped off imaginary sweat from her forehead. "Did you curse her?"

"No way! All I did was to push her away." The blouse muffled her reply. "I called myself a fool. Maybe she thought it was her."

"Nancy was so angry at you; I couldn't believe it."

"Why the smile?" Efe demanded. Jane, who had darted outside, now stood at the door with a smirk.

Jane smiled wider, "I heard out there that Nancy loves this guy in her class, but he's only interested in you…"

"Hey, tell us more." Nneka adjusted herself on the bed.

"I don't know more. Maybe Efe does…" Jane sneaked another teasing look at her.

Efe wiped her palms together. "My hands are clean o…"

"You have too many admirers, abi?" Jane joked.

They all laughed, and Efe wondered who it was. Her most recent toaster was Kevwe. Did this mean he told other people about her? When he hadn't said anything except greet her? Trust UniBen students, once one person heard it, the news travelled real fast. She would've rather heard it from him, instead of like this. She threw down the ruined blouse, and left the room with Nneka.

"But what Nancy did was terrible." Nneka said, breaking into her thoughts. "Shame on her! Are you to blame if she cannot land a boyfriend? Do you think it's your new guy who's behind it? What's his name again…?"

"It's Kevwe, and I think he must be the one too."

Nneka stopped immediately. "Is he an Engineering student?"

Efe lifted her shoulders in a shrug. Since the last time they met Kevwe, she hadn't spoken to him much. Usually, when they saw around the campus, it was 'hello' and 'bye'. "The thing is I don't even know. You saw us last week on Omage Street."

"Yes, I remember him better. You gave him a wrong name."

Efe laughed again; she'd thought it would be one of those chance encounters. "Please don't blame me. Anyway, he's been the only one after me since this semester started…"

"I like Kevwe, he's fine. Will you agree if he asks for a date?"

"Slow down jo," Efe replied, "We'll wait and see. It's like everyone knows he likes me, he's lucky I like him too…"

"Now you're talking." Nneka laughed. "But don't let Nancy hear those words."

"Na who born me? The exams are around the corner, and I don't want any injuries. I just thank God for Abosede; what could I have done otherwise?"

"She grabbed you by the collar, and you flapped your arms..."

Efe laughed at the picture Nneka made. "Can you recall how she pushed me to the wall, and then held you off with just one hand? Both of us are flyweights o..."

"And Nancy is the heavyweight champion, Mike Tyson," Nneka retorted.

Efe laughed as the humor of the situation struck her. Tears of mirth streaked her cheeks as Nneka gesticulated, speaking like a commentator in a boxing match.

"First, the opponents in the ring, Nancy and Abosede, take turns to say how strong they are. Efe enters, and Nancy the champion jumps on her. Nneka Okeke comes in as referee, and the champion further displays her strength."

Efe joined in, making the sound of a ringing bell. "Gbagaun!"

"Round two! First opponent Abosede jumps into the fray again." Nneka intoned. "Two fast slaps and the champion is defeated."

They laughed all the way to class, talking about the event.

4

Benin City. August 30, 1999. 11pm.

Kevwe had been reading for some time when the sound of a familiar voice close by intruded on his consciousness. It had rained earlier in the day, and a chill breeze came in through the open windows of the main library.

Outside, the day was darkening, and inside, only an occasional noise broke the silence of the large room; a cough from a student walking in, the rattle of a pen, the scrape of books on the wooden table tops. Now and again, some whispers could be heard, but they were soon shushed. Kevwe took a break from the textbook before him, sat up and listened.

The voice came again from the other side of the partition, and he placed it. It was Efe Sagay; a little husky, but distinctive and well-modulated. Efe kept her tone low as she asked a question. The topic was Accounts, and Kevwe listened as someone replied. This sounded like a good point to interrupt, so he stood and peered over the partition. The pleased surprise on Efe's face when he greeted them spread a smile across his face.

"Let me know when you're ready to leave," Kevwe said, addressing both Efe and Nneka who was there with her. "I'll walk you girls home."

"Okay," Efe said without hesitation, making his heart soar.

After the chance meeting with Efe and Nneka a month ago, Kevwe scouted all the major reading rooms in the campus. His primary aim was to read, but he also wanted to read where he might see Efe. Kevwe had continued seeing Efe from afar, but they never got beyond hello. And now his luck had changed while he was in the main library of all places, with exams in progress.

Kevwe sat back down, smiled to himself and thanked his stars. Three hours later, Efe and Nneka stood, and Kevwe packed up his own textbooks to follow them.

They fell into step on the way leading to the off-campus hostels.

"You're new, aren't you?" Nneka was the first to speak. "I don't think I've seen you around the school before this semester."

"You're right, I transferred from UniLag in June," Kevwe replied. His gaze was on Efe who walked between them. He feasted his eyes on her profile, but she looked ahead as if she wasn't interested in the conversation.

"How do you like our school?" Nneka asked.

"So-so," Kevwe replied.

"What's your faculty?"

"Engineering. I'm in the Electrical and Electronics department," Kevwe replied. More questions came in quick succession from Nneka, and he realized she was a talkative one. "What about you girls?" he finally asked.

"Management," Nneka said. "First year in business admin."

Kevwe filed the snippet of information away, wanting Efe to speak too. As if she had heard his wishes, she asked for his level.

"After exams, I'll be in my final year," he answered with pride, pleased she wasn't aloof from the conversation as he thought.

"Are you looking forward to the big world of engineering?" she asked with a smile.

"So-so," Kevwe replied, grinning. Her normal cheerful nature seemed to have broken through her shyness, like a butterfly breaking off its cocoon. He could feel himself fall for her even more at that moment.

"But I can't wait to get out," he said, "Except I'll miss seeing fine girls like you." The girls started laughing. "Maybe you won't understand because you're Jambites."

"Not anymore o." Nneka laughed. "If you look well, you'll see the next set already in school, and enjoying the campus life."

"What's there to enjoy? Not when you've spent six years in school and still haven't finished a five-year degree."

"We've been lucky," Efe said, "We've not experienced any ASUU strikes yet."

"And I hope you never do." Kevwe smiled at her.

They chatted about the issue of staff strikes in universities till they got to the hostel.

Benin City, October 24, 1999. 11am

Efe returned to school two weeks into the new semester, eager to see Kevwe again. He'd given her a lovely success card the day after the library meeting, and they'd seen a few more times before she traveled. As the two-month long vacation had dragged on, she'd thought of him a lot.

Now she unpacked her luggage and got ready for the hairdressing salon, hoping she would see him on the way. She pushed some books, and a magazine to pass the time at the salon, into her handbag.

"Don't tell me you're going to study?" Jane asked.

Efe laughed, "Books will have to wait for a while o."

"What are those for then?" Joan asked.

"Oh, I'm returning them to a friend on my way back from the salon." She waved her hairdressing kit at the two identical faces looking at her. "Ovie will take me to her cousin's."

"Why didn't you braid your hair at home like you usually do?" Jane gestured at the loose bun on top of Efe's head.

"I missed my appointment because of some work I had to do for my mother," Efe replied.

"Alright,' they both replied at the same time.

"Are you ready?" Ovie asked from the door as if on cue.

"OK, see you later then," Efe said to her room mates before closing the door.

"Thanks for coming over," she murmured to Ovie as they fell into step down the stairs. They had bumped into each other earlier on her way from the bus park back to school. When Efe mentioned needing one, Ovie had insisted her cousin had the best salon.

"It's no problem. But sha, we'll do another TDB. That's the only payment I want."

Efe laughed. "Ovie!"

"Yes now, abi?" Ovie laughed with her. "It's for both of our own good. You're talking as if you did not enjoy the one you did with me last semester sef."

Efe wanted to remind her of the experience with Dr. Eboche, but Ovie spoke before she could.

"Ehen, you've met my boyfriend, Nosa, haven't you?" Ovie's large breasts heaved with effort at their pace.

"What about him?" Efe had met him once when she'd been visiting Ovie with Nneka, and they had all spent some time chatting.

"He said I should warn you about your Kevwe, that new guy who came around last semester..."

"He's not my guy! Ah ah! There's nothing between us o, before one tatafo carries the news to my parents in Warri."

"Haba, wetin you mean now?" Ovie eyeballed her.

Efe laughed to appease her. "Anyway, what about Kevwe?"

Ovie's voice lowered, "They talk say he be secret cult member!"

Efe drew back, eyebrows raised. "I don't believe you."

"Dey there. Don't say I didn't warn you o," Ovie replied, as she kept on walking. "Nosa said he's in one of the most dangerous ones. The school had to be shut down last year because of them."

"Are you sure?" Efe asked, weakened by the implication of Kevwe being a cult guy, and deciding her idea of dating him had to be discarded. Anything to do with cults scared her. She knew of the several measures adopted to curb cultism, one of which was the expulsion of any cultist who was caught. And Kevwe had joined their school in the second semester. Could it be because he was expelled for cultism and had to leave UniLag?

"Speak of the devil," Ovie muttered.

Efe didn't know what to do when she saw Kevwe walking towards them. Should she pretend not to have seen him, or walk by with a smile? He would expect her to chat, but Ovie's news changed things. Efe looked straight ahead, but stumbled when he greeted her. Ovie hissed her name with a subtle nudge. Cold with fear, Efe kept walking till a hand tapped her shoulder.

"Efe, didn't you hear me?" Kevwe asked.

She felt stuck, knowing she must say something, even as her heart raced a mile a minute like a mouse in a cage. If he was truly a cult guy, she didn't want to annoy him.

She avoided his eyes. "Oh, I didn't know it was you." The excuse made no sense, but it was the only thing that came to mind.

"That's fine. How are you? When did you get back?"

"Today," she said, smiling at where his face should be. "Sorry, I have to run, or I'll miss the appointment to braid my hair."

"All right, I will come over to your room later..."

"I'm not sure when I'll be around, but it's OK." As she spoke, she turned away, hoping he got the message.

5

Benin City. October 24, 1999. 5pm

Kevwe had been to female hostels before; in fact, he had been here to see Efe a couple of times last semester. But today he felt self conscious. He was dressed in jeans, a checkered shirt and Timberland high-top boots his brother had sent over during the holidays, but he still worried he might fail to meet whatever standards Efe expected.

After starting a casual friendship with Efe last semester, he'd been ready to bare his mind and ask for a relationship this time. However, their meeting along the road earlier in the day had put a different spin on things. Had she tried to ignore him - or had she truly not seen him? Maybe she had met someone else during the vacation. He knocked on the door with his mind still roiling.

Her roommate opened up the door, cutting short his thoughts.

"Hi Jane," he greeted, as he walked into the room.

At the desk, another Jane looked up from a book and answered, "Hi, Kevwe, how were your holidays?"

Kevwe did a double take as his eyes flew back to the doorway to see the one who had opened up smiling at him. He whistled, amazed to realize they were identical twins. He'd assumed Efe had only one roommate, who always disappeared whenever he came. He'd called the one he saw Jane the few occasions they met, and no one had corrected him.

"Wow," he said again when they were seated opposite him. "You're so identical, no difference at all." He settled comfortably on Efe's bed. "Which one is Jane?"

"I am," they both replied and laughed. After some light teasing, he told them he was also a twin. They talked some more, and he found some kind of relief from not having to see Efe immediately. Fifteen minutes passed before he asked of her whereabouts.

"She came back in the morning, and then left for the salon. She's been gone for hours now, so I'm sure she'll be back soon." Jane replied.

Minutes later, Efe stood at the door. "Kevwe," she whispered, "You're here?"

He couldn't stop the smile which bloomed on his face. "I've been here for a while. I told you I would come." She seemed frozen at the door, and he got the feeling again she didn't want him.

Efe came in and closed the door behind her. Her heart had stopped when she saw him. She had tried without success not to think about him while having her hair braided. He'd said he would come, but she had hoped it wasn't today.

Kevwe stood when she came further into the room, but she motioned him back. "Please sit. I'll join the twins."

"Your hair looks lovely and different," he complimented.

Jane and Joan agreed with him, running their hands through the long strands. Efe tried to engage them in conversation, but the twins soon made their excuses and left. Efe looked at Kevwe in silence, the information from Ovie weighing heavy on her mind. How would she bring it up – or should she?

"It's great seeing you again," Kevwe finally said. To be honest, he'd been thrilled when he saw her on the road. With Efe before him, the doubts that had plagued him after the earlier brief meeting disappeared. He wouldn't say it of course, but he felt like hugging her. Absences truly made the heart fonder because he'd been waiting for her since school resumed two weeks ago.

"How come you didn't return in time?" he asked.

"You talk like the newcomer you are," Efe replied, forcing a laugh. She didn't want him to feel her unease, but still the nerves caused her to babble.

"Lectures don't commence till at least about two weeks into the semester. In the second semester, a week may be enough, but this is the first semester and admission and registration may take up to a month before lectures begin fully." She had said all this in one breath, unable to stop till she ran out of air.

Kevwe laughed. He simply loved watching her speak. A smile lingered on his lips. His smile widened as he concluded he must have misread her reaction when they met earlier.

"How were your holidays?" Efe asked. She appeared embarrassed by his smiles, and got busy opening a packet of digestive biscuits. She took the opposite bed and placed the plate of biscuits between them.

"So-so," Kevwe replied with a shrug of his shoulders, still smiling, "You know how it is with us guys; we have to make business arrangements."

Kevwe reached for the album on her bedside table. He'd looked at it last semester but wanted to see if there were some new photos from the vacation. There were, most in the studio, but some with her family in outdoor shots. He wasn't surprised she looked breathtaking in all of them. He looked up with an even wider smile.

"You know, Efe, you never said where you and your folks stay."

"You never asked," Efe replied.

Kevwe waited for her to say more, but the words that came next weren't what he expected.

"Do you belong to a cult?"

"What!" Kevwe sprang up from the bed at the question.

Efe was silent, only wiping at her nose.

Kevwe became serious. Cultism held a grim fascination among his mates, and he shouldn't be surprised she had heard the rumors about him. Wale had warned him last semester such talk would come up because of his transfer.

"Efe, look at me."

She looked up but didn't meet his eyes.

"I'll tell you the truth now, and I hope you'll accept it over anything you may hear. I am not a cult guy; never have been, never will be."

Kevwe was worried when Efe wouldn't look at him "Then why did you leave UniLag in the middle of a session?" she probed.

Kevwe peered at her averted face before answering. "UniLag had so many issues with student riots and lecturers' strikes. Also, my dad has heart problems, and my mum prefers I stay with them. So right now I live in my parent's house."

Efe nodded throughout his speech, until the last sentence. She looked at him, and then away, pressing her nostrils together.

"What's the problem?" Kevwe asked. He'd noticed fiddling with her nose was a nervous tic she couldn't hide.

"No... no," Efe stammered, "It's just... I thought... you know... you said you lived on BCPA..."

"I do sometimes," he said, glad she was so open about her issues with him. "I also share a flat with Wale, and I stay there when it's too busy or during exams."

"That explains it," Efe said, relief written all over her. She looked into his eyes and smiled.

He smiled back at her, glad to have his address out of the way. "Now will you tell me where you live?"

"We moved to Warri recently from Sapele."

"Where do you people live?" His voice was eager. "My aunt lives in Warri, and I sometimes visit her."

"We're on Airport Road, Effurun," she said.

"My aunt lives in Okumagba Layout now... hmm... I'll visit you one of these days. 'Warri no dey carry last'," he hailed, "Have you heard of it? What of 'Area'?"

"Of course," Efe laughed as she repeated the phrases, fists raised.

"Ahhh, you be real Warri pikin." He couldn't avoid the next topic. "I hope the recent crisis in the city did not affect your family?"

She looked down and sighed. "No, we live on the other side of town, but it was traumatic. "My sister had nightmares, and I'm glad the violence is over."

It was obvious the senseless destruction in Warri depressed her. Kevwe spoke softly, "I mostly heard about the fights on the radio and television. My aunt also complained of hearing gunshots and explosions all the time. She had to move in with another uncle for a while, but she's home now."

Kevwe had heard the violence was a fall-out from the elections, and that things had calmed down a lot. "From the news, the new president did his best. He visited the place, as did the governor."

"I'm glad your aunt's fine," Efe said. "I sometimes wonder why the Warri ethnic groups can't live in peace. Sapele is diverse too, but elections were peaceful there."

Kevwe was drawn in by the compassion in her eyes. She was certainly making a place for herself in his heart. He told himself to focus as she spoke further.

"I think everyone is a bit more settled now; the curfew helped a lot. My father is a lecturer at the Petroleum Institute, but he can't wait for us to leave Warri. If possible, he would like us to leave the country entirely."

"I don't blame them. It can get crazy in Nigeria sometimes."

Efe sighed, "I'm happy things have quieted down now."

When she looked up, their gazes locked and Kevwe tried to still his racing heart. The physical attraction between them heated his skin, and he knew she could feel it too. He smiled when she broke off her gaze and topped up his drink.

"What about you?" she asked. "Where do you live?"

"My parents live in the GRA, here in Benin; so holidays don't quite feel like vacations. We stayed in Victoria Island Lagos for a long while, but packed down here to Benin when my dad retired last year." Kevwe put some biscuits in his mouth. "Why not have some?" He gestured at the saucer, smiling at Efe.

She declined. "That's why you just transferred last semester."

"Mmm," Kevwe agreed with a nod, "And now I'm here with you." Efe looked like a goddess in his eyes. He liked the look of smiling expectation and soft desire on her face, and decided there and then to pursue this to the end.

6

Benin City. November 8, 1999. 7pm

Two weeks after her talk with Kevwe, Efe was in the lecture hall when Joan came in and leaned close, whispering in her ear.

"Are you serious?" Efe shouted, and then hid her face as she everyone in the class stared at her in annoyance at the disturbance. She packed up her books and followed Joan. Her roommate walked off to another reading room while Efe dashed the other way, and made her way to Nneka's room in Edegbe hostel.

She tiptoed through the open door and threw her books on the nearest bed. Nneka, with her back to the door, turned with a jump. They fell into each other's arms screaming. When they separated, they looked up and down at each other.

"You look amazing," Efe said, "How was your holiday?"

"I'll tell you later," Nneka said with a wink, folding her clothes. "What about yours?"

"So-so, my dear," she said, flicking her hand. She'd learnt the phrase from spending so much time with Kevwe. "Nigeria is always the same."

"You mean nothing happened? Nneka waggled her eyebrows. "No new boyfriends?"

"Ha, you know me better now," Efe protested, standing up to help fold the clothes. She had been waiting to share her news with Nneka and could wait some more.

Nneka laughed. "Mmm... listen, I think things have changed a bit. Maybe it's time to start paying attention to boys. I turned down one guy before I left. He's twenty-seven, rich, responsible and the son of my dad's friend. My mum didn't let me rest."

"Your mother knows about your toasters?"

"She knows some of them. This one in particular came through her, so she was the architect, so to say. My mother harped on how old I was, how it was time to look for the right husband, and I should stop rejecting guys, left, right and center. I told her I was just twenty and not yet in the market. My flight to the US was only a few days later, and I was happy to leave."

Efe sighed. She sure wasn't yet ready for any man-talk with her parents. Luckily, she'd not yet turned down anybody they knew. Her mum only mentioned marriage once in a while. "Now tell me what happened in America. It's unlike you to be secretive."

"Wouldn't you just like to know? Nneka asked in return.

"Of course..." Nneka always liked building the suspense, but her gist was worth it. Efe waved her on, sitting closer.

"OK...OK," Nneka said. "The aunt I stayed with told me about this guy who's a student. His name is Dozie. He lives in a different state from my aunt, but he's from my town in Anambra. She showed me his picture, and I spoke with him on the phone twice. He sounded delicious, come and hear *'fone'*. He said he'll call me again, so make I dey wait. Anyway, it's your turn. What's happening in school?"

"It's all about the secret cults o. Do you know the latest?"

"What is it this time? Was anyone killed again?"

"No... but cult members were asked to come forward and renounce their involvement in their secret societies. And that's not all. There's a new government initiative. We have a new anti-cult group with military members. Also, all staff and students must sign an undertaking to show they do not belong to cults. I've done mine, and you will have to do the same before you'll be allowed to register for the new session."

"Wow, school must have been entertaining since then..."

"You'll get to see some of it yourself. And also..." Efe wiped at her nose.

Nneka laughed, pointing. "I recognize that! You've been holding back on me. Is it Kevwe?"

Efe's smiled and nodded, looking anywhere but at Nneka.

"OK, spill before you burst. When did you come back?"

"I came back about a week ago," Efe said. "Kevwe came to visit me the same day."

Efe felt shy about confiding in Nneka. She turned away and folded more clothes. She had seen Kevwe several times since his first visit, and her feelings for him grew each time. "We've spent more time together, and I like him."

"Mmm, so you'll become lovers with him?"

"No..." Efe protested, "We're just friends."

"Sounds like 'boyfriend' to me, but it's not bad o. He's perfect husband material."

"Nneka! Who's saying anything about marriage now?"

"Let me tell you what my mother would say if she knew." Nneka wagged a finger. "Kevwe is in his final year, a serious and responsible guy. And he has..." She paused till she got Efe's full attention, "educated parents!"

"You're so funny," Efe said. She had thought Nneka would say money. "Besides I've not seen him in the last two days, so maybe he's just like the others."

"He better not be, not after you've accepted him."

Efe laughed. "I think Kevwe's real, sha. I don't know why, but I trust him. Do you know Ovie told me he was part of a secret cult?"

"No way!" Nneka jumped to her feet.

Efe readjusted her position on the bed and moved forward. "He denied it when I asked and like I said, I trust him."

"You don't think he's lying to you?"

Efe shook her head. "He wouldn't do that. And I will find out sooner or later, right? Anyway, I'm taking it slow for now."

The way Kevwe looked at her sent butterflies flitting in her stomach, but it also grounded her. He didn't ogle her body even as she felt the attraction between them was mutual. He spoke in a quiet and confident manner which did not detract from his natural flair for humor. He made her laugh often, and also found her jokes funny.

They also shared a lot of interests in common, and he was always encouraging her to be more dedicated to her academics. Her parents would love him, though she worried about how to introduce the idea to them. Kevwe had not asked outright, but she knew he would be her boyfriend one day.

Benin City. November 10, 1999. 4pm

Kevwe was alone in his Edmorton hostel flat a month after school resumed. He still had the place to himself, though he mostly only studied, slept or entertained friends there before heading home. A knock came and he went to open the door.

"Wale!" he hailed.

Wale sauntered in, and dropped his luggage in one corner, "Kevwe the Great," he called. "Man, it's good to see you, yeah?"

Kevwe extended his arm, and Wale responded with their usual handshake and a hug. They unpacked his stuff, and moved to the bedroom where Wale sat, and Kevwe stretched out on the bed. It felt right to have his flat mate around. "So you decided to return?"

"You resumed the first week?" Wale asked, raising his brows.

"I'm just the JJC you called me the other day, but I won't make the same mistake again. Come, let's hear about your holidays. What happened? Did you have a good rest?"

"Good rest? Rest was not in the dictionary." Wale stood up, shaking his head. "I worked full time at the old man's place, and that's twelve-hour days, yeah, even on Saturdays."

"Not bad," Kevwe said, smiling.

"Did you say, not bad?" Wale asked, "See, I want to become a manager after graduation, but my dad is against it. He says he's been too soft on me, and I need to toughen up, yeah? So I have to start from the lowest rung of the ladder, and move up only as fast as I worked hard. That is bad, yeah?"

Kevwe chuckled as Wale continued. "The old man forced me to work off some of the stages now. There was no other way around the issue, so I had to take him up on it, yeah?"

Kevwe chuckled outright.

"This is no joke, man, so just stop those noises." His friend stood up and came ovcr to hit him on the shoulder. "I say the man worked me as if I were a slave; even messengers got more rest than I did."

Kevwe continued to laugh. "Was that why you stayed this long?" he asked, "No wonder you look so slim."

"Others have said it suits me." Wale went to his seat with a shrug and adjusted his T-shirt over his shoulders. "Now tell me about your vacation."

"Well, my dad quizzed me about my plans for the future and I said I intended to run my own company. He says it's best to work for myself, and he helped me to get started."

"You're starting up a company?"

"Yeah, man… so you can imagine my vacation. I had to travel to Abuja, and I was there for about a month with the dad. He made things a lot easier as I rushed from the Corporate Affairs Commission to several ministries, trying to put things in order. Thank God, everything is now in control."

"You're now a managing director, yeah? Kevwe, the boss."

"MD, Executive Director, Chairman, you can call me all of the above…" Kevwe was proud of himself. He had made some connections and one or two contracts.

"How's Abuja? I've heard a lot about that city, yeah? When the old man was a minister, things were run from Lagos, so I've never been there."

"Man, Abuja looks like it's not part of Nigeria." Kevwe stood and moved to the small table-top fridge. "What will you take?"

"There's brandy, yeah? Give me some, and coke."

"No beer today?" Kevwe asked. He got the drinks ready and handed Wale one.

"As I was saying, some of the locations on Victoria Island and Ikoyi can compare a little, but what makes Abuja different is the plan. Wide roads, streets cleaned often and another glaring thing. Unlike here in Benin or Lagos, there are very few cars or okadas on the roads. Beggars are also scarce in the city center; I think my dad said there's a law against them."

"They can't try that in Lagos." Wale laughed.

"What I like about Lagos which Abuja doesn't have are beaches." Kevwe poured more cola into his glass and drank.

"I don't miss Lagos at all; I'll take Ilorin any day. But tell me more about Abuja, what's the area like, yeah? I'm thinking to ask my dad to work my youth service posting to the North. Maybe I'll tell him to make it Abuja."

"That's true; we have to start thinking about youth service. Anyway, the cityscape is incredible. Driving up into Abuja, you see Zuma Rock, this massive hill with a man's face. Aso Rock frames the National Assembly and the president's residence like a picture. Man, you should see it yourself. Each time I went to the Federal Secretariat, I would just stare at all those buildings. Construction continues across the city, and I hope to get some business there."

They exchanged another handshake, and Wale sat back with a low belch. "You did well with your company, yeah?"

Kevwe relaxed too. He smiled at the future he could already see in his mind's eye. Career aside, he had not mentioned that the instant he got to Abuja, he'd dreamed of bringing Efe with him to see it. It wouldn't be bad too to settle there one day together.

7

Benin City. November 22, 1999. 6pm

Kevwe stood in the kitchen of his flat, bouncing on the soles of his feet. He just couldn't relax. Efe was in the living-room, and they were alone again. When she had accepted his invitation to visit him on her own today, he'd been excited and hopeful.

They had seen several times since school resumed, but he hadn't been able to get her in the right mood where he could ask her what had been on his mind for months now. He wiped his damp palms on his jeans, brought out the cooler of fried meat he had cajoled from his mother that morning, and put some in a small saucer. He took a deep breath and picked up the plate.

"There you are," Kevwe said when he found her in the bedroom, and tried to see the two large mattresses on the floor through her eyes. At least, a desk and chair flanked the wall, and the room was neat.

"This is a nice flat," she murmured on the way to the living room.

"Thanks. It's small, but it's enough for us." Kevwe sounded nervous, and hated the silence that stretched between them. Contrary to what he'd told Wale sometime ago, this wasn't easy at all. In his head, he revised again how to broach the topic.

Efe took a piece of meat from the plate he set on the coffee table and bit into it, looking down at her feet.

"Efe," his voice cracked, so he cleared his throat. Kevwe knew Efe was shy, but it didn't help him now. He was afraid she would reject his advances. "Efe, why don't you look at me?"

Efe spoke, her voice coming low and fast, "Kevwe, I know you want to start off where you stopped last semester. I feel I should first tell you that I'm the wrong person for you. I'm simply not interested in such things."

Kevwe felt his heart slow, and then begin to race, and he rubbed his sweaty palms together.

"I want to concentrate on my books alone. I know you want us to be closer, but I don't need any distraction from me and you."

"Is it wrong?" Efe was right. He did want them to be closer.

"No, I'm not saying it is, but please you have to understand me too. I don't think it's wise as students." Efe knew she was not up to the stage of handling a relationship without losing her composure. She liked Kevwe, but he also threw her off balance. It felt good knowing he also cared for her, but she wanted to be careful.

"Efe, listen. You are not a child anymore," Kevwe interrupted, "so let me make this clear. I want us to be close friends." It was true they'd known each other for just a few months, and he hadn't seen her at all for some of these months while they were on break. But she already had a part of his heart.

"Is that so impossible?" he continued before she could speak, "Also, if our relationship matures into anything else, we'll work out where to take it from there."

Kevwe saw the doubts play over her face, and tried to convince her she could call all the shots, and nothing could go wrong. He urged her to trust his words and insisted that since he was in his final year, he was more settled and if she gave them a chance, it could be the beginning of something great.

"Efe, I think I'm in love with you," he declared.

Efe opened her mouth to say something, but he went first. "Okay, okay… I know I joked about it last semester, but now I'm serious."

"When guys on campus say those words, they're usually trying to deceive a girl." Efe said, and told him about one of the twins, who had been undone by those three words, adding on a firm note, "They only want one thing from us girls."

"Has your heart ever been broken?" Kevwe asked.

"No..." Efe laughed, "I just want it to remain that way, in one piece." She was very attracted to Kevwe, but she was scared of where it all would lead. Already their short relationship had its fair share of ups and down. First, giving him a fake name, getting in a fight, and then finding he might be involved with cults and could hurt her if she refused him. Now, those were all resolved, but the future was unknown. Could she handle their mutual desire? Would he allow her decide the speed and direction of a deeper relationship?

"I promise I'll never break your heart, and I won't ask anything you're not ready to give."

They sat in silence for a while. Kevwe knew it would come to this today, and feared he would lose her altogether if she turned him down. While his heart pounded a tattoo in his chest, he gave her all the time she needed to make her decision.

"Efe, I'm not asking for a reply now, only that you don't turn me away. Think about it."

"Well, I can't refuse. But I don't want it to exceed the boundaries of a platonic relationship."

Her small voice hooked, and then reeled in his emotions. Kevwe felt a burst of happiness flare within him. At least, she had not sent him away with his tail between his legs like others. They had started something, and he looked forward to a closer relationship with her.

"I've told you to trust me,"

"I hope you never let down my trust," Efe told him in a lightened mood, and he went to put away the used plates.

Kevwe stepped aside to let Efe go before him out of the narrow gateway; she had suggested they take a walk to inspect the new hostel being erected on campus. As they approached the site, he walked behind, admiring her green blouse and the rounded backside in her jeans. She was everything he admired in a woman, and he couldn't wait till she became his girlfriend.

He suspected the walk was because she didn't want to be cooped up in his small flat, alone with him and a mattress. The chemistry between them was undeniable, though nothing had been said. He increased his pace to catch up with her, and with a smile, he swung her up in the air.

She laughed out loud, clutching the arms about her waist.

"Put me down," she begged, screaming when he swung her around one more time before putting her on her feet.

They swayed together, laughing, until she regained her balance, and then they walked around the unfinished buildings.

"So what of Nneka?" he asked.

"Entertaining her flat mates? She has these great stories from America. Last year, she went with her mum for the summer, but she went alone this time. I wish I had the same opportunity."

"So, you are one of those who believe our dear country Nigeria doesn't measure up to developed countries," Kevwe teased. "Who hunger for constant electricity?"

"But it's true," Efe cut in, protesting. "Who no like better things? Why else are we among the underdeveloped nations?"

"Developing, not underdeveloped," he corrected.

"You can call it anything," she replied. "I told you my parents register for the visa lottery every year, right?" She waited till he nodded for her to continue. "Now I'm over eighteen, they continue to apply separately for me, and I can't wait to go to America."

Efe dreamed of travelling abroad. She knew her parents couldn't afford it, and so the immigration lottery was their main hope. Nigeria was so unstable, and it affected everything. Nothing was worse than living in Warri at this time, with so many bad things happening.

While her family was her sanctuary, she feared something might happen to them one day. Maybe she would feel better when they moved to Lagos, but that would not change the fact she would have better chances in life if she acquired her education abroad.

"The thing is," she said, "I wouldn't spend all my life there, but I wish to complete my education in America. I want to travel and live abroad for some time. I want to experience it all."

Kevwe noted the earnestness in her voice, and how she had opened up more than she had ever done before. He wasn't the biggest fan of immigrating to another country, but he could understand how some might prefer it.

"Hmm… you remember my brother who's in the States?"

"Yes, you mentioned him last semester,"

"We're the only children of our parents and twins too. You have to see pictures of Ofure. I don't have any recent ones of us together because it's been so long since he came to visit but I can bring an album of when we were younger if you want, or we can go to my parents' place."

Efe laughed at his thinly disguised ploy to invite her to his parents' house. Kevwe was a private person, and only shared details of his life on a need to know basis. Their friendship was close; she didn't gossip about everything with him like she did with Nneka, but she felt butterflies and felt her muscles turn to mush when she was in his arms.

This had happened a few other times, and now she preferred not to be alone with him for long. She had been to his flat a couple of times now, but going to his parents' house was on another level altogether.

She was pleased he wanted her in his private life, but she wasn't ready yet. Maybe she would go to his parents' house soon, but now, she would much rather talk about his brother and how it was, studying abroad.

"So why didn't you go too?" Efe was curious.

"It was more like, remain there," Kevwe corrected. "My parents were diplomats, and when they were away, they left us in Nigeria, either with relatives or in boarding houses. However, when they were sent to the States, they took us with them. We both completed our high school there, and then applied to college."

"College? That is not the same as secondary school, is it?"

Kevwe smiled. "Americans use college to mean university. Anyway, my parents were only stationed there for three years before they had to return to Nigeria. I preferred to come with them, and study here. My brother wanted to come too, but because of his profession, I persuaded him against it."

"I can see you call all the shots..." Efe teased.

"No o," Kevwe laughed. "Though Ofure is the younger one, you wouldn't know. He's more stubborn than I am, but let's just say we understand each other."

"Ofure is his name?"

"It's Kerhi, but he prefers his second name, Akpofure, Ofure for short."

"Ofure's good, but 'Kevwe and Kerhi' sounds more 'twinny'."

"It does, right? That's the reason we can't stand it. I think only girls do the let's match everything because we're twins."

Efe's eyes twinkled. "So what's your twin doing there now?"

"Becoming a doctor, and that's why he had to stay. It's much better studying medicine abroad; they have all the right equipment. He had also already been accepted in a good school. He has some years to go before he finally returns to Nigeria, since he will do his residency there too."

Efe nodded, and then asked, "How come you're in different fields? Most twins, like Jane and Joan, study the same courses and even have the same grades."

"I can't answer that question now. You have to wait till Ofure comes back, he's the intelligent one."

Kevwe laughed with her as they continued chatting, and deeper emotions for this funny, beautiful young woman continued to bloom within him.

8

Benin City. February 14, 2000.

"I'm so tired," Efe said, "I just want to go to the hostel and have some rest."

"Let's go for a stroll. Please…" Kevwe sat down beside her and stroked her bare arm.

She looked at him and then out the doors. The sun shone with intensity, and she debated whether to refuse. Her lectures for the day were over, and Kevwe had come to spend time with her. The eager look in his eyes and the questions she'd been meaning to ask decided her. She wanted to know how he felt about her.

Today she would decide how she wanted to continue with this relationship. They'd been seeing each other regularly for the past few months, and all their friends knew them together. But nothing was defined. She winced as she stood and then frowned at her hard and unyielding seat. As they strolled out of the lecture hall, she brushed her braids behind her ears and tugged down her blouse.

When they got to the door, she rifled through her handbag, found and popped on her sunglasses. On the road, the sun, behind them now, was about to set over the treetops. Its rays played on the houses and threw liquid patterns on the waving grasses by the roadside. They took the lane weaving through the campus, leading off to the hostels.

Soon, they turned off the road, and Kevwe steered her to a table in front of Ochino's. A tall, muscular woman swooped on them when they were seated. She called Kevwe by name and fussed over them before finally taking their orders. Efe ordered a bottle of soft drink. Kevwe wanted her to ask for something else, maybe pepper-soup, but she declined. The drinks were brought by a waitress, who also wiped the table before she left them alone.

Efe thought of a way to bring up her question but drew a blank, so she asked for food instead, to give them time. Kevwe said something which made her laugh and she studied his face. The occasions they'd spent together so far had been fun; they had made her realize she liked Kevwe and did not want to lose him without giving their relationship a chance. The time passed and the evening wore on as they talked.

The lighted signpost cast a glow on the dark street when they left the restaurant. On the street of her hostel, she was surprised when Kevwe drew her into an alley. She peered into his shadowed face scared about what would happen.

"It would be good to know how you feel about me," he said, teeth flashing. "Do you think we could have something more?"

He must have read her thoughts because this was exactly what had been on her mind too. She didn't even know what they had now.

"Well... you asked for friendship, right?"

"I think we're beyond that," Kevwe whispered, "and now I want you to be my girlfriend for real. Will you be my Valentine?"

Efe lowered her eyelids. Her heartbeat raced, and she folded her fingers into her moist palms. "I like you, Kevwe." When she raised her face and searched his, she saw how her expressiveness had moved him. Her fists softened, and she allowed her feelings roll off her lips like a confession. "I like you a lot."

She was only afraid she was too young, and would not be able to keep up with him or match his experience.

Kevwe drew her close and wrapped an arm around her waist. "I know you think you're too young, but that only means we have a lot of time. I see a rich future with both of us together, and I'm planning for it, for two of us. Are you with me?"

"I just don't know," Efe said. Sometimes she didn't know how to speak about the boundaries that would make her more comfortable being with him. He was like a magnet she couldn't stay away from, at the same time such attraction had its consequences.

"Look at me." Kevwe stared into her eyes, "I wouldn't do anything you didn't want me to do. I just want to know my plans are not in vain. Are we a couple?"

Efe continued looking at him and then her eyes fell to her twisting fingers. No guy had ever rattled her like this, and none understood her like him. Kevwe held a part of her already. It would be a big shame if she missed what might be the best experience of her life just because she was scared. She nodded with a bent head. His hand, which had been stroking her hair moved to her nape. He brought up the other one and placed it on her cheek, raising her face.

"May I?" Kevwe asked.

She saw his eyes sparkle with anticipation, and she knew what was about to happen. The way he looked at her melted her heart. She couldn't think of anyone else with whom she'd rather do this. She nodded and closed her eyes.

The kiss was a butterfly brush. He kissed both corners of her lips tenderly before finally covering her lips with his. Efe kissed him with her whole being, pouring all her feelings into the kiss. He licked at her lips till she opened them.

He sucked on the softness of her tongue and ran his over her teeth and the recesses of her mouth. He came to her lips again, biting and sucking on them. She soon ended the kiss, pulling away to place her head on his shoulders and hold him as if afraid to let go.

Benin City. August 8, 2000.

Efe wished there was a way to turn back time. Dating Kevwe was lots of fun and their relationship had become tighter over the months. He had even mentioned several times he wanted to marry her. Each time she had brushed it off, not wanting to become too expectant and then get disappointed. She knew if he were serious, she wouldn't hesitate in saying yes, because she had fallen in love with him during the past months. It was less than two weeks since the anniversary of when they met.

But now the second semester exams had started, and for final year students, they came some weeks before the rest of the students. For Kevwe, they were his finals - the degree exams that in UniBen, could determine whether you graduated or got an extra year.

After buying two beautiful cards to wish him success, she did all she could to make sure everything went well. As the first week of the degree exams passed and she didn't see him, Efe dreaded his leaving. She knew he was just busy and needed to concentrate, but that did not make her miss him any less.

Kevwe had vowed not to let her feel it, said he wouldn't leave off sending letters and making her sure of his unchanging love. He loved sending and receiving mail, and he hoped she would reciprocate. Efe wasn't sure if she could match his love of letters, but she would always reply any letters Kevwe sent her. Kevwe had also told her not to allow their separation affect her performance, and Efe had promised to do her best.

But studying had become less attractive than chatting with her roommates, sleeping or staying in bed. Now, a week before her exams, she flipped through a magazine while thinking of their first real kiss. No matter how many more times they kissed, she would never forget their Valentine kiss.

She also recalled times spent at joints around campus or in the town proper, the times spent in Hall 2 and the library, reading together or just chatting in the hot, damp night air. These memories would stay with her when he went away.

She was alone in the room so when a knock came, she went to open the door. A smile broke over her face when she saw Kevwe in the evening light, and she flew into his arms for a long bear hug.

"How were your exams?" she asked at last.

"I've missed you," Kevwe said, feasting his sore eyes on her. Their different schedules in the past week had meant they'd spent the whole exam period apart.

"Are you prepared for exams?" he asked when they were seated.

"So-so." Her exams started next week. "What are your plans?"

"I have to leave Benin for Lagos in about a week. Our set leaves for orientation camp with the early batch, so I need to sort out my new business before going to Ekiti in August."

A sad silence fell after his speech.

"Again?" he asked, "We've been over this, so why tears?"

A lump the size of a big ball of *Eba* clogged her throat. Efe turned and buried her face in his broad shoulders, sobs racking her. "Kevwe, please don't leave me. I don't want you to go...."

"Sweetheart, you have to stop crying. You know I can't stand it." Kevwe brought out his handkerchief, and used it to wipe the tears. "Please stop these tears, they're breaking my heart. I promise I'll always be here for you OK?"

Efe looked at his earnest face, and the security he had begun to represent for her enfolded her. This was a guy who loved her, and he always showed it whenever he could. He believed in her, and supported her in everything, and she didn't want to lose him or what they had together. Her fear was that when he left, the distance would destroy their trust for each, or he would find someone else. She felt fresh tears spill over, but he wrapped his arms around her before she could turn away.

9

Benin City. August 12, 2000.

Kevwe wiped away her tears and offered Efe the shopping bag she had overlooked when he entered.

"This is for you." He tried to catch her gaze, but she looked away as she collected the bag. Opening it, she exclaimed in delight, and she took out a vase of flowers, a bottle of perfume and two beautiful cards. She placed all of them on the desk, and then came over to hug him again, tightly.

The first card contained beautiful words wishing her success, and she gave him a peck after reading. She didn't mind when he turned his face, and their lips clung in a sweet kiss that threatened to last forever. Efe savored the kiss, the sweet and slow meeting of tongues before finally breaking it off to open the other card.

The words were handwritten, and she read them out loud:

I've lost count of the hours
I've lost track of the days
I've lost tally of the months
I've lost even my mind
Thinking about going away
Still I know, I could never lose
The memories we made together
The laughter we shared together
So, though I still have to go
I know I'll always love you

"You wrote this yourself?" Tears in her eyes, she raised her face, and at the expression on Kevwe's face, they became a stream down her face.

"Yes," Kevwe replied.

Efe walked to the opposite end of the room and turned her back. She loved his card, but his coming absence rocked her more.

"Efe, please stop crying." Kevwe came to stand behind her.

"Hey... hey..." He placed his hands on her shoulders and led her to the bed. He sat down close beside her, all thc while murmuring soft endearments into her ears.

"Efe, listen. I won't leave you, okay? I will leave school, but I won't desert you. We've gone beyond that. I love you, and I would like to marry you. Haven't I told you so?" he asked.

"You did," she replied, head bent. "But..."

"But you didn't take me serious," he completed for her. "Well, you better do. Ofure knew about you from the beginning, and I've just told my mum. If it all goes as I plan, we'll get married when you graduate."

"But you're still leaving," Efe said in a halting voice.

"It's just a short separation. I know my dad can ensure I get redeployed to Benin. As for camp, I'll send letters every day till I return."

"You forget we'll have left school for the holidays by then," Efe reminded.

"Oh yes! Not to worry. I already have your Warri address. I'll surely write, and then when school resumes, we'll talk about you seeing my folks if that's okay by you?"

"Yes," Efe said, sniffing and wiping her nose.

"Promise me you won't forget me once I'm out of sight,"

She looked him in the eye, "I love you, Kevwe. There's no way I could ever love another person but you. You are my love, and I want you to be my first love, my last love, and my only love. I can't leave you and I won't ever forget you."

Kevwe was so surprised, he couldn't say a word. He chose to kiss her, passionately exploring the corners of her mouth with his tongue. She kissed him back just as hard, her arms wrapped around him. He broke off to catch his breath.

"I love you Efe, and I will love you forever," he said, pushing till he lay over her on the narrow bed. To keep his weight away, he leaned on his elbows, but she twined her arms round his shoulders, and cushioned him on her curves.

"I'm too heavy for you," he whispered.

"I don't mind," she murmured too, not crying anymore. But her eyes were still wet as she pulled his head down. He met her halfway, returning the kiss full measure, sharing her taste.

He groaned and switched their positions, so he was beneath her. He hugged her and rubbed his palms against her back as their tongues caressed each other. The kiss could have gone on for long minutes or just seconds, but when they pulled away they were both panting. She scooted down till their legs tangled, and her head was against his chest.

"Your heart beat is quite fast," she teased, rubbing her palm where his chest heaved. "Maybe we should kiss again."

"Maybe we should leave before I kiss you, and we can't stop ourselves. I swear, each time we kiss it's like I'm dancing *atilogu*; you've seen that dance?" He laughed against her ear, pushing till she stood. He levered himself up too.

Efe straightened her dress, not meeting his eyes.

"You don't have to be shy with me," he whispered, laughing. "Let's go to Campus Sheraton and have some drinks, OK?"

Efe washed her face, put on fresh powder, and they soon left.

Benin City. August 20, 2000

"Man, what's bugging you?" Kevwe was in the bedroom when Osas sauntered in and slumped on the bed, ignoring the hand he extended for a handshake "What's up?"

"I should ask you," Osas replied with a sniff, "Who could've guessed you'd reject us for of a girl? Wale warned me."

Just then the door opened again, and Kevwe looked up at Wale, who stood there smirking. "What did you tell him?"

"You're neglecting us for her."

"Did I speak with water in my mouth?"

Wale and Osas spoke together, leaving Kevwe confused. He didn't like Wale spreading stories about him, but at the same time, he did not want to hurt Osas's feelings. "What do you mean?"

They stared at him and then they burst out laughing. Osas stood, raising his hands, palms forward. High fives over, Kevwe shook hands with Wale, and Osas slumped on the bed again. Kevwe turned, straddling the chair next to him.

"So now we've confirmed how Efe has taken you over, tell me all about it. Will you get her before we graduate and leave? You know what I mean?" Osas traced a crude hand gesture, and his brows waggled.

"You and your dirty mind," Kevwe laughed.

Wale asked for details, and Kevwe leaned back on the study desk behind him, smiling at the guys who were closest to him in the entire campus. He wasn't used to sharing his feelings, and he looked away. He'd told them when he'd been after Efe, but things were different now. "Not that I don't want to be with Efe that way o, but I can wait. I'm in love with that babe."

"Love eh... love eh," Wale sang, clapping in time, "love eh..."

Kevwe rolled his eyes up to the ceiling, "Stop it," he laughed.

"I don't think your head is screwed on right, yeah?"

"I hope you're not carried away by her pretty face," Osas said.

Kevwe sobered. "Osas, you know me better. Na Efe fine pass all the girls for this UniBen?"

"But she still fine sha."

Wale chipped in, "I would have thought these last few weeks in school with exams over would be for the final flings, yeah? Before one has to go into the world and become a responsible adult with one dull desk job."

"Not with a girl like Efe. She's a real gem, and I don't want to misuse her or lose her..."

"That rhymed too, yeah?" Mockery dripped from Wale.

"Yeah," Kevwe mimicked, "and I'm going to marry her."

"What?" Osas screamed, but Wale said nothing.

"You don't think I mean it?" Kevwe laughed at the face Wale made. "Efe is the one for me, I just know it."

"Don't you think it is too early to know?" Osas asked.

"What about her? Does she feel the same way? Wale asked. "She's just in Year Two, yeah?" He shook his head. "Is she even twenty yet?"

"Soon," Kevwe shifted forward. "See, I'm not saying we'll marry immediately. I have to graduate and she has to, too. But I don't intend to lose her to anyone else."

"Hmmm…" his friends did not sound convinced.

"I have it all planned. She'll be mine."

10

Benin City. August 27, 2000.

Kevwe saw Efe every day until the driver came to collect his belongings. He didn't go with their driver but stayed till Efe had finished her exams for the day. As he stood beside the car his parents had just bought him, he thought of the weeks ahead and a shadow crossed his face. Not that he feared to lose Efe, but he imagined how they would cope with the separation.

As he checked his wristwatch, a hubbub from the direction of the hall signaled the end of exams. Soon, Efe and Nneka walked towards him with smiles on their faces. At least, it showed the first paper of their exam had not been a disaster for either of them.

"Hi! Kevwe, did you decide to wait for us?"

"Yeah, I wanted to make sure..." Kevwe didn't get to finish.

"I'm afraid I have to say goodbye now," Nneka continued, "I've arranged to meet some of my friends at Toseton in five minutes and so I have to run." She glanced at her watch.

"Then let me drop you off," Kevwe offered, wondering if she avoided his gaze. So close, her smile also seemed false.

"No need." Nneka rushed on, "Goodbye, you've been a real friend." She hugged him tight before she escaped.

When Kevwe got into the car, Efe was in the passenger seat, wiping her eyes. Kevwe offered her his handkerchief, and she placed it over her face. When he began to sniff and make crying noises, Efe looked at him and laughed, and he started the engine, glad to have brought a smile to her face.

He drove them to Prest Motel for an early dinner, which turned out to be a silent affair. The restaurant was one of the best on campus, but the food tasted like sawdust in his mouth. Efe seemed lost in her thoughts, just like he was. He wondered how she would cope without him and knew he would miss her too.

If anyone had told him on that first day when he saw Efe walking along the street with Nneka he would feel like this two years later, he would have laughed them to scorn. His plan for this stage in his life had been to get decent grades and build up his wealth. A serious relationship would only come after his brother had returned, and they would seek wives together. Efe had changed it all, and he didn't regret it one bit.

"I'll be leaving for Lagos tomorrow, and from there I'll go on down to the youth service orientation camp in Ado-Ekiti." They were now parked in front of her hostel after dinner, and they had been sitting in the car now for several minutes when he spoke.

"When?" Efe whispered. She could feel the tears again.

"Next month," Kevwe said. Their words were punctuated with long silences, but he just could not ask her to go so he could drive home. "I know you'll be in Warri; can I come and visit you there?" Kevwe smiled at Efe, willing her to face him. When she did, he was silenced by the slow tears making their way down her cheeks. With his chest clogging up and his heart like a stone dropped into a still pond, he put an arm around her shoulders and drew her to him. Her head fit into his neck, and her arms tightened around his waist as she burrowed closer.

"I love you so much Kevwe," he heard her whisper.

"I love you too, a lot," he replied. He tilted her face up and placed his lips on hers. It was a soft kiss, meant to give and receive solace. She reciprocated and they spent the next five minutes wrapped in each other's arms, their lips clinging.

When he finally couldn't bear it anymore, Kevwe told her in a voice made gruff by passion and tears it was time to go. He drove off feeling as if he should damn the rest of his future and stay behind in UniBen for her. He knew the night would be the longest they had ever spent. Efe and her roommates would get no sleep if she kept crying like that, and neither would he.

◆◆◆

Warri. September 28, 2000.

Efe couldn't stop thinking of Kevwe. She was back at home with her family, and had received a couple of letters from him, but she still missed him like mad. As she daydreamed about him while her fingers braided Alero, her younger sister's hair, she was interrupted by Gbubemi's call from downstairs.

"Efe! Efe!"

"What is it?" She continued weaving, knowing her ten-year old brother, loved pranks. She wouldn't be surprised if his call meant nothing, or it was to ruin her concentration.

A few moments later, Gbubemi put his head in the door and frowned. "I know you find it hard to take me serious, but you have a visitor, a man, downstairs."

"Where is Mum?" Efe asked with suspicion.

"She's in the kitchen, but I'm sure she'll soon come to check," he replied, adding, "I think the man is one of your many admirers o."

Efe chased him out with a comb, put some powder on her face and skipped downstairs. At the foot of the stairs, her eyes went wide with surprise at the person sitting comfortably in their sitting room. Her scream was not diminished by the presence of her mother, who stood at kitchen the door with arms folded.

"Kevwe!" She jumped down the stairs and stood before him in the next second. Her lips felt as if they would tear if they smiled wider, but her mother's glare reminded Efe she could not throw herself into his arms like she wished, so she settled for a hug. "I'm so glad to see you!"

Kevwe was pleased by the overjoyed look on her face at his surprise visit. His smile vied with hers in his own happiness.

"He informs me he knows you from school." Mrs. Sagay moved to the sitting room and took the double couch facing the television.

Efe perched on the arm of Kevwe's chair after he sat down. "He's Kevwe Mukoro, a great friend… I told you about him..."

"Oh, my dear, how are you?" her mum enthused. "How is your service so far?"

"Everything is alright, ma." Kevwe was glad Efe had told her mum about him. He smiled because she looked as if she was in support of the relationship.

"Efe, go and bring him something," her mum commanded. She faced Kevwe, and Efe knew he was about to get some tough questions. Efe guessed her mum had thought Kevwe was just another school boy. Her mum had not expressed this much interest during their brief talk soon after she arrived home.

Efe left through a door leading off the sitting room, and returned with a saucer containing a wedge of fruitcake and a bottle of chilled soft drink. In the kitchen, she'd heard her mum extracting Kevwe's details - his life and his hometown, down to his village. When she came in, he talked about his parents, saying they were retired. Efe set the items on the table in front of him and sat in the opposite chair.

Once her mum excused herself and went into the kitchen, Efe ran to Kevwe's chair and hugged him, giving him a discreet kiss in the process. Pulling away, they looked at each other, their eyes speaking volumes. She'd missed him so much.

"So you're only 'glad' to see me? Don't you still love me? Kevwe whispered, his hand lingering on her waist.

Efe gave him a deep kiss in reply and then sat again on the arm of his chair. "I'm overjoyed to see you. Is that better? And thanks, thanks, thanks... for the cards and letters. Now tell me all about your orientation camp; I know your letters were just a summary."

"At camp, only thoughts of you kept me going."

Kevwe narrated some of his experiences, telling her about the bugle which woke them up so early it was painful, and about climbing ropes. It sounded like fun, and she asked to see photos of him in uniform soon. He also described marching under the sun and rain and about his platoon and their strange commander called 'Banger Banger'. As she laughed, her parents came in from opposites sides of the room. Her father came in from the front door and her mum from the kitchen. Efe sprang to her feet immediately.

"Hey, welcome darling," her mum greeted, embracing her dad and whispering something to him. Her dad's face had tightened on seeing Efe with a strange man, but he relaxed a bit more as he came into the sitting room. He sat down on one of the chairs, and Efe went to pull off his shoes, taking the shoes and his briefcase out of the room.

"Good evening sir," Kevwe greeted. "Welcome," he added after an instant of tense silence. Efe's father, Mr. Sagay was of average height, dark and quite stocky.

Mr. Sagay looked him over, "What's your name, young man?"

"Kevwe Mukoro," Kevwe stated, trying to sound more confident than he felt. Mr. Sagay was dressed in a safari suit and reminded Kevwe of the lecturers he'd left behind in UniBen. Soon, Efe returned, and he drew strength from her wide eyes and her smile.

"Hmm," Mr Sagay said again looking from the tip of Kevwe's head, down his well-cut three-piece suit to the toes of his Italian shoes. "What brings you to Warri?"

"I came to see Efe, sir. My aunt also lives in Okumagba."

Her mum motioned Efe to come with her and leave the men alone. She dragged her feet as she followed her mum into the kitchen.

"What do you think, Mum?" Efe asked, once the door was shut. The steam from the banga soup on the cooker flavored the small space. Mrs. Sagay did not reply as she stirred some bitter-leaf into the simmering sauce and asked Efe to fill the electric kettle. Finally, she dropped the spoon, smiled and drew Efe closer.

"Do you really like him?"

Efe looked down, "I think I love him, Mum."

Mrs. Sagay laughed. Efe was her first daughter, and she wanted her happy, as long as her husband approved. She believed everything would be fine, by the grace of God. Efe had made a superb choice with this young man. He looked quite conscientious, already had his own company and was from a respectable family too. He even had family in Sapele, so enquiries would not be difficult to organize.

"I think Kevwe's okay," she said.

"You do? Thanks, Mum," Efe said, hugging her mum.

In the sitting room, Kevwe went through an interrogation much more stressful than the one from Efe's mum. When Mr. Sagay seemed satisfied, he invited Kevwe to lunch.

"Thank you sir, but I've got to be leaving."

"All right," her dad said, and called aloud, "Efe…"

When Efe came out, he told her to see Kevwe off and come back immediately to attend to his food. "Do you hear me?"

They only squeezed hands before he got in his car, promising to see her the next day, when they would have more time together.

11

Benin City. November 11, 2000.

Efe resumed for her third year in a much happier mood.

During Kevwe's brief stay in Warri, they'd gone to the Shell Sports Club with her younger siblings. They had also gone for dinner at the Wellington Hotel in Effurun.

It turned out he had some problems about being redeployed to Benin after leaving the camp. She wasn't too happy about, so they discussed ways to keep in touch while he was away. Her dad frowned at them over the rim of his reading glasses when they got home by 9 o'clock, but had exchanged some pleasantries with Kevwe.

Now, Efe walked into her hostel room humming her favourite tune, 'The Only One', by BB Winans and Eternal. The song had been at the top of the British charts some years ago, and the radio stations still played it. A knock sounded on the door, and she went to open it. It was Nneka, her face beaming.

"Halloo ... and welcome back!" Jumping up, she gave Nneka a massive hug, and then she closed the door. Settling on the bed, Efe continued folding her clothes into the room's shared closet.

"How was your vacation? Any marriage proposals?"

"How did you know?" Nneka asked, taking a packet of cream crackers from the cupboard. "An irritating line-up of suitors wouldn't let me rest. Mmm… I tried to rebuff them, but they all had the green light from my parents to present themselves o. Worst of all, most of them were from my town. Ehen, you remember that student I told you about, the guy I spoke with while I was at my aunt's place in America last vacation?"

Efe nodded, waiting for Nneka to finish a mouthful of crackers.

"His parents want to get him a Nigerian wife, and he says it's no one but me. My hands and my legs are clean. I wash my hands of them all." Nneka stood up and swept each hand across the opposite arm, from shoulder to wrist, as though ridding herself of dirt.

Efe laughed till tears flowed from her eyes. "You outrageous girl, I thought you liked Dozie. He called you a few times last semester, didn't he? All the way from America."

Nneka denied she liked him, protesting they had not met each other and that she was not ready for a long-distance marriage. Efe understood because her relationship with Kevwe since he moved to Ekiti State was hard enough as it was. She missed him so much sometimes and wished she could call him every day.

She went on to tell Nneka about Kevwe's visit during the holidays, and how caring he was despite the long distance between them, always sending letters or calling. Nneka wanted to hear everything including the plans Kevwe had for them if it turned out Efe's parents and her family won the visa lottery which they had applied for again.

Efe confided they hoped to get married, and the talk moved to wedding colors amidst much laughter. From then on, Kevwe came often to visit her in school, at least once a month. He had not been able to redeploy his youth service assignment to Benin and now worked with the Ekiti State Ministry of Power and Steel.

He also continued seeking out small contracts for his new cooler manufacturing business. Most times he came, he took her out to one of their favorite bars and then back to the hostel, they would share a long goodnight kiss in the car.

"I wish we could stay here forever," Kevwe said on one of those visits, placing his head against the car seat. She leaned back too, and he stroked her hair against the headrest.

Efe traced the outline of his lips. She remembered the pleasure she'd found in those lips several times and reached out to hug him.

"I love you," she whispered into his ear.

He took her hand in his and kissed her fingertips, then her palm. She smiled, not having expected such a sweet, gentle gesture.

"I love you too," he replied, staring into her eyes.

Efe touched her lips to his and was not surprised this time when he turned it into a deep kiss. His eyes were open, and she felt as if she could drown in their liquid brown depths. His love and passion for her were written there.

Efe could feel a flood of sweet passion; unlike anything she had ever felt before, running through her veins. She shut her eyes and gave herself in to it. As the kiss intensified, she opened her lips and wrapped her arms round his neck.

His mouth was hot, and the kiss tasted of the wine they had earlier. Every time they were together, each time they kissed, she wished it would never end. This was the most exciting feeling she knew. He broke the kiss but kept his face close. She hugged him till it felt as if every inch of their skin touched. At that moment, nothing made her happier than being in the arms of the man she loved.

However, Efe was also frustrated having to make out only in the car with Kevwe whenever he visited. When he nuzzled her neck, she knew it was a prelude for them to stop. She looked at him under her lashes, wondering whether it was time to go further.

"Come inside," she finally whispered into his ear.

"Are you sure," he asked, searching her eyes.

"Yes, just for a while. The twins travelled."

Kevwe felt like a teenager as Efe stepped out of the car giggling. He killed the engine and followed her. He didn't know what to expect, but he still checked his wallet to be sure there were some condoms. The atmosphere hinted at something serious. He wasn't sure she was ready for sex yet, with all it entailed and well, some protection wouldn't hurt if they did decide to go all the way.

Inside her room, they flowed into each other's arms. Efe moaned and her head dropped on Kevwe's shoulder as he slipped his arms under her fitted blouse, and rubbed her back.

When his hands moved to her front, the sensations running over her body became exquisite. He pressed open-mouthed kisses on her forehead and her ears. Aching to touch him too, she wrapped her hands around him. Kevwe pushed her down on the bed, one of his hands gliding over her thighs.

More sweet and drugging kisses followed as they both explored each other's bodies with hands and lips. When Kevwe put his full weight on her, his arousal pressing urgently into her thigh, she noticed her blouse was completely unbuttoned, her skirt riding around her hips, and felt the last of her resistance slipping away. Eyes closed, she brought his face to hers for a long kiss, wishing it would never end. When he pulled away, Efe remained that way, knowing he was right there.

"Can you help me put this on?" Kevwe's voice brought her out of the lull.

Efe opened her eyes and turned to him, looking away instantly in panic. A condom strained halfway down his erection and sweat beaded his shirtless torso. It was as if a bucket of ice water had been dashed in her face, draining her passion. She caught hold of one of Kevwe's hands which again stroked her intimately, and said in a low, husky voice, "Kevwe, I think we should stop now."

Kevwe lay beside her, and his hips moved involuntarily against hers. "I thought you wanted this... Efe," he moaned in longing, "I need you now..."

"I'm not ready. Please Kevwe." Efe fought her feelings.

He took a deep breath and let it go with a gust. Sanity returned to both of them as he rolled away. Efe breathed again.

Kevwe sat up on the other side of the bed with his head bowed and scratched his head. He looked at her. Efe had pulled down her skirt and buttoned her blouse. She felt like sinking into the ground as she watched him remove the condom and begin to put on his clothes. She knew it was better that they had stopped now. She wouldn't have been able to look at him the next day if they'd continued.

"I'm sorry," she said when he was fully dressed.

"I guess we both are," Kevwe said, smile tight. He stood but didn't meet her gaze. His heart raced, and his erection felt trapped in his underwear. He stretched and adjusted his trousers.

"I have to go now."

"I'm really sorry," Efe said again.

At the door, Kevwe stopped and glanced at her. An awkward silence stretched between them, and Efe stroked her nose.

"See you next month? I'll call you when I get to Ado."

She looked up at him in relief. "OK."

Efe did not sleep much that night, and for the first time since they became friends, she couldn't bring herself to confide in Nneka the next morning. The feelings were too new, too intimate; too... she didn't know the words to use in describing how she felt.

However, even though she couldn't talk about it, she didn't seem able to put it out of her mind. The day's lectures passed in a blur, she talked, joked with her friends, but the experience with Kevwe remained at the front of her mind.

Every spare moment after that day found her thinking. Sometimes she smiled dreamily over the memory of her near sex experience, at other times she frowned. Still she kept the dilemma to herself. Her immediate problem was whether she could stop the way she felt if she found herself in such a situation with Kevwe again.

Their wedding was planned for after her youth service, when his brother would be around, and that was two years in the future. Did she intend they would both remain celibate in the interval? If so, then how was she to tell Kevwe so it would not be an issue?

She asked herself the same question several times. Other questions also began pop into her mind at oddest moments. Should she stop any form of intimacy between them, or should she just allow nature take its course? Was there a way to ensure such situations never arose again? Did she even want them to stop?

She realized what she feared more than anything else was an unplanned pregnancy. It wasn't as if she cherished her virginity that much, and she trusted Kevwe would not abandon her.

These thoughts ran through her mind when reading, during lectures, especially when she was alone. Then she made up her mind, one day Kevwe came to visit her, not to stress over whatever would happen. She knew Kevwe would not do anything she wasn't ready for or didn't want to do.

That day, after going to Mr. Biggs, they dropped Nneka off at the hostel and went on to a nightclub. She spent most of the night wondering if he would make a move on her, but he didn't. When he dropped her off at the hostel later with just a chaste kiss, she didn't know whether to be relieved or annoyed.

12

Benin City. July 3, 2001

On his first visit that month, Kevwe surprised Efe by requesting they go to Hotel Doris Dey, a prestigious hotel in the city. They had enjoyed their first visit there, and over another sumptuous dinner, they discussed plans for his business. After dinner, they moved to the nightclub and the conversation turned to her school life, and future plans. Kevwe excused himself to see the DJ and soon some R&B music pervaded the air. As the tape continued, Efe realized it had exactly the same selection of tunes she loved playing in her room every time. It was an unbeatable collection of her favorites in the top fifty hits of the past years.

When they finished their drinks, he led her to the dance floor. There, they stood close together as they danced dreamily round the dance floor. Kevwe was a superior dancer and simply allowed her body move with his. She was carried away by the feeling of love as 'A Whole New World' played in the background. Kevwe's hands circled her, his left palm warm on the small of her back.

"We fit together very well, don't you think?" he whispered.

She nodded, they fit together much more than she'd ever thought. They had danced several times before, but tonight was different. Heat raced along her nerve endings as she inhaled the clean smell of him, laced with his usual cologne.

Efe was sorry when it was time for the live band to start, and they returned to their seats. Kevwe excused himself and again she watched him weave his way to the band. He said a few things while pointing at her and the band members all nodded. He came back to his seat and held her hand across the small table.

"Sweetheart, there's something I wish to ask you." As she made to speak, he shushed her. "Hear me out, okay?"

She nodded, eyes fixed on him.

"Efe, you know I love you. It's been two years since we met. It's over a year since I asked you to be my special friend and you accepted. Over this period, our relationship has grown. I want us to take this to the next level. I want us to promise our future together."

Efe remained silent. It was true she loved him, and she knew he did love her. They'd had their ups and downs but had weathered them better than most of her friends, like Nosa and Ovie, who had split up since he graduated. But wasn't she too young to promise the rest of her life to someone else? She was not even yet twenty-one.

"Kevwe, but we're both so young."

"I'm not so young anymore, Efe. I'm twenty-six, and I have my own business. I know you're young and have most of your life ahead, but we can take this first step now. There's no doubt in my mind. I need you, Efe." He stared intently into her eyes. "I want to spend the rest of my life with you, to wake up in the morning and see you, to go to bed at night looking at you. I want you to be the mother of my children. I know I'll not find another person who suits me the same way you do."

The emotions choked her and Efe looked down at her fingers. She didn't know why she hesitated. Though she was yet to meet his parents, her family knew him and liked him. He was the only serious boyfriend she had ever had. When he looked at her, she tingled at places she didn't know could feel.

She sneaked a look at him from under her lashes as his deep voice twined into her thoughts, "I promise to marry only you. You will be the only woman in my life. I want you to promise me the same. Please say yes."

Warmth infused her face at his words, and she answered softly, "Yes Kevwe, yes, I promise."

She meant her words with every piece of her. Kevwe had shown her what devotion meant; much more then the sensual images which flooded her mind. She could spend hours with him talking, and not get bored. He chose her over his friends anytime. And yes, she also knew he desired her, and they would have a great sex life.

"You'll never regret it, I promise." He let out a sigh of relief and came to kneel beside her, kissing her fingers one after the other. When he got to the third, he slipped on the most beautiful promissory ring she'd ever seen. A small stone winked in the middle of a narrow band of gold. She had not expected he would go this far, and tears rushed into her eyes.

"I love it so much," she breathed, locking her arms around his neck.

The people around their table who had noticed the proposal clapped then. The band leader stood and cleared his throat. "This song is dedicated to Miss Efe Sagay, the most beautiful girl for Mr. Mukoro, and if I may say so, the most beautiful lady in this room. The song is titled "Heart and Soul, all I promise to you."

As the slow number started, Kevwe drew her to her feet, and with a brief kiss, he led her to the dance floor. The whole house applauded before other couples joined them on the floor.

Benin City. August 8, 2001

Not minding the cloudy weather, Kevwe made his way down to Benin for the first time that month. It was all over the news that violence had broken out in Warri again, and he wanted to see Efe and make sure she and her family were safe. After dropping his things at his parents' place, he called on Wale, and together with Efe and Nneka, they went off to Oluku Junction.

There, they settled in one of the bars, eating peppered snails and drinking palm wine while discussing politics and school. There was a heated debate on the Warri crisis by the group beside them and soon insults flew.

"Lazy amphibians," one said, shaking his fist. "Itsekiri are all liars and traitors! Na me talk am, una dey too greedy."

"Urhobo nko?" another asked. "You ingrates and fortune-hunters, you want to be middlemen, so you can eat from both sides of your mouth!"

"No mind am, e no dey shame."

"Me no dey shame? Damned mulatto! Is it not your mother's wantonness that gave birth to you and all the other half caste Itsekiri children?"

"I go box your mouth, wretched Urhobo man, if you mention my mother again!"

The mudslinging degenerated to fighting, and Kevwe decided it was time to go. He dropped Wale, who had to retake his finals, at the old flat, then Nneka at her hostel. When they got to Osasogie, Efe made to say goodnight.

"Don't go yet," Kevwe said. "Tell me more about the riots in Warri. I heard about them all the way from Ado, that it was caused by a new local government headquarters."

Efe pursed her lips. "Yes, it was that sort of thing," she said. "I don't know if all this tribal politics will ever stop."

She'd heard some people say the Itsekiri were dominating the new local government council, and the Urhobo are not happy. She thought the Ijaw were also involved, but wasn't sure. The fighting spread from Okumagba Avenue, and it had lasted two days before the Effurun Battalion soldiers stopped it.

The unnecessary loss of life and property for her were the crux of the matter, and which she felt not enough people were paying attention to.

"My mum's shop burnt down and she lost everything inside. Some say she was lucky..."

Kevwe hissed. "Lucky, they say? I can't believe the extent of our acceptance of these things. Has the government set up an inquiry to find out the culprits?"

Efe shook her head. "This makes my parents even more eager to leave the country."

"I don't blame them. Did they apply in the current visa lottery?"

"Yes." Efe replied. "But my father is fed up. He's on his Ph. D now and wants to get transferred to Lagos, and my mother can't wait to leave too." After some silence, Efe asked, "Do you think we should worry about this whole Urhobo and Itsekiri thing?"

"You mean about us? Did your parents say anything?"

"No... I was just wondering. What about yours?" The quarrelling men at the Oluku joint had made her realize being from the same town with Kevwe, with the same culture, might not be enough for people for whom tribal affiliations ranked higher. She truly wanted to be with Kevwe, and it scared her that a situation like this which was totally out of their control could affect their relationship.

"My dad was a diplomat, so he's above this kind of parochial stuff. As for me, I wouldn't care even if you were from Mars because I love you."

"I love you too." Efe kissed his cheek, reassured, and smiled. "I have to go now."

He brushed away the curtain of her braided hair and kissed her soundly on the lips. "I will be here next week. See you then?"

She nodded and stepped out of the car.

After that, Kevwe continued going to Benin regularly, only cutting back while Efe prepared for her third year finals. National service would soon be done, and since he didn't want to live with his parents when he returned, Efe helped him hunt for a place that would be their first apartment.

After one such search, he told her he would be going to Lagos for some business, but he would be back before the month ended. More important, he said, was he wanted to take her home and introduce her to his parents as his fiancée.

13

Benin City. October 26, 2001.

Two weeks after accepting Kevwe's request to meet his parents, Efe stood beside her bed staring at the discarded dresses, blouses and trousers that covered most of it. After promising to marry him, she couldn't have turned him down. He'd been thrilled when she accepted, and said they would be staying at the family house for the whole weekend.

Immediately he dropped her off, Efe had rushed straight to Nneka's hostel. Ovie was there too, and they both tried to calm her. They reminded her she had been to the house in GRA before and met his mother a few times. She fired back she was always with other people, and had insisted Kevwe introduce her as just one of his school mates. After that, they agreed with her that meeting the parents-in-law was never straightforward and that made her even more nervous.

Since then, she worried about Kevwe's parents, and how they would receive her as a potential daughter in law. What if they didn't like each other? What if his mother hated her? What if they didn't get on well? His father was extremely travelled and educated; would he think her too young and inexperienced, and their marriage plans foolish?

Sometimes she wondered if they had been too hasty to promise to marry each other without involving the parents. But Kevwe said this wasn't like a proper engagement, he just wanted them to be sure of each other.

"Efe Sagay," Nneka called, coming into the hostel room as Efe stared at herself in the mirror. "I saw Kevwe downstairs. Do you know he's waiting?"

"Yes, Jane told me." Efe tugged at the pale pink T-shirt she wore and pulled it over her blue jeans. "Do you think this is okay?"

"It looks great. Now go on with you, I'll clear the others up later."

"Thanks." Efe gathered her already packed bags and hugged her friend. "Wish me luck," she said going out of the room.

Nneka followed behind, laughing. "My fingers are crossed, but it'll be fine."

Efe knew her friend thought she worried too much. Nneka and Ovie agreed that since Kevwe's parents had been diplomats, they were likely to be liberal, and would welcome her more than any other kind of parents. But it didn't stop her heart from racing as she slid into the Honda Prelude Kevwe had come with and popped her bags over the seats.

He leaned across and gave her a small kiss on the cheek.

"Why did you keep me waiting? Don't you know how much I missed your beautiful looks?"

"Welcome, sweetheart, I'm sorry," she said as Nneka put the rest of the luggage in the back, and then they were on their way.

"Here we are," Kevwe informed her half an hour later. The house was in the GRA, off Gabriel Igbinedion Way, and not too far from the golf course. It was a two-storied structure with a pillared portico and netted casement windows. Sunlight glinted off the water in a swimming pool on the far side of the house. Kevwe smiled at her, and butterflies started a wild dance in Efe's stomach.

"Relax," he told her. He jumped out and came to open her door.

That was the gentleman she loved in him. She remembered a night they'd gone for a party. The evening had been warm, and she'd worn a sleeveless black gown whose swirling hem just got to beneath her knees. By the time it was ten, the weather had changed, and become chilly. Kevwe had removed his blazer and draped it over her shoulders. The other girls had looked on in envy till they'd left around midnight.

Efe got out and allowed the landscaped compound, the neat lawns and flower runners to soothe her. She helped him with the bags, and a flight of concrete steps led them to the solid front door.

Kevwe pressed the doorbell, and a uniformed maid opened it. "Welcome, Master Kevwe."

"Thanks, Eno," Kevwe gestured at Efe's bags and added, "Take those to the guest room, okay?"

The girl moved towards an ornate staircase, and Kevwe led Efe into the sitting room where both his parents watched television. Her knees shook. She had never met both of them at the same time before. With Kevwe's palm supporting her elbow, she picked up her feet and stepped forward.

"Good evening, Mum, Dad," Kevwe said, "This is Efe."

Efe bent low at the knees as she said her own greetings. For a long moment, tension stretched as they studied her. His father inspected every inch of her skin, always returning to her face. Efe wiped her forehead in case she had picked up something.

"Please sit down my dear, you're welcome." It was Kevwe's mother who finally spoke. She smiled as she got to her feet. She was a matronly looking woman and wore a light George wrapper and blouse patterned with peacock feathers.

"Thank you, ma." Efe walked to the nearest settee, mystified at the welcome. His father still considered her as if she were a piece of meat he would not purchase. She shook the thoughts out of her head and focused on Kevwe.

He hugged his mother and shook hands with his dad.

"How was your trip?" Chief Mukoro finally asked.

He had a deep voice which surprised her because he was rather thin and spare. His head was covered with sparse grey hair and was set forward on his shoulders by a long neck which gave him a slight stoop. He wore a lace dashiki and plain trousers with dark beads round both wrists. Some of his fingers sparkled with rings too.

"Everything went well," Kevwe sat beside Efe on the settee.

"You're welcome," his mother said again. "We've heard a lot about you," she said to Efe. "You'll spend the weekend, right?"

"Yes ma, thank you so much." Efe looked sideways at Kewve's father and was shocked at the disdain in the man's eyes.

"Efe, your name is misleading," he said. "You could be Bini or Urhobo, but I don't think so. What's your full name?"

"My name is Toritsefe Sagay, sir." Sitting up straight, Efe understood the hostility was because of her tribe. The stare when they arrived had been seeking a tribal mark. "My parents are from Sapele. We live in Warri now."

"Why am I not surprised?" Chief Mukoro stood up and stared at Efe from head to toe again. "Damned Itsekiri."

His lips thinned, and his nostrils flared. Large teeth flashed as he ran his tongue over the upper row twice, sucking his teeth in a hissing manner each time.

"Tega, please." Kevwe's mother said.

He ignored her, sucked on his teeth one last time and then marched out of the room. Efe stared in silence at his father's retreating figure and then looked over at Kevwe.

Kevwe was shocked. Was her ethnicity that important to his father? His parents had known about Efe this last year because he told his mother once he started youth service about a girl in university he was serious with. He knew she'd passed it on to his father who, though he hadn't pried, had sometimes teased him about the campus romance. He'd never shown any sort of hostility. Now he hadn't even bothered with a welcome before going off into a tribal rant. Kevwe looked at his mum in enquiry.

"Mmm... Efe, please don't take it personal," Kevwe's mother assured before she turned to him. "Kevwe, your father has been in a very bad mood since morning, so I don't think it's your girl."

Efe thought the excuse was a cover-up for her husband.

Kevwe turned to her. "Let's accept what my mum said. It's not about you. My father is not usually like this. In fact, he's never like this. By tomorrow, I know you'll see a difference. Meanwhile, come upstairs, I'll show you to your room, and you can change for supper. It's been delayed till eight for us."

He stood up while talking, and Efe rose with him.

"You're welcome my dear. Relax, okay?"

"Thank you, ma."

As she clambered the stairs, her mind whirled. She had not expected to run into problems with his father, and not about tribalism. In a large room, Kevwe excused himself with a brief kiss and hurried assurances. The room was well furnished but didn't lift her spirits, not even after she cleansed and freshened up her face. His father's hostile reaction had spoiled the day. Who would have thought such an educated man was tribalistic?

Supper was a strained affair. Kevwe's father maintained a tense silence that prevented everyone else from expressing themselves. Even the servants knew something was amiss, they crept in noiselessly with the dishes, staring at Efe with pity as they moved around the dining room. Depressed and annoyed, her mood wasn't lifted by Kevwe's smile across the table.

After the meal, they retired to the living room. His father spoke now, but, not to her. Tired of being rebuffed each time she tried to join the talk, Efe asked to be excused pleading a long day of lectures. Kevwe walked her to the bedroom and left after a short while, promising to mollify his father on her behalf.

Efe woke to a cockerel crowing outside her window, but a look at her watch showed it was far from dawn. She turned over and found she needed to go to the toilet. Getting out of bed, she tied a patterned wrapper over her short nightgown and walked down the corridor to the shared toilet. On her way back to the room, a cough stopped her in her tracks. It was Kevwe's father.

"Good morning, sir," Efe instinctively tugged up her wrapper as she knelt, and averted her eyes in respect.

"You say you're Itsekiri? Don't you know there's a problem between the Urhobo and the Itsekiri in Warri right now?"

Efe nodded, "I do sir…"

"And what do you think about it, eh? Just a few months ago, you Itsekiri murdered some more Urhobo people in your continuing apartheid against us. I know you children of nowadays put no stock by your history, but let me make this clear to you. We may both be from Sapele, but we're not the same at all!"

Efe flinched at the forceful tone.

"Kevwe is from a ruling house of the Okpe Kingdom, and stands to inherit my place as a representative of the Urhobo people in Sapele. I am a chief and cannot in all fairness allow this relationship between you and my son to continue."

"But sir…" her eyes widened as the man pointed a be-ringed finger at her.

"I've got just a little to say, but if you're wise you'll heed my words. A word, they say, is enough for the wise."

All early morning cobwebs cleared from her brain at his increasingly angry tirade.

"It is better you know this sooner than later. I cannot accept you as my daughter-in-law. You can only become Kevwe's wife over my dead body. I don't care how long it takes and what it involves, all I know is that you will not have him. You will never marry my son. So, if you know what's good for you, just leave him alone now."

Efe was dumbfounded. She had worried about Kevwe's mother and hadn't considered his father would be the problem. How wrong she had been…

"I hope you're listening?" he asked. "If you persist in the relationship, I'll let you see the dark side of an Urhobo man. Accept my advice now and stay away. Be wise."

With that, he strode along the corridor and walked into a room at the end, slamming the door behind him.

Efe stumbled into the room assigned to her and slumped on the pillow. Who could have known Kevwe's father was such a staunch traditionalist? And instead of peace between their warring ethnic groups, he would prefer the divide and rule option? He had spoken to her, small her, with such venom and malice, and she was really scared of what he could do to harm her.

She didn't think it would be physical, but maybe he could turn Kevwe against her. She trusted in Kevwe's love and wanted to believe he would stand by her, but who knew?

She couldn't return to sleep, and spent the next hour tossing till at last, she got out of bed. She would tell Kevwe everything once they were alone. Her heart pounded as she walked down the corridor again to take her bath, but she returned to her room without incident.

When she joined Kevwe and his mother at the breakfast table downstairs, she was still filled with trepidation at the thought of how to face her antagonist. Greeting them both, she sat next to Kevwe, and he pecked her on her cheek.

"How was your night, my dear?" his mother asked, smiling at them. "And call me Mum," she continued. "You'll soon be our daughter." A maid trundled in a trolley with two plates of eggs and toast and a teapot.

"Exactly," Chief Mukoro declared, coming into the room. "Efe will be the daughter you've always wanted."

Efe looked up to make sure she heard correctly as the maid placed a plate before her, and filled her mug with steaming tea.

"Eat, my dear," Kevwe's father said, gesturing at the food.

Efe looked at him. The amazing turn-around made her question the earlier warning. She didn't know whether to offer thanks or check the food for ground glass.

"Thank you, sir," she said, hesitantly biting into the food.

"Call me Dad," Chief Mukoro added.

Efe blinked, not knowing what to think of this new persona. She wondered what had occurred, since their earlier encounter in the corridor, to change his mind. Whatever it was, she appreciated it. She would not look the gift horse in the mouth right now.

Later in the morning, Kevwe wanted to play tennis and she joined him. His parents watched from the sidelines. Around midday, after Kevwe had sent her chasing around the courts with his quick serves and dexterous moves, they decided to wash off in the pool.

An hour later, he told her they would be going to Randekhi Royal Hotel and she went upstairs to change into a suitable outfit. Afterwards, they went to look at some more of the apartments he hoped to rent when he came back from youth service. They managed to see only two before finally having to return to the house.

Alone on the balcony upstairs, Efe brought up the subject. "What do you think of the relationship between the Itsekiri and Urhobo in Warri?"

Kevwe looked at her. "What do you mean?"

"They're killing each other and burning up houses."

"Well, I don't know for sure. Efe, you have to remember, the power tussle has been on for decades..."

"We weren't here then!" she almost shouted. His father's words burned in her head. They had to take their differences more seriously than they had. His father had let her know in no uncertain terms, and she wanted Kevwe to understand too.

"Is this about my father's attitude?"

"Yes! He hates that I'm Itsekiri."

"But he's changed now. Didn't he ask you to call him Dad?"

"I don't know if it's genuine. This morning, he..."

A squeak announced the sliding door to the balcony, and Efe was scared his father had overheard her. When she turned, it was Eno who had come to interrupt them.

"Master Kevwe, madam say to call you for dinner."

The dinner turned out more relaxed than the previous day and this time Efe spent a longer time with them in the sitting room where they watched the network news by nine. But when she retired to bed, she could not sleep, puzzling over the behavior of Kevwe's father, and the disconnection between yesterday and today.

She couldn't help wondering what had triggered his hostile outburst in the corridor last night and the changed attitude at breakfast and for the rest of the day. That was what she had wanted to point out to Kevwe. There was no ready answer, and she decided she would continue the discussion with him the next day. She finally drifted off to sleep on the soft and comfortable bed, to the lulling sound of the air conditioner.

The following morning, they all had an early breakfast and went for church service at the cathedral. A sumptuous lunch of yellow starch and banga soup followed soon after they returned. Kevwe drove her back to campus much later, after she had exchanged goodbyes with his parents.

It was only when she closed the door and dropped her bags she realized she had forgotten to tell him about his father's warning. She decided that maybe there wasn't really any need.

14

Benin City. December 16, 2001.

After pressing the bell, Efe stood with her arms wrapped around her body, dripping onto the mat lettered WELCOME in front of Kevwe's door. He had been visiting his twin brother in the United States for a month and was supposed to return today.

After the visit to his parents, they hadn't been able to spend a lot of time together, with Efe soon busy with half-semester exams. Kevwe travelled while she was in Warri with her family, so Efe wanted them to spend some quality time together before she had to go home for Christmas. She prayed he was in; it would be serious if he were not.

"Efe… Efe, what is it?" Kevwe asked in dismay once he opened the door.

"Nothing." She clenched her teeth, unable to meet his eyes.

"Oh my God!" Kevwe scooped her up and carried her straight into the bathroom.

"What happened to you?" he questioned again, after he'd put her on the covered toilet seat. He ran a hot bath for her and as the bucket filled, steam rose and merged in a cloud hovering over them.

"I'll tell you later," Efe whispered. She was soaked through, and goose-bumps lined her skin. As she bent to remove her shoes, shivers racked her body, and when she tried to control then, her teeth chattered the more.

"Can you undress by yourself?" Kevwe asked.

"Yes," Efe replied, and he left her alone to take her bath, closing the door behind him. When he knocked on it later, Efe was out of the tub and wrapped in a large, fluffy towel. Though still cold, she was a bit more composed as she opened the door and stepped out into the bedroom.

"Feeling better? Put this on," Kevwe commanded, handing her his biggest sweater. "I'll go and get the hot cocoa drink I prepared."

When he left, Efe put on the sweater and walked into the sitting room. Immediately Kevwe saw her, he burst out laughing.

"What's so amusing?" Efe queried.

He continued smiling, "You're the one making me laugh."

Efe looked down at herself and laughed too. It was a funny sight. The sweater got past her knees, and the long sleeves hung down her sides with no sign of her hands and fingers.

"But I love the way you look in my clothes," Kevwe said in a thick voice, his eyes moving all over her. He handed her the cup of cocoa and cleared his throat before speaking again. "Tell me what happened..."

Efe sipped the hot drink and began to choke.

"I put in some brandy to chase the cold away," Kevwe explained, rubbing her back.

Efe took another sip before she answered the question. The brandy warmed her like liquid fire and seemed to make the cocoa slip faster down her throat.

"Nothing much. We finished the stock of your mum's frozen food, and I wanted to surprise you by getting here earlier to cook something. But the taxi developed a fault along the way, and I had to wait for over an hour for the driver to go for a mechanic before we could continue. Then just after Edokpolor Grammar School, the vehicle broke down again. Seeing the clouds heavy with rain, I decided to finish the journey on foot. However, before I could take more than a couple of steps, the heavens opened and there I was, drenched immediately," she concluded.

"Double wahala," Kevwe murmured in sympathy. "The funny thing is, it doesn't even usually rain so much in January."

"The rain didn't last for long sha, but it was heavy..."

"Well, it is better you're here now," Kevwe said. "I was so tired after the flight that I took an airport taxi. When the rain started, I wondered how I was going to collect you since my car is still at the airport. I hope you're fine though?"

"I feel much better. Let me go and prepare some food for us."

"First I want to show you something, come on."

He beckoned and followed him into the bedroom. Hc sat on the bed, and she moved to perch lotus style beside him. Kevwe opened the sturdy box and brought out a beautifully wrapped packet. Handing it over, he shifted closer opposite her and nodded.

"Open it."

Efe untied the ribbon, tore the wrapping and separated the two boxes inside. The item in the first one robbed her of speech. There was a silver bracelet decorated with two amethyst hearts pierced with one golden arrow. The second contained a Cartier watch.

"Turn it over," he urged.

On the back was engraved, "Kevwe LOVES Efe."

She scrambled into his lap, dropping the gifts and their boxes on the bed. They kissed for a long time, but Kevwe pushed her off when he felt he couldn't handle more without wanting to go further. When she mumbled in protest, he held her at arm's length.

"Efe, I love you and I would do anything for you. Let's not get carried away now. We have our whole lives together, remember?" He also didn't want to take their lovemaking further because there was no condom in the house, but no need to tell her. He was happy the way she enjoyed being intimate with him. Her reaction always thrilled him, and he could hold off his arousal just by watching her pleasure.

"Now where were we?" he asked.

Efe moved from the bed to the carpeted floor and opened the luggage box, which contained designer labels like Chanel, Tommy Hilfiger, Dior, Elizabeth Arden and others in clothes, perfumes, and cosmetics. There was a box of Nine-West shoes with a smaller package and some cards.

"For Nneka," he said when she held up a package. "Some of the others are for your family; I'm sure Gbubemi will like the Tommy shirt."

"Oh, he'll be ecstatic," Efe said as she flipped through the cards, "and I'm sure Nneka will be delighted too. Thanks again."

"You're welcome." Kevwe was glad she liked the gifts he had selected. His rescheduled flight and the rain had almost spoilt their day, but they'd been able to salvage it. He smiled. "If you're ready, let's find something to eat."

"Oh no! You don't have to do anything," Efe protested. "You've had your shine," she smiled at him, "I still have to make my surprise for you. Just go and rest, okay? I'll wake you up when I'm ready." She sent him into the bedroom, and Kevwe went, humming. She strutted into the kitchen feeling like a queen.

Warri, January 27, 2002. 3pm

Kevwe had been kept busy starting his business. Several contracts from the construction projects in Abuja meant he frequently shuttled between Benin and the new Federal Capital. However, after renewed violence in Warri some weeks after Christmas when Efe was already in school, he made out time to drive her home for a visit. She wanted to see her parents and be reassured everyone was safe. She first went upstairs to spend some time with her mother and Alero, before joining Kevwe who remained with her father and Gbubemi in the living room.

"Gbubemi, change the channel to the NTA," Mr. Sagay said, pointing to the television. A few minutes later, a talking head appeared on the screen.

"Large numbers of people have been fleeing ethnic violence in Delta State. Reports say at least ten homes were set ablaze in Warri."

"Did I not just talk about this?" Mr. Sagay said to no one in particular. "Gbubemi, increase the volume." He sat forward as the news report continued, complete with pictures. The clip of the news anchorwoman changed to videos of the outcome of some of the violence. There were people in hospital or temporary shelters, vandalized shops and cars, burnt tires in the middle of the road and roofless houses with black splotches on their sides.

"We passed that area yesterday," Gbubemi shouted, "on our way from school."

Their father ordered him to shut up, and Efe noted the tension in the room as the news continued with interviews of some people from both sides of the divide on the issue.

One Urhobo man complained, "The Itsekiri bias the rest of the country against the Urhobo to gain advantages in employment, politics and representation. Now they also want the Olu of Warri to remain the paramount Chief in Delta State. It's the same deviousness that won them the chairman of the local government position."

Efe noticed her father shaking his head throughout the speech as she caught Kevwe's eye. The next person to speak was an academic at the state university.

"He's the professor supervising my doctoral degree," Mr. Sagay said to Kevwe.

The professor continued, "Nigeria is a mixture of ethnic nationalities, each with its homeland. There are the Hausa, Yoruba, Igbo, Kanuri, Ibibio, Isoko, small and big. This homeland issue is crucial in Nigeria because our diverse peoples have roots, traditions, myths and cultures peculiar to them. It gives a belonging and people know what they are and where they are. Are the Itsekiri, because they are a micro minority, not entitled to their own homelands? Pressed by the Urhobo from the land, and the Ijaw from the rivers, will they have no homeland on the ground?"

"Good question, but will the trouble-makers answer?" Kevwe wondered what that meant as he watched Mr. Sagay nod then hiss as another man ranted on the TV.

"We need to get our own share of political power, our share of the oil money. During the transition elections, the Itsekiri had more roles in the Midwest region when the new state was created. In spite of their small size, they want to lord it over us - and they think it will continue forever?"

The man spewed more rhetoric, but Mr. Sagay ordered Gbubemi to turn off the TV. Kevwe felt the agitation from his future father-in-law reach him in waves. It was times like this he wished he and Efe weren't from different ethnic groups, at least not ones currently at each other's throats. He wasn't surprised when Mr. Sagay turned to him.

"What are your father's thoughts on this?" he asked, before also addressing Efe, "Are you sure you're welcome in their home?"

"Of course sir, yessir," Kevwe replied, taking up the hand Efe put beside him.

"It's going to be OK, Dad," Efe added, She recalled the first strange reception Kevwe's father had given her, but she pushed it to the rear of her mind. She had met his parents one more time since then, and they had all got along well.

"I'm glad to hear that," her father looked at Kevwe. "I know your father was a diplomat, but you never can tell with these things."

"You said 'trouble-makers' earlier, sir. Who did you mean?" Kevwe knew that Efe's father often preached peace between their tribes and wondered if the current violence had not tipped the man's usual patience to think all Urhobo demons and the Itsekiri, saints.

"Oh, you have them everywhere, on all sides." Mr. Sagay settled himself and looked at them all before clearing his throat. "Take the debate on the title, Olu of Warri. Some Urhobo and Ijaw hypocrites want to reject what their grandfathers accepted in 1952. They have homelands o, but it pained them that this small area was given to the Itsekiri. I won't bore you with the carnage they caused then."

Efe tuned out while her father recounted the history of the Niger Delta peoples. His thesis was on the subject, and this particular discussion was often repeated. She was just happy everyone was safe and unharmed.

"What about the governor?" Kevwe asked, "I would think he'd do something to repair relations between the warring factions if he wants to be re-elected."

Mr. Sagay shook his head, "Since you ask me, I have to say the governor is part of the problem in Warri, not part of its solution. As far as I know, the Itsekiri, to a man, have no confidence in him."

Her father started again, describing peace parleys where he felt the governor could have done better, or where the government had done nothing at all. It all flowed over her head.

"Please Dad, enough of politics." Efe decided to cut in, winking at Kevwe. "We'll soon be heading to school."

Mr. Sagay turned on Kevwe with a piercing stare. "As far as you both assure me there's no problem with your parents?"

Kevwe and Efe smiled at each other, before they turned as one to her father. His prospective father-in-law appeared mollified, and Efe asked Kevwe to talk about the contract he got to design the cooling system of a new building in Abuja.

It had been fascinating listening to her father talk, but Kevwe was also relieved they cleared the hurdle of ethnic tensions. He didn't mind discussing other things with Mr. Sagay and young Gbubemi, who immediately bombarded him with questions on Engineering.

15

Benin. February 20, 2002. 11am

Kevwe was home to collect the usual Tupperware of frozen food his mother got ready for him on weekends when his father's agitated voice got his attention. He peered into the sitting room and noticed their new family friend, Mr. Edewor, was there too.

"Good morning Dad, Mr. Edewor…"

"Did you hear the latest news from Warri?"

"Is there an outbreak of violence?" Kevwe immediately thought of Efe and her family, hoping they were safe.

"Maybe not physically, but they've started with their lies again. They say this over and over, that Urhobo were slaves to Itsekiri. How is that possible? We all arrived there at the same time!" His father waved him to a seat, "I want you listen to Edewor, sit."

Kevwe recalled his discussion with Mr. Sagay and decided to listen to the other side. It was a rare occasion to discuss ethnic politics with his father, most other times, their discussions focused on the federal government, appointments into the diplomatic service or on business, the boards his father sat on and contacts for Kevwe's company. But since her father's questions the other day, he sometimes wondered what exactly his father thought of Efe being Itsekiri. The knee-jerk hostility to her on their first meeting could not be entirely baseless. Kevwe sat down and faced Mr. Edewor.

"Well, they had this Brazilian professor lecture on the Itsekiri and ownership of Warri. I was there at the Palmgrove Motel, and I tell you it was a farce..."

"Kevwe, do you see what I'm saying now? They're the ones oppressing us, killing us and yet they'll cry wolf to the outside world. Is that not trouble they want?"

Kevwe calmed his shouting father. "Dad, please, your heart."

"His heart is fine," Mr. Edewor said. "Kevwe, I know you're disconnected from your roots, but this is imperative since you're a chief-to-be. Do you know Urhobo children are forced to learn Itsekiri in Warri schools? Imagine!" Mr. Edewor snapped his fingers. "And they learn it as their mother tongue o, because Itsekiri cooked up census figures to say they're the dominant tribe in the State."

Kevwe glared at the man whom his father befriended at the Urhobo Congress meeting he joined last year. Mr. Edewor must be behind this recent fixation with Itsekiri-Urhobo differences, and he was always fuelling the flames.

"Dad, I don't see any reason for you to be worked up," Kevwe said, turning to his father. "I thought the Urhobo outside of Warri were not involved in the case? And Mr. Sagay said all the Itsekiri want is peace. We're supposed to be brothers…"

"Don't quote that man to me," his father sneered. "We're not brothers anything! Not when they want to separate us from our kin in the homelands. My sister in Okumagba barely escaped with her life this January! How am I to remain aloof? No way!"

"My son," Mr. Edewor said in a more moderate tone. "A brother will not want to suppress the other. The Itsekiri leaders use rigged election and census results to raise a campaign of calumny against Urhobo interests. You should know that by now."

"Tell him, maybe he will listen to you." His father's knees shook.

Kevwe had not seen this side of his father often, but it was obviously an issue close to his heart. He listened more closely as Mr. Edewor spoke.

"They gain monopoly with forged data, and then lord it over us. It's time for Urhobo everywhere to rise to the challenge. We have to speak with one voice at all levels of government to get our due. Chief, do I speak your mind?"

"Yes, of course. But it's not the main thing. As I said, I'm more bothered by the wanton loss of lives on our side. We need to speak with a united voice, and show we're not the troublemakers Itsekiri make us out to be."

"I agree Dad, but our voice must be for peace..."

"Peace should not make us weak," Mr. Edewor snapped.

"While the bargaining goes on, who protects our people in the villages? What of all the casualties from 1952 till today? We cannot continue dying in silence," his father muttered.

"I don't know Dad, but I don't think violence is an option." Kevwe felt the leaderships of both sides could work it out, and maybe the government had to step in too. He looked up and was shocked to see the disdain on his dad's face.

"You want to sit on the fence, right? I know it's all because of that girl." He turned to his friend. "I heard about this Efe and thought, she must be a good Urhobo girl. But don't be fooled by the name, she's Itsekiri!" He turned to Kevwe, "And here you want to quote her father to me, they are all bad news!"

"Is it because she's Itsekiri?" Kevwe asked, "Why, Dad? You know I've decided to marry Efe, and now you come up with this?" He frowned, anger flaring in him. It was now certain his dad's outburst to Efe last August was more than a bad mood, but out of a grouse against her entire ethnic group.

"Oho. It has already come to marriage?" Edewor crooked a grin.

A thin smile curved his father's lips. "He proposed before introducing her to us o."

"My dear young man, young people make mistakes by jumping into things when they're not ready," Edewor said. "Do you know Itsekiri women are fickle? It's rare for them to stay with one man, and they will leave you at the slightest excuse..."

"We've been together close to three years and I have no reason to doubt Efe." Kevwe turned to meet his father's gaze without flinching. "We're getting married."

His father tapped an index finger on his narrow chin, "Kevwe, I would have liked to say the marriage would not happen in my lifetime, because what face would I use to look at the other chiefs, and my ancestors? But I'll only warn you to reconsider."

"You're taking it too easy," Edewor said to his father, as if Kevwe was not there. "I know we used to intermarry with them, but in these times, no child of mine will marry an Itsekiri with my knowledge. It can't happen! If necessary, I'll snub the traditional rites and refuse to grant my blessing. One has to use more force with these modern children, they think their education trumps our culture."

Kevwe watched Mr. Edewor, who it was clear now was indeed an instigator, wondering to what extent his father shared the same thoughts. Before he turned to his father, Kevwe bit his tongue, to stop from telling Edewor to mind his business.

"Is that what you'll do, Dad?"

"You're my son, Kevwe. If you've made up your mind, I won't be an obstacle."

Kevwe hated that Mr. Edewor was there as he would have loved to continue the discussion with his father. Still this wasn't a terrible point on which to end it for now.

"Thank you Dad, I have to go now." Kevwe stood, shaking hands with both men before striding out of the room.

◆◆◆

Benin City. March 9, 2002.

Since the New Year, the preparation for her final year seminar had taken up most of Efe's time. There was so much material to read and even more to research. Still she made out time each Saturday to visit the NITEL office and make calls to her family. She was fortunate her parents now had a phone in the house unlike when they had lived in Sapele. She'd been a boarding house student in secondary school then and had to depend on the slow postal service to get messages to and from her parents. Now she stood in the queue and waited for a turn at the payphones, coins ready.

"Hello?"

It was her father who picked the phone instead of her mum. "Good morning, Dad."

"Efe, how are you?"

Her father spoke in a serious tone and her mind raced, wondering if something wrong at home.

"I want to talk to you about something before you greet the others. Do you remember the visa lottery we all applied for last year? You won it!" A thread of excitement weaved through his usual monotone.

Efe screamed, "Are you serious, Dad?"

"Would I be joking?"

It took a lot to get her father excited, so she laughed with him, and her siblings shouted in the background. She knew they couldn't wait to talk to her, and she laughed again. Her heart sped up as she looked around the hall at the people staring at her. She smiled and tried not to squeal her exciting news to them.

"This is God-sent, Efe," her father started again after he'd quieted the others. "I hope you realize what it means to the family too. You know how long we've been applying for an American visa for the whole family. It just so happens you won instead, but it's good all the same. Your mother and I discussed it last night. We know you're still young, but you're mature enough to go alone."

It had felt great to win something, but now the reality broke on her. Her dad's words flowed on while she tried to gather her scattered thoughts. She would be separated from her family, and she had to leave Nigeria where she had Kevwe and her friends for company. She wondered what Kevwe would have to say about this. How would she break it to him? Did she honestly want to go and leave him? It didn't look so impressive anymore.

"Efe, are you there?"

She shook her head and gripped the receiver tight, her palms sweating. "Yes, Dad. So what are the next steps?"

"Like I said earlier, you're mature enough to travel on your own. We trust we've brought you up well. Your mother has some relations who will host you when you get to America. You'll continue your education over there."

"Do you mean I have to abandon my degree here?"

"Yes. Nigerian degrees are rarely recognized abroad, so it doesn't matter. The earlier you go the better. You can start a new summer program when you're settled with your aunt in Florida."

"It doesn't make sense, Dad. UniBen is one of the best universities in Nigeria. I've discussed this before with some classmates. They said qualifications from our school are recognized anywhere in the world. I have just a few months to round up my degree. If they don't accept it in the States, I can keep it for when I return. If they do accept it, then I can go ahead and do a masters degree or something."

Her father remained silent for a moment, making her happy he was listening at all. Most of the time, he acted the know-it-all parent and treated her like a child. She couldn't tell him the real reason she needed more time and hoped the school excuse worked. She heard him exchange whispers with her mother before he spoke again.

"I want to discuss this further with your mother. We'll talk to you on the matter before long, OK?"

"All right, Dad… can I speak with the others now?"

Her younger brother came on, and she bore his teases. Her mother reminded her to discuss the issue with Kevwe before Saturday, and Efe knew her next stop after the phone conversation.

16

Benin. March 9, 2002

Kevwe's was in the sitting-room of his new apartment when Efe arrived from NITEL, and speaking with her family.

"Hi, sweetie." He kissed her on the lips.

She returned it fully, and they fell on the sofa laughing.

Kevwe rolled till she was over him. "How's your family? And what's making you so happy? Is it them or is it me?"

Efe laughed, "We won the visa lottery!"

"Oh wow! Congratulations." He hugged her.

"Thank you. I'm so happy..."

Before she finished, he picked her up and jumped to his feet. In the small space of the apartment, he twirled her around till he was dizzy. She laughed and clung to his neck.

When he slumped on the sofa, Efe rained small kisses on his face. Kevwe stopped smiling, sitting up so she slipped off his thighs. "Who won, did you say?"

"I won." She frowned when he stood. "Kevwe, what's wrong?"

"Oh nothing, I thought at first you said your parents won the visa." Kevwe couldn't help but wonder what would happen to their plans. He wanted to remain happy for her, so he pushed the thing that niggled at him away.

"Well, you know my parents have been applying for this since I was a child."

"That's true." Kevwe raised his eyebrows, "Were they disappointed you won?"

"No o. You should've seen how they all rejoiced and were excited for me. I just got off from speaking with them on the phone."

"So will they allow you to go? They can't leave you to go alone, can they?" For him, this was where things got sticky.

"I don't think they'll object at all." she replied as she moved to sit beside him.

"I think you're too young." Kevwe knew he was more emotional than logical, but it was the only argument that occurred to him. He didn't want to state baldly that he just did not want her to go.

She faced him. "I'm not so young; I'll be twenty-two this year. My father suggested I leave immediately."

"What?" Kevwe gaped.

"He's of the opinion that the earlier I go the better. I don't think that's so good; I'll miss you of course, but he pointed out I can start my education afresh and finish before too long. And he's right, I can have my masters in five years."

"But you're in your final year here already." His heart raced. He could feel her slipping out of his reach, and he couldn't bear it.

"I suggested to my dad that I finish my degree here before leaving, so I can have more options. But I don't know what they'll decide. He said he'll discuss with my mum and let me know."

"When?"

"Oh, I'll speak to them on the phone again next Saturday. But you know, the more I think about it, the more excited I become. I just feel as if I should leave immediately."

Efe had a starry look in her eyes that told him she was not fully there with him, and her voice was equally dreamy.

"I remember the stories Nneka told me about America, about how the schools are always on schedule. I want to experience what it's like to have uninterrupted electricity, water, and peace – unlike in Warri, where there has been fighting in the streets every year since we moved there."

"What about me?"

Efe speech slowed down for the first time since she came in. "But we can remain in touch. You like writing letters, so that's not a problem. I'll reply them and tell you my experiences. Also, UniBen has just put up their internet. Over there it's everywhere. I hear there are internet mails..."

"I know about emails," Kevwe snapped, a tight feeling growing in his chest. "But what about our plans? We agreed to get married soon, didn't we? We've been discussing this since last year."

Efe was silent. She had only discussed these plans with her mother who had said they should keep them from her dad till she graduated. She knew her dad wouldn't even want to hear about them now, with her winning the visa. He had his own plans for her to get educated in the States and live there; at least till she was a citizen and could help her younger ones immigrate too if they wanted. She was torn in two as she stood, and paced the small room.

"I don't know... My dad has all these plans."

"You promised to marry me, you accepted my ring!"

"I know, but that was before this visa came. I never thought this would happen or that our plans would clash like this."

"Efe listen, I can talk to your parents. But I want to understand what you want." He blocked her way. "Are we still getting married?"

"Of course, we'll still get married," she stopped pacing and faced him, "only not next year. I need time after I travel to settle down..."

"Must you travel?" Her eyes widened in denial, but he continued, "I'm serious. I promise to give you the best here in Nigeria."

Efe shook her head as she interrupted him. "I have to travel! My parents have invested a lot of time, effort and money into this visa lottery thing. It will break their heart if I say I want to reject the green card that comes with my win."

Kevwe stood, his chest filling up quickly with fear, and then anger. He did not want to lose her. "Efe, you have to choose between your parents and me. Between winning the visa, and our plans to get married and settle down here. We can also have a great life here you know? You've not seen Abuja, it's beautiful. We can move there. It's all part of my vision, to establish my company and start a family with you here. You agreed with me then."

"I did, but now I'm confused." She covered her face with her hands. "I just wanted you to be happy for me."

"OK, let me ask you a few questions." Kevwe strode over and gripped her shoulders. "If you travel abroad now or when you graduate, when will you return?"

"Five years at the least."

"You insist on travelling next year, say we get married next year before you do. Are you ready for a long-distance marriage?"

"Maybe you could join me? I know your American visa will allow you to." Efe peeped through her fingers. She knew he wouldn't agree to the suggestion.

"Don't be childish! You already know what I'll say. Ofure is the one to stay abroad. I like it here in Nigeria, and our parents wish for me to stay close to them."

She loved Kevwe, and she also liked the idea of having a future in Nigeria together, but how could he ask her to turn her back on such an opportunity as this? Efe shook off his arms, standing straighter. And how dare he call her childish?

"Kevwe, I think you're being selfish here. What about me and what I want? What about my parents' wishes?"

"You have to decide by yourself." Kevwe stepped back and turned away. He'd never wanted to be caught in the middle of her choices, but here they were. They had come from fearing they would be split by the differences between their ethnic groups, to being divided by their own personal dreams.

He'd known how much her parents wanted to travel, but it had never been a main source of worry for him. Lotteries were so unpredictable, and a large percentage of the millions who applied for the American visa never won. Also, he'd trusted more and more in the love Efe had for him as their relationship matured, especially when she took his ring.

"Efe, I love you, and I want you to stay in Nigeria and marry me. But it has to come from your heart."

Efe remained silent, torn up inside between conflicting emotions. When she looked up, his face was closed. It didn't look as if he wanted any negotiation. She wished to be with him, but she couldn't deny the lure of travelling abroad. How she wished she could have them both without any stress.

Kevwe turned away, not wanting to quarrel anymore, but knowing he couldn't stay with her and not say anything. "I planned to come see you later. I'm travelling to Lagos tomorrow."

She flounced over to the sofa and slung her handbag over her shoulder. "How long are you away for?"

"I'll go with my father's driver and will return in a week."

"Alright, I'll speak with my parents again on Saturday." He was clearly not in the mood for more talk now. Maybe the break would be for the best, and everything would be sorted out.

Kevwe stared at her for a few long minutes. He remembered what his father's friend said about fickle Itsekiri women. He bit his tongue and pushed the angry words tottering on his lips away. He snatched up his car keys, jangling them as he marched towards the door.

Benin City. March 22, 2002.

Efe paced her room in slow strides, worry for Kevwe creasing her brows. It was almost two weeks after Kevwe went to Lagos, and she just knew something was wrong. For days now she felt cold to her bones anytime she thought about him. A knock on the door disturbed her reverie, and Nneka peeped before coming into the room.

"Twins told me something was wrong, what is it?

After her last telephone appointment with her parents, Efe had become worried when Sunday passed with no word from Kevwe. Before then, she'd only been mildly vexed he had been out of town for several days and had not called her through the mobile phone operator in front of her hostel at least once like he usually did.

On their disagreement about her visa, she'd been waiting to tell him that no matter what her parents said, she would insist on postponing her trip, at least till after graduation. She'd spoken about it to her parents and also raised the issue of marriage plans with her mother, who promised they would speak further when next Efe called.

"Nneka, I just don't know." Efe felt tears track down her cheeks, "Kevwe said he'd be in Benin two days ago but I haven't seen him. He also hasn't called since he's been away."

"But it's too early to be so anxious," Nneka said. "You'll still hear from him."

"He could have called," Efe replied. "He usually does when business delays him."

"It might be he couldn't get through…"

"Yesterday, I tried calling his GSM with one of the kiosks outside, but the call wasn't going through, saying 'the number does not exist, is unavailable or is switched off'."

"I think you're worried like this because of the disagreement you guys had the last time, abi?" Nneka continued. "I don't think he would cut you off just like that."

Efe smeared the tears across her eyes declaring she would go to Kevwe's house after her phone call to Warri the next day. She was there by noon, but all her knocks went unanswered. Several minutes later, the door in the opposite flat opened. Five kids crowded against the metal burglary-proof gate shielding the door.

"Nobody lives there," piped up the only girl.

"What do you mean?" Efe asked, frowning as she spoke. The child couldn't be right. "I was here just two weeks ago."

"Since then, nobody lives there anymore," a boy, who looked the oldest, explained.

Efe could see the others whispering to each other as they stared at her with wide eyes. The boy moved to close the door, but the girl held it. "Some people came yesterday and packed up everything there."

Efe collapsed against the nearest wall when the door shut. Her eyes blinked rapidly as she tried to regain control. What had happened to Kevwe? As she walked to the road, she imagined the worst that could have happened. Confusion consumed her, and she didn't know when she started crying.

After some time, she mopped her tears and ran her fingers through her hair, deciding that she needed to go directly to the campus. She didn't have the patience to wait for a taxi, so she hailed an *okada* she saw on the street. The motorbike took her to Nneka's hostel, where she found Nneka in the room with Ovie and a couple more of their other friends. She dragged both girls downstairs.

"Efe, what is it?" Ovie asked with a frown. "See as you just disturb our enjoyment, eh?"

"I have a problem." Efe declared in a loud tone.

"Is it Kevwe again?"

"That's the problem o. I went to his place and all his stuff had been moved away…"

"He packed without telling you? These Urhobo boys sef."

"Kevwe cannot do that." Nneka was having none of it.

"I tell you, I know these area boys pass you o, dem cunny well well," Ovie replied.

"It's not true. We've known this guy for more than two years." Nneka turned to Efe. "You said you felt something was wrong; maybe Kevwe's ill."

Ovie shook her head but remained quiet.

"Do you think I should go to their house in GRA?" Efe asked. She didn't feel very comfortable going, but there was no other option.

Nneka nodded. "Go tomorrow."

17

Benin City. March 24, 2002. 11am

Efe missed church that Sunday, and boarded a taxi instead to take her to the GRA residence of Kevwe's parents. When she got to the house, everywhere was quiet, which was not unusual. She paid the driver at the gate and watched him drive away, wondering how she would get to school if Kevwe was not home. She trudged along the drive and up the front stairs where one of the maids opened the door as if she had been waiting. Efe was surprised to see the maid's tears. Fresh drops accompanied her words.

"Madam no dey here, she traveled…"

"Who is that?" Kevwe's dad spoke from behind the door.

"It is Master Kevwe's...." the girl stammered.

Kevwe's dad entered the doorway. "You!"

"Good afternoon, sir," Efe greeted, watching as his glare sent the maid scurrying.

"Stupid girl." Chief Mukoro barked, adding something else in another language. The girl crept off in the direction of the kitchen and Efe pitied her. It seemed she wasn't the only one who got the sharp edge of the man's tongue.

"Why are you here?" he asked when the maid was gone.

"I'd like to see Kevwe. His GSM phone is not going through, and his place in Upper Lawani has been cleared. I'm afraid…"

He laughed. "No need to be afraid, my son is fine."

"Oh, thank God." Efe felt so relieved, she smiled too. "I wanted to tell him that my parents have agreed for us to postpone my trip. My mother will speak to my father about our marriage if we fix it for next year…"

All mirth left his face. "I warned you earlier to leave my son alone, didn't I? How dare you come to my house to tell me about stupid marriage plans? What temerity!"

"Sorry sir." Efe was lost for words. Kevwe's dad reverting to the man she first met made her stammer, "I-I… didn't…"

"Listen, this is the last time I'll say this." Chief Mukoro said, and shook a be-ringed finger at her. "Kevwe says he doesn't want you anymore. I told him why Itsekiri people cannot be trusted, and he has finally seen the light. He has changed his phone number and packed out of his house. Now, leave him alone!"

His words hit her like stones, leaving burning nicks in their wake. "But…"

"But what?" he pushed his face closer to hers. "Kevwe doesn't want you. You're not good enough for him. He can't see where you fit into his future, and that's it."

"Please sir, I don't understand…"

"Did I not warn you from the beginning?" he sneered, his breath heating up the shrinking space between then. "I won't live to see my son marry from a people that kill so heartlessly. Thank God Kevwe has seen sense."

"I'm sorry, but can I see Kevwe, talk to him…"

The force of the door cut her off as it slammed in her face.

Efe trekked all the way to campus like one in a daze, calling on Nneka, who then followed her to her room. By the time they got there, Nneka knew the whole story.

Two days later, Efe still refused to leave the shroud of her sheets.

"Why? Why? How can it end this way? If Kevwe had to reject me, at least he could do it to my face." She sobbed, tears trickling from her eyes. Joan sat beside her, her own eyes red-rimmed.

Nneka signaled Jane to bring a basin of water, "Efe, it's enough; stop crying. Remember, exams start next week..."

"You don't know how I feel, or you wouldn't be saying that," Efe cried. "No crying will be enough, and of what good are exams if Kevwe has broken up with me?" She scrubbed at her nose. "Kevwe was everything to me, my past and my future. I loved him with my very soul. How could I continue life without him?"

Jane stood there with the water basin, her lids heavy with tears. "Efe, please don't say that, stop crying. We've been over this." Jane said. Joan sniffled in the background.

"Stop crying, Efe, you'll make yourself sick." Nneka said.

Efe sat up, "I want to go home, my mother will…"

"If you continue crying, do you think your parents will allow you return to school when they see you like this?"

"It may be for the best. Why would I want to come back to this place again?" Efe started crying again, "How can I come back where I may see Kevwe with someone else, or hear news of his wedding? You know how Benin is such a small place."

"It may not come to that…"

"I swear I will just die if it happens." Deep sobs welled up in her throat again as if to strangle her. "Nneka, I swear… I will. After three years with Kevwe, that would be the worst thing. Why should I remain in this country? Eh, tell me, why?"

Jane and Joan's sobs mingled, and they ran out of the room, tears gushing down their cheeks. Ovie came in soon after.

"What is this I hear? I saw the twins on my way here."

"Kevwe may have broken up with Efe…"

Efe looked up to her. "Is there any doubt about it? His father told me. I'd been hoping he would call, but he hasn't."

"So he couldn't face you to tell you himself?" Ovie demanded as she sat. "I saw him today, and he wouldn't talk to me too…"

"You saw Kevwe, today?" Efe sat straight. Time seemed to move in slow motion, and she felt dizzy for a while.

"Yes. On my way to First Bank, I saw him at UBA Akpakpava, near the roundabout. When I said hi, he ignored me. Maybe he thought I knew about the break-up ..."

"Are you sure it was him you saw?" Efe clutched her chest. The ache in her pounding heart was real.

"I'm sure. You know how I complain about his habit of jangling his keys all the time as if he's the only one who has a car. It was the sound that caught my attention, and he was with another girl."

Efe stopped thinking, her breathing also seemed to cease. All the blood in every single part of her body drained to her heart, making it expand, and it pushed against her ribs as if to burst loose. Efe sprang out of bed, screaming in fear.

"Efe stop it, stop it right now!"

She came to her senses to find Nneka and Ovie restraining her on the bed. Two girls were at the door, but Ovie went and pushed them away. Her ears rang and her eyes felt hot with piercing pain. One thought seized her mind, echoing in her head over and again until everything blurred together. Kevwe had another girl. Nneka and Ovie murmured above her head, but they sounded far away. Efe wondered if she was going mad. She closed her eyes and blanked her mind, but the thought refused to go.

"He has another girl. Nneka did you hear? Kevwe had another girl." Efe talked more to herself than to the others. "Do you know what sent him away from me? I didn't tell you earlier but now I will. He had wanted to make love to me I refused. He pretended to accept it but I now know better. I stopped him, so I'm the one who pushed him into the arms of another girl. He should have told me, I would have agreed…"

"Efe please pull yourself together," Ovie said, "Isn't it better you didn't agree, with the way things have turned out?"

"But it wouldn't have been like this if I did." Fresh tears rolled down her cheeks. Efe thought now his father's tribal disdain was a secondary reason. Kevwe already knew he didn't want her. Or could Kevwe teamed up with his father to get his way, since his mother liked her,? The simple truth was he'd found another girl.

"It's not the end of the world…" Nneka said, wrapping her arms around Efe.

Efe shifted for Ovie to join them on the bed, and as tears from the other girls fell on her face and neck, she knew she had to put her emotions in check. She had to get ready for the worst.

"Efe, what are you going to do?" Nneka must have read her mind.

"I will go to America…"

"You changed your mind because of this? I thought you decided to get your first degree here in UniBen before travelling."

"Ovie, I can't stay in this town knowing Kevwe is dating another girl. I can't even stay in this country, and I won't!"

"OK, relax. At least your parents won't object."

"You have to call them first," Nneka added, "and talk to your mum. She'll understand if you explain what happened with Kevwe."

Efe nodded, and then shook her head from side to side.

"What is it?" Nneka asked.

"I still don't understand. Kevwe promised, he promised he'd marry me." Efe stretched out her left hand. "Isn't this ring proof of it?" The sobs racked her body again.

Benin City. April 5, 2002. 2pm

Efe sat in the back seat of the chartered taxi, hypnotized by the wiper's frantic movement. The slow rain which started as they left the hostel now lashed at the windscreen of the taxi, and the wipers were doing their best to clear them off. It was a week since she had gone to the Mukoros, and she was on her way there again. Nneka had insisted she had to go one final time.

Her parents had agreed for her to come back to Warri, and start processing her green card. While her mother knew of Kevwe's betrayal, she had passed off her return to her dad as obedience to his earlier idea. He couldn't come to pick her up as usual, but he had chartered a taxi to bring her home. A couple of suitcases and a large duffel bag were in the boot, and the taxi was to drive her to Warri after the trip to Kevwe's parents.

"Madam o, we don reach the address." The driver broke her trance.

Efe shook her head and ran her thumb and index finger across both eyelids. The storm had turned the afternoon to gloom. "Wait for me here abeg, I may be long."

Efe opened the car door, shook out her compact umbrella and dashed through the rain up the front stairs. Chief Mukoro himself opened the door to her, dressed for going out, and accompanied by a man she'd not seen before but who smirked at the sight of her dripping at the door. Both men wore hats with feathers sticking out and long necklaces of coral beads around their necks. She guessed the car she'd seen idling on the driveway must be waiting for them.

"That's the girl." Chief Mukoro nudged his friend. "She's the Itsekiri girl who won't let us rest."

The other man smirked even wider. Like Kevwe's dad, he was dressed in a cream lace long sleeved top with wrist cuffs and slits down the sides. Instead of the plain trousers, he carried the end of a trailing George wrapper and a carved walking stick.

"Let's allow her in, out of the rain," he suggested.

Both men preceded her into the sitting room. The house seemed to bustle more than she'd ever seen it. The sound of activity wafted from the direction of the kitchen. Efe followed the men and sat down where she was directed. Kevwe's dad shut the door behind her and sat down on his favorite chair.

"What more do you want?"

"I want to see Kevwe. I'm leaving Benin..."

Chief Mukoro laughed. "Good riddance to bad rubbish."

Efe slid to her knees. The tears had pooled in her eyes, but she tried to hold them. It couldn't end like this. "Please, I want to see him, hear it from him..."

"What part of 'he doesn't want you anymore' or 'leave him alone' can't you understand?" He rushed on before she could speak. "Even after he cut himself off from you, you want to see him again? For what? Tell me why? Why you want to put him to the trouble of telling you face to face he's finished with you? Get this into your thick skull. Kevwe has another girl."

Efe was frozen in place by the harsh words.

"A more befitting girl I chose for him myself..."

Efe jerked in pain. He had confirmed what Ovie said, but she refused to believe it. "Kevwe wouldn't reject me. He can't betray me."

The other man who had remained silent spoke, "You think you've snared him with your *ebele koko meyo*?"

"Edewor, my children were fortified at birth! *Akpobrisi* will reward those who try anything," Chief Mukoro said, turning to Efe, "This one will not be his death. I have warned her. There will be no wanton Itsekiri in this house!"

"Itsekiri!" the man called Edewor sneered. "They are all brazen. Bootlickers and sycophants..." The role of Edewor seemed to be to pour petrol on the fire. Efe just ignored him and fixed her gaze on Kevwe's father.

Chief Mukoro stood. "You won't get my son. Now leave."

"I can't leave, I won't!" Efe stood too. She pulled off the narrow ring on her left hand. "Kevwe gave me this, if he didn't want to marry me anymore, he would've taken it."

"Give me the ring," Chief Mukoro was unsmiling.

Efe stepped back. "No… no, I won't…"

"What is this?" Kevwe's mother came into the room and closed the door. She looked at Efe in surprise and addressed her husband. "I thought you had left. Aren't you late?"

"We met her at the door; she came to return her ring."

At this point, Edewor got up and left the room.

"I came to see Kevwe." Efe corrected Chief Mukoro.

"You can't," Kevwe's mum said. "I mean, he's not… he can't..."

Efe felt all the muscles in her body go passive. Even her heart seemed to slow. She blinked her eyes to keep them open. So this was true after all. "Noo… I… don't… he—"

Chief Mukoro cut off her stumbled speech; he didn't want this to drag. He knew his wife would say nothing, and the girl must continue to misunderstand. He wanted her out of the house as soon as possible before Ofure returned.

"Give the ring to her. You've heard it. Kevwe doesn't want to see you. He just doesn't want you, period."

Efe walked like a zombie and placed the small token in the woman's open palm. She saw the pity in the eyes of Kevwe's mother and her heart, which had been strung together by buried hope, was torn apart in that instant. All the arteries in her body felt charged as if they would burst out of her skin. She dashed towards the door held open by Kevwe's dad, ignoring Edewor who stood by the front door.

She gasped for breath as she came to the gaping doorway. A flash of lightning revealed a raging storm. The driving rain washed down the front stairs, and damp air blew past her. The crack of the following thunder galvanized her. She shook out the umbrella, gathered her skirt and ran out into the cold arms of the weather. She missed her footing on the wet steps when the wind snatched her umbrella, but she plunged on, the wind lashing at her face, her clothes and her hair.

The storm attacked her, trying to tear her body apart, but the job had already been done. She was both physically and emotionally defeated from the inside, and nothing more could affect her. Blinded by rain and tears and dripping water, she stumbled into the taxi, arms wrapped around her body.

She huddled in the seat, shivering as the car lurched towards the open gates. They were met by the full beam of another car. The sight of the car's occupants almost had her joining the pool of water at her feet. It was Kevwe's car, and he was driving it with a girl in the passenger seat. Shame and finality washed over her, and she slid lower in her seat as the taxi rattled onto Sapele Road.

PRAISE FOR A LOVE REKINDLED

"...a moving love tale of first love, the challenges of tribal biases and the importance of hope, persistence and forgiveness – critical ingredients for every relationship to survive."

Lara Daniels, author of *Love at Dawn*

"Reading [this] is like holding up a cloth of kente: each piece rich with history and beauty. With confidence and deftness, Nkem Akin weaves a riveting brocade of friendship, heartache, and love..."

Uche Umez, author of *Tears in her Eyes*

"....a romance novel that affirms one's belief in true love and that it truly does conquer all. It also proves that though external forces can cause a delay, they cannot kill love."

Folake Taylor, author of *The Only Way is Up*

PRAISE FOR A HEART TO MEND

"…the beauty of this book is that there is redemption for all…in tandem with the title cover, that there can indeed be mended hearts."
- Ify Malo, USA

"Written by a Nigerian….with Nigerian characters and setting, A Heart to Mend is a fun and fast read."
Pamela Stitch, African Loft Magazine

Peoples of all cultures face the same emotional issues when it comes to relationships – this is Nkem Akin's message in her debut novel." Belinda Otas, New African Woman Magazine

Acknowledgements

I am grateful to the following people who helped me to polish up this manuscript and my writing craft as a whole; - Members of the Eastside Writers Meetup Group in Seattle Washington, who read excerpts and gave useful critique; - those who commented on and gave feedback on my blog; for their encouragement.

I am highly indebted to my editor, Tola Odejayi, who with eagle eyes and a compassionate pen, draws out the best in me. It is a pleasure working with you to spin the sweetest stories.

For pointing out what was wrong and sometimes, how to get it right, I thank the beta readers of one of the several drafts of this novel including Neefemi, Kiru Taye, Juanita and Shenaim, whose fantastic comments guided the book process.

For showing me such awesome love and support, and helping with the distribution of my first book, A Heart to Mend, I thank all my family and in-laws, the Okotcha and Akinsoto families, far and near. Ada, Fumnanya and Chi were very encouraging with their words as they gave early thumbs up to one of the drafts of this novel. Thanks to Fumns for telling me she cried while reading the book. You made my day.

Finally and chiefly, I thank my husband, who inspires me with his love and makes me believe in romance every day. You give me the wings with which to fly. I love you.

ABOUT THE AUTHOR

Nkem was born and raised in Enugu, Nigeria, where she spent most of her time, studying, reading and daydreaming or climbing trees and playing with the boys. She has a master's degree in Public Health Research and now works full time in an academic medical center.

She is Nigerian and believes in the use of the internet and social media to promote the book industry and literacy levels in the country. Between 2010 and 2020, she founded and managed Naijastores.com, a free website for those that read, write or publish Nigerian stories.

CPSIA information can be obtained
at www.ICGtesting.com
Printed in the USA
BVHW051000300123
657433BV00018B/620